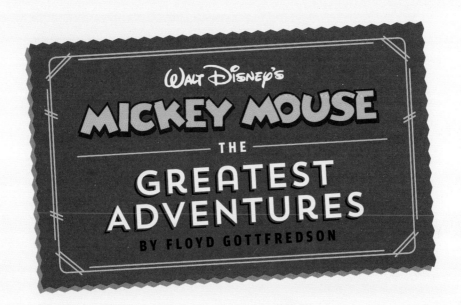

Walt Disney's

MICKEY MOUSE

THE

GREATEST ADVENTURES

BY FLOYD GOTTFREDSON

Fantagraphics Books, Inc. | 7563 Lake City Way NE | Seattle WA 98115 | (800) 657-1100

Visit us at fantagraphics.com. Follow us on Twitter at @fantagraphics and on Facebook at facebook.com/fantagraphics.

First printing: December 2018

ISBN 978-1-68396-122-2

Printed in China

Library of Congress Control Number: 2018936466

PUBLISHER . . . . GARY GROTH

SENIOR EDITOR . . . . J. MICHAEL CATRON

ARCHIVAL EDITOR . . . . DAVID GERSTEIN

DESIGN . . . . JACOB COVEY

PRODUCTION . . . . PAUL BARESH

COLOR EDITOR . . . . SEAN DAVID WILLIAMS

ASSOCIATE PUBLISHER . . . . ERIC REYNOLDS

The stories in this volume were originally serialized as daily newspaper comic strip adventures.

"Mickey Mouse in Death Valley," April 1–September 22, 1930

"The Picnic," January 5-10, 1931

"Island in the Sky," November 30, 1936–April 3, 1937

"The Gleam," January 19–May 2, 1942

"Mickey Mouse and Goofy's Rocket," September 9-21, 1946

"The Atombrella and the Rhyming Man," April 30–October 9, 1948

"Mickey's Dangerous Double," March 2–June 20, 1953

These stories were created during an earlier time and may include cartoon violence, historically dated content, or gags that depict smoking, drinking, gunplay, or ethnic stereotypes. We present them here with their original flaws and a caution to the reader that they reflect a bygone era.

There have been many previous attempts to publish a high quality, completely restored, and fully colored version of "Mickey Mouse in Death Valley," Floyd Gottfredson's first *Mickey Mouse* story.

We hope you enjoy the completed version that, at long last, appears in these pages for the first time anywhere. But we could not have realized this accomplishment without the work that was begun for those earlier efforts.

Thus, the Archival Editor would like to dedicate this book to the late Bill Blackbeard and Cole Johnson; and to Byron Erickson, Bob Foster, David Seidman, Cris Palomino, Marco Barlotti, John Clark, Gary Leach, Susan Daigle-Leach, Travis Seitler, Ken Shue, Iliana Lopez, and Miguel Pujol.

Some of us have waited more than 25 years for this moment. Here it is!

Walt Disney's
MICKEY MOUSE
THE
GREATEST ADVENTURES

BY FLOYD GOTTFREDSON

FANTAGRAPHICS BOOKS, SEATTLE

California

Magazine of Pacific Business
March 1937 • 25 Cents
In Two Parts—PART ONE

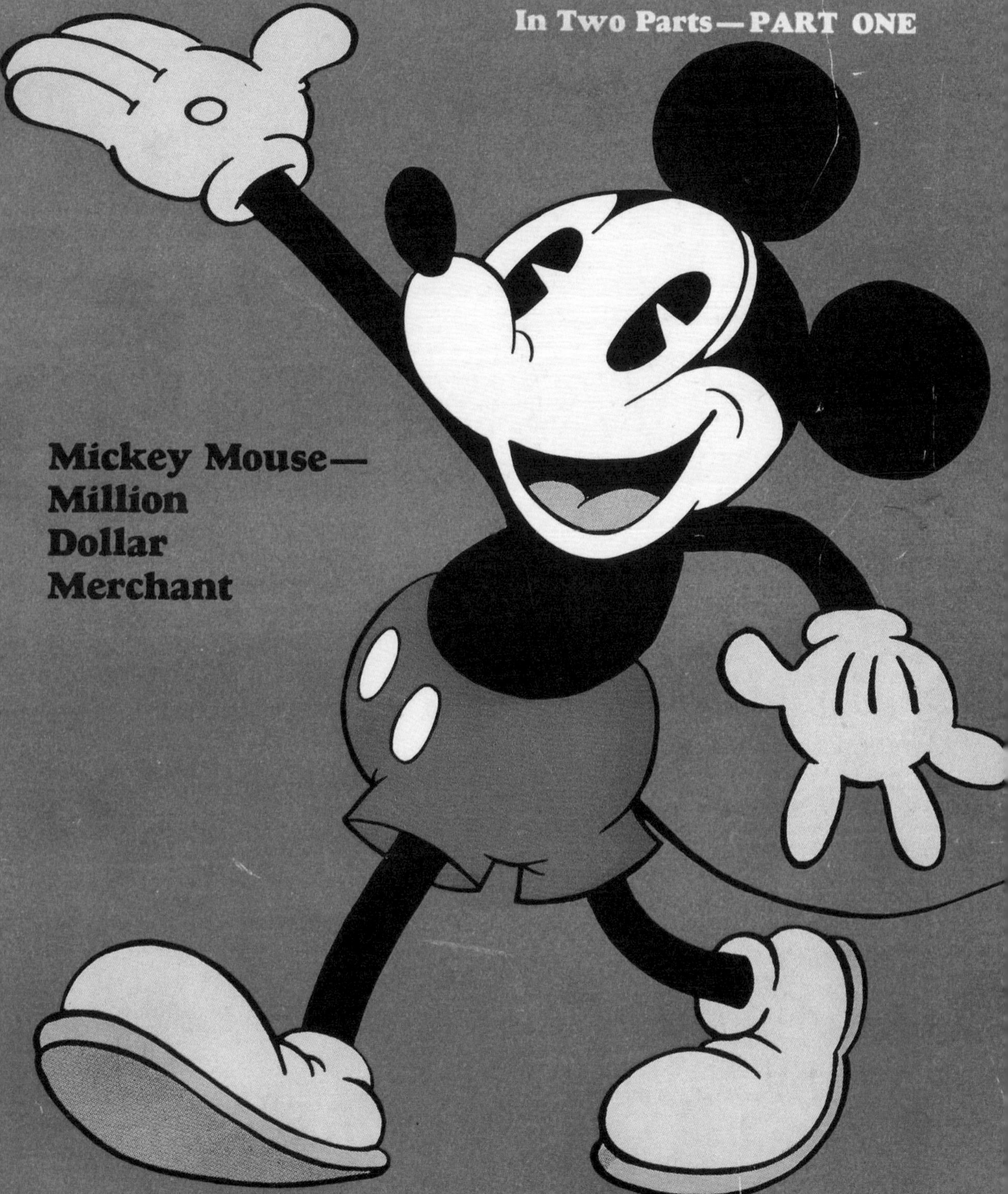

**Mickey Mouse—
Million
Dollar
Merchant**

nperial Valle[redacted] • Qui ksilver • Wild [redacted]l

FLOYD GOTTFREDSON: WALT DISNEY'S MOUSE MAN

Foreword by David Gerstein

WE ALL KNOW DISNEY'S GOLDEN AGE "started with a mouse." *The* Mouse, actually. But today, for Disney fans of a certain age, Mickey Mouse is regarded as more of an icon than a character. His cheerful visage brings to mind nostalgic comic books and video games full of comfortable, but repetitive good-versus-evil stories. Such stories have their fans, it's true. Yet if you ask those fans who their favorite Disney character is, the answer they will often give is "Donald Duck!"

For after the grumpy, hilarious edginess of Donald and Uncle Scrooge as portrayed by Carl Barks and, later, Don Rosa, in their brilliant comic book stories, Mickey Mouse as those fans think they know him — as a dependable crime-buster and small-town celebrity — might seem a little too basic and predictable.

But is this Mickey the only Mickey? Long before Donald Duck was the Donald of Barks and Rosa (among others) — a *different* Mickey Mouse was Disney's greatest, most important comics star. That earlier version of Mickey, like his successor, was often propelled into fights against crime — but with a personality as rich as Sherlock's own. *That* Mickey's character and charisma made for much more memorable mysteries. *That*

Mickey boasted an endearing attitude at once positive and cynical. *That* Mickey was inquisitive, adventurous, trailblazing, selfless — and funny.

That Mickey was the work of cartoonist Floyd Gottfredson, and *this* Mickey collection is *that* Mickey's book.

A go-getter just like his star, Gottfredson (1905–1986) persevered through a childhood pockmarked with tragedy. At the age of 11, young Floyd shot himself in the arm while hunting and never fully healed. Struggling to move forward after the accident, the invalid boy put himself through an art correspondence course. With his injury limiting the movement of his wrist, Gottfredson learned to draw by moving his entire upper arm — causing his art to be characterized by broad, dashing lines and raw energy.

At the same time, Gottfredson got hooked on Horatio Alger adventure novels: stirring stories of plucky young heroes forging their way in an unforgiving world. Soon, Gottfredson did the same by finding a job that was not too hard on his weakened arm — he became a projectionist for a movie theater. The job exposed Gottfredson to the likes of Charlie Chaplin, Buster Keaton, and Harold Lloyd — more plucky young heroes.

In the late 1920s, Gottfredson moved his family to Los Angeles, hoping to find a career as a newspaper cartoonist. But another kind of cartooning job presented itself. Gottfredson found California theaters featuring a new, plucky, animated star — one created by Walt Disney and Ub Iwerks.

Mickey Mouse excited Gottfredson from the moment he saw him, and so Gottfredson applied to the Disney studio to become a comic strip artist. But in late 1929, Walt didn't need another strip artist. He already had Iwerks and staff illustrator Win Smith drawing the new *Mickey Mouse* daily strip for King Features Syndicate. Nor did Walt need a writer. At the start, Walt wrote the strip himself. But Walt did put Gottfredson to work — as an animation assistant.

Then opportunity knocked. In January 1930, Iwerks left Disney. Walt asked Smith, who was already inking the strip, to also pencil *Mickey Mouse* — and soon after, to write it as well. Rather than do all the work, Smith quit. Gottfredson was asked to take over the daily *Mickey Mouse* for a few weeks until Walt could find another talent.

Those "few weeks" turned into decades — because Gottfredson developed a tone, a technique, and a characterization of Mickey that kept readers coming back. "Mickey Mouse in Death Valley" (1930), the story that was then running when Gottfredson took over, began the process: Walt himself established Mickey as an inquisitive youth nosing his way into a risky treasure hunt. But it is Gottfredson's Mickey who, relishing the challenge, proclaims, "I'm a one-way guy and that's forward." Mickey's trailblazing in the Wild West reflects the Horatio Alger heroes of Gottfredson's boyhood. Mickey's selfless defense of Minnie's safety is stirring. "Remember," he bluffs the bad guys, "you're dealing with Mickey Mouse!"

On the strengths of all this funny fighting spirit, Gottfredson's *Mickey Mouse* fast became one of the most popular 1930s comic strips. It was also vitally influential on how fans perceived Disney characters. Moviegoers only got to see a dozen new Mickey Mouse cartoons every year, but they could read Mickey's comics every day. And where Mickey went every day, so did his gang: Gottfredson's characterizations of hopeful Minnie, egotistical Horace, and über-eccentric Goofy became as beloved as his two-fisted Mickey.

Of course, being beloved by readers didn't make Mickey's lot any easier. In this book's "Island in the Sky" (1936–1937), Air Force Captain Doberman tasks Mickey with investigating Dr. Einmug, a scientist whose powers threaten the planet. But while Mickey's past experience has won him Doberman's respect, Einmug treats Mickey like an unreliable kid. Gottfredson often called his Mickey a "Mouse Against the World" — circumstances made him an underdog.

The animated Mickey did not stay an underdog. From the mid-1930s, he became a more authoritative and reserved figure on screen, while the ever-raffish Donald grabbed more of the screen time. This made Gottfredson's strip more important as a source of Mickey stories and by World War II, it provided the most active version of Mickey that fans got to see.

The war shook up both Mickey's environment and Gottfredson's. Gottfredson had been penciler, plotter, and part-time writer of *Mickey Mouse* since 1930, sharing the duties with scripters Ted Osborne and Merrill De Maris. But Gottfredson was also manager of Disney's Comic Strip Department — and his workload grew too heavy. Thus, in 1943, Gottfredson hired an ambitious radio writer, Bill Walsh (1913–1975), to take over as *Mickey* plotter — and the final era of Gottfredson's Mickey adventures began.

As an idea man, Walsh favored science fiction and fantasy — opining that "a little too much realism goes a long way." In keeping with this philosophy, Walsh co-created wild strip characters like Eega Beeva, Mickey's wacky time-traveling friend, and the Rhyming Man, a verse-prone enemy spy who co-stars in this book's "The Atombrella and the Rhyming Man." Apart from his penchant for poetry, the Rhyming Man boasts a threatening sort of schizophrenia, and his story, on some level, is schizophrenic, too. As thrilling as Walsh and Gottfredson get — Mickey and Eega are fighting for the fate of the planet! — they move from location to location so fast that wacky co-stars seem to disarmingly pile on: a dignified trained ape comes, a boy genius goes. The technique spilled into later stories, too. In 1955, when Gottfredson was asked to stop making adventure serials, one might sense that his Mickey was actually relieved.

Perhaps the stage was set, then, for that nostalgic-era Mickey whom Donald's fans look back on so fondly.

Luckily, the end of Gottfredson's adventure serials was not the end of his adventurous, inquisitive, selfless, trailblazing, funny Mickey Mouse. As a curious youth and embattled fighter, Mickey marches on today in modern comics by comics creators such as Andrea "Casty" Castellan, Byron Erickson, Noel Van Horn, and others whose work is often based directly on Gottfredson's. As Gottfredson himself put it in later years, the Mickey who "was my very exciting and satisfying companion … is very much alive and well. Long may he reign!"

This special collection offers you the chance to enjoy the best stories from Gottfredson's own reign.

OPPOSITE: Floyd Gottfredson at his drawing board in 1951, two decades into his work on the *Mickey Mouse* daily strip. Image courtesy Disney Publishing Worldwide.

P.VI: Cover by Floyd Gottfredson for *California* magazine, March 1937. (Mickey likely drawn circa 1933.) Image courtesy Hake's Americana.

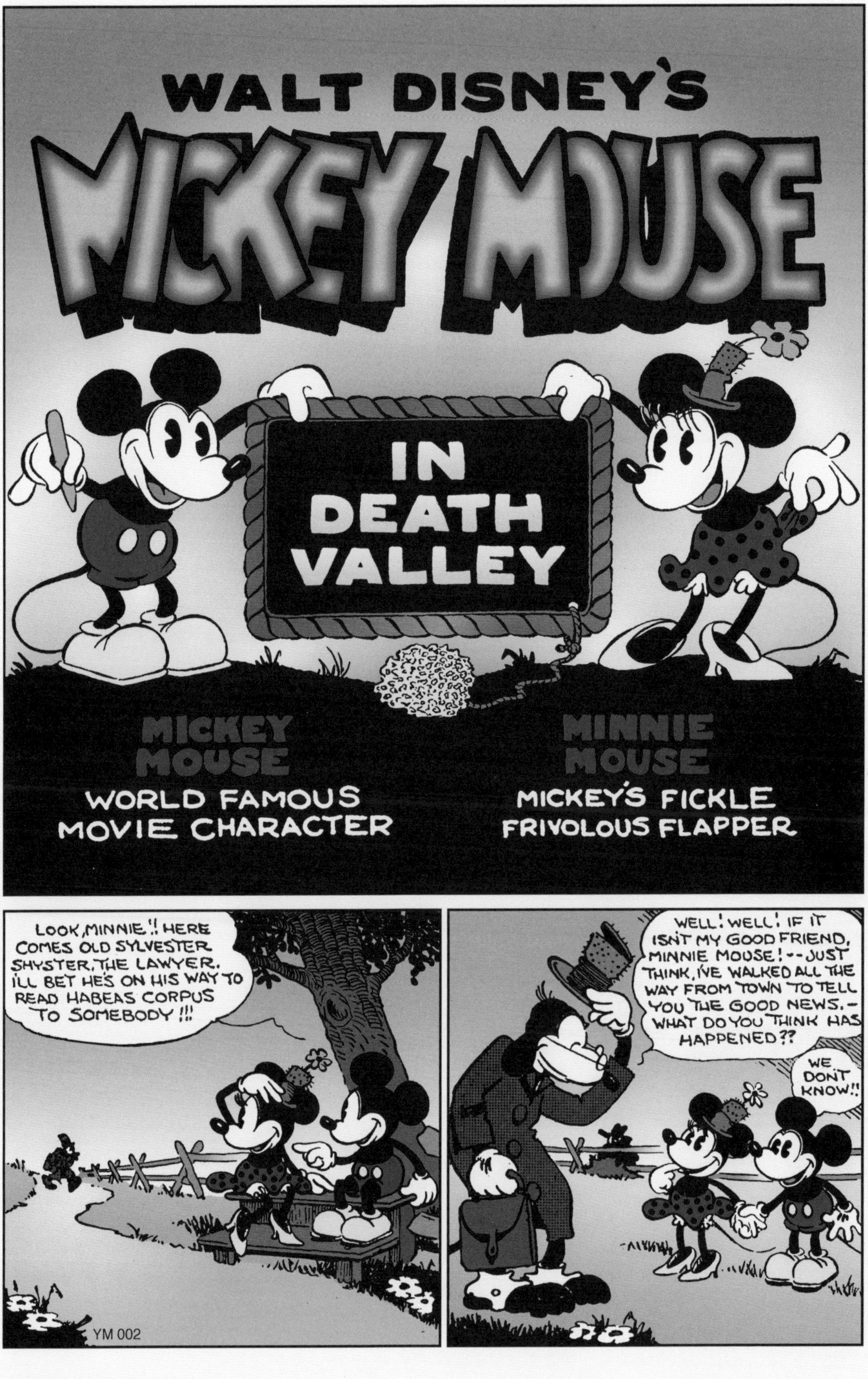
WALT DISNEY'S
MICKEY MOUSE
IN DEATH VALLEY
MICKEY MOUSE
WORLD FAMOUS MOVIE CHARACTER
MINNIE MOUSE
MICKEY'S FICKLE FRIVOLOUS FLAPPER
LOOK, MINNIE!! HERE COMES OLD SYLVESTER SHYSTER, THE LAWYER. I'LL BET HE'S ON HIS WAY TO READ HABEAS CORPUS TO SOMEBODY!!!
YM 002
WELL! WELL! IF IT ISN'T MY GOOD FRIEND, MINNIE MOUSE! -- JUST THINK, I'VE WALKED ALL THE WAY FROM TOWN TO TELL YOU THE GOOD NEWS. - WHAT DO YOU THINK HAS HAPPENED??
WE DON'T KNOW!!

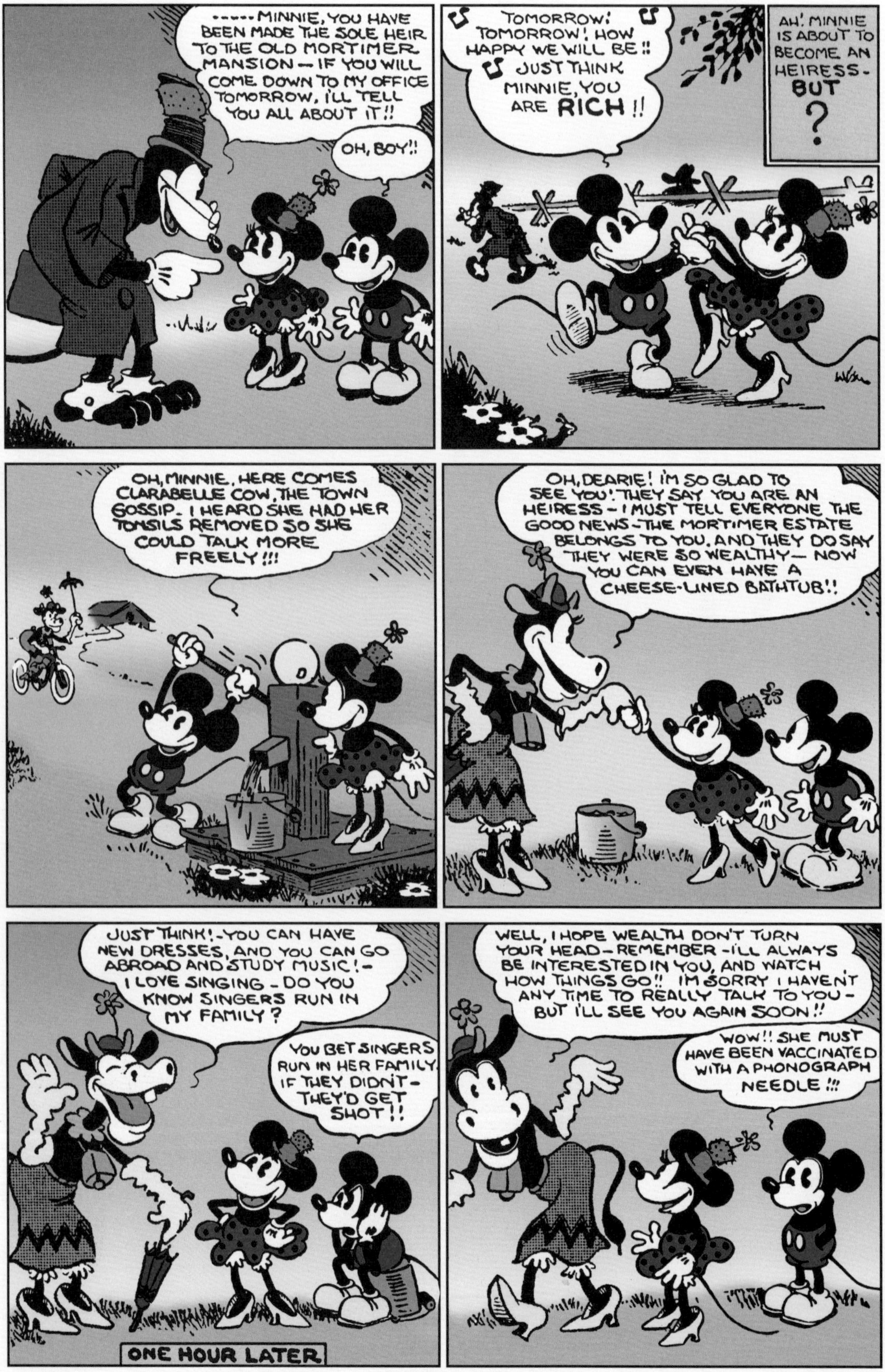
-----MINNIE, YOU HAVE BEEN MADE THE SOLE HEIR TO THE OLD MORTIMER MANSION — IF YOU WILL COME DOWN TO MY OFFICE TOMORROW, I'LL TELL YOU ALL ABOUT IT!!
OH, BOY!!
TOMORROW! TOMORROW! HOW HAPPY WE WILL BE!! JUST THINK MINNIE, YOU ARE RICH!!
AH! MINNIE IS ABOUT TO BECOME AN HEIRESS- BUT ?
OH, MINNIE, HERE COMES CLARABELLE COW, THE TOWN GOSSIP. I HEARD SHE HAD HER TONSILS REMOVED SO SHE COULD TALK MORE FREELY!!!
OH, DEARIE! I'M SO GLAD TO SEE YOU! THEY SAY YOU ARE AN HEIRESS - I MUST TELL EVERYONE THE GOOD NEWS - THE MORTIMER ESTATE BELONGS TO YOU, AND THEY DO SAY THEY WERE SO WEALTHY— NOW YOU CAN EVEN HAVE A CHEESE-LINED BATHTUB!!
JUST THINK! - YOU CAN HAVE NEW DRESSES, AND YOU CAN GO ABROAD AND STUDY MUSIC! - I LOVE SINGING - DO YOU KNOW SINGERS RUN IN MY FAMILY?
YOU BET SINGERS RUN IN HER FAMILY. IF THEY DIDN'T - THEY'D GET SHOT!!
ONE HOUR LATER
WELL, I HOPE WEALTH DON'T TURN YOUR HEAD - REMEMBER - I'LL ALWAYS BE INTERESTED IN YOU, AND WATCH HOW THINGS GO!! I'M SORRY I HAVEN'T ANY TIME TO REALLY TALK TO YOU - BUT I'LL SEE YOU AGAIN SOON!!
WOW!! SHE MUST HAVE BEEN VACCINATED WITH A PHONOGRAPH NEEDLE!!!

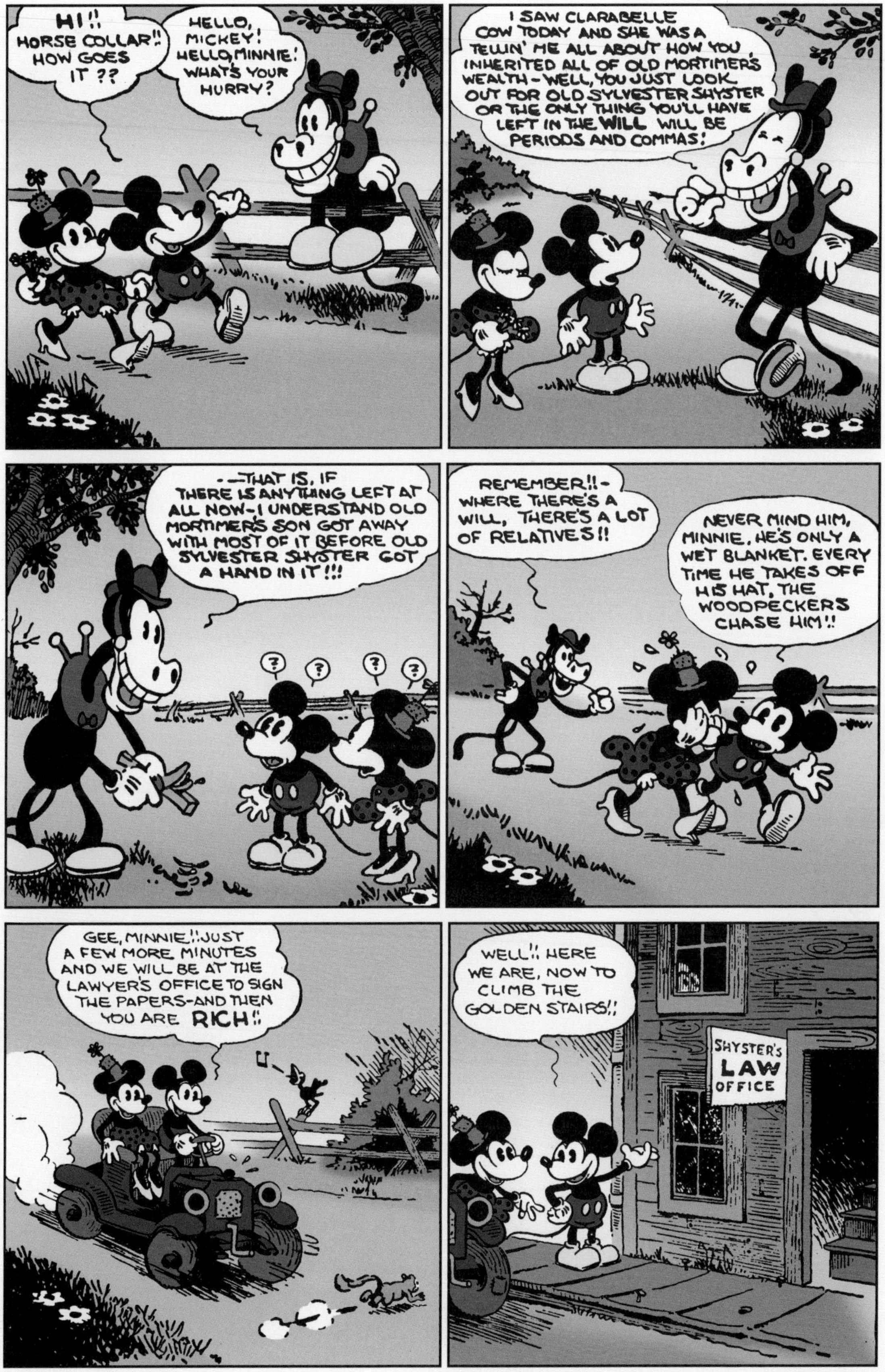
HI!! HORSE COLLAR!! HOW GOES IT ??
HELLO, MICKEY! HELLO, MINNIE! WHAT'S YOUR HURRY?
I SAW CLARABELLE COW TODAY AND SHE WAS A TELLIN' ME ALL ABOUT HOW YOU INHERITED ALL OF OLD MORTIMER'S WEALTH - WELL, YOU JUST LOOK OUT FOR OLD SYLVESTER SHYSTER OR THE ONLY THING YOU'LL HAVE LEFT IN THE WILL WILL BE PERIODS AND COMMAS!
--THAT IS, IF THERE IS ANYTHING LEFT AT ALL NOW - I UNDERSTAND OLD MORTIMER'S SON GOT AWAY WITH MOST OF IT BEFORE OLD SYLVESTER SHYSTER GOT A HAND IN IT!!!
REMEMBER!! - WHERE THERE'S A WILL, THERE'S A LOT OF RELATIVES!!
NEVER MIND HIM, MINNIE. HE'S ONLY A WET BLANKET. EVERY TIME HE TAKES OFF HIS HAT, THE WOODPECKERS CHASE HIM!!
GEE, MINNIE!! JUST A FEW MORE MINUTES AND WE WILL BE AT THE LAWYER'S OFFICE TO SIGN THE PAPERS-AND THEN YOU ARE RICH!!
WELL!! HERE WE ARE, NOW TO CLIMB THE GOLDEN STAIRS!!
SHYSTER'S LAW OFFICE

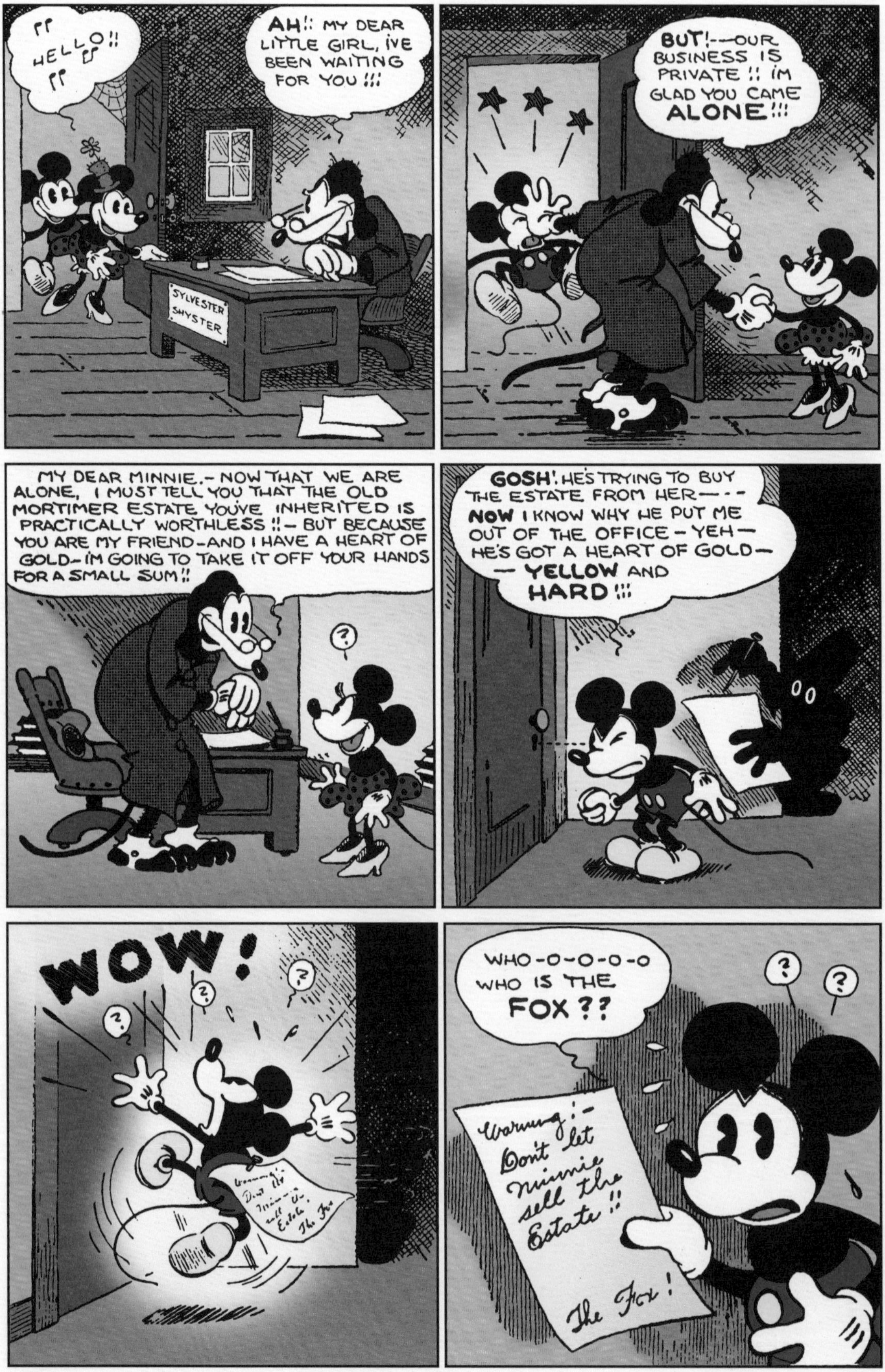
"HELLO!!"
AH!! MY DEAR LITTLE GIRL, I'VE BEEN WAITING FOR YOU!!!
SYLVESTER SHYSTER
BUT!--OUR BUSINESS IS PRIVATE!! I'M GLAD YOU CAME ALONE!!!
MY DEAR MINNIE.- NOW THAT WE ARE ALONE, I MUST TELL YOU THAT THE OLD MORTIMER ESTATE YOU'VE INHERITED IS PRACTICALLY WORTHLESS!!- BUT BECAUSE YOU ARE MY FRIEND-AND I HAVE A HEART OF GOLD-I'M GOING TO TAKE IT OFF YOUR HANDS FOR A SMALL SUM!!
GOSH! HE'S TRYING TO BUY THE ESTATE FROM HER--- NOW I KNOW WHY HE PUT ME OUT OF THE OFFICE - YEH - HE'S GOT A HEART OF GOLD- - YELLOW AND HARD!!!
WOW!
WHO-O-O-O-O WHO IS THE FOX??
Warning!- Don't let minnie sell the Estate!! The Fox!

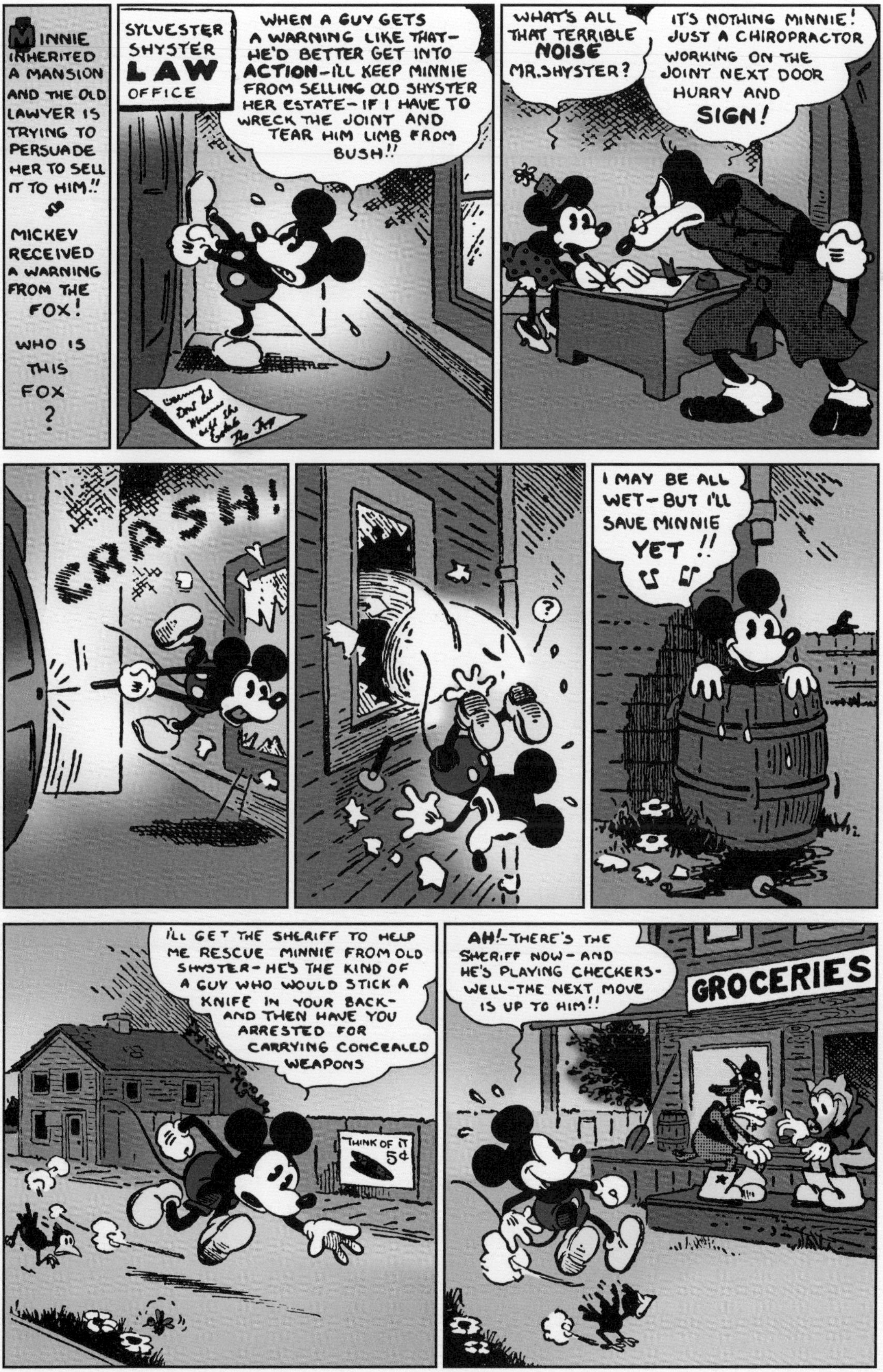
MINNIE INHERITED A MANSION AND THE OLD LAWYER IS TRYING TO PERSUADE HER TO SELL IT TO HIM!!
MICKEY RECEIVED A WARNING FROM THE FOX!
WHO IS THIS FOX ?
SYLVESTER SHYSTER LAW OFFICE
WHEN A GUY GETS A WARNING LIKE THAT— HE'D BETTER GET INTO ACTION—I'LL KEEP MINNIE FROM SELLING OLD SHYSTER HER ESTATE—IF I HAVE TO WRECK THE JOINT AND TEAR HIM LIMB FROM BUSH!!
WHAT'S ALL THAT TERRIBLE NOISE MR. SHYSTER?
IT'S NOTHING MINNIE! JUST A CHIROPRACTOR WORKING ON THE JOINT NEXT DOOR HURRY AND SIGN!
CRASH!
?
I MAY BE ALL WET—BUT I'LL SAVE MINNIE YET!!
I'LL GET THE SHERIFF TO HELP ME RESCUE MINNIE FROM OLD SHYSTER—HE'S THE KIND OF A GUY WHO WOULD STICK A KNIFE IN YOUR BACK— AND THEN HAVE YOU ARRESTED FOR CARRYING CONCEALED WEAPONS
THINK OF IT 5¢
AH!—THERE'S THE SHERIFF NOW—AND HE'S PLAYING CHECKERS— WELL—THE NEXT MOVE IS UP TO HIM!!
GROCERIES

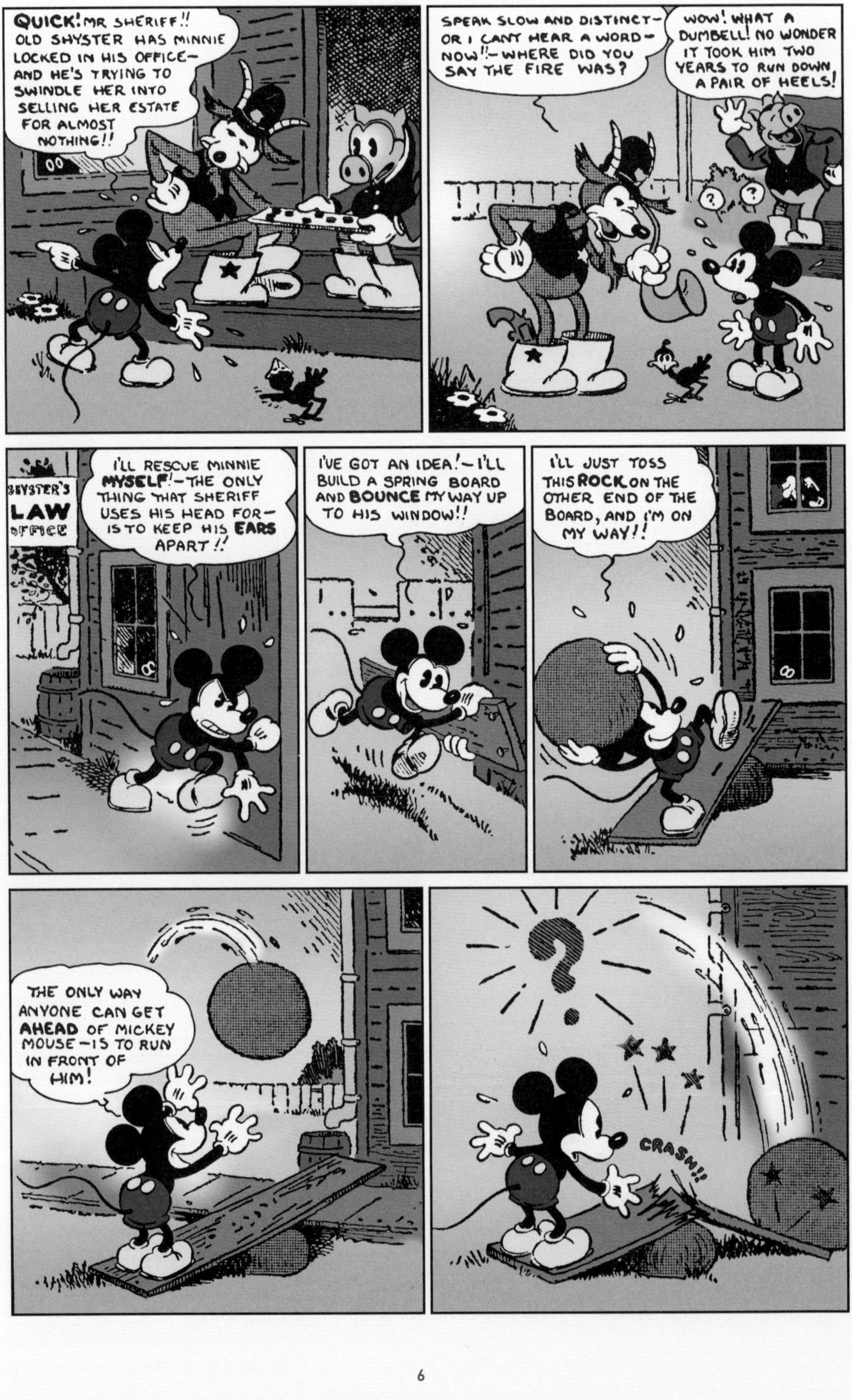
QUICK! MR SHERIFF!! OLD SHYSTER HAS MINNIE LOCKED IN HIS OFFICE— AND HE'S TRYING TO SWINDLE HER INTO SELLING HER ESTATE FOR ALMOST NOTHING!!
SPEAK SLOW AND DISTINCT— OR I CANT HEAR A WORD— NOW!!—WHERE DID YOU SAY THE FIRE WAS?
WOW! WHAT A DUMBELL! NO WONDER IT TOOK HIM TWO YEARS TO RUN DOWN A PAIR OF HEELS!
SHYSTER'S LAW OFFICE
I'LL RESCUE MINNIE MYSELF!—THE ONLY THING THAT SHERIFF USES HIS HEAD FOR— IS TO KEEP HIS EARS APART!!
I'VE GOT AN IDEA!—I'LL BUILD A SPRING BOARD AND BOUNCE MY WAY UP TO HIS WINDOW!!
I'LL JUST TOSS THIS ROCK ON THE OTHER END OF THE BOARD, AND I'M ON MY WAY!!
THE ONLY WAY ANYONE CAN GET AHEAD OF MICKEY MOUSE—IS TO RUN IN FRONT OF HIM!
CRASH!!

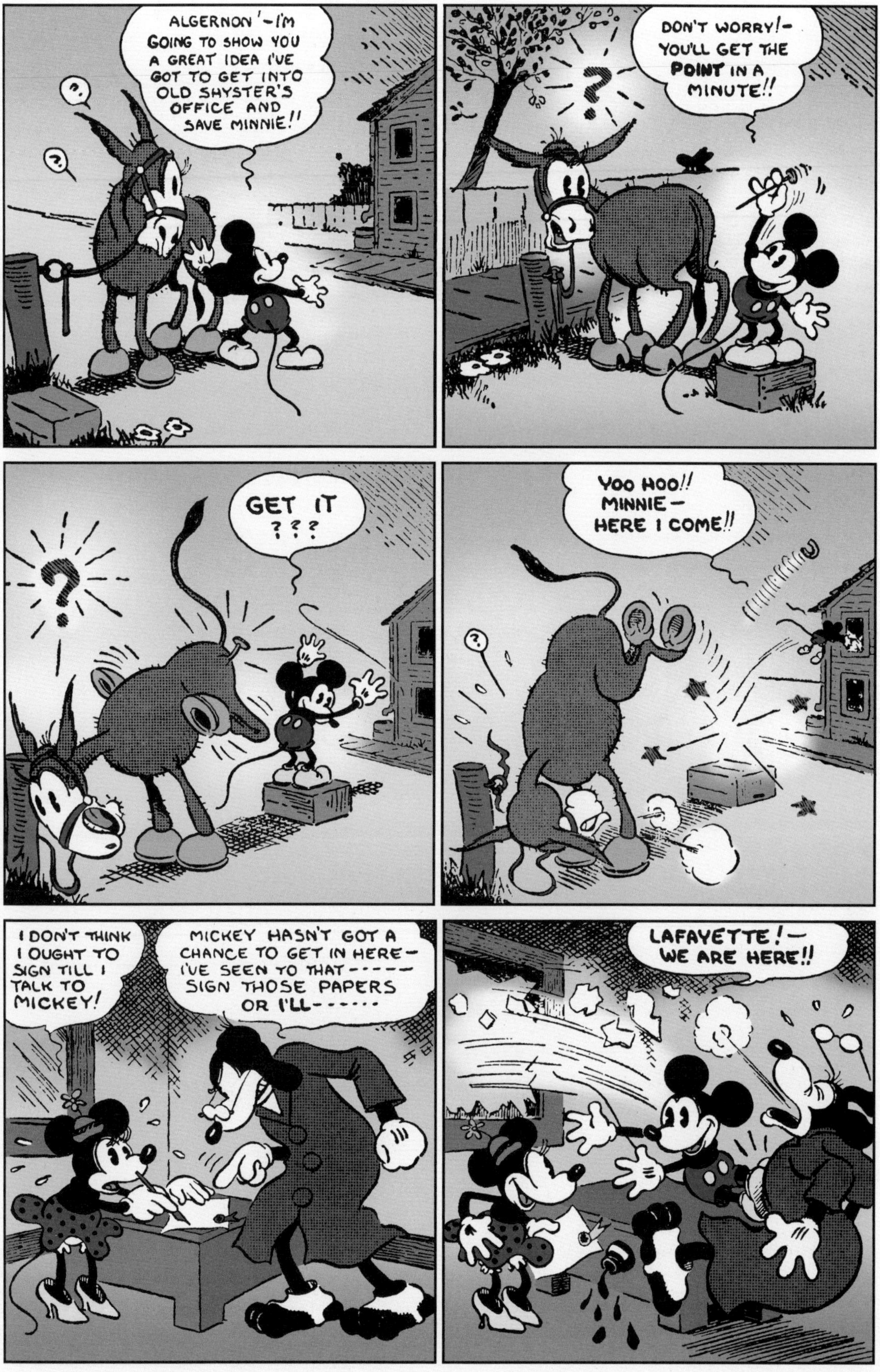

?
?
ALGERNON'—I'M GOING TO SHOW YOU A GREAT IDEA I'VE GOT TO GET INTO OLD SHYSTER'S OFFICE AND SAVE MINNIE!!
?
DON'T WORRY!—YOU'LL GET THE POINT IN A MINUTE!!
?
GET IT ???
YOO HOO!! MINNIE—HERE I COME!!
?
I DON'T THINK I OUGHT TO SIGN TILL I TALK TO MICKEY!
MICKEY HASN'T GOT A CHANCE TO GET IN HERE—I'VE SEEN TO THAT-----SIGN THOSE PAPERS OR I'LL-----
LAFAYETTE!—WE ARE HERE!!

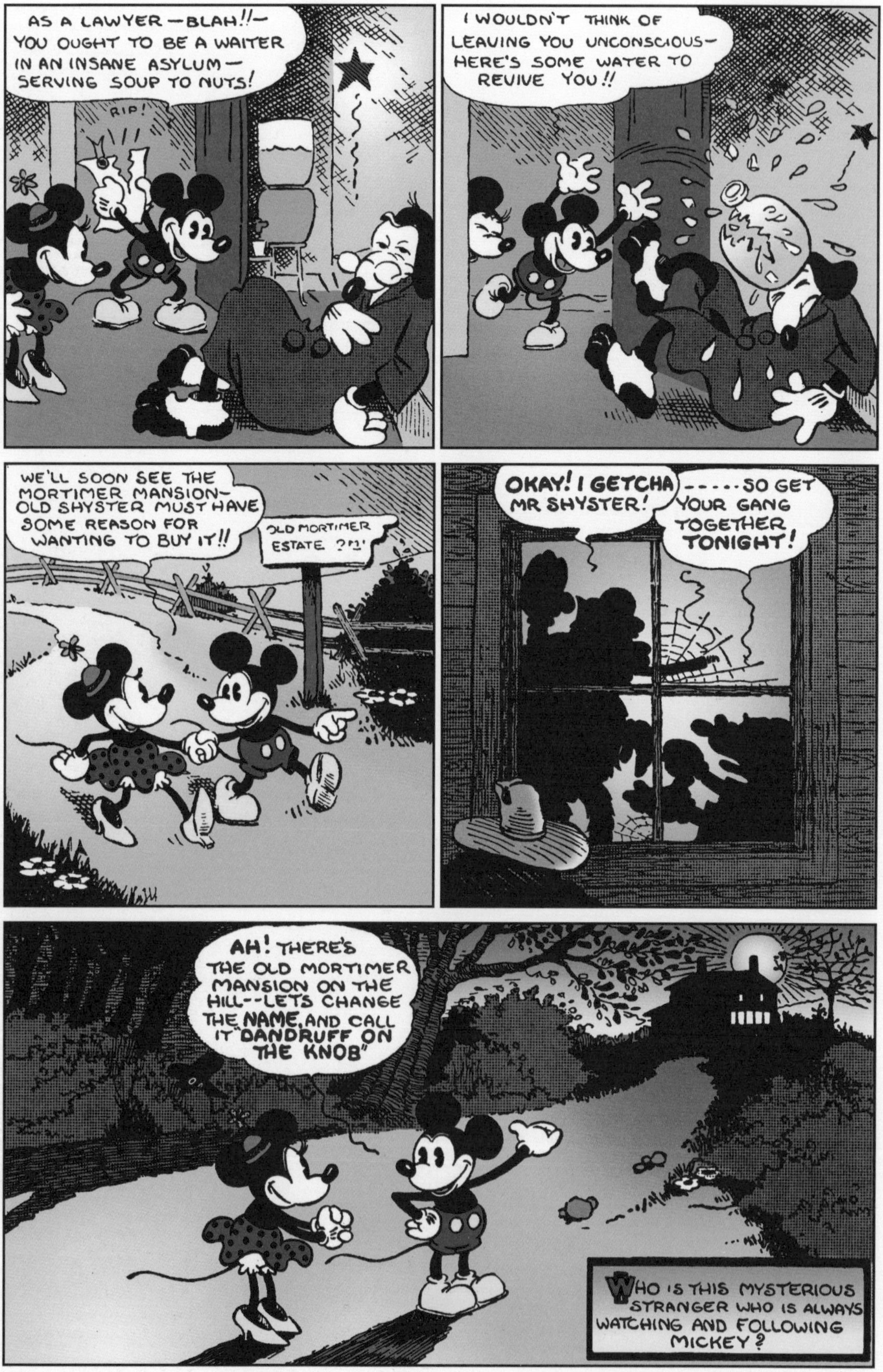
AS A LAWYER—BLAH!!—
YOU OUGHT TO BE A WAITER IN AN INSANE ASYLUM—SERVING SOUP TO NUTS!
RIP!
I WOULDN'T THINK OF LEAVING YOU UNCONSCIOUS—HERE'S SOME WATER TO REVIVE YOU!!
WE'LL SOON SEE THE MORTIMER MANSION—OLD SHYSTER MUST HAVE SOME REASON FOR WANTING TO BUY IT!!
OLD MORTIMER ESTATE
OKAY! I GETCHA MR SHYSTER!
----SO GET YOUR GANG TOGETHER TONIGHT!
AH! THERE'S THE OLD MORTIMER MANSION ON THE HILL--LETS CHANGE THE NAME, AND CALL IT "DANDRUFF ON THE KNOB"
WHO IS THIS MYSTERIOUS STRANGER WHO IS ALWAYS WATCHING AND FOLLOWING MICKEY?

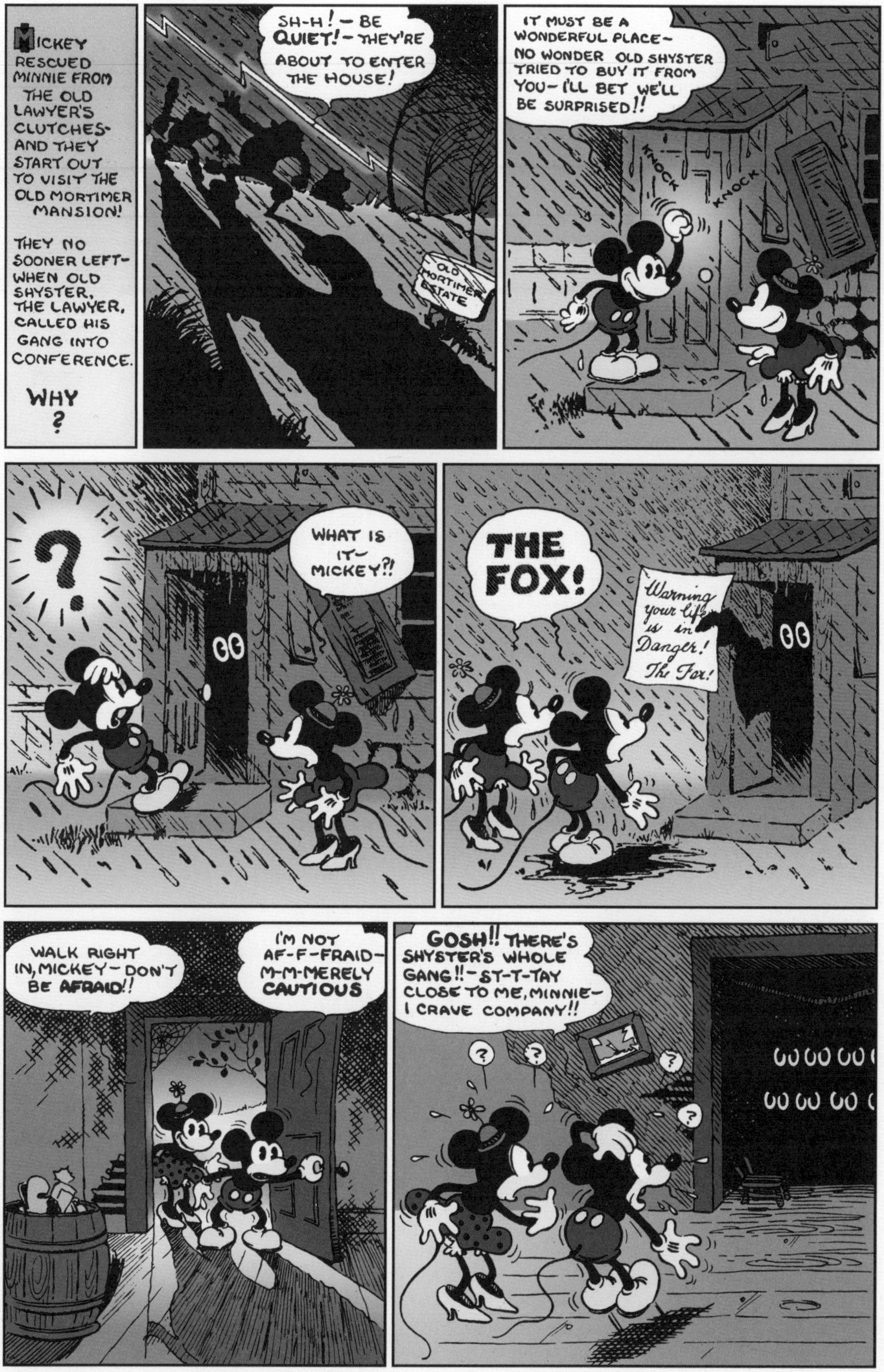
MICKEY RESCUED MINNIE FROM THE OLD LAWYER'S CLUTCHES- AND THEY START OUT TO VISIT THE OLD MORTIMER MANSION!
THEY NO SOONER LEFT- WHEN OLD SHYSTER, THE LAWYER, CALLED HIS GANG INTO CONFERENCE.
WHY ?
SH-H! - BE QUIET! - THEY'RE ABOUT TO ENTER THE HOUSE!
OLD MORTIMER ESTATE
IT MUST BE A WONDERFUL PLACE- NO WONDER OLD SHYSTER TRIED TO BUY IT FROM YOU- I'LL BET WE'LL BE SURPRISED!!
KNOCK
KNOCK
?
WHAT IS IT- MICKEY?!
THE FOX!
Warning your life is in Danger! The Fox!
WALK RIGHT IN, MICKEY- DON'T BE AFRAID!!
I'M NOT AF-F-FRAID- M-M-MERELY CAUTIOUS
GOSH!! THERE'S SHYSTER'S WHOLE GANG!!-ST-T-TAY CLOSE TO ME, MINNIE- I CRAVE COMPANY!!

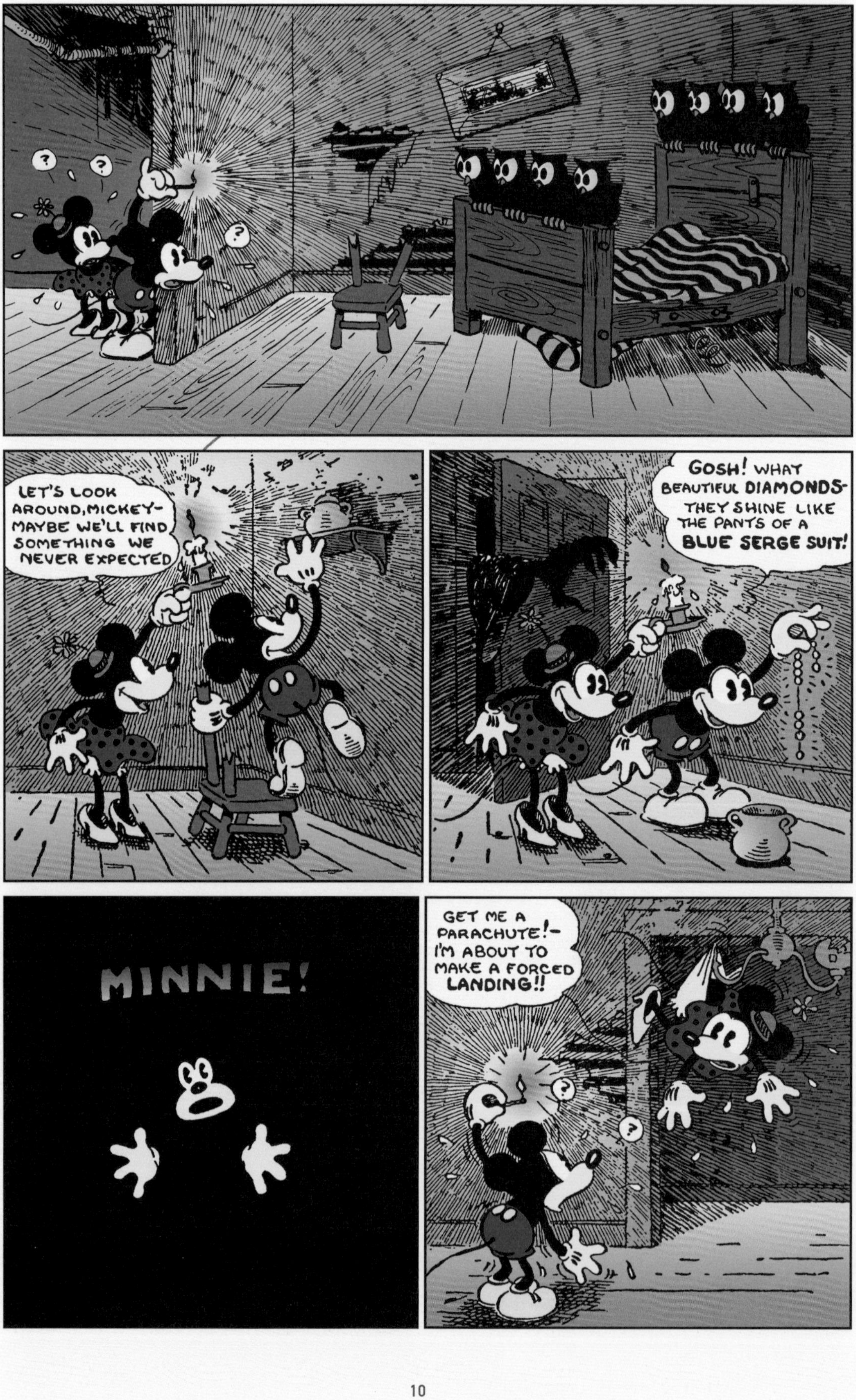
LET'S LOOK AROUND, MICKEY— MAYBE WE'LL FIND SOMETHING WE NEVER EXPECTED
GOSH! WHAT BEAUTIFUL DIAMONDS— THEY SHINE LIKE THE PANTS OF A BLUE SERGE SUIT!
MINNIE!
GET ME A PARACHUTE!— I'M ABOUT TO MAKE A FORCED LANDING!!

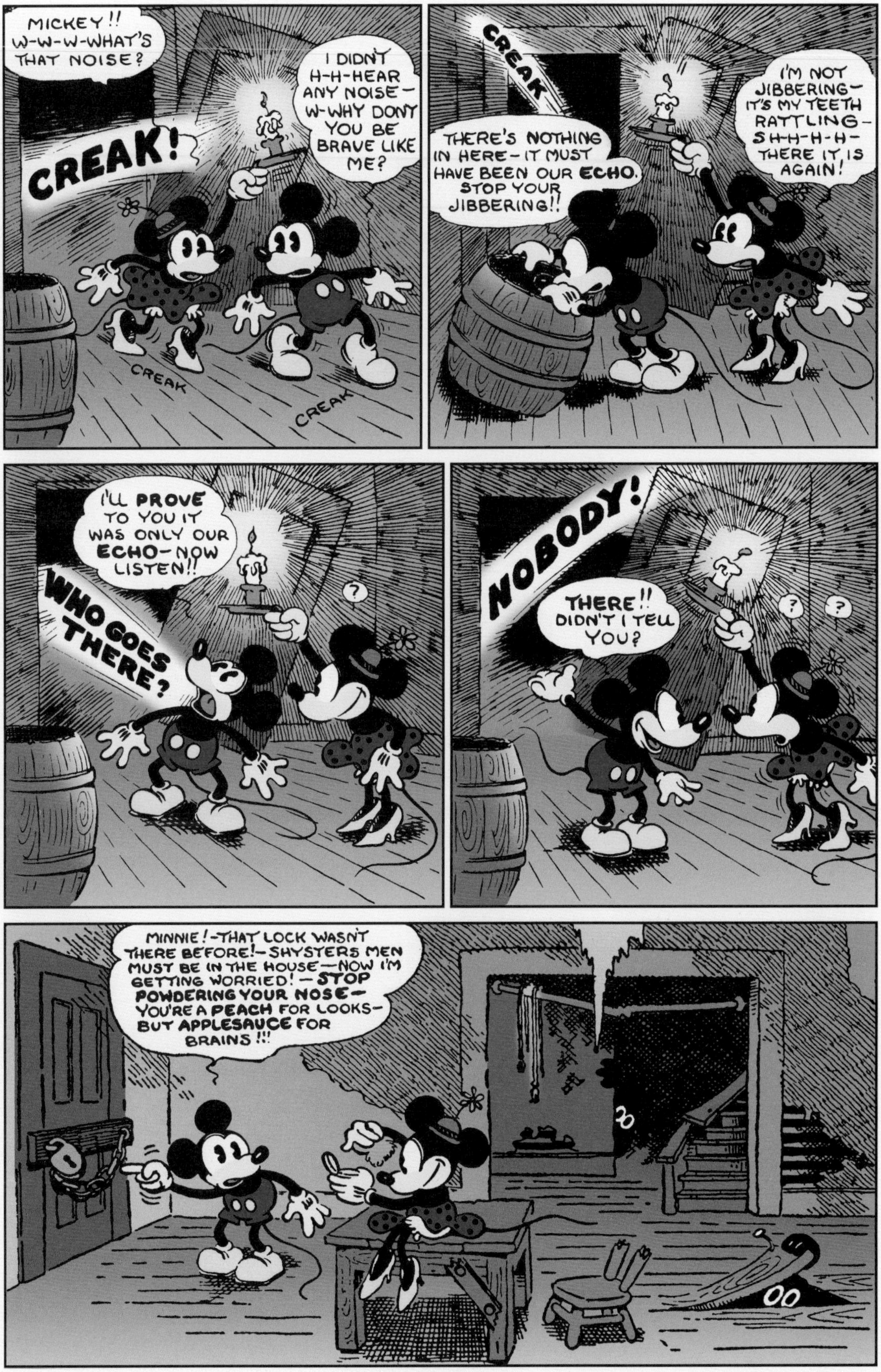
MICKEY!! W-W-W-WHAT'S THAT NOISE?
I DIDN'T H-H-HEAR ANY NOISE— W-WHY DON'T YOU BE BRAVE LIKE ME?
CREAK!
CREAK
CREAK
CREAK
THERE'S NOTHING IN HERE—IT MUST HAVE BEEN OUR ECHO. STOP YOUR JIBBERING!!
I'M NOT JIBBERING— IT'S MY TEETH RATTLING— S-H-H-H-H— THERE IT IS AGAIN!
I'LL PROVE TO YOU IT WAS ONLY OUR ECHO—NOW LISTEN!!
WHO GOES THERE?
?
NOBODY!
THERE!! DIDN'T I TELL YOU?
? ?
MINNIE!—THAT LOCK WASN'T THERE BEFORE!—SHYSTERS MEN MUST BE IN THE HOUSE—NOW I'M GETTING WORRIED!—STOP POWDERING YOUR NOSE— YOU'RE A PEACH FOR LOOKS— BUT APPLESAUCE FOR BRAINS!!!

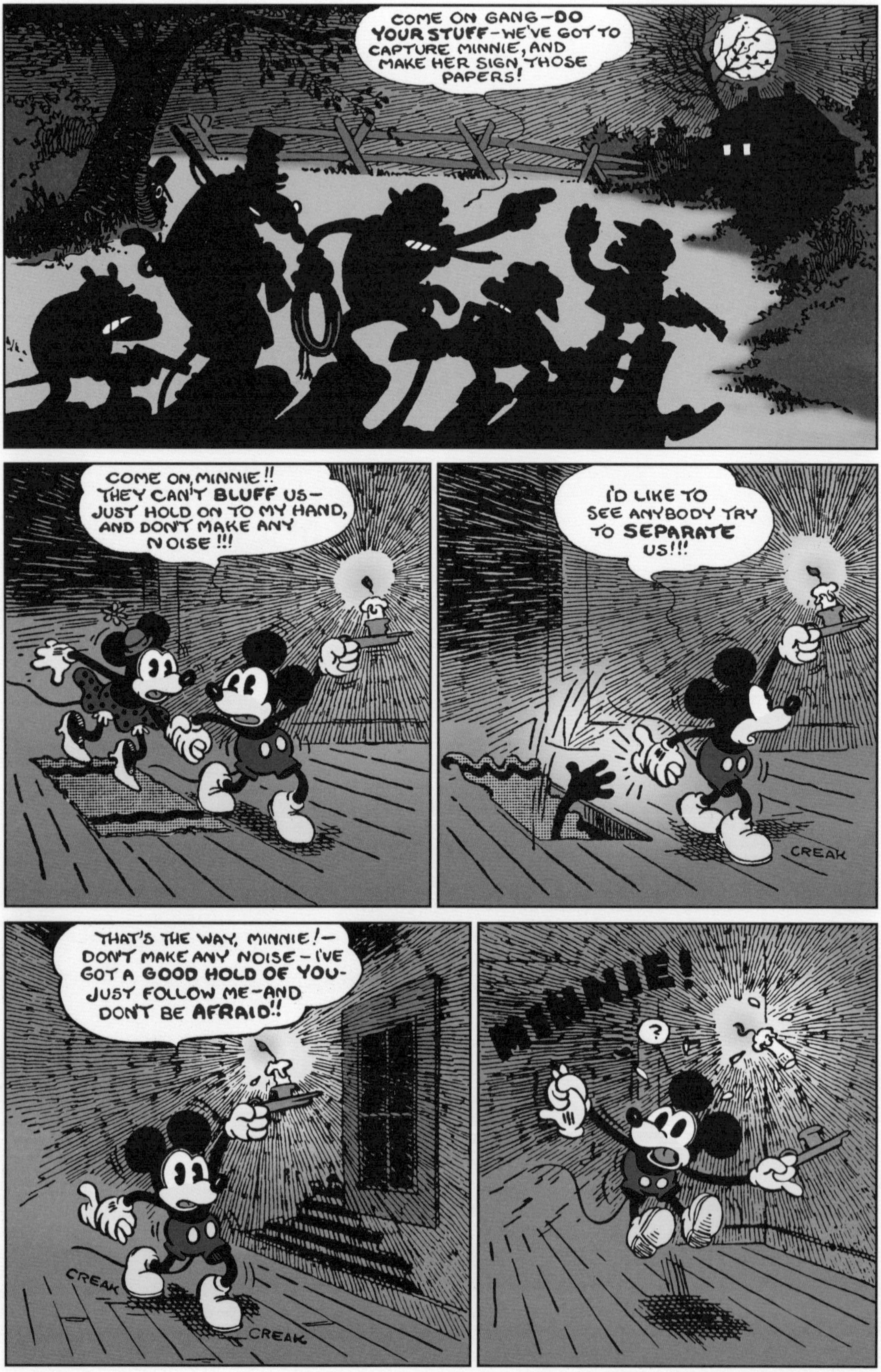
COME ON GANG—DO YOUR STUFF—WE'VE GOT TO CAPTURE MINNIE, AND MAKE HER SIGN THOSE PAPERS!
COME ON, MINNIE!! THEY CAN'T BLUFF US—JUST HOLD ON TO MY HAND, AND DON'T MAKE ANY NOISE!!!
I'D LIKE TO SEE ANYBODY TRY TO SEPARATE US!!!
CREAK
THAT'S THE WAY, MINNIE!—DON'T MAKE ANY NOISE—I'VE GOT A GOOD HOLD OF YOU—JUST FOLLOW ME—AND DON'T BE AFRAID!!
CREAK
CREAK
MINNIE!

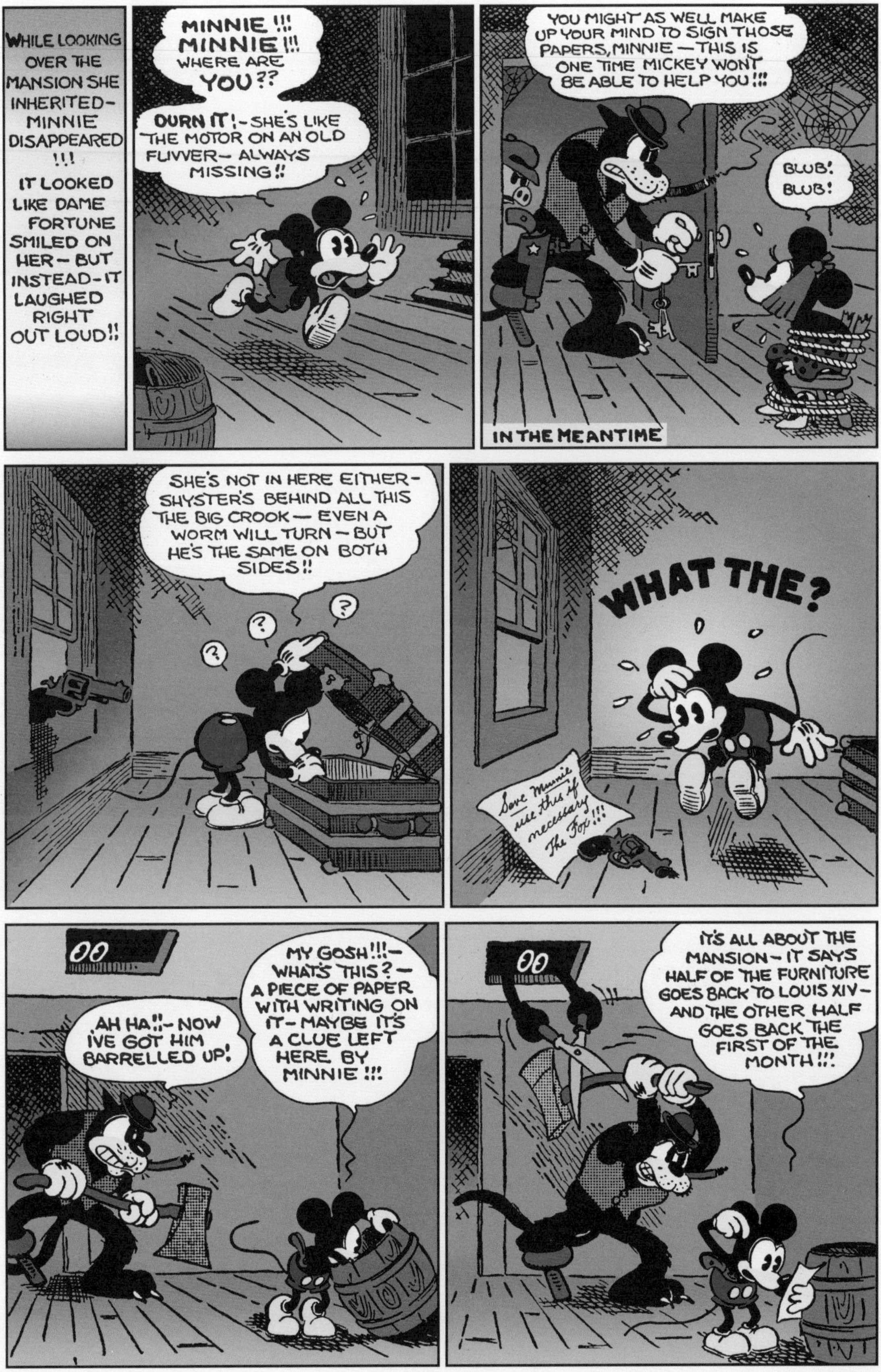
WHILE LOOKING OVER THE MANSION SHE INHERITED- MINNIE DISAPPEARED !!! IT LOOKED LIKE DAME FORTUNE SMILED ON HER- BUT INSTEAD- IT LAUGHED RIGHT OUT LOUD!!
MINNIE !!! MINNIE !!! WHERE ARE YOU??
DURN IT!- SHE'S LIKE THE MOTOR ON AN OLD FLIVVER- ALWAYS MISSING!!
IN THE MEANTIME
YOU MIGHT AS WELL MAKE UP YOUR MIND TO SIGN THOSE PAPERS, MINNIE — THIS IS ONE TIME MICKEY WONT BE ABLE TO HELP YOU!!!
BLUB! BLUB!
SHE'S NOT IN HERE EITHER- SHYSTER'S BEHIND ALL THIS THE BIG CROOK — EVEN A WORM WILL TURN — BUT HE'S THE SAME ON BOTH SIDES!!
WHAT THE?
Save Minnie use this if necessary The Fox!!!
AH HA!!- NOW I'VE GOT HIM BARRELLED UP!
MY GOSH!!!- WHAT'S THIS?- A PIECE OF PAPER WITH WRITING ON IT- MAYBE IT'S A CLUE LEFT HERE BY MINNIE!!!
IT'S ALL ABOUT THE MANSION- IT SAYS HALF OF THE FURNITURE GOES BACK TO LOUIS XIV- AND THE OTHER HALF GOES BACK THE FIRST OF THE MONTH!!!

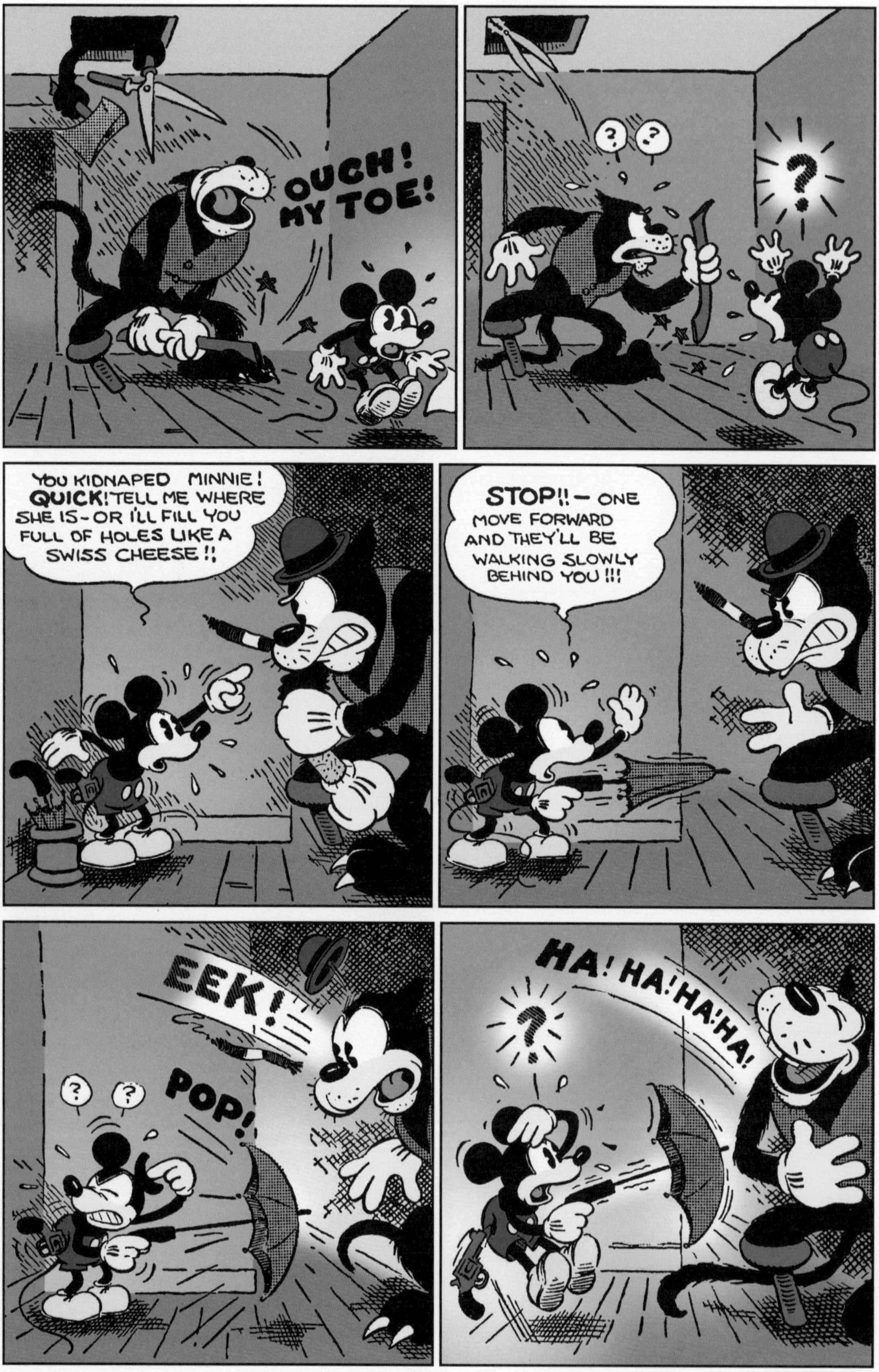
OUCH! MY TOE!
YOU KIDNAPED MINNIE! QUICK! TELL ME WHERE SHE IS-OR I'LL FILL YOU FULL OF HOLES LIKE A SWISS CHEESE!!
STOP!!-ONE MOVE FORWARD AND THEY'LL BE WALKING SLOWLY BEHIND YOU!!!
EEK!
POP!
HA! HA! HA! HA! HA!

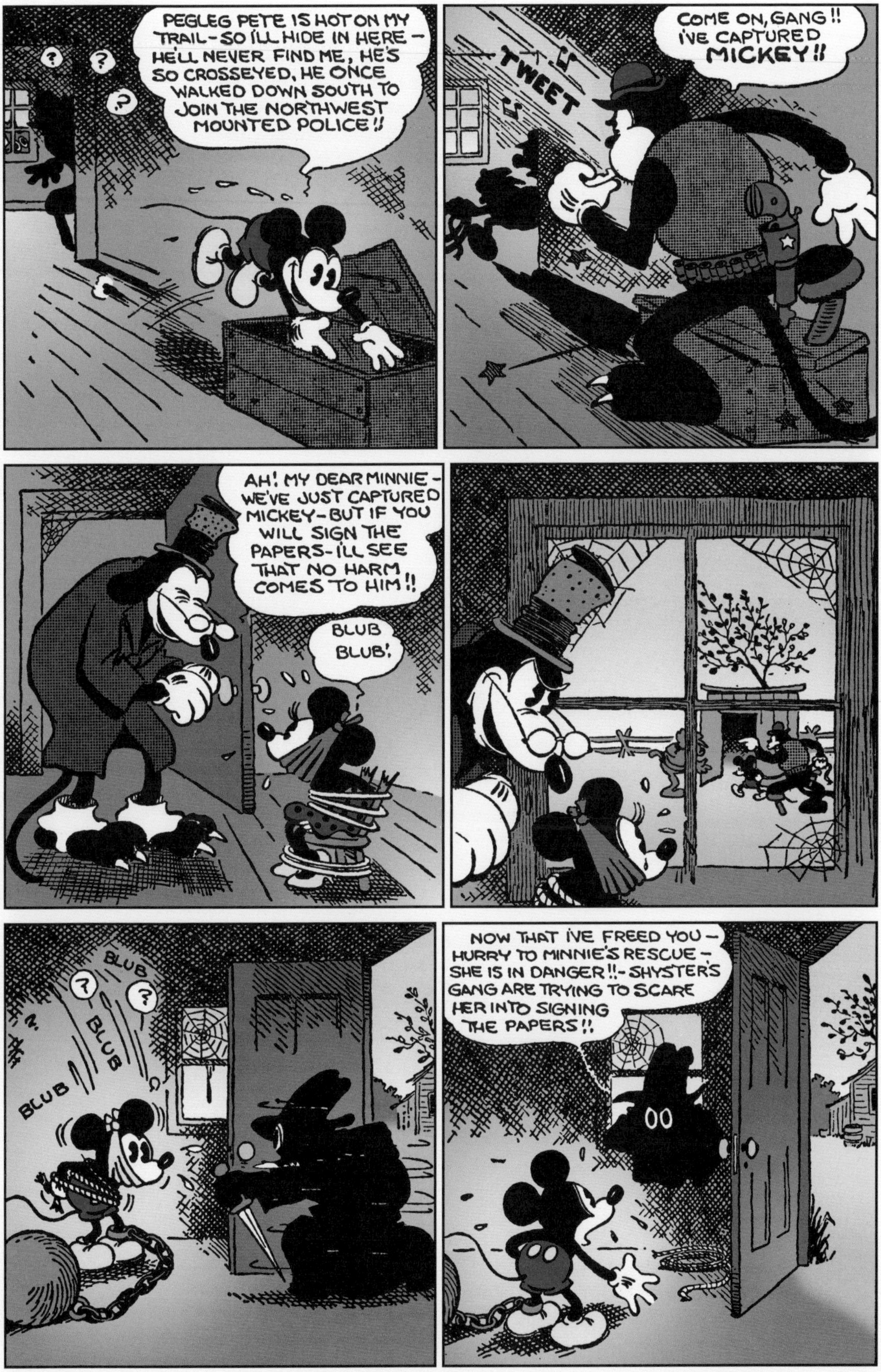
PEGLEG PETE IS HOT ON MY TRAIL-SO I'LL HIDE IN HERE-HE'LL NEVER FIND ME, HE'S SO CROSSEYED, HE ONCE WALKED DOWN SOUTH TO JOIN THE NORTHWEST MOUNTED POLICE!!
TWEET
COME ON, GANG!! I'VE CAPTURED MICKEY!!
AH! MY DEAR MINNIE-WE'VE JUST CAPTURED MICKEY-BUT IF YOU WILL SIGN THE PAPERS-I'LL SEE THAT NO HARM COMES TO HIM!!
BLUB BLUB!
BLUB
BLUB
BLUB
BLUB
NOW THAT I'VE FREED YOU-HURRY TO MINNIE'S RESCUE-SHE IS IN DANGER!!-SHYSTER'S GANG ARE TRYING TO SCARE HER INTO SIGNING THE PAPERS!!

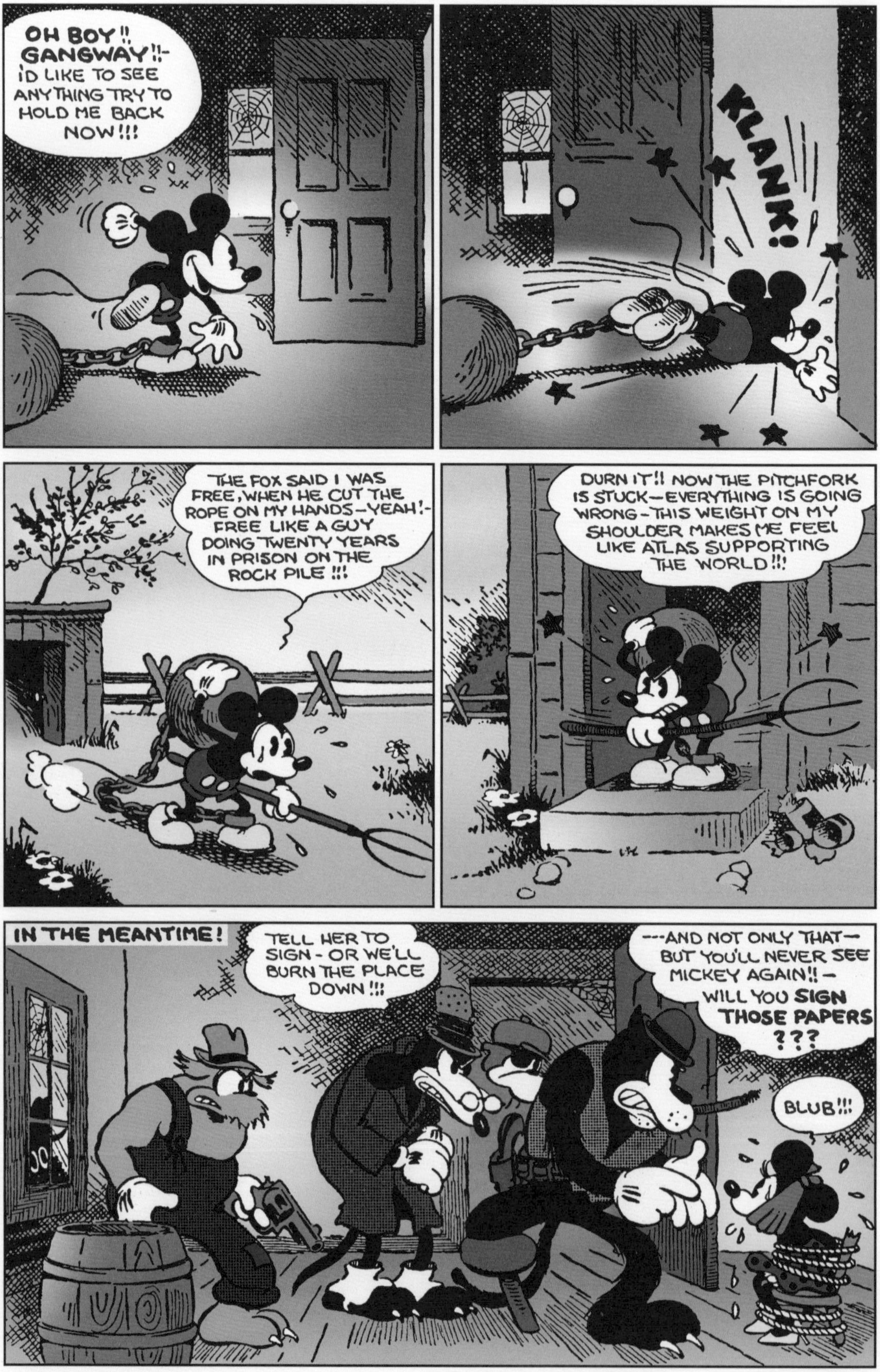
OH BOY!! GANGWAY!!- I'D LIKE TO SEE ANYTHING TRY TO HOLD ME BACK NOW!!!
KLANK!
THE FOX SAID I WAS FREE, WHEN HE CUT THE ROPE ON MY HANDS—YEAH!- FREE LIKE A GUY DOING TWENTY YEARS IN PRISON ON THE ROCK PILE!!!
DURN IT!! NOW THE PITCHFORK IS STUCK—EVERYTHING IS GOING WRONG—THIS WEIGHT ON MY SHOULDER MAKES ME FEEL LIKE ATLAS SUPPORTING THE WORLD!!!
IN THE MEANTIME!
TELL HER TO SIGN - OR WE'LL BURN THE PLACE DOWN!!!
---AND NOT ONLY THAT— BUT YOU'LL NEVER SEE MICKEY AGAIN!! — WILL YOU SIGN THOSE PAPERS???
BLUB!!!

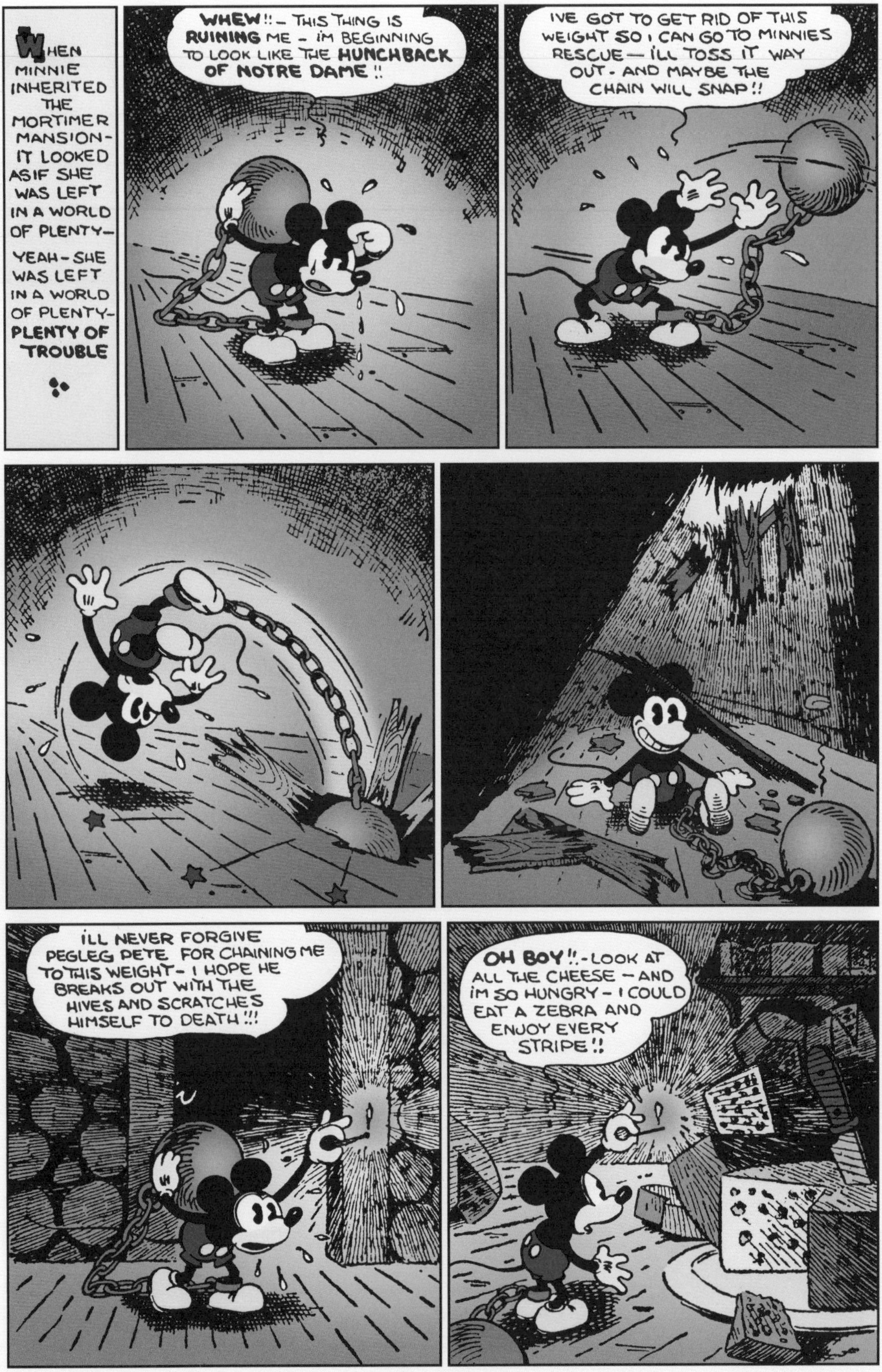
WHEN MINNIE INHERITED THE MORTIMER MANSION- IT LOOKED ASIF SHE WAS LEFT IN A WORLD OF PLENTY-
YEAH- SHE WAS LEFT IN A WORLD OF PLENTY- PLENTY OF TROUBLE
WHEW!! - THIS THING IS RUINING ME - IM BEGINNING TO LOOK LIKE THE HUNCHBACK OF NOTRE DAME!!
IVE GOT TO GET RID OF THIS WEIGHT SO I CAN GO TO MINNIES RESCUE— ILL TOSS IT WAY OUT - AND MAYBE THE CHAIN WILL SNAP!!
ILL NEVER FORGIVE PEGLEG PETE FOR CHAINING ME TO THIS WEIGHT- I HOPE HE BREAKS OUT WITH THE HIVES AND SCRATCHES HIMSELF TO DEATH!!!
OH BOY!!.-LOOK AT ALL THE CHEESE - AND IM SO HUNGRY - I COULD EAT A ZEBRA AND ENJOY EVERY STRIPE!!

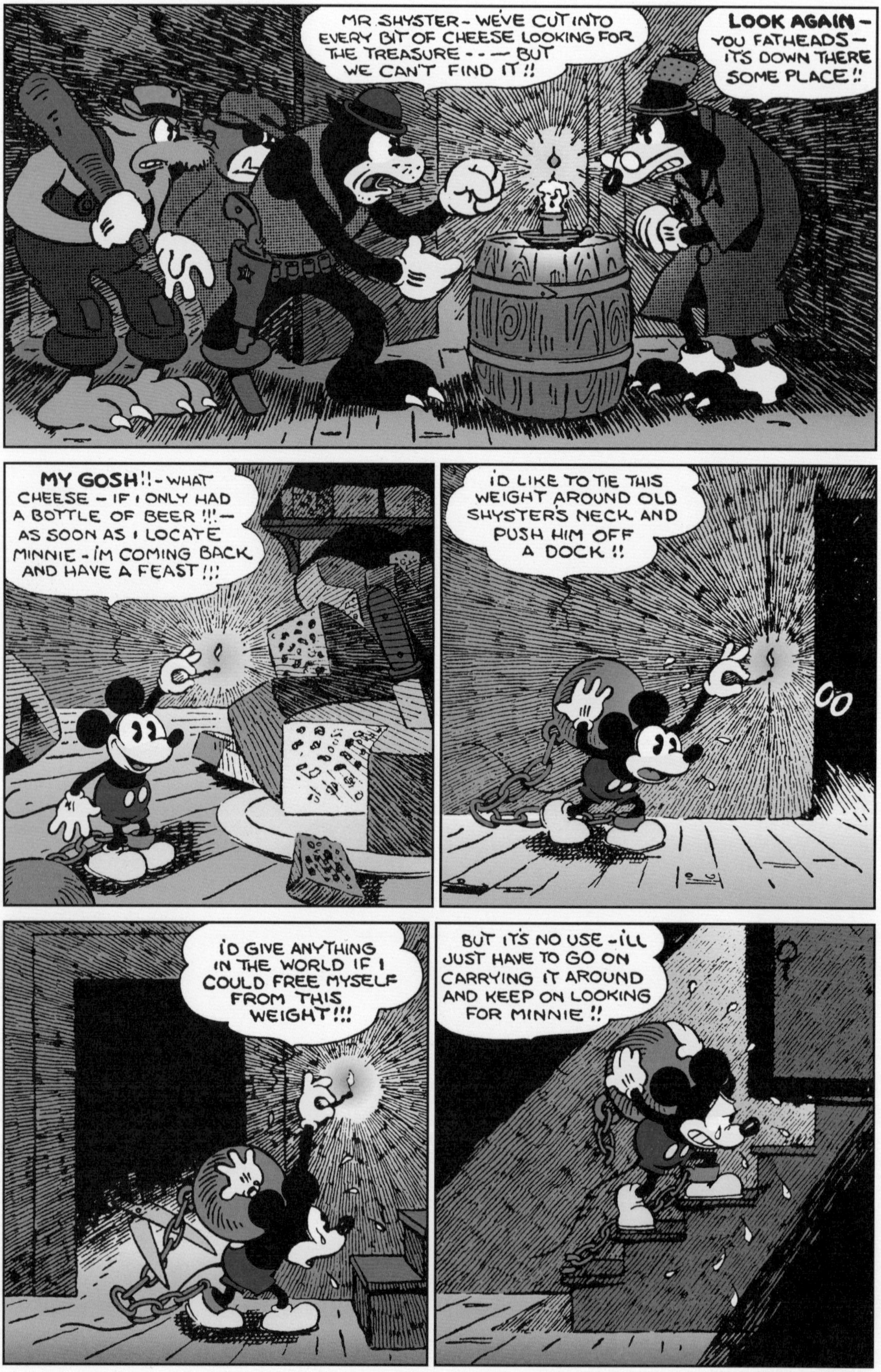
MR. SHYSTER - WE'VE CUT INTO EVERY BIT OF CHEESE LOOKING FOR THE TREASURE - - - BUT WE CAN'T FIND IT !!
LOOK AGAIN - YOU FATHEADS - IT'S DOWN THERE SOME PLACE !!
MY GOSH !! - WHAT CHEESE - IF I ONLY HAD A BOTTLE OF BEER !!! - AS SOON AS I LOCATE MINNIE - I'M COMING BACK AND HAVE A FEAST !!!
I'D LIKE TO TIE THIS WEIGHT AROUND OLD SHYSTER'S NECK AND PUSH HIM OFF A DOCK !!
OO
I'D GIVE ANYTHING IN THE WORLD IF I COULD FREE MYSELF FROM THIS WEIGHT !!!
BUT IT'S NO USE - I'LL JUST HAVE TO GO ON CARRYING IT AROUND AND KEEP ON LOOKING FOR MINNIE !!

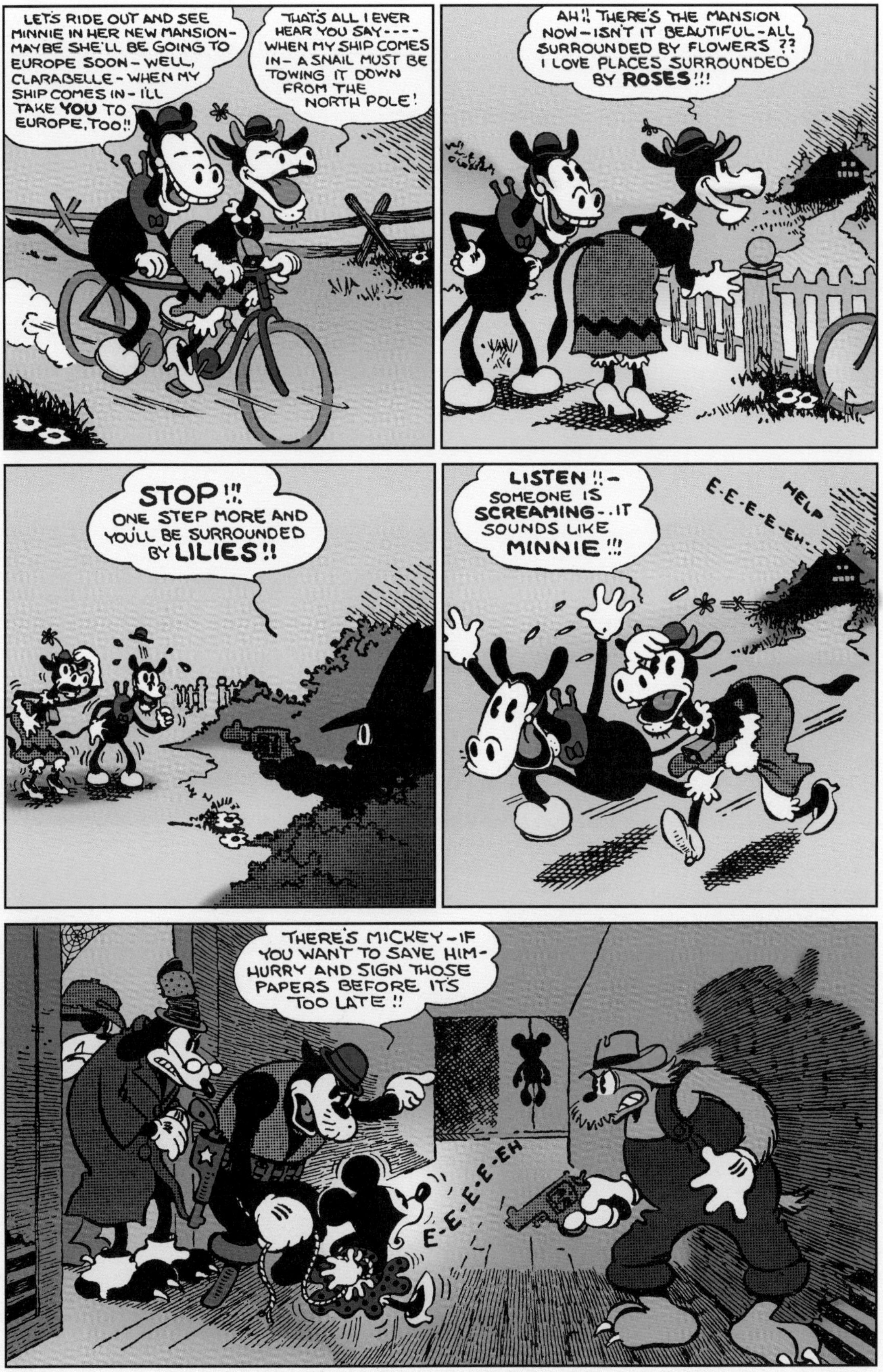
LET'S RIDE OUT AND SEE MINNIE IN HER NEW MANSION- MAYBE SHE'LL BE GOING TO EUROPE SOON - WELL, CLARABELLE - WHEN MY SHIP COMES IN - I'LL TAKE **YOU** TO EUROPE, TOO!!
THAT'S ALL I EVER HEAR YOU SAY---- WHEN MY SHIP COMES IN - A SNAIL MUST BE TOWING IT DOWN FROM THE NORTH POLE!
AH!! THERE'S THE MANSION NOW - ISN'T IT BEAUTIFUL - ALL SURROUNDED BY FLOWERS?? I LOVE PLACES SURROUNDED BY **ROSES**!!!
STOP!!! ONE STEP MORE AND YOU'LL BE SURROUNDED BY **LILIES**!!
LISTEN!! - SOMEONE IS **SCREAMING**-.IT SOUNDS LIKE **MINNIE**!!!
E-E-E-E-EH--
HELP
THERE'S MICKEY - IF YOU WANT TO SAVE HIM - HURRY AND SIGN THOSE PAPERS BEFORE IT'S TOO LATE!!
E-E-E-E-EH

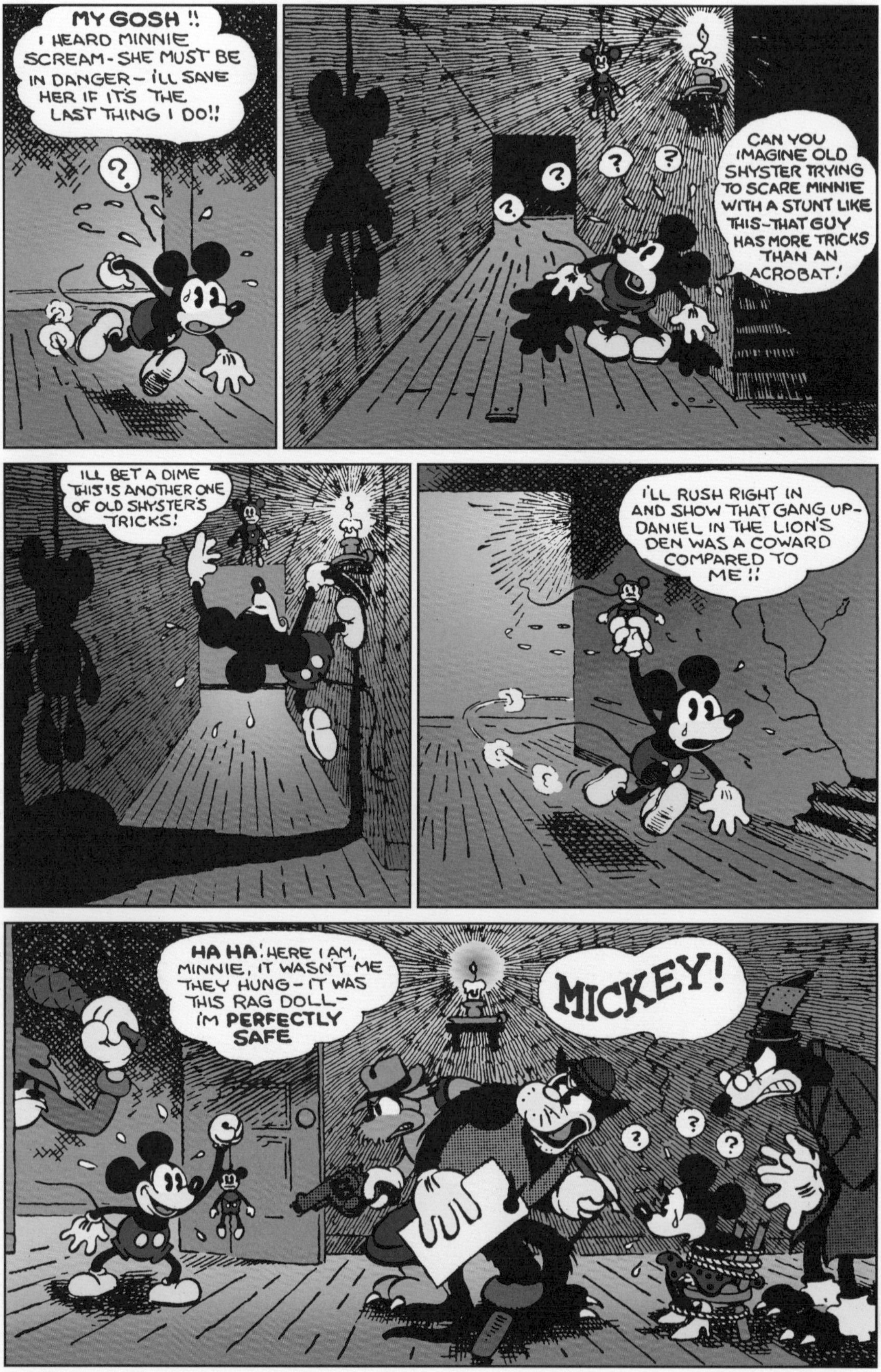
MY GOSH !! I HEARD MINNIE SCREAM - SHE MUST BE IN DANGER - I'LL SAVE HER IF IT'S THE LAST THING I DO!!
CAN YOU IMAGINE OLD SHYSTER TRYING TO SCARE MINNIE WITH A STUNT LIKE THIS - THAT GUY HAS MORE TRICKS THAN AN ACROBAT!
I'LL BET A DIME THIS IS ANOTHER ONE OF OLD SHYSTER'S TRICKS!
I'LL RUSH RIGHT IN AND SHOW THAT GANG UP - DANIEL IN THE LION'S DEN WAS A COWARD COMPARED TO ME!!
HA HA! HERE I AM, MINNIE, IT WASN'T ME THEY HUNG - IT WAS THIS RAG DOLL - I'M PERFECTLY SAFE
MICKEY!

WHEN MINNIE INHERITED OLD MORTIMER'S MANSION IT LOOKED LIKE EVERYTHING WAS GOING TO BE ROSY
- BUT -
OLD SHYSTER AND HIS GANG ARE PROVING TO BE A LOT OF THORNS!
LEMME AT HIM! HE MAY BE THE APPLE OF MINNIE'S EYE—BUT HE'LL SOON BE APPLESAUCE!
HERE I AM MINNIE! I TOLD YOU I'D COME OUT ALL RIGHT!
I FOOLED THEM AGAIN! OLD SHYSTER AND HIS GANG ARE GOOD EXAMPLES OF HOW LONG MEN CAN LIVE WITHOUT BRAINS!
I'LL GET YOU AWAY FROM OLD SHYSTER'S GANG, MINNIE! THOSE GUYS ARE SO DANGEROUS THEY OUGHT TO CARRY RED LANTERNS!
NOW THAT WE'RE AWAY FROM THAT HOUSE NOTHING IN THE WORLD CAN SEPARATE US!

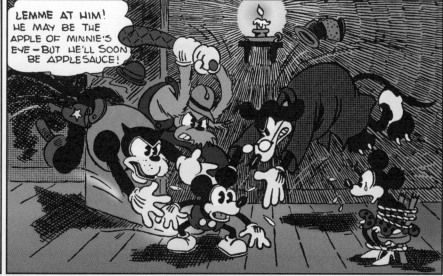

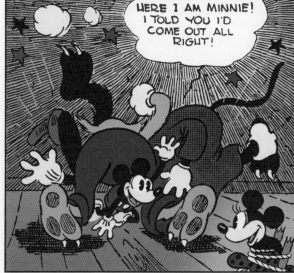

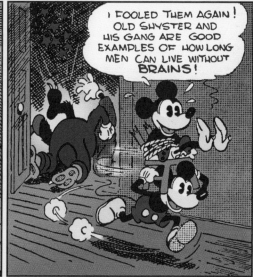

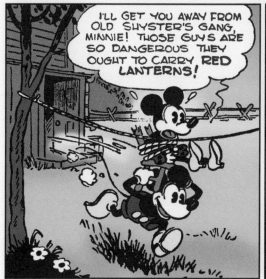

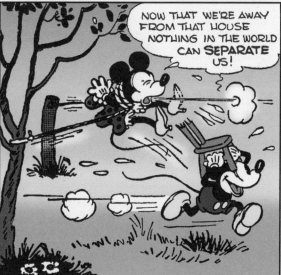

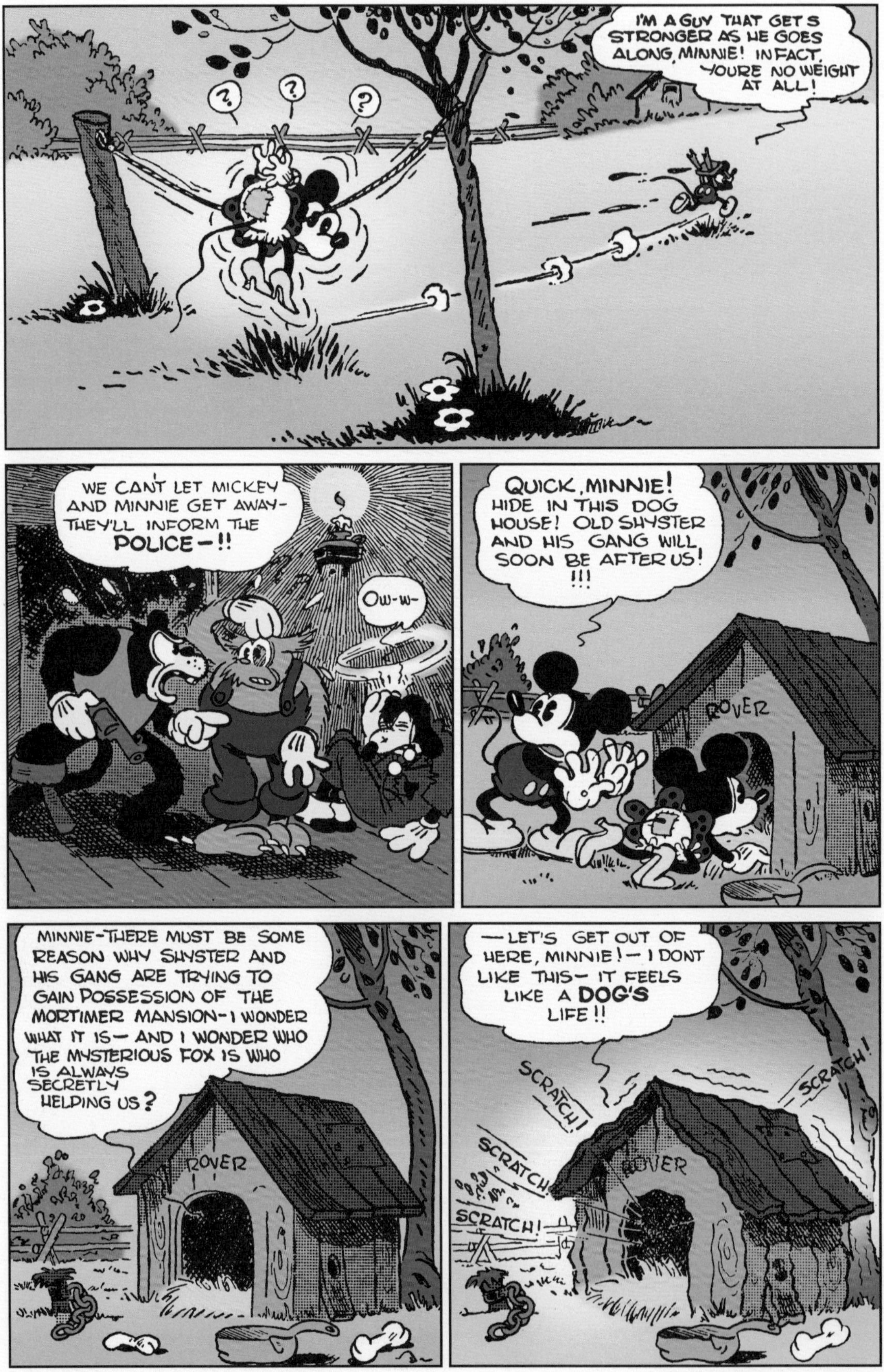
?
?
?
I'M A GUY THAT GETS STRONGER AS HE GOES ALONG, MINNIE! IN FACT, YOU'RE NO WEIGHT AT ALL!
WE CAN'T LET MICKEY AND MINNIE GET AWAY- THEY'LL INFORM THE POLICE-!!
OW-W-
QUICK, MINNIE! HIDE IN THIS DOG HOUSE! OLD SHYSTER AND HIS GANG WILL SOON BE AFTER US! !!!
ROVER
MINNIE-THERE MUST BE SOME REASON WHY SHYSTER AND HIS GANG ARE TRYING TO GAIN POSSESSION OF THE MORTIMER MANSION-I WONDER WHAT IT IS- AND I WONDER WHO THE MYSTERIOUS FOX IS WHO IS ALWAYS SECRETLY HELPING US?
ROVER
—LET'S GET OUT OF HERE, MINNIE!— I DONT LIKE THIS— IT FEELS LIKE A DOG'S LIFE!!
SCRATCH!
SCRATCH!
SCRATCH
SCRATCH!
ROVER

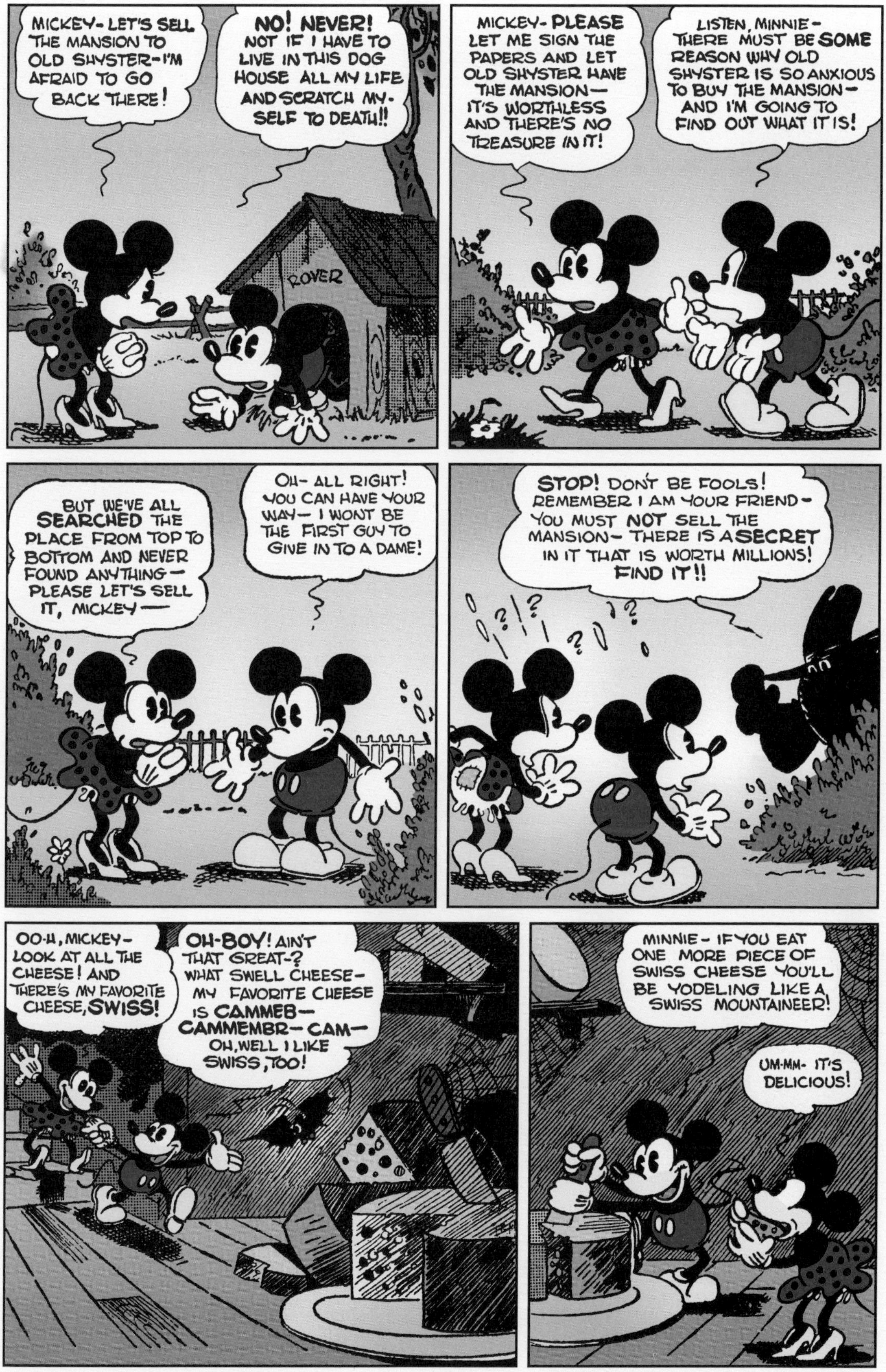
MICKEY- LET'S SELL THE MANSION TO OLD SHYSTER-I'M AFRAID TO GO BACK THERE!
NO! NEVER! NOT IF I HAVE TO LIVE IN THIS DOG HOUSE ALL MY LIFE AND SCRATCH MY-SELF TO DEATH!!
ROVER
MICKEY- PLEASE LET ME SIGN THE PAPERS AND LET OLD SHYSTER HAVE THE MANSION— IT'S WORTHLESS AND THERE'S NO TREASURE IN IT!
LISTEN, MINNIE- THERE MUST BE SOME REASON WHY OLD SHYSTER IS SO ANXIOUS TO BUY THE MANSION- AND I'M GOING TO FIND OUT WHAT IT IS!
BUT WE'VE ALL SEARCHED THE PLACE FROM TOP TO BOTTOM AND NEVER FOUND ANYTHING- PLEASE LET'S SELL IT, MICKEY—
OH- ALL RIGHT! YOU CAN HAVE YOUR WAY- I WONT BE THE FIRST GUY TO GIVE IN TO A DAME!
STOP! DON'T BE FOOLS! REMEMBER I AM YOUR FRIEND- YOU MUST NOT SELL THE MANSION- THERE IS A SECRET IN IT THAT IS WORTH MILLIONS! FIND IT!!
OO-H, MICKEY- LOOK AT ALL THE CHEESE! AND THERE'S MY FAVORITE CHEESE, SWISS!
OH-BOY! AIN'T THAT GREAT-? WHAT SWELL CHEESE- MY FAVORITE CHEESE IS CAMMEB— CAMMEMBR— CAM— OH, WELL I LIKE SWISS, TOO!
MINNIE- IF YOU EAT ONE MORE PIECE OF SWISS CHEESE YOU'LL BE YODELING LIKE A SWISS MOUNTAINEER!
UM-MM- IT'S DELICIOUS!

U-UH—WHAT'S THIS? I NEARLY CHOKED ON IT! IT'S -IT'S A PAPER OR SOMETHING—!!!
WHY—IT'S A MAP! IT SHOWS THE LOCATION OF—OF A SECRET GOLD MINE YOUR UNCLE MORTIMER OWNS OUT WEST IN DEATH VALLEY!!! THIS MUST BE WHAT OLD SHYSTER AND HIS GANG ARE AFTER!!
OH—MICKEY!
OH, BOY! WASN'T THAT A LUCKY BREAK—FINDING THIS MAP SHOWING YOUR UNCLE'S GOLD MINE! WE'RE OFF FOR DEATH VALLEY!
SO!
GIMME THAT MAP—OR THIS WILL BE YOUR DEATH VALLEY!!
EEK!
HA! HA! ME HEARTIES—WE'RE OFF FOR DEATH VALLEY! WE'LL LEAVE YOU LOCKED IN THIS CELLAR—DEATH VALLEY IS NO PLACE FOR YOU TWO—YOU MIGHT GET SUN-BURNED!!
!
COME BACK AND FIGHT LIKE MEN—YOU COWARDS!!!
OH MICKEY—WHAT ARE WE GOING TO DO NOW?
IS THIS THE END?
WHO WILL EVER FIND THEM IN THIS DISMAL HOLE?

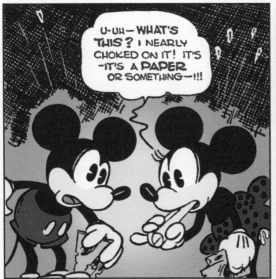

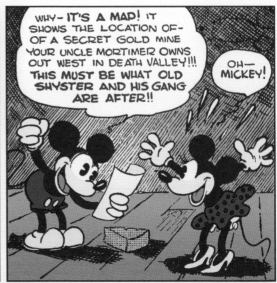

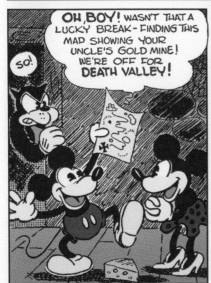

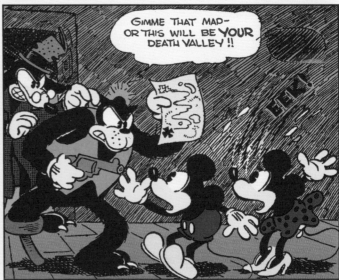

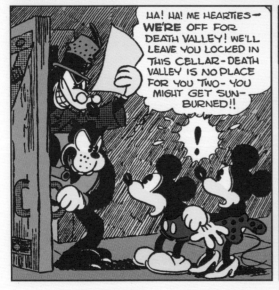

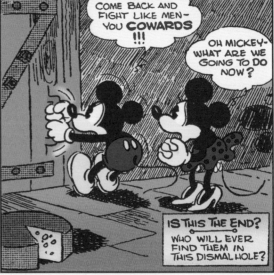

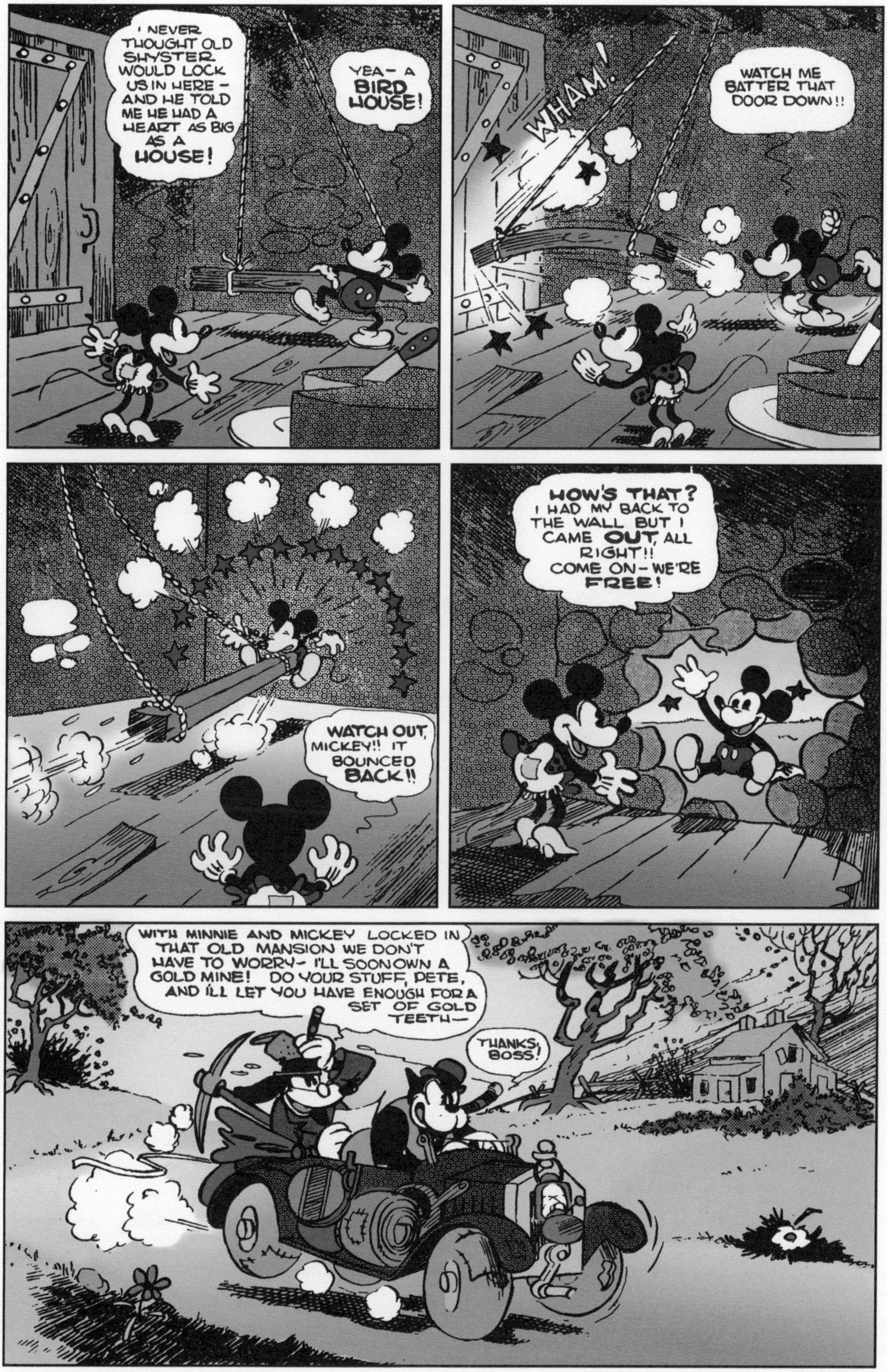
I NEVER THOUGHT OLD SHYSTER WOULD LOCK US IN HERE - AND HE TOLD ME HE HAD A HEART AS BIG AS A HOUSE!
YEA- A BIRD HOUSE!
WHAM!
WATCH ME BATTER THAT DOOR DOWN!!
WATCH OUT, MICKEY!! IT BOUNCED BACK!!
HOW'S THAT? I HAD MY BACK TO THE WALL BUT I CAME OUT, ALL RIGHT!! COME ON- WE'RE FREE!
WITH MINNIE AND MICKEY LOCKED IN THAT OLD MANSION WE DON'T HAVE TO WORRY- I'LL SOON OWN A GOLD MINE! DO YOUR STUFF, PETE, AND I'LL LET YOU HAVE ENOUGH FOR A SET OF GOLD TEETH—
THANKS, BOSS!

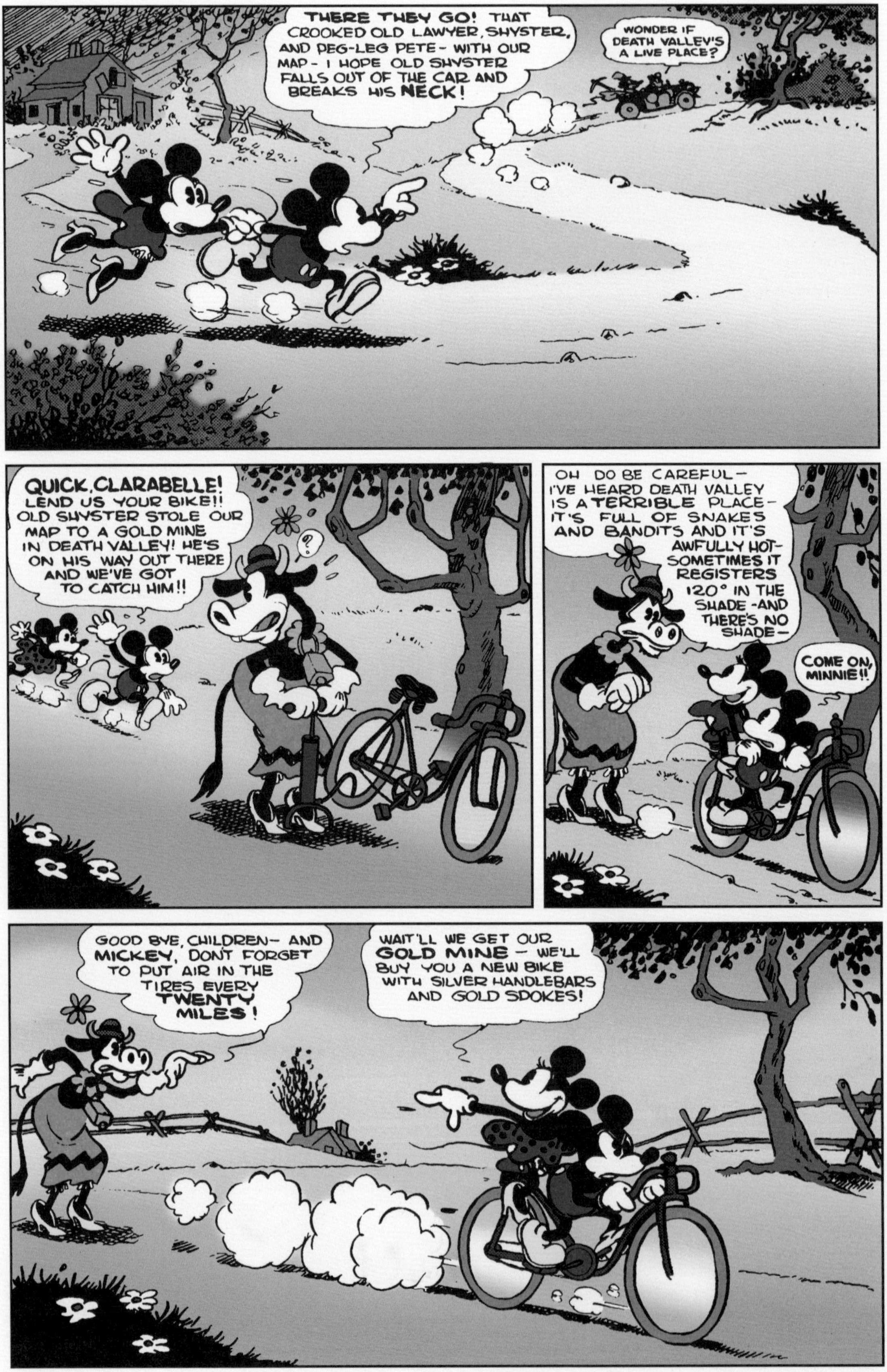
THERE THEY GO! THAT CROOKED OLD LAWYER, SHYSTER, AND PEG-LEG PETE - WITH OUR MAP - I HOPE OLD SHYSTER FALLS OUT OF THE CAR AND BREAKS HIS NECK!
WONDER IF DEATH VALLEY'S A LIVE PLACE?
QUICK, CLARABELLE! LEND US YOUR BIKE!! OLD SHYSTER STOLE OUR MAP TO A GOLD MINE IN DEATH VALLEY! HE'S ON HIS WAY OUT THERE AND WE'VE GOT TO CATCH HIM!!
?
OH DO BE CAREFUL - I'VE HEARD DEATH VALLEY IS A TERRIBLE PLACE - IT'S FULL OF SNAKES AND BANDITS AND IT'S AWFULLY HOT - SOMETIMES IT REGISTERS 120° IN THE SHADE - AND THERE'S NO SHADE -
COME ON, MINNIE!!
GOOD BYE, CHILDREN - AND MICKEY, DON'T FORGET TO PUT AIR IN THE TIRES EVERY TWENTY MILES!
WAIT'LL WE GET OUR GOLD MINE - WE'LL BUY YOU A NEW BIKE WITH SILVER HANDLEBARS AND GOLD SPOKES!

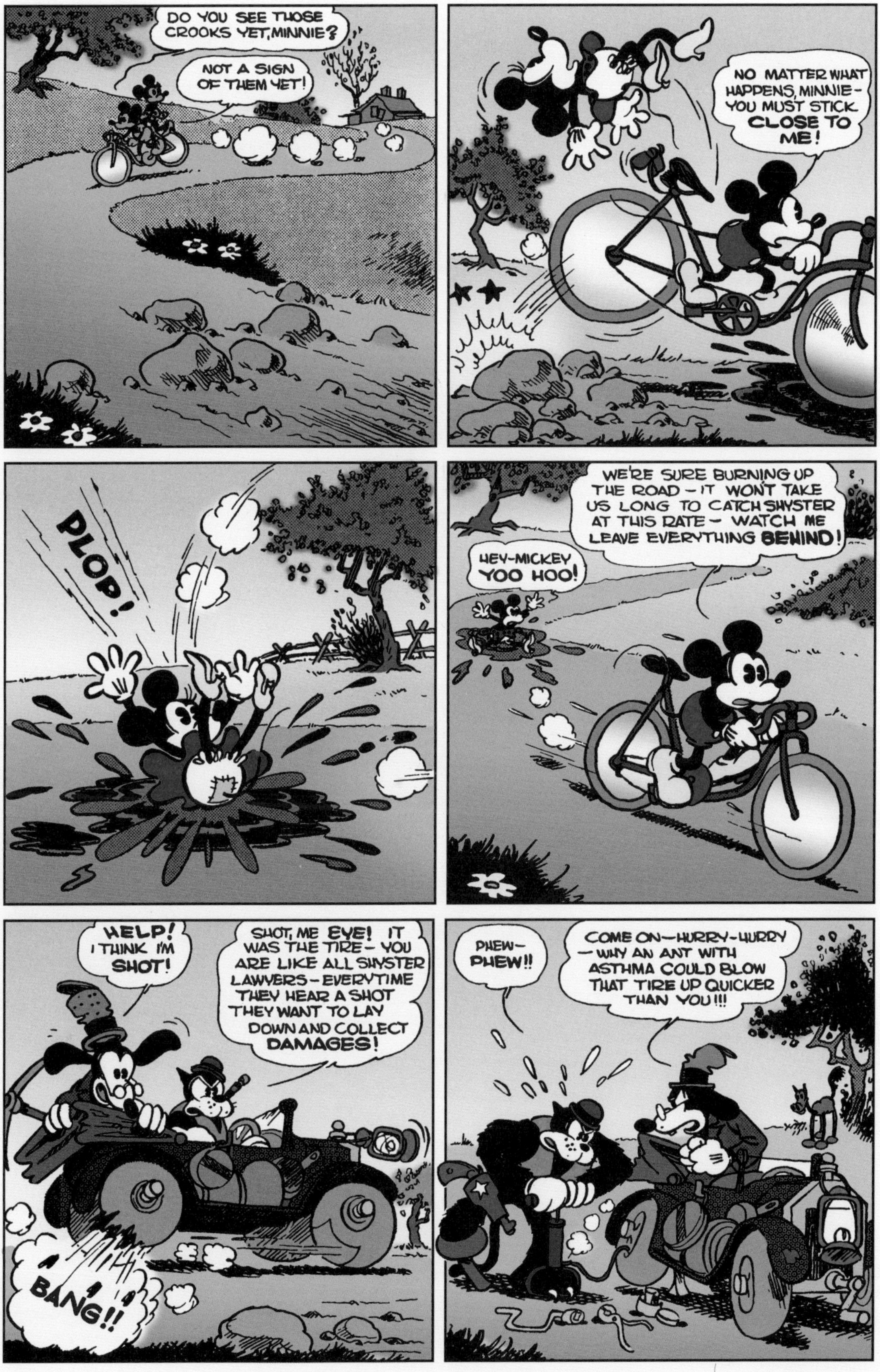
DO YOU SEE THOSE CROOKS YET, MINNIE?
NOT A SIGN OF THEM YET!
NO MATTER WHAT HAPPENS, MINNIE - YOU MUST STICK CLOSE TO ME!
PLOP!
WE'RE SURE BURNING UP THE ROAD - IT WON'T TAKE US LONG TO CATCH SHYSTER AT THIS RATE - WATCH ME LEAVE EVERYTHING BEHIND!
HEY-MICKEY YOO HOO!
HELP! I THINK I'M SHOT!
SHOT, ME EYE! IT WAS THE TIRE - YOU ARE LIKE ALL SHYSTER LAWYERS - EVERYTIME THEY HEAR A SHOT THEY WANT TO LAY DOWN AND COLLECT DAMAGES!
BANG!!
PHEW- PHEW!!
COME ON - HURRY - HURRY - WHY AN ANT WITH ASTHMA COULD BLOW THAT TIRE UP QUICKER THAN YOU!!!

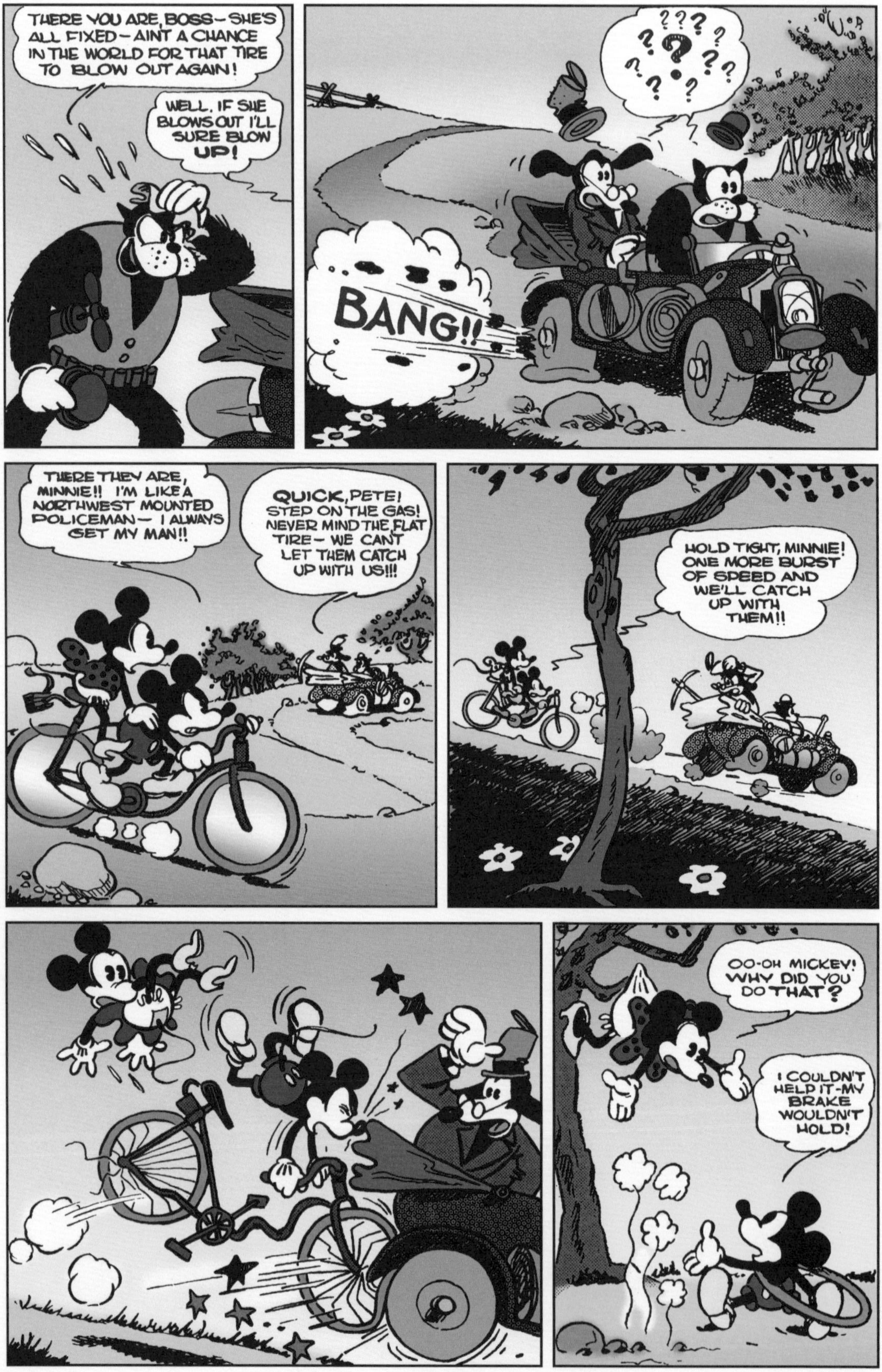
THERE YOU ARE, BOSS- SHE'S ALL FIXED- AINT A CHANCE IN THE WORLD FOR THAT TIRE TO BLOW OUT AGAIN!
WELL, IF SHE BLOWS OUT I'LL SURE BLOW UP!
???
BANG!!
THERE THEY ARE, MINNIE!! I'M LIKE A NORTHWEST MOUNTED POLICEMAN- I ALWAYS GET MY MAN!!
QUICK, PETE! STEP ON THE GAS! NEVER MIND THE FLAT TIRE- WE CAN'T LET THEM CATCH UP WITH US!!!
HOLD TIGHT, MINNIE! ONE MORE BURST OF SPEED AND WE'LL CATCH UP WITH THEM!!
OO-OH MICKEY! WHY DID YOU DO THAT?
I COULDN'T HELP IT-MY BRAKE WOULDN'T HOLD!

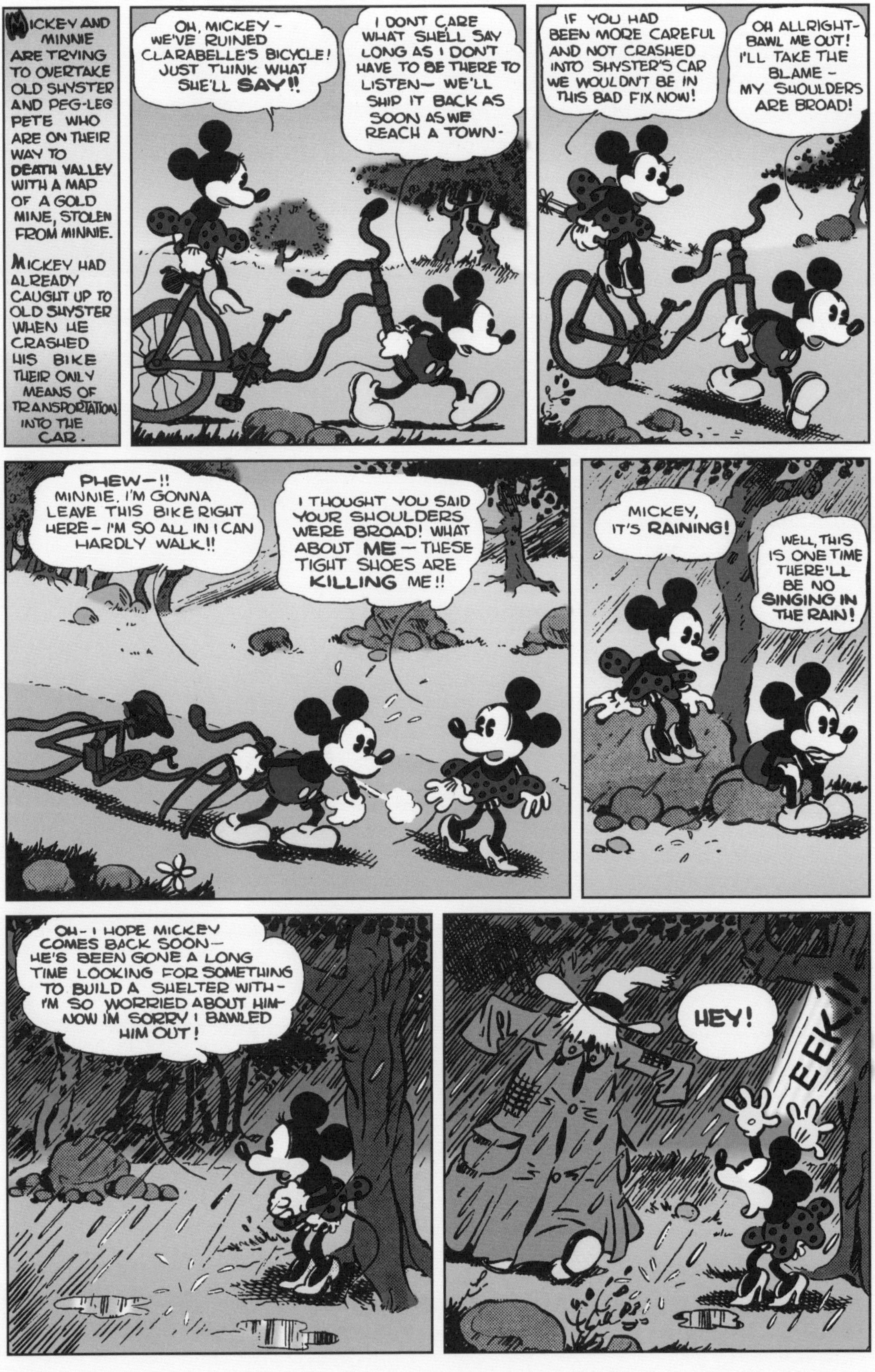
MICKEY AND MINNIE ARE TRYING TO OVERTAKE OLD SHYSTER AND PEG-LEG PETE WHO ARE ON THEIR WAY TO DEATH VALLEY WITH A MAP OF A GOLD MINE, STOLEN FROM MINNIE.
MICKEY HAD ALREADY CAUGHT UP TO OLD SHYSTER WHEN HE CRASHED HIS BIKE THEIR ONLY MEANS OF TRANSPORTATION, INTO THE CAR.
OH, MICKEY - WE'VE RUINED CLARABELLE'S BICYCLE! JUST THINK WHAT SHE'LL SAY!!
I DONT CARE WHAT SHE'LL SAY LONG AS I DON'T HAVE TO BE THERE TO LISTEN— WE'LL SHIP IT BACK AS SOON AS WE REACH A TOWN-
IF YOU HAD BEEN MORE CAREFUL AND NOT CRASHED INTO SHYSTER'S CAR WE WOULDN'T BE IN THIS BAD FIX NOW!
OH ALLRIGHT- BAWL ME OUT! I'LL TAKE THE BLAME - MY SHOULDERS ARE BROAD!
PHEW—!! MINNIE, I'M GONNA LEAVE THIS BIKE RIGHT HERE - I'M SO ALL IN I CAN HARDLY WALK!!
I THOUGHT YOU SAID YOUR SHOULDERS WERE BROAD! WHAT ABOUT ME — THESE TIGHT SHOES ARE KILLING ME!!
MICKEY, IT'S RAINING!
WELL, THIS IS ONE TIME THERE'LL BE NO SINGING IN THE RAIN!
OH- I HOPE MICKEY COMES BACK SOON— HE'S BEEN GONE A LONG TIME LOOKING FOR SOMETHING TO BUILD A SHELTER WITH- I'M SO WORRIED ABOUT HIM- NOW IM SORRY I BAWLED HIM OUT!
HEY!
EEK!

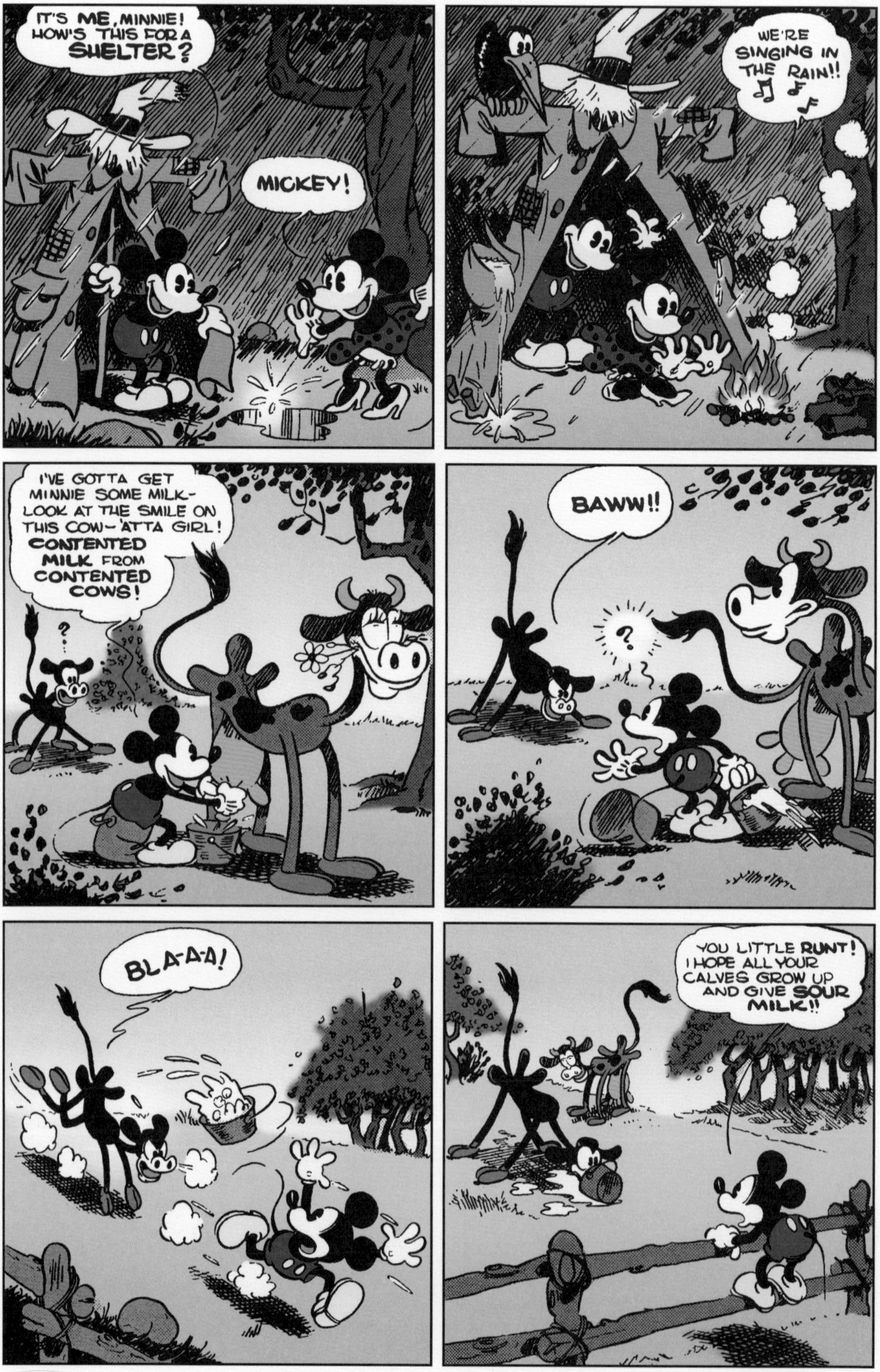
IT'S ME, MINNIE! HOW'S THIS FOR A SHELTER?
MICKEY!
WE'RE SINGING IN THE RAIN!!
I'VE GOTTA GET MINNIE SOME MILK- LOOK AT THE SMILE ON THIS COW- 'ATTA GIRL! CONTENTED MILK FROM CONTENTED COWS!
?
BAWW!!
?
BLA-A-A!
YOU LITTLE RUNT! I HOPE ALL YOUR CALVES GROW UP AND GIVE SOUR MILK!!

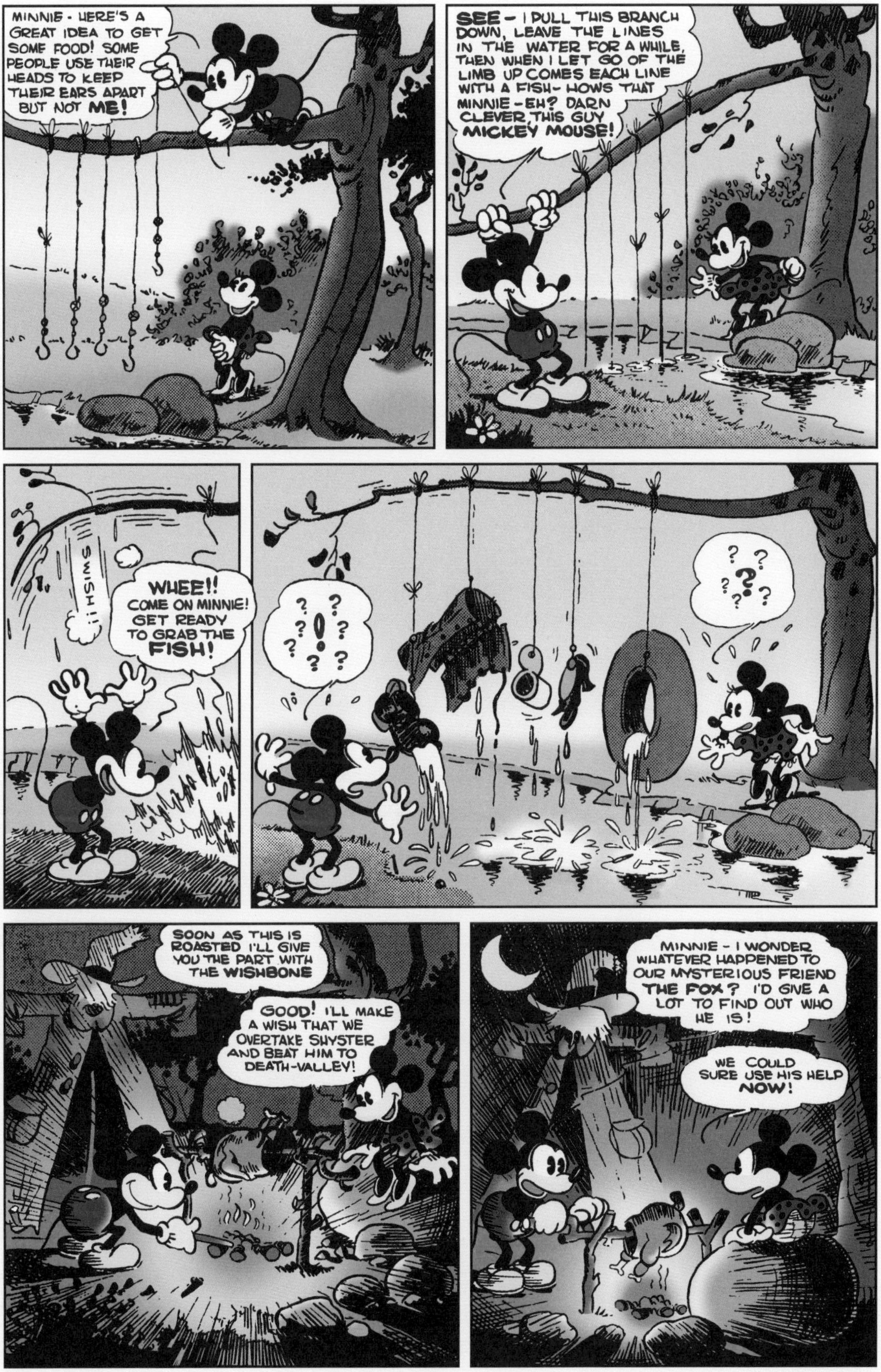
MINNIE - HERE'S A GREAT IDEA TO GET SOME FOOD! SOME PEOPLE USE THEIR HEADS TO KEEP THEIR EARS APART BUT NOT ME!
SEE - I PULL THIS BRANCH DOWN, LEAVE THE LINES IN THE WATER FOR A WHILE, THEN WHEN I LET GO OF THE LIMB UP COMES EACH LINE WITH A FISH- HOWS THAT MINNIE - EH? DARN CLEVER THIS GUY MICKEY MOUSE!
SWISH!!
WHEE!! COME ON MINNIE! GET READY TO GRAB THE FISH!
? ? ? ! ? ? ? ?
? ? ? ? ? ?
SOON AS THIS IS ROASTED I'LL GIVE YOU THE PART WITH THE WISHBONE
GOOD! I'LL MAKE A WISH THAT WE OVERTAKE SHYSTER AND BEAT HIM TO DEATH-VALLEY!
MINNIE - I WONDER WHATEVER HAPPENED TO OUR MYSTERIOUS FRIEND THE FOX? I'D GIVE A LOT TO FIND OUT WHO HE IS!
WE COULD SURE USE HIS HELP NOW!

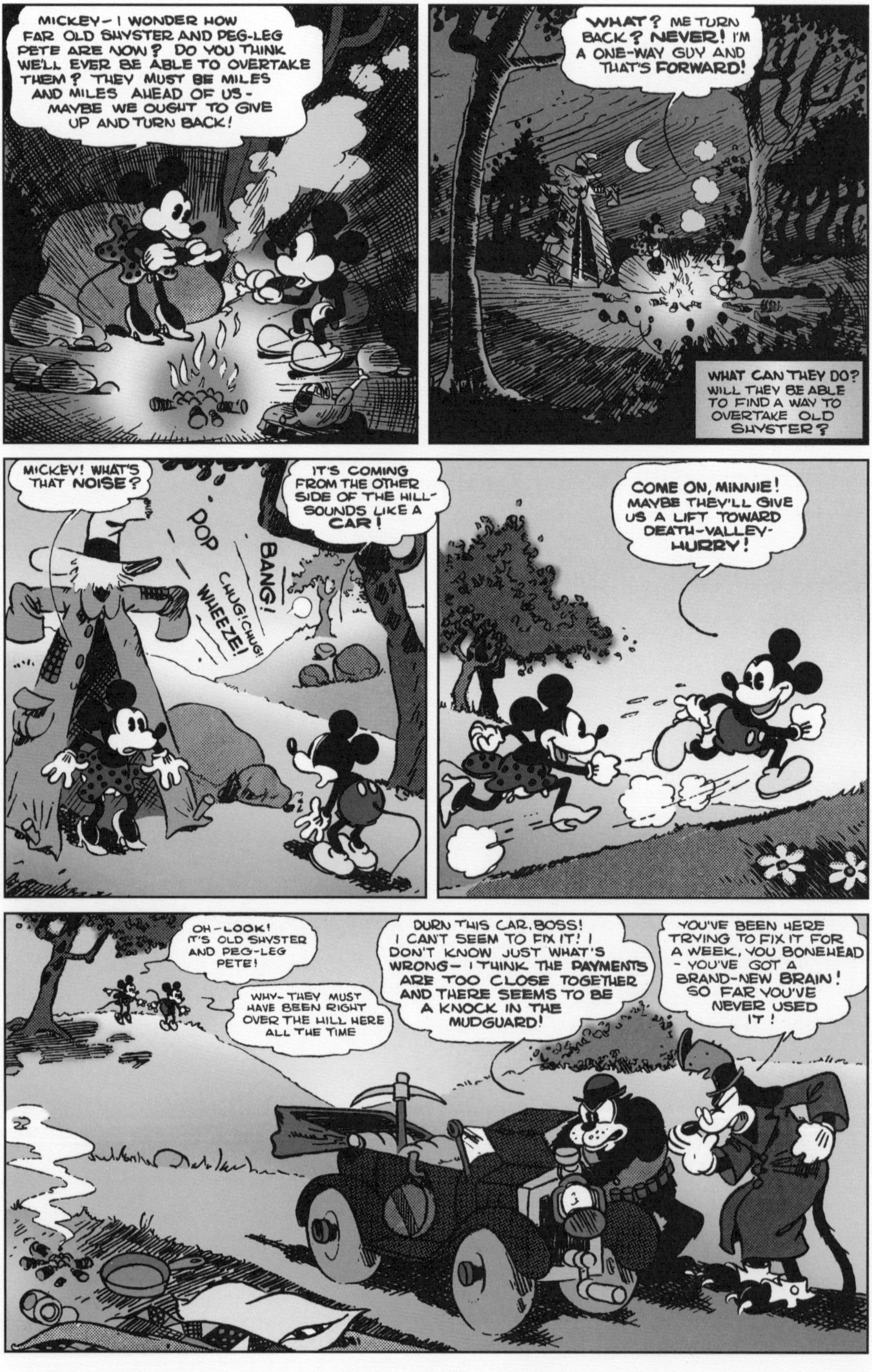
MICKEY- I WONDER HOW FAR OLD SHYSTER AND PEG-LEG PETE ARE NOW? DO YOU THINK WE'LL EVER BE ABLE TO OVERTAKE THEM? THEY MUST BE MILES AND MILES AHEAD OF US- MAYBE WE OUGHT TO GIVE UP AND TURN BACK!
WHAT? ME TURN BACK? NEVER! I'M A ONE-WAY GUY AND THAT'S FORWARD!
WHAT CAN THEY DO? WILL THEY BE ABLE TO FIND A WAY TO OVERTAKE OLD SHYSTER?
MICKEY! WHAT'S THAT NOISE?
POP
BANG!
CHUG! CHUG!
WHEEZE!
IT'S COMING FROM THE OTHER SIDE OF THE HILL- SOUNDS LIKE A CAR!
COME ON, MINNIE! MAYBE THEY'LL GIVE US A LIFT TOWARD DEATH-VALLEY- HURRY!
OH-LOOK! IT'S OLD SHYSTER AND PEG-LEG PETE!
WHY- THEY MUST HAVE BEEN RIGHT OVER THE HILL HERE ALL THE TIME
DURN THIS CAR, BOSS! I CAN'T SEEM TO FIX IT! I DON'T KNOW JUST WHAT'S WRONG- I THINK THE PAYMENTS ARE TOO CLOSE TOGETHER AND THERE SEEMS TO BE A KNOCK IN THE MUDGUARD!
YOU'VE BEEN HERE TRYING TO FIX IT FOR A WEEK, YOU BONEHEAD - YOU'VE GOT A BRAND-NEW BRAIN! SO FAR YOU'VE NEVER USED IT!

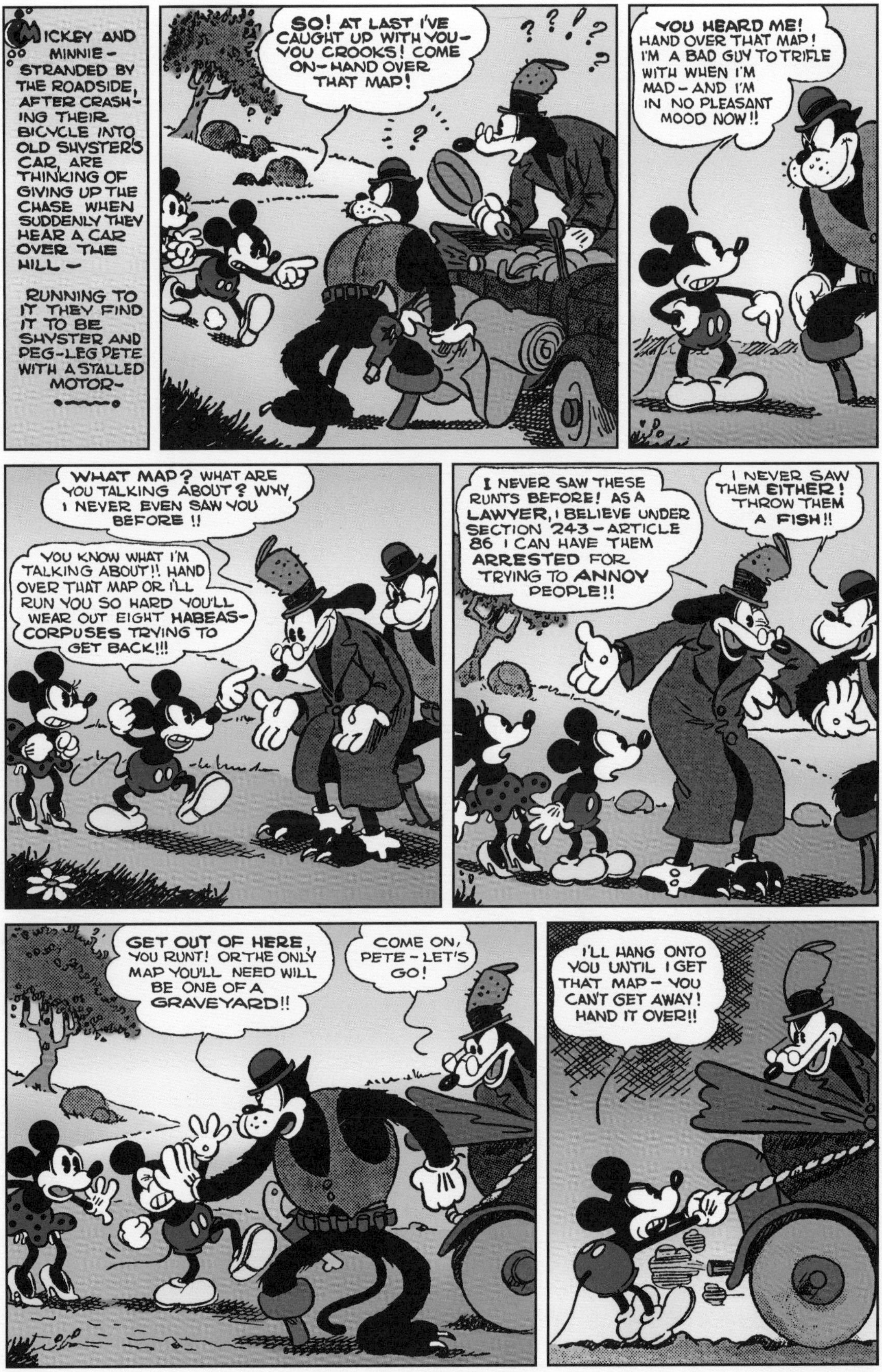
MICKEY AND MINNIE – STRANDED BY THE ROADSIDE, AFTER CRASHING THEIR BICYCLE INTO OLD SHYSTER'S CAR, ARE THINKING OF GIVING UP THE CHASE WHEN SUDDENLY THEY HEAR A CAR OVER THE HILL –
RUNNING TO IT THEY FIND IT TO BE SHYSTER AND PEG-LEG PETE WITH A STALLED MOTOR –
SO! AT LAST I'VE CAUGHT UP WITH YOU – YOU CROOKS! COME ON – HAND OVER THAT MAP!
? ? ! ?
YOU HEARD ME! HAND OVER THAT MAP! I'M A BAD GUY TO TRIFLE WITH WHEN I'M MAD – AND I'M IN NO PLEASANT MOOD NOW!!
WHAT MAP? WHAT ARE YOU TALKING ABOUT? WHY, I NEVER EVEN SAW YOU BEFORE!!
YOU KNOW WHAT I'M TALKING ABOUT!! HAND OVER THAT MAP OR I'LL RUN YOU SO HARD YOU'LL WEAR OUT EIGHT HABEAS-CORPUSES TRYING TO GET BACK!!!
I NEVER SAW THESE RUNTS BEFORE! AS A LAWYER, I BELIEVE UNDER SECTION 243 – ARTICLE 86 I CAN HAVE THEM ARRESTED FOR TRYING TO ANNOY PEOPLE!!
I NEVER SAW THEM EITHER! THROW THEM A FISH!!
GET OUT OF HERE, YOU RUNT! OR THE ONLY MAP YOU'LL NEED WILL BE ONE OF A GRAVEYARD!!
COME ON, PETE – LET'S GO!
I'LL HANG ONTO YOU UNTIL I GET THAT MAP – YOU CAN'T GET AWAY! HAND IT OVER!!

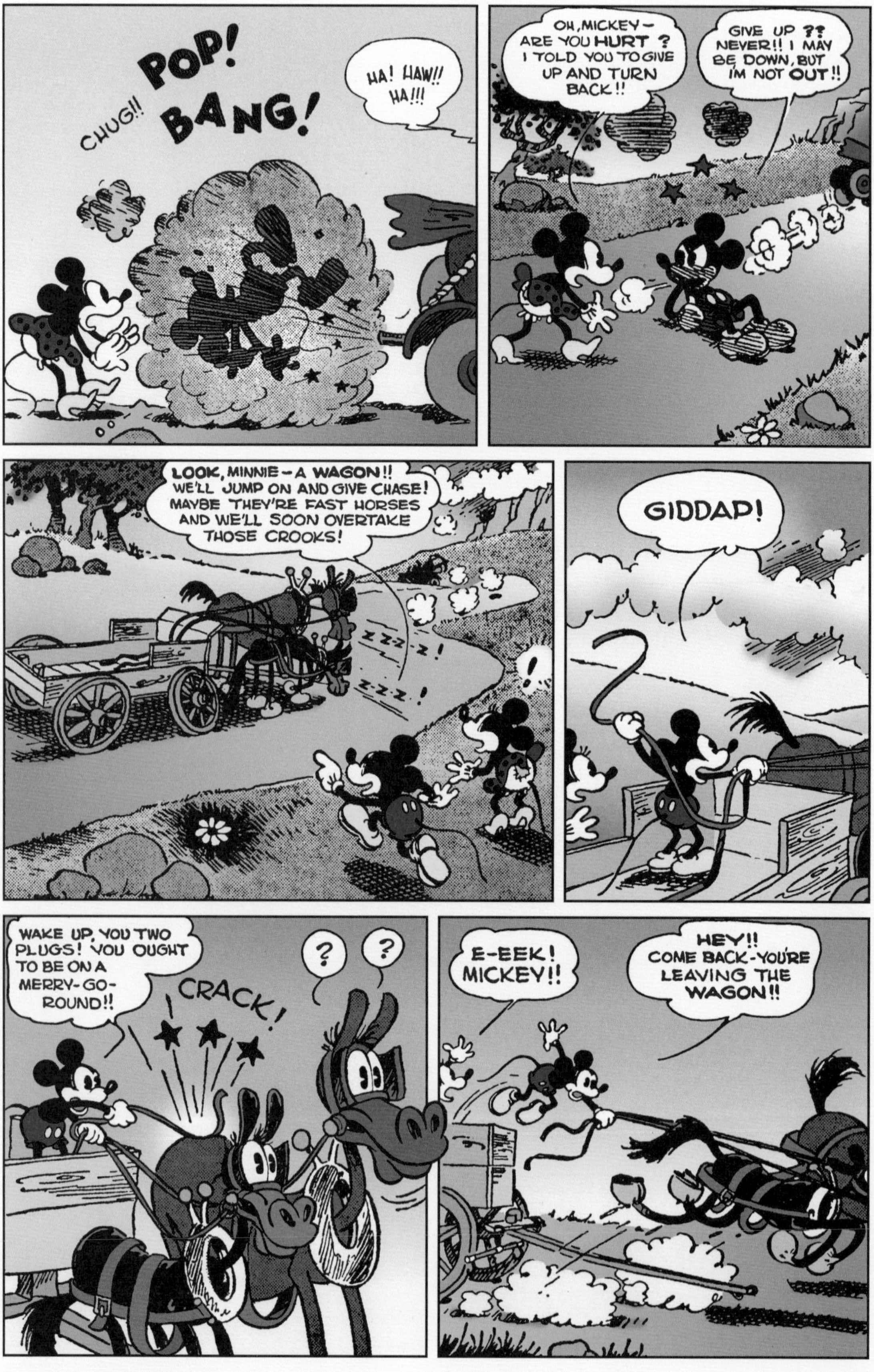
CHUG!!
POP!
BANG!
HA! HAW!! HA!!!
OH, MICKEY— ARE YOU HURT ? I TOLD YOU TO GIVE UP AND TURN BACK!!
GIVE UP ?? NEVER!! I MAY BE DOWN, BUT I'M NOT OUT!!
LOOK, MINNIE—A WAGON!! WE'LL JUMP ON AND GIVE CHASE! MAYBE THEY'RE FAST HORSES AND WE'LL SOON OVERTAKE THOSE CROOKS!
Z-Z-Z-Z!
Z-Z-Z!
!
GIDDAP!
WAKE UP, YOU TWO PLUGS! YOU OUGHT TO BE ON A MERRY-GO-ROUND!!
CRACK!
?
?
E-EEK! MICKEY!!
HEY!! COME BACK-YOU'RE LEAVING THE WAGON!!

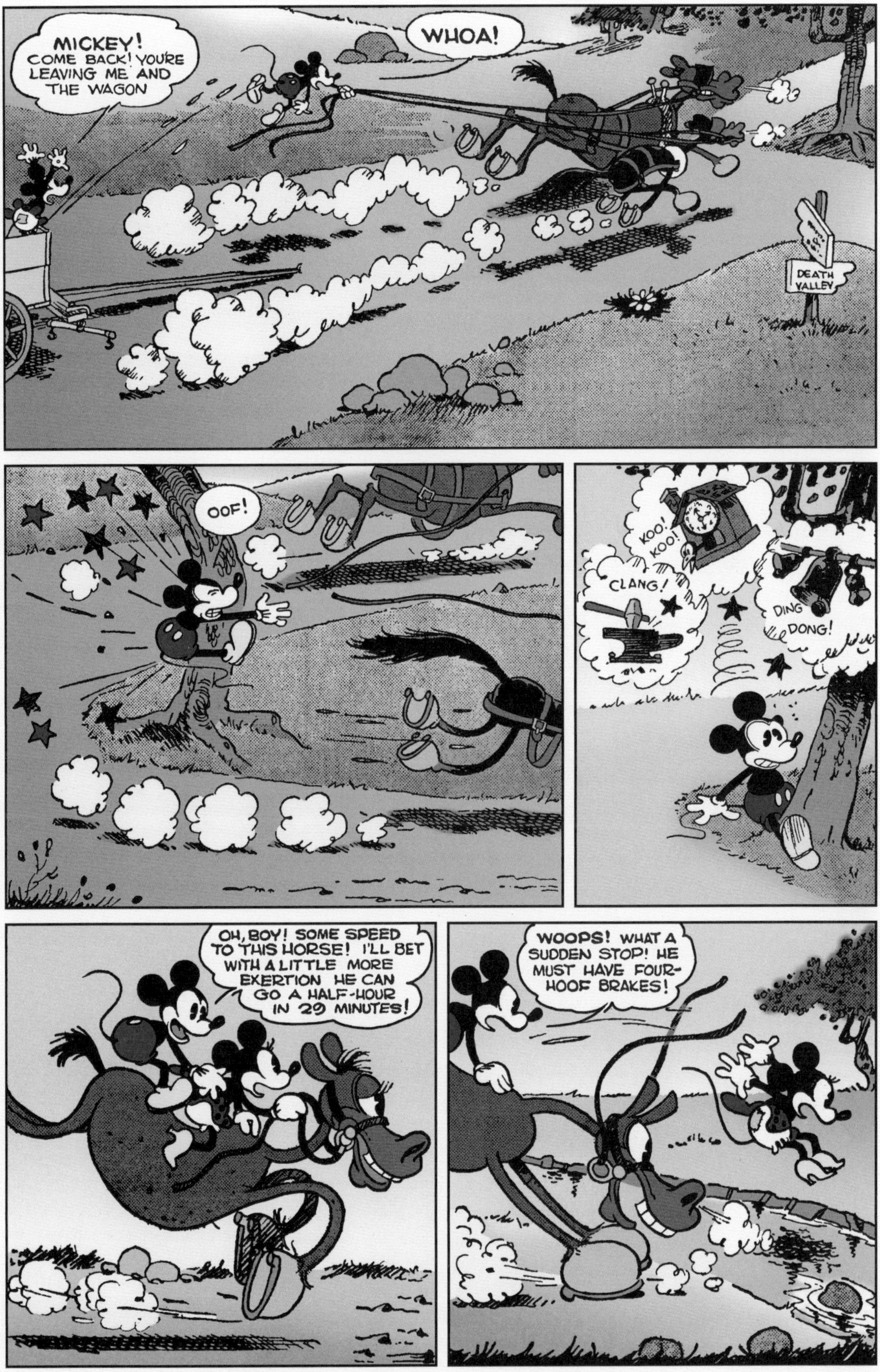
MICKEY! COME BACK! YOU'RE LEAVING ME AND THE WAGON
WHOA!
DEATH VALLEY
OOF!
KOO! KOO!
CLANG!
DING DONG!
OH, BOY! SOME SPEED TO THIS HORSE! I'LL BET WITH A LITTLE MORE EXERTION HE CAN GO A HALF-HOUR IN 29 MINUTES!
WOOPS! WHAT A SUDDEN STOP! HE MUST HAVE FOUR-HOOF BRAKES!

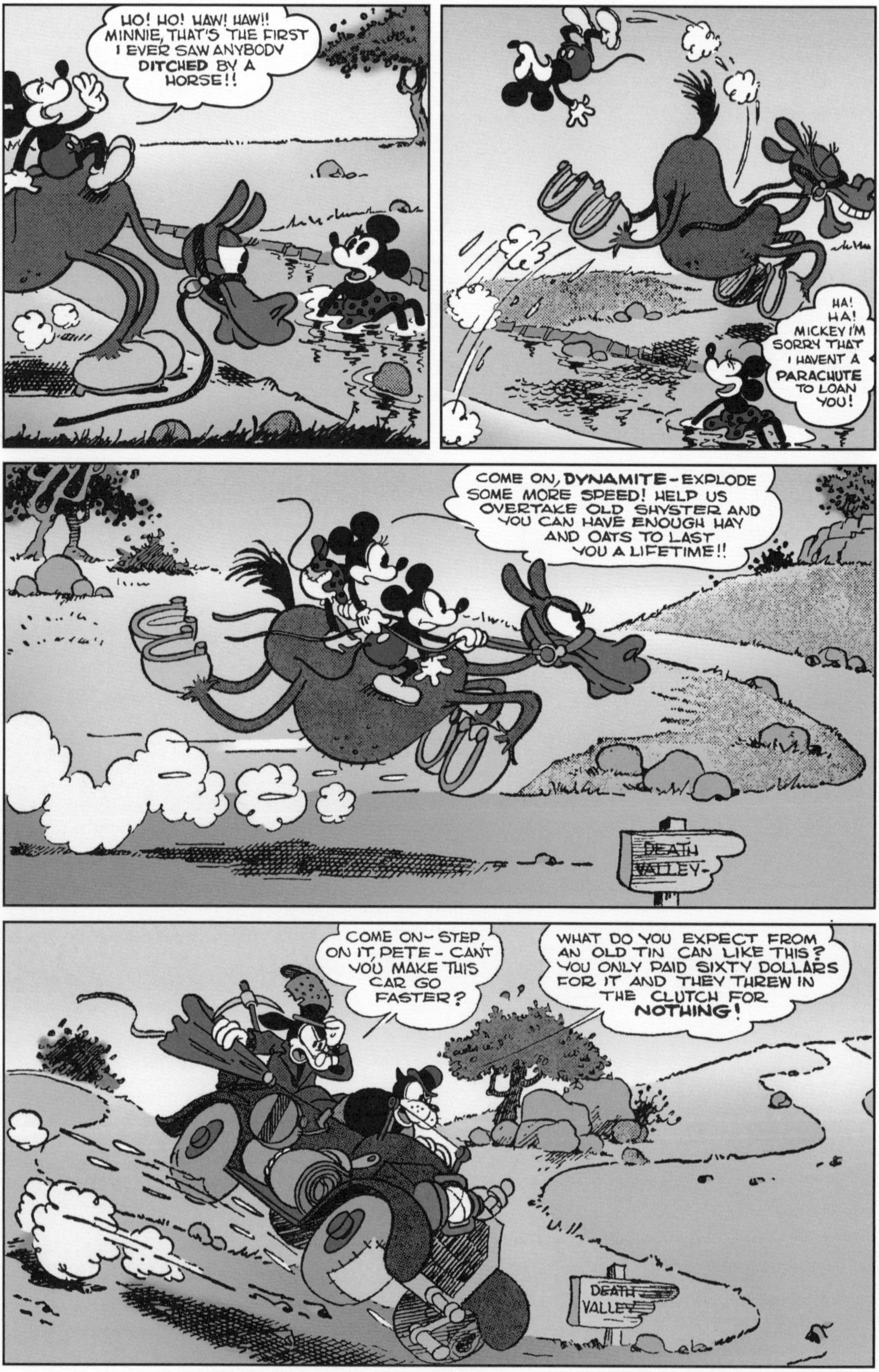
HO! HO! HAW! HAW!!
MINNIE, THAT'S THE FIRST I EVER SAW ANYBODY DITCHED BY A HORSE!!
HA! HA! MICKEY I'M SORRY THAT I HAVENT A PARACHUTE TO LOAN YOU!
COME ON, DYNAMITE - EXPLODE SOME MORE SPEED! HELP US OVERTAKE OLD SHYSTER AND YOU CAN HAVE ENOUGH HAY AND OATS TO LAST YOU A LIFETIME!!
DEATH VALLEY
COME ON - STEP ON IT, PETE - CAN'T YOU MAKE THIS CAR GO FASTER?
WHAT DO YOU EXPECT FROM AN OLD TIN CAN LIKE THIS? YOU ONLY PAID SIXTY DOLLARS FOR IT AND THEY THREW IN THE CLUTCH FOR NOTHING!
DEATH VALLEY

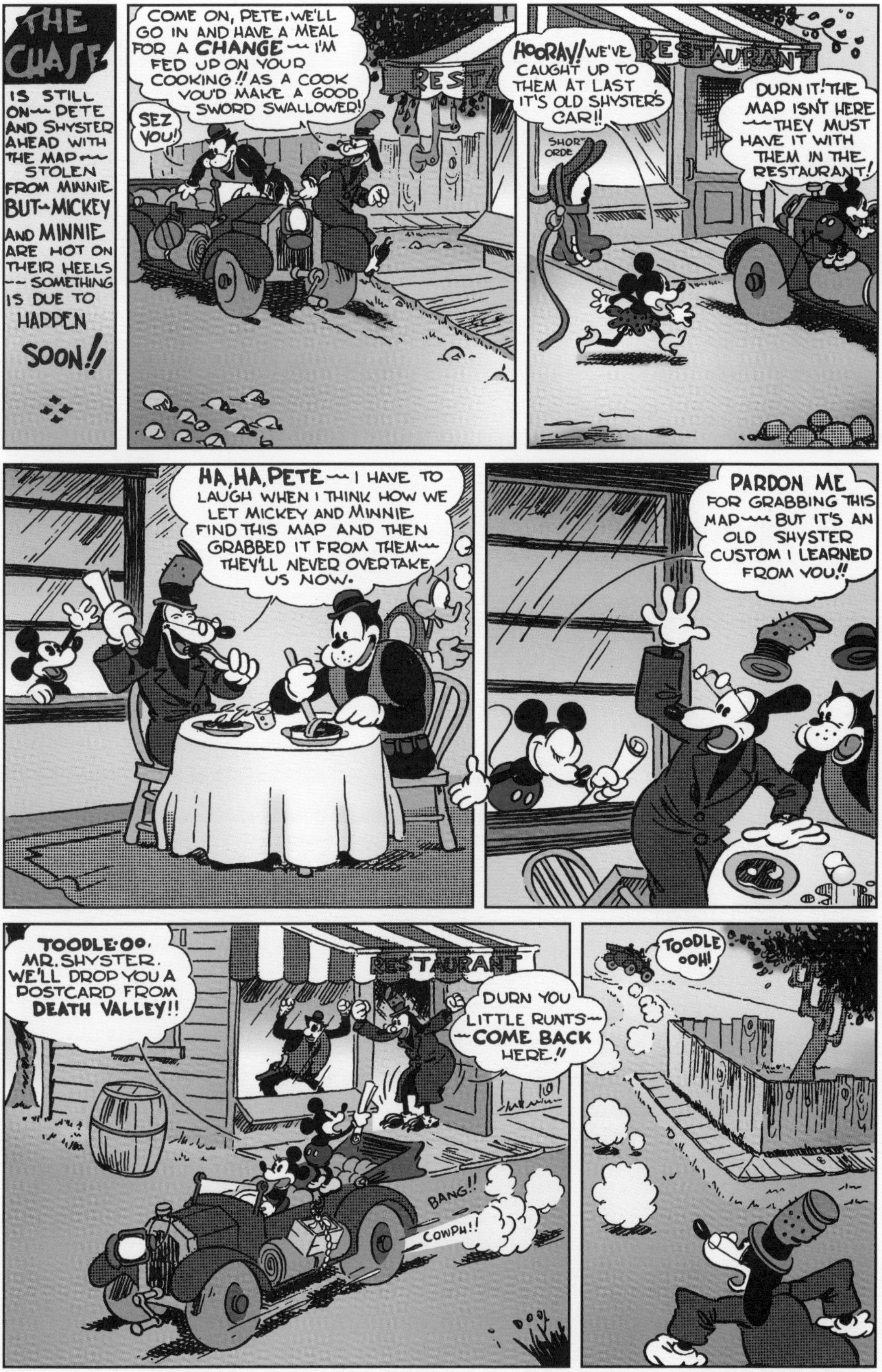
THE CHASE
IS STILL ON—PETE AND SHYSTER AHEAD WITH THE MAP—STOLEN FROM MINNIE BUT—MICKEY AND MINNIE ARE HOT ON THEIR HEELS—SOMETHING IS DUE TO HAPPEN SOON!!
COME ON, PETE, WE'LL GO IN AND HAVE A MEAL FOR A CHANGE—I'M FED UP ON YOUR COOKING!! AS A COOK YOU'D MAKE A GOOD SWORD SWALLOWER!
SEZ YOU!
RESTA
HOORAY!! WE'VE CAUGHT UP TO THEM AT LAST IT'S OLD SHYSTER'S CAR!!
RESTAURANT
SHORT ORDE
DURN IT! THE MAP ISN'T HERE—THEY MUST HAVE IT WITH THEM IN THE RESTAURANT!
HA, HA, PETE—I HAVE TO LAUGH WHEN I THINK HOW WE LET MICKEY AND MINNIE FIND THIS MAP AND THEN GRABBED IT FROM THEM—THEY'LL NEVER OVERTAKE US NOW.
PARDON ME FOR GRABBING THIS MAP—BUT IT'S AN OLD SHYSTER CUSTOM I LEARNED FROM YOU!!
TOODLE-OO, MR. SHYSTER. WE'LL DROP YOU A POSTCARD FROM DEATH VALLEY!!
RESTAURANT
DURN YOU LITTLE RUNTS—COME BACK HERE!!
BANG!!
COWPH!!
TOODLE OOH!

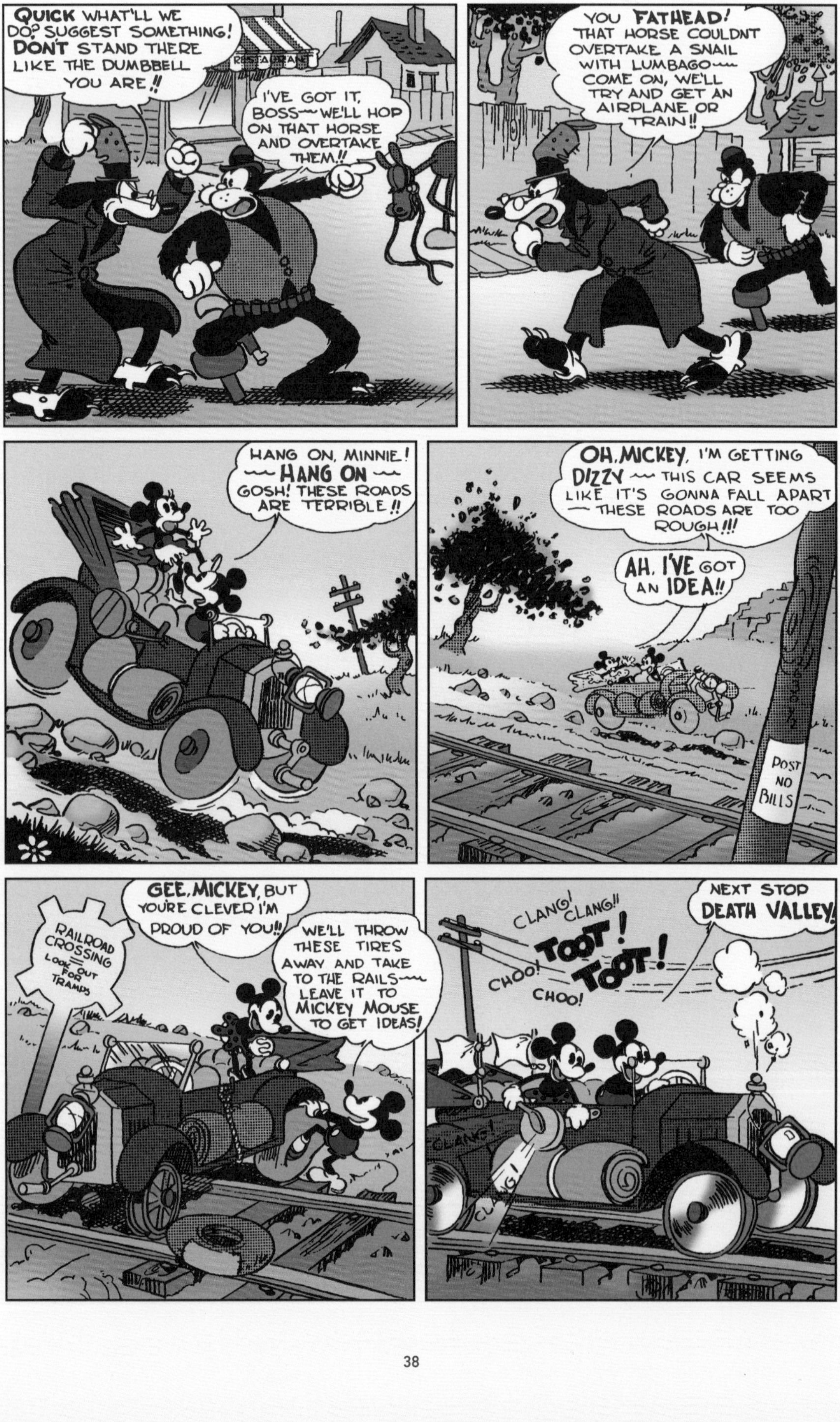
QUICK WHAT'LL WE DO? SUGGEST SOMETHING! DON'T STAND THERE LIKE THE DUMBBELL YOU ARE!!
RESTAURANT
I'VE GOT IT, BOSS — WE'LL HOP ON THAT HORSE AND OVERTAKE THEM!!
YOU FATHEAD! THAT HORSE COULDNT OVERTAKE A SNAIL WITH LUMBAGO — COME ON, WE'LL TRY AND GET AN AIRPLANE OR TRAIN!!
HANG ON, MINNIE! — HANG ON — GOSH! THESE ROADS ARE TERRIBLE!!
OH, MICKEY, I'M GETTING DIZZY — THIS CAR SEEMS LIKE IT'S GONNA FALL APART — THESE ROADS ARE TOO ROUGH!!!
AH, I'VE GOT AN IDEA!!
POST NO BILLS
GEE, MICKEY, BUT YOU'RE CLEVER I'M PROUD OF YOU!!
RAILROAD CROSSING LOOK OUT FOR TRAMPS
WE'LL THROW THESE TIRES AWAY AND TAKE TO THE RAILS — LEAVE IT TO MICKEY MOUSE TO GET IDEAS!
CLANG! CLANG!!
TOOT! TOOT!
CHOO! CHOO!
NEXT STOP DEATH VALLEY!
CLANG!

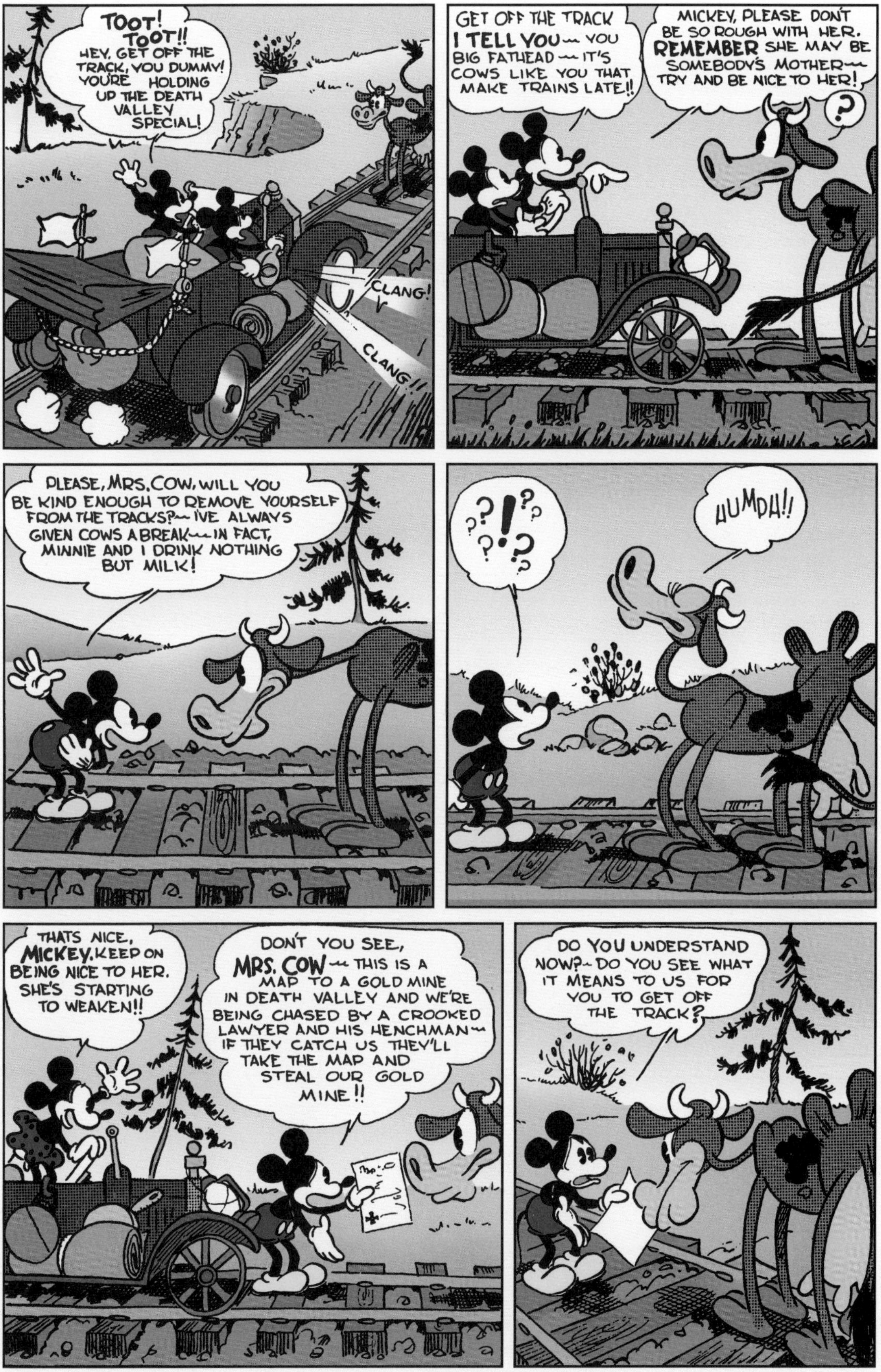
TOOT! TOOT!! HEY, GET OFF THE TRACK, YOU DUMMY! YOU'RE HOLDING UP THE DEATH VALLEY SPECIAL!
CLANG!
CLANG!!
GET OFF THE TRACK I TELL YOU — YOU BIG FATHEAD — IT'S COWS LIKE YOU THAT MAKE TRAINS LATE!!
MICKEY, PLEASE DON'T BE SO ROUGH WITH HER. REMEMBER SHE MAY BE SOMEBODY'S MOTHER— TRY AND BE NICE TO HER!
?
PLEASE, MRS. COW, WILL YOU BE KIND ENOUGH TO REMOVE YOURSELF FROM THE TRACKS?— I'VE ALWAYS GIVEN COWS A BREAK— IN FACT, MINNIE AND I DRINK NOTHING BUT MILK!
??!??
UUMPH!!
THATS NICE, MICKEY, KEEP ON BEING NICE TO HER. SHE'S STARTING TO WEAKEN!!
DON'T YOU SEE, MRS. COW — THIS IS A MAP TO A GOLD MINE IN DEATH VALLEY AND WE'RE BEING CHASED BY A CROOKED LAWYER AND HIS HENCHMAN — IF THEY CATCH US THEY'LL TAKE THE MAP AND STEAL OUR GOLD MINE!!
DO YOU UNDERSTAND NOW?— DO YOU SEE WHAT IT MEANS TO US FOR YOU TO GET OFF THE TRACK?

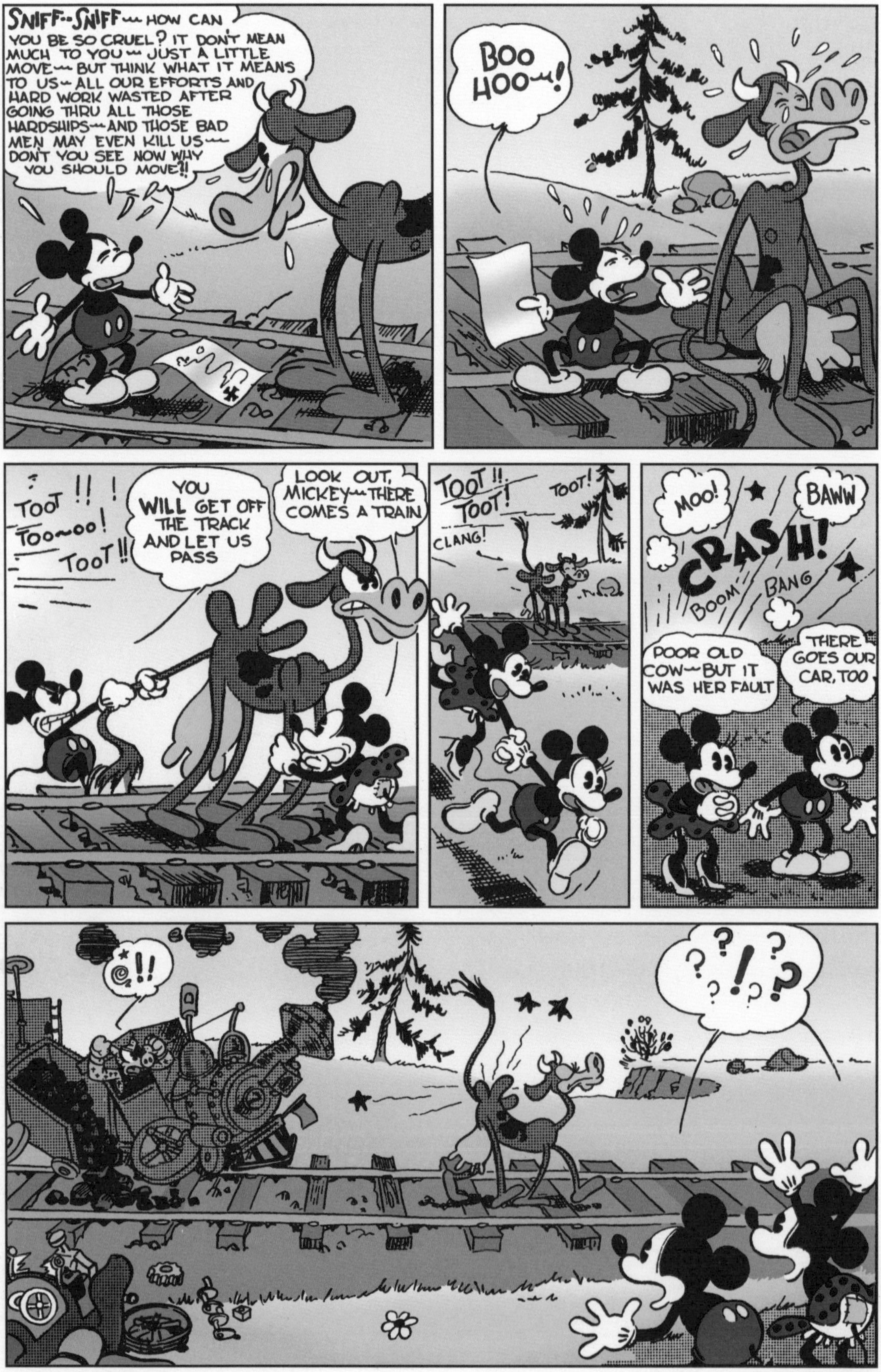
SNIFF--SNIFF-- HOW CAN YOU BE SO CRUEL? IT DON'T MEAN MUCH TO YOU-- JUST A LITTLE MOVE-- BUT THINK WHAT IT MEANS TO US-- ALL OUR EFFORTS AND HARD WORK WASTED AFTER GOING THRU ALL THOSE HARDSHIPS--AND THOSE BAD MEN MAY EVEN KILL US-- DON'T YOU SEE NOW WHY YOU SHOULD MOVE?!!
BOO HOO--!
TOOT !! !
TOO-oo!
TOOT!!
YOU WILL GET OFF THE TRACK AND LET US PASS
LOOK OUT, MICKEY--THERE COMES A TRAIN
TOOT!! TOOT!
TOOT!
CLANG!
MOO!
BAWW
CRASH!
BOOM
BANG
POOR OLD COW--BUT IT WAS HER FAULT
THERE GOES OUR CAR, TOO
!!
? ? ! ? ? ? ?

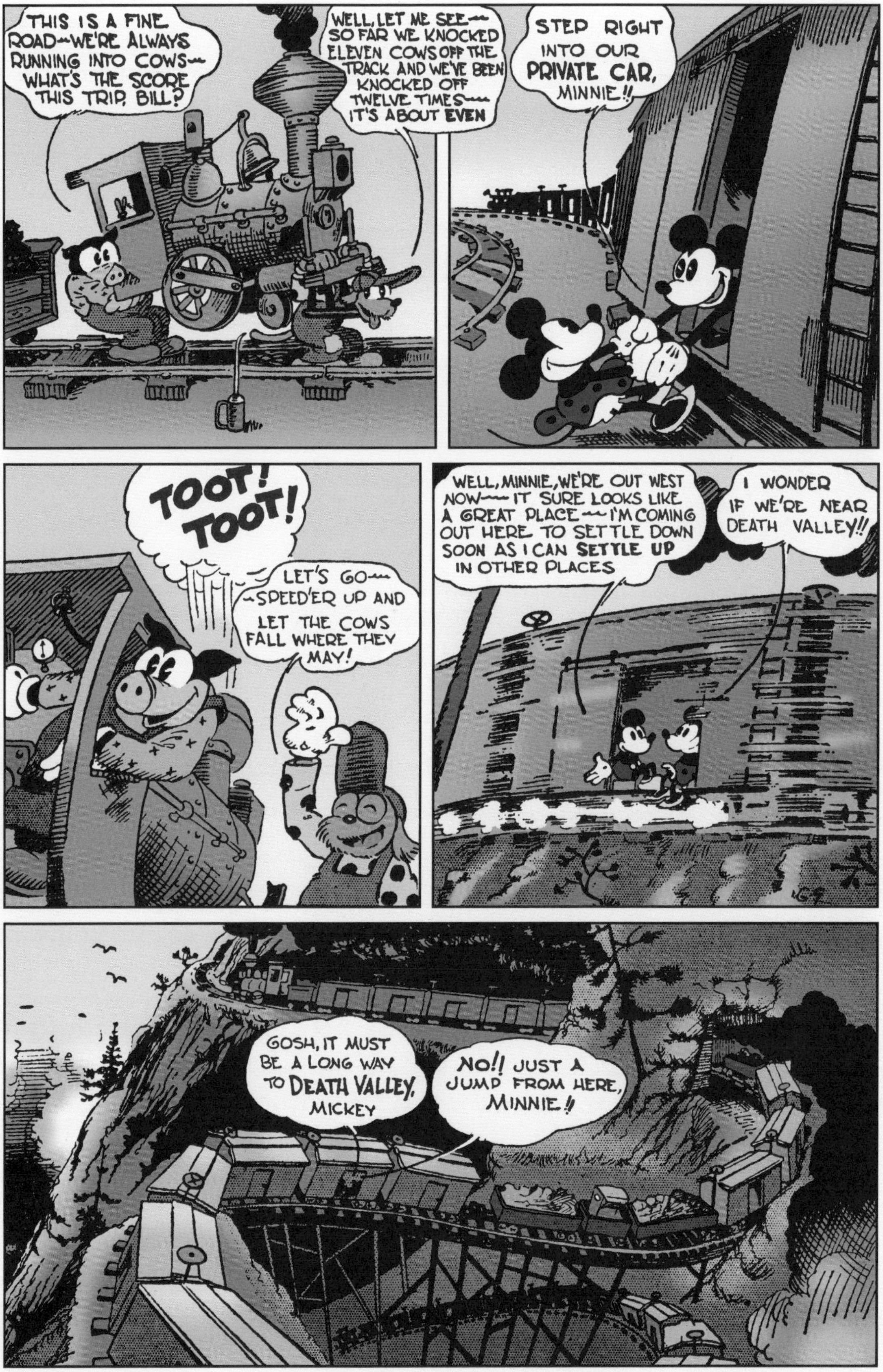
THIS IS A FINE ROAD—WE'RE ALWAYS RUNNING INTO COWS— WHAT'S THE SCORE THIS TRIP, BILL?
WELL, LET ME SEE— SO FAR WE KNOCKED ELEVEN COWS OFF THE TRACK AND WE'VE BEEN KNOCKED OFF TWELVE TIMES— IT'S ABOUT EVEN
STEP RIGHT INTO OUR PRIVATE CAR, MINNIE!!
TOOT! TOOT!
LET'S GO— SPEED'ER UP AND LET THE COWS FALL WHERE THEY MAY!
WELL, MINNIE, WE'RE OUT WEST NOW— IT SURE LOOKS LIKE A GREAT PLACE— I'M COMING OUT HERE TO SETTLE DOWN SOON AS I CAN SETTLE UP IN OTHER PLACES
I WONDER IF WE'RE NEAR DEATH VALLEY!!
GOSH, IT MUST BE A LONG WAY TO DEATH VALLEY, MICKEY
NO!! JUST A JUMP FROM HERE, MINNIE!!

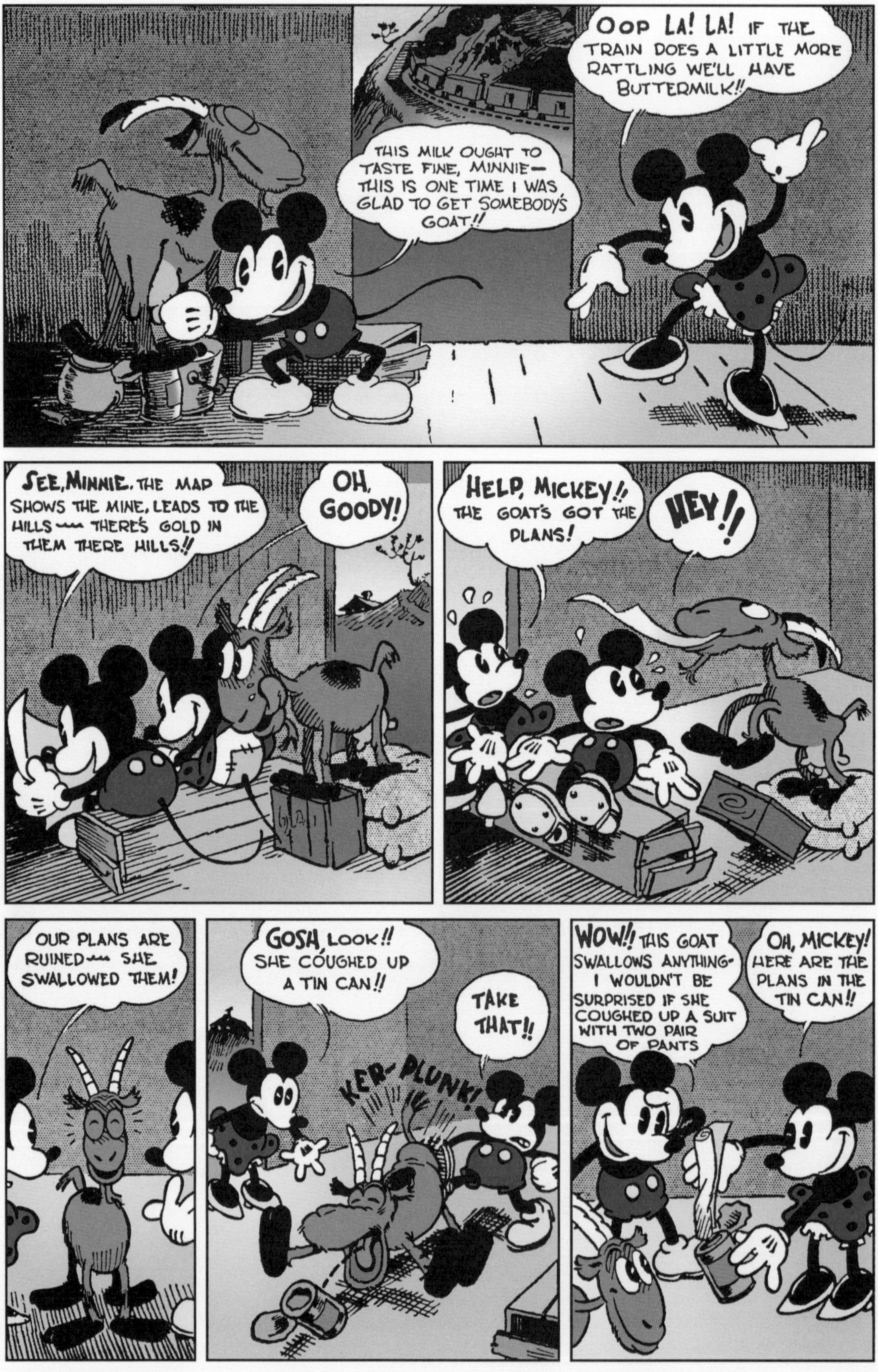
THIS MILK OUGHT TO TASTE FINE, MINNIE— THIS IS ONE TIME I WAS GLAD TO GET SOMEBODY'S GOAT!!
OOP LA! LA! IF THE TRAIN DOES A LITTLE MORE RATTLING WE'LL HAVE BUTTERMILK!!
SEE, MINNIE. THE MAP SHOWS THE MINE, LEADS TO THE HILLS — THERE'S GOLD IN THEM THERE HILLS!!
OH, GOODY!
HELP, MICKEY!! THE GOAT'S GOT THE PLANS!
HEY!!
OUR PLANS ARE RUINED — SHE SWALLOWED THEM!
GOSH, LOOK!! SHE COUGHED UP A TIN CAN!!
TAKE THAT!!
KER-PLUNK!
WOW!! THIS GOAT SWALLOWS ANYTHING- I WOULDN'T BE SURPRISED IF SHE COUGHED UP A SUIT WITH TWO PAIR OF PANTS
OH, MICKEY! HERE ARE THE PLANS IN THE TIN CAN!!

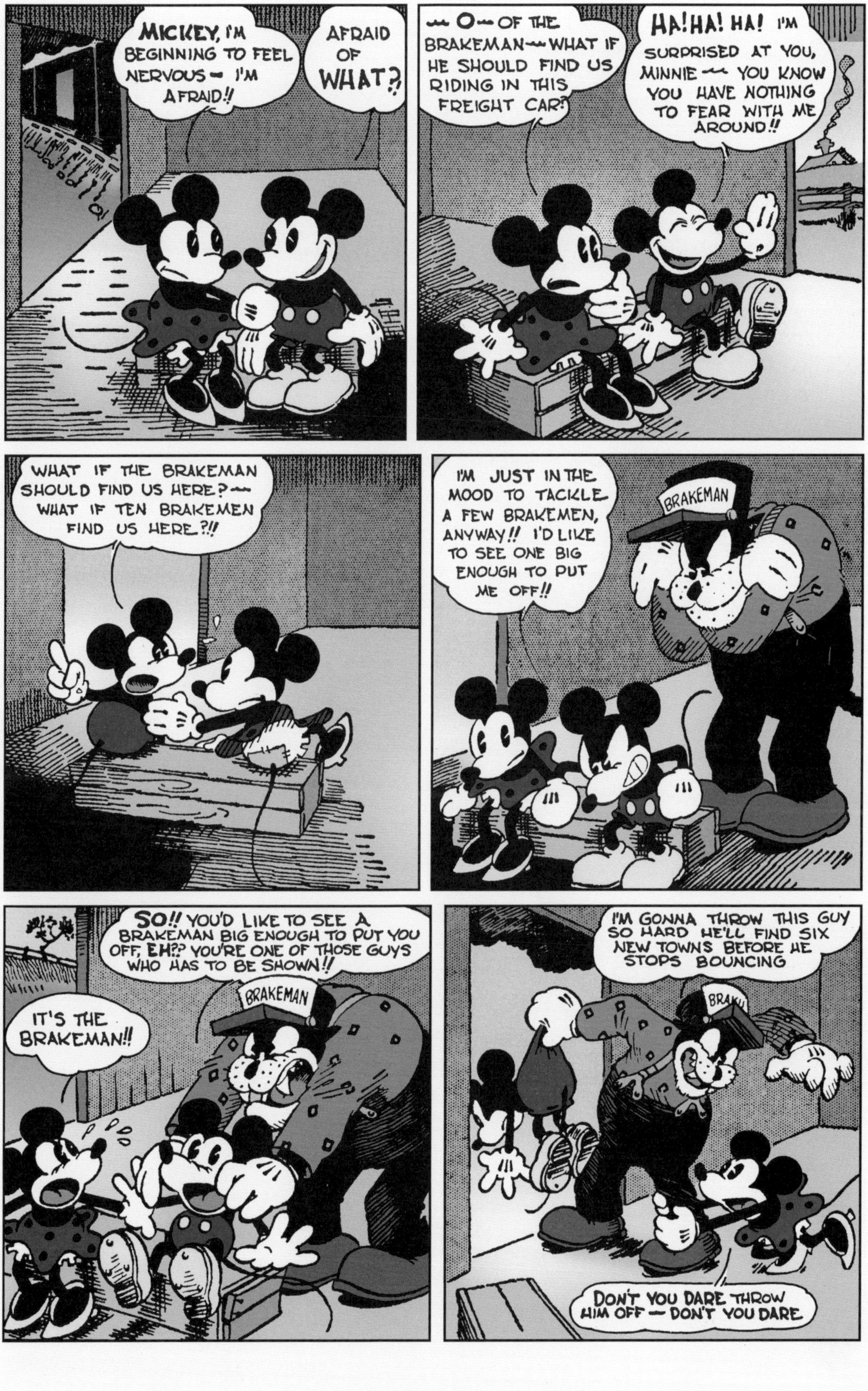
MICKEY, I'M BEGINNING TO FEEL NERVOUS — I'M AFRAID!!
AFRAID OF WHAT?!
— O — OF THE BRAKEMAN — WHAT IF HE SHOULD FIND US RIDING IN THIS FREIGHT CAR?
HA! HA! HA! I'M SURPRISED AT YOU, MINNIE — YOU KNOW YOU HAVE NOTHING TO FEAR WITH ME AROUND!!
WHAT IF THE BRAKEMAN SHOULD FIND US HERE? — WHAT IF TEN BRAKEMEN FIND US HERE?!!
I'M JUST IN THE MOOD TO TACKLE A FEW BRAKEMEN, ANYWAY!! I'D LIKE TO SEE ONE BIG ENOUGH TO PUT ME OFF!!
BRAKEMAN
SO!! YOU'D LIKE TO SEE A BRAKEMAN BIG ENOUGH TO PUT YOU OFF, EH!? YOU'RE ONE OF THOSE GUYS WHO HAS TO BE SHOWN!!
BRAKEMAN
IT'S THE BRAKEMAN!!
I'M GONNA THROW THIS GUY SO HARD HE'LL FIND SIX NEW TOWNS BEFORE HE STOPS BOUNCING
DON'T YOU DARE THROW HIM OFF — DON'T YOU DARE

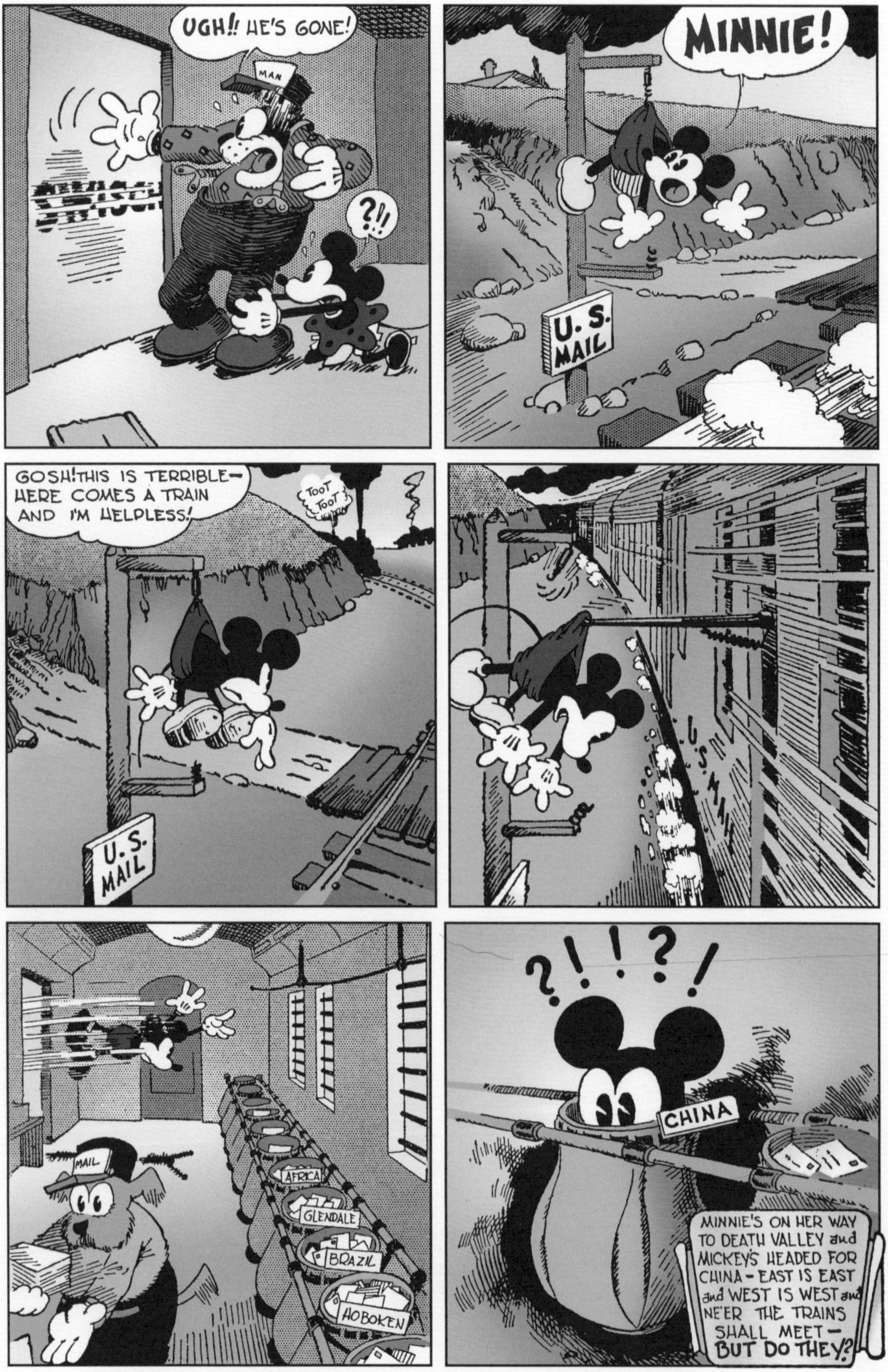
UGH!! HE'S GONE!
MAN
?!!
MINNIE!
U.S. MAIL
GOSH! THIS IS TERRIBLE— HERE COMES A TRAIN AND I'M HELPLESS!
TOOT TOOT
U.S. MAIL
U.S. MAIL
MAIL
AFRICA
GLENDALE
BRAZIL
HOBOKEN
?!!?!
CHINA
MINNIE'S ON HER WAY TO DEATH VALLEY and MICKEY'S HEADED FOR CHINA — EAST IS EAST and WEST IS WEST and NE'ER THE TRAINS SHALL MEET— BUT DO THEY?

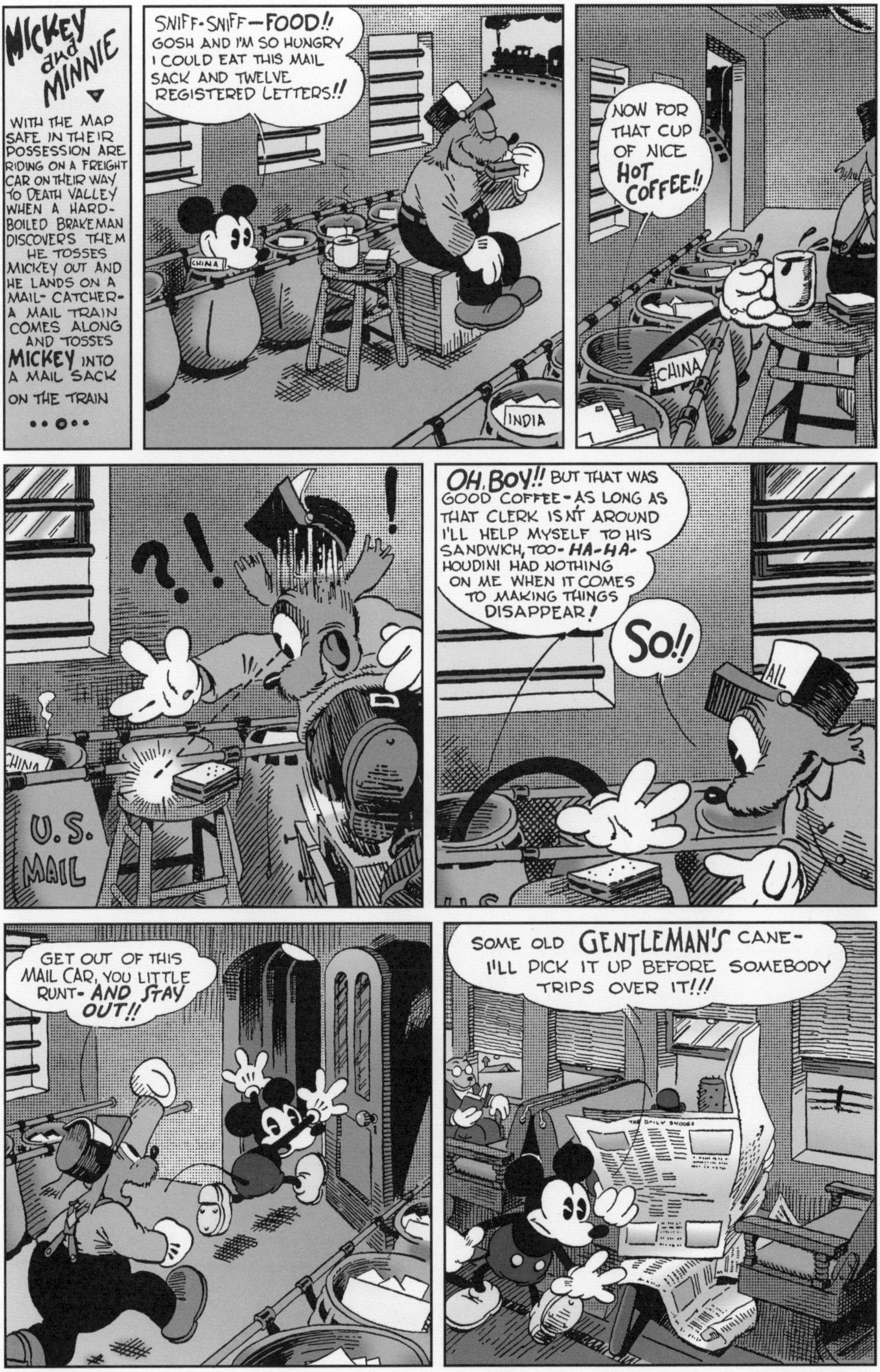
MICKEY and MINNIE
WITH THE MAP SAFE IN THEIR POSSESSION ARE RIDING ON A FREIGHT CAR ON THEIR WAY TO DEATH VALLEY WHEN A HARD-BOILED BRAKEMAN DISCOVERS THEM HE TOSSES MICKEY OUT AND HE LANDS ON A MAIL-CATCHER- A MAIL TRAIN COMES ALONG AND TOSSES MICKEY INTO A MAIL SACK ON THE TRAIN
SNIFF-SNIFF—FOOD!! GOSH AND I'M SO HUNGRY I COULD EAT THIS MAIL SACK AND TWELVE REGISTERED LETTERS!!
CHINA
INDIA
NOW FOR THAT CUP OF NICE HOT COFFEE!!
CHINA
?!!
!
CHINA
U.S. MAIL
OH, BOY!! BUT THAT WAS GOOD COFFEE-AS LONG AS THAT CLERK ISN'T AROUND I'LL HELP MYSELF TO HIS SANDWICH, TOO-HA-HA-HOUDINI HAD NOTHING ON ME WHEN IT COMES TO MAKING THINGS DISAPPEAR!
SO!!
GET OUT OF THIS MAIL CAR, YOU LITTLE RUNT-AND STAY OUT!!
SOME OLD GENTLEMAN'S CANE-I'LL PICK IT UP BEFORE SOMEBODY TRIPS OVER IT!!!

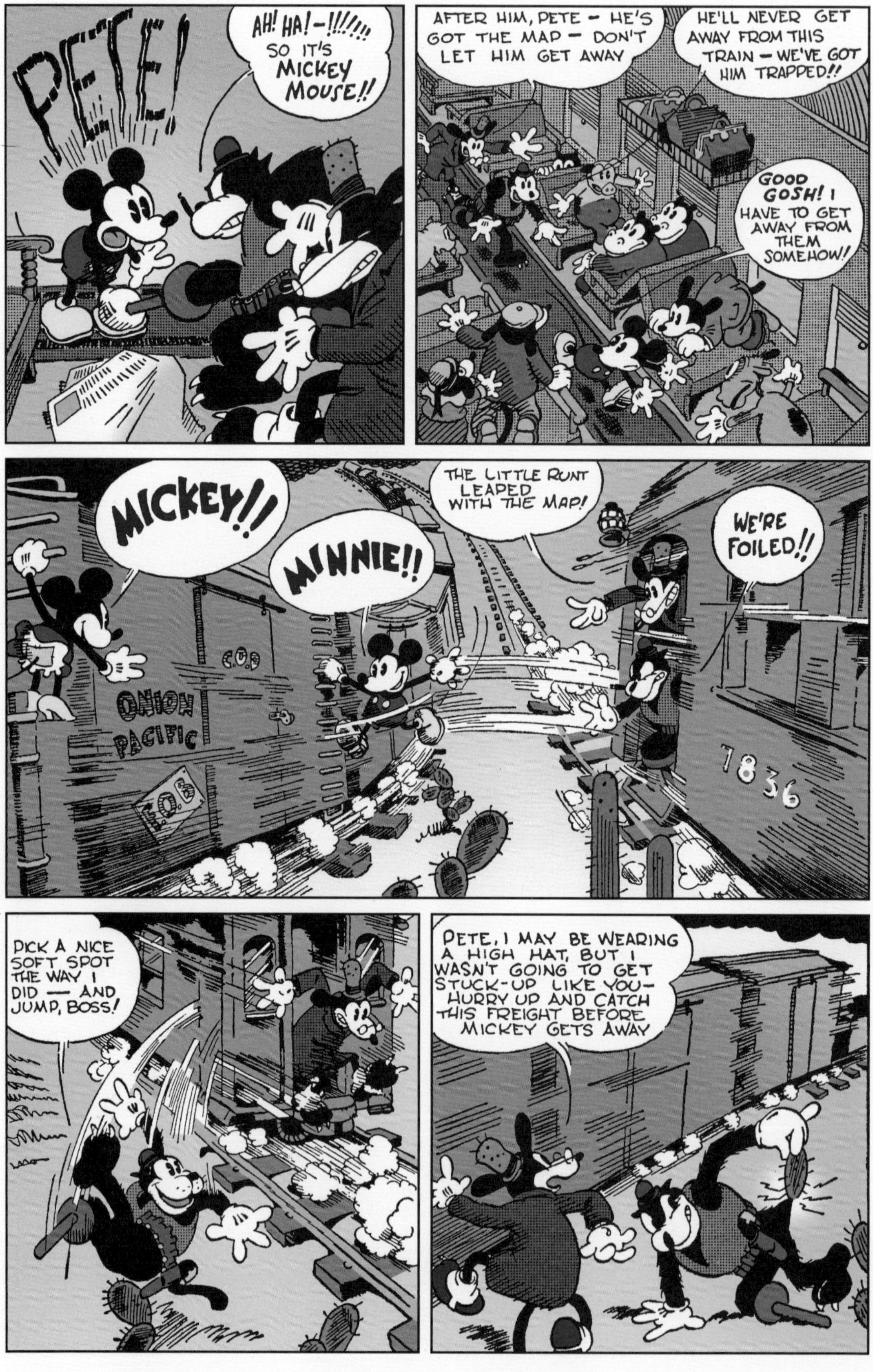
PETE!
AH! HA!-!!!!!!! SO IT'S MICKEY MOUSE!!
AFTER HIM, PETE - HE'S GOT THE MAP - DON'T LET HIM GET AWAY
HE'LL NEVER GET AWAY FROM THIS TRAIN - WE'VE GOT HIM TRAPPED!!
GOOD GOSH! I HAVE TO GET AWAY FROM THEM SOMEHOW!!
MICKEY!!
MINNIE!!
THE LITTLE RUNT LEAPED WITH THE MAP!
WE'RE FOILED!!
C.O.D
ONION PACIFIC
C.O.D
7836
PICK A NICE SOFT SPOT THE WAY I DID — AND JUMP, BOSS!
PETE, I MAY BE WEARING A HIGH HAT, BUT I WASN'T GOING TO GET STUCK-UP LIKE YOU- HURRY UP AND CATCH THIS FREIGHT BEFORE MICKEY GETS AWAY

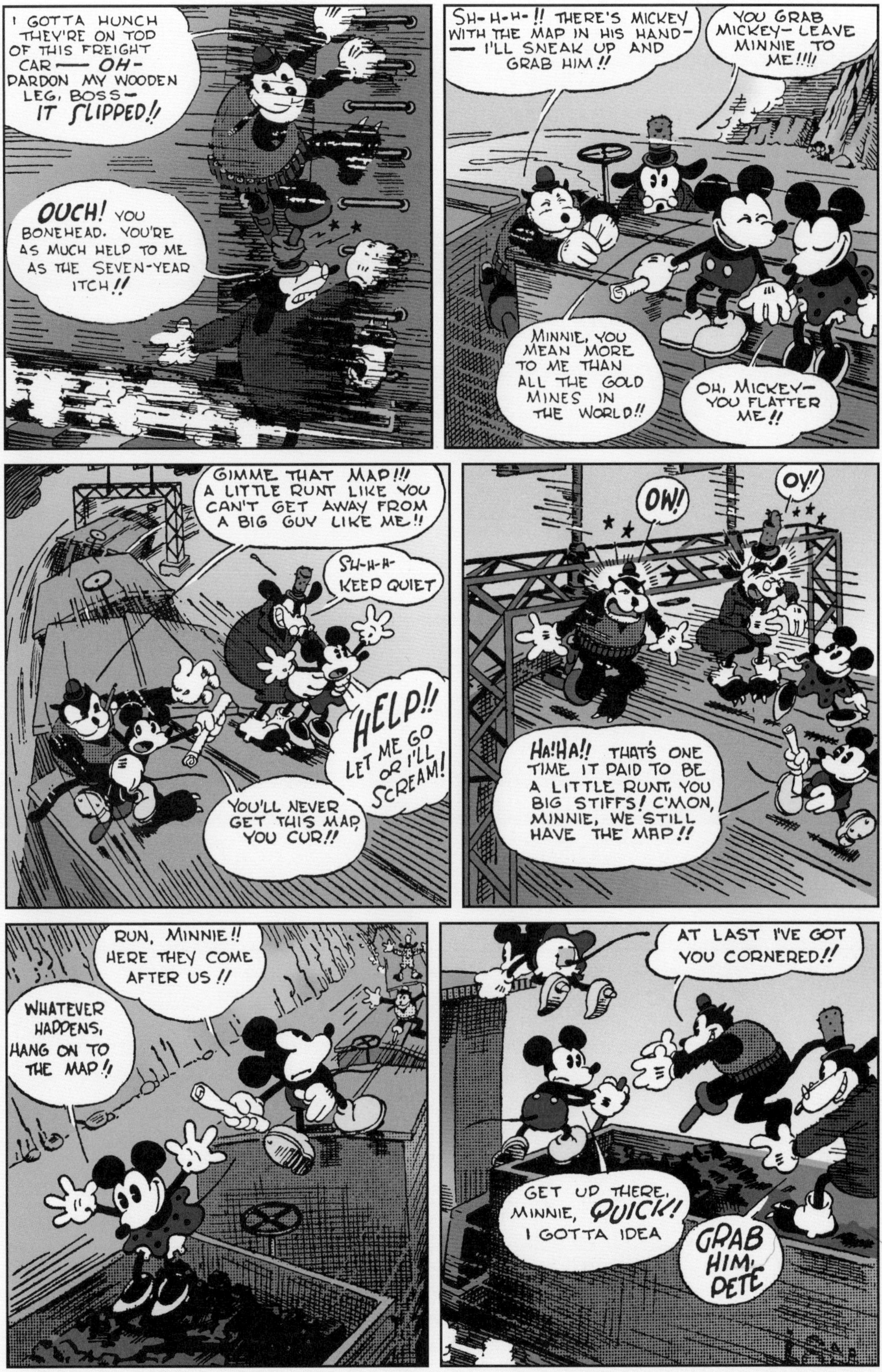
I GOTTA HUNCH THEY'RE ON TOP OF THIS FREIGHT CAR — OH-PARDON MY WOODEN LEG, BOSS— IT SLIPPED!!
OUCH! YOU BONEHEAD. YOU'RE AS MUCH HELP TO ME AS THE SEVEN-YEAR ITCH!!
SH-H-H-!! THERE'S MICKEY WITH THE MAP IN HIS HAND— — I'LL SNEAK UP AND GRAB HIM!!
YOU GRAB MICKEY— LEAVE MINNIE TO ME!!!!
MINNIE, YOU MEAN MORE TO ME THAN ALL THE GOLD MINES IN THE WORLD!!
OH, MICKEY— YOU FLATTER ME!!
GIMME THAT MAP!!! A LITTLE RUNT LIKE YOU CAN'T GET AWAY FROM A BIG GUY LIKE ME!!
SH-H-H- KEEP QUIET
HELP!! LET ME GO OR I'LL SCREAM!
YOU'LL NEVER GET THIS MAP, YOU CUR!!
OW!
OY!
HA!HA!! THAT'S ONE TIME IT PAID TO BE A LITTLE RUNT, YOU BIG STIFFS! C'MON, MINNIE, WE STILL HAVE THE MAP!!
RUN, MINNIE!! HERE THEY COME AFTER US!!
WHATEVER HAPPENS, HANG ON TO THE MAP!!
AT LAST I'VE GOT YOU CORNERED!!
GET UP THERE, MINNIE, QUICK! I GOTTA IDEA
GRAB HIM, PETE

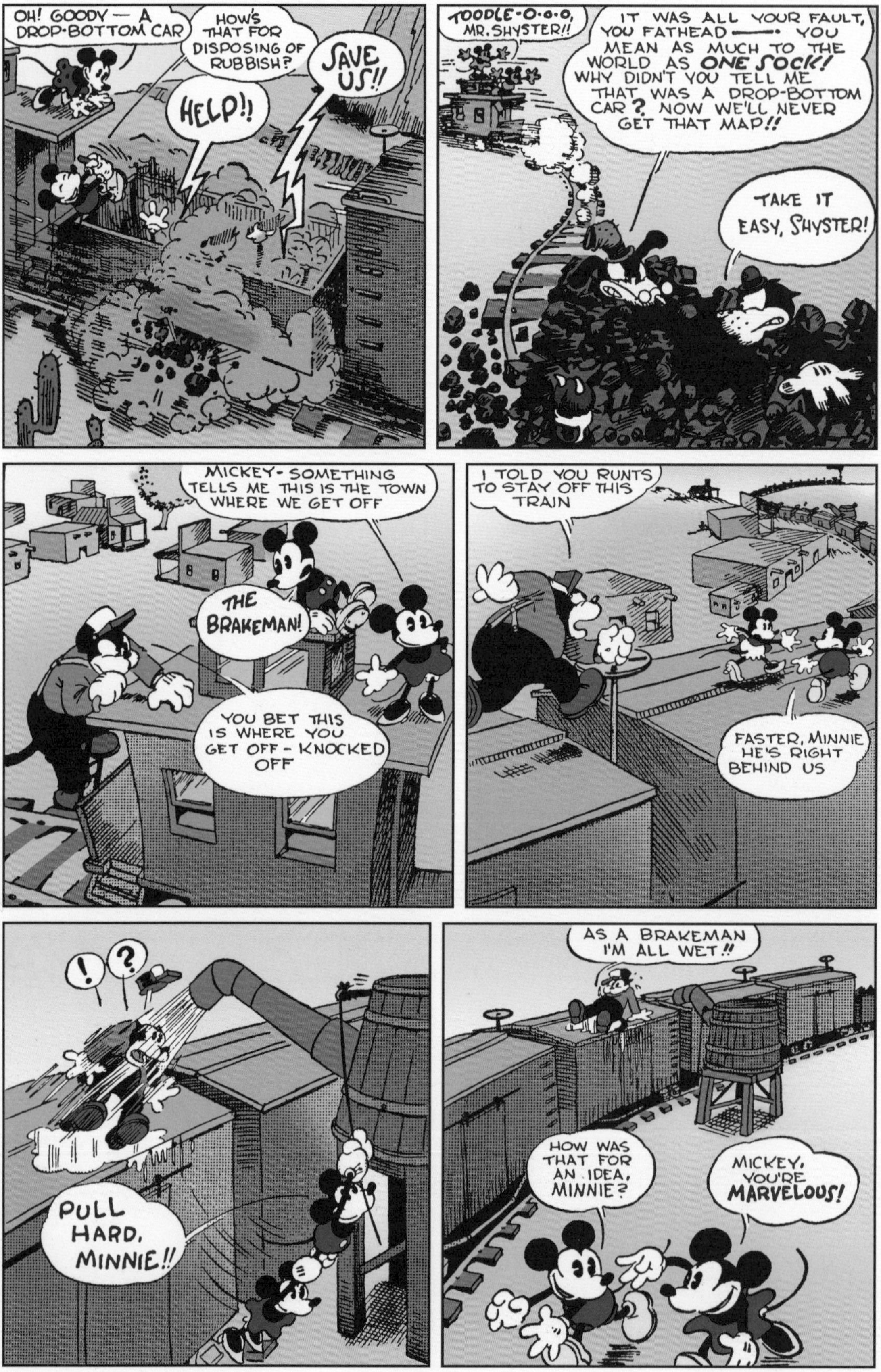
OH! GOODY — A DROP-BOTTOM CAR
HOW'S THAT FOR DISPOSING OF RUBBISH?
SAVE US!!
HELP!!
TOODLE-O-O-O, MR. SHYSTER!!
IT WAS ALL YOUR FAULT, YOU FATHEAD — YOU MEAN AS MUCH TO THE WORLD AS ONE SOCK!! WHY DIDN'T YOU TELL ME THAT WAS A DROP-BOTTOM CAR? NOW WE'LL NEVER GET THAT MAP!!
TAKE IT EASY, SHYSTER!
MICKEY - SOMETHING TELLS ME THIS IS THE TOWN WHERE WE GET OFF
THE BRAKEMAN!
YOU BET THIS IS WHERE YOU GET OFF - KNOCKED OFF
I TOLD YOU RUNTS TO STAY OFF THIS TRAIN
FASTER, MINNIE HE'S RIGHT BEHIND US
!
?
PULL HARD, MINNIE!!
AS A BRAKEMAN I'M ALL WET!!
HOW WAS THAT FOR AN IDEA, MINNIE?
MICKEY, YOU'RE MARVELOUS!

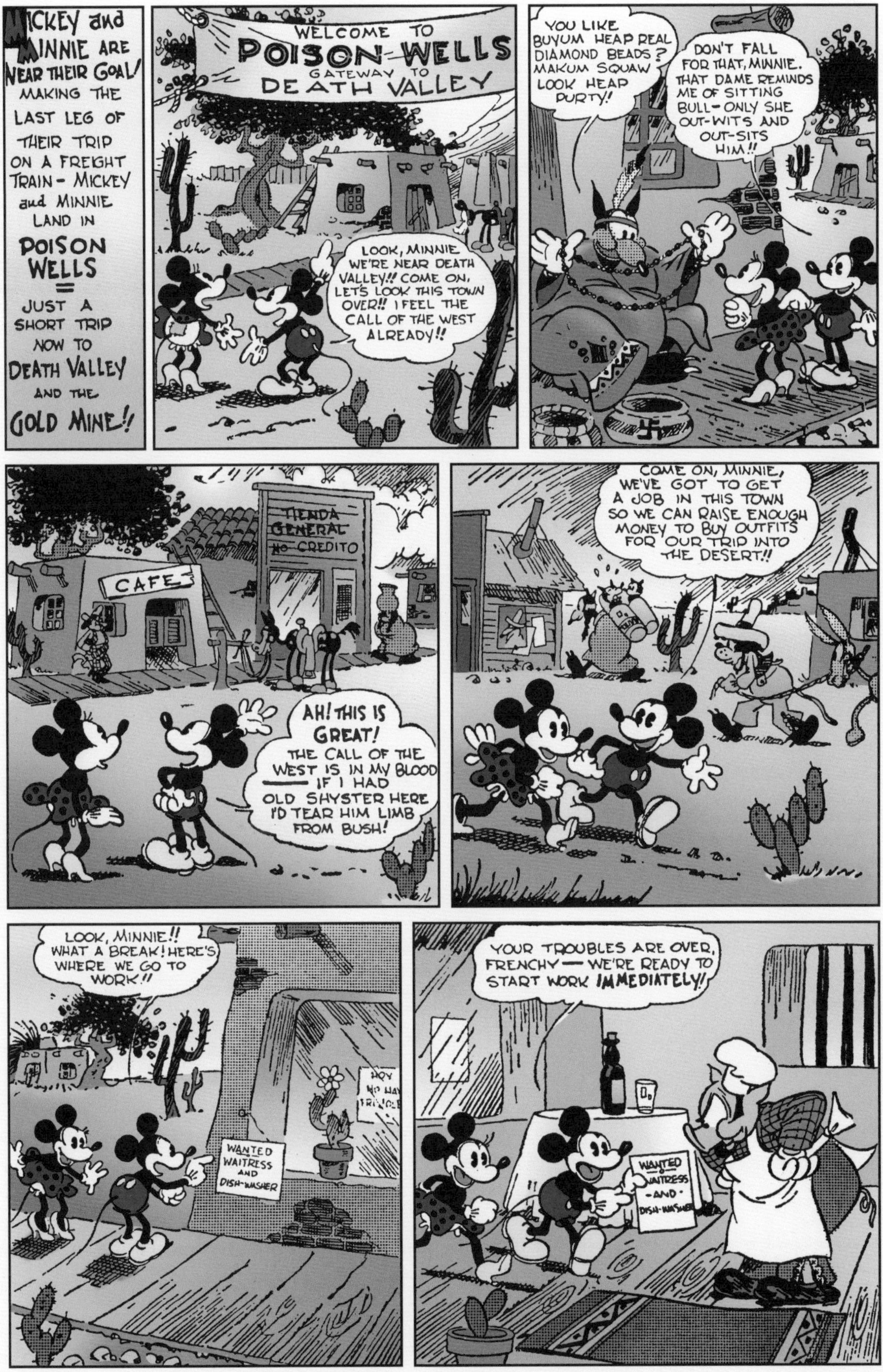
MICKEY and MINNIE ARE NEAR THEIR GOAL! MAKING THE LAST LEG OF THEIR TRIP ON A FREIGHT TRAIN – MICKEY and MINNIE LAND IN POISON WELLS = JUST A SHORT TRIP NOW TO DEATH VALLEY AND THE GOLD MINE!!
WELCOME TO POISON WELLS GATEWAY TO DEATH VALLEY
LOOK, MINNIE WE'RE NEAR DEATH VALLEY!! COME ON, LET'S LOOK THIS TOWN OVER!! I FEEL THE CALL OF THE WEST ALREADY!!
YOU LIKE BUYUM HEAP REAL DIAMOND BEADS? MAKUM SQUAW LOOK HEAP PURTY!
DON'T FALL FOR THAT, MINNIE. THAT DAME REMINDS ME OF SITTING BULL – ONLY SHE OUT-WITS AND OUT-SITS HIM!!
TIENDA GENERAL NO CREDITO
CAFE
AH! THIS IS GREAT! THE CALL OF THE WEST IS IN MY BLOOD — IF I HAD OLD SHYSTER HERE I'D TEAR HIM LIMB FROM BUSH!
COME ON, MINNIE, WE'VE GOT TO GET A JOB IN THIS TOWN SO WE CAN RAISE ENOUGH MONEY TO BUY OUTFITS FOR OUR TRIP INTO THE DESERT!!
LOOK, MINNIE!! WHAT A BREAK! HERE'S WHERE WE GO TO WORK!!
WANTED WAITRESS AND DISH-WASHER
YOUR TROUBLES ARE OVER, FRENCHY — WE'RE READY TO START WORK IMMEDIATELY!
WANTED WAITRESS -AND- DISH-WASHER

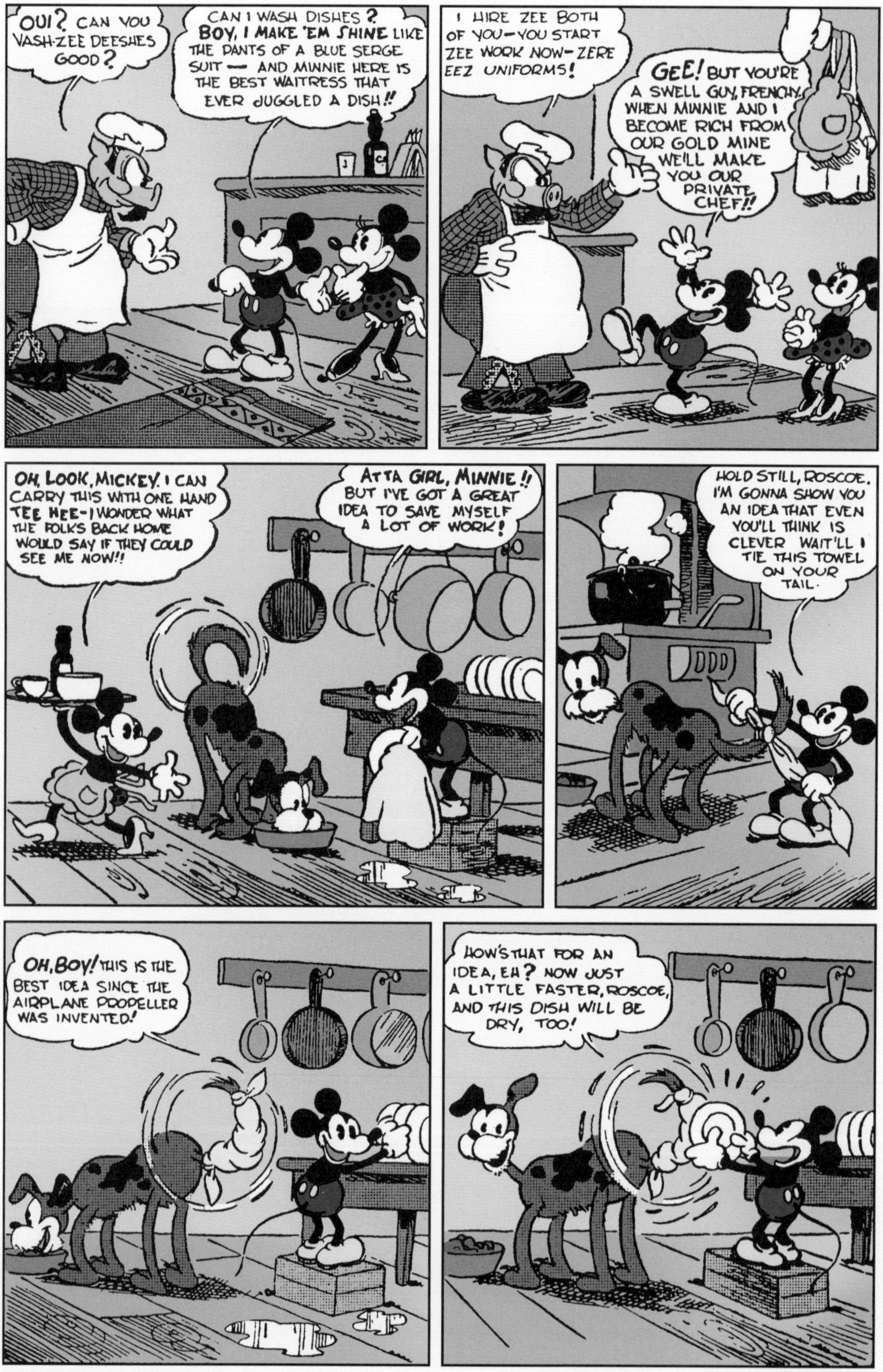
OUI? CAN YOU VASH-ZEE DEESHES GOOD?
CAN I WASH DISHES? BOY, I MAKE 'EM SHINE LIKE THE PANTS OF A BLUE SERGE SUIT — AND MINNIE HERE IS THE BEST WAITRESS THAT EVER JUGGLED A DISH!!
I HIRE ZEE BOTH OF YOU—YOU START ZEE WORK NOW—ZERE EEZ UNIFORMS!
GEE! BUT YOU'RE A SWELL GUY, FRENCHY. WHEN MINNIE AND I BECOME RICH FROM OUR GOLD MINE WE'LL MAKE YOU OUR PRIVATE CHEF!!
OH, LOOK, MICKEY. I CAN CARRY THIS WITH ONE HAND TEE HEE—I WONDER WHAT THE FOLKS BACK HOME WOULD SAY IF THEY COULD SEE ME NOW!!
ATTA GIRL, MINNIE!! BUT I'VE GOT A GREAT IDEA TO SAVE MYSELF A LOT OF WORK!
HOLD STILL, ROSCOE. I'M GONNA SHOW YOU AN IDEA THAT EVEN YOU'LL THINK IS CLEVER WAIT'LL I TIE THIS TOWEL ON YOUR TAIL.
OH, BOY! THIS IS THE BEST IDEA SINCE THE AIRPLANE PROPELLER WAS INVENTED!
HOW'S THAT FOR AN IDEA, EH? NOW JUST A LITTLE FASTER, ROSCOE, AND THIS DISH WILL BE DRY, TOO!

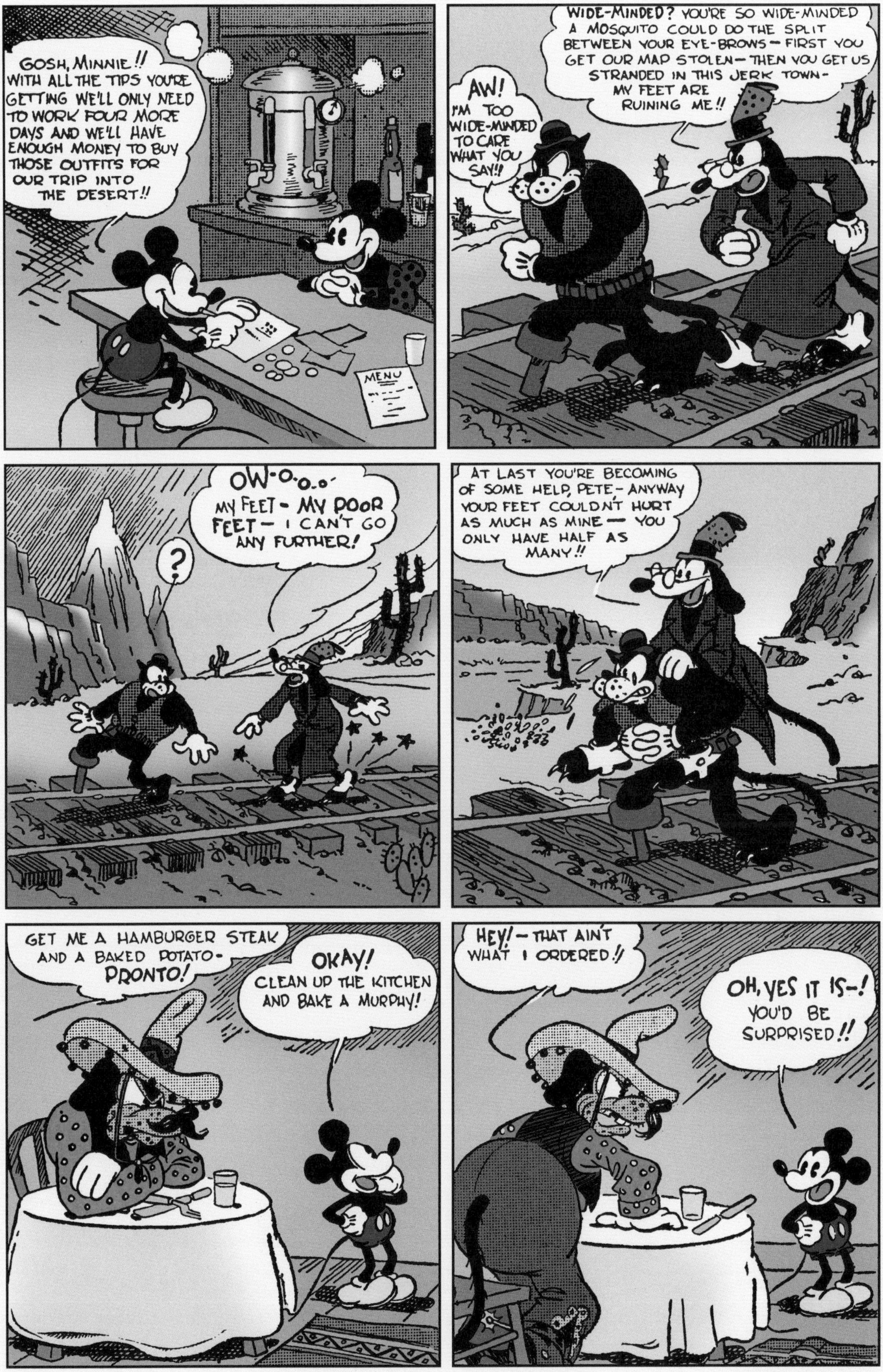
GOSH, MINNIE!! WITH ALL THE TIPS YOU'RE GETTING WE'LL ONLY NEED TO WORK FOUR MORE DAYS AND WE'LL HAVE ENOUGH MONEY TO BUY THOSE OUTFITS FOR OUR TRIP INTO THE DESERT!!
WIDE-MINDED? YOU'RE SO WIDE-MINDED A MOSQUITO COULD DO THE SPLIT BETWEEN YOUR EYE-BROWS—FIRST YOU GET OUR MAP STOLEN—THEN YOU GET US STRANDED IN THIS JERK TOWN—MY FEET ARE RUINING ME!!
AW! I'M TOO WIDE-MINDED TO CARE WHAT YOU SAY!!
OW-O-O-O-
MY FEET—MY POOR FEET—I CAN'T GO ANY FURTHER!
?
AT LAST YOU'RE BECOMING OF SOME HELP, PETE—ANYWAY YOUR FEET COULDN'T HURT AS MUCH AS MINE—YOU ONLY HAVE HALF AS MANY!!
GET ME A HAMBURGER STEAK AND A BAKED POTATO—PRONTO!
OKAY! CLEAN UP THE KITCHEN AND BAKE A MURPHY!
HEY!—THAT AIN'T WHAT I ORDERED!!
OH, YES IT IS—! YOU'D BE SURPRISED!!

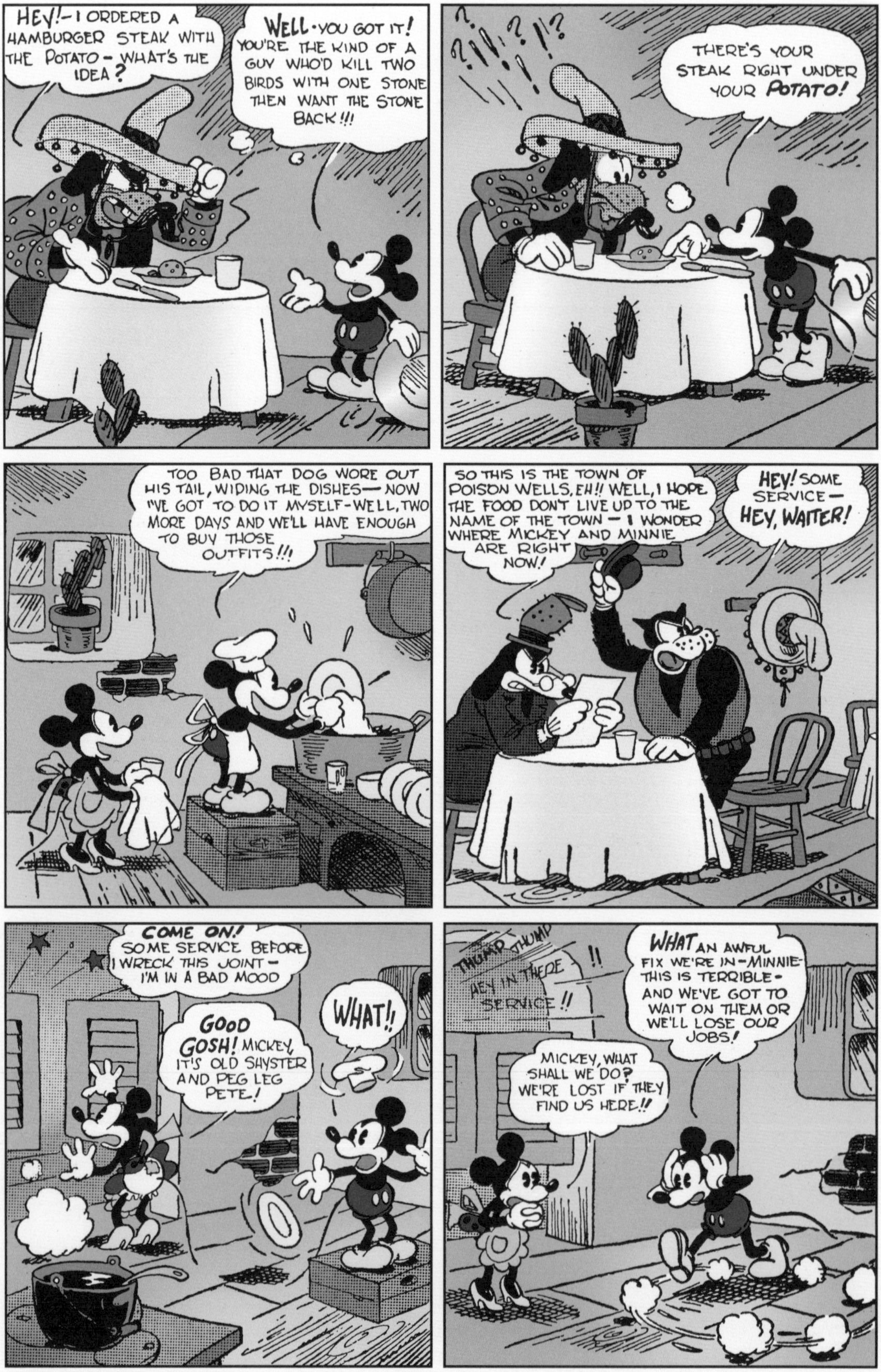
HEY!—I ORDERED A HAMBURGER STEAK WITH THE POTATO—WHAT'S THE IDEA?
WELL—YOU GOT IT! YOU'RE THE KIND OF A GUY WHO'D KILL TWO BIRDS WITH ONE STONE THEN WANT THE STONE BACK!!!
?!!?!!?
THERE'S YOUR STEAK RIGHT UNDER YOUR POTATO!
TOO BAD THAT DOG WORE OUT HIS TAIL, WIPING THE DISHES—NOW I'VE GOT TO DO IT MYSELF—WELL, TWO MORE DAYS AND WE'LL HAVE ENOUGH TO BUY THOSE OUTFITS!!!
SO THIS IS THE TOWN OF POISON WELLS, EH!! WELL, I HOPE THE FOOD DON'T LIVE UP TO THE NAME OF THE TOWN—I WONDER WHERE MICKEY AND MINNIE ARE RIGHT NOW!
HEY! SOME SERVICE—HEY, WAITER!
COME ON! SOME SERVICE BEFORE I WRECK THIS JOINT—I'M IN A BAD MOOD
GOOD GOSH! MICKEY, IT'S OLD SHYSTER AND PEG LEG PETE!
WHAT!!
THUMP THUMP
HEY IN THERE SERVICE!!
!!
WHAT AN AWFUL FIX WE'RE IN—MINNIE THIS IS TERRIBLE—AND WE'VE GOT TO WAIT ON THEM OR WE'LL LOSE OUR JOBS!
MICKEY, WHAT SHALL WE DO? WE'RE LOST IF THEY FIND US HERE!!

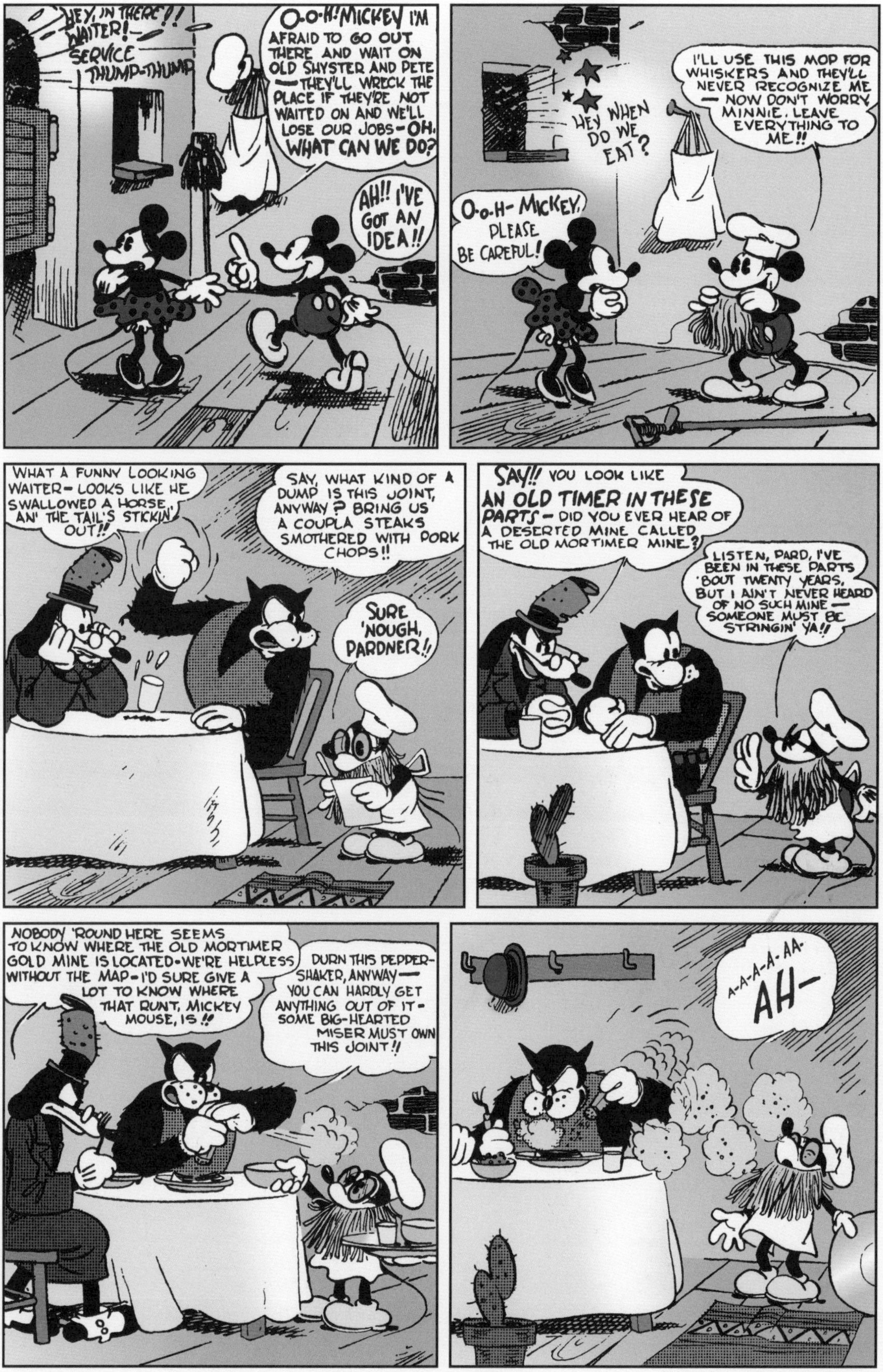
HEY, IN THERE!! WAITER!— SERVICE
THUMP-THUMP
O-O-H! MICKEY I'M AFRAID TO GO OUT THERE AND WAIT ON OLD SHYSTER AND PETE —THEY'LL WRECK THE PLACE IF THEY'RE NOT WAITED ON AND WE'LL LOSE OUR JOBS—OH. WHAT CAN WE DO?
AH!! I'VE GOT AN IDEA!!
HEY WHEN DO WE EAT?
I'LL USE THIS MOP FOR WHISKERS AND THEY'LL NEVER RECOGNIZE ME — NOW DON'T WORRY, MINNIE. LEAVE EVERYTHING TO ME!!
O-o-H- MICKEY, PLEASE BE CAREFUL!
WHAT A FUNNY LOOKING WAITER— LOOKS LIKE HE SWALLOWED A HORSE, AN' THE TAIL'S STICKIN' OUT!!
SAY, WHAT KIND OF A DUMP IS THIS JOINT, ANYWAY? BRING US A COUPLA STEAKS SMOTHERED WITH PORK CHOPS!!
SURE 'NOUGH, PARDNER!!
SAY!! YOU LOOK LIKE AN OLD TIMER IN THESE PARTS— DID YOU EVER HEAR OF A DESERTED MINE CALLED THE OLD MORTIMER MINE?
LISTEN, PARD, I'VE BEEN IN THESE PARTS 'BOUT TWENTY YEARS, BUT I AIN'T NEVER HEARD OF NO SUCH MINE— SOMEONE MUST BE STRINGIN' YA!!
NOBODY 'ROUND HERE SEEMS TO KNOW WHERE THE OLD MORTIMER GOLD MINE IS LOCATED—WE'RE HELPLESS WITHOUT THE MAP—I'D SURE GIVE A LOT TO KNOW WHERE THAT RUNT, MICKEY MOUSE, IS!!
DURN THIS PEPPER-SHAKER, ANYWAY— YOU CAN HARDLY GET ANYTHING OUT OF IT— SOME BIG-HEARTED MISER MUST OWN THIS JOINT!!
A-A-A-A-A-AA-AH—

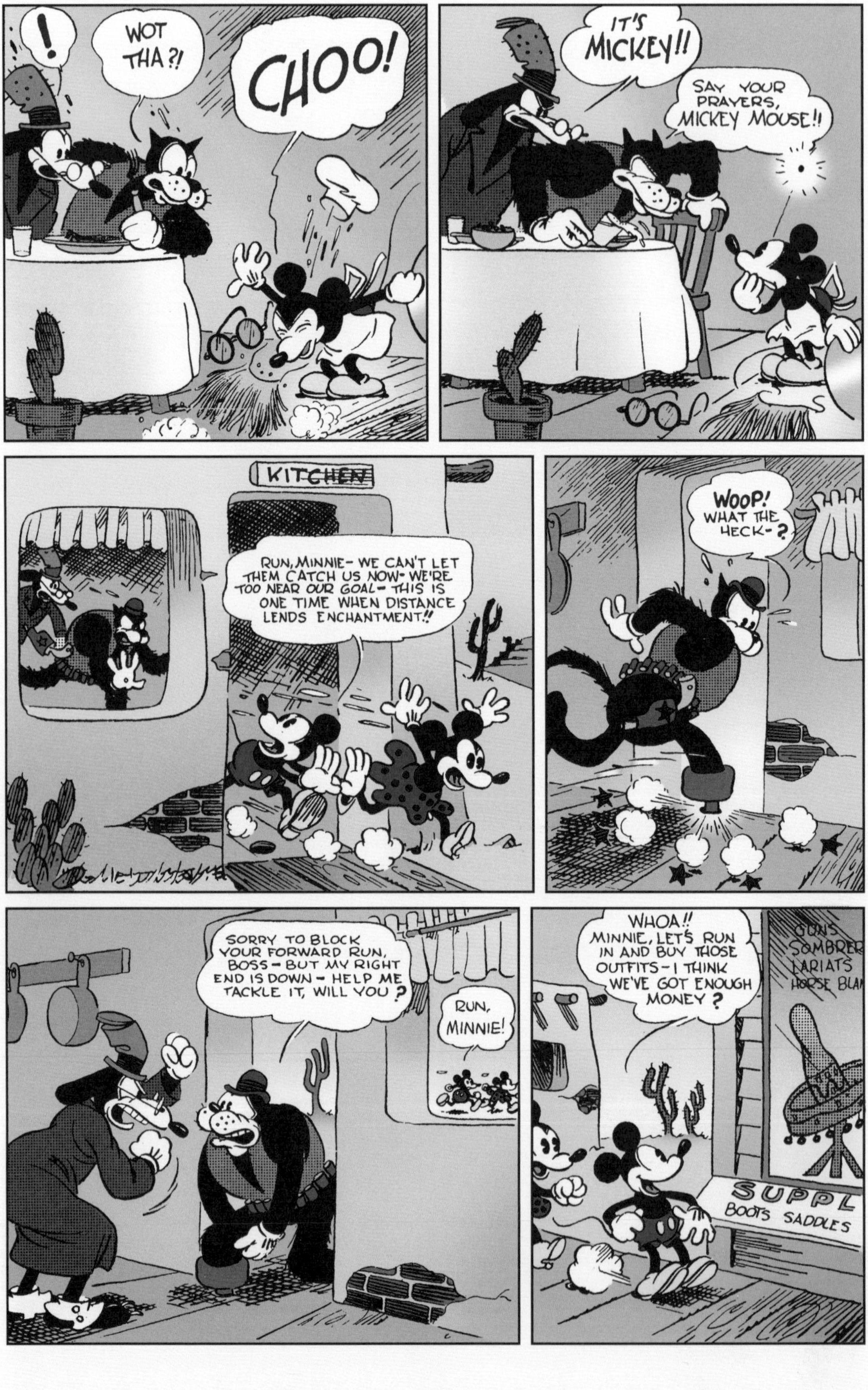
!
WOT THA ?!
CHOO!
IT'S MICKEY!!
SAY YOUR PRAYERS, MICKEY MOUSE!!
KITCHEN
RUN, MINNIE- WE CAN'T LET THEM CATCH US NOW- WE'RE TOO NEAR OUR GOAL- THIS IS ONE TIME WHEN DISTANCE LENDS ENCHANTMENT!!
WOOP! WHAT THE HECK-?
SORRY TO BLOCK YOUR FORWARD RUN, BOSS - BUT MY RIGHT END IS DOWN - HELP ME TACKLE IT, WILL YOU?
RUN, MINNIE!
WHOA!! MINNIE, LET'S RUN IN AND BUY THOSE OUTFITS - I THINK WE'VE GOT ENOUGH MONEY?
SOMBRER
LARIATS
SUPPL
BOOTS SADDLES

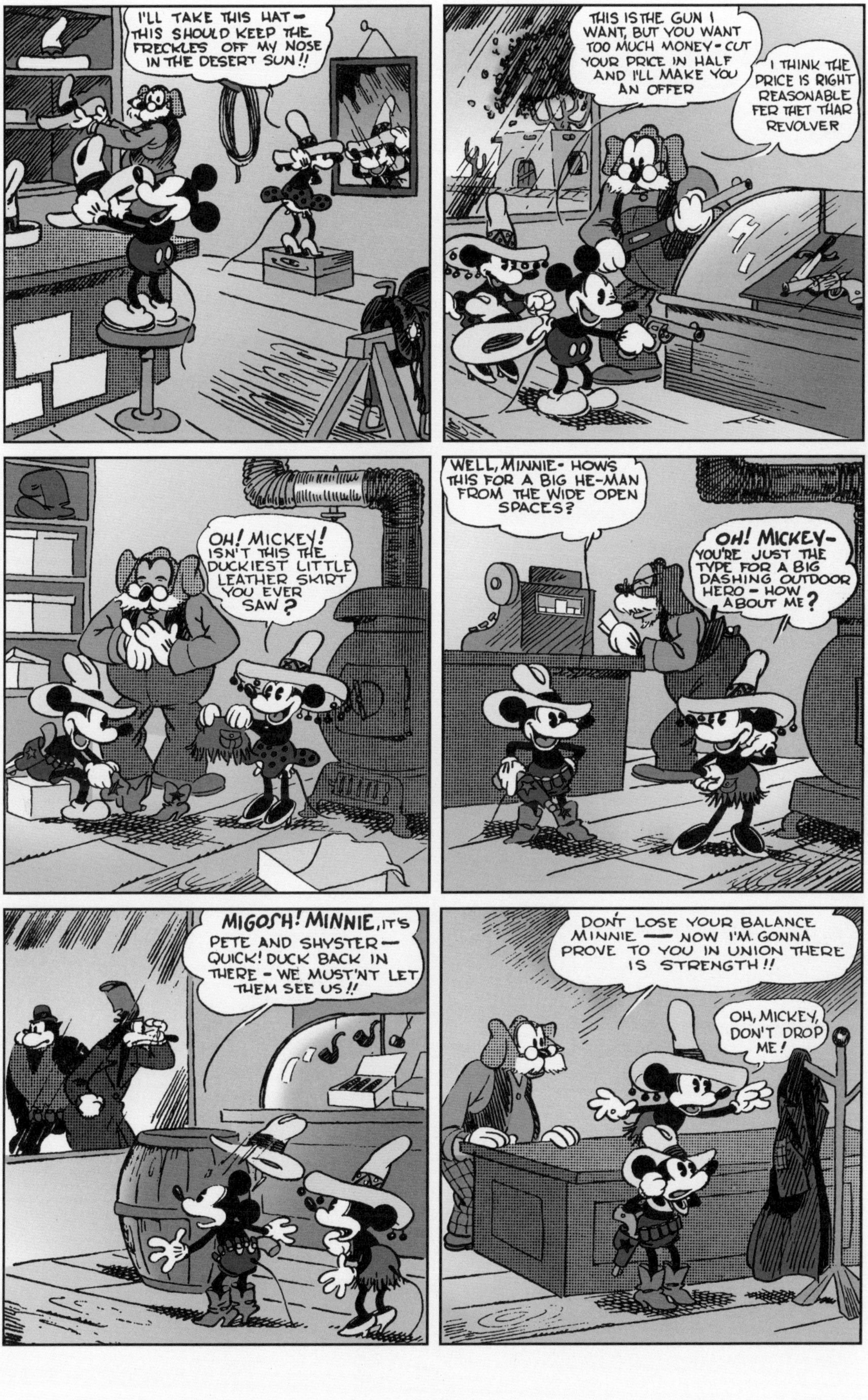
I'LL TAKE THIS HAT— THIS SHOULD KEEP THE FRECKLES OFF MY NOSE IN THE DESERT SUN!!
THIS IS THE GUN I WANT, BUT YOU WANT TOO MUCH MONEY — CUT YOUR PRICE IN HALF AND I'LL MAKE YOU AN OFFER
I THINK THE PRICE IS RIGHT REASONABLE FER THET THAR REVOLVER
OH! MICKEY! ISN'T THIS THE DUCKIEST LITTLE LEATHER SKIRT YOU EVER SAW?
WELL, MINNIE- HOWS THIS FOR A BIG HE-MAN FROM THE WIDE OPEN SPACES?
OH! MICKEY- YOU'RE JUST THE TYPE FOR A BIG DASHING OUTDOOR HERO — HOW ABOUT ME?
MIGOSH! MINNIE, IT'S PETE AND SHYSTER— QUICK! DUCK BACK IN THERE — WE MUST'NT LET THEM SEE US!!
DON'T LOSE YOUR BALANCE MINNIE — NOW I'M GONNA PROVE TO YOU IN UNION THERE IS STRENGTH!!
OH, MICKEY, DON'T DROP ME!

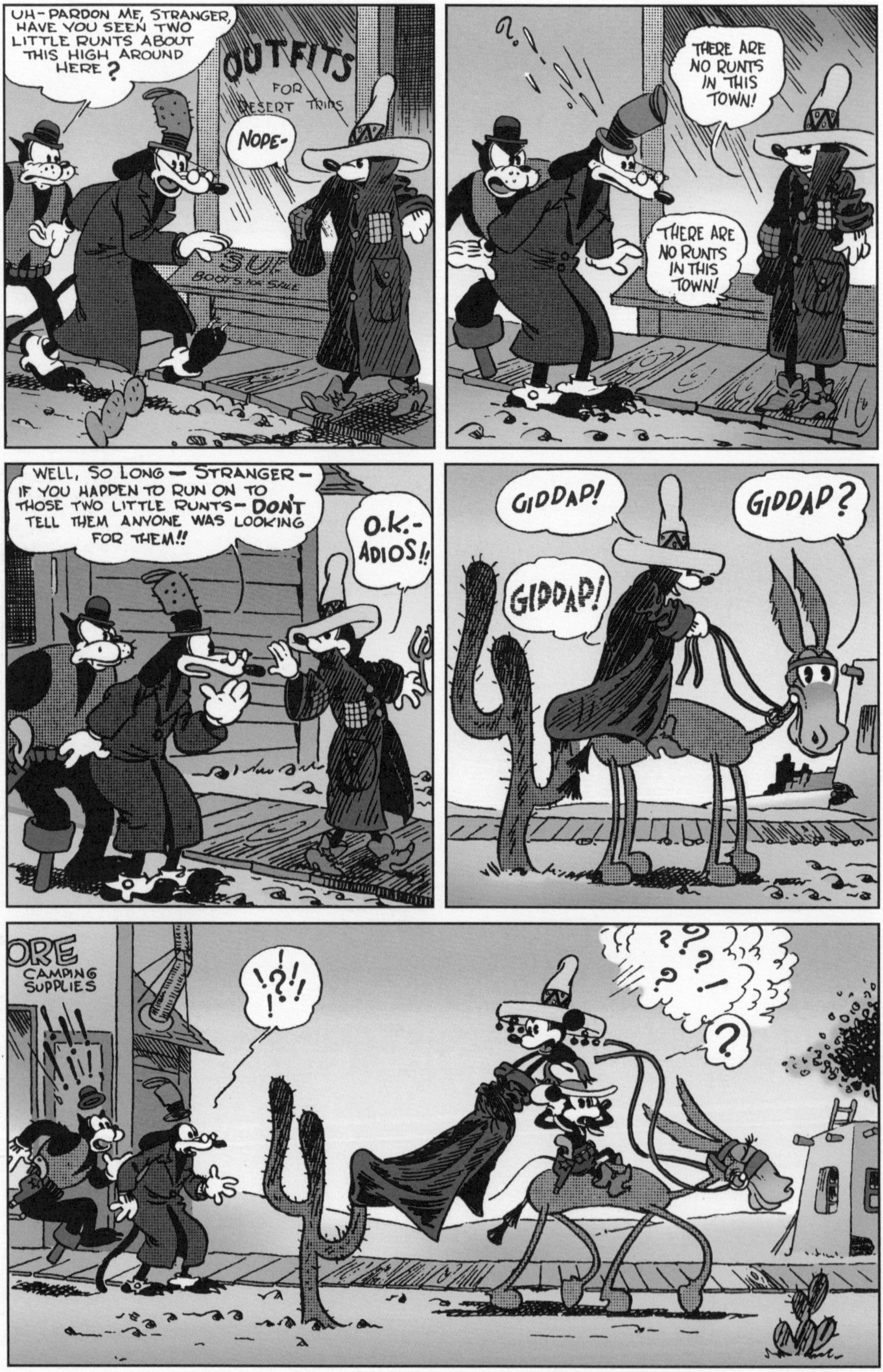
UH-PARDON ME, STRANGER, HAVE YOU SEEN TWO LITTLE RUNTS ABOUT THIS HIGH AROUND HERE?
OUTFITS FOR DESERT TRIPS
NOPE-
BOOTS for SALE
THERE ARE NO RUNTS IN THIS TOWN!
THERE ARE NO RUNTS IN THIS TOWN!
WELL, SO LONG — STRANGER — IF YOU HAPPEN TO RUN ON TO THOSE TWO LITTLE RUNTS — DON'T TELL THEM ANYONE WAS LOOKING FOR THEM!!
O.K.- ADIOS!!
GIDDAP!
GIDDAP?
GIDDAP!
ORE
CAMPING SUPPLIES
!?!!
?

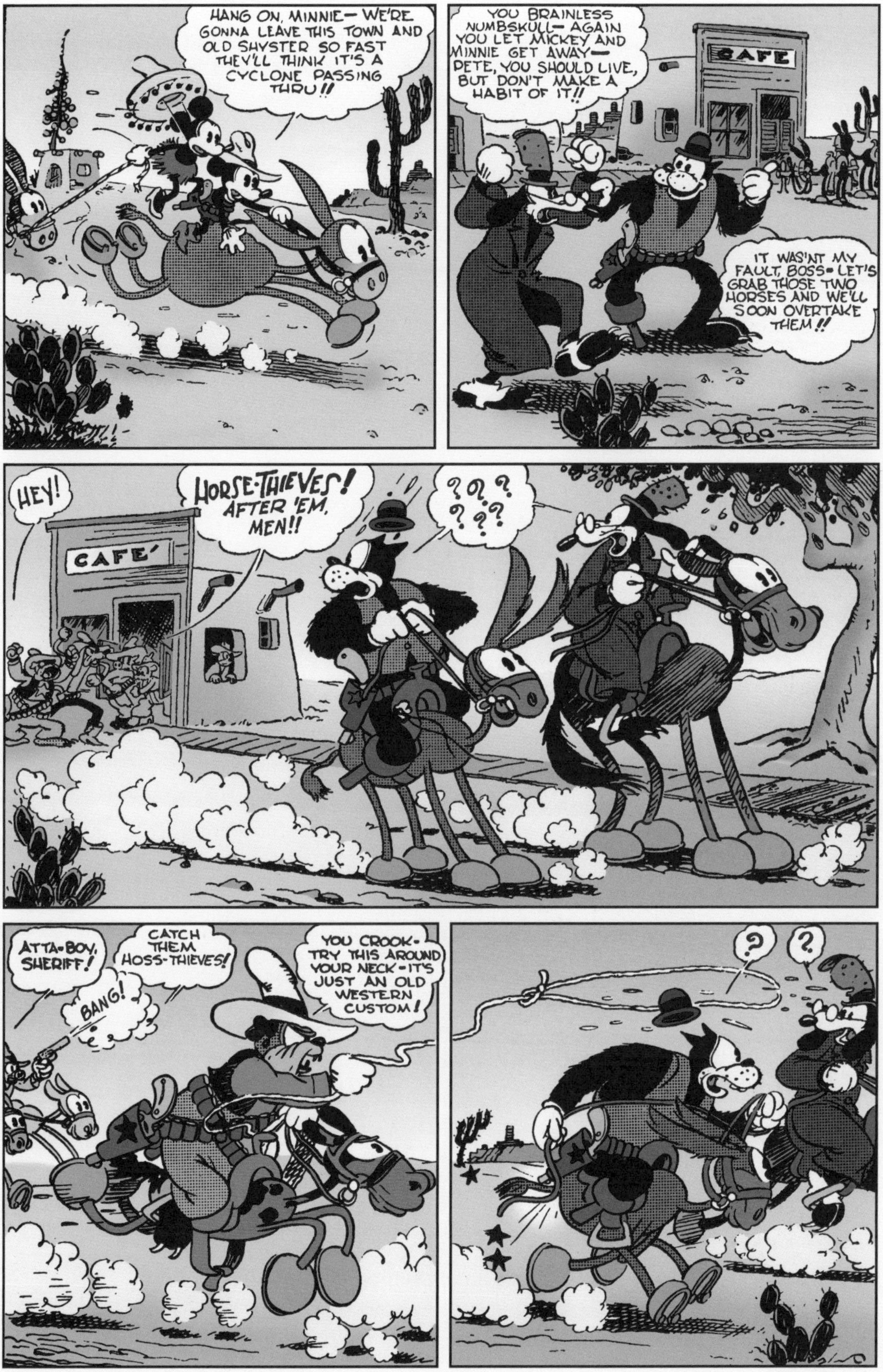
HANG ON, MINNIE— WE'RE GONNA LEAVE THIS TOWN AND OLD SHYSTER SO FAST THEY'LL THINK IT'S A CYCLONE PASSING THRU!!
YOU BRAINLESS NUMBSKULL— AGAIN YOU LET MICKEY AND MINNIE GET AWAY— PETE, YOU SHOULD LIVE, BUT DON'T MAKE A HABIT OF IT!!
CAFE
IT WAS'NT MY FAULT, BOSS• LET'S GRAB THOSE TWO HORSES AND WE'LL SOON OVERTAKE THEM!!
HEY!
CAFE'
HORSE-THIEVES! AFTER 'EM, MEN!!
??? ???
ATTA-BOY, SHERIFF!
CATCH THEM HOSS-THIEVES!
BANG!
YOU CROOK- TRY THIS AROUND YOUR NECK- IT'S JUST AN OLD WESTERN CUSTOM!
?
?

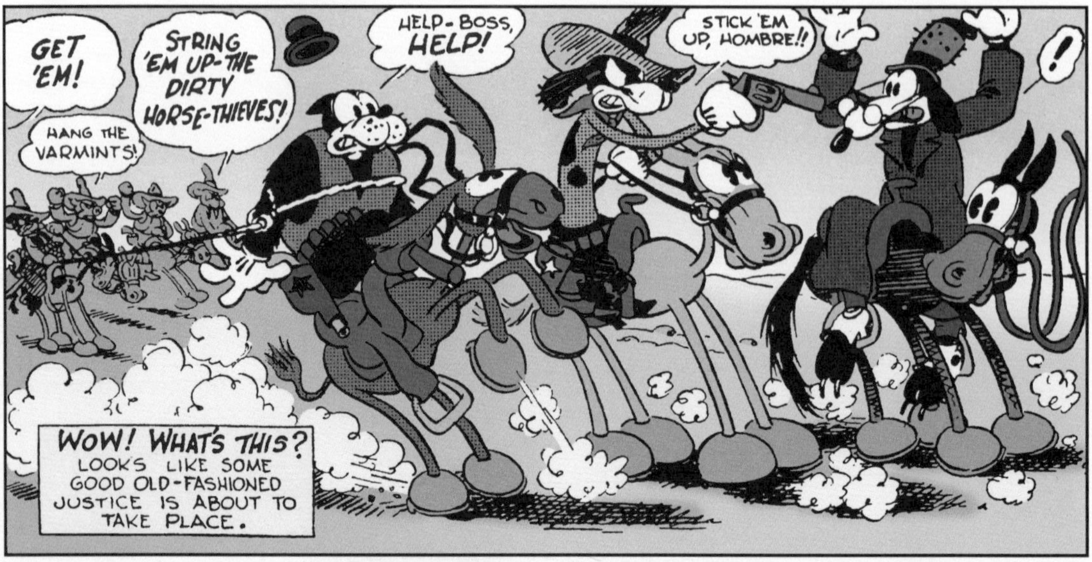
GET 'EM!
HANG THE VARMINTS!
STRING 'EM UP-THE DIRTY HORSE-THIEVES!
HELP-BOSS, HELP!
STICK 'EM UP, HOMBRE!!
!
WOW! WHAT'S THIS? LOOK'S LIKE SOME GOOD OLD-FASHIONED JUSTICE IS ABOUT TO TAKE PLACE.

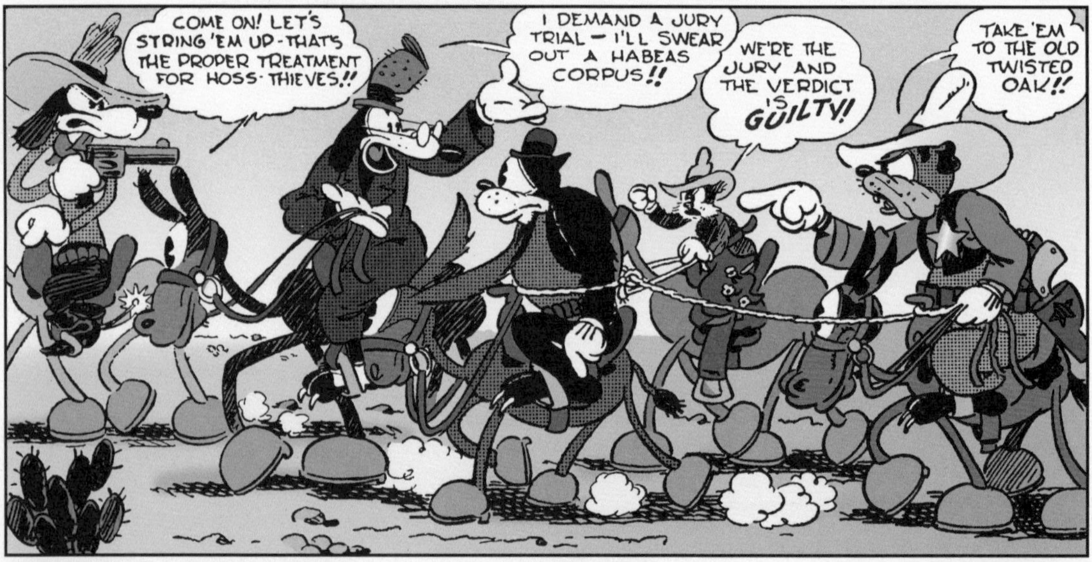
COME ON! LET'S STRING 'EM UP-THAT'S THE PROPER TREATMENT FOR HOSS-THIEVES!!
I DEMAND A JURY TRIAL-I'LL SWEAR OUT A HABEAS CORPUS!!
WE'RE THE JURY AND THE VERDICT IS GUILTY!
TAKE 'EM TO THE OLD TWISTED OAK!!

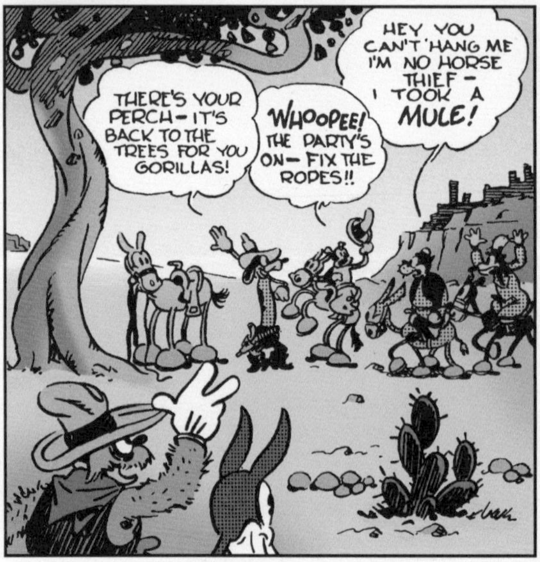
THERE'S YOUR PERCH-IT'S BACK TO THE TREES FOR YOU GORILLAS!
WHOOPEE! THE PARTY'S ON-FIX THE ROPES!!
HEY YOU CAN'T HANG ME I'M NO HORSE THIEF-I TOOK A MULE!

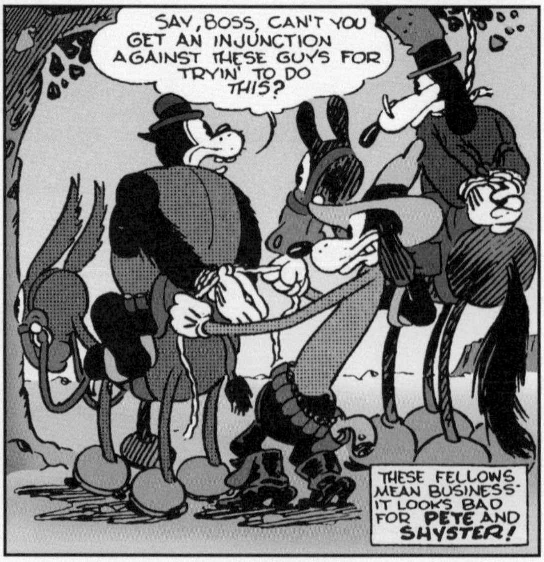
SAY, BOSS, CAN'T YOU GET AN INJUNCTION AGAINST THESE GUYS FOR TRYIN' TO DO THIS?
THESE FELLOWS MEAN BUSINESS-IT LOOKS BAD FOR PETE AND SHYSTER!

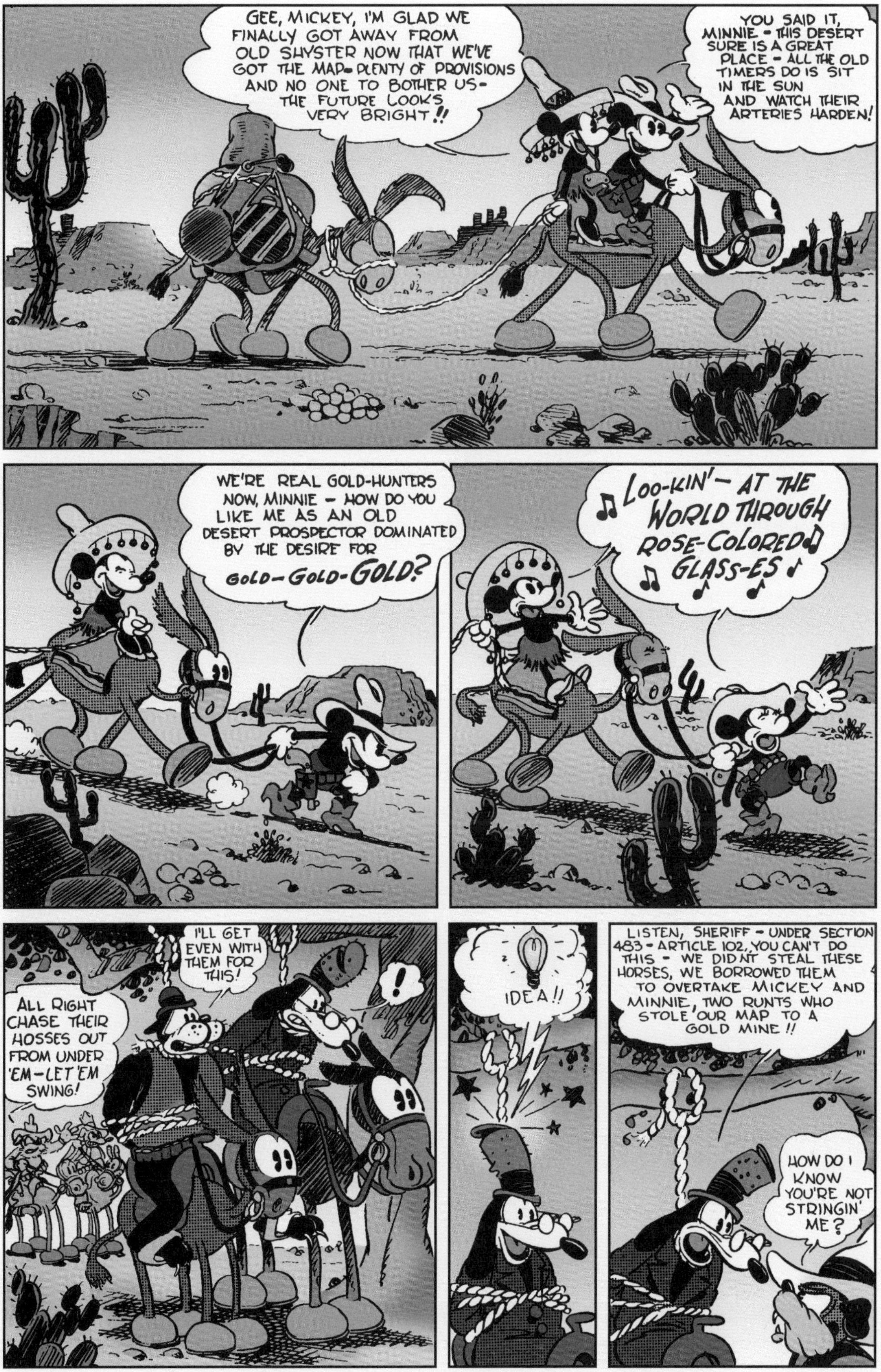
GEE, MICKEY, I'M GLAD WE FINALLY GOT AWAY FROM OLD SHYSTER NOW THAT WE'VE GOT THE MAP- PLENTY OF PROVISIONS AND NO ONE TO BOTHER US- THE FUTURE LOOKS VERY BRIGHT!!
YOU SAID IT, MINNIE - THIS DESERT SURE IS A GREAT PLACE - ALL THE OLD TIMERS DO IS SIT IN THE SUN AND WATCH THEIR ARTERIES HARDEN!
WE'RE REAL GOLD-HUNTERS NOW, MINNIE - HOW DO YOU LIKE ME AS AN OLD DESERT PROSPECTOR DOMINATED BY THE DESIRE FOR GOLD-GOLD-GOLD?
LOO-KIN'- AT THE WORLD THROUGH ROSE-COLORED GLASS-ES
I'LL GET EVEN WITH THEM FOR THIS!
ALL RIGHT CHASE THEIR HOSSES OUT FROM UNDER 'EM-LET 'EM SWING!
!
IDEA!!
LISTEN, SHERIFF - UNDER SECTION 483 - ARTICLE 102, YOU CAN'T DO THIS - WE DIDN'T STEAL THESE HORSES, WE BORROWED THEM TO OVERTAKE MICKEY AND MINNIE, TWO RUNTS WHO STOLE OUR MAP TO A GOLD MINE!!
HOW DO I KNOW YOU'RE NOT STRINGIN' ME?

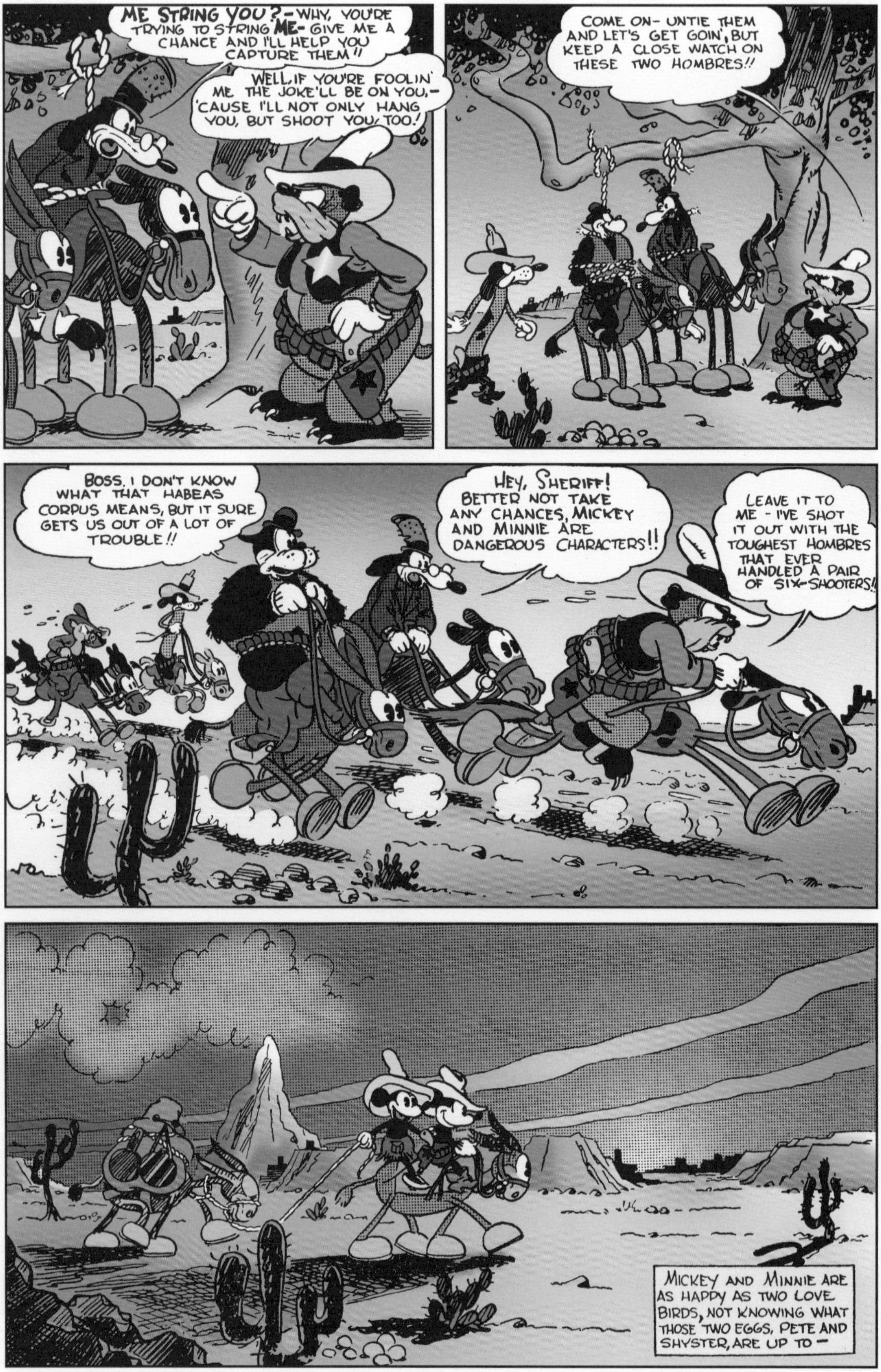
ME STRING YOU?–WHY, YOU'RE TRYING TO STRING ME–GIVE ME A CHANCE AND I'LL HELP YOU CAPTURE THEM!!
WELL,IF YOU'RE FOOLIN' ME THE JOKE'LL BE ON YOU,–'CAUSE I'LL NOT ONLY HANG YOU, BUT SHOOT YOU, TOO!
COME ON– UNTIE THEM AND LET'S GET GOIN', BUT KEEP A CLOSE WATCH ON THESE TWO HOMBRES!!
BOSS, I DON'T KNOW WHAT THAT HABEAS CORPUS MEANS, BUT IT SURE GETS US OUT OF A LOT OF TROUBLE!!
HEY, SHERIFF! BETTER NOT TAKE ANY CHANCES, MICKEY AND MINNIE ARE DANGEROUS CHARACTERS!!
LEAVE IT TO ME – I'VE SHOT IT OUT WITH THE TOUGHEST HOMBRES THAT EVER HANDLED A PAIR OF SIX-SHOOTERS!!
MICKEY AND MINNIE ARE AS HAPPY AS TWO LOVE BIRDS, NOT KNOWING WHAT THOSE TWO EGGS, PETE AND SHYSTER, ARE UP TO–

WHAT HAS HAPPENED
—TO DATE—

OUR GALLANT LITTLE HERO, "MICKEY MOUSE", IS WITH HIS SWEETHEART, "MINNIE." ONE DAY WHEN SHE RECEIVES WORD THAT SHE HAS BEEN MADE SOLE HEIR TO THE CHEESE FACTORY AND OLD MANSION OF HER LATE UNCLE, "MORTIMER MOUSE!" THE ESTATE IS UNDER THE GUARDIANSHIP OF A CROOKED OLD LAWYER, "SYLVESTER SHYSTER".

"MICKEY"

"MINNIE"

WHO, KNOWING THAT THE OLD MANSION CONTAINS VALUABLE INFORMATION CONCERNING A SECRET TREASURE LEFT BY OLD MORTIMER, TRIES TO BUY THE ESTATE FROM MINNIE. THINKING THE MANSION WORTHLESS MINNIE IS ABOUT TO SELL WHEN—

A MAP, MINNIE— A MAP TO A GOLD MINE!

OH, MICKEY!

SUDDENLY A MYSTERIOUS STRANGER, "THE FOX", APPEARS ON THE SCENE AND TELLS MINNIE NOT TO SELL— SHE THEREFORE REFUSES OLD SHYSTER'S OFFER AND SHE AND MICKEY TAKE POSSESSION OF THE MANSION. AFTER A SERIES OF ADVENTURES IN WHICH OLD SHYSTER'S HENCHMAN, PEG-LEG PETE, TRIES TO FORCE MINNIE TO SELL THE MANSION, MICKEY AND MINNIE FIND IN THE CELLAR A MAP OF A GOLD MINE IN DEATH VALLEY WHICH OLD SHYSTER IS REALLY AFTER —

SYLVESTER SHYSTER. A CROOKED LAWYER— THE KIND OF A GUY WHO'D STICK A KNIFE IN YOUR BACK THEN HAVE YOU ARRESTED FOR CARRYING CONCEALED WEAPONS.

"PEG-LEG PETE," OLD SHYSTER'S HENCHMAN FIENDISH BUT DUMB.

"THE FOX," A MYSTERIOUS FRIEND TO MICKEY AND MINNIE···? WHO IS HE? WHAT IS HE? NO ONE KNOWS.

TAKING THE MAP THEY STRIKE OUT FOR DEATH VALLEY AND ARE PURSUED BY OLD SHYSTER. BEFORE GOING INTO THE DESERT MICKEY AND MINNIE EQUIP THEMSELVES AS PROSPECTORS AND START OUT FOR THE MINE.

BOTH ARE HAPPY AND THRILLED WITH THE SPIRIT OF ADVENTURE ALL UNAWARE THAT—

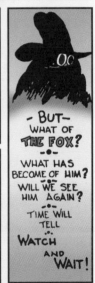

— BUT— WHAT OF THE FOX?
—·—
WHAT HAS BECOME OF HIM?
—·—
WILL WE SEE HIM AGAIN?
—·—
TIME WILL TELL
WATCH AND WAIT!

— SHYSTER AND PETE HAVE ENLISTED THE AID OF A WESTERN SHERIFF AND POSSE BY MAKING THEM BELIEVE THAT MICKEY STOLE THE MAP— AND ARE NOW HOTLY PURSUING MICKEY AND MINNIE ACROSS THE DESERT

SO YOU REFUSE TO MOVE, EH?— SO YOU DON'T UNDERSTAND WHEN I SAY MOVE—WELL YOU'LL SOON GET THE POINT!!

YOU BALKY OLD THING! I'VE A GOOD MIND TO RING YOUR EARS!!

NOW MOVE!!

SOCK!

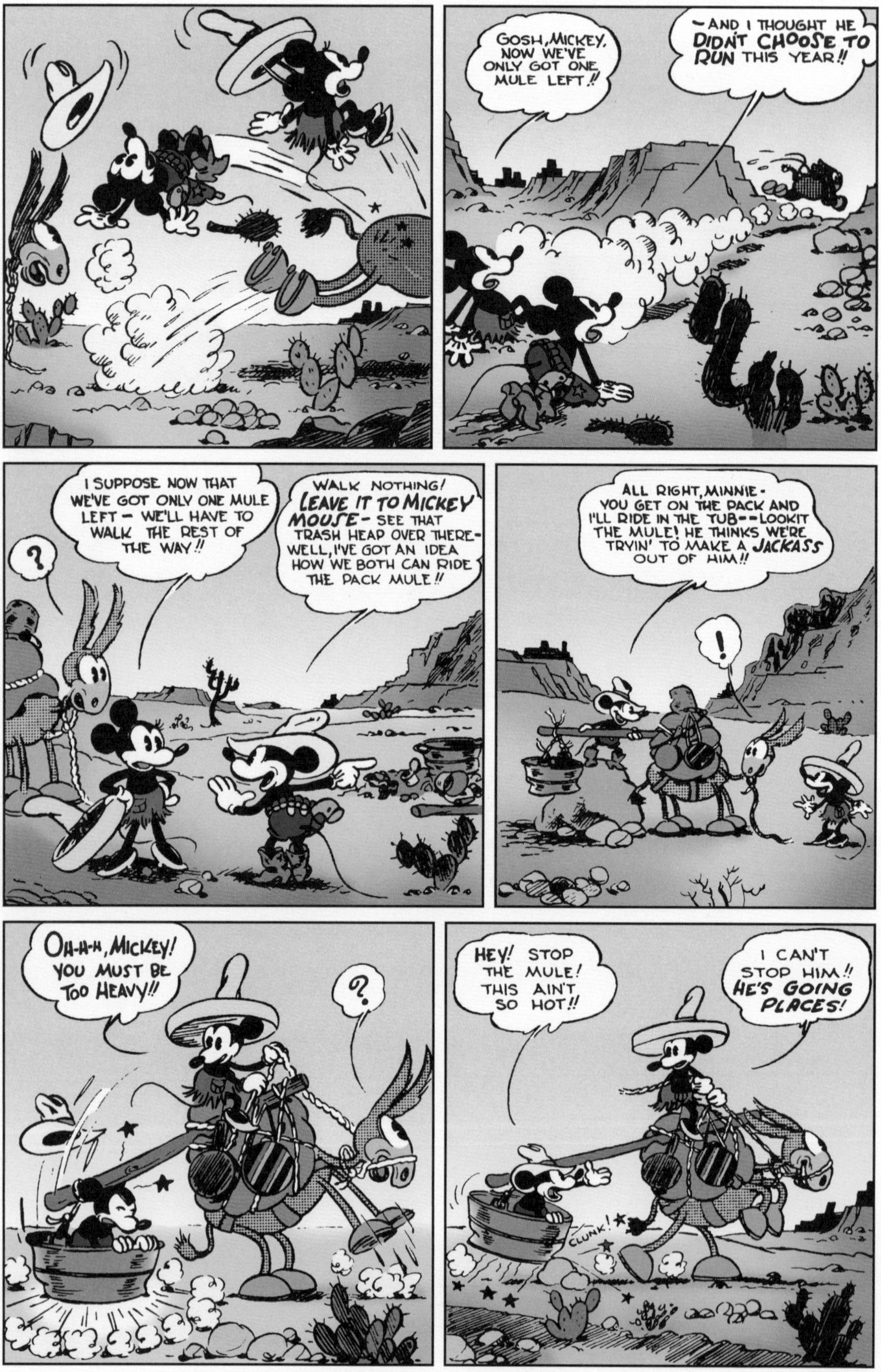
GOSH, MICKEY, NOW WE'VE ONLY GOT ONE MULE LEFT!!
–AND I THOUGHT HE DIDN'T CHOOSE TO RUN THIS YEAR!!
?
I SUPPOSE NOW THAT WE'VE GOT ONLY ONE MULE LEFT – WE'LL HAVE TO WALK THE REST OF THE WAY!!
WALK NOTHING! LEAVE IT TO MICKEY MOUSE – SEE THAT TRASH HEAP OVER THERE – WELL, I'VE GOT AN IDEA HOW WE BOTH CAN RIDE THE PACK MULE!!
ALL RIGHT, MINNIE – YOU GET ON THE PACK AND I'LL RIDE IN THE TUB – – LOOKIT THE MULE! HE THINKS WE'RE TRYIN' TO MAKE A JACKASS OUT OF HIM!!
!
OH-H-H, MICKEY! YOU MUST BE TOO HEAVY!!
?
HEY! STOP THE MULE! THIS AIN'T SO HOT!!
I CAN'T STOP HIM!! HE'S GOING PLACES!
CLUNK!

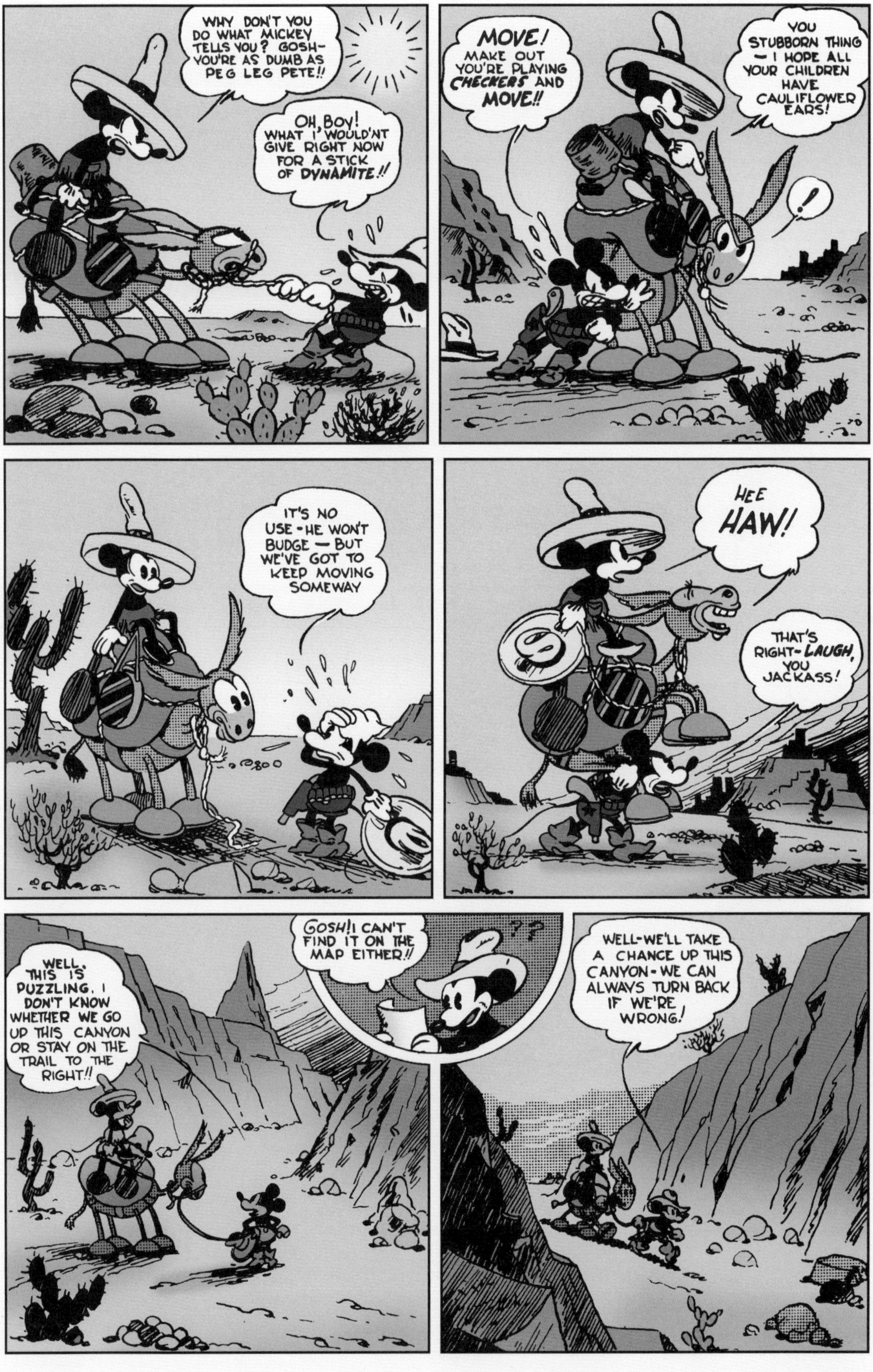
WHY DON'T YOU DO WHAT MICKEY TELLS YOU? GOSH- YOU'RE AS DUMB AS PEG LEG PETE!!
OH, BOY! WHAT I' WOULD'NT GIVE RIGHT NOW FOR A STICK OF DYNAMITE!!
MOVE! MAKE OUT YOU'RE PLAYING CHECKERS AND MOVE!!
YOU STUBBORN THING - I HOPE ALL YOUR CHILDREN HAVE CAULIFLOWER EARS!
!
IT'S NO USE-HE WON'T BUDGE - BUT WE'VE GOT TO KEEP MOVING SOMEWAY
HEE HAW!
THAT'S RIGHT-LAUGH, YOU JACKASS!
WELL, THIS IS PUZZLING. I DON'T KNOW WHETHER WE GO UP THIS CANYON OR STAY ON THE TRAIL TO THE RIGHT!!
GOSH! I CAN'T FIND IT ON THE MAP EITHER!!
??
WELL-WE'LL TAKE A CHANCE UP THIS CANYON-WE CAN ALWAYS TURN BACK IF WE'RE WRONG!

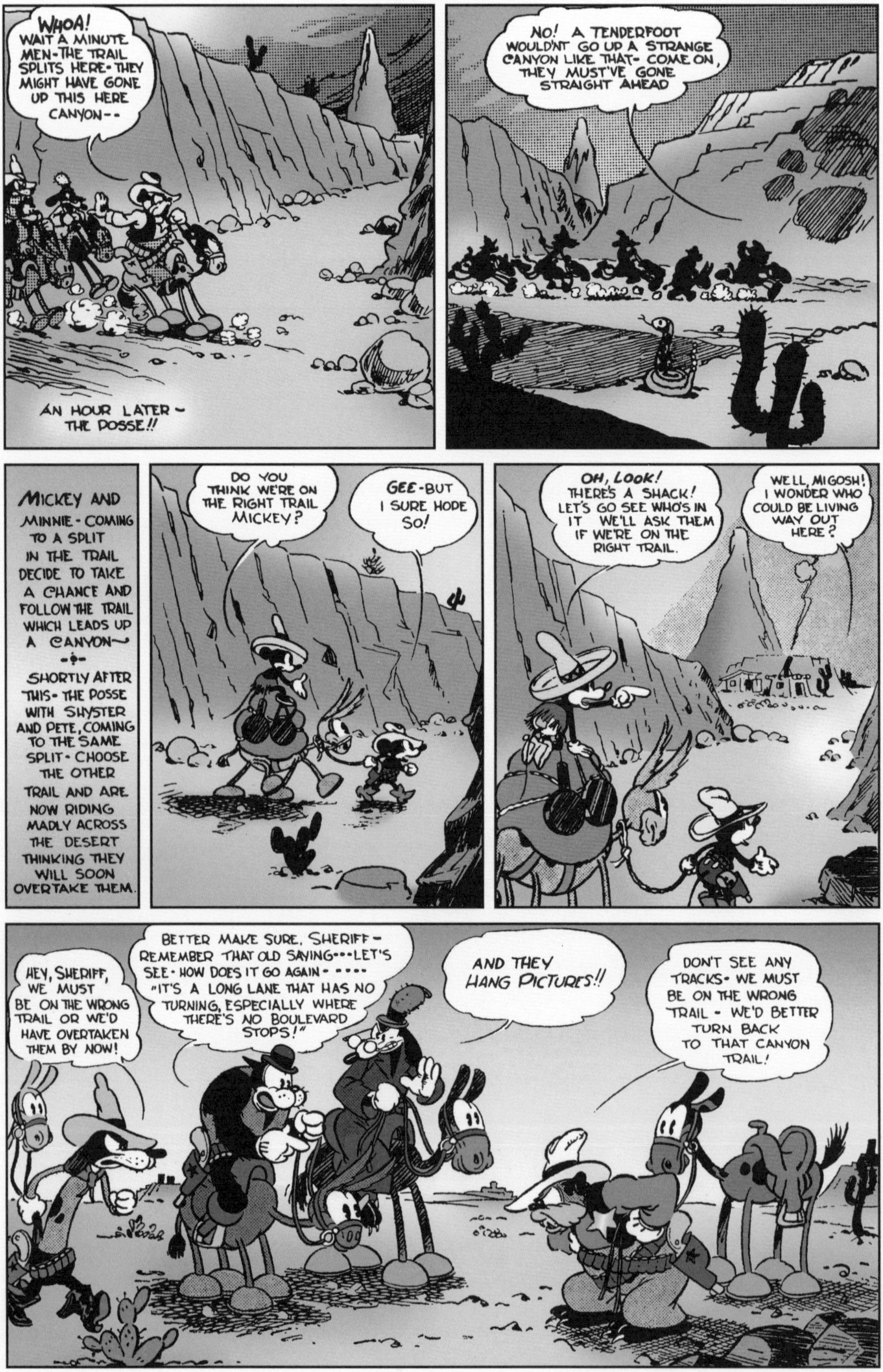
WHOA!
WAIT A MINUTE MEN-THE TRAIL SPLITS HERE-THEY MIGHT HAVE GONE UP THIS HERE CANYON--
AN HOUR LATER - THE POSSE!!
NO! A TENDERFOOT WOULD'NT GO UP A STRANGE CANYON LIKE THAT- COME ON, THEY MUST'VE GONE STRAIGHT AHEAD
MICKEY AND MINNIE-COMING TO A SPLIT IN THE TRAIL DECIDE TO TAKE A CHANCE AND FOLLOW THE TRAIL WHICH LEADS UP A CANYON~
SHORTLY AFTER THIS-THE POSSE WITH SHYSTER AND PETE, COMING TO THE SAME SPLIT-CHOOSE THE OTHER TRAIL AND ARE NOW RIDING MADLY ACROSS THE DESERT THINKING THEY WILL SOON OVERTAKE THEM.
DO YOU THINK WE'RE ON THE RIGHT TRAIL MICKEY?
GEE-BUT I SURE HOPE SO!
OH, LOOK! THERE'S A SHACK! LET'S GO SEE WHO'S IN IT WE'LL ASK THEM IF WE'RE ON THE RIGHT TRAIL.
WELL, MIGOSH! I WONDER WHO COULD BE LIVING WAY OUT HERE?
HEY, SHERIFF, WE MUST BE ON THE WRONG TRAIL OR WE'D HAVE OVERTAKEN THEM BY NOW!
BETTER MAKE SURE, SHERIFF-REMEMBER THAT OLD SAYING---LET'S SEE-HOW DOES IT GO AGAIN-----"IT'S A LONG LANE THAT HAS NO TURNING, ESPECIALLY WHERE THERE'S NO BOULEVARD STOPS!"
AND THEY HANG PICTURES!!
DON'T SEE ANY TRACKS-WE MUST BE ON THE WRONG TRAIL - WE'D BETTER TURN BACK TO THAT CANYON TRAIL!

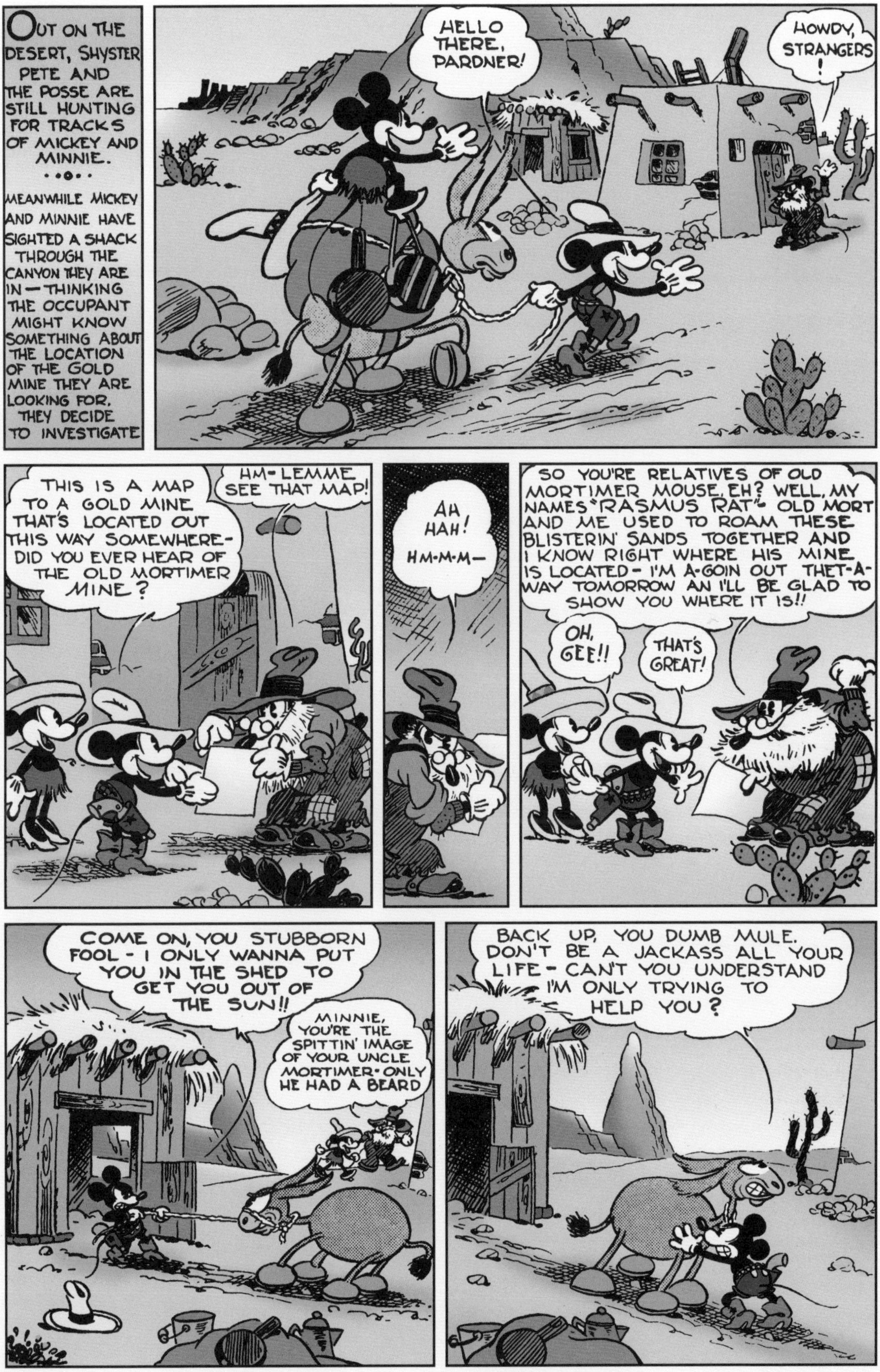
OUT ON THE DESERT, SHYSTER PETE AND THE POSSE ARE STILL HUNTING FOR TRACKS OF MICKEY AND MINNIE.
•••
MEANWHILE MICKEY AND MINNIE HAVE SIGHTED A SHACK THROUGH THE CANYON THEY ARE IN—THINKING THE OCCUPANT MIGHT KNOW SOMETHING ABOUT THE LOCATION OF THE GOLD MINE THEY ARE LOOKING FOR. THEY DECIDE TO INVESTIGATE
HELLO THERE, PARDNER!
HOWDY, STRANGERS!
THIS IS A MAP TO A GOLD MINE THAT'S LOCATED OUT THIS WAY SOMEWHERE-DID YOU EVER HEAR OF THE OLD MORTIMER MINE?
HM-LEMME SEE THAT MAP!
AH HAH! HM-M-M—
SO YOU'RE RELATIVES OF OLD MORTIMER MOUSE, EH? WELL, MY NAMES "RASMUS RAT"- OLD MORT AND ME USED TO ROAM THESE BLISTERIN' SANDS TOGETHER AND I KNOW RIGHT WHERE HIS MINE IS LOCATED- I'M A-GOIN OUT THET-A-WAY TOMORROW AN I'LL BE GLAD TO SHOW YOU WHERE IT IS!!
OH, GEE!!
THAT'S GREAT!
COME ON, YOU STUBBORN FOOL - I ONLY WANNA PUT YOU IN THE SHED TO GET YOU OUT OF THE SUN!!
MINNIE, YOU'RE THE SPITTIN' IMAGE OF YOUR UNCLE MORTIMER- ONLY HE HAD A BEARD
BACK UP, YOU DUMB MULE. DON'T BE A JACKASS ALL YOUR LIFE - CAN'T YOU UNDERSTAND I'M ONLY TRYING TO HELP YOU?

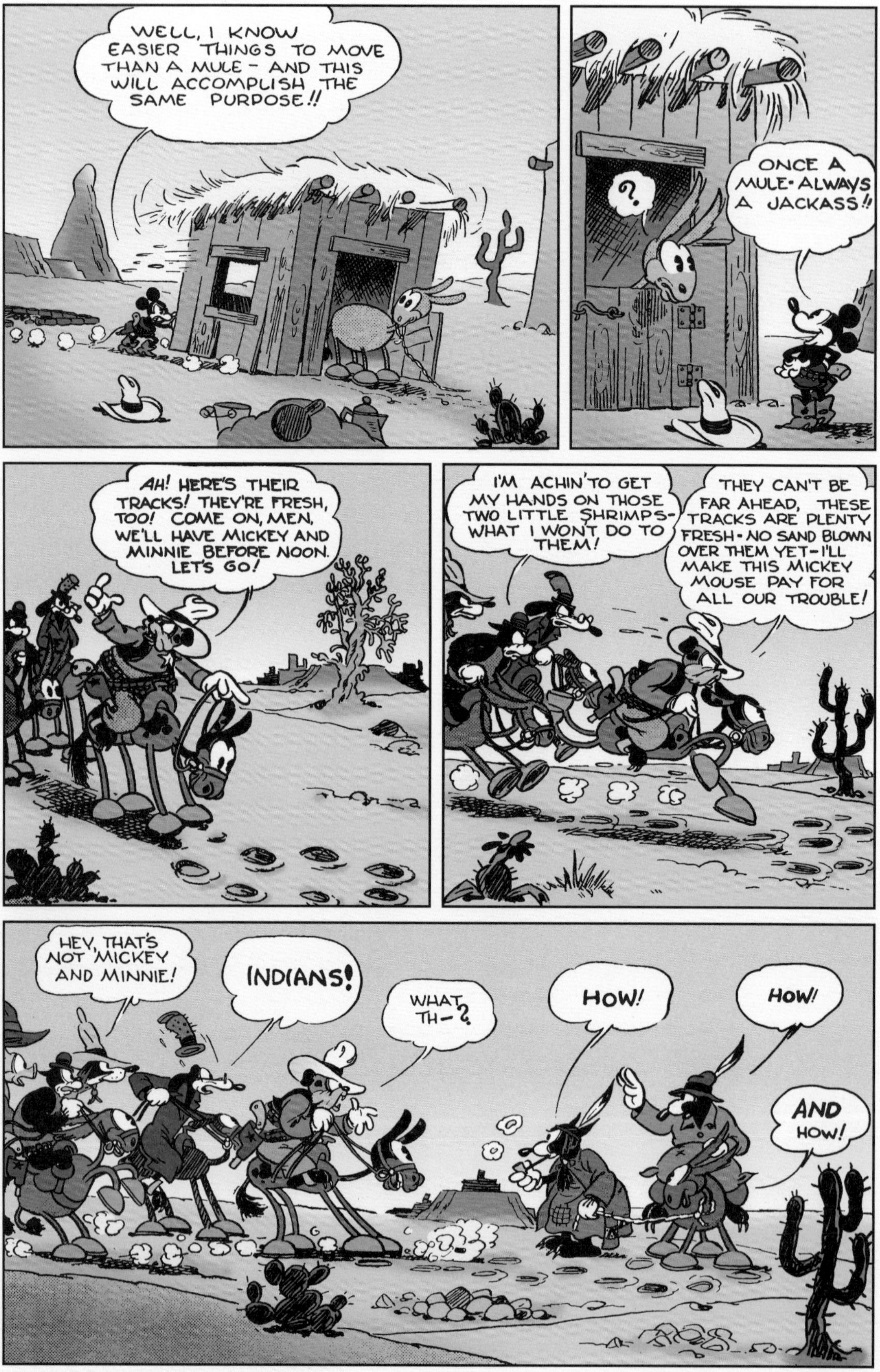
WELL, I KNOW EASIER THINGS TO MOVE THAN A MULE - AND THIS WILL ACCOMPLISH THE SAME PURPOSE!!
?
ONCE A MULE-ALWAYS A JACKASS!!
AH! HERE'S THEIR TRACKS! THEY'RE FRESH, TOO! COME ON, MEN, WE'LL HAVE MICKEY AND MINNIE BEFORE NOON. LET'S GO!
I'M ACHIN' TO GET MY HANDS ON THOSE TWO LITTLE SHRIMPS-WHAT I WON'T DO TO THEM!
THEY CAN'T BE FAR AHEAD, THESE TRACKS ARE PLENTY FRESH - NO SAND BLOWN OVER THEM YET-I'LL MAKE THIS MICKEY MOUSE PAY FOR ALL OUR TROUBLE!
HEY, THAT'S NOT MICKEY AND MINNIE!
INDIANS!
WHAT TH-?
HOW!
HOW!
AND HOW!

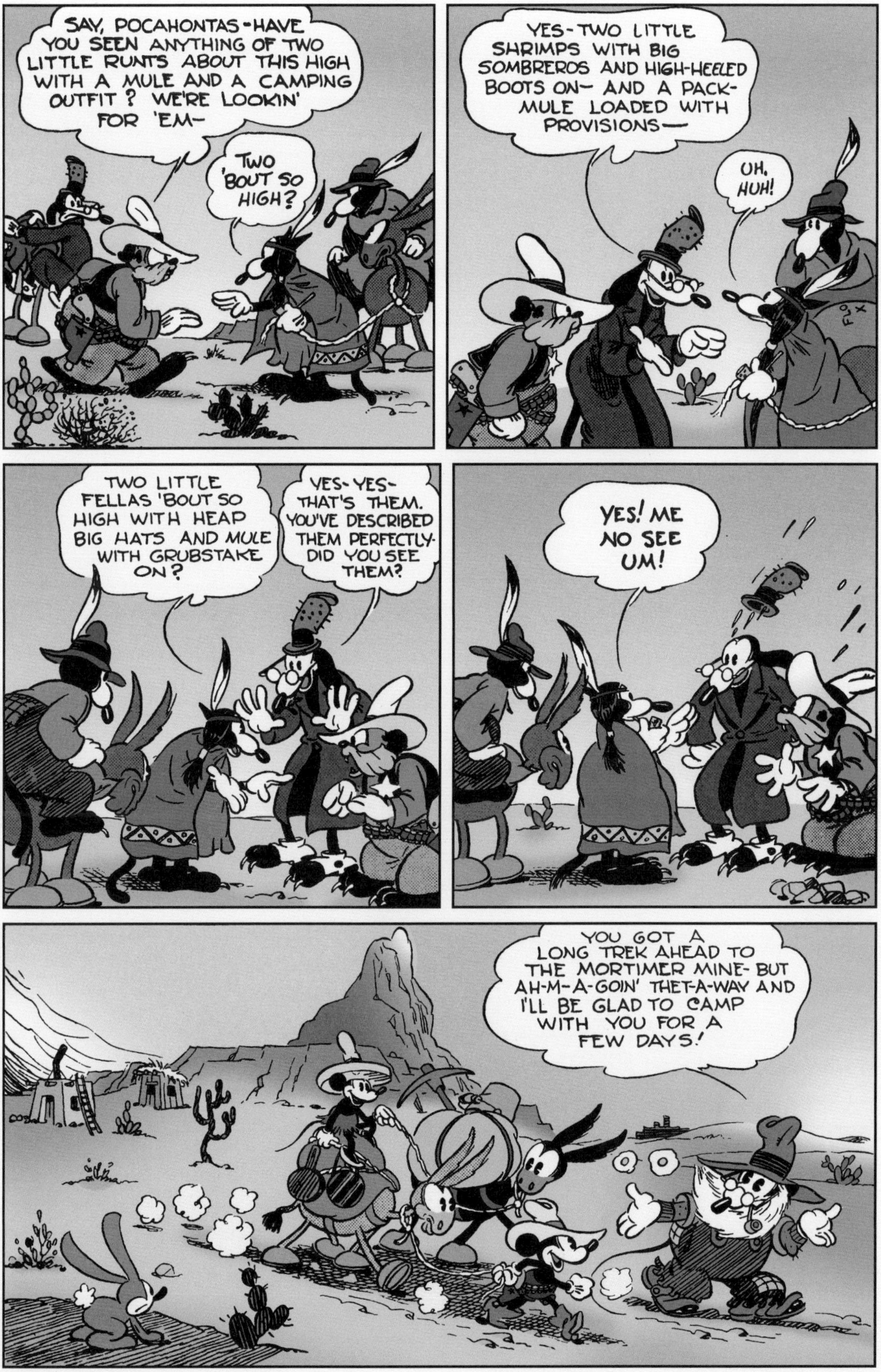
SAY, POCAHONTAS-HAVE YOU SEEN ANYTHING OF TWO LITTLE RUNTS ABOUT THIS HIGH WITH A MULE AND A CAMPING OUTFIT? WE'RE LOOKIN' FOR 'EM—
TWO 'BOUT SO HIGH?
YES-TWO LITTLE SHRIMPS WITH BIG SOMBREROS AND HIGH-HEELED BOOTS ON— AND A PACK-MULE LOADED WITH PROVISIONS—
UH, HUH!
TWO LITTLE FELLAS 'BOUT SO HIGH WITH HEAP BIG HATS AND MULE WITH GRUBSTAKE ON?
YES-YES-THAT'S THEM. YOU'VE DESCRIBED THEM PERFECTLY-DID YOU SEE THEM?
YES! ME NO SEE UM!
YOU GOT A LONG TREK AHEAD TO THE MORTIMER MINE- BUT AH-M-A-GOIN' THET-A-WAY AND I'LL BE GLAD TO CAMP WITH YOU FOR A FEW DAYS!

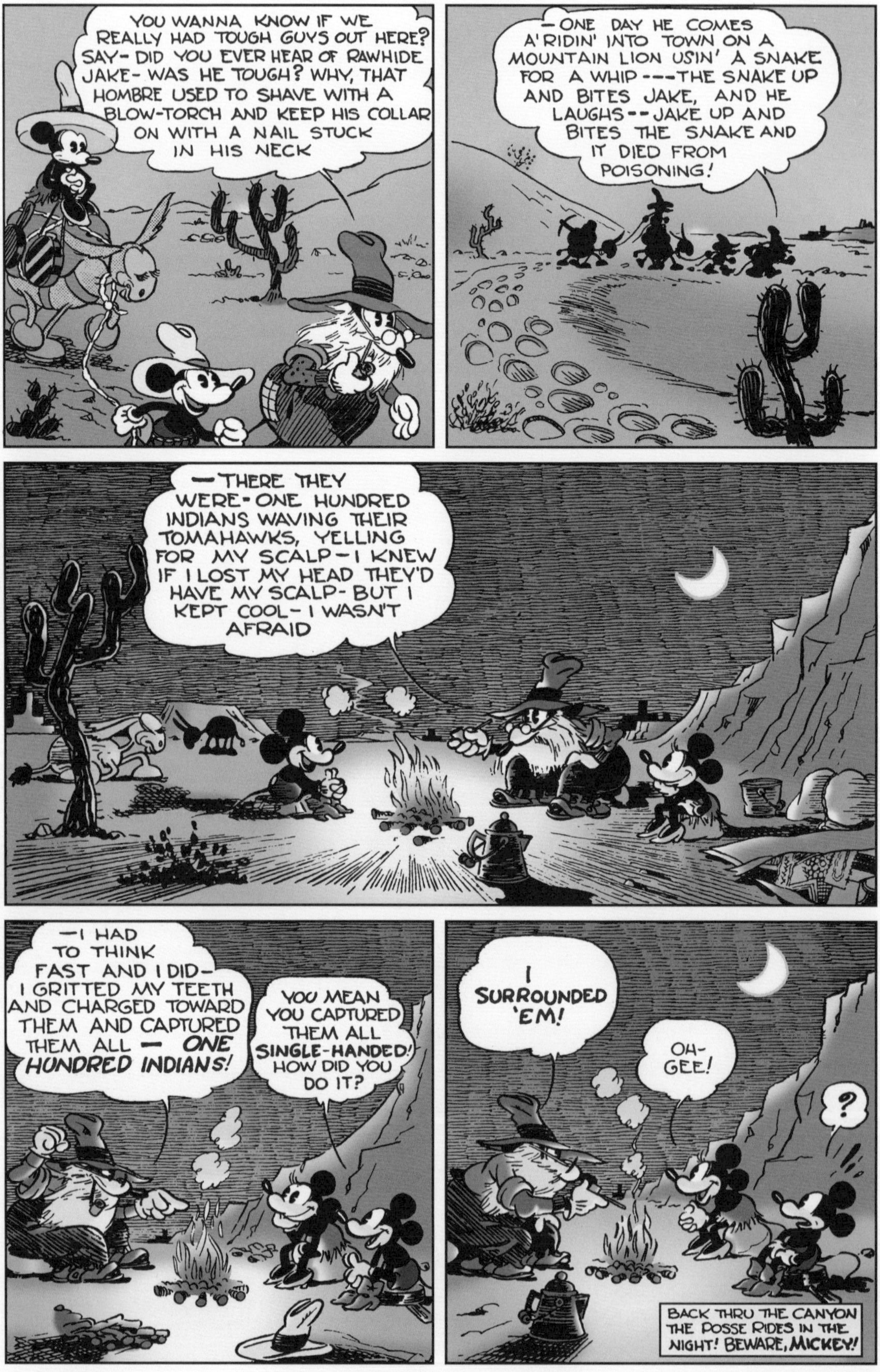
YOU WANNA KNOW IF WE REALLY HAD TOUGH GUYS OUT HERE? SAY- DID YOU EVER HEAR OF RAWHIDE JAKE- WAS HE TOUGH? WHY, THAT HOMBRE USED TO SHAVE WITH A BLOW-TORCH AND KEEP HIS COLLAR ON WITH A NAIL STUCK IN HIS NECK
—ONE DAY HE COMES A'RIDIN' INTO TOWN ON A MOUNTAIN LION USIN' A SNAKE FOR A WHIP---THE SNAKE UP AND BITES JAKE, AND HE LAUGHS--JAKE UP AND BITES THE SNAKE AND IT DIED FROM POISONING!
—THERE THEY WERE- ONE HUNDRED INDIANS WAVING THEIR TOMAHAWKS, YELLING FOR MY SCALP—I KNEW IF I LOST MY HEAD THEY'D HAVE MY SCALP- BUT I KEPT COOL- I WASN'T AFRAID
—I HAD TO THINK FAST AND I DID- I GRITTED MY TEETH AND CHARGED TOWARD THEM AND CAPTURED THEM ALL — ONE HUNDRED INDIANS!
YOU MEAN YOU CAPTURED THEM ALL SINGLE-HANDED! HOW DID YOU DO IT?
I SURROUNDED 'EM!
OH- GEE!
?
BACK THRU THE CANYON THE POSSE RIDES IN THE NIGHT! BEWARE, MICKEY!

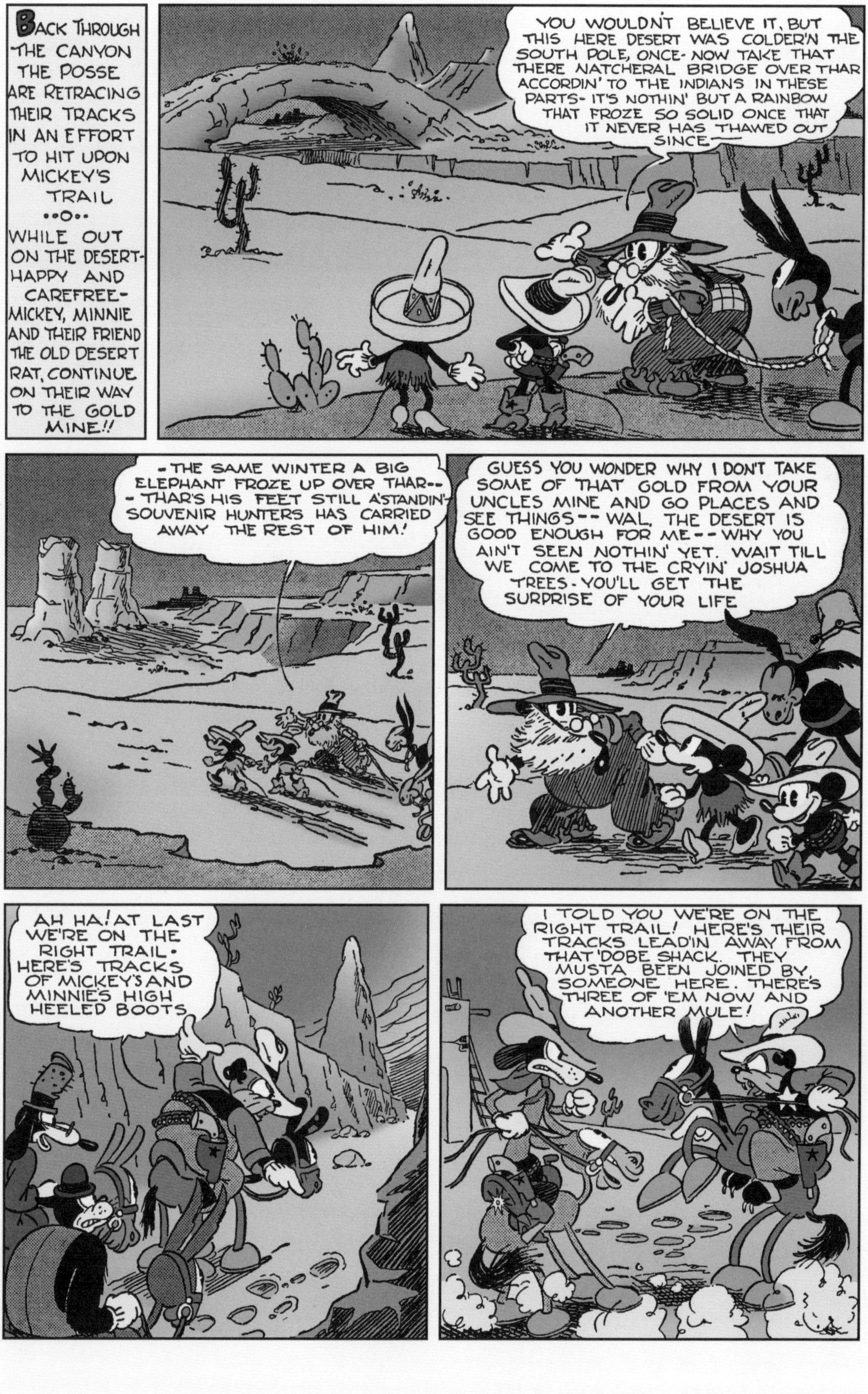
BACK THROUGH THE CANYON THE POSSE ARE RETRACING THEIR TRACKS IN AN EFFORT TO HIT UPON MICKEY'S TRAIL
•○•
WHILE OUT ON THE DESERT- HAPPY AND CAREFREE- MICKEY, MINNIE AND THEIR FRIEND THE OLD DESERT RAT, CONTINUE ON THEIR WAY TO THE GOLD MINE!!
YOU WOULDN'T BELIEVE IT, BUT THIS HERE DESERT WAS COLDER'N THE SOUTH POLE, ONCE- NOW TAKE THAT THERE NATCHERAL BRIDGE OVER THAR ACCORDIN' TO THE INDIANS IN THESE PARTS- IT'S NOTHIN' BUT A RAINBOW THAT FROZE SO SOLID ONCE THAT IT NEVER HAS THAWED OUT SINCE—
-THE SAME WINTER A BIG ELEPHANT FROZE UP OVER THAR-- -THAR'S HIS FEET STILL A'STANDIN'- SOUVENIR HUNTERS HAS CARRIED AWAY THE REST OF HIM!
GUESS YOU WONDER WHY I DON'T TAKE SOME OF THAT GOLD FROM YOUR UNCLES MINE AND GO PLACES AND SEE THINGS-- WAL, THE DESERT IS GOOD ENOUGH FOR ME-- WHY YOU AIN'T SEEN NOTHIN' YET. WAIT TILL WE COME TO THE CRYIN' JOSHUA TREES- YOU'LL GET THE SURPRISE OF YOUR LIFE
AH HA! AT LAST WE'RE ON THE RIGHT TRAIL- HERE'S TRACKS OF MICKEY'S AND MINNIE'S HIGH HEELED BOOTS
I TOLD YOU WE'RE ON THE RIGHT TRAIL! HERE'S THEIR TRACKS LEAD'IN AWAY FROM THAT 'DOBE SHACK. THEY MUSTA BEEN JOINED BY SOMEONE HERE. THERE'S THREE OF 'EM NOW AND ANOTHER MULE!

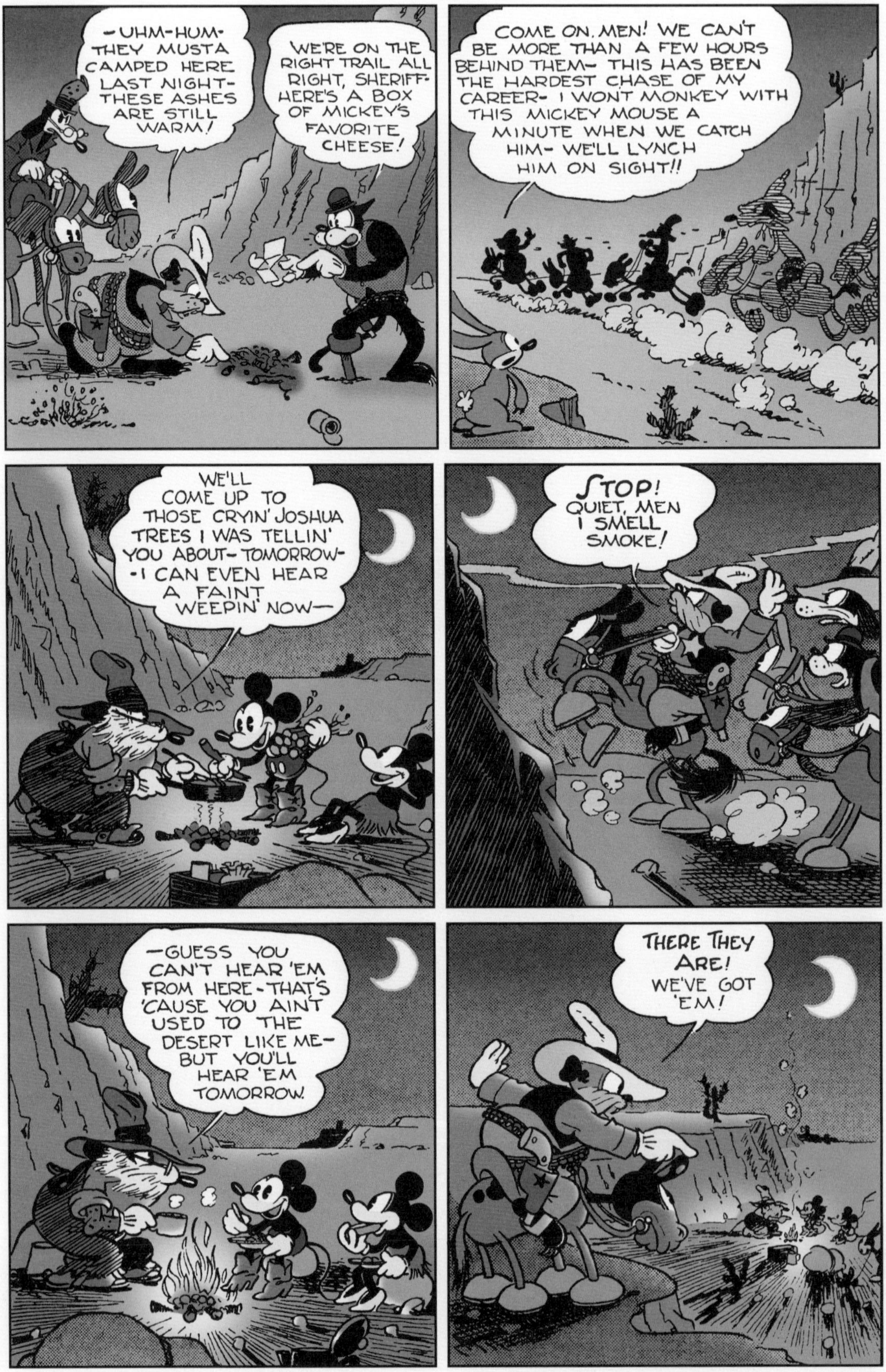
-UHM-HUM- THEY MUSTA CAMPED HERE LAST NIGHT- THESE ASHES ARE STILL WARM!
WE'RE ON THE RIGHT TRAIL ALL RIGHT, SHERIFF- HERE'S A BOX OF MICKEY'S FAVORITE CHEESE!
COME ON, MEN! WE CAN'T BE MORE THAN A FEW HOURS BEHIND THEM- THIS HAS BEEN THE HARDEST CHASE OF MY CAREER- I WON'T MONKEY WITH THIS MICKEY MOUSE A MINUTE WHEN WE CATCH HIM- WE'LL LYNCH HIM ON SIGHT!!
WE'LL COME UP TO THOSE CRYIN' JOSHUA TREES I WAS TELLIN' YOU ABOUT- TOMORROW- -I CAN EVEN HEAR A FAINT WEEPIN' NOW—
STOP! QUIET, MEN I SMELL SMOKE!
-GUESS YOU CAN'T HEAR 'EM FROM HERE- THAT'S 'CAUSE YOU AIN'T USED TO THE DESERT LIKE ME- BUT YOU'LL HEAR 'EM TOMORROW.
THERE THEY ARE! WE'VE GOT 'EM!

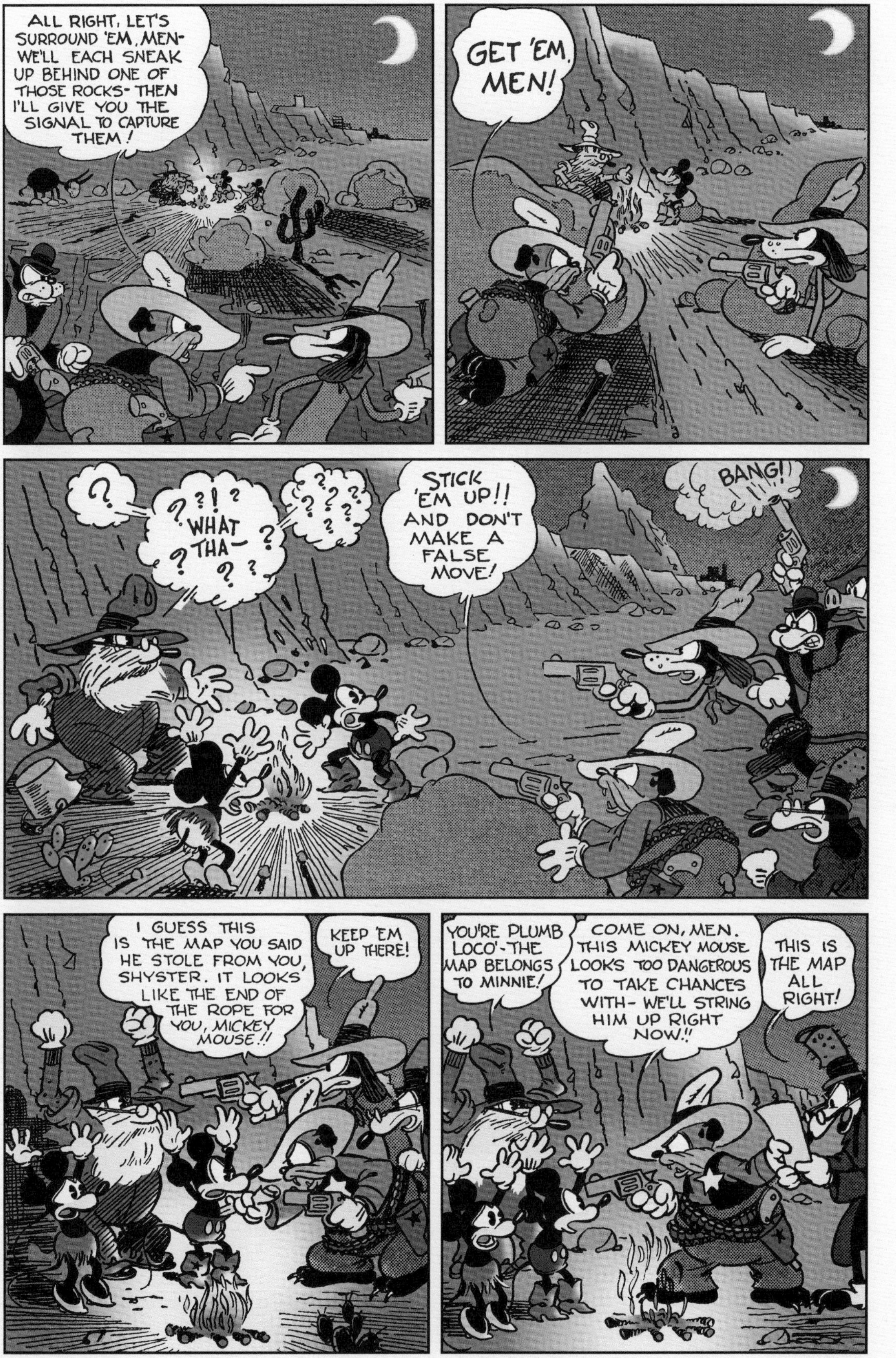
ALL RIGHT, LET'S SURROUND 'EM, MEN- WE'LL EACH SNEAK UP BEHIND ONE OF THOSE ROCKS- THEN I'LL GIVE YOU THE SIGNAL TO CAPTURE THEM!
GET 'EM, MEN!
?
? ?! ? WHAT THA- ? ? ? ?
? ? ? ? ? ?
STICK 'EM UP!! AND DON'T MAKE A FALSE MOVE!
BANG!!
I GUESS THIS IS THE MAP YOU SAID HE STOLE FROM YOU, SHYSTER. IT LOOKS LIKE THE END OF THE ROPE FOR YOU, MICKEY MOUSE!!
KEEP 'EM UP THERE!
YOU'RE PLUMB LOCO'-THE MAP BELONGS TO MINNIE!
COME ON, MEN. THIS MICKEY MOUSE LOOKS TOO DANGEROUS TO TAKE CHANCES WITH- WE'LL STRING HIM UP RIGHT NOW!!
THIS IS THE MAP ALL RIGHT!

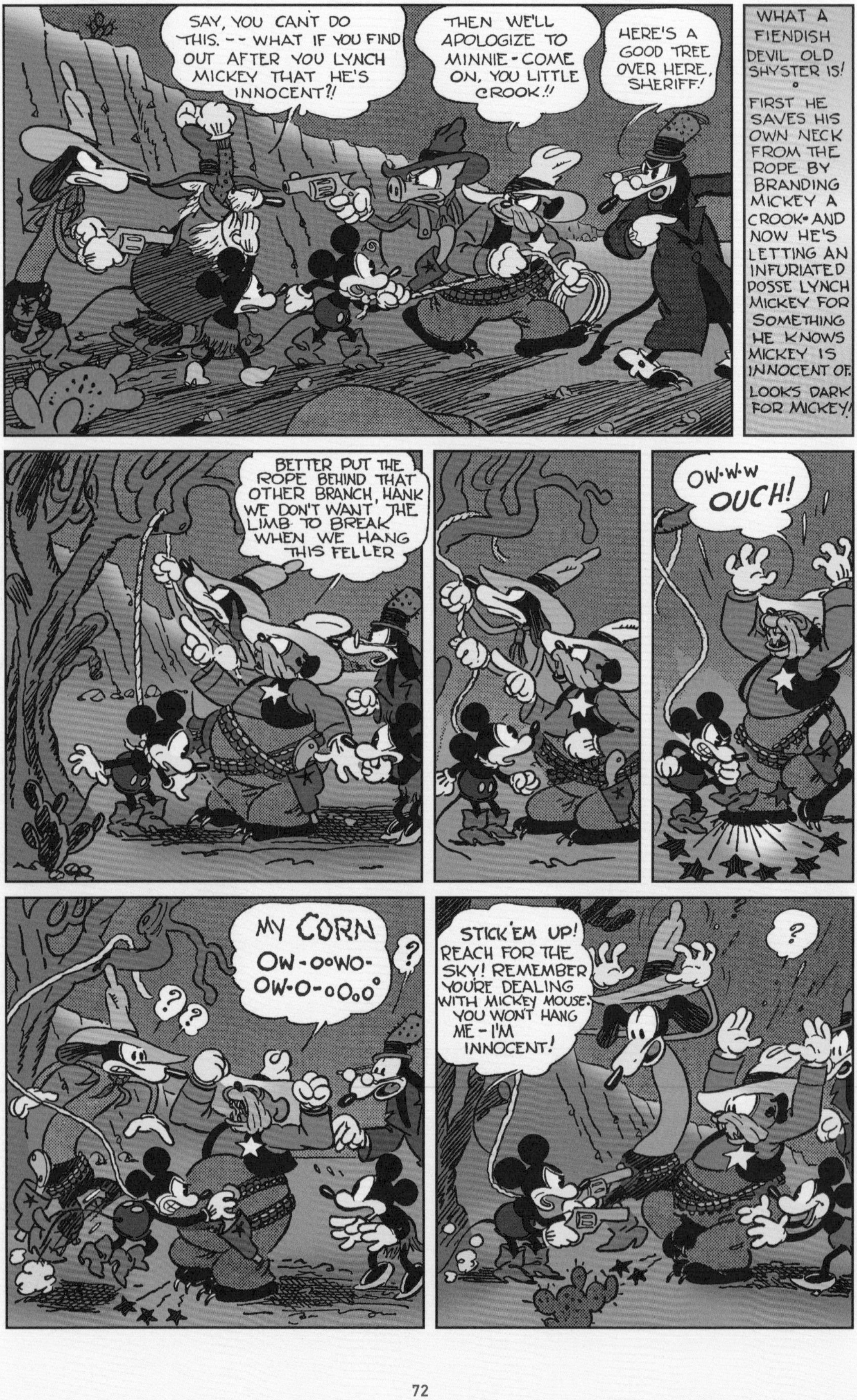
SAY, YOU CAN'T DO THIS. -- WHAT IF YOU FIND OUT AFTER YOU LYNCH MICKEY THAT HE'S INNOCENT?!
THEN WE'LL APOLOGIZE TO MINNIE - COME ON, YOU LITTLE CROOK!!
HERE'S A GOOD TREE OVER HERE, SHERIFF!
WHAT A FIENDISH DEVIL OLD SHYSTER IS!
FIRST HE SAVES HIS OWN NECK FROM THE ROPE BY BRANDING MICKEY A CROOK• AND NOW HE'S LETTING AN INFURIATED POSSE LYNCH MICKEY FOR SOMETHING HE KNOWS MICKEY IS INNOCENT OF.
LOOKS DARK FOR MICKEY!
BETTER PUT THE ROPE BEHIND THAT OTHER BRANCH, HANK WE DON'T WANT THE LIMB TO BREAK WHEN WE HANG THIS FELLER
OW•W•W OUCH!
MY CORN OW-OOWO-OW-O-OOOO
??
?
STICK'EM UP! REACH FOR THE SKY! REMEMBER YOU'RE DEALING WITH MICKEY MOUSE. YOU WON'T HANG ME - I'M INNOCENT!
?

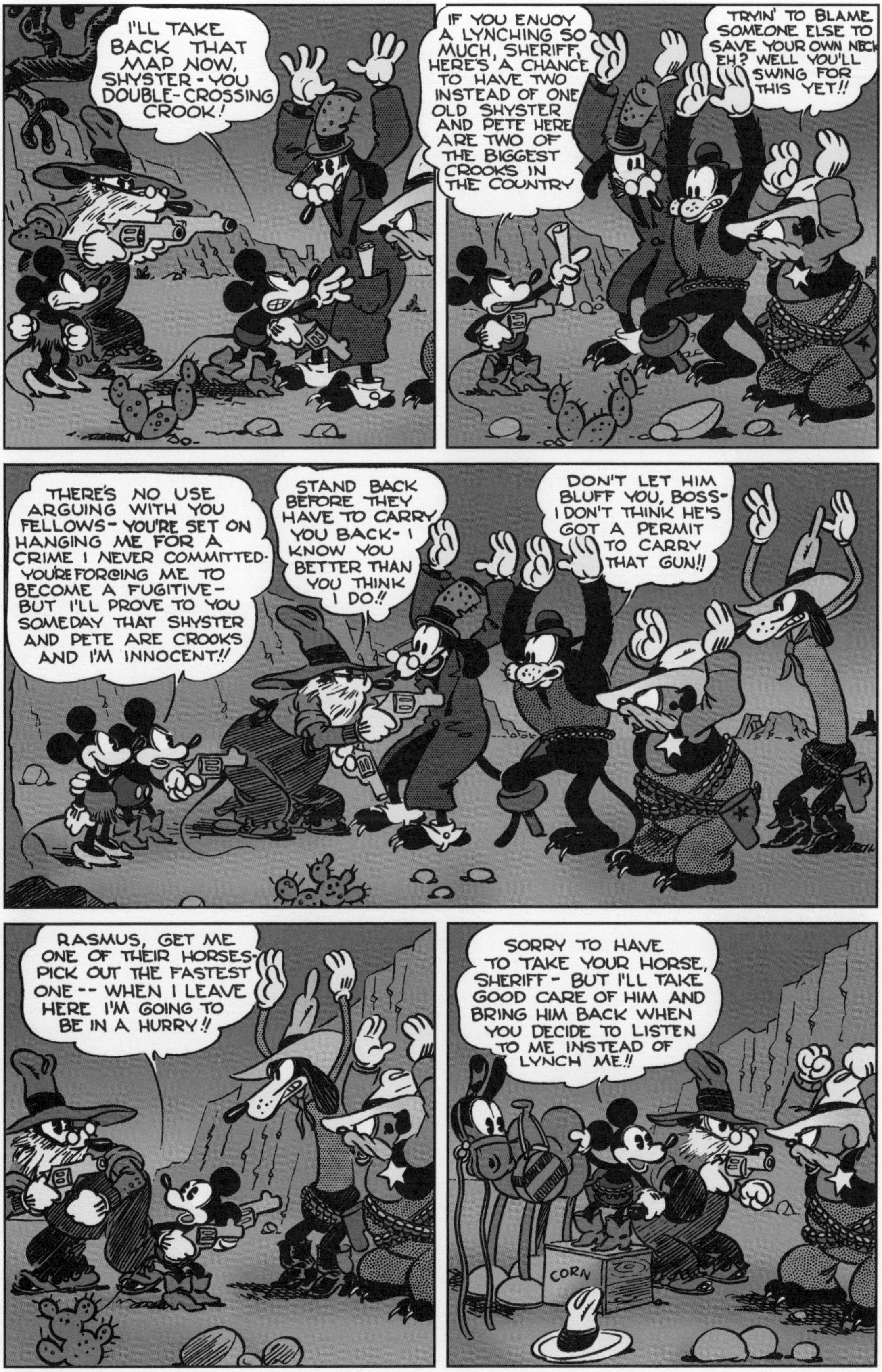
I'LL TAKE BACK THAT MAP NOW, SHYSTER - YOU DOUBLE-CROSSING CROOK!
IF YOU ENJOY A LYNCHING SO MUCH, SHERIFF, HERE'S A CHANCE TO HAVE TWO INSTEAD OF ONE OLD SHYSTER AND PETE HERE ARE TWO OF THE BIGGEST CROOKS IN THE COUNTRY
TRYIN' TO BLAME SOMEONE ELSE TO SAVE YOUR OWN NECK EH? WELL YOU'LL SWING FOR THIS YET!!
THERE'S NO USE ARGUING WITH YOU FELLOWS- YOU'RE SET ON HANGING ME FOR A CRIME I NEVER COMMITTED- YOU'RE FORCING ME TO BECOME A FUGITIVE- BUT I'LL PROVE TO YOU SOMEDAY THAT SHYSTER AND PETE ARE CROOKS AND I'M INNOCENT!!
STAND BACK BEFORE THEY HAVE TO CARRY YOU BACK- I KNOW YOU BETTER THAN YOU THINK I DO!!
DON'T LET HIM BLUFF YOU, BOSS- I DON'T THINK HE'S GOT A PERMIT TO CARRY THAT GUN!!
RASMUS, GET ME ONE OF THEIR HORSES- PICK OUT THE FASTEST ONE -- WHEN I LEAVE HERE I'M GOING TO BE IN A HURRY!!
SORRY TO HAVE TO TAKE YOUR HORSE, SHERIFF - BUT I'LL TAKE GOOD CARE OF HIM AND BRING HIM BACK WHEN YOU DECIDE TO LISTEN TO ME INSTEAD OF LYNCH ME!!
CORN

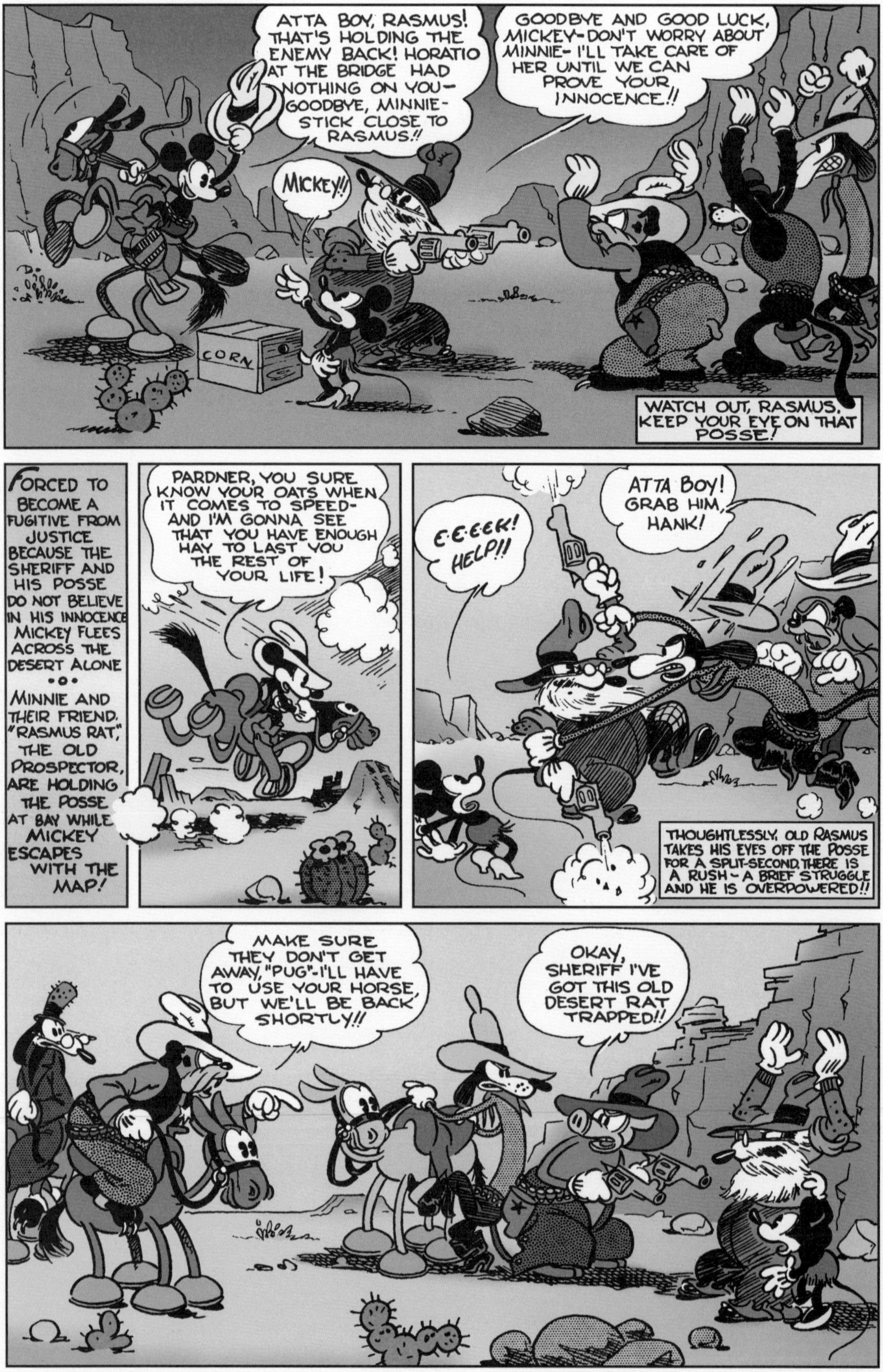
ATTA BOY, RASMUS! THAT'S HOLDING THE ENEMY BACK! HORATIO AT THE BRIDGE HAD NOTHING ON YOU— GOODBYE, MINNIE— STICK CLOSE TO RASMUS.!!
GOODBYE AND GOOD LUCK, MICKEY— DON'T WORRY ABOUT MINNIE— I'LL TAKE CARE OF HER UNTIL WE CAN PROVE YOUR INNOCENCE.!!
MICKEY!!
CORN
WATCH OUT, RASMUS, KEEP YOUR EYE ON THAT POSSE!
FORCED TO BECOME A FUGITIVE FROM JUSTICE BECAUSE THE SHERIFF AND HIS POSSE DO NOT BELIEVE IN HIS INNOCENCE MICKEY FLEES ACROSS THE DESERT ALONE
•O•
MINNIE AND THEIR FRIEND, "RASMUS RAT," THE OLD PROSPECTOR, ARE HOLDING THE POSSE AT BAY WHILE MICKEY ESCAPES WITH THE MAP!
PARDNER, YOU SURE KNOW YOUR OATS WHEN IT COMES TO SPEED— AND I'M GONNA SEE THAT YOU HAVE ENOUGH HAY TO LAST YOU THE REST OF YOUR LIFE!
E-E-E-EK! HELP!!
ATTA BOY! GRAB HIM, HANK!
THOUGHTLESSLY, OLD RASMUS TAKES HIS EYES OFF THE POSSE FOR A SPLIT-SECOND. THERE IS A RUSH— A BRIEF STRUGGLE AND HE IS OVERPOWERED!!
MAKE SURE THEY DON'T GET AWAY, "PUG"— I'LL HAVE TO USE YOUR HORSE, BUT WE'LL BE BACK SHORTLY!!
OKAY, SHERIFF I'VE GOT THIS OLD DESERT RAT TRAPPED!!

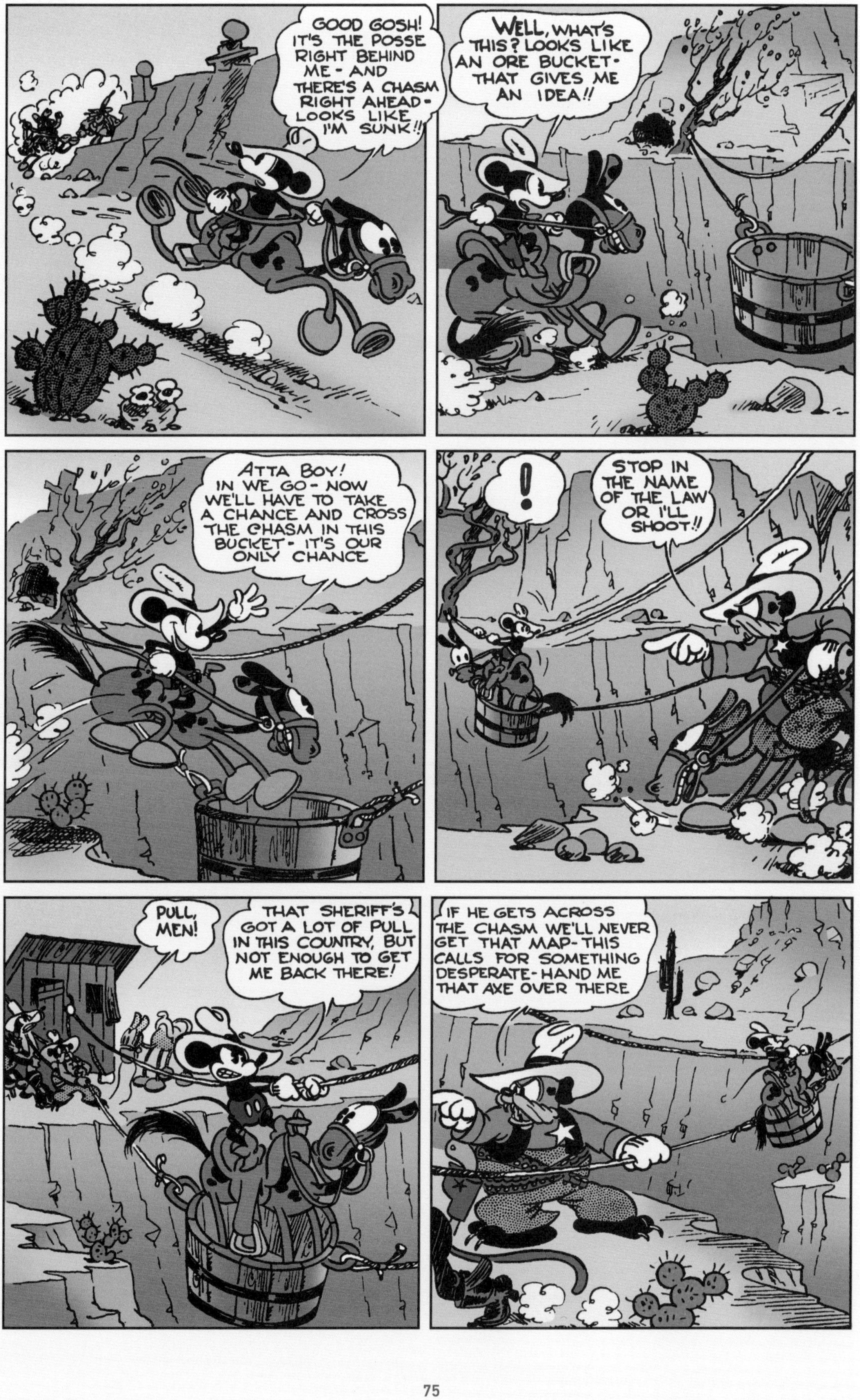
GOOD GOSH! IT'S THE POSSE RIGHT BEHIND ME - AND THERE'S A CHASM RIGHT AHEAD - LOOKS LIKE I'M SUNK!!
WELL, WHAT'S THIS? LOOKS LIKE AN ORE BUCKET - THAT GIVES ME AN IDEA!!
ATTA BOY! IN WE GO - NOW WE'LL HAVE TO TAKE A CHANCE AND CROSS THE CHASM IN THIS BUCKET - IT'S OUR ONLY CHANCE
!
STOP IN THE NAME OF THE LAW OR I'LL SHOOT!!
PULL, MEN!
THAT SHERIFF'S GOT A LOT OF PULL IN THIS COUNTRY, BUT NOT ENOUGH TO GET ME BACK THERE!
IF HE GETS ACROSS THE CHASM WE'LL NEVER GET THAT MAP - THIS CALLS FOR SOMETHING DESPERATE - HAND ME THAT AXE OVER THERE

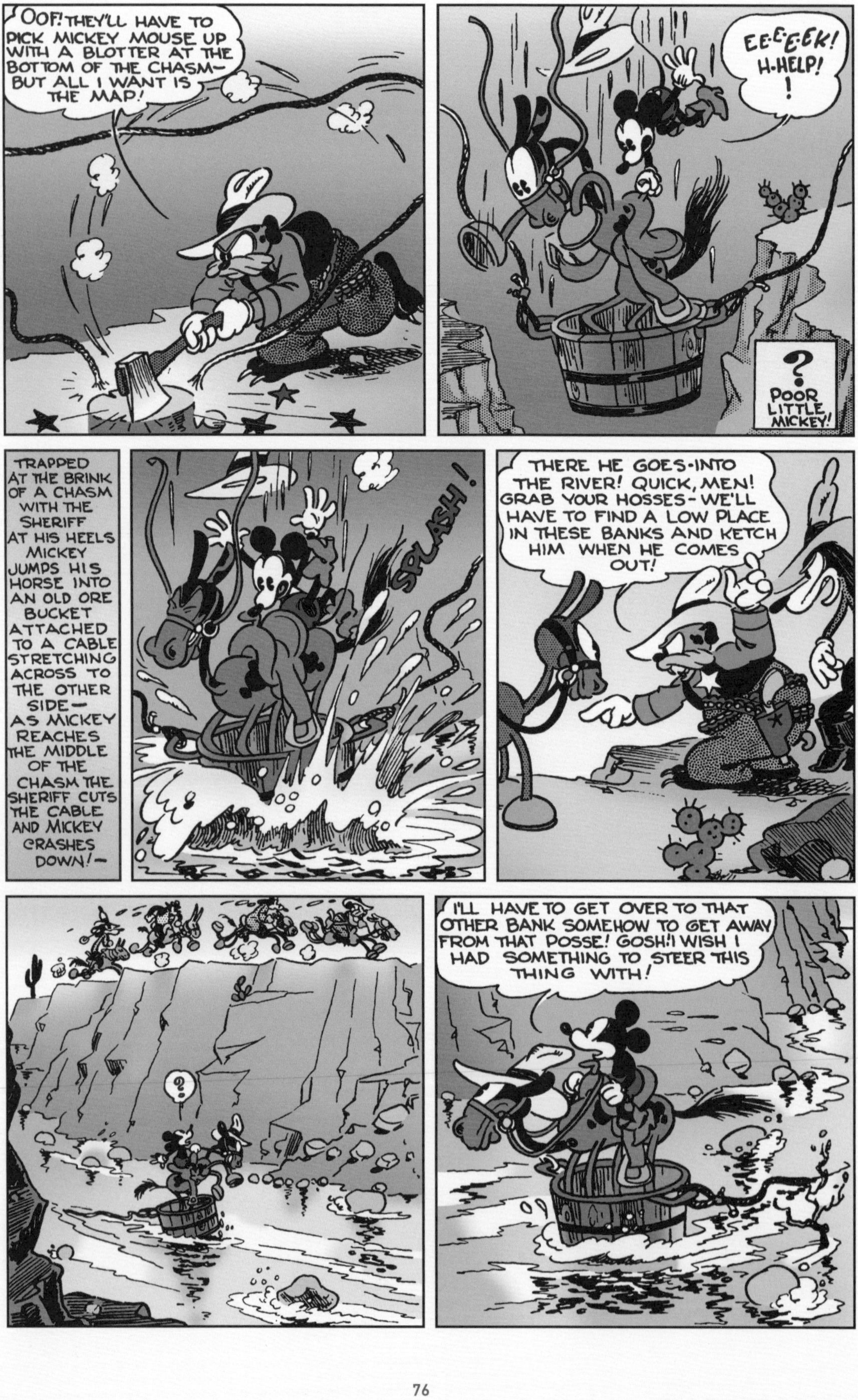
OOF! THEY'LL HAVE TO PICK MICKEY MOUSE UP WITH A BLOTTER AT THE BOTTOM OF THE CHASM— BUT ALL I WANT IS THE MAP!
EE-E-E-EK! H-HELP! !
? POOR LITTLE MICKEY!
TRAPPED AT THE BRINK OF A CHASM WITH THE SHERIFF AT HIS HEELS MICKEY JUMPS HIS HORSE INTO AN OLD ORE BUCKET ATTACHED TO A CABLE STRETCHING ACROSS TO THE OTHER SIDE— AS MICKEY REACHES THE MIDDLE OF THE CHASM THE SHERIFF CUTS THE CABLE AND MICKEY CRASHES DOWN!—
SPLASH!
THERE HE GOES-INTO THE RIVER! QUICK, MEN! GRAB YOUR HOSSES- WE'LL HAVE TO FIND A LOW PLACE IN THESE BANKS AND KETCH HIM WHEN HE COMES OUT!
?
I'LL HAVE TO GET OVER TO THAT OTHER BANK SOMEHOW TO GET AWAY FROM THAT POSSE! GOSH! I WISH I HAD SOMETHING TO STEER THIS THING WITH!

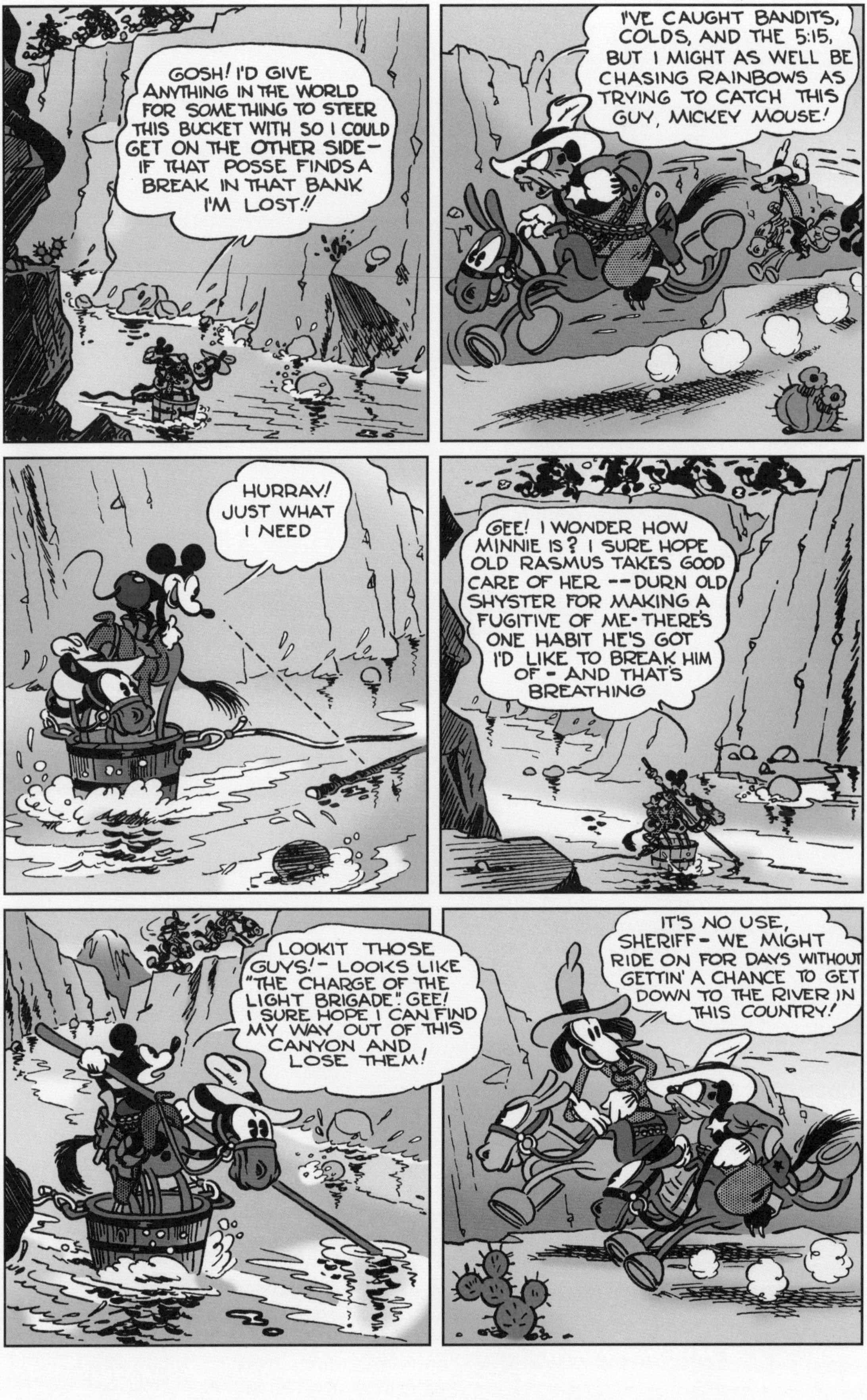
GOSH! I'D GIVE ANYTHING IN THE WORLD FOR SOMETHING TO STEER THIS BUCKET WITH SO I COULD GET ON THE OTHER SIDE- IF THAT POSSE FINDS A BREAK IN THAT BANK I'M LOST!!
I'VE CAUGHT BANDITS, COLDS, AND THE 5:15, BUT I MIGHT AS WELL BE CHASING RAINBOWS AS TRYING TO CATCH THIS GUY, MICKEY MOUSE!
HURRAY! JUST WHAT I NEED
GEE! I WONDER HOW MINNIE IS? I SURE HOPE OLD RASMUS TAKES GOOD CARE OF HER -- DURN OLD SHYSTER FOR MAKING A FUGITIVE OF ME- THERE'S ONE HABIT HE'S GOT I'D LIKE TO BREAK HIM OF - AND THAT'S BREATHING
LOOKIT THOSE GUYS!- LOOKS LIKE "THE CHARGE OF THE LIGHT BRIGADE." GEE! I SURE HOPE I CAN FIND MY WAY OUT OF THIS CANYON AND LOSE THEM!
IT'S NO USE, SHERIFF- WE MIGHT RIDE ON FOR DAYS WITHOUT GETTIN' A CHANCE TO GET DOWN TO THE RIVER IN THIS COUNTRY!

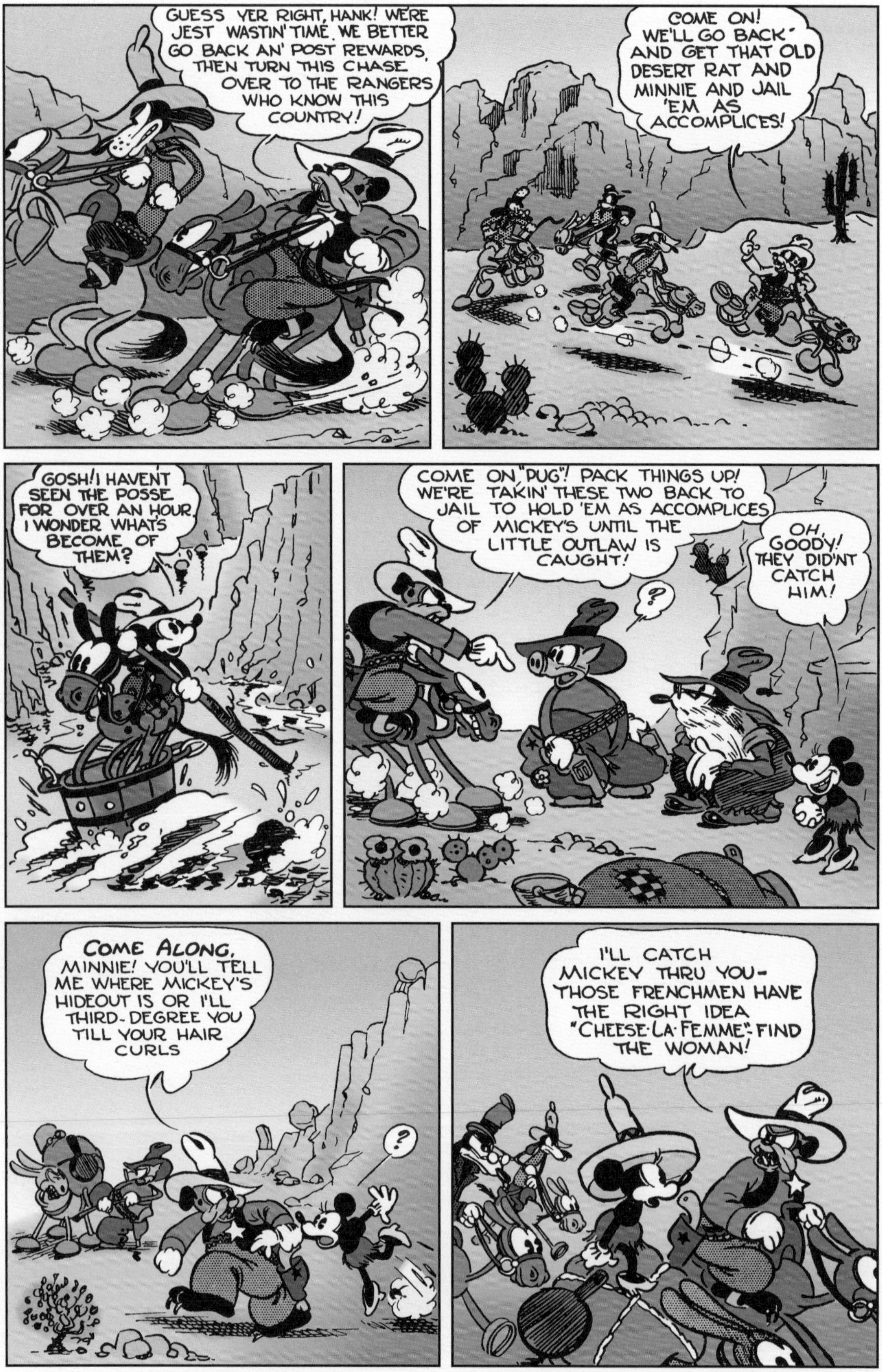
GUESS YER RIGHT, HANK! WE'RE JEST WASTIN' TIME. WE BETTER GO BACK AN' POST REWARDS, THEN TURN THIS CHASE OVER TO THE RANGERS WHO KNOW THIS COUNTRY!
COME ON! WE'LL GO BACK AND GET THAT OLD DESERT RAT AND MINNIE AND JAIL 'EM AS ACCOMPLICES!
GOSH! I HAVENT SEEN THE POSSE FOR OVER AN HOUR. I WONDER WHAT'S BECOME OF THEM?
COME ON, "PUG"! PACK THINGS UP! WE'RE TAKIN' THESE TWO BACK TO JAIL TO HOLD 'EM AS ACCOMPLICES OF MICKEY'S UNTIL THE LITTLE OUTLAW IS CAUGHT!
?
OH, GOODY! THEY DID'NT CATCH HIM!
COME ALONG, MINNIE! YOU'LL TELL ME WHERE MICKEY'S HIDEOUT IS OR I'LL THIRD-DEGREE YOU TILL YOUR HAIR CURLS
?
I'LL CATCH MICKEY THRU YOU- THOSE FRENCHMEN HAVE THE RIGHT IDEA "CHEESE-LA-FEMME"- FIND THE WOMAN!

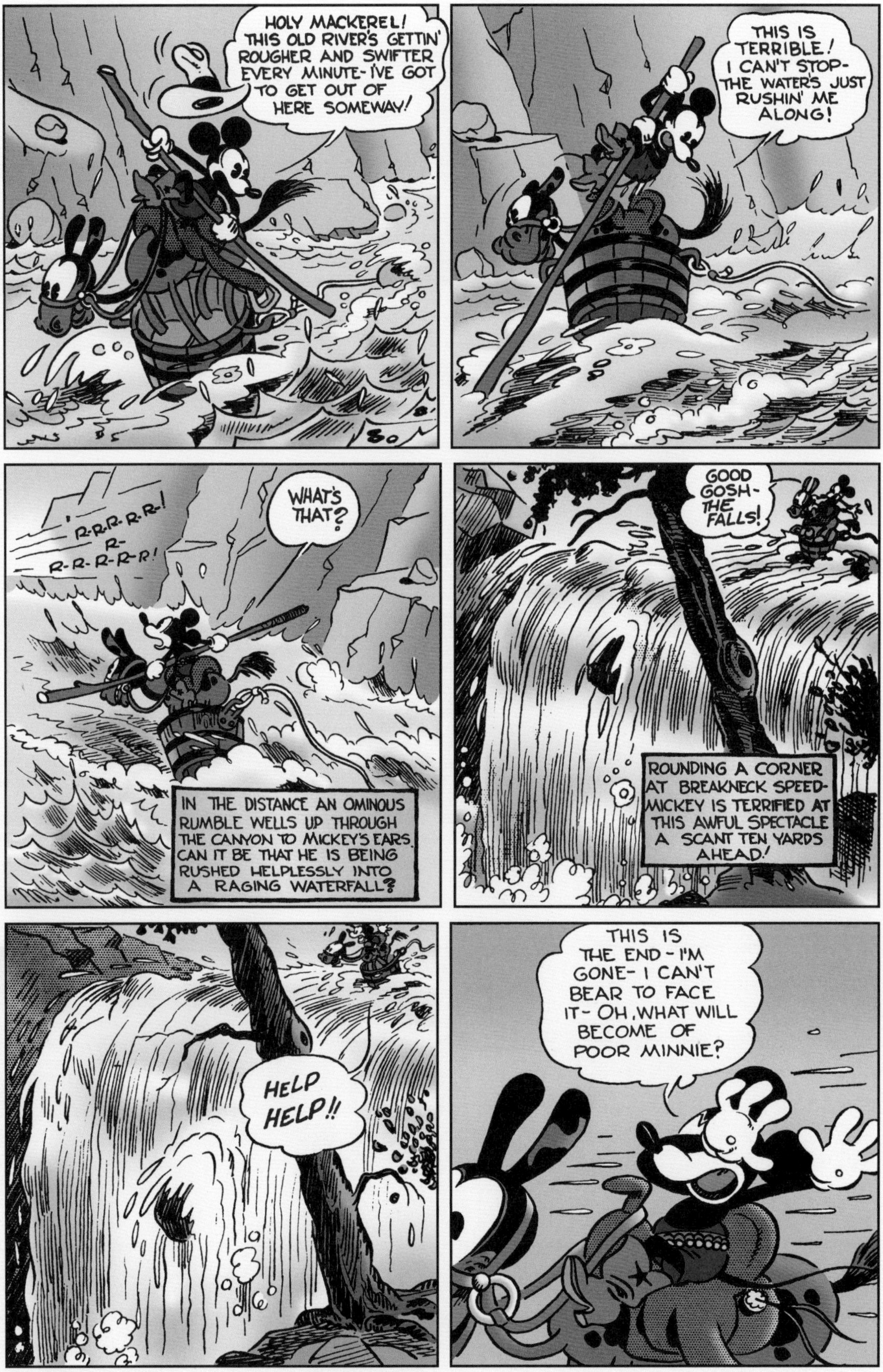
HOLY MACKEREL! THIS OLD RIVER'S GETTIN' ROUGHER AND SWIFTER EVERY MINUTE- I'VE GOT TO GET OUT OF HERE SOMEWAY!
THIS IS TERRIBLE! I CAN'T STOP- THE WATER'S JUST RUSHIN' ME ALONG!
R-R-R-R-R-! R- R-R-R-R-R!
WHAT'S THAT?
IN THE DISTANCE AN OMINOUS RUMBLE WELLS UP THROUGH THE CANYON TO MICKEY'S EARS. CAN IT BE THAT HE IS BEING RUSHED HELPLESSLY INTO A RAGING WATERFALL?
GOOD GOSH- THE FALLS!
ROUNDING A CORNER AT BREAKNECK SPEED- MICKEY IS TERRIFIED AT THIS AWFUL SPECTACLE A SCANT TEN YARDS AHEAD!
HELP HELP!!
THIS IS THE END- I'M GONE- I CAN'T BEAR TO FACE IT- OH, WHAT WILL BECOME OF POOR MINNIE?

Giving up the chase for Mickey temporarily the posse returns to "Poison Wells" with Minnie and Rasmus.

The Sheriff decides to put Minnie in jail thinking 'it will scare her into telling where Mickey is

YOU'LL BE SORRY FOR THIS!

WE'RE NOT JAILIN' YOU - SEE - BUT MIND YOU, DON'T LEAVE THIS TOWN OR WE'LL STRING YOU UP FOR IT - WE'RE HOLDIN' MINNIE FOR A LITTLE INFORMATION WE HAPPEN TO WANT!!

COME ON! YOU'RE GOIN' TO JAIL UNTIL YOU TELL US WHERE THAT CROOK MICKEY IS - YOU'RE JUST A BANDIT'S MOLL.

HELP! RASMUS! MICKEY!

JAIL

OH - PLEASE - PLEASE, MR. OFFICER - DON'T LEAVE ME IN HERE ALONE - I - I'M - S-S-SCARED.

SNIFF! SNIFF! OH, MICKEY WHERE ARE YOU?

BUT WHAT OF MICKEY?

WAS HE CRUSHED IN THE POUNDING WATERS AT THE BOTTOM OF THE FALLS

PERHAPS WE SHALL KNOW MONDAY

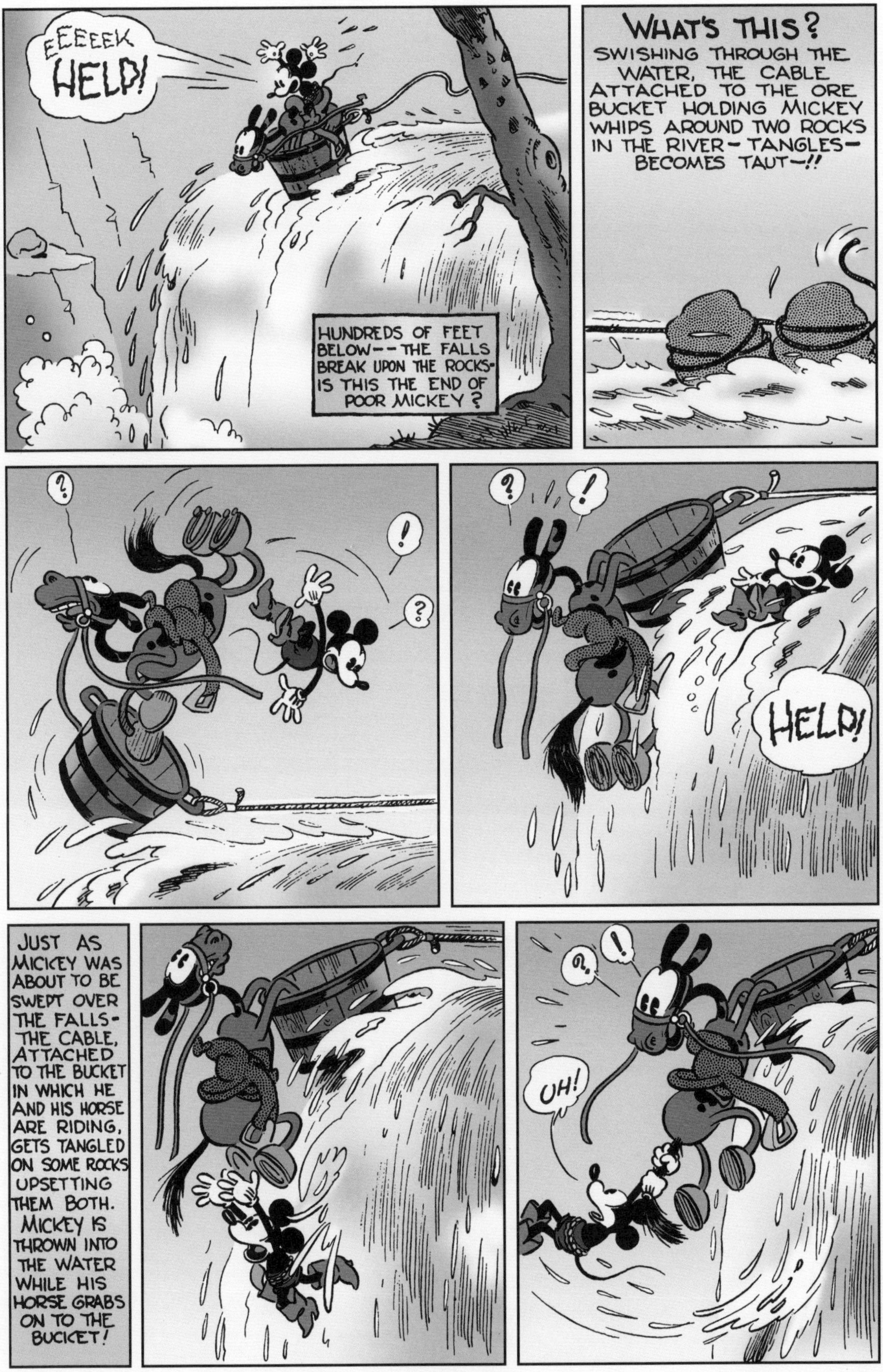
EEEEEK HELP!
HUNDREDS OF FEET BELOW-- THE FALLS BREAK UPON THE ROCKS- IS THIS THE END OF POOR MICKEY?
WHAT'S THIS? SWISHING THROUGH THE WATER, THE CABLE ATTACHED TO THE ORE BUCKET HOLDING MICKEY WHIPS AROUND TWO ROCKS IN THE RIVER - TANGLES- BECOMES TAUT-!!
?
!
?
?
!
HELP!
JUST AS MICKEY WAS ABOUT TO BE SWEPT OVER THE FALLS- THE CABLE, ATTACHED TO THE BUCKET IN WHICH HE AND HIS HORSE ARE RIDING, GETS TANGLED ON SOME ROCKS UPSETTING THEM BOTH. MICKEY IS THROWN INTO THE WATER WHILE HIS HORSE GRABS ON TO THE BUCKET!
?
!
UH!

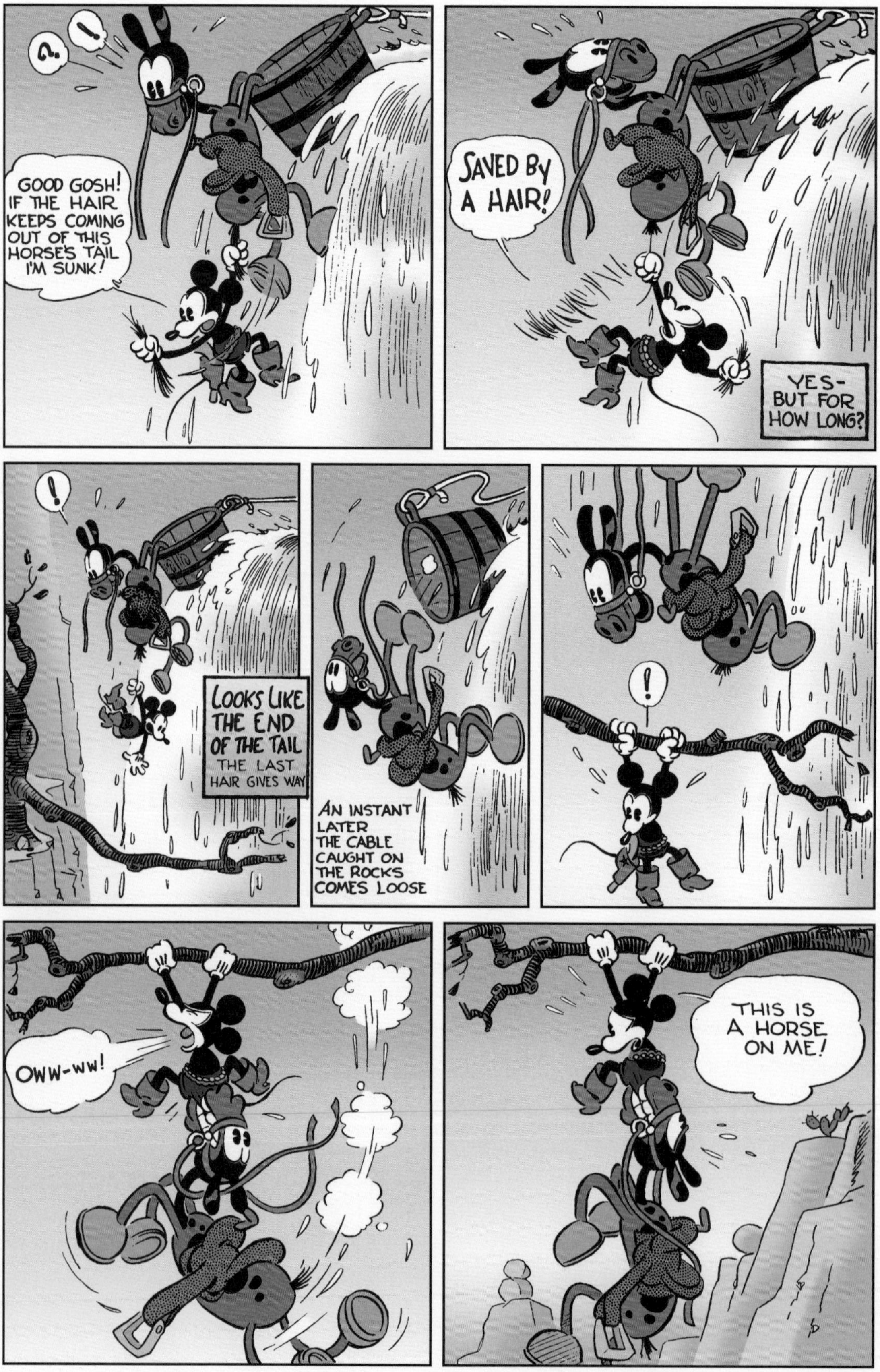
?
!
GOOD GOSH! IF THE HAIR KEEPS COMING OUT OF THIS HORSE'S TAIL I'M SUNK!
SAVED BY A HAIR!
YES- BUT FOR HOW LONG?
!
LOOKS LIKE THE END OF THE TAIL
THE LAST HAIR GIVES WAY
AN INSTANT LATER THE CABLE CAUGHT ON THE ROCKS COMES LOOSE
!
OWW-WW!
THIS IS A HORSE ON ME!

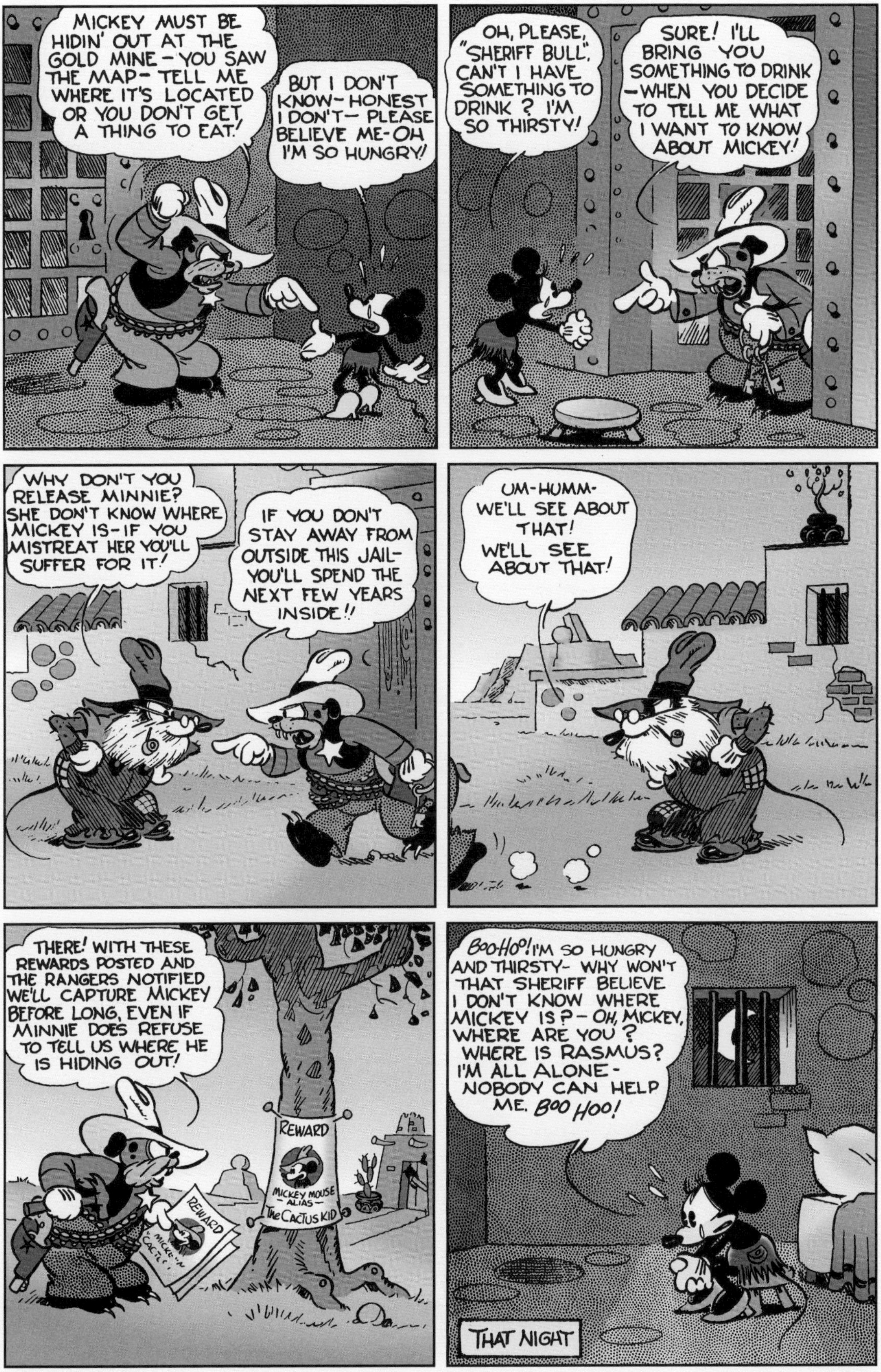
MICKEY MUST BE HIDIN' OUT AT THE GOLD MINE- YOU SAW THE MAP- TELL ME WHERE IT'S LOCATED OR YOU DON'T GET A THING TO EAT!
BUT I DON'T KNOW- HONEST I DON'T- PLEASE BELIEVE ME- OH I'M SO HUNGRY!
OH, PLEASE, "SHERIFF BULL", CAN'T I HAVE SOMETHING TO DRINK ? I'M SO THIRSTY!
SURE! I'LL BRING YOU SOMETHING TO DRINK -WHEN YOU DECIDE TO TELL ME WHAT I WANT TO KNOW ABOUT MICKEY!
WHY DON'T YOU RELEASE MINNIE? SHE DON'T KNOW WHERE MICKEY IS- IF YOU MISTREAT HER YOU'LL SUFFER FOR IT!
IF YOU DON'T STAY AWAY FROM OUTSIDE THIS JAIL- YOU'LL SPEND THE NEXT FEW YEARS INSIDE!!
UM-HUMM- WE'LL SEE ABOUT THAT! WE'LL SEE ABOUT THAT!
THERE! WITH THESE REWARDS POSTED AND THE RANGERS NOTIFIED WE'LL CAPTURE MICKEY BEFORE LONG, EVEN IF MINNIE DOES REFUSE TO TELL US WHERE HE IS HIDING OUT!
REWARD
MICKEY MOUSE ALIAS The CACTUS KID
REWARD
BOO-HOO! I'M SO HUNGRY AND THIRSTY- WHY WON'T THAT SHERIFF BELIEVE I DON'T KNOW WHERE MICKEY IS? - OH, MICKEY, WHERE ARE YOU ? WHERE IS RASMUS? I'M ALL ALONE- NOBODY CAN HELP ME. BOO HOO!
THAT NIGHT

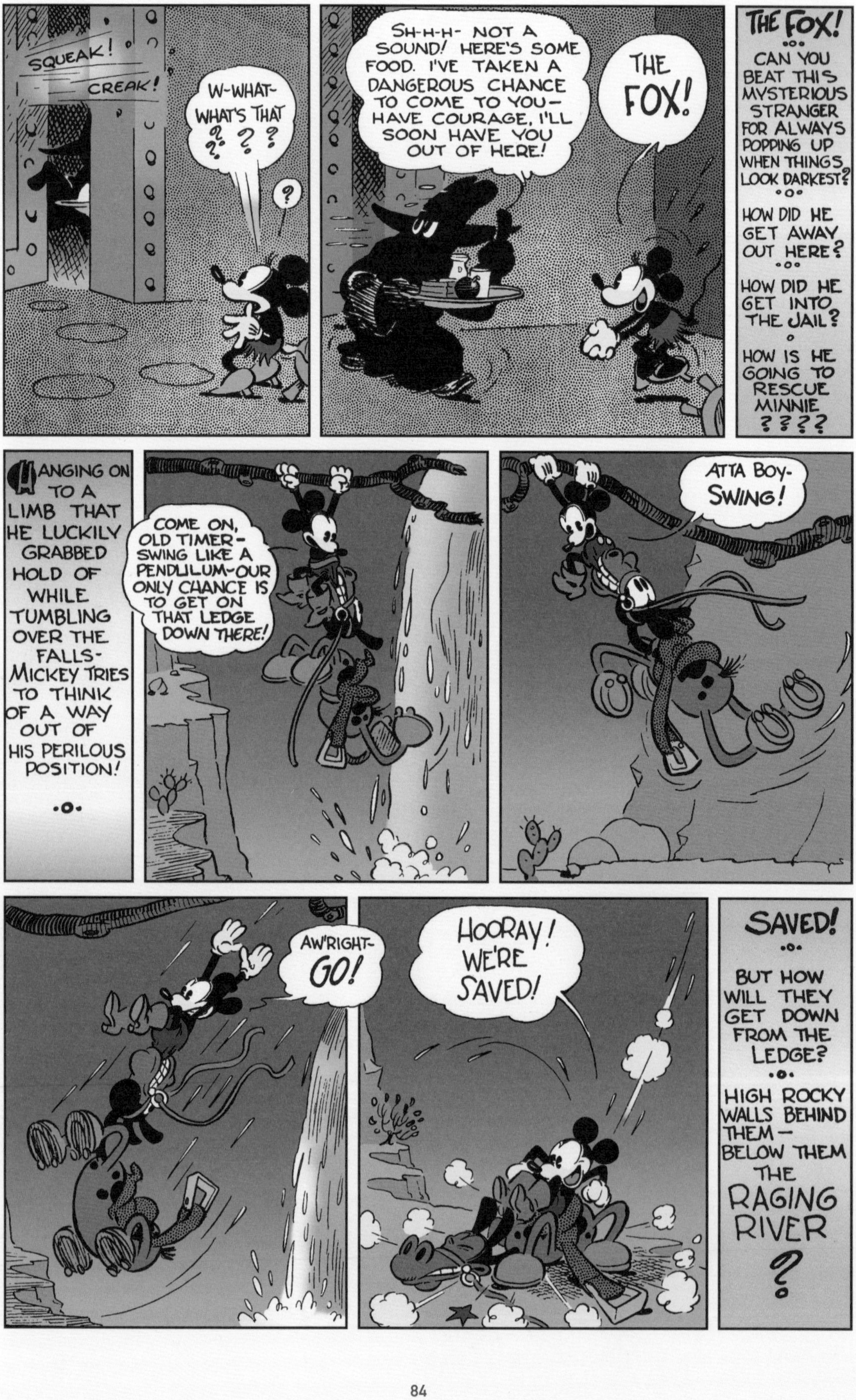
SQUEAK!
CREAK!
W-WHAT- WHAT'S THAT ? ? ?
?
SH-H-H- NOT A SOUND! HERE'S SOME FOOD. I'VE TAKEN A DANGEROUS CHANCE TO COME TO YOU- HAVE COURAGE, I'LL SOON HAVE YOU OUT OF HERE!
THE FOX!
THE FOX! CAN YOU BEAT THIS MYSTERIOUS STRANGER FOR ALWAYS POPPING UP WHEN THINGS LOOK DARKEST?
HOW DID HE GET AWAY OUT HERE?
HOW DID HE GET INTO THE JAIL?
HOW IS HE GOING TO RESCUE MINNIE ????
HANGING ON TO A LIMB THAT HE LUCKILY GRABBED HOLD OF WHILE TUMBLING OVER THE FALLS- MICKEY TRIES TO THINK OF A WAY OUT OF HIS PERILOUS POSITION!
COME ON, OLD TIMER- SWING LIKE A PENDULUM-OUR ONLY CHANCE IS TO GET ON THAT LEDGE DOWN THERE!
ATTA BOY- SWING!
AW'RIGHT- GO!
HOORAY! WE'RE SAVED!
SAVED!
BUT HOW WILL THEY GET DOWN FROM THE LEDGE?
HIGH ROCKY WALLS BEHIND THEM— BELOW THEM THE RAGING RIVER
?

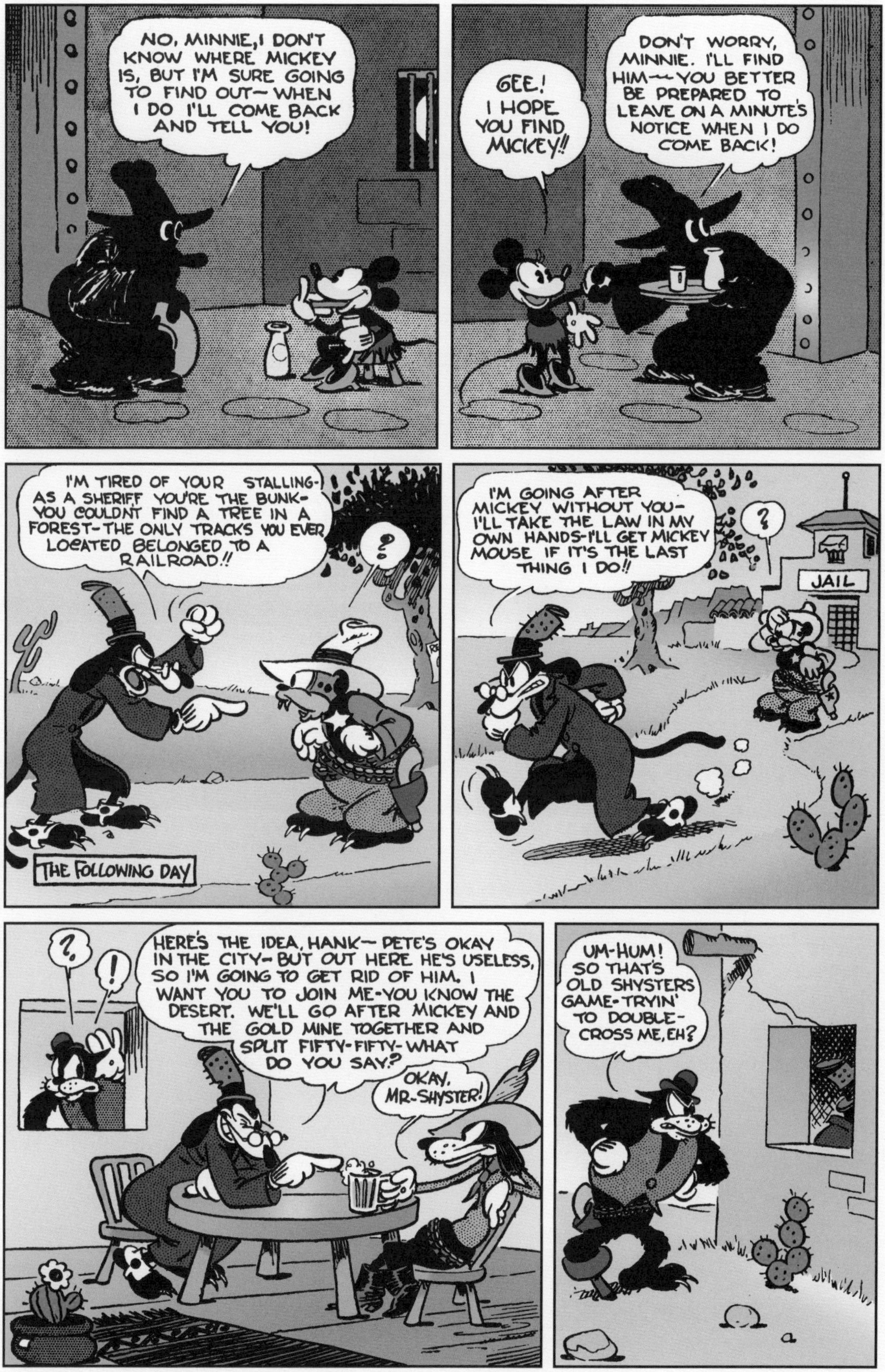
NO, MINNIE, I DON'T KNOW WHERE MICKEY IS, BUT I'M SURE GOING TO FIND OUT— WHEN I DO I'LL COME BACK AND TELL YOU!
GEE! I HOPE YOU FIND MICKEY!!
DON'T WORRY, MINNIE. I'LL FIND HIM—YOU BETTER BE PREPARED TO LEAVE ON A MINUTE'S NOTICE WHEN I DO COME BACK!
I'M TIRED OF YOUR STALLING- AS A SHERIFF YOU'RE THE BUNK- YOU COULDN'T FIND A TREE IN A FOREST- THE ONLY TRACKS YOU EVER LOCATED BELONGED TO A RAILROAD!!
?
THE FOLLOWING DAY
I'M GOING AFTER MICKEY WITHOUT YOU- I'LL TAKE THE LAW IN MY OWN HANDS-I'LL GET MICKEY MOUSE IF IT'S THE LAST THING I DO!!
?
JAIL
?
!
HERE'S THE IDEA, HANK— PETE'S OKAY IN THE CITY- BUT OUT HERE HE'S USELESS, SO I'M GOING TO GET RID OF HIM. I WANT YOU TO JOIN ME-YOU KNOW THE DESERT. WE'LL GO AFTER MICKEY AND THE GOLD MINE TOGETHER AND SPLIT FIFTY-FIFTY- WHAT DO YOU SAY?
OKAY, MR-SHYSTER!
UM-HUM! SO THAT'S OLD SHYSTERS GAME-TRYIN' TO DOUBLE-CROSS ME, EH?

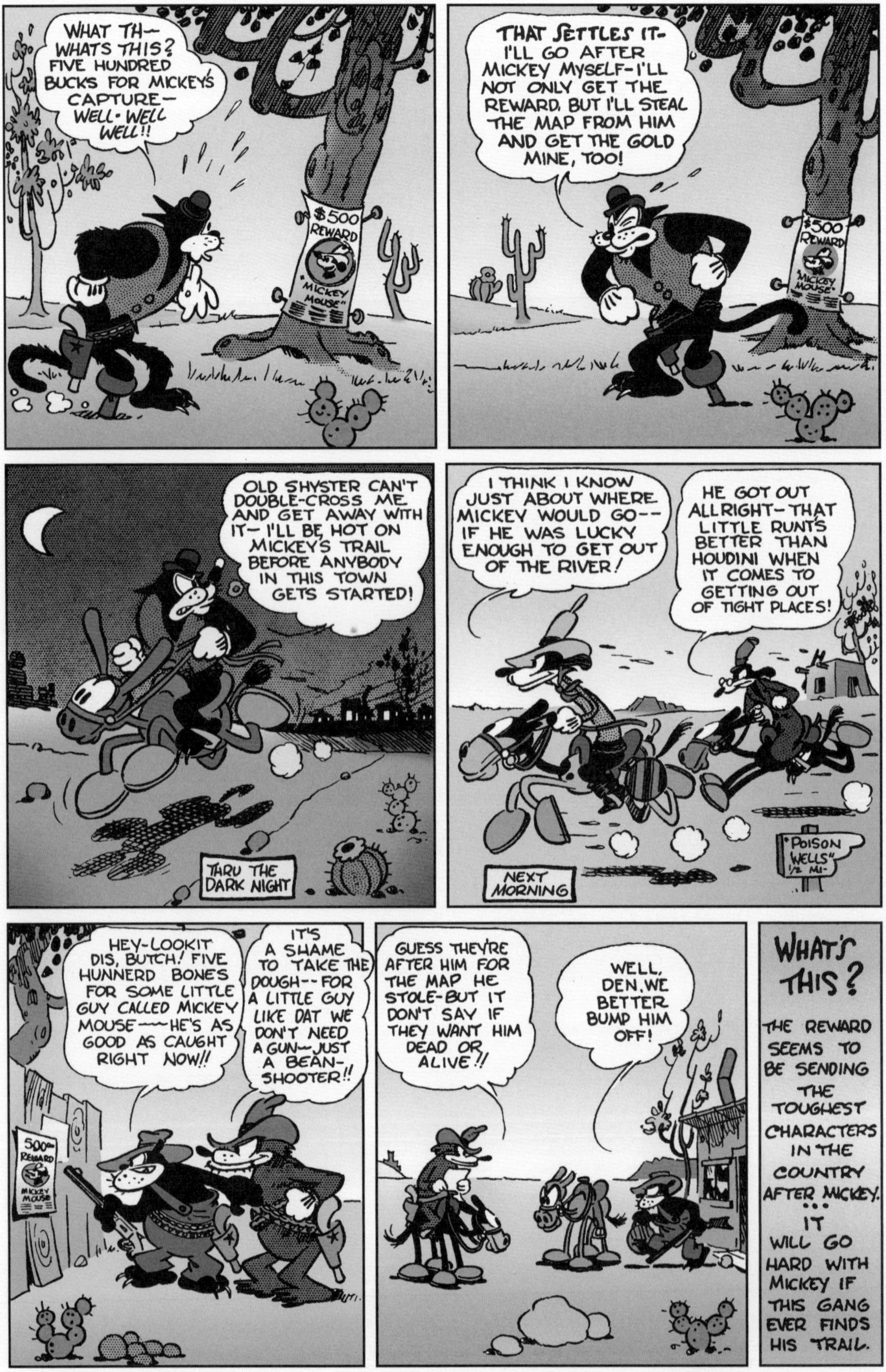
WHAT TH— WHATS THIS? FIVE HUNDRED BUCKS FOR MICKEY'S CAPTURE— WELL-WELL WELL!!
$500 REWARD
"MICKEY MOUSE"
THAT SETTLES IT- I'LL GO AFTER MICKEY MYSELF-I'LL NOT ONLY GET THE REWARD, BUT I'LL STEAL THE MAP FROM HIM AND GET THE GOLD MINE, TOO!
$500 REWARD
"MICKEY MOUSE"
OLD SHYSTER CAN'T DOUBLE-CROSS ME AND GET AWAY WITH IT- I'LL BE HOT ON MICKEY'S TRAIL BEFORE ANYBODY IN THIS TOWN GETS STARTED!
THRU THE DARK NIGHT
I THINK I KNOW JUST ABOUT WHERE MICKEY WOULD GO-- IF HE WAS LUCKY ENOUGH TO GET OUT OF THE RIVER!
HE GOT OUT ALLRIGHT- THAT LITTLE RUNT'S BETTER THAN HOUDINI WHEN IT COMES TO GETTING OUT OF TIGHT PLACES!
NEXT MORNING
"POISON WELLS" 1/2 MI.
HEY-LOOKIT DIS, BUTCH! FIVE HUNNERD BONES FOR SOME LITTLE GUY CALLED MICKEY MOUSE—HE'S AS GOOD AS CAUGHT RIGHT NOW!!
IT'S A SHAME TO TAKE THE DOUGH--FOR A LITTLE GUY LIKE DAT WE DON'T NEED A GUN—JUST A BEAN-SHOOTER!!
500 REWARD MICKEY MOUSE
GUESS THEY'RE AFTER HIM FOR THE MAP HE STOLE-BUT IT DON'T SAY IF THEY WANT HIM DEAD OR ALIVE!!
WELL, DEN, WE BETTER BUMP HIM OFF!
WHAT'S THIS?
THE REWARD SEEMS TO BE SENDING THE TOUGHEST CHARACTERS IN THE COUNTRY AFTER MICKEY...
IT WILL GO HARD WITH MICKEY IF THIS GANG EVER FINDS HIS TRAIL.

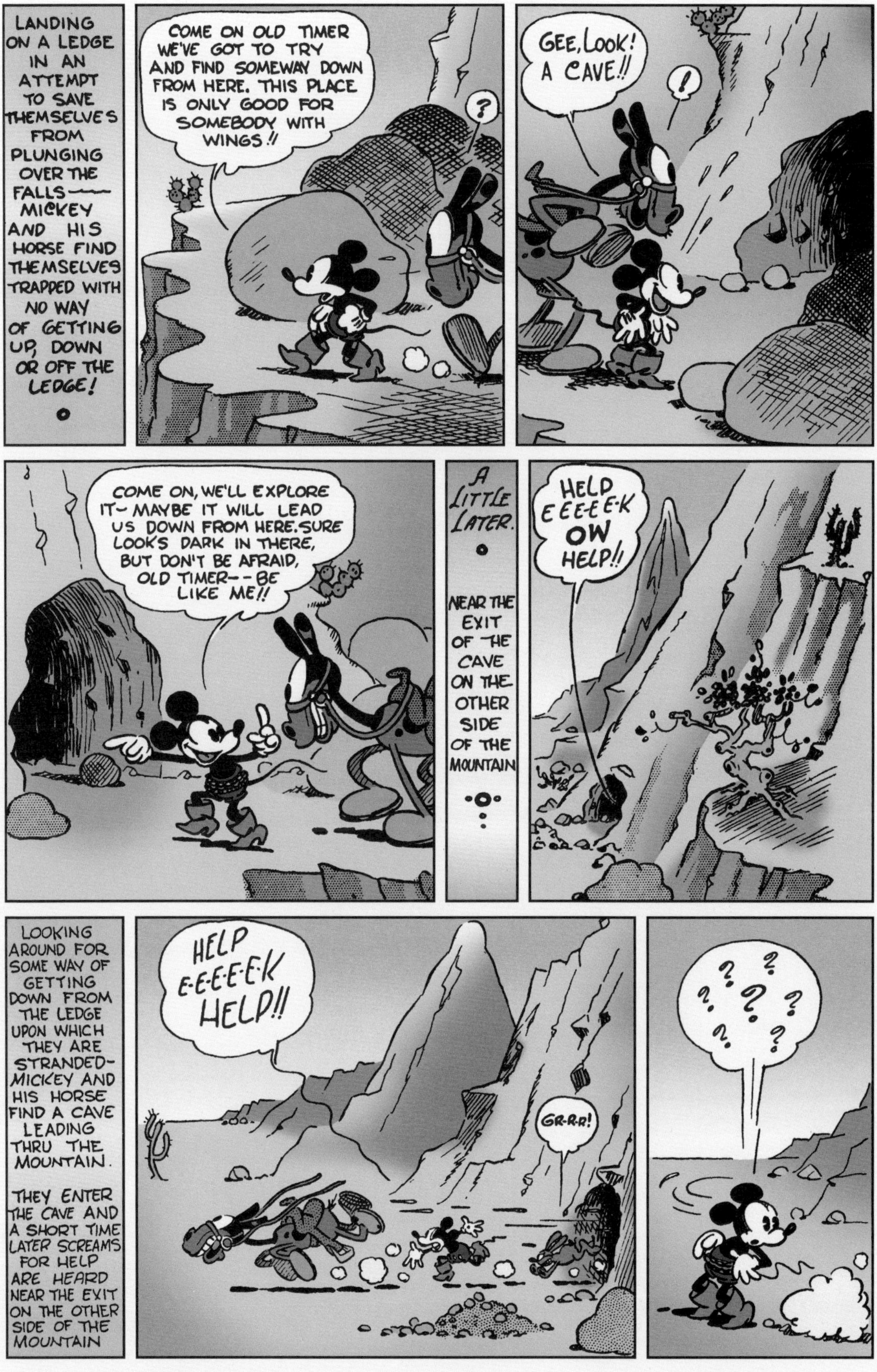
LANDING ON A LEDGE IN AN ATTEMPT TO SAVE THEMSELVES FROM PLUNGING OVER THE FALLS— MICKEY AND HIS HORSE FIND THEMSELVES TRAPPED WITH NO WAY OF GETTING UP, DOWN OR OFF THE LEDGE!
COME ON OLD TIMER WE'VE GOT TO TRY AND FIND SOMEWAY DOWN FROM HERE. THIS PLACE IS ONLY GOOD FOR SOMEBODY WITH WINGS!!
?
GEE, LOOK! A CAVE!!
!
COME ON, WE'LL EXPLORE IT— MAYBE IT WILL LEAD US DOWN FROM HERE. SURE LOOKS DARK IN THERE, BUT DON'T BE AFRAID, OLD TIMER-- BE LIKE ME!!
A LITTLE LATER.
NEAR THE EXIT OF THE CAVE ON THE OTHER SIDE OF THE MOUNTAIN
HELP EEE-E-E-K OW HELP!!
LOOKING AROUND FOR SOME WAY OF GETTING DOWN FROM THE LEDGE UPON WHICH THEY ARE STRANDED- MICKEY AND HIS HORSE FIND A CAVE LEADING THRU THE MOUNTAIN.
THEY ENTER THE CAVE AND A SHORT TIME LATER SCREAMS FOR HELP ARE HEARD NEAR THE EXIT ON THE OTHER SIDE OF THE MOUNTAIN
HELP E-E-E-E-E-K HELP!!
GR-R-R!
? ? ? ? ? ? ?

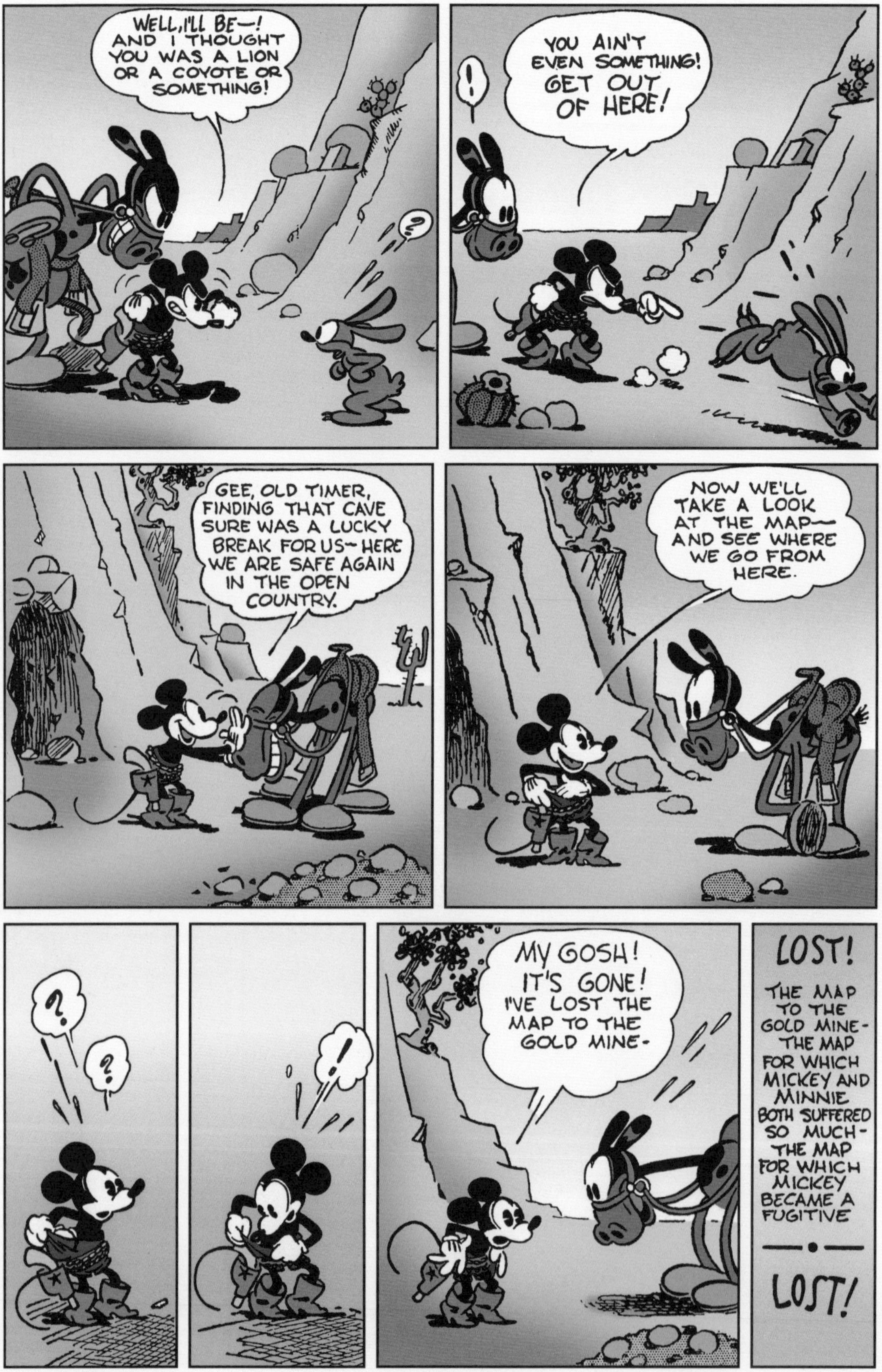
WELL, I'LL BE—! AND I THOUGHT YOU WAS A LION OR A COYOTE OR SOMETHING!
?
!
YOU AIN'T EVEN SOMETHING! GET OUT OF HERE!
GEE, OLD TIMER, FINDING THAT CAVE SURE WAS A LUCKY BREAK FOR US— HERE WE ARE SAFE AGAIN IN THE OPEN COUNTRY.
NOW WE'LL TAKE A LOOK AT THE MAP— AND SEE WHERE WE GO FROM HERE.
?
?
!
MY GOSH! IT'S GONE! I'VE LOST THE MAP TO THE GOLD MINE-
LOST!
THE MAP TO THE GOLD MINE- THE MAP FOR WHICH MICKEY AND MINNIE BOTH SUFFERED SO MUCH- THE MAP FOR WHICH MICKEY BECAME A FUGITIVE
LOST!

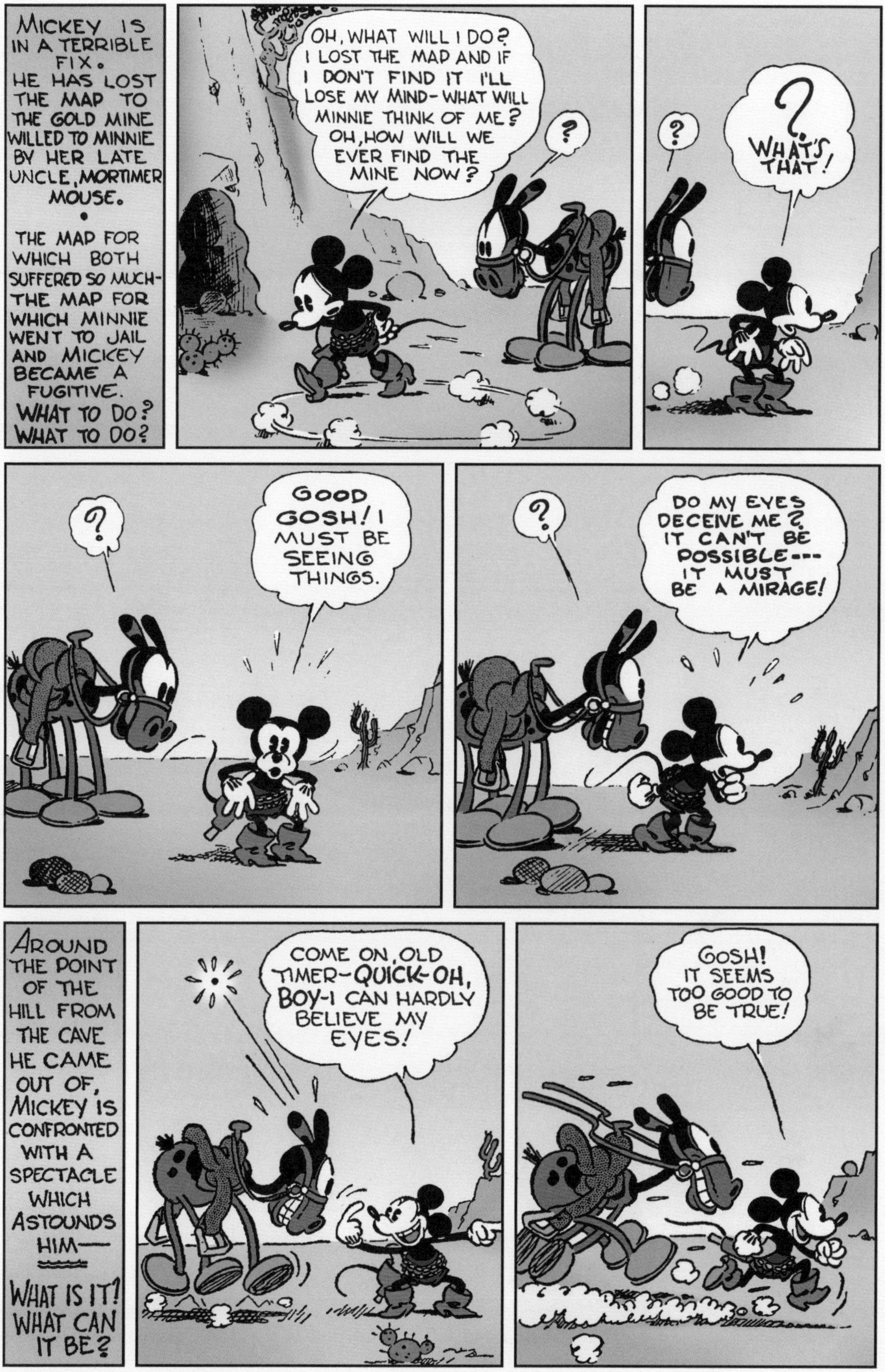
MICKEY IS IN A TERRIBLE FIX. HE HAS LOST THE MAP TO THE GOLD MINE WILLED TO MINNIE BY HER LATE UNCLE, MORTIMER MOUSE.
THE MAP FOR WHICH BOTH SUFFERED SO MUCH- THE MAP FOR WHICH MINNIE WENT TO JAIL AND MICKEY BECAME A FUGITIVE. WHAT TO DO? WHAT TO DO?
OH, WHAT WILL I DO? I LOST THE MAP AND IF I DON'T FIND IT I'LL LOSE MY MIND- WHAT WILL MINNIE THINK OF ME? OH, HOW WILL WE EVER FIND THE MINE NOW?
?
?
? WHAT'S THAT!
?
GOOD GOSH! I MUST BE SEEING THINGS.
?
DO MY EYES DECEIVE ME? IT CAN'T BE POSSIBLE--- IT MUST BE A MIRAGE!
AROUND THE POINT OF THE HILL FROM THE CAVE HE CAME OUT OF, MICKEY IS CONFRONTED WITH A SPECTACLE WHICH ASTOUNDS HIM—
WHAT IS IT! WHAT CAN IT BE?
COME ON, OLD TIMER- QUICK- OH, BOY- I CAN HARDLY BELIEVE MY EYES!
GOSH! IT SEEMS TOO GOOD TO BE TRUE!

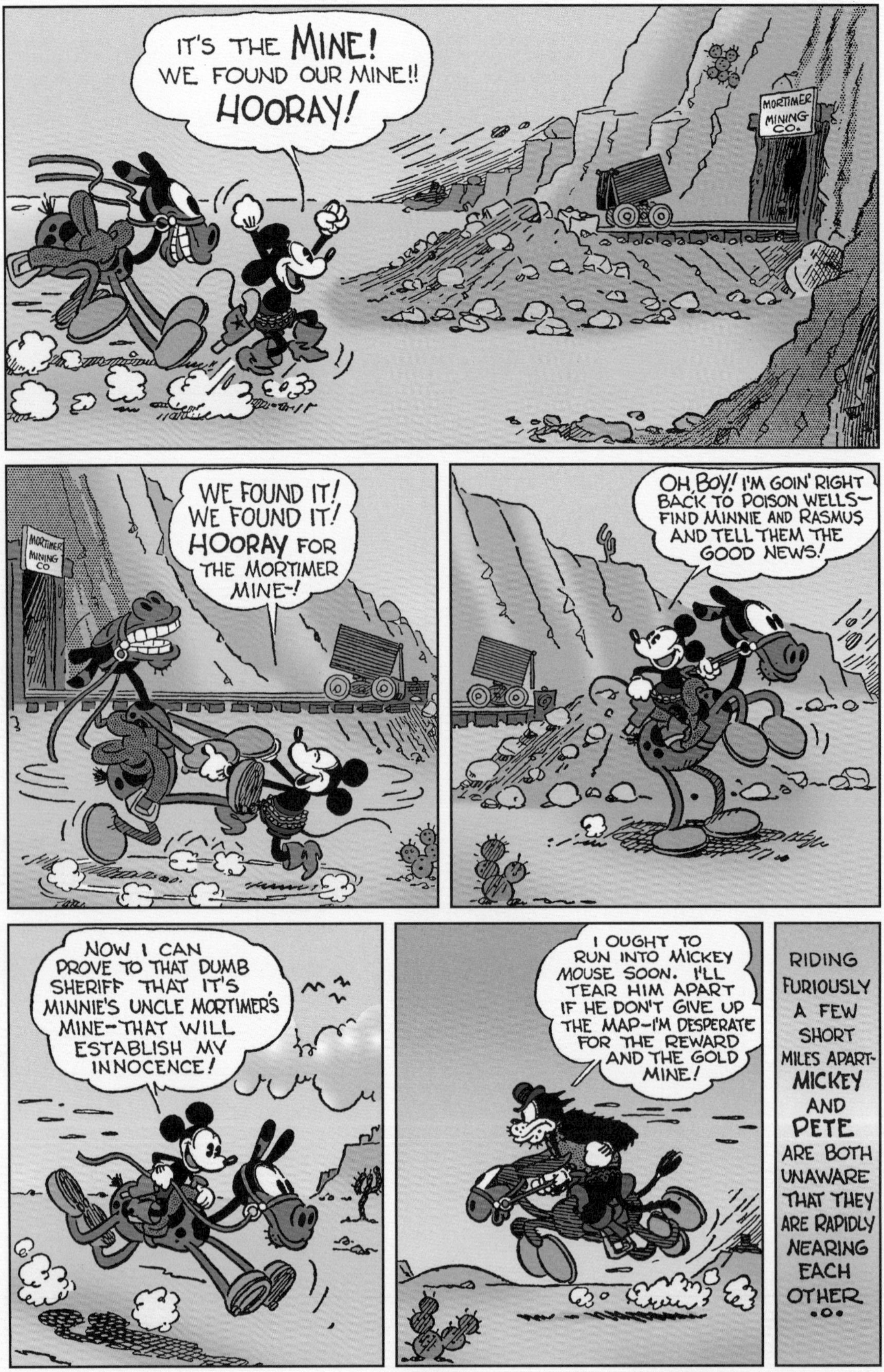
IT'S THE MINE! WE FOUND OUR MINE!! HOORAY!
MORTIMER MINING CO.
MORTIMER MINING CO
WE FOUND IT! WE FOUND IT! HOORAY FOR THE MORTIMER MINE-!
OH, BOY! I'M GOIN' RIGHT BACK TO POISON WELLS— FIND MINNIE AND RASMUS AND TELL THEM THE GOOD NEWS!
NOW I CAN PROVE TO THAT DUMB SHERIFF THAT IT'S MINNIE'S UNCLE MORTIMER'S MINE—THAT WILL ESTABLISH MY INNOCENCE!
I OUGHT TO RUN INTO MICKEY MOUSE SOON. I'LL TEAR HIM APART IF HE DON'T GIVE UP THE MAP—I'M DESPERATE FOR THE REWARD AND THE GOLD MINE!
RIDING FURIOUSLY A FEW SHORT MILES APART— MICKEY AND PETE ARE BOTH UNAWARE THAT THEY ARE RAPIDLY NEARING EACH OTHER •O•

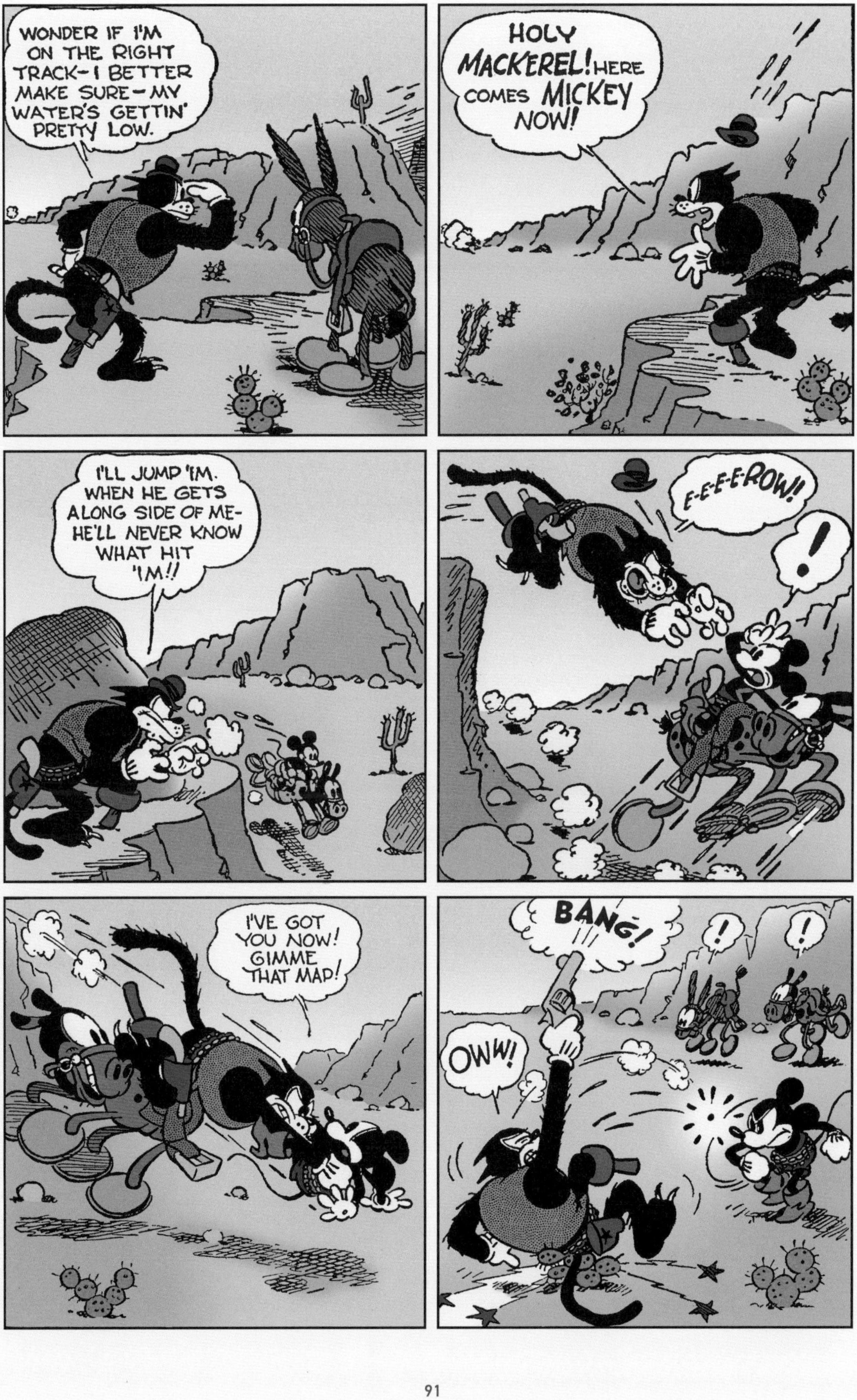
WONDER IF I'M ON THE RIGHT TRACK- I BETTER MAKE SURE- MY WATER'S GETTIN' PRETTY LOW.
HOLY MACKEREL! HERE COMES MICKEY NOW!
I'LL JUMP 'IM. WHEN HE GETS ALONG SIDE OF ME- HE'LL NEVER KNOW WHAT HIT 'IM!!
E-E-E-E-ROW!
!
I'VE GOT YOU NOW! GIMME THAT MAP!
BANG!
!
!
OWW!

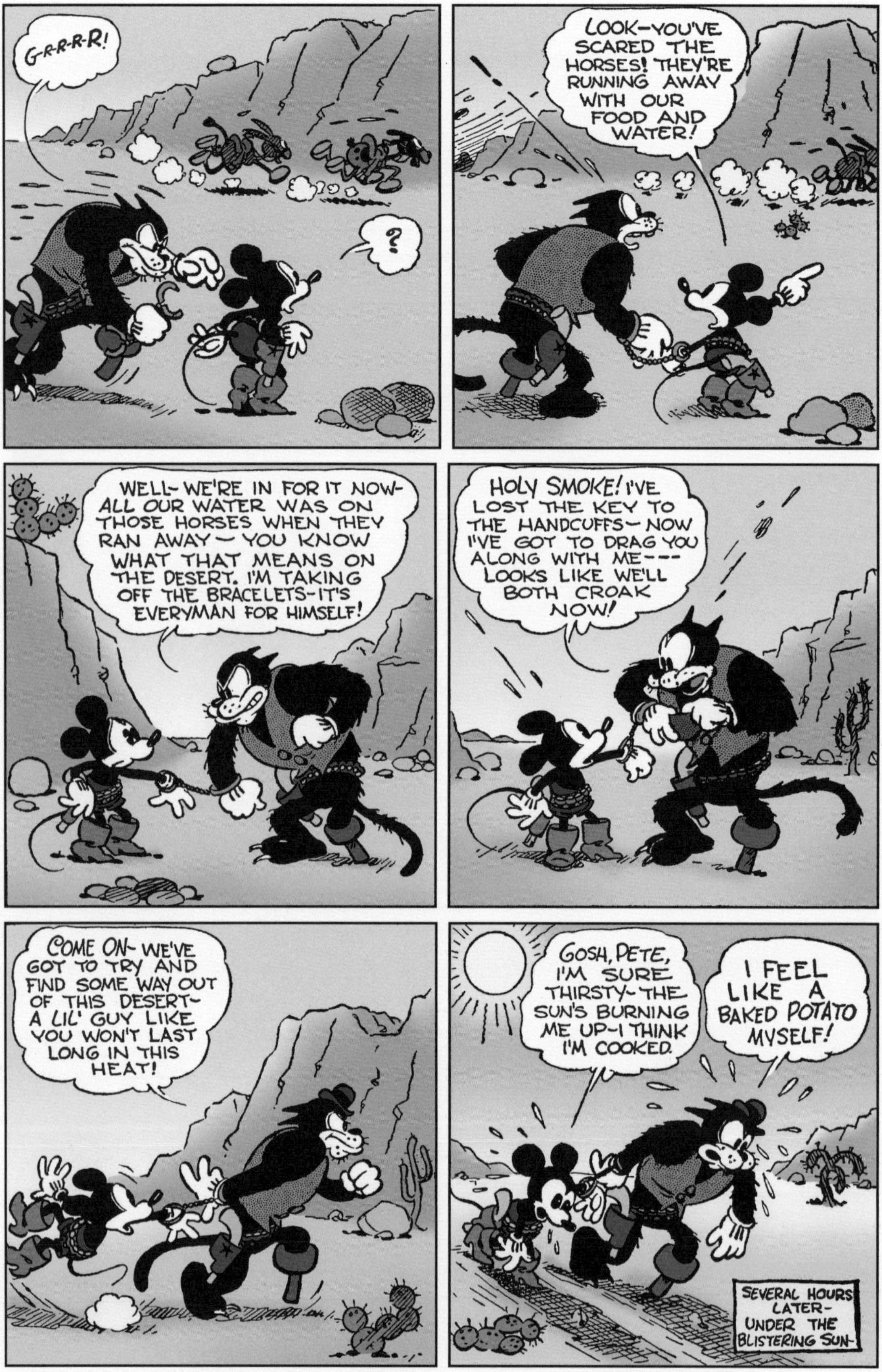
G-R-R-R-R!
?
LOOK—YOU'VE SCARED THE HORSES! THEY'RE RUNNING AWAY WITH OUR FOOD AND WATER!
WELL- WE'RE IN FOR IT NOW- ALL OUR WATER WAS ON THOSE HORSES WHEN THEY RAN AWAY — YOU KNOW WHAT THAT MEANS ON THE DESERT. I'M TAKING OFF THE BRACELETS-IT'S EVERYMAN FOR HIMSELF!
HOLY SMOKE! I'VE LOST THE KEY TO THE HANDCUFFS— NOW I'VE GOT TO DRAG YOU ALONG WITH ME--- LOOKS LIKE WE'LL BOTH CROAK NOW!
COME ON- WE'VE GOT TO TRY AND FIND SOME WAY OUT OF THIS DESERT- A LIL' GUY LIKE YOU WON'T LAST LONG IN THIS HEAT!
SEVERAL HOURS LATER- UNDER THE BLISTERING SUN-
GOSH, PETE, I'M SURE THIRSTY- THE SUN'S BURNING ME UP-I THINK I'M COOKED.
I FEEL LIKE A BAKED POTATO MYSELF!

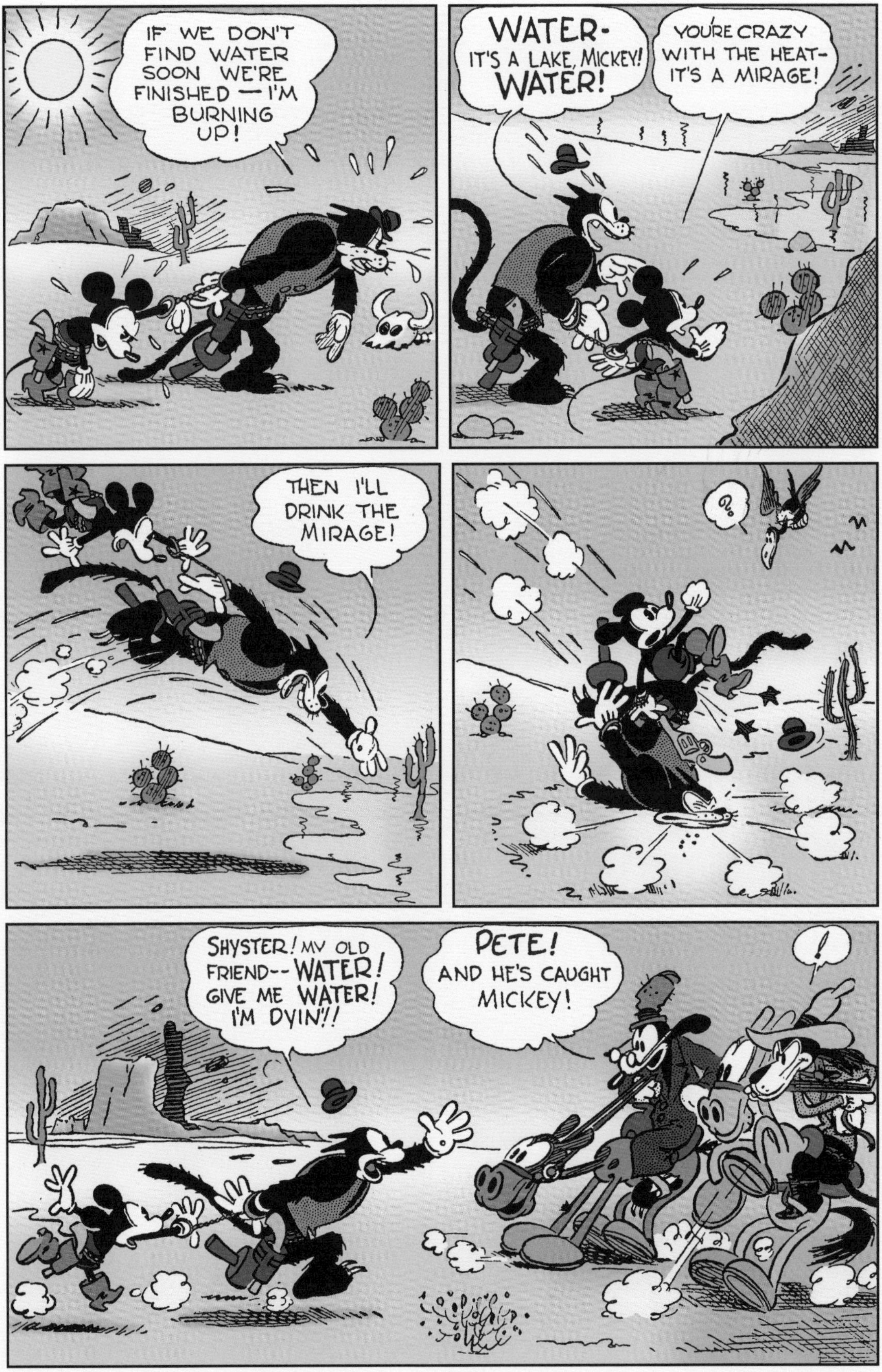
IF WE DON'T FIND WATER SOON WE'RE FINISHED — I'M BURNING UP!
WATER- IT'S A LAKE, MICKEY! WATER!
YOU'RE CRAZY WITH THE HEAT- IT'S A MIRAGE!
THEN I'LL DRINK THE MIRAGE!
?
SHYSTER! MY OLD FRIEND-- WATER! GIVE ME WATER! I'M DYIN'!!
PETE! AND HE'S CAUGHT MICKEY!
!

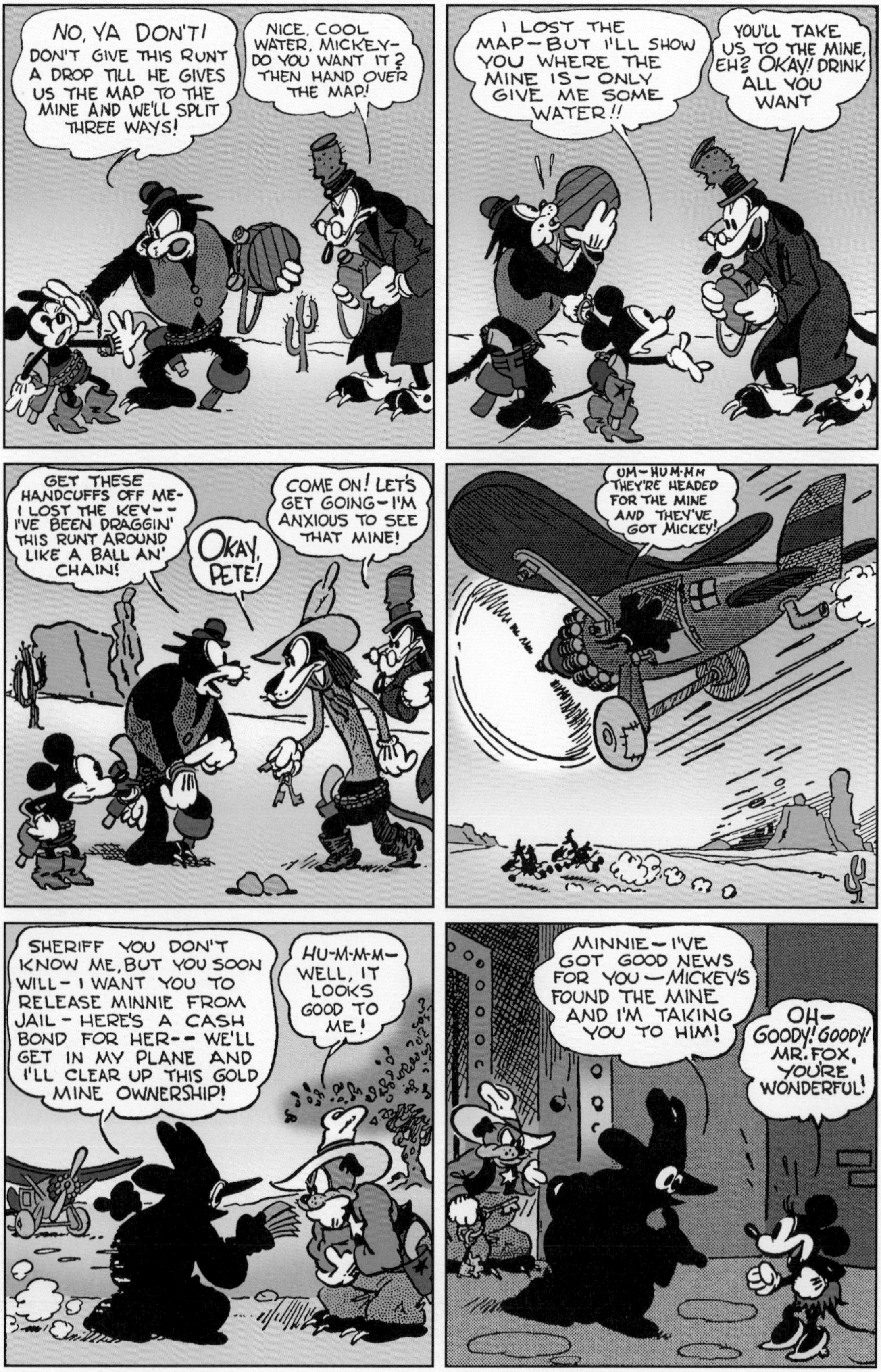
NO, YA DON'T! DON'T GIVE THIS RUNT A DROP TILL HE GIVES US THE MAP TO THE MINE AND WE'LL SPLIT THREE WAYS!
NICE, COOL WATER, MICKEY- DO YOU WANT IT? THEN HAND OVER THE MAP!
I LOST THE MAP—BUT I'LL SHOW YOU WHERE THE MINE IS—ONLY GIVE ME SOME WATER!!
YOU'LL TAKE US TO THE MINE, EH? OKAY! DRINK ALL YOU WANT
GET THESE HANDCUFFS OFF ME- I LOST THE KEY-- I'VE BEEN DRAGGIN' THIS RUNT AROUND LIKE A BALL AN' CHAIN!
OKAY, PETE!
COME ON! LET'S GET GOING—I'M ANXIOUS TO SEE THAT MINE!
UM-HUM-MM THEY'RE HEADED FOR THE MINE AND THEY'VE GOT MICKEY!
SHERIFF YOU DON'T KNOW ME, BUT YOU SOON WILL- I WANT YOU TO RELEASE MINNIE FROM JAIL—HERE'S A CASH BOND FOR HER-- WE'LL GET IN MY PLANE AND I'LL CLEAR UP THIS GOLD MINE OWNERSHIP!
HU-M-M-M- WELL, IT LOOKS GOOD TO ME!
MINNIE—I'VE GOT GOOD NEWS FOR YOU—MICKEY'S FOUND THE MINE AND I'M TAKING YOU TO HIM!
OH-GOODY! GOODY! MR. FOX, YOU'RE WONDERFUL!

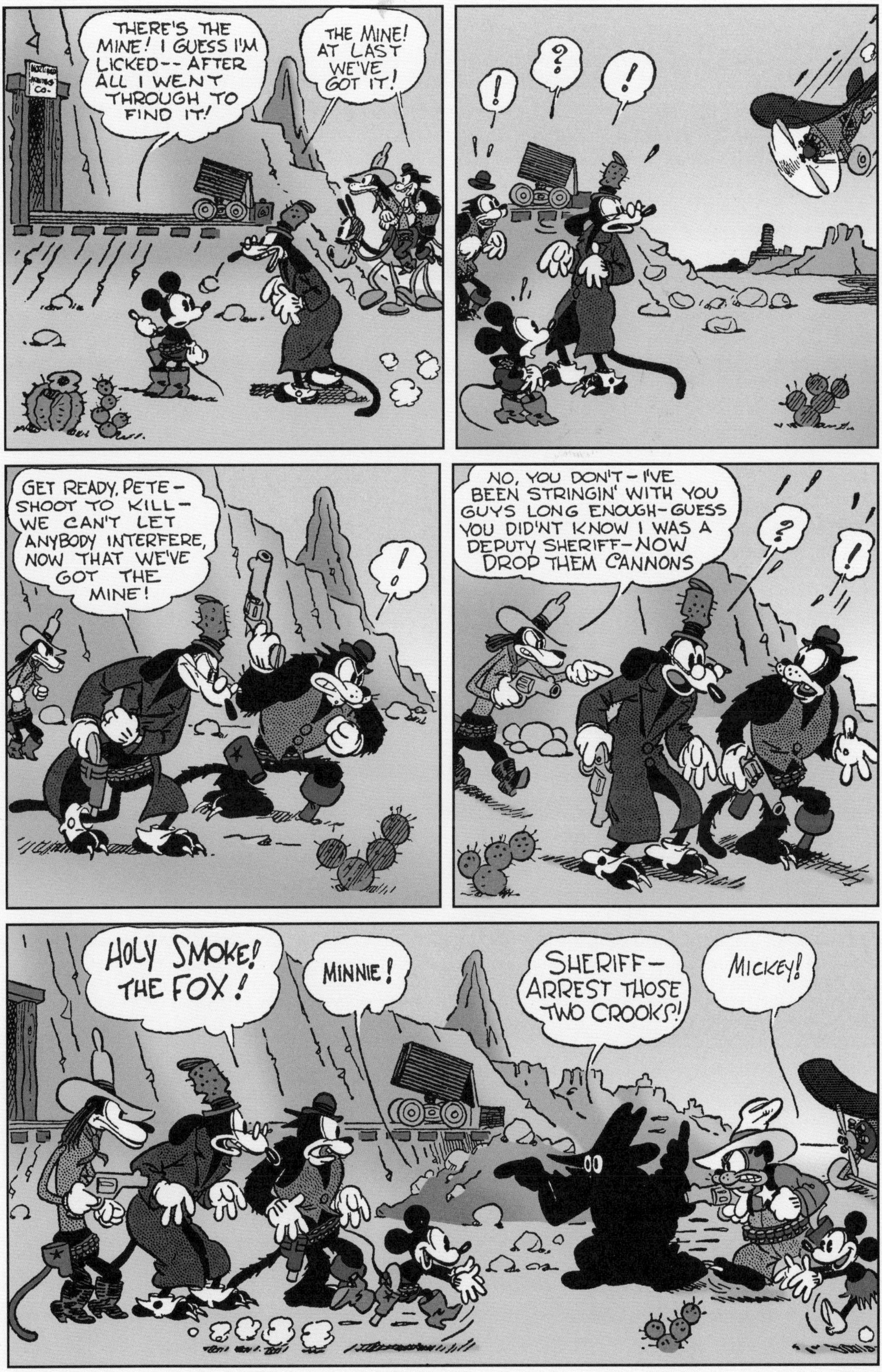
THERE'S THE MINE! I GUESS I'M LICKED-- AFTER ALL I WENT THROUGH TO FIND IT!
THE MINE! AT LAST WE'VE GOT IT!
!
?
!
GET READY, PETE - SHOOT TO KILL - WE CAN'T LET ANYBODY INTERFERE, NOW THAT WE'VE GOT THE MINE!
!
NO, YOU DON'T - I'VE BEEN STRINGIN' WITH YOU GUYS LONG ENOUGH - GUESS YOU DID'NT KNOW I WAS A DEPUTY SHERIFF - NOW DROP THEM CANNONS
?
!
HOLY SMOKE! THE FOX!
MINNIE!
SHERIFF - ARREST THOSE TWO CROOKS!
MICKEY!

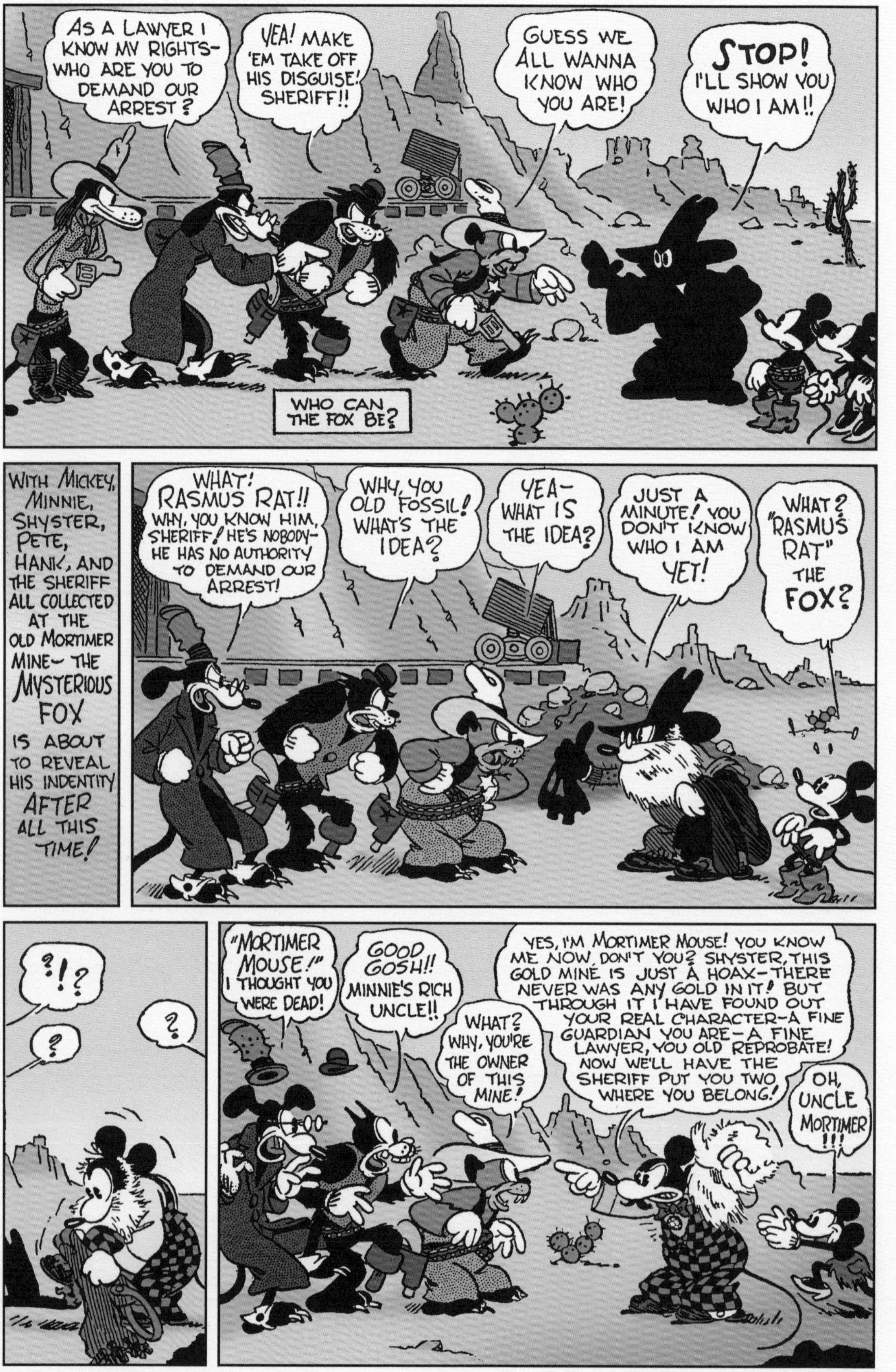
AS A LAWYER I KNOW MY RIGHTS- WHO ARE YOU TO DEMAND OUR ARREST?
YEA! MAKE 'EM TAKE OFF HIS DISGUISE! SHERIFF!!
GUESS WE ALL WANNA KNOW WHO YOU ARE!
STOP! I'LL SHOW YOU WHO I AM!!
WHO CAN THE FOX BE?
WITH MICKEY, MINNIE, SHYSTER, PETE, HANK, AND THE SHERIFF ALL COLLECTED AT THE OLD MORTIMER MINE- THE MYSTERIOUS FOX IS ABOUT TO REVEAL HIS INDENTITY AFTER ALL THIS TIME!
WHAT! RASMUS RAT!! WHY, YOU KNOW HIM, SHERIFF! HE'S NOBODY- HE HAS NO AUTHORITY TO DEMAND OUR ARREST!
WHY, YOU OLD FOSSIL! WHAT'S THE IDEA?
YEA- WHAT IS THE IDEA?
JUST A MINUTE! YOU DON'T KNOW WHO I AM YET!
WHAT? "RASMUS RAT" THE FOX?
?!?
?
?
"MORTIMER MOUSE!" I THOUGHT YOU WERE DEAD!
GOOD GOSH!! MINNIE'S RICH UNCLE!!
WHAT? WHY, YOU'RE THE OWNER OF THIS MINE!
YES, I'M MORTIMER MOUSE! YOU KNOW ME NOW, DON'T YOU? SHYSTER, THIS GOLD MINE IS JUST A HOAX- THERE NEVER WAS ANY GOLD IN IT! BUT THROUGH IT I HAVE FOUND OUT YOUR REAL CHARACTER- A FINE GUARDIAN YOU ARE- A FINE LAWYER, YOU OLD REPROBATE! NOW WE'LL HAVE THE SHERIFF PUT YOU TWO WHERE YOU BELONG!
OH, UNCLE MORTIMER!!!

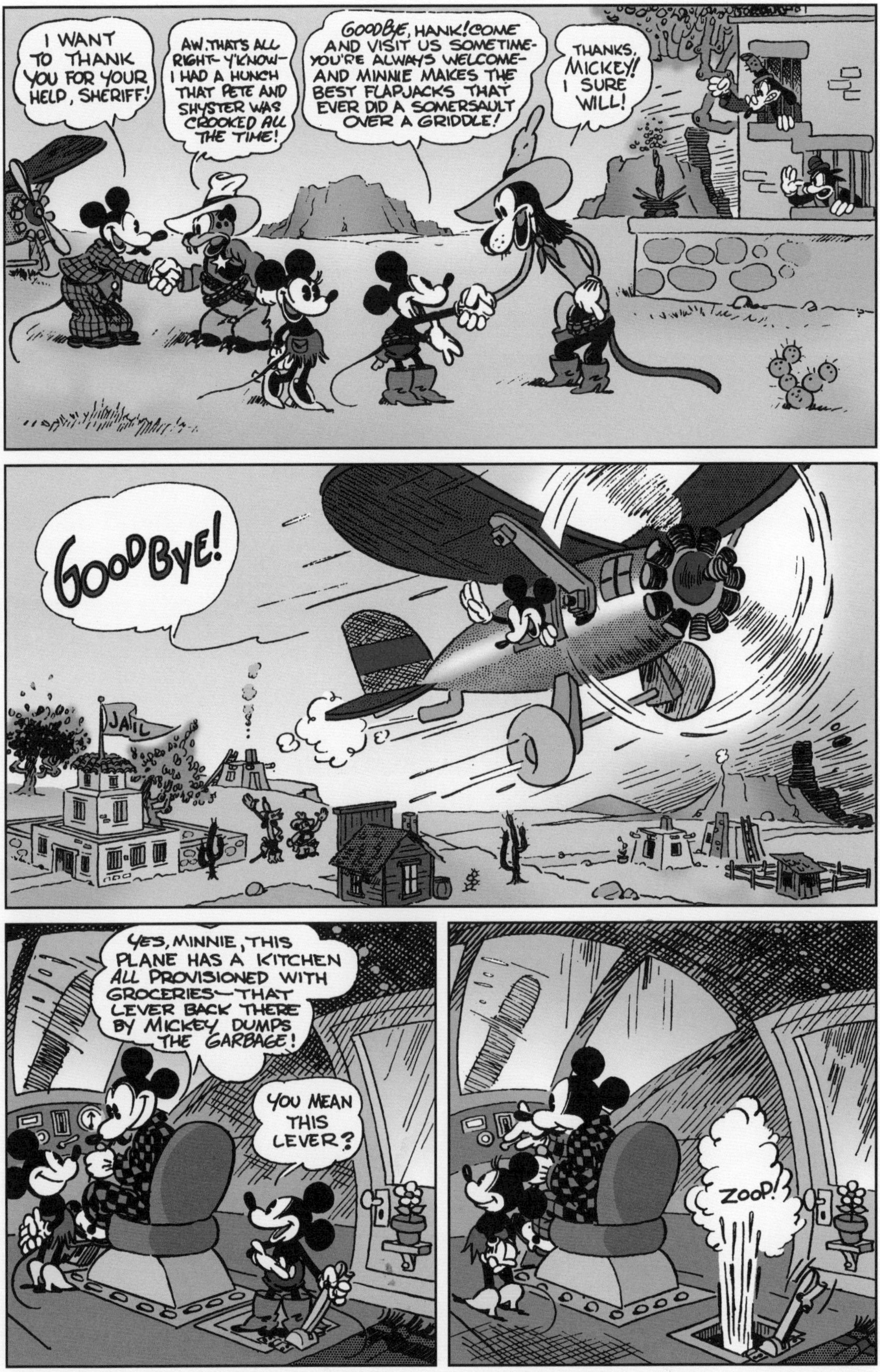
I WANT TO THANK YOU FOR YOUR HELP, SHERIFF!
AW. THAT'S ALL RIGHT– Y'KNOW– I HAD A HUNCH THAT PETE AND SHYSTER WAS CROOKED ALL THE TIME!
GOODBYE, HANK! COME AND VISIT US SOMETIME– YOU'RE ALWAYS WELCOME– AND MINNIE MAKES THE BEST FLAPJACKS THAT EVER DID A SOMERSAULT OVER A GRIDDLE!
THANKS, MICKEY! I SURE WILL!
GOODBYE!
JAIL
YES, MINNIE, THIS PLANE HAS A KITCHEN ALL PROVISIONED WITH GROCERIES– THAT LEVER BACK THERE BY MICKEY DUMPS THE GARBAGE!
YOU MEAN THIS LEVER?
ZOOP!

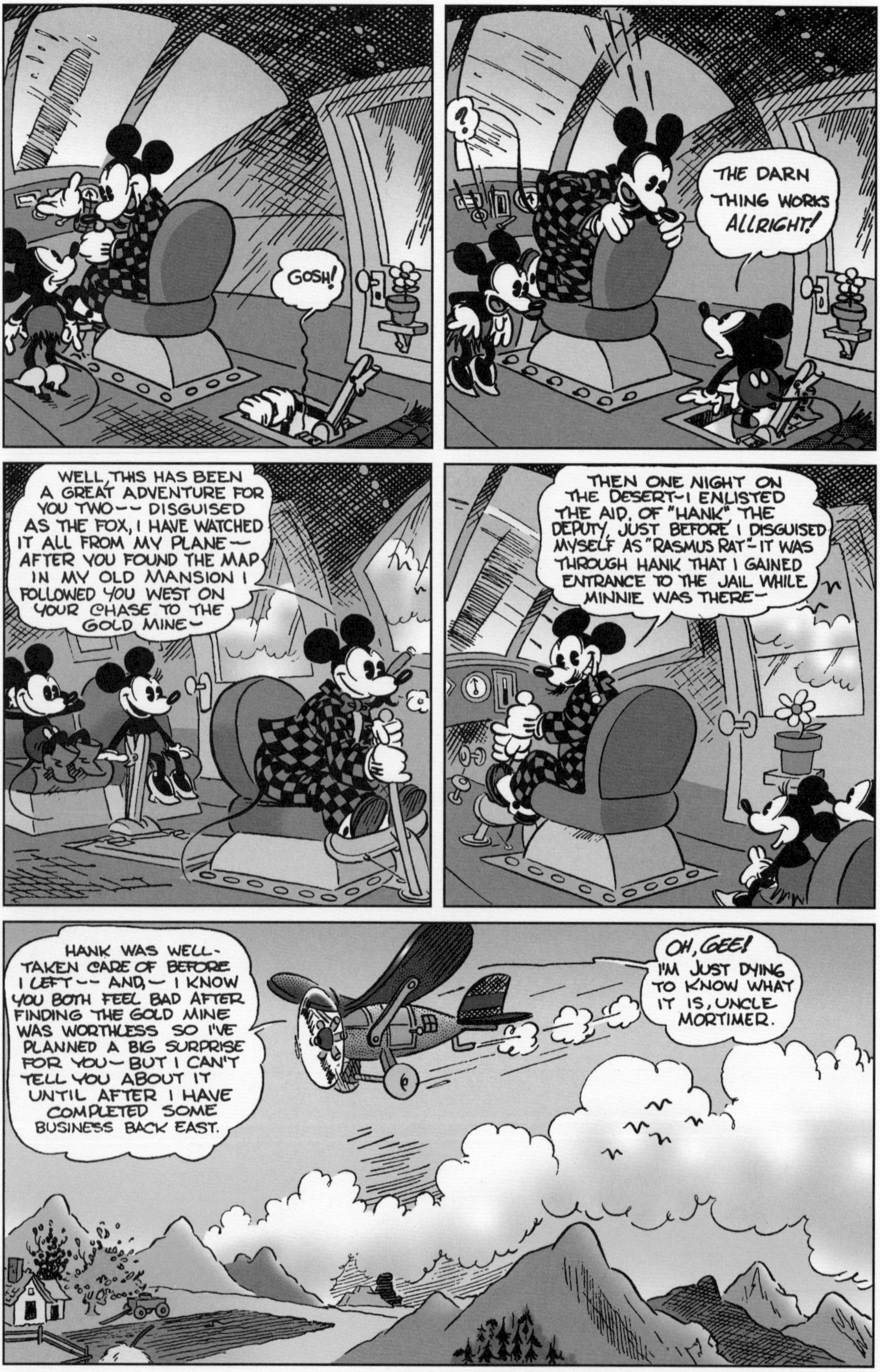
GOSH!
THE DARN THING WORKS ALLRIGHT!
WELL, THIS HAS BEEN A GREAT ADVENTURE FOR YOU TWO-- DISGUISED AS THE FOX, I HAVE WATCHED IT ALL FROM MY PLANE— AFTER YOU FOUND THE MAP IN MY OLD MANSION I FOLLOWED YOU WEST ON YOUR CHASE TO THE GOLD MINE—
THEN ONE NIGHT ON THE DESERT-I ENLISTED THE AID, OF "HANK" THE DEPUTY, JUST BEFORE I DISGUISED MYSELF AS "RASMUS RAT"-IT WAS THROUGH HANK THAT I GAINED ENTRANCE TO THE JAIL WHILE MINNIE WAS THERE—
HANK WAS WELL-TAKEN CARE OF BEFORE I LEFT -- AND,— I KNOW YOU BOTH FEEL BAD AFTER FINDING THE GOLD MINE WAS WORTHLESS SO I'VE PLANNED A BIG SURPRISE FOR YOU— BUT I CAN'T TELL YOU ABOUT IT UNTIL AFTER I HAVE COMPLETED SOME BUSINESS BACK EAST.
OH, GEE! I'M JUST DYING TO KNOW WHAT IT IS, UNCLE MORTIMER.

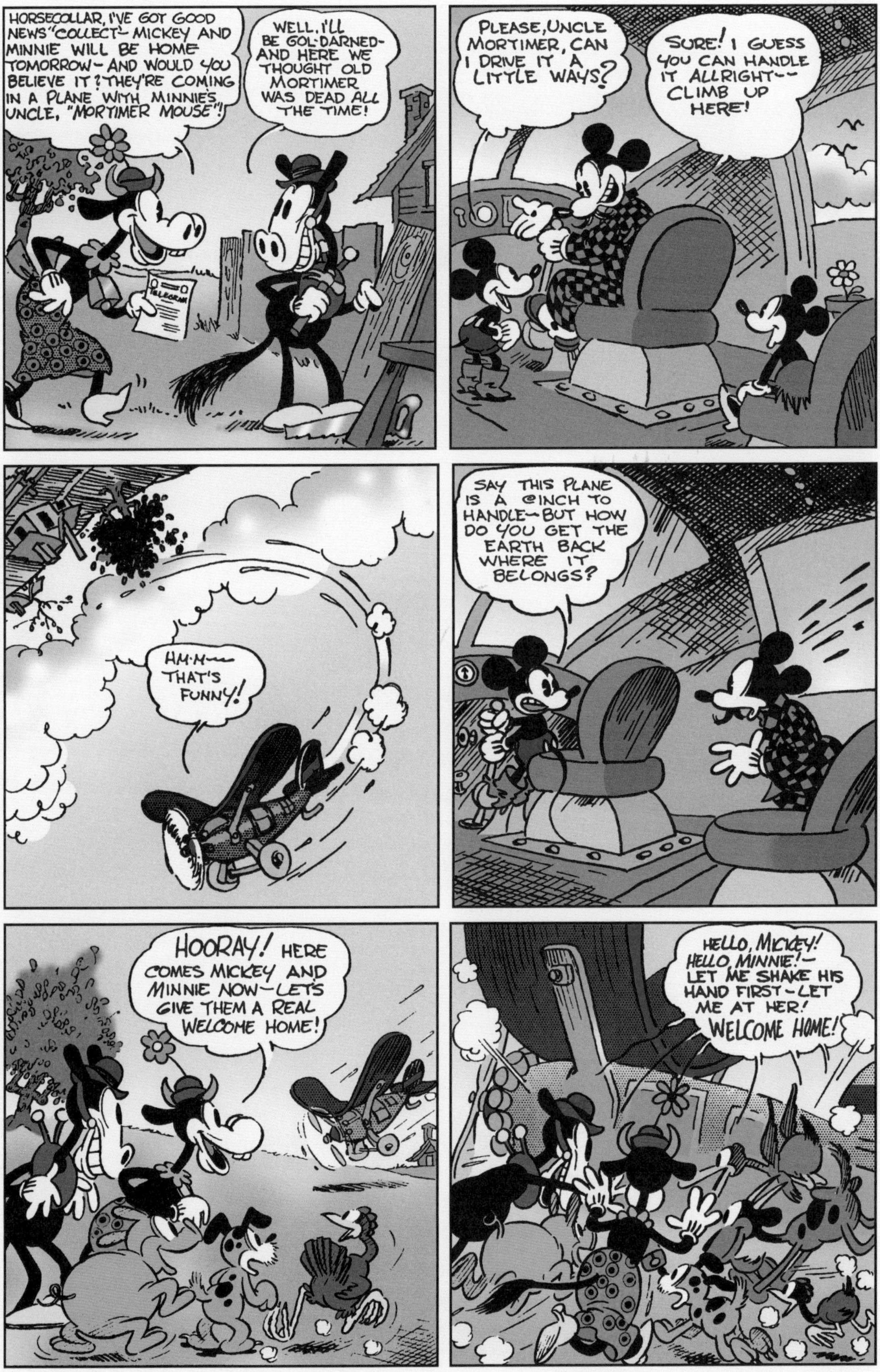
HORSECOLLAR, I'VE GOT GOOD NEWS "COLLECT"- MICKEY AND MINNIE WILL BE HOME TOMORROW- AND WOULD YOU BELIEVE IT? THEY'RE COMING IN A PLANE WITH MINNIE'S UNCLE, "MORTIMER MOUSE"!
WELL, I'LL BE GOL-DARNED- AND HERE WE THOUGHT OLD MORTIMER WAS DEAD ALL THE TIME!
TELEGRAM
PLEASE, UNCLE MORTIMER, CAN I DRIVE IT A LITTLE WAYS?
SURE! I GUESS YOU CAN HANDLE IT ALLRIGHT-- CLIMB UP HERE!
HM-M-- THAT'S FUNNY!
SAY THIS PLANE IS A CINCH TO HANDLE- BUT HOW DO YOU GET THE EARTH BACK WHERE IT BELONGS?
HOORAY! HERE COMES MICKEY AND MINNIE NOW- LET'S GIVE THEM A REAL WELCOME HOME!
HELLO, MICKEY! HELLO, MINNIE!- LET ME SHAKE HIS HAND FIRST- LET ME AT HER! WELCOME HOME!

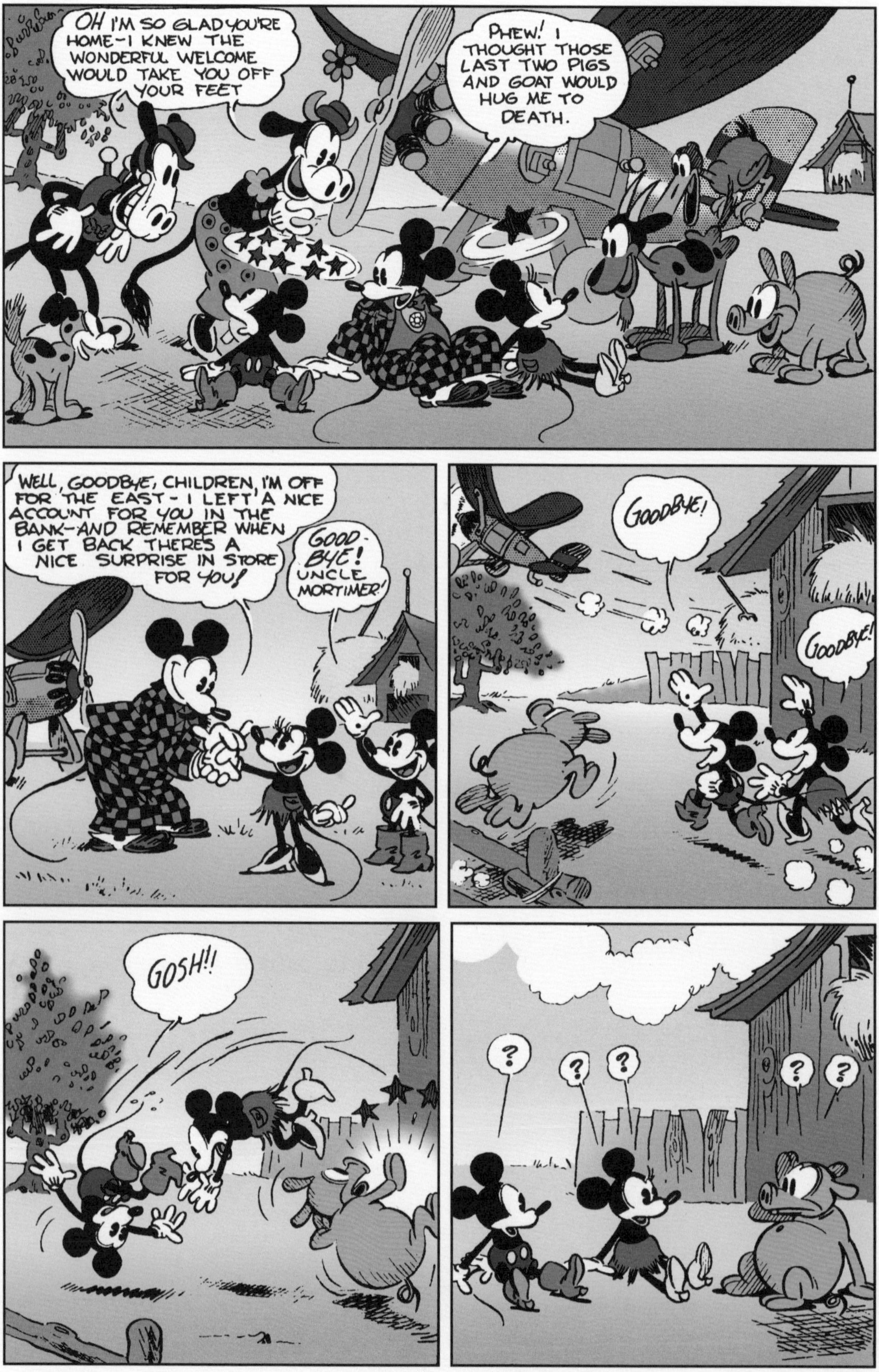
OH I'M SO GLAD YOU'RE HOME-I KNEW THE WONDERFUL WELCOME WOULD TAKE YOU OFF YOUR FEET
PHEW! I THOUGHT THOSE LAST TWO PIGS AND GOAT WOULD HUG ME TO DEATH.
WELL, GOODBYE, CHILDREN, I'M OFF FOR THE EAST - I LEFT A NICE ACCOUNT FOR YOU IN THE BANK-AND REMEMBER WHEN I GET BACK THERE'S A NICE SURPRISE IN STORE FOR YOU!
GOOD-BYE! UNCLE MORTIMER!
GOODBYE!
GOODBYE!
GOSH!!
?
?
?
?
?

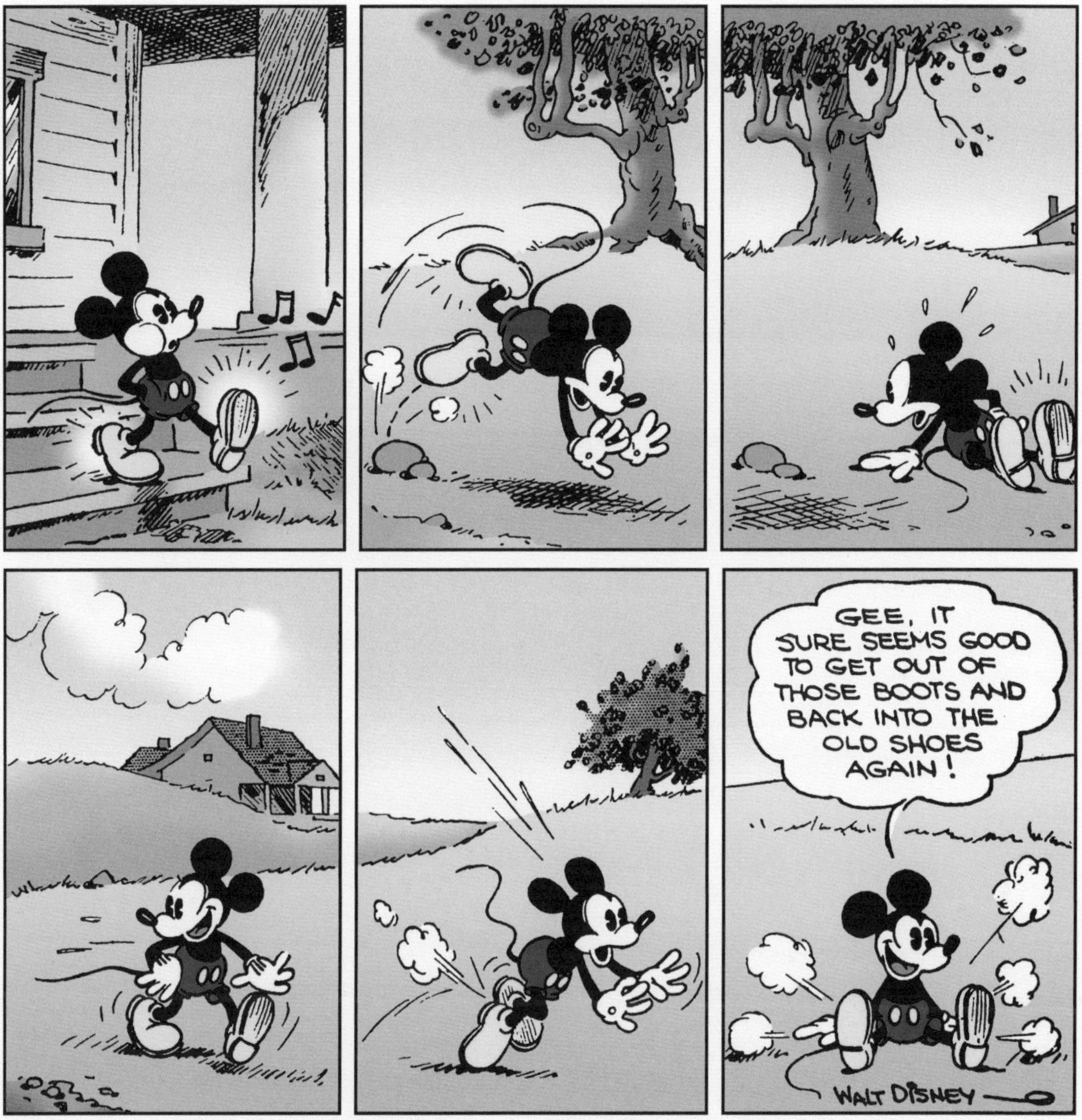
GEE, IT SURE SEEMS GOOD TO GET OUT OF THOSE BOOTS AND BACK INTO THE OLD SHOES AGAIN!
WALT DISNEY

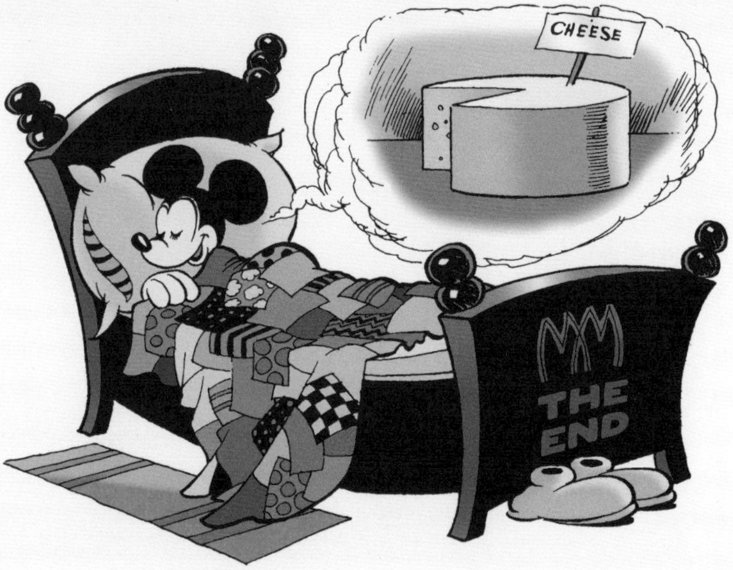
CHEESE
THE END

Gobs of Good Wishes
Mickey Mouse

Me too
Butch

Mickey's tough pal Butch — seen here in the suit of armor — was the first of many ongoing characters created by Gottfredson. Born in late 1930, Butch would go on to feature as a costumed character in the "Mickey Mouse Idea" (1931), the first licensed Disney stage show, and then in this giveaway "photo" created by Gottfredson's team to promote the daily strip. Readers could write in to the Disney studio to receive copies of the image; an unexpected avalanche of mail was achieved.

Fan card image and photo courtesy Walt Disney Archives.

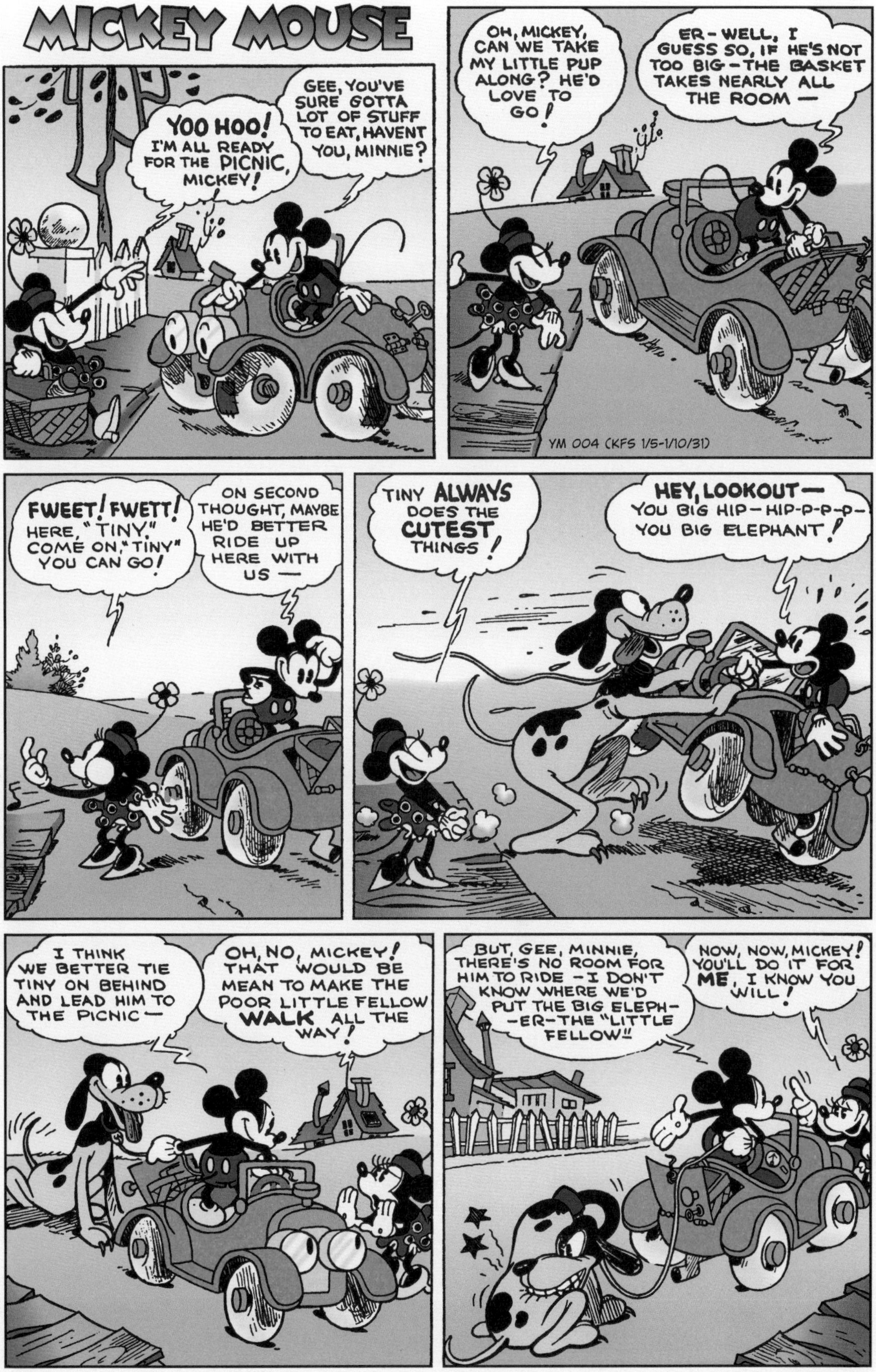
MICKEY MOUSE
YOO HOO! I'M ALL READY FOR THE PICNIC, MICKEY!
GEE, YOU'VE SURE GOTTA LOT OF STUFF TO EAT, HAVENT YOU, MINNIE?
OH, MICKEY, CAN WE TAKE MY LITTLE PUP ALONG? HE'D LOVE TO GO!
ER-WELL, I GUESS SO, IF HE'S NOT TOO BIG-THE BASKET TAKES NEARLY ALL THE ROOM—
YM 004 (KFS 1/5-1/10/31)
FWEET! FWETT! HERE, "TINY." COME ON, "TINY" YOU CAN GO!
ON SECOND THOUGHT, MAYBE HE'D BETTER RIDE UP HERE WITH US—
TINY ALWAYS DOES THE CUTEST THINGS!
HEY, LOOKOUT— YOU BIG HIP-HIP-P-P-P- YOU BIG ELEPHANT!
I THINK WE BETTER TIE TINY ON BEHIND AND LEAD HIM TO THE PICNIC—
OH, NO, MICKEY! THAT WOULD BE MEAN TO MAKE THE POOR LITTLE FELLOW WALK ALL THE WAY!
BUT, GEE, MINNIE, THERE'S NO ROOM FOR HIM TO RIDE—I DON'T KNOW WHERE WE'D PUT THE BIG ELEPH- -ER-THE "LITTLE FELLOW!"
NOW, NOW, MICKEY! YOU'LL DO IT FOR ME, I KNOW YOU WILL!

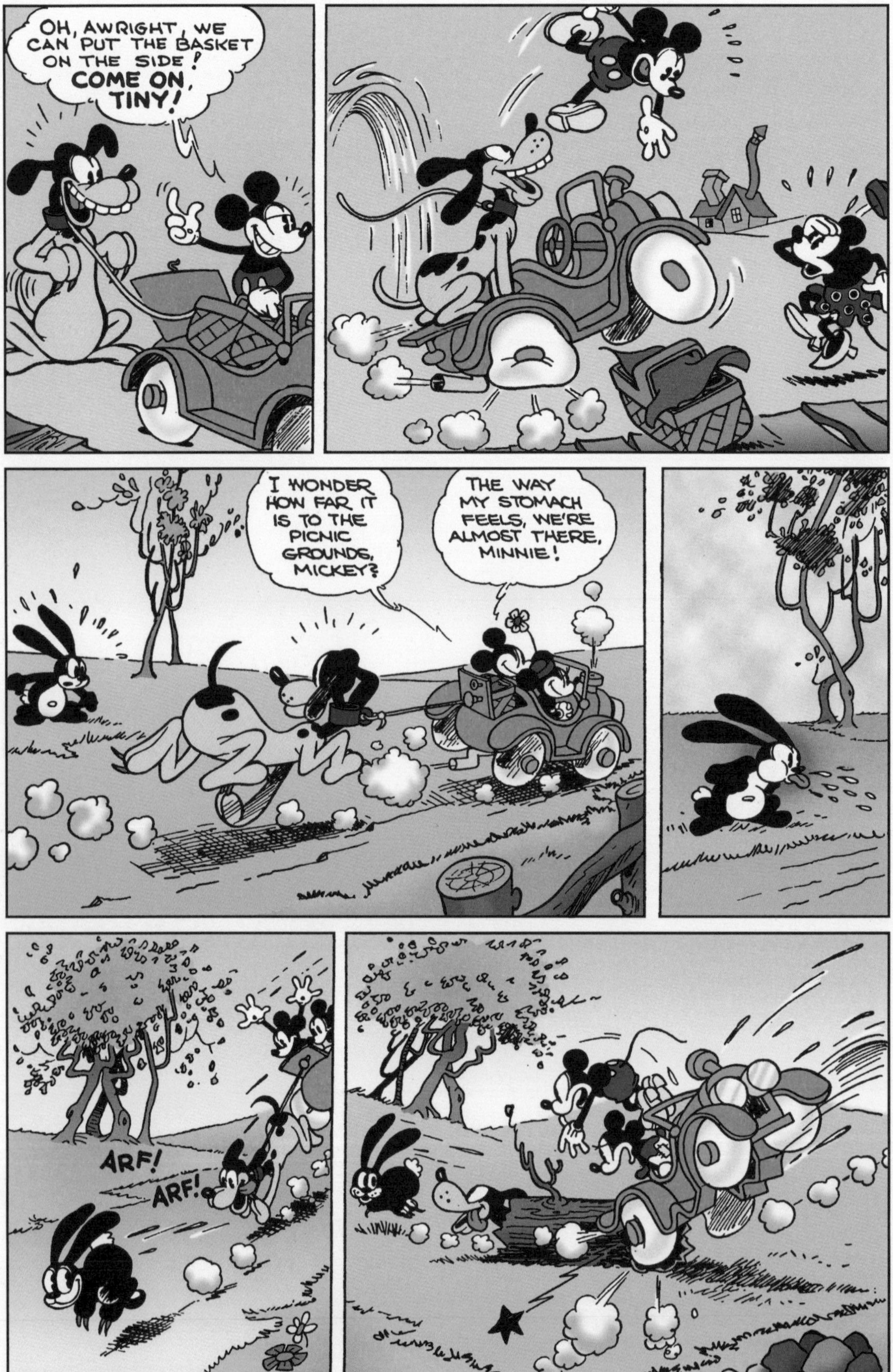
OH, AWRIGHT, WE CAN PUT THE BASKET ON THE SIDE! COME ON, TINY!
I WONDER HOW FAR IT IS TO THE PICNIC GROUNDS, MICKEY?
THE WAY MY STOMACH FEELS, WE'RE ALMOST THERE, MINNIE!
ARF!
ARF!

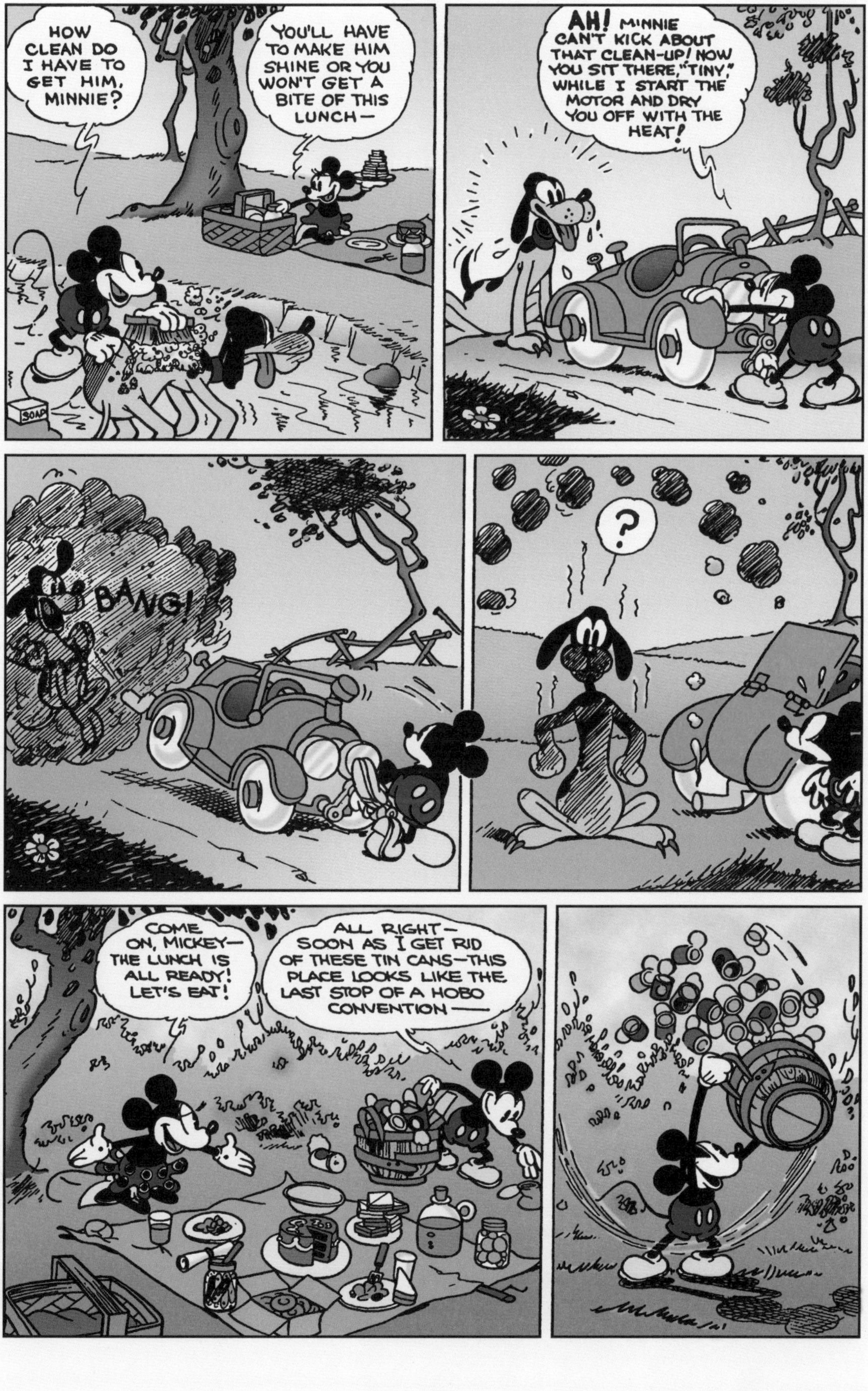
HOW CLEAN DO I HAVE TO GET HIM, MINNIE?
YOU'LL HAVE TO MAKE HIM SHINE OR YOU WON'T GET A BITE OF THIS LUNCH—
SOAP
AH! MINNIE CAN'T KICK ABOUT THAT CLEAN-UP! NOW YOU SIT THERE, "TINY," WHILE I START THE MOTOR AND DRY YOU OFF WITH THE HEAT!
BANG!
?
COME ON, MICKEY— THE LUNCH IS ALL READY! LET'S EAT!
ALL RIGHT— SOON AS I GET RID OF THESE TIN CANS—THIS PLACE LOOKS LIKE THE LAST STOP OF A HOBO CONVENTION——

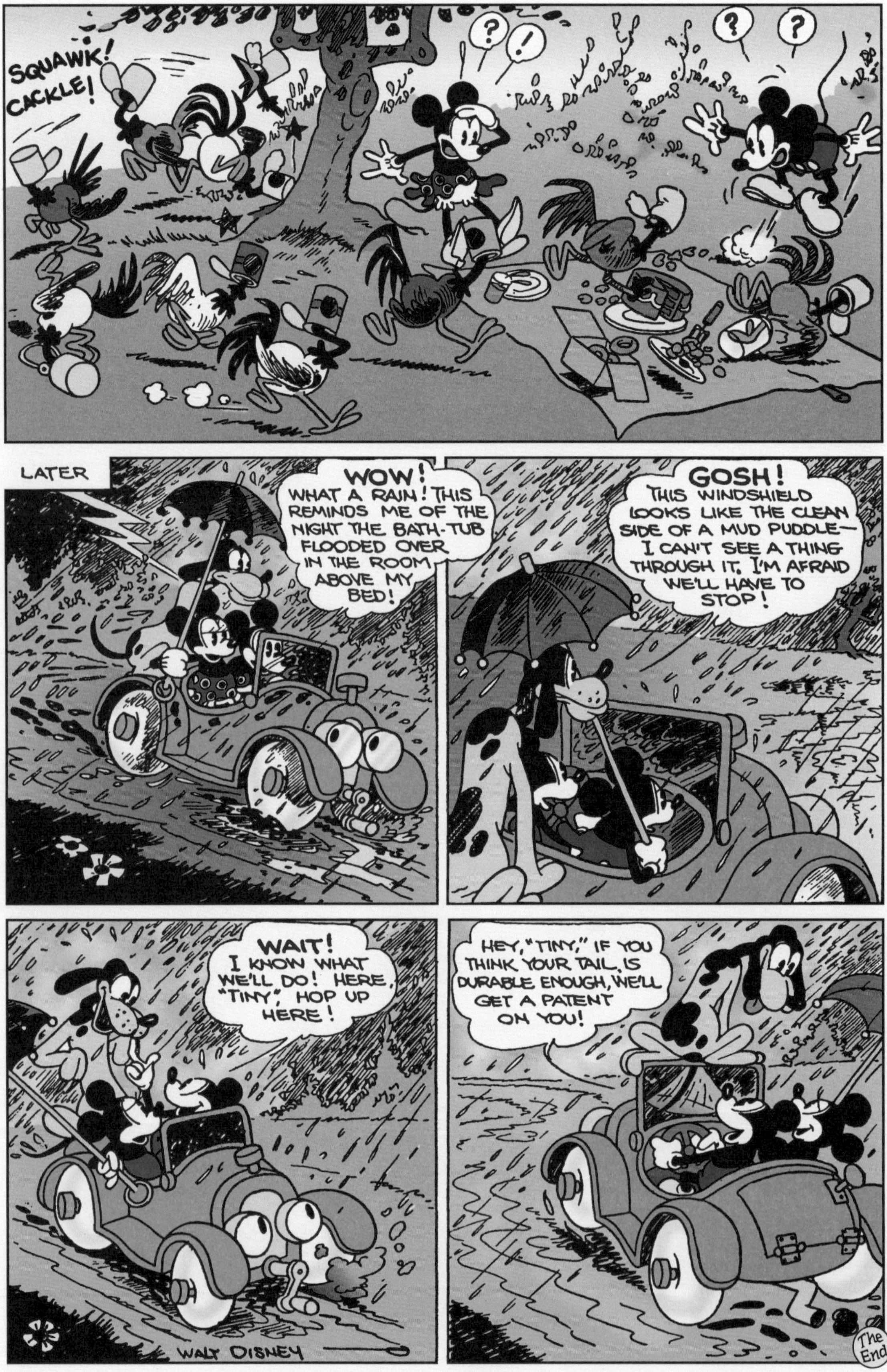
SQUAWK! CACKLE!
?
!
?
?
LATER
WOW! WHAT A RAIN! THIS REMINDS ME OF THE NIGHT THE BATH-TUB FLOODED OVER IN THE ROOM ABOVE MY BED!
GOSH! THIS WINDSHIELD LOOKS LIKE THE CLEAN SIDE OF A MUD PUDDLE— I CAN'T SEE A THING THROUGH IT. I'M AFRAID WE'LL HAVE TO STOP!
WAIT! I KNOW WHAT WE'LL DO! HERE, "TINY", HOP UP HERE!
WALT DISNEY
HEY, "TINY," IF YOU THINK YOUR TAIL IS DURABLE ENOUGH, WE'LL GET A PATENT ON YOU!
The End

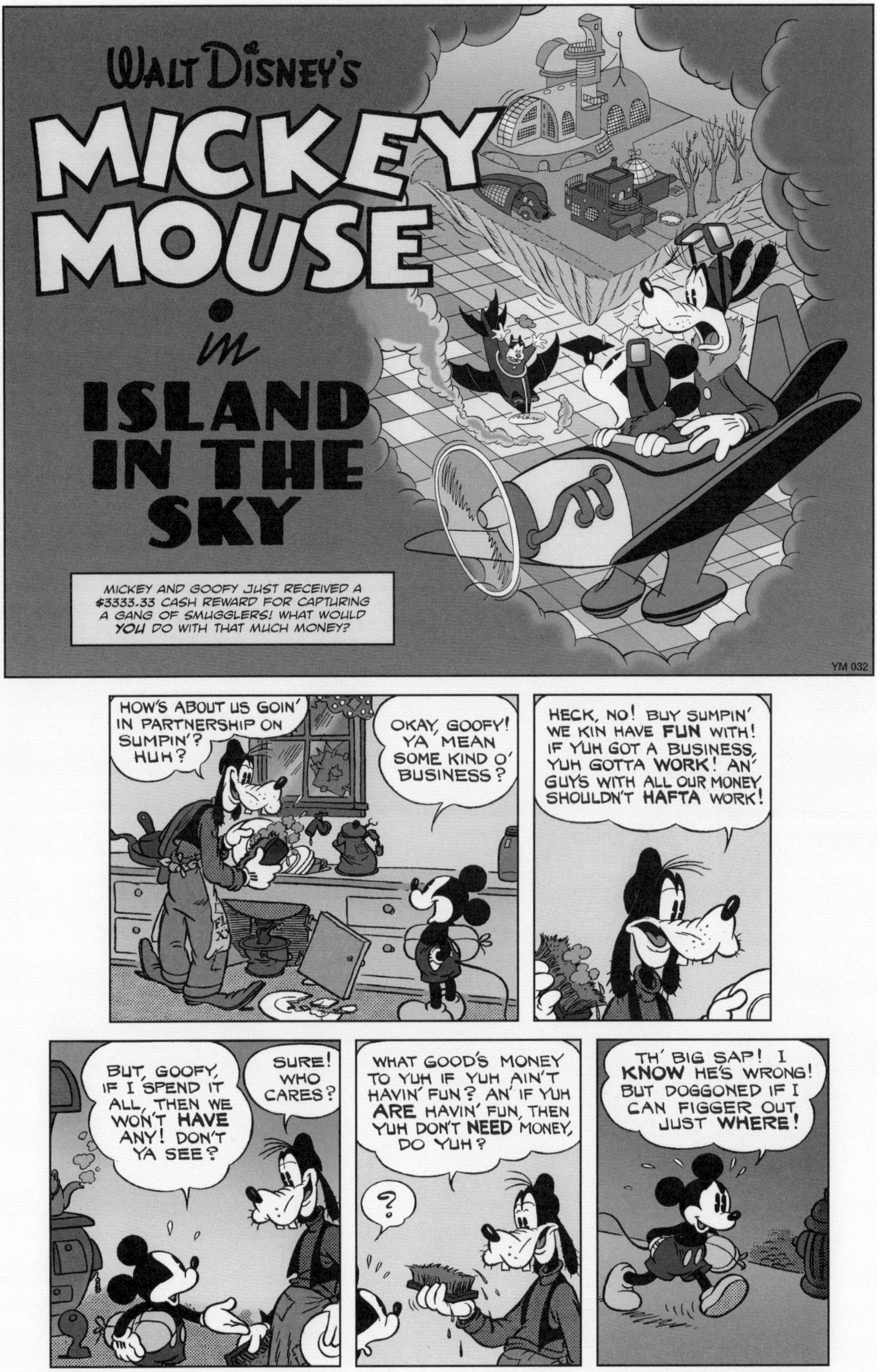
WALT DISNEY'S
MICKEY MOUSE
in
ISLAND IN THE SKY
MICKEY AND GOOFY JUST RECEIVED A $3333.33 CASH REWARD FOR CAPTURING A GANG OF SMUGGLERS! WHAT WOULD YOU DO WITH THAT MUCH MONEY?
YM 032
HOW'S ABOUT US GOIN' IN PARTNERSHIP ON SUMPIN'? HUH?
OKAY, GOOFY! YA MEAN SOME KIND O' BUSINESS?
HECK, NO! BUY SUMPIN' WE KIN HAVE FUN WITH! IF YUH GOT A BUSINESS, YUH GOTTA WORK! AN' GUYS WITH ALL OUR MONEY SHOULDN'T HAFTA WORK!
BUT, GOOFY, IF I SPEND IT ALL, THEN WE WON'T HAVE ANY! DON'T YA SEE?
SURE! WHO CARES?
WHAT GOOD'S MONEY TO YUH IF YUH AIN'T HAVIN' FUN? AN' IF YUH ARE HAVIN' FUN, THEN YUH DON'T NEED MONEY, DO YUH?
?
TH' BIG SAP! I KNOW HE'S WRONG! BUT DOGGONED IF I CAN FIGGER OUT JUST WHERE!

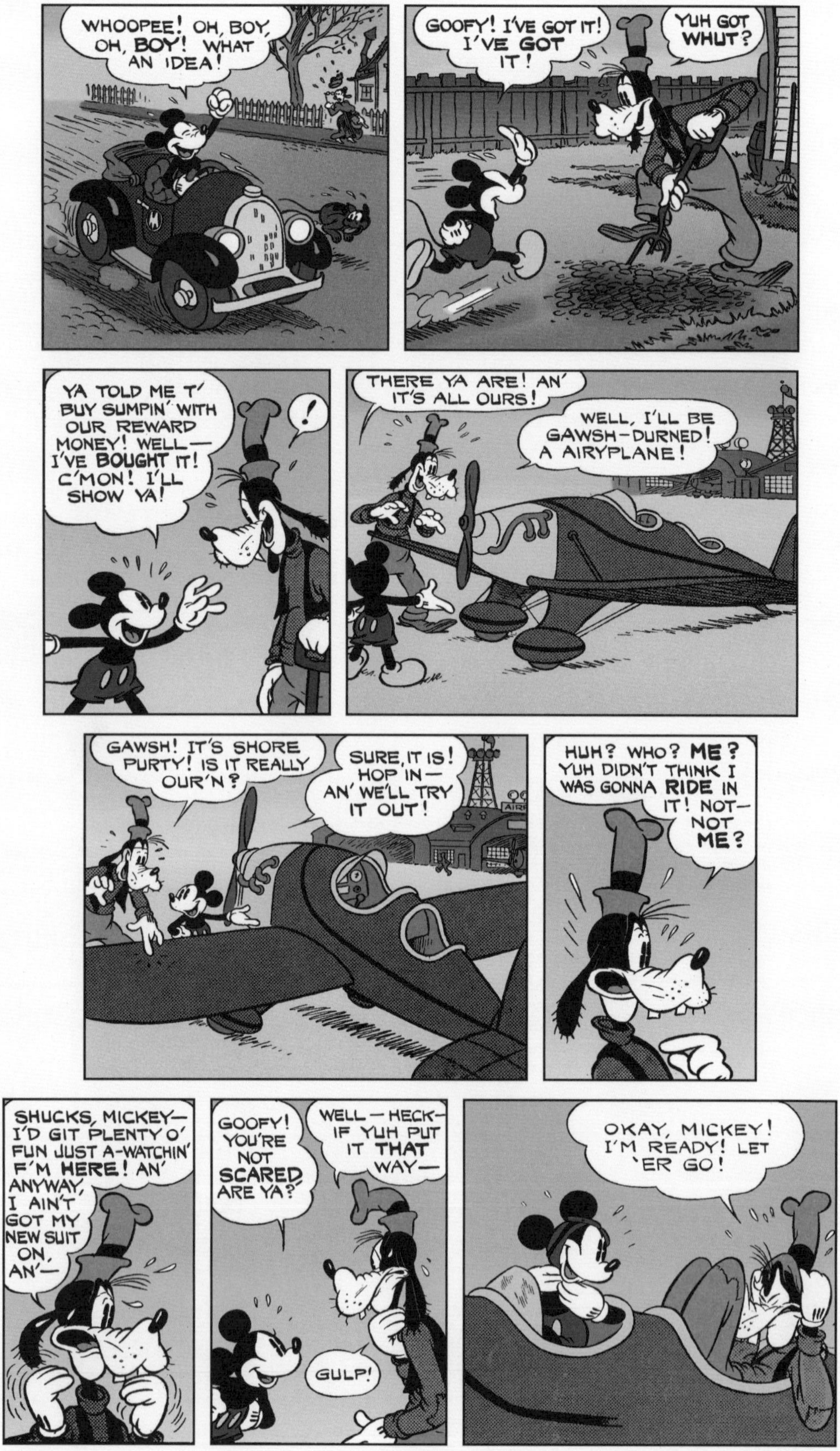
WHOOPEE! OH, BOY, OH, BOY! WHAT AN IDEA!
GOOFY! I'VE GOT IT! I'VE GOT IT!
YUH GOT WHUT?
YA TOLD ME T' BUY SUMPIN' WITH OUR REWARD MONEY! WELL— I'VE BOUGHT IT! C'MON! I'LL SHOW YA!
!
THERE YA ARE! AN' IT'S ALL OURS!
WELL, I'LL BE GAWSH-DURNED! A AIRYPLANE!
GAWSH! IT'S SHORE PURTY! IS IT REALLY OUR'N?
SURE, IT IS! HOP IN— AN' WE'LL TRY IT OUT!
HUH? WHO? ME? YUH DIDN'T THINK I WAS GONNA RIDE IN IT! NOT— NOT ME?
SHUCKS, MICKEY— I'D GIT PLENTY O' FUN JUST A-WATCHIN' F'M HERE! AN' ANYWAY, I AIN'T GOT MY NEW SUIT ON, AN'—
GOOFY! YOU'RE NOT SCARED ARE YA?
WELL—HECK— IF YUH PUT IT THAT WAY—
GULP!
OKAY, MICKEY! I'M READY! LET 'ER GO!

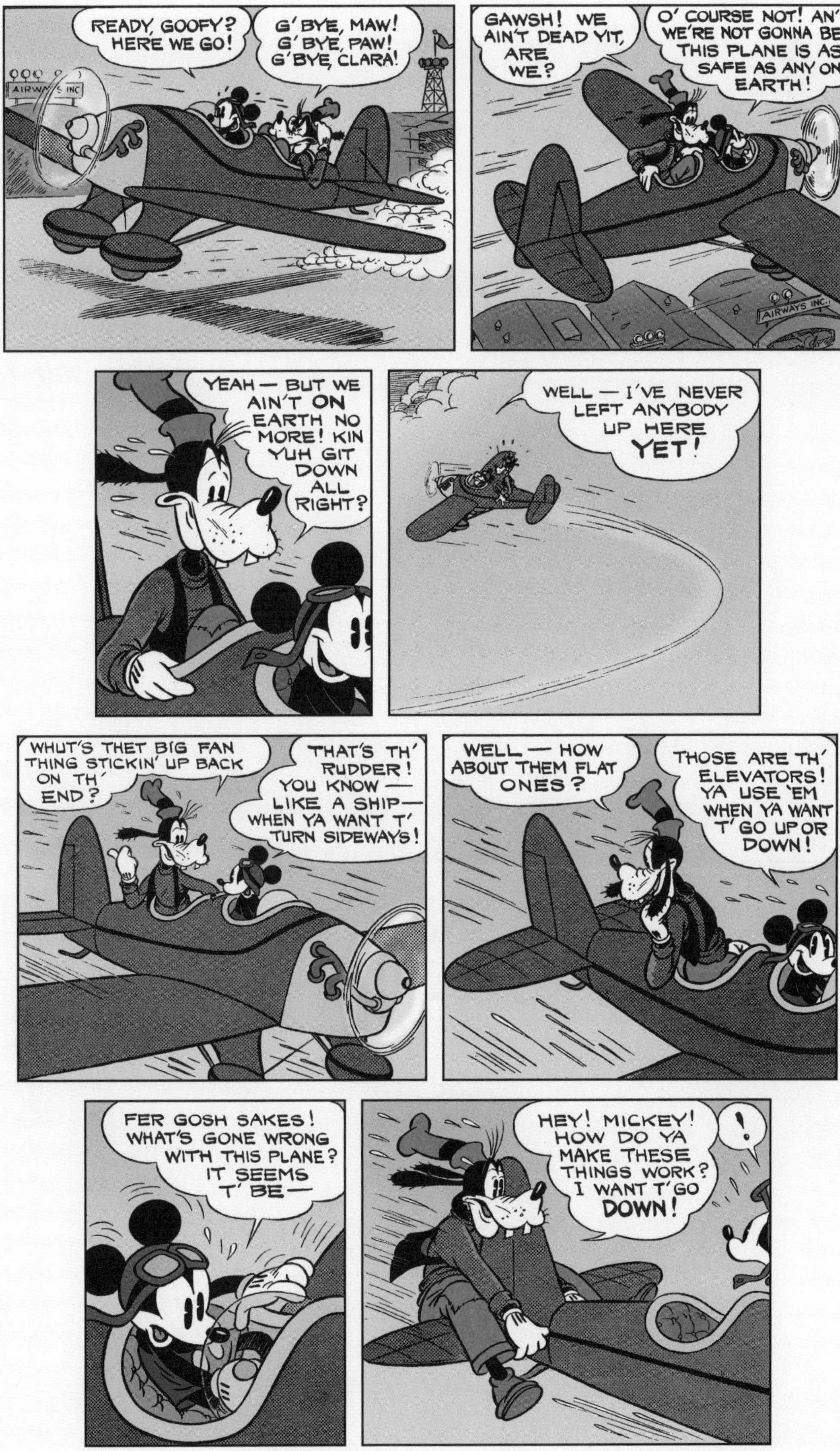
READY, GOOFY? HERE WE GO!
G' BYE, MAW! G' BYE, PAW! G' BYE, CLARA!
AIRWAYS INC
GAWSH! WE AIN'T DEAD YIT, ARE WE?
O' COURSE NOT! AN' WE'RE NOT GONNA BE! THIS PLANE IS AS SAFE AS ANY ON EARTH!
AIRWAYS INC.
YEAH — BUT WE AIN'T ON EARTH NO MORE! KIN YUH GIT DOWN ALL RIGHT?
WELL — I'VE NEVER LEFT ANYBODY UP HERE YET!
WHUT'S THET BIG FAN THING STICKIN' UP BACK ON TH' END?
THAT'S TH' RUDDER! YOU KNOW — LIKE A SHIP — WHEN YA WANT T' TURN SIDEWAYS!
WELL — HOW ABOUT THEM FLAT ONES?
THOSE ARE TH' ELEVATORS! YA USE 'EM WHEN YA WANT T' GO UP OR DOWN!
FER GOSH SAKES! WHAT'S GONE WRONG WITH THIS PLANE? IT SEEMS T' BE—
HEY! MICKEY! HOW DO YA MAKE THESE THINGS WORK? I WANT T' GO DOWN!
!

THE TWO PARTNERS, MICKEY AND GOOFY, HAVE JUST TAKEN A TRIAL SPIN IN THEIR NEW AIRPLANE

HOW DO YA FEEL, GOOFY?

ALL RIGHT, I GUESS!

I JEST WANT TUH THANK YUH FER BOTH O' THEM RIDES!

WHADDAYA MEAN, BOTH OF 'EM? YA ONLY HAD ONE!

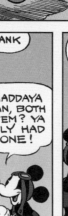

NOPE! YER WRONG! I'VE JEST TAKEN MUH FIRST ONE AN' MUH LAST ONE!

LOOK WHAT I GOT FOR YA! TRY 'EM ON, AN' SEE IF THEY FIT!

GAWSH! I LOOK JEST LIKE A AVIATOR!

BOY! THEY'RE SWELL! IT'S SURE TOO BAD WE'VE GOTTA SEND 'EM BACK!

SEND 'EM BACK? WHY? AIN'T THEY MINE?

YEAH! SURE! BUT YA SAID YA WEREN'T GOIN' UP IN OUR PLANE ANY MORE, SO IT'D BE SILLY T' KEEP 'EM! YOU WON'T NEED 'EM!

SHUCKS! CAN'T YUH TAKE A JOKE? I'M NOT ONLY GOIN' UP — I'M GONNA LEARN HOW TUH FLY!

WITH TWO SETS OF CONTROLS IN THEIR PLANE, MICKEY IS GIVING GOOFY HIS FIRST FLYING LESSON!

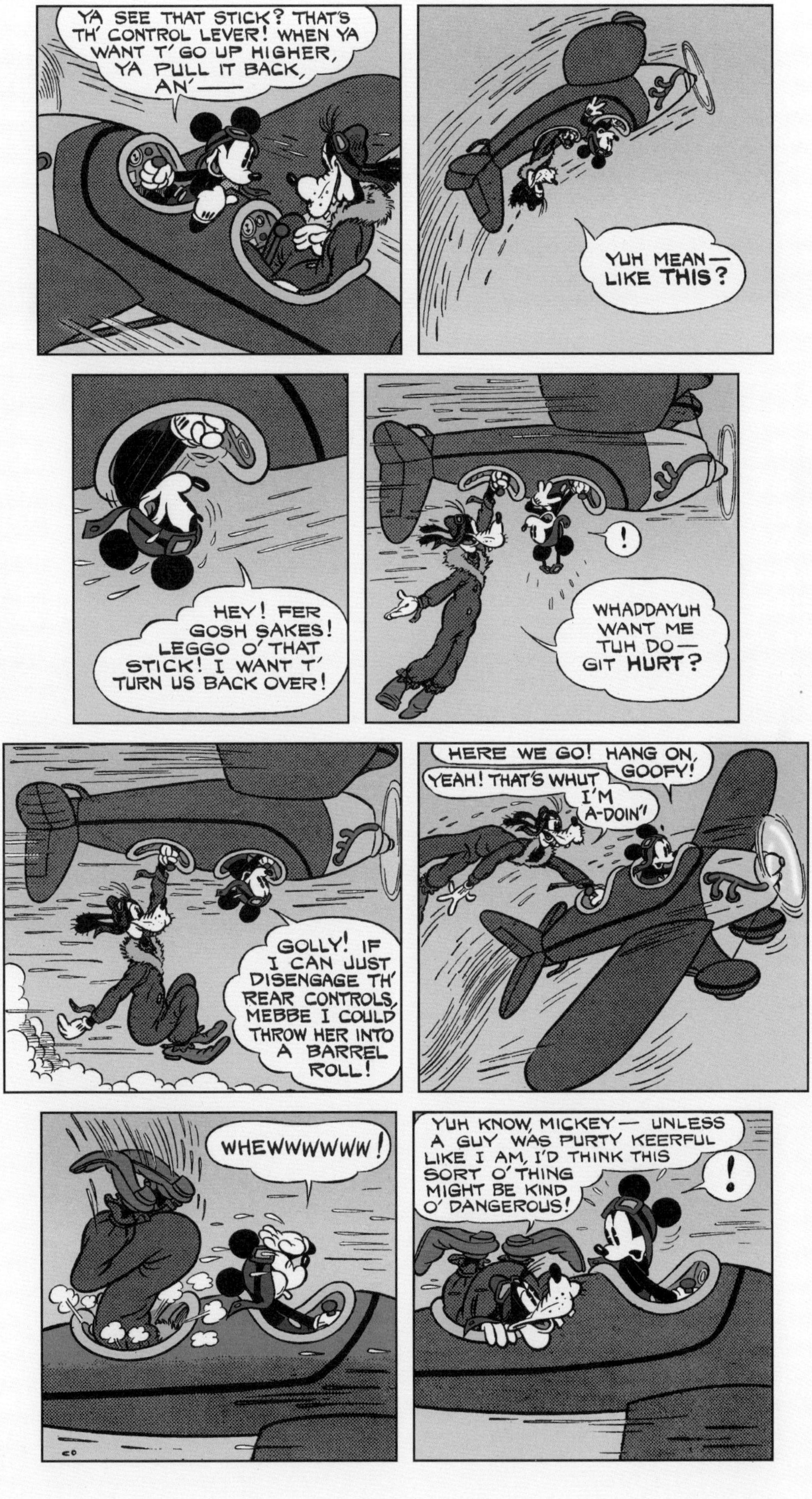
YA SEE THAT STICK? THAT'S TH' CONTROL LEVER! WHEN YA WANT T' GO UP HIGHER, YA PULL IT BACK, AN'——
YUH MEAN— LIKE THIS?
HEY! FER GOSH SAKES! LEGGO O' THAT STICK! I WANT T' TURN US BACK OVER!
!
WHADDAYUH WANT ME TUH DO— GIT HURT?
GOLLY! IF I CAN JUST DISENGAGE TH' REAR CONTROLS, MEBBE I COULD THROW HER INTO A BARREL ROLL!
HERE WE GO! HANG ON, GOOFY!
YEAH! THAT'S WHUT I'M A-DOIN'!
WHEWWWWWW!
YUH KNOW, MICKEY— UNLESS A GUY WAS PURTY KEERFUL LIKE I AM, I'D THINK THIS SORT O' THING MIGHT BE KIND O' DANGEROUS!
!

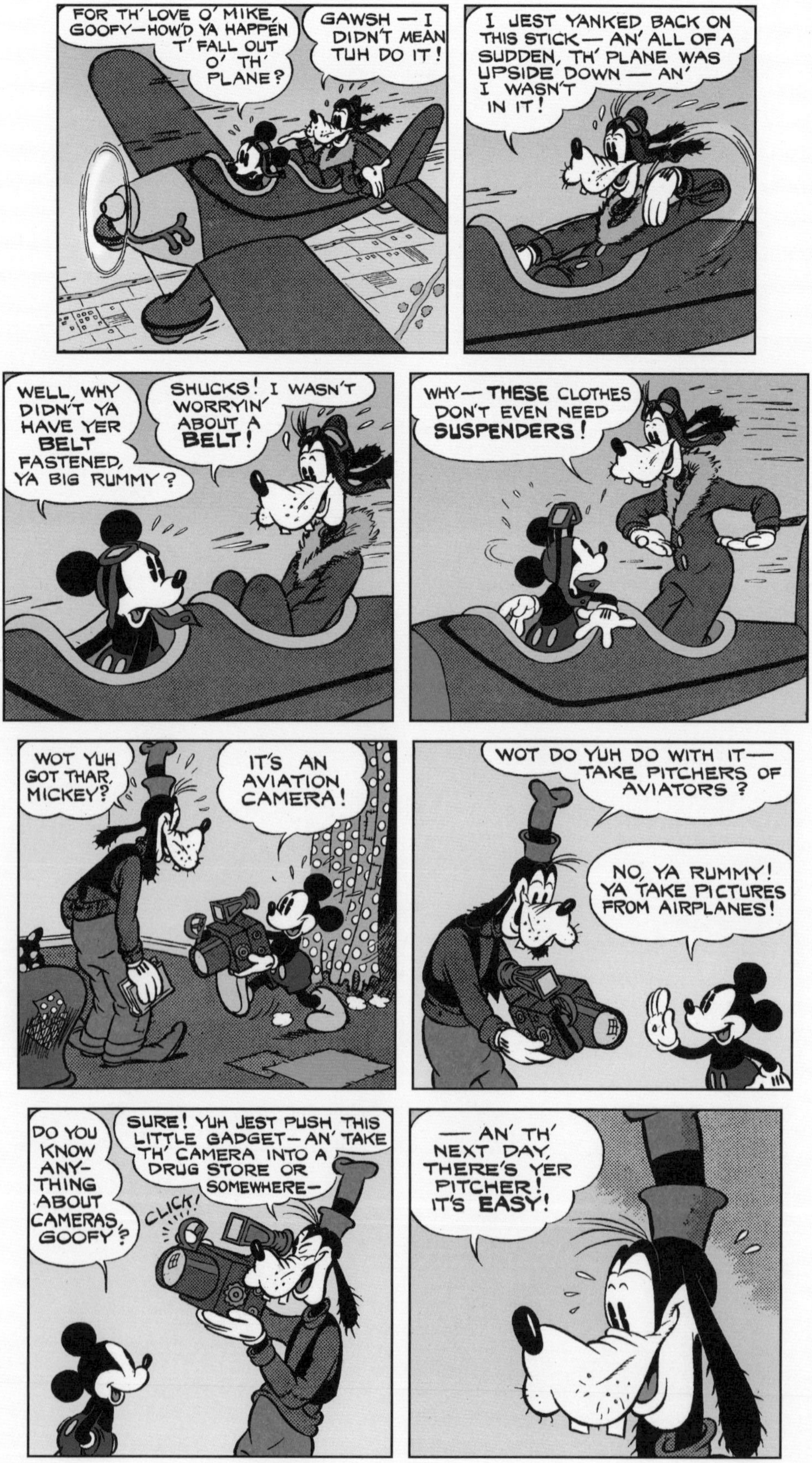
FOR TH' LOVE O' MIKE, GOOFY—HOW'D YA HAPPEN T' FALL OUT O' TH' PLANE?
GAWSH — I DIDN'T MEAN TUH DO IT!
I JEST YANKED BACK ON THIS STICK— AN' ALL OF A SUDDEN, TH' PLANE WAS UPSIDE DOWN — AN' I WASN'T IN IT!
WELL, WHY DIDN'T YA HAVE YER BELT FASTENED, YA BIG RUMMY?
SHUCKS! I WASN'T WORRYIN' ABOUT A BELT!
WHY— THESE CLOTHES DON'T EVEN NEED SUSPENDERS!
WOT YUH GOT THAR, MICKEY?
IT'S AN AVIATION CAMERA!
WOT DO YUH DO WITH IT— TAKE PITCHERS OF AVIATORS?
NO, YA RUMMY! YA TAKE PICTURES FROM AIRPLANES!
DO YOU KNOW ANY-THING ABOUT CAMERAS, GOOFY?
SURE! YUH JEST PUSH THIS LITTLE GADGET— AN' TAKE TH' CAMERA INTO A DRUG STORE OR SOMEWHERE—
CLICK!
— AN' TH' NEXT DAY, THERE'S YER PITCHER! IT'S EASY!

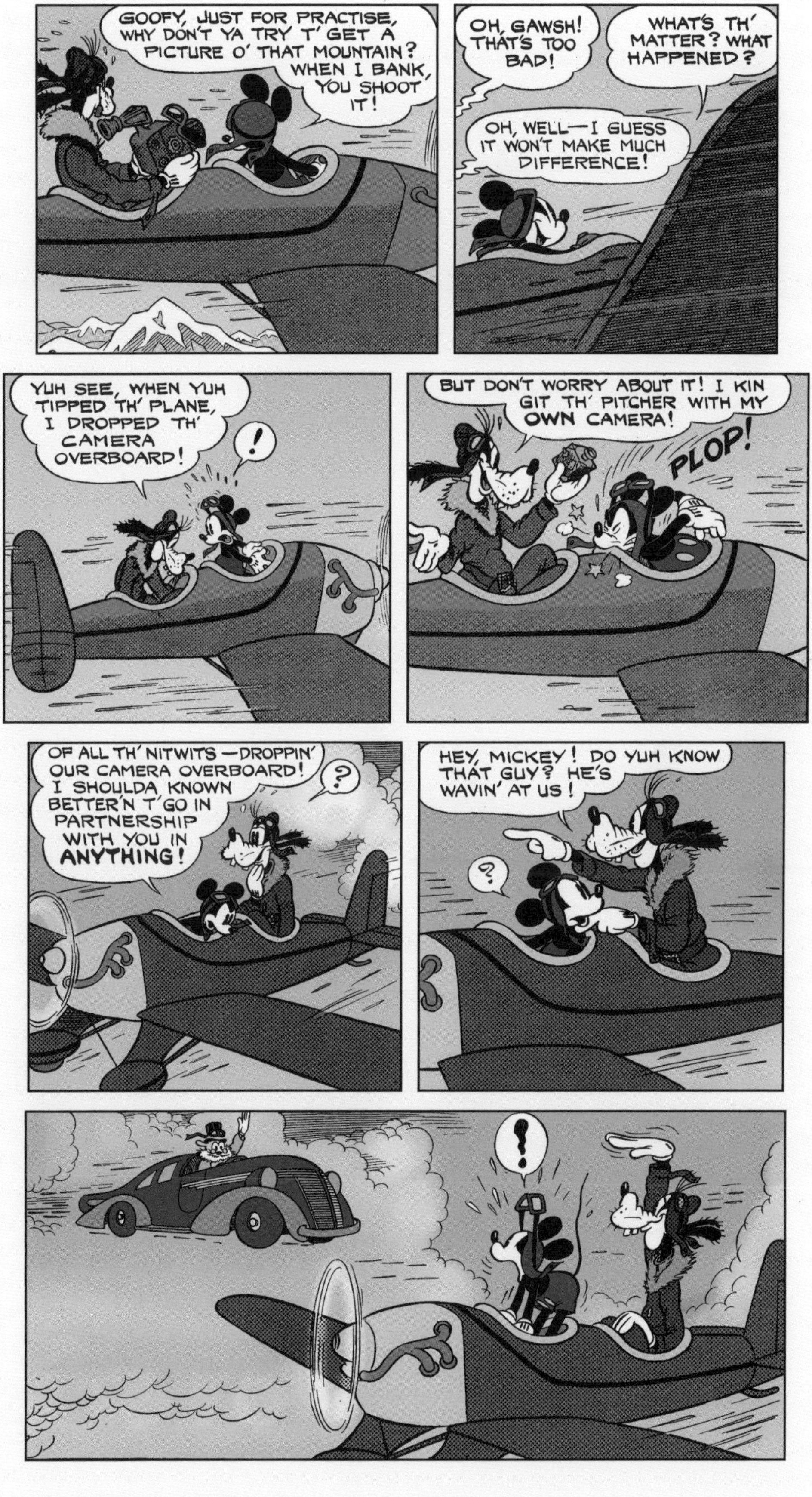
GOOFY, JUST FOR PRACTISE, WHY DON'T YA TRY T' GET A PICTURE O' THAT MOUNTAIN? WHEN I BANK, YOU SHOOT IT!
OH, GAWSH! THAT'S TOO BAD!
WHAT'S TH' MATTER? WHAT HAPPENED?
OH, WELL—I GUESS IT WON'T MAKE MUCH DIFFERENCE!
YUH SEE, WHEN YUH TIPPED TH' PLANE, I DROPPED TH' CAMERA OVERBOARD!
!
BUT DON'T WORRY ABOUT IT! I KIN GIT TH' PITCHER WITH MY OWN CAMERA!
PLOP!
OF ALL TH' NITWITS—DROPPIN' OUR CAMERA OVERBOARD! I SHOULDA KNOWN BETTER'N T' GO IN PARTNERSHIP WITH YOU IN ANYTHING!
?
HEY, MICKEY! DO YUH KNOW THAT GUY? HE'S WAVIN' AT US!
?
!

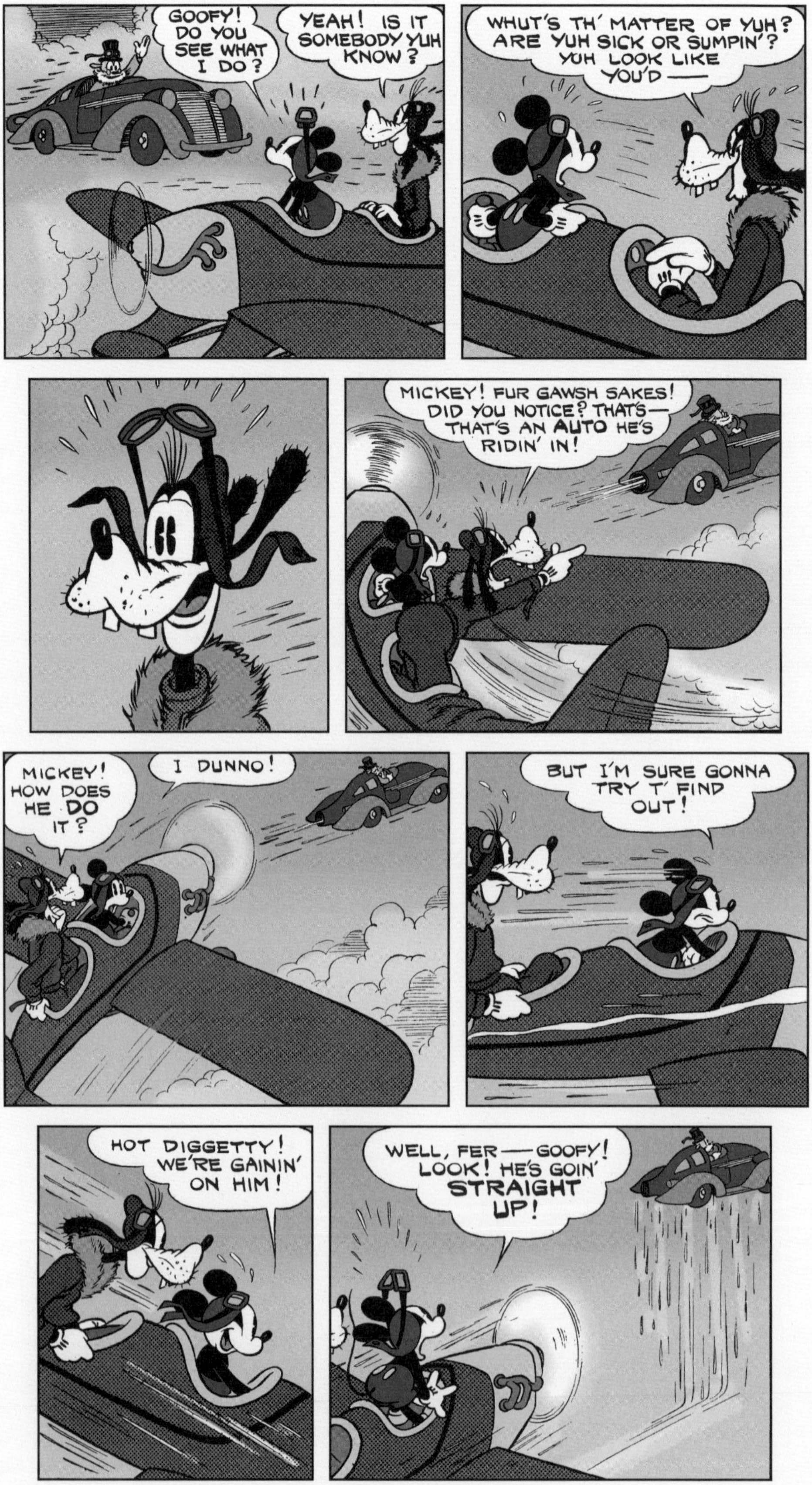
GOOFY! DO YOU SEE WHAT I DO?
YEAH! IS IT SOMEBODY YUH KNOW?
WHUT'S TH' MATTER OF YUH? ARE YUH SICK OR SUMPIN'? YUH LOOK LIKE YOU'D ——
MICKEY! FUR GAWSH SAKES! DID YOU NOTICE? THAT'S— THAT'S AN AUTO HE'S RIDIN' IN!
MICKEY! HOW DOES HE DO IT?
I DUNNO!
BUT I'M SURE GONNA TRY T' FIND OUT!
HOT DIGGETTY! WE'RE GAININ' ON HIM!
WELL, FER— GOOFY! LOOK! HE'S GOIN' STRAIGHT UP!

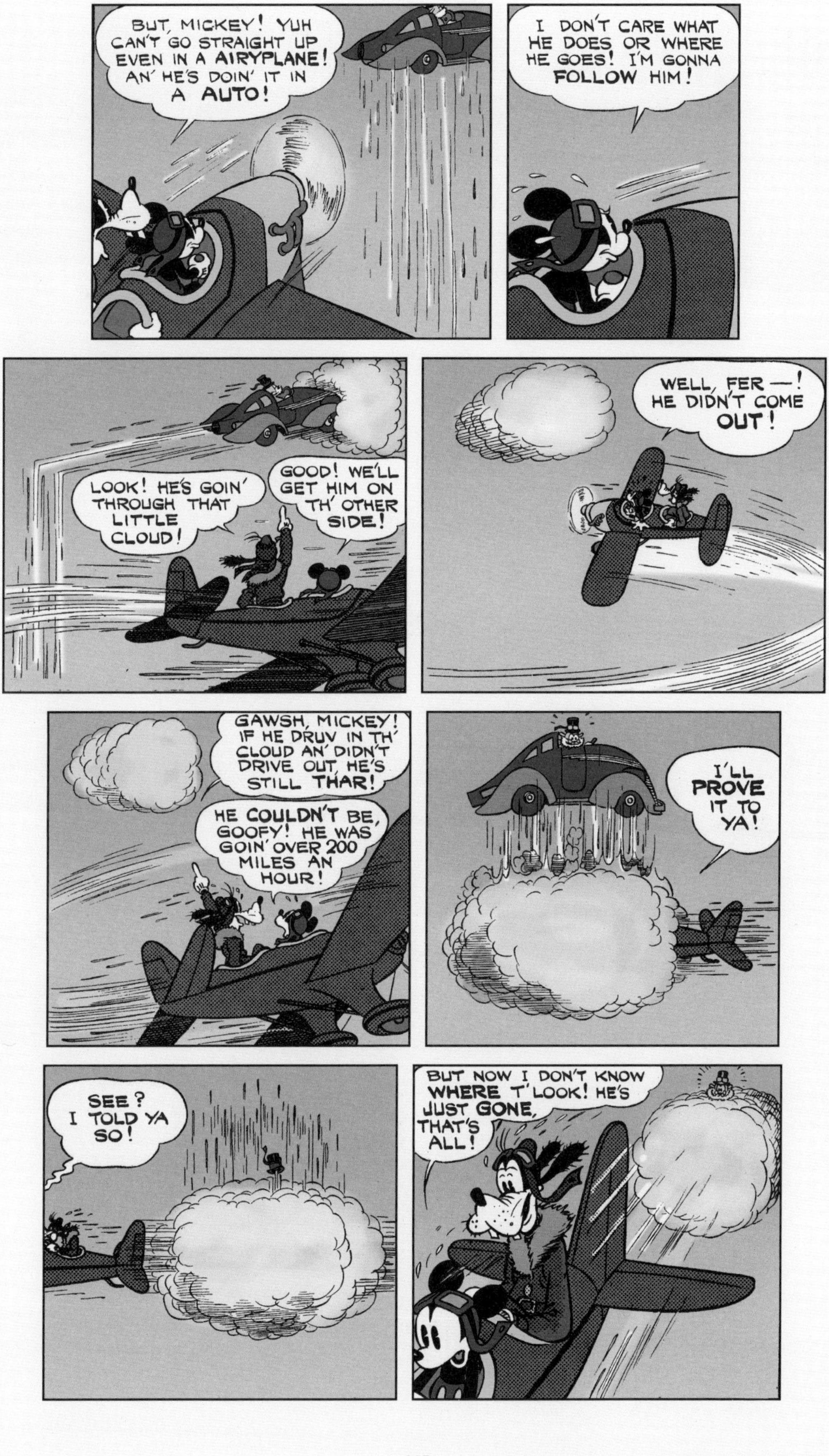
BUT, MICKEY! YUH CAN'T GO STRAIGHT UP EVEN IN A AIRYPLANE! AN' HE'S DOIN' IT IN A AUTO!
I DON'T CARE WHAT HE DOES OR WHERE HE GOES! I'M GONNA FOLLOW HIM!
LOOK! HE'S GOIN' THROUGH THAT LITTLE CLOUD!
GOOD! WE'LL GET HIM ON TH' OTHER SIDE!
WELL, FER —! HE DIDN'T COME OUT!
GAWSH, MICKEY! IF HE DRUV IN TH' CLOUD AN' DIDN'T DRIVE OUT, HE'S STILL THAR!
HE COULDN'T BE, GOOFY! HE WAS GOIN' OVER 200 MILES AN HOUR!
I'LL PROVE IT TO YA!
SEE? I TOLD YA SO!
BUT NOW I DON'T KNOW WHERE T' LOOK! HE'S JUST GONE, THAT'S ALL!

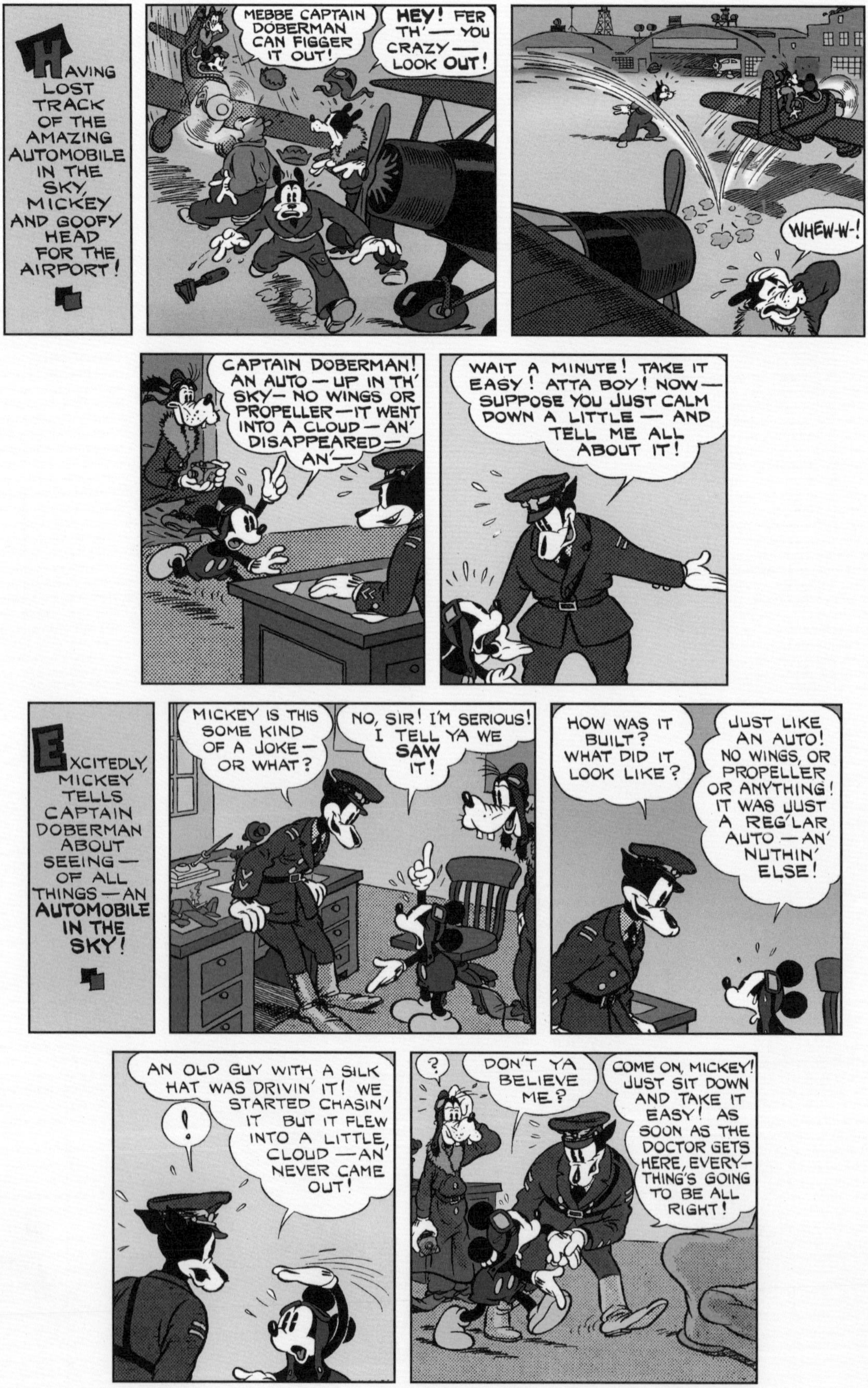
HAVING LOST TRACK OF THE AMAZING AUTOMOBILE IN THE SKY, MICKEY AND GOOFY HEAD FOR THE AIRPORT!
MEBBE CAPTAIN DOBERMAN CAN FIGGER IT OUT!
HEY! FER TH'— YOU CRAZY— LOOK OUT!
WHEW-W-!
CAPTAIN DOBERMAN! AN AUTO — UP IN TH' SKY— NO WINGS OR PROPELLER — IT WENT INTO A CLOUD — AN' DISAPPEARED — AN'—
WAIT A MINUTE! TAKE IT EASY! ATTA BOY! NOW— SUPPOSE YOU JUST CALM DOWN A LITTLE — AND TELL ME ALL ABOUT IT!
EXCITEDLY, MICKEY TELLS CAPTAIN DOBERMAN ABOUT SEEING — OF ALL THINGS — AN AUTOMOBILE IN THE SKY!
MICKEY IS THIS SOME KIND OF A JOKE — OR WHAT?
NO, SIR! I'M SERIOUS! I TELL YA WE SAW IT!
HOW WAS IT BUILT? WHAT DID IT LOOK LIKE?
JUST LIKE AN AUTO! NO WINGS, OR PROPELLER OR ANYTHING! IT WAS JUST A REG'LAR AUTO — AN' NUTHIN' ELSE!
AN OLD GUY WITH A SILK HAT WAS DRIVIN' IT! WE STARTED CHASIN' IT BUT IT FLEW INTO A LITTLE CLOUD — AN' NEVER CAME OUT!
!
?
DON'T YA BELIEVE ME?
COME ON, MICKEY! JUST SIT DOWN AND TAKE IT EASY! AS SOON AS THE DOCTOR GETS HERE, EVERYTHING'S GOING TO BE ALL RIGHT!

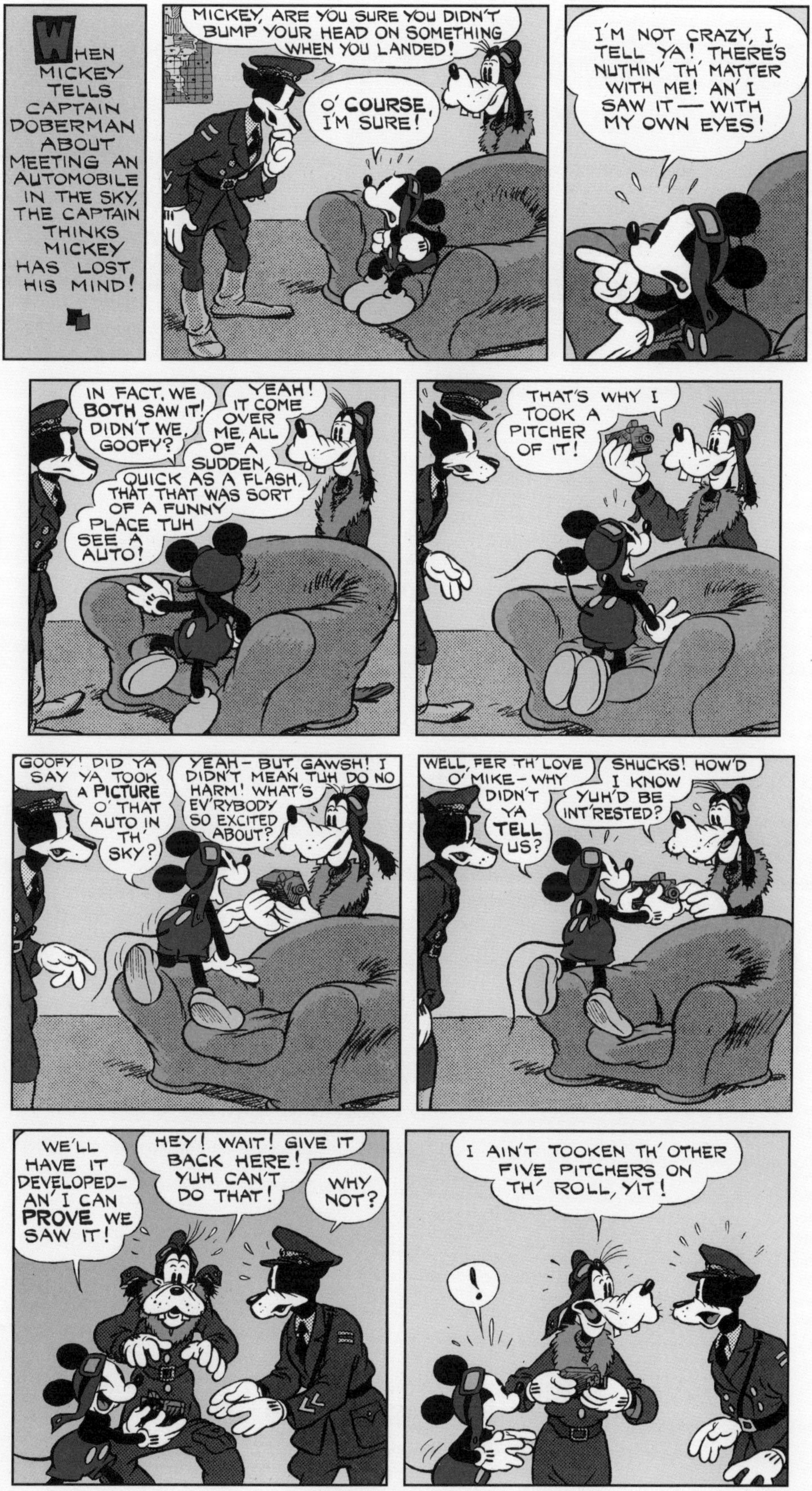
WHEN MICKEY TELLS CAPTAIN DOBERMAN ABOUT MEETING AN AUTOMOBILE IN THE SKY, THE CAPTAIN THINKS MICKEY HAS LOST HIS MIND!
MICKEY, ARE YOU SURE YOU DIDN'T BUMP YOUR HEAD ON SOMETHING WHEN YOU LANDED!
O' COURSE, I'M SURE!
I'M NOT CRAZY, I TELL YA! THERE'S NUTHIN' TH' MATTER WITH ME! AN' I SAW IT — WITH MY OWN EYES!
IN FACT, WE BOTH SAW IT! DIDN'T WE, GOOFY?
YEAH! IT COME OVER ME, ALL OF A SUDDEN, QUICK AS A FLASH, THAT THAT WAS SORT OF A FUNNY PLACE TUH SEE A AUTO!
THAT'S WHY I TOOK A PITCHER OF IT!
GOOFY! DID YA SAY YA TOOK A PICTURE O' THAT AUTO IN TH' SKY?
YEAH - BUT, GAWSH! I DIDN'T MEAN TUH DO NO HARM! WHAT'S EV'RYBODY SO EXCITED ABOUT?
WELL, FER TH' LOVE O' MIKE - WHY DIDN'T YA TELL US?
SHUCKS! HOW'D I KNOW YUH'D BE INT'RESTED?
WE'LL HAVE IT DEVELOPED - AN' I CAN PROVE WE SAW IT!
HEY! WAIT! GIVE IT BACK HERE! YUH CAN'T DO THAT!
WHY NOT?
I AIN'T TOOKEN TH' OTHER FIVE PITCHERS ON TH' ROLL, YIT!
!

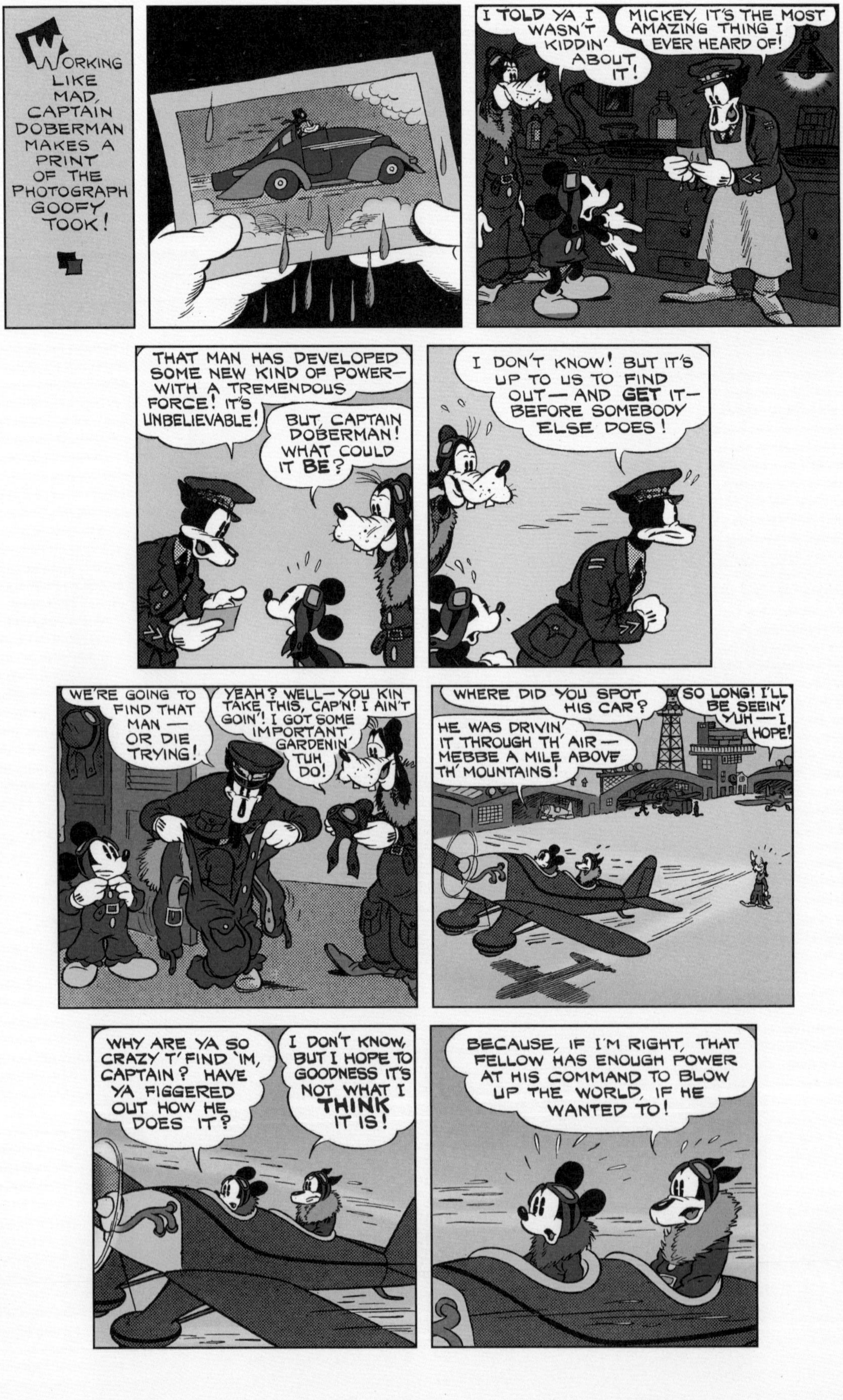
WORKING LIKE MAD, CAPTAIN DOBERMAN MAKES A PRINT OF THE PHOTOGRAPH GOOFY TOOK!
I TOLD YA I WASN'T KIDDIN' ABOUT IT!
MICKEY, IT'S THE MOST AMAZING THING I EVER HEARD OF!
THAT MAN HAS DEVELOPED SOME NEW KIND OF POWER— WITH A TREMENDOUS FORCE! IT'S UNBELIEVABLE!
BUT, CAPTAIN DOBERMAN! WHAT COULD IT BE?
I DON'T KNOW! BUT IT'S UP TO US TO FIND OUT— AND GET IT— BEFORE SOMEBODY ELSE DOES!
WE'RE GOING TO FIND THAT MAN — OR DIE TRYING!
YEAH? WELL— YOU KIN TAKE THIS, CAP'N! I AIN'T GOIN'! I GOT SOME IMPORTANT GARDENIN' TUH DO!
WHERE DID YOU SPOT HIS CAR?
HE WAS DRIVIN' IT THROUGH TH' AIR— MEBBE A MILE ABOVE TH' MOUNTAINS!
SO LONG! I'LL BE SEEIN' YUH — I HOPE!
WHY ARE YA SO CRAZY T' FIND 'IM, CAPTAIN? HAVE YA FIGGERED OUT HOW HE DOES IT?
I DON'T KNOW, BUT I HOPE TO GOODNESS IT'S NOT WHAT I THINK IT IS!
BECAUSE, IF I'M RIGHT, THAT FELLOW HAS ENOUGH POWER AT HIS COMMAND TO BLOW UP THE WORLD, IF HE WANTED TO!

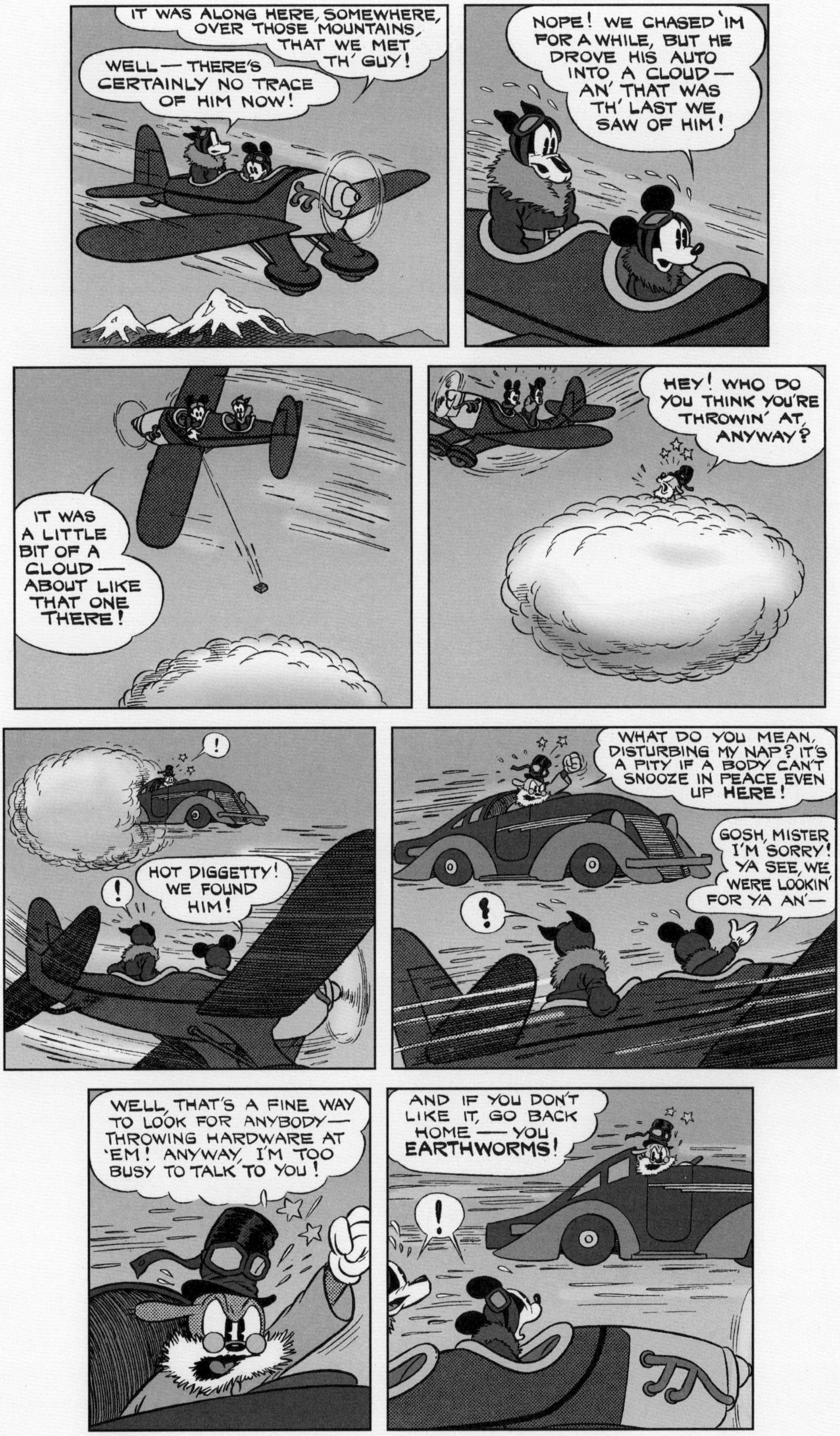
IT WAS ALONG HERE, SOMEWHERE, OVER THOSE MOUNTAINS, THAT WE MET TH' GUY!
WELL — THERE'S CERTAINLY NO TRACE OF HIM NOW!
NOPE! WE CHASED 'IM FOR A WHILE, BUT HE DROVE HIS AUTO INTO A CLOUD — AN' THAT WAS TH' LAST WE SAW OF HIM!
IT WAS A LITTLE BIT OF A CLOUD — ABOUT LIKE THAT ONE THERE!
HEY! WHO DO YOU THINK YOU'RE THROWIN' AT, ANYWAY?
!
HOT DIGGETTY! WE FOUND HIM!
!
WHAT DO YOU MEAN, DISTURBING MY NAP? IT'S A PITY IF A BODY CAN'T SNOOZE IN PEACE EVEN UP HERE!
GOSH, MISTER I'M SORRY! YA SEE, WE WERE LOOKIN' FOR YA AN'—
!
WELL, THAT'S A FINE WAY TO LOOK FOR ANYBODY — THROWING HARDWARE AT 'EM! ANYWAY, I'M TOO BUSY TO TALK TO YOU!
AND IF YOU DON'T LIKE IT, GO BACK HOME — YOU EARTHWORMS!
!

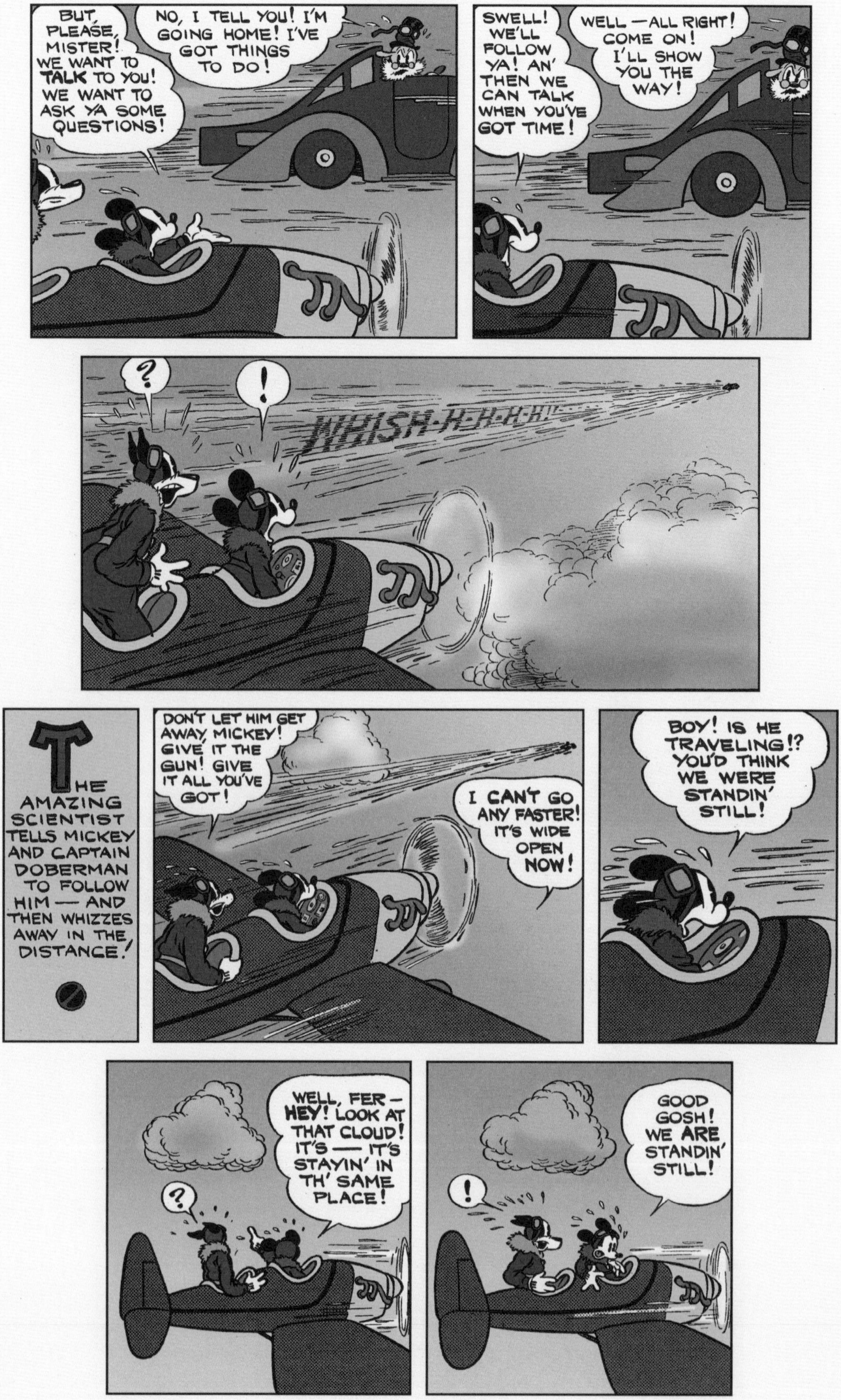
BUT, PLEASE, MISTER! WE WANT TO TALK TO YOU! WE WANT TO ASK YA SOME QUESTIONS!
NO, I TELL YOU! I'M GOING HOME! I'VE GOT THINGS TO DO!
SWELL! WE'LL FOLLOW YA! AN' THEN WE CAN TALK WHEN YOU'VE GOT TIME!
WELL — ALL RIGHT! COME ON! I'LL SHOW YOU THE WAY!
?
!
WHISH-H-H-H-H!
THE AMAZING SCIENTIST TELLS MICKEY AND CAPTAIN DOBERMAN TO FOLLOW HIM — AND THEN WHIZZES AWAY IN THE DISTANCE!
DON'T LET HIM GET AWAY, MICKEY! GIVE IT THE GUN! GIVE IT ALL YOU'VE GOT!
I CAN'T GO ANY FASTER! IT'S WIDE OPEN NOW!
BOY! IS HE TRAVELING!? YOU'D THINK WE WERE STANDIN' STILL!
?
WELL, FER — HEY! LOOK AT THAT CLOUD! IT'S — IT'S STAYIN' IN TH' SAME PLACE!
!
GOOD GOSH! WE ARE STANDIN' STILL!

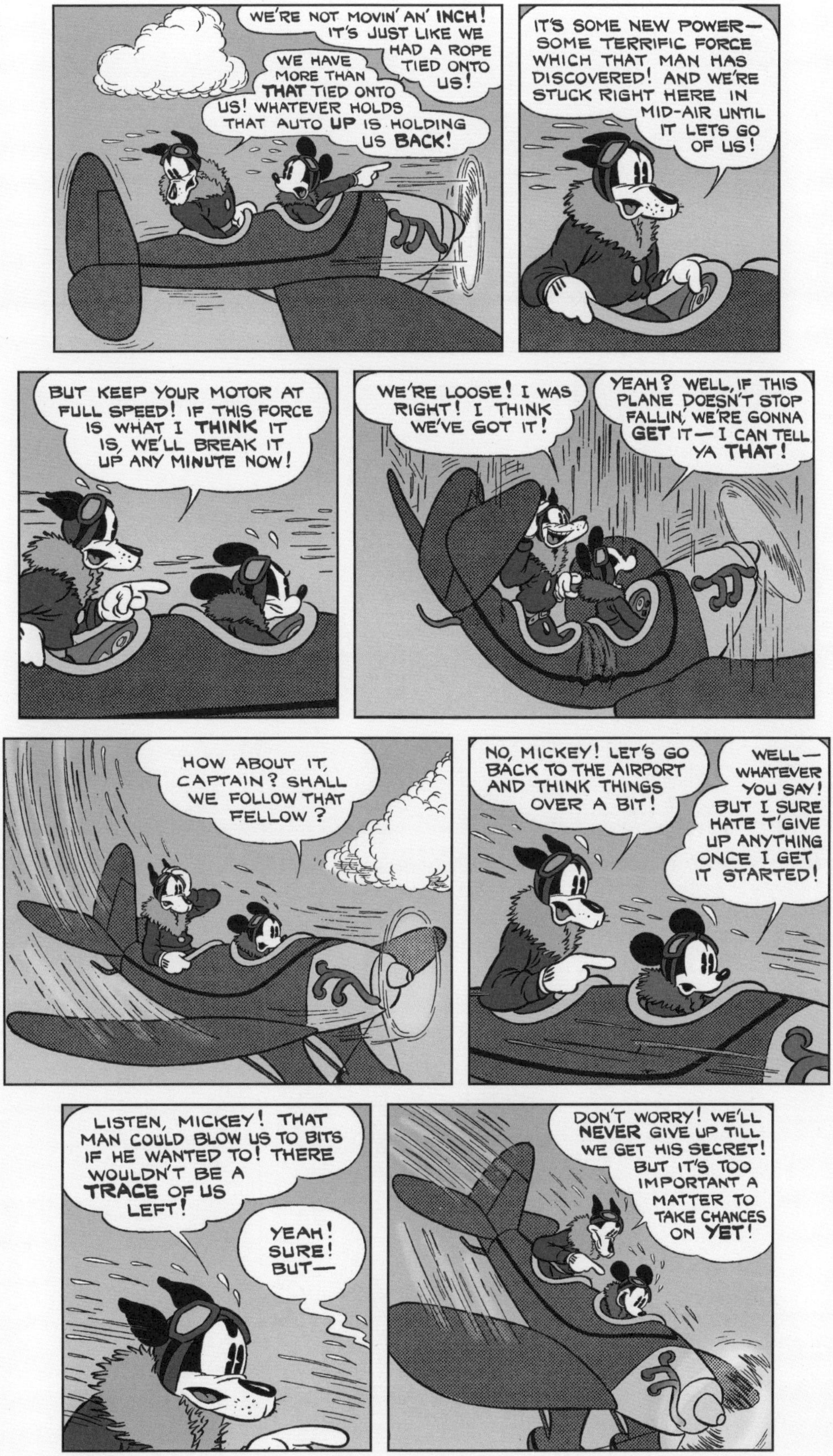
WE'RE NOT MOVIN' AN' INCH! IT'S JUST LIKE WE HAD A ROPE TIED ONTO US!
WE HAVE MORE THAN THAT TIED ONTO US! WHATEVER HOLDS THAT AUTO UP IS HOLDING US BACK!
IT'S SOME NEW POWER— SOME TERRIFIC FORCE WHICH THAT MAN HAS DISCOVERED! AND WE'RE STUCK RIGHT HERE IN MID-AIR UNTIL IT LETS GO OF US!
BUT KEEP YOUR MOTOR AT FULL SPEED! IF THIS FORCE IS WHAT I THINK IT IS, WE'LL BREAK IT UP ANY MINUTE NOW!
WE'RE LOOSE! I WAS RIGHT! I THINK WE'VE GOT IT!
YEAH? WELL, IF THIS PLANE DOESN'T STOP FALLIN', WE'RE GONNA GET IT— I CAN TELL YA THAT!
HOW ABOUT IT, CAPTAIN? SHALL WE FOLLOW THAT FELLOW?
NO, MICKEY! LET'S GO BACK TO THE AIRPORT AND THINK THINGS OVER A BIT!
WELL— WHATEVER YOU SAY! BUT I SURE HATE T'GIVE UP ANYTHING ONCE I GET IT STARTED!
LISTEN, MICKEY! THAT MAN COULD BLOW US TO BITS IF HE WANTED TO! THERE WOULDN'T BE A TRACE OF US LEFT!
YEAH! SURE! BUT—
DON'T WORRY! WE'LL NEVER GIVE UP TILL WE GET HIS SECRET! BUT IT'S TOO IMPORTANT A MATTER TO TAKE CHANCES ON YET!

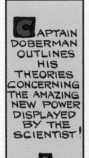

CAPTAIN DOBERMAN OUTLINES HIS THEORIES CONCERNING THE AMAZING NEW POWER DISPLAYED BY THE SCIENTIST!

I THOUGHT AT FIRST IT MIGHT BE SOME IMPOSSIBLE FORCE LIKE THOSE YOU READ ABOUT IN THE FUNNY PAPERS! BUT I DISCARDED THAT THEORY RIGHT AWAY!

YEAH! SURE! NATURALLY!

AS YOU KNOW, THERE IS A TERRIFIC POWER IN RADIUM — BUT IT ACTS SLOWLY, OVER THOUSANDS OF YEARS! WELL, HE MAY HAVE DISCOVERED HOW TO EXTRACT ALL THAT POWER IMMEDIATELY!

GOSH! DO YA THINK THAT'S IT?

SUCH A FORCE COULD EASILY DO EVERYTHING WE HAVE SEEN — BUT I FAVOR STILL A THIRD EXPLANATION!

I BELIEVE THAT SOMEHOW HE HAS INVENTED A METHOD OF LINING UP ATOMS— SO THAT ALL OF THEM PULL IN THE SAME DIRECTION AT THE SAME TIME!

IF SO, MICKEY— HIS POWER IS ABSOLUTELY UNLIMITED! AN' WE'VE GOT TO STOP HIM!

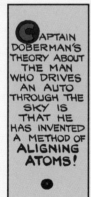

CAPTAIN DOBERMAN'S THEORY ABOUT THE MAN WHO DRIVES AN AUTO THROUGH THE SKY IS THAT HE HAS INVENTED A METHOD OF ALIGNING ATOMS!

IT IS SOMETHING ON WHICH SCIENTISTS HAVE BEEN WORKING FOR MANY YEARS— BUT WITHOUT SUCCESS!

YEAH! I REMEMBER READIN' ABOUT IT IN A NEWSPAPER ARTICLE!

BUT WHY DO YA THINK IT WAS THAT INSTEAD O' RADIUM?

BECAUSE OF THE WAY OUR PLANE ACTED WHEN THE MYSTERIOUS FORCE WAS HOLDING US BACK!

THE AGITATION CAUSED BY THE WHIRLING PROPELLER AND OUR RACING MOTOR THREW THE ATOMS OUT OF LINE — AND DOWN WE CAME! SEE?

IF IT HAD BEEN RADIUM WE'D BE UP THERE YET!

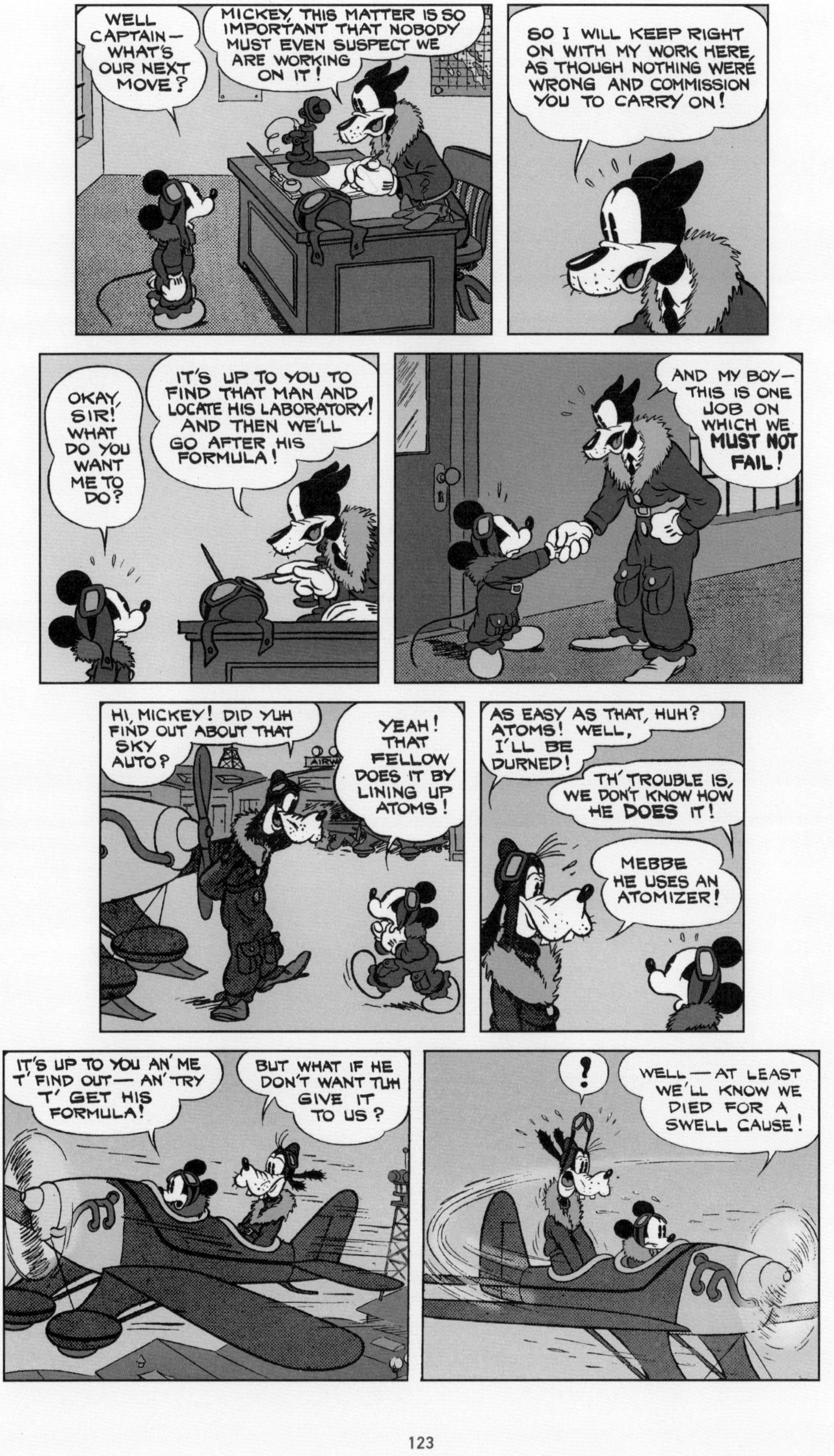
WELL CAPTAIN— WHAT'S OUR NEXT MOVE?
MICKEY, THIS MATTER IS SO IMPORTANT THAT NOBODY MUST EVEN SUSPECT WE ARE WORKING ON IT!
SO I WILL KEEP RIGHT ON WITH MY WORK HERE, AS THOUGH NOTHING WERE WRONG AND COMMISSION YOU TO CARRY ON!
OKAY, SIR! WHAT DO YOU WANT ME TO DO?
IT'S UP TO YOU TO FIND THAT MAN AND LOCATE HIS LABORATORY! AND THEN WE'LL GO AFTER HIS FORMULA!
AND MY BOY— THIS IS ONE JOB ON WHICH WE MUST NOT FAIL!
HI, MICKEY! DID YUH FIND OUT ABOUT THAT SKY AUTO?
YEAH! THAT FELLOW DOES IT BY LINING UP ATOMS!
AS EASY AS THAT, HUH? ATOMS! WELL, I'LL BE DURNED!
TH' TROUBLE IS, WE DON'T KNOW HOW HE DOES IT!
MEBBE HE USES AN ATOMIZER!
IT'S UP TO YOU AN' ME T' FIND OUT— AN' TRY T' GET HIS FORMULA!
BUT WHAT IF HE DON'T WANT TUH GIVE IT TO US?
?
WELL— AT LEAST WE'LL KNOW WE DIED FOR A SWELL CAUSE!

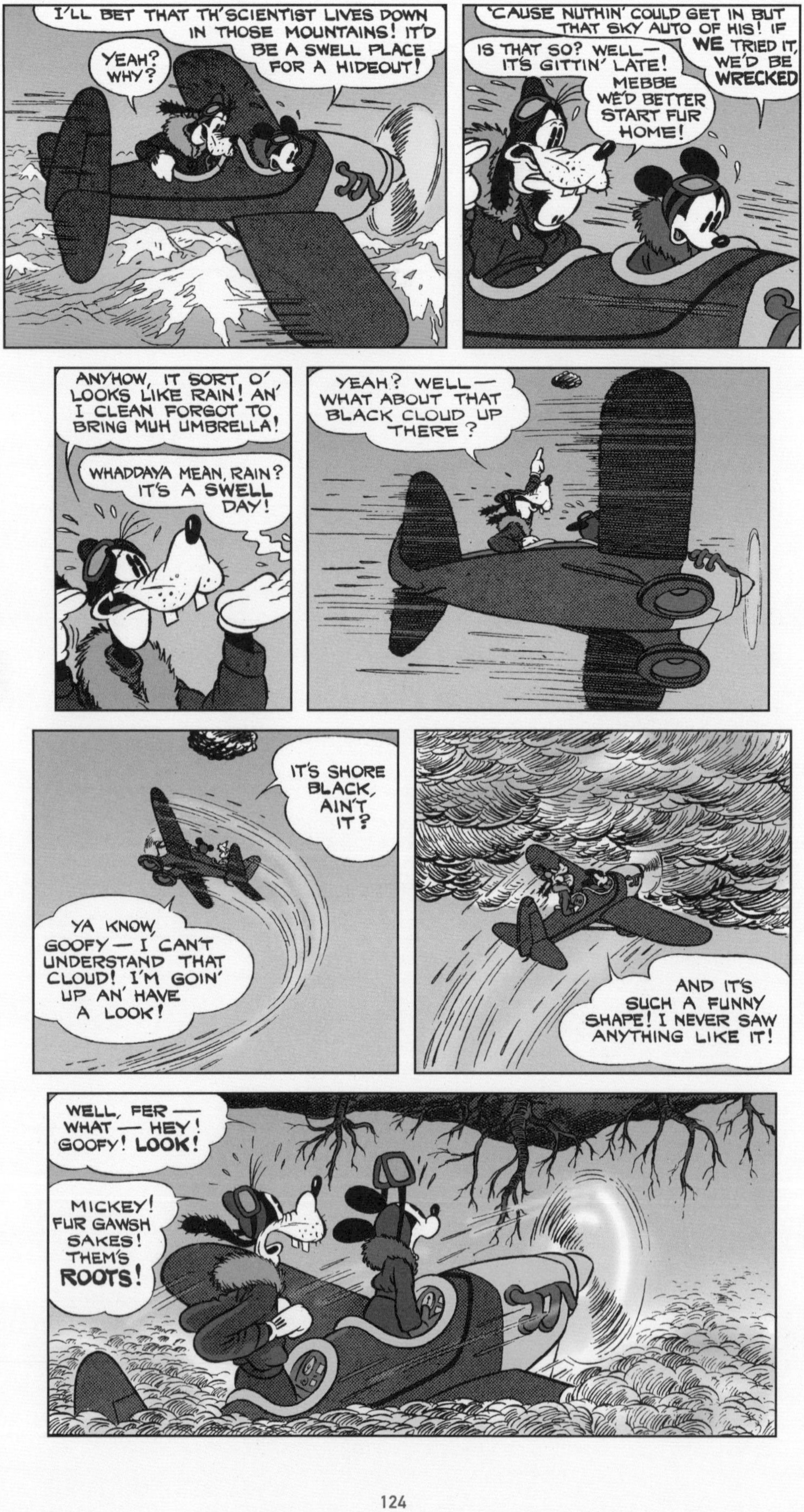
I'LL BET THAT TH' SCIENTIST LIVES DOWN IN THOSE MOUNTAINS! IT'D BE A SWELL PLACE FOR A HIDEOUT!
YEAH? WHY?
'CAUSE NUTHIN' COULD GET IN BUT THAT SKY AUTO OF HIS! IF WE TRIED IT, WE'D BE WRECKED
IS THAT SO? WELL— IT'S GITTIN' LATE! MEBBE WE'D BETTER START FUR HOME!
ANYHOW, IT SORT O' LOOKS LIKE RAIN! AN' I CLEAN FORGOT TO BRING MUH UMBRELLA!
WHADDAYA MEAN, RAIN? IT'S A SWELL DAY!
YEAH? WELL— WHAT ABOUT THAT BLACK CLOUD UP THERE?
IT'S SHORE BLACK, AIN'T IT?
YA KNOW, GOOFY— I CAN'T UNDERSTAND THAT CLOUD! I'M GOIN' UP AN' HAVE A LOOK!
AND IT'S SUCH A FUNNY SHAPE! I NEVER SAW ANYTHING LIKE IT!
WELL, FER— WHAT— HEY! GOOFY! LOOK!
MICKEY! FUR GAWSH SAKES! THEM'S ROOTS!

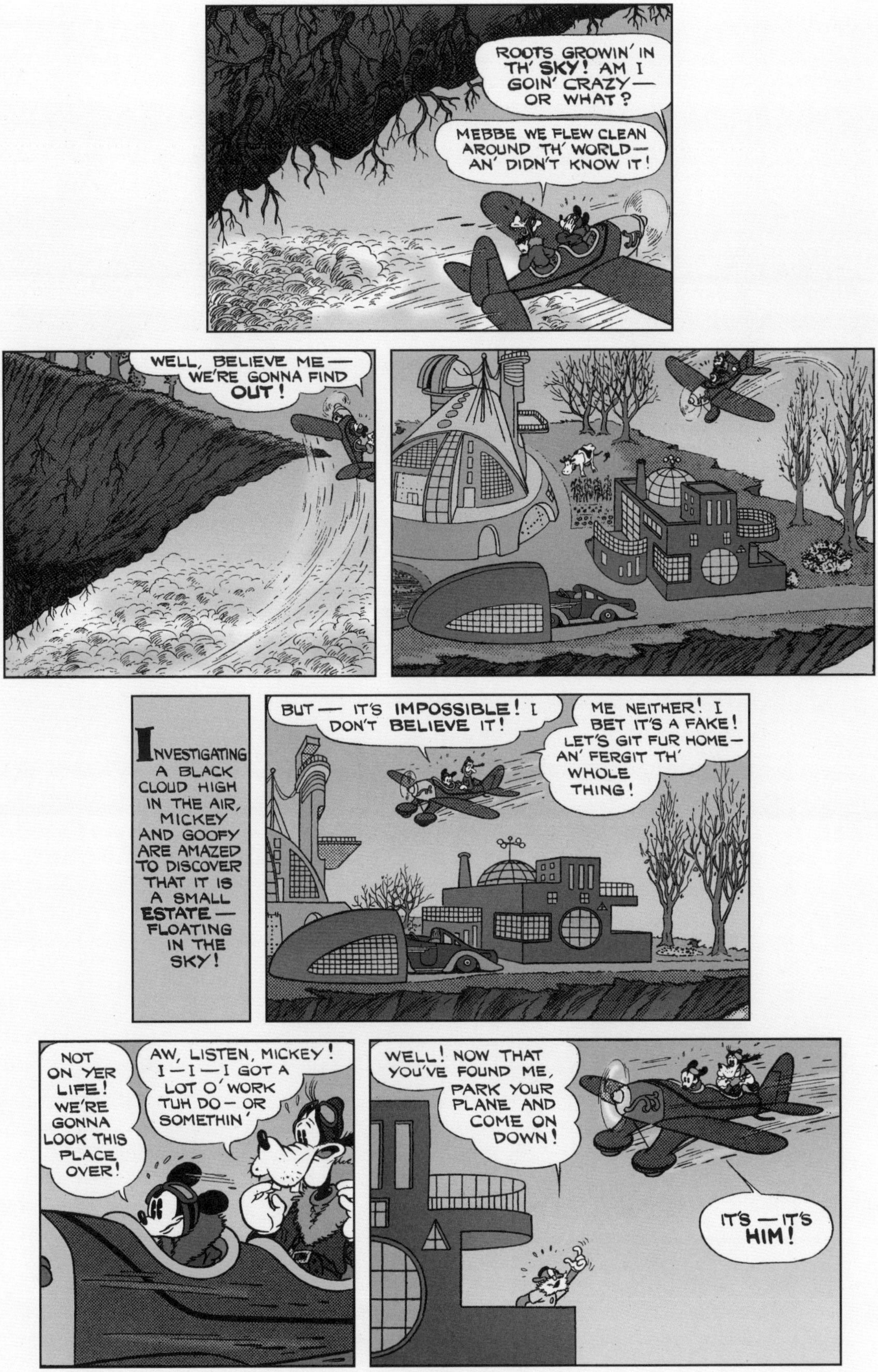
ROOTS GROWIN' IN TH' SKY! AM I GOIN' CRAZY— OR WHAT?
MEBBE WE FLEW CLEAN AROUND TH' WORLD— AN' DIDN'T KNOW IT!
WELL, BELIEVE ME— WE'RE GONNA FIND OUT!
INVESTIGATING A BLACK CLOUD HIGH IN THE AIR, MICKEY AND GOOFY ARE AMAZED TO DISCOVER THAT IT IS A SMALL ESTATE— FLOATING IN THE SKY!
BUT— IT'S IMPOSSIBLE! I DON'T BELIEVE IT!
ME NEITHER! I BET IT'S A FAKE! LET'S GIT FUR HOME— AN' FERGIT TH' WHOLE THING!
NOT ON YER LIFE! WE'RE GONNA LOOK THIS PLACE OVER!
AW, LISTEN, MICKEY! I—I—I GOT A LOT O' WORK TUH DO— OR SOMETHIN'
WELL! NOW THAT YOU'VE FOUND ME, PARK YOUR PLANE AND COME ON DOWN!
IT'S—IT'S HIM!

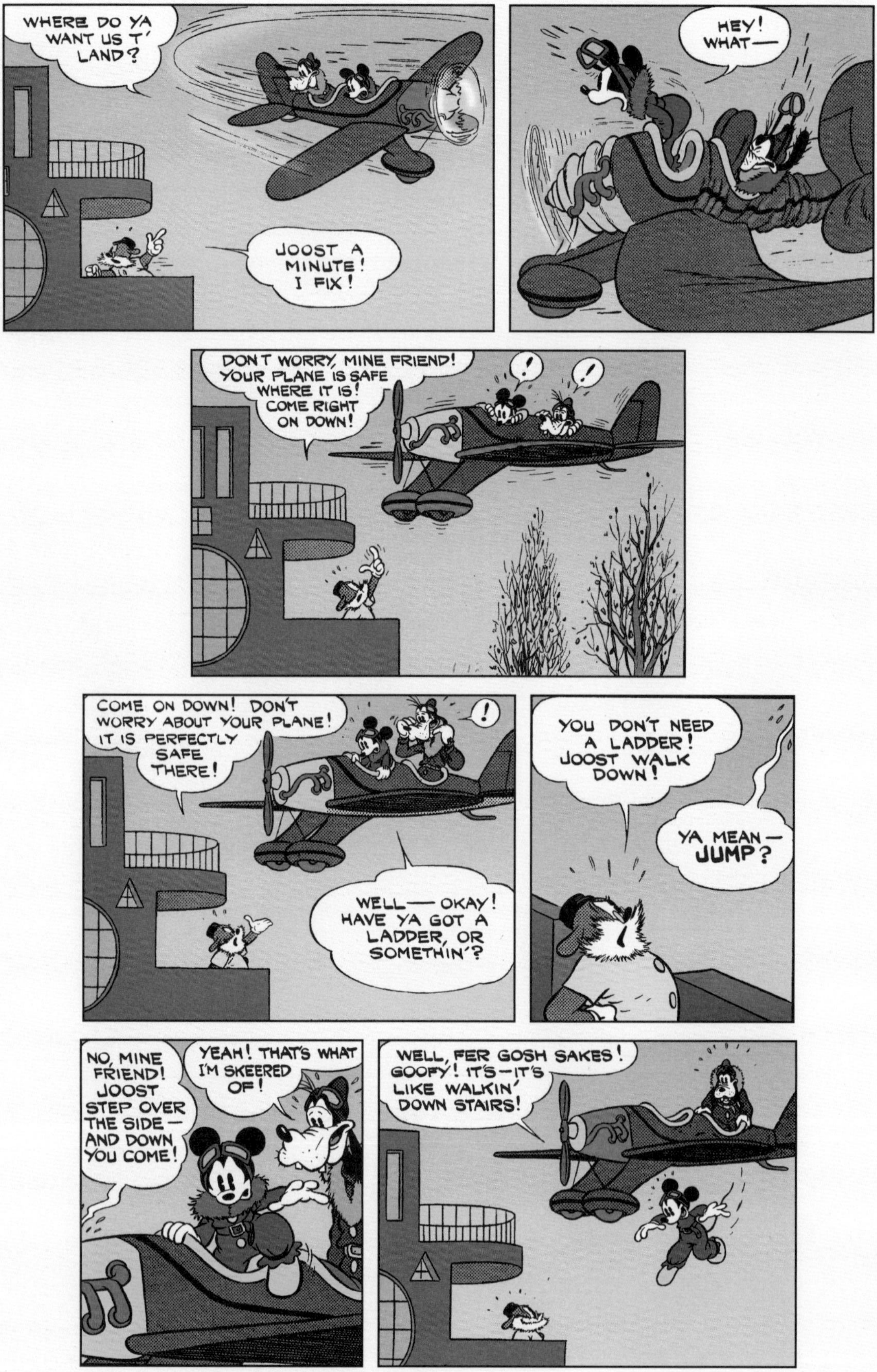
WHERE DO YA WANT US T' LAND?
JOOST A MINUTE! I FIX!
HEY! WHAT—
DON'T WORRY, MINE FRIEND! YOUR PLANE IS SAFE WHERE IT IS! COME RIGHT ON DOWN!
!
!
COME ON DOWN! DON'T WORRY ABOUT YOUR PLANE! IT IS PERFECTLY SAFE THERE!
!
WELL—OKAY! HAVE YA GOT A LADDER, OR SOMETHIN'?
YOU DON'T NEED A LADDER! JOOST WALK DOWN!
YA MEAN— JUMP?
NO, MINE FRIEND! JOOST STEP OVER THE SIDE— AND DOWN YOU COME!
YEAH! THAT'S WHAT I'M SKEERED OF!
WELL, FER GOSH SAKES! GOOFY! IT'S—IT'S LIKE WALKIN' DOWN STAIRS!

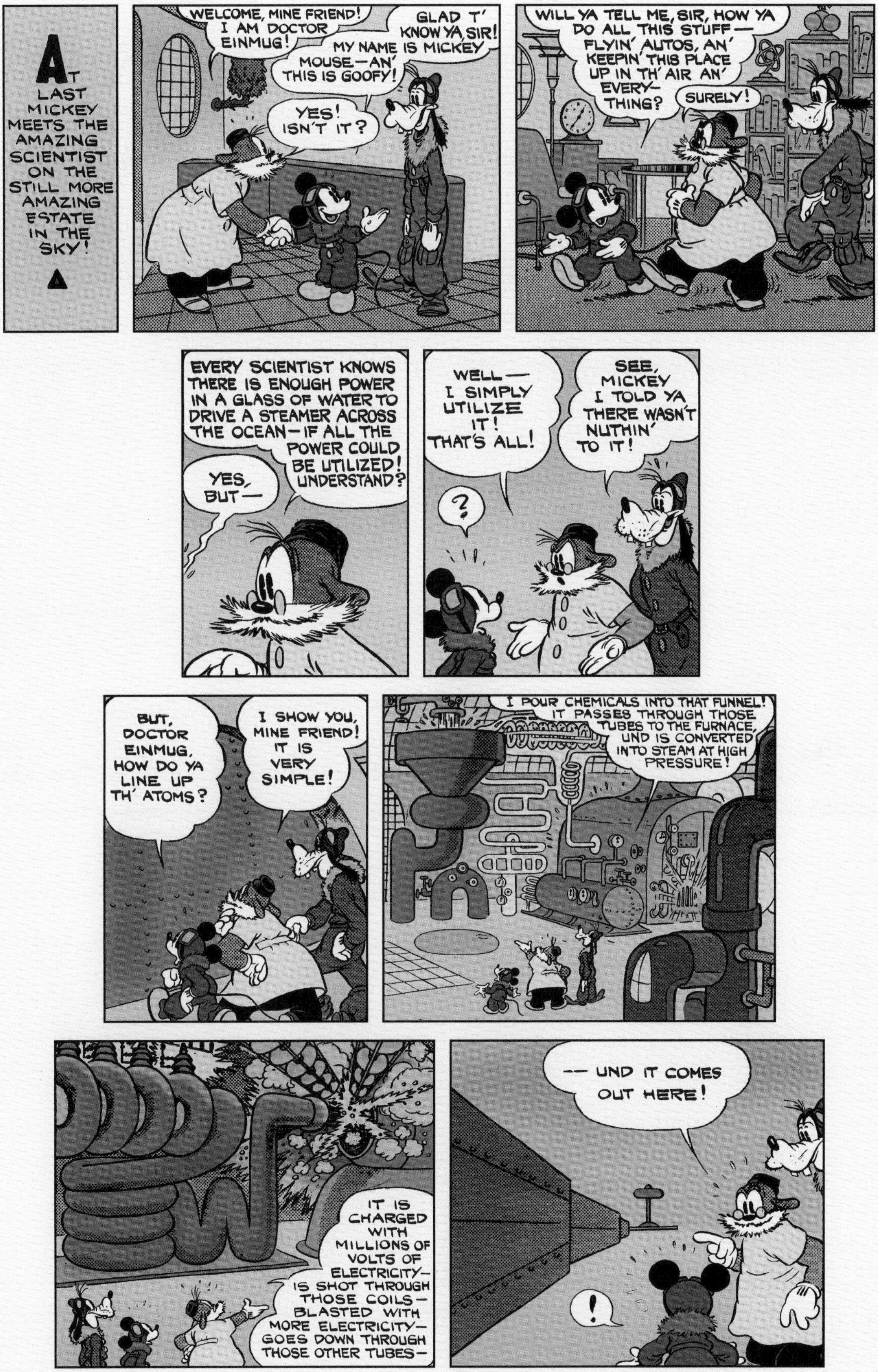
At last Mickey meets the amazing scientist on the still more amazing estate in the sky!
WELCOME, MINE FRIEND! I AM DOCTOR EINMUG!
GLAD T' KNOW YA, SIR! MY NAME IS MICKEY MOUSE—AN' THIS IS GOOFY!
YES! ISN'T IT?
WILL YA TELL ME, SIR, HOW YA DO ALL THIS STUFF—FLYIN' AUTOS, AN' KEEPIN' THIS PLACE UP IN TH' AIR AN' EVERY-THING?
SURELY!
EVERY SCIENTIST KNOWS THERE IS ENOUGH POWER IN A GLASS OF WATER TO DRIVE A STEAMER ACROSS THE OCEAN—IF ALL THE POWER COULD BE UTILIZED! UNDERSTAND?
YES, BUT—
WELL—I SIMPLY UTILIZE IT! THAT'S ALL!
SEE, MICKEY I TOLD YA THERE WASN'T NUTHIN' TO IT!
?
BUT, DOCTOR EINMUG, HOW DO YA LINE UP TH' ATOMS?
I SHOW YOU, MINE FRIEND! IT IS VERY SIMPLE!
I POUR CHEMICALS INTO THAT FUNNEL! IT PASSES THROUGH THOSE TUBES TO THE FURNACE, UND IS CONVERTED INTO STEAM AT HIGH PRESSURE!
IT IS CHARGED WITH MILLIONS OF VOLTS OF ELECTRICITY—IS SHOT THROUGH THOSE COILS—BLASTED WITH MORE ELECTRICITY—GOES DOWN THROUGH THOSE OTHER TUBES—
—— UND IT COMES OUT HERE!
!

GOSH, DOCTOR EINMUG! MY GOVERNMENT WOULD PAY YOU A MILLION DOLLARS FOR YOUR DISCOVERY!

POOF! CHICKENFOOD! SOME FOREIGNERS OFFERED ME A **BILLION**!

SOME FOREIGNERS? YA MEAN— SOMEBODY **ELSE** KNOWS ABOUT IT?

OF COURSE! BUT I HAVE MONEY! I NEED NO MORE! ALL I WANT IS A QUIET PLACE TO WORK! I AM A SCIENTIST— NOT A BANKER!

BUT— WHAT DID YOU TELL 'EM?

THOSE AGENTS! THEY BOTHERED ME! THEY PESTERED ME! I COULDN'T WORK! I COULDN'T EVEN SLEEP!

I TOLD THEM NODDING! I JOOST MOVED MINE LABORATORY UP HERE IN THE SKY— WHERE I CAN WORK IN PEACE!

DR. EINMUG, WHAT ARE YOU GONNA DO WITH YOUR DISCOVERY?

I CAN DO NODDING! I AM HELPLESS!

WHADDAYA MEAN— HELPLESS?

MR. MOUSE, WITH MY ATOMIC FORCE, EVERYBODY IN THE WORLD COULD BE RICH— AND HAPPY!

SURE! THEN WHY HOLD IT BACK? WHY NOT TURN IT LOOSE?

BECAUSE THEY WOULDN'T BE! INSTEAD OF USING IT FOR INDUSTRY AND PEACE, THEY WOULD USE IT FOR **WAR**!

INSTEAD OF **HELPING** PEOPLE, IT WOULD **KILL THEM**! IT ISS AWFUL! I COULDN'T **BEAR** IT!

BOO-- BOO HOO HOO!! SNIFF— SNIFF!

SO! YOU ARE LAUGHING AT ME, IS IT? FOR WHY? DO YOU T'INK I HAVE NO FEELINGS?

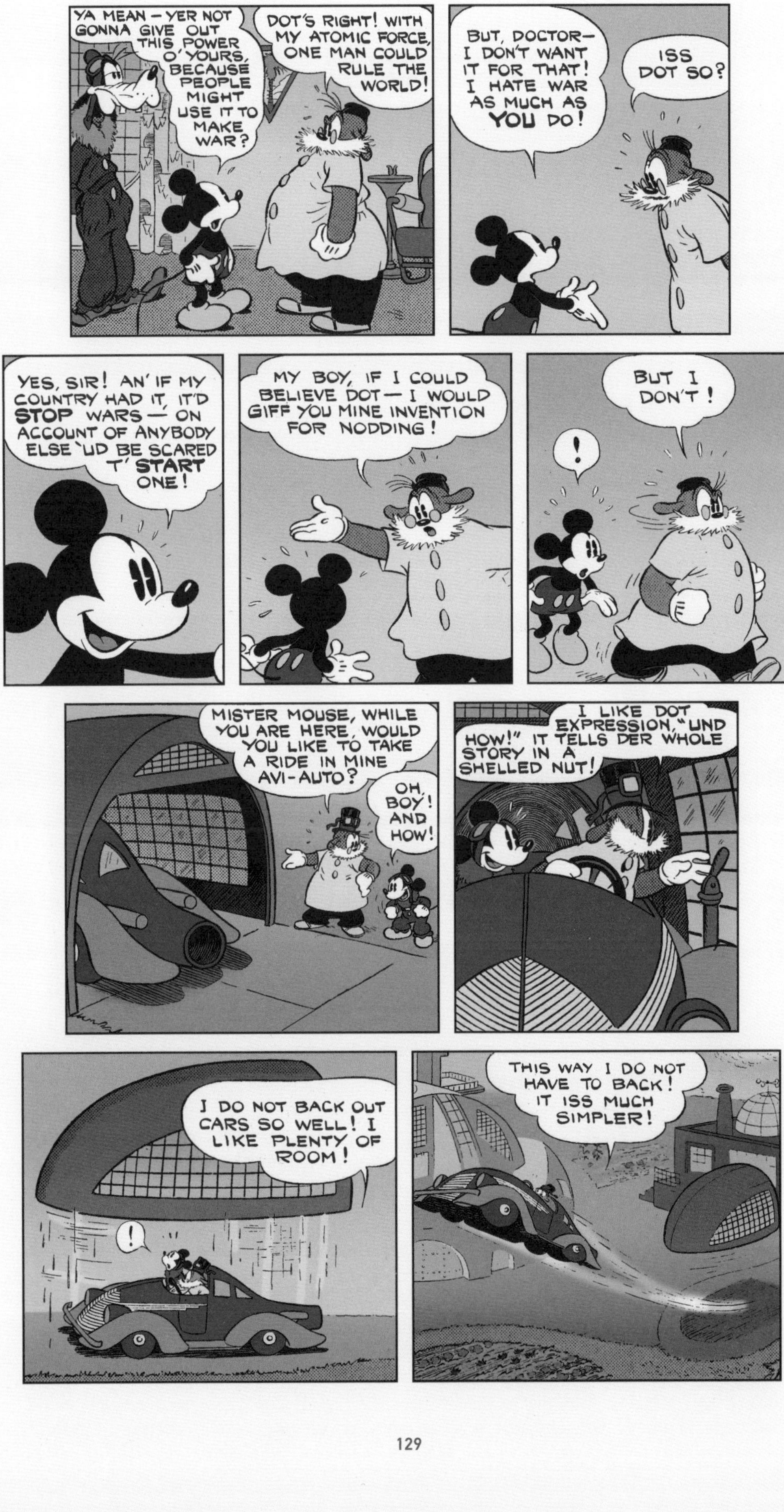
YA MEAN – YER NOT GONNA GIVE OUT THIS POWER O' YOURS, BECAUSE PEOPLE MIGHT USE IT TO MAKE WAR?
DOT'S RIGHT! WITH MY ATOMIC FORCE, ONE MAN COULD RULE THE WORLD!
BUT, DOCTOR– I DON'T WANT IT FOR THAT! I HATE WAR AS MUCH AS YOU DO!
ISS DOT SO?
YES, SIR! AN' IF MY COUNTRY HAD IT, IT'D STOP WARS – ON ACCOUNT OF ANYBODY ELSE 'UD BE SCARED T' START ONE!
MY BOY, IF I COULD BELIEVE DOT – I WOULD GIFF YOU MINE INVENTION FOR NODDING!
BUT I DON'T!
!
MISTER MOUSE, WHILE YOU ARE HERE, WOULD YOU LIKE TO TAKE A RIDE IN MINE AVI-AUTO?
OH, BOY! AND HOW!
I LIKE DOT EXPRESSION, "UND HOW!" IT TELLS DER WHOLE STORY IN A SHELLED NUT!
I DO NOT BACK OUT CARS SO WELL! I LIKE PLENTY OF ROOM!
!
THIS WAY I DO NOT HAVE TO BACK! IT ISS MUCH SIMPLER!

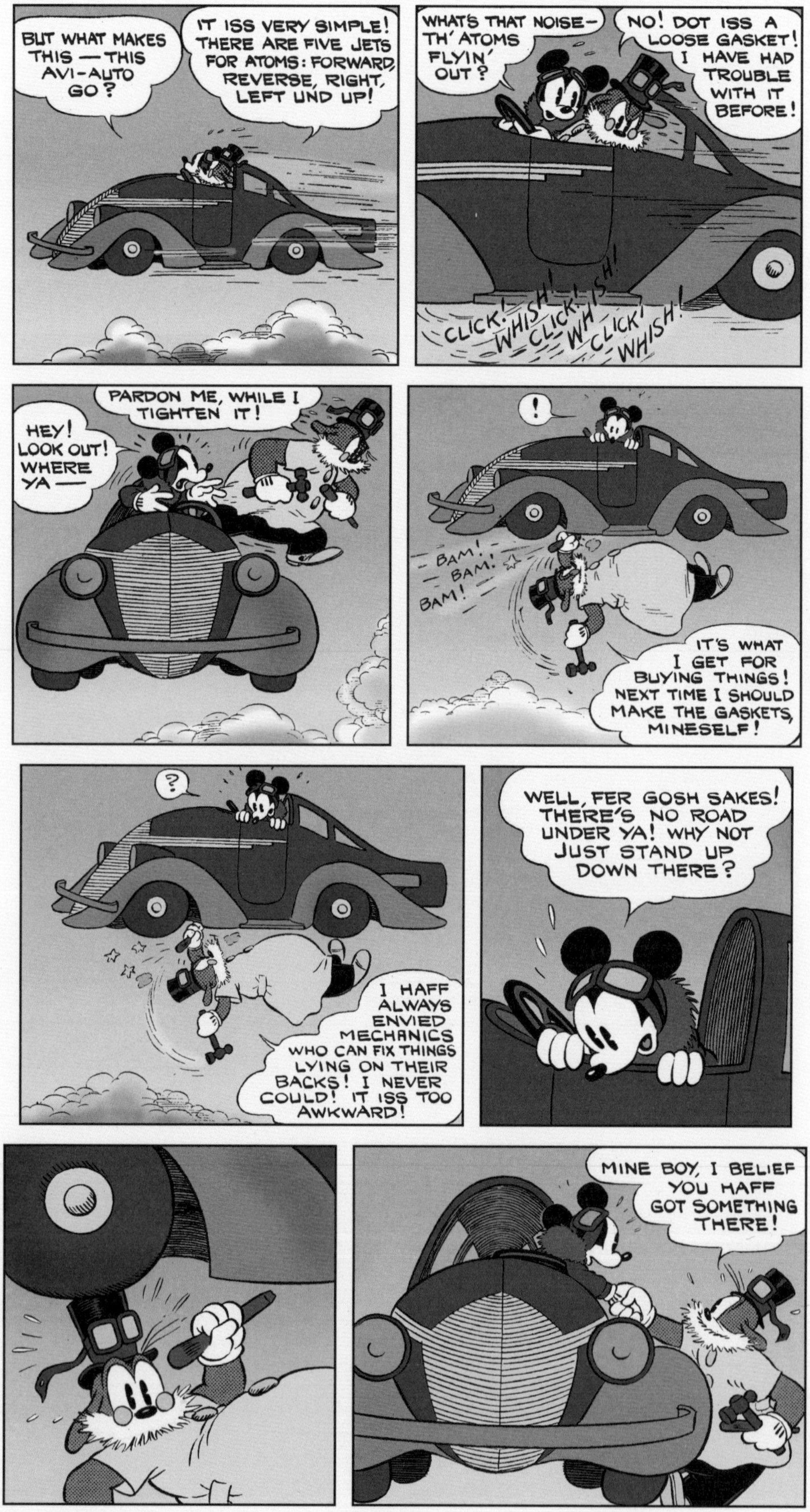
BUT WHAT MAKES THIS — THIS AVI-AUTO GO?
IT ISS VERY SIMPLE! THERE ARE FIVE JETS FOR ATOMS: FORWARD, REVERSE, RIGHT, LEFT UND UP!
WHAT'S THAT NOISE— TH' ATOMS FLYIN' OUT?
NO! DOT ISS A LOOSE GASKET! I HAVE HAD TROUBLE WITH IT BEFORE!
CLICK! WHISH! CLICK! WHISH! CLICK! WHISH!
PARDON ME, WHILE I TIGHTEN IT!
HEY! LOOK OUT! WHERE YA —
!
BAM! BAM! BAM!
IT'S WHAT I GET FOR BUYING THINGS! NEXT TIME I SHOULD MAKE THE GASKETS, MINESELF!
?
I HAFF ALWAYS ENVIED MECHANICS WHO CAN FIX THINGS LYING ON THEIR BACKS! I NEVER COULD! IT ISS TOO AWKWARD!
WELL, FER GOSH SAKES! THERE'S NO ROAD UNDER YA! WHY NOT JUST STAND UP DOWN THERE?
MINE BOY, I BELIEF YOU HAFF GOT SOMETHING THERE!

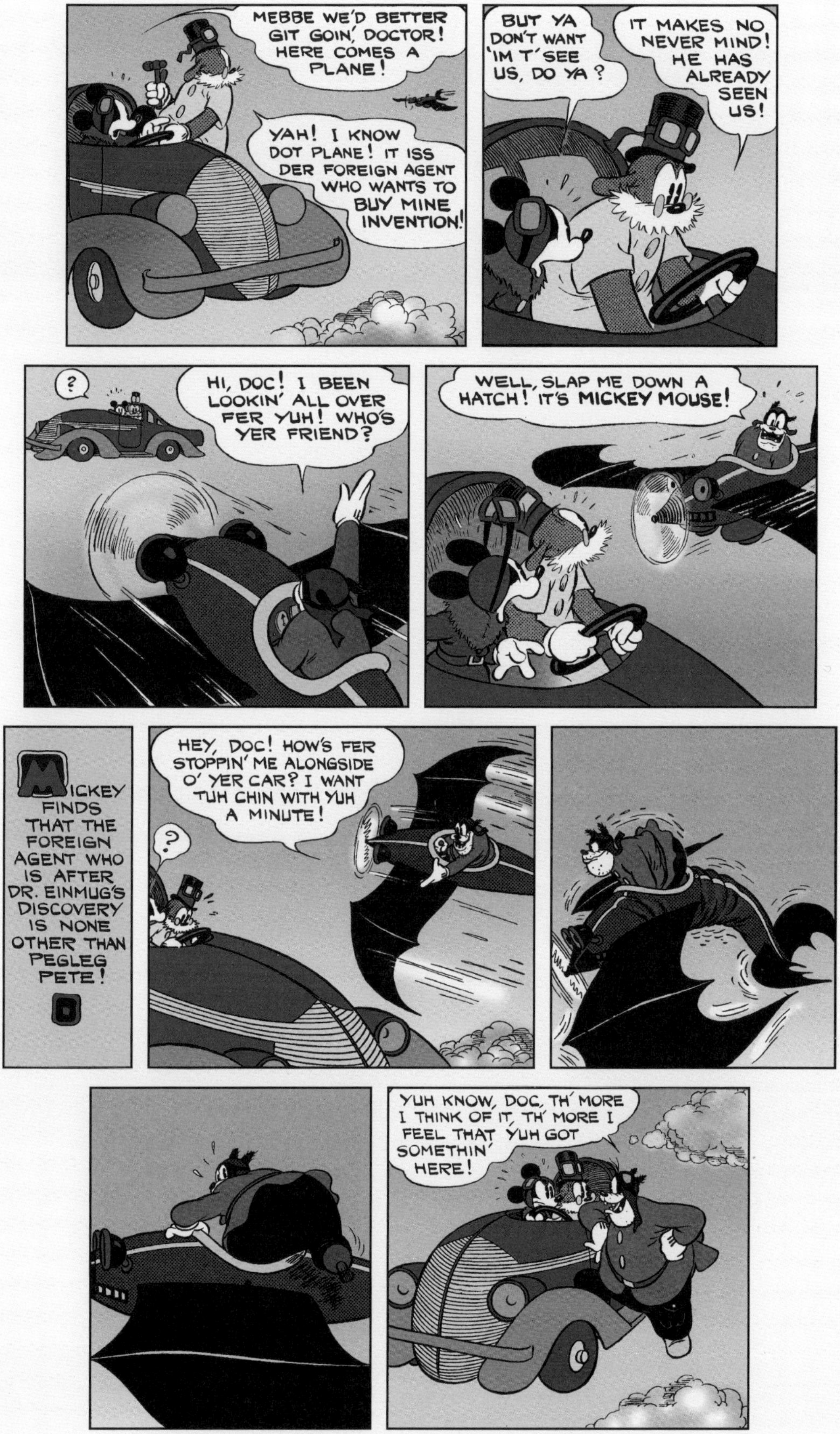
MEBBE WE'D BETTER GIT GOIN', DOCTOR! HERE COMES A PLANE!
YAH! I KNOW DOT PLANE! IT ISS DER FOREIGN AGENT WHO WANTS TO BUY MINE INVENTION!
BUT YA DON'T WANT 'IM T' SEE US, DO YA?
IT MAKES NO NEVER MIND! HE HAS ALREADY SEEN US!
?
HI, DOC! I BEEN LOOKIN' ALL OVER FER YUH! WHO'S YER FRIEND?
WELL, SLAP ME DOWN A HATCH! IT'S MICKEY MOUSE!
MICKEY FINDS THAT THE FOREIGN AGENT WHO IS AFTER DR. EINMUG'S DISCOVERY IS NONE OTHER THAN PEGLEG PETE!
HEY, DOC! HOW'S FER STOPPIN' ME ALONGSIDE O' YER CAR? I WANT TUH CHIN WITH YUH A MINUTE!
?
YUH KNOW, DOC, TH' MORE I THINK OF IT, TH' MORE I FEEL THAT YUH GOT SOMETHIN' HERE!

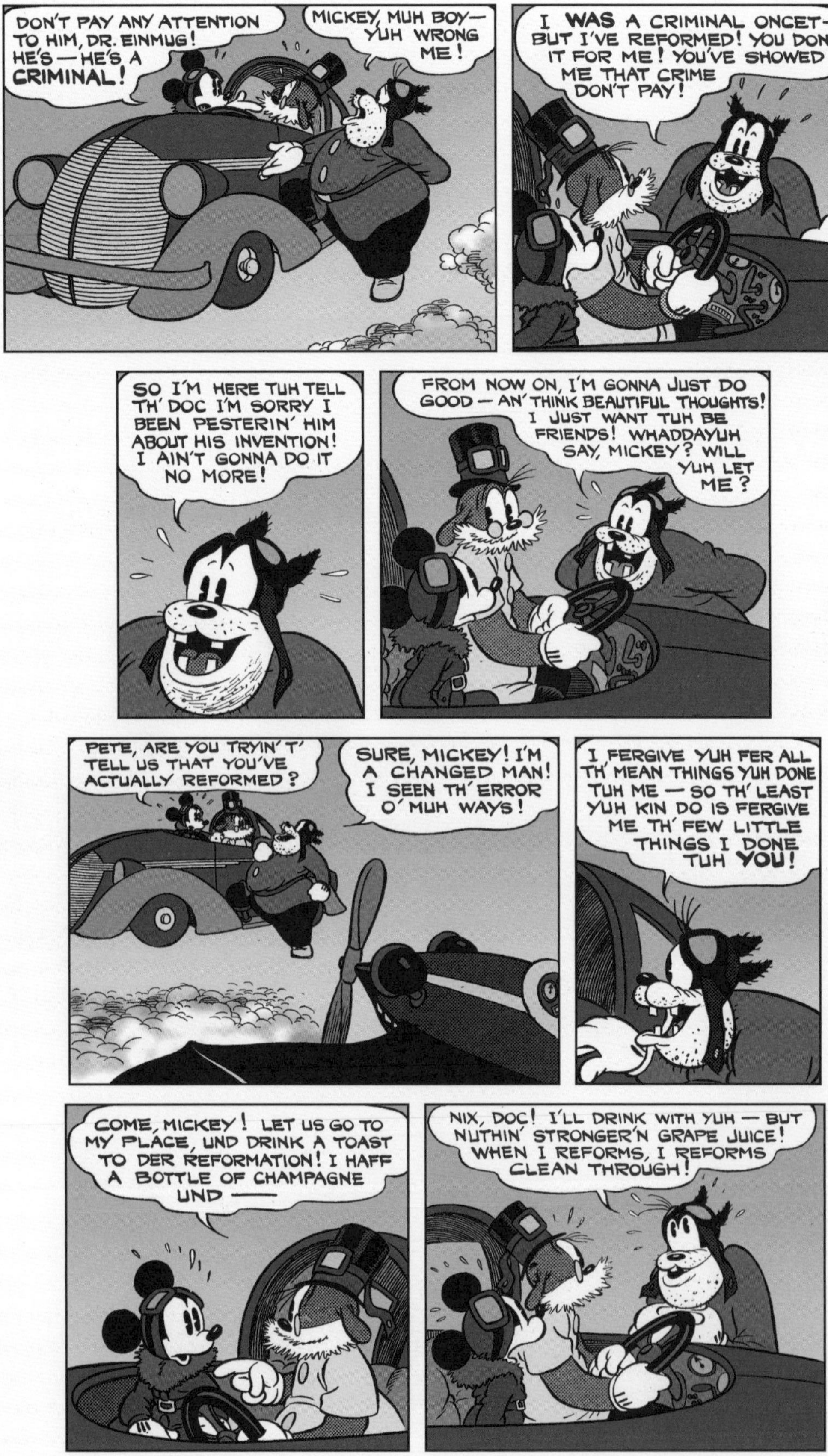
DON'T PAY ANY ATTENTION TO HIM, DR. EINMUG! HE'S — HE'S A CRIMINAL!
MICKEY, MUH BOY— YUH WRONG ME!
I WAS A CRIMINAL ONCET— BUT I'VE REFORMED! YOU DONE IT FOR ME! YOU'VE SHOWED ME THAT CRIME DON'T PAY!
SO I'M HERE TUH TELL TH' DOC I'M SORRY I BEEN PESTERIN' HIM ABOUT HIS INVENTION! I AIN'T GONNA DO IT NO MORE!
FROM NOW ON, I'M GONNA JUST DO GOOD — AN' THINK BEAUTIFUL THOUGHTS! I JUST WANT TUH BE FRIENDS! WHADDAYUH SAY, MICKEY? WILL YUH LET ME?
PETE, ARE YOU TRYIN' T' TELL US THAT YOU'VE ACTUALLY REFORMED?
SURE, MICKEY! I'M A CHANGED MAN! I SEEN TH' ERROR O' MUH WAYS!
I FERGIVE YUH FER ALL TH' MEAN THINGS YUH DONE TUH ME — SO TH' LEAST YUH KIN DO IS FERGIVE ME TH' FEW LITTLE THINGS I DONE TUH YOU!
COME, MICKEY! LET US GO TO MY PLACE, UND DRINK A TOAST TO DER REFORMATION! I HAFF A BOTTLE OF CHAMPAGNE UND ——
NIX, DOC! I'LL DRINK WITH YUH — BUT NUTHIN' STRONGER'N GRAPE JUICE! WHEN I REFORMS, I REFORMS CLEAN THROUGH!

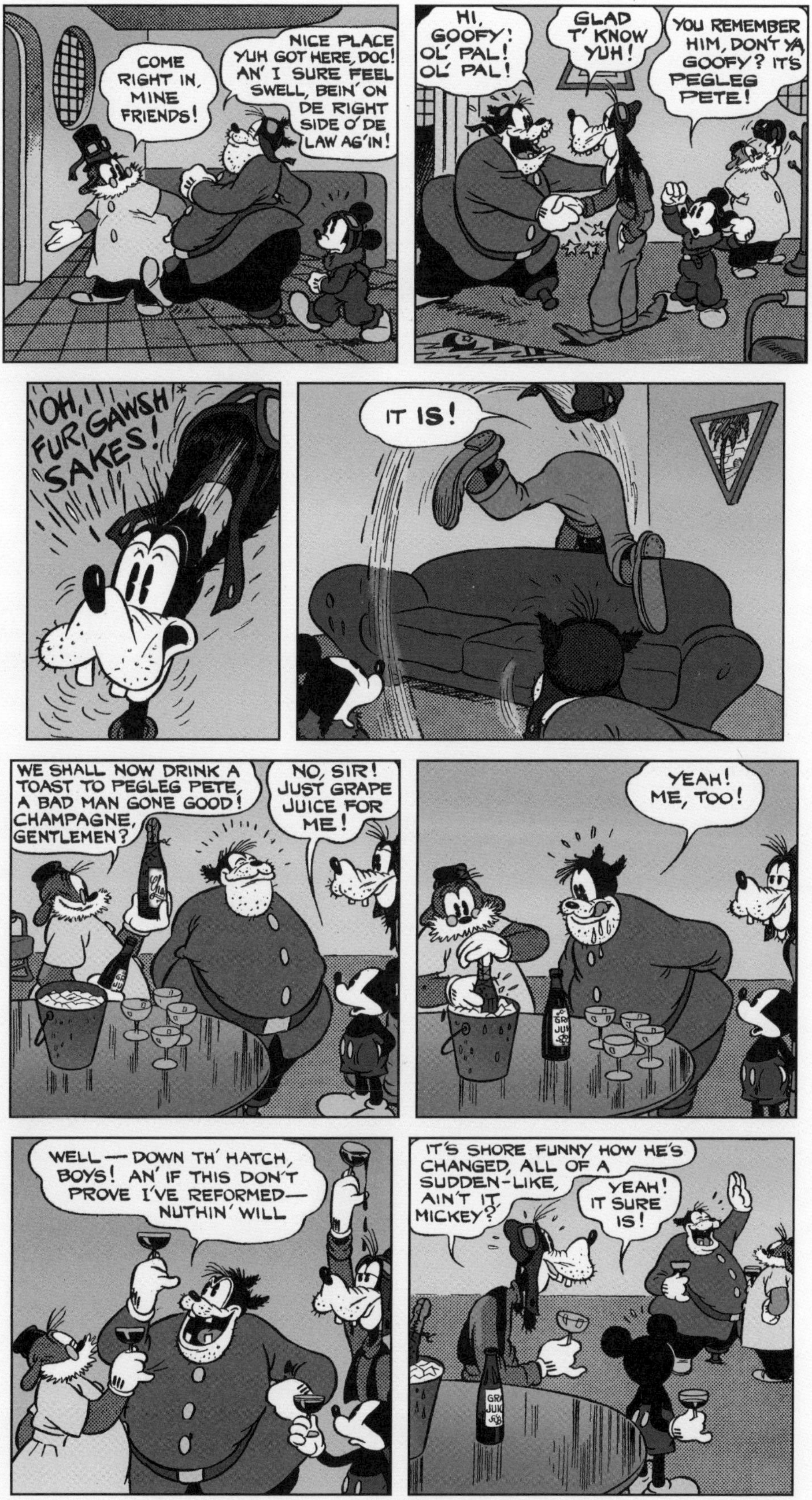
COME RIGHT IN, MINE FRIENDS!
NICE PLACE YUH GOT HERE, DOC! AN' I SURE FEEL SWELL, BEIN' ON DE RIGHT SIDE O' DE LAW AG'IN!
HI, GOOFY! OL' PAL! OL' PAL!
GLAD T' KNOW YUH!
YOU REMEMBER HIM, DON'T YA, GOOFY? IT'S PEGLEG PETE!
OH, FUR GAWSH* SAKES!
IT IS!
WE SHALL NOW DRINK A TOAST TO PEGLEG PETE, A BAD MAN GONE GOOD! CHAMPAGNE, GENTLEMEN?
NO, SIR! JUST GRAPE JUICE FOR ME!
YEAH! ME, TOO!
WELL — DOWN TH' HATCH, BOYS! AN' IF THIS DON'T PROVE I'VE REFORMED — NUTHIN' WILL
IT'S SHORE FUNNY HOW HE'S CHANGED, ALL OF A SUDDEN-LIKE, AIN'T IT, MICKEY?
YEAH! IT SURE IS!

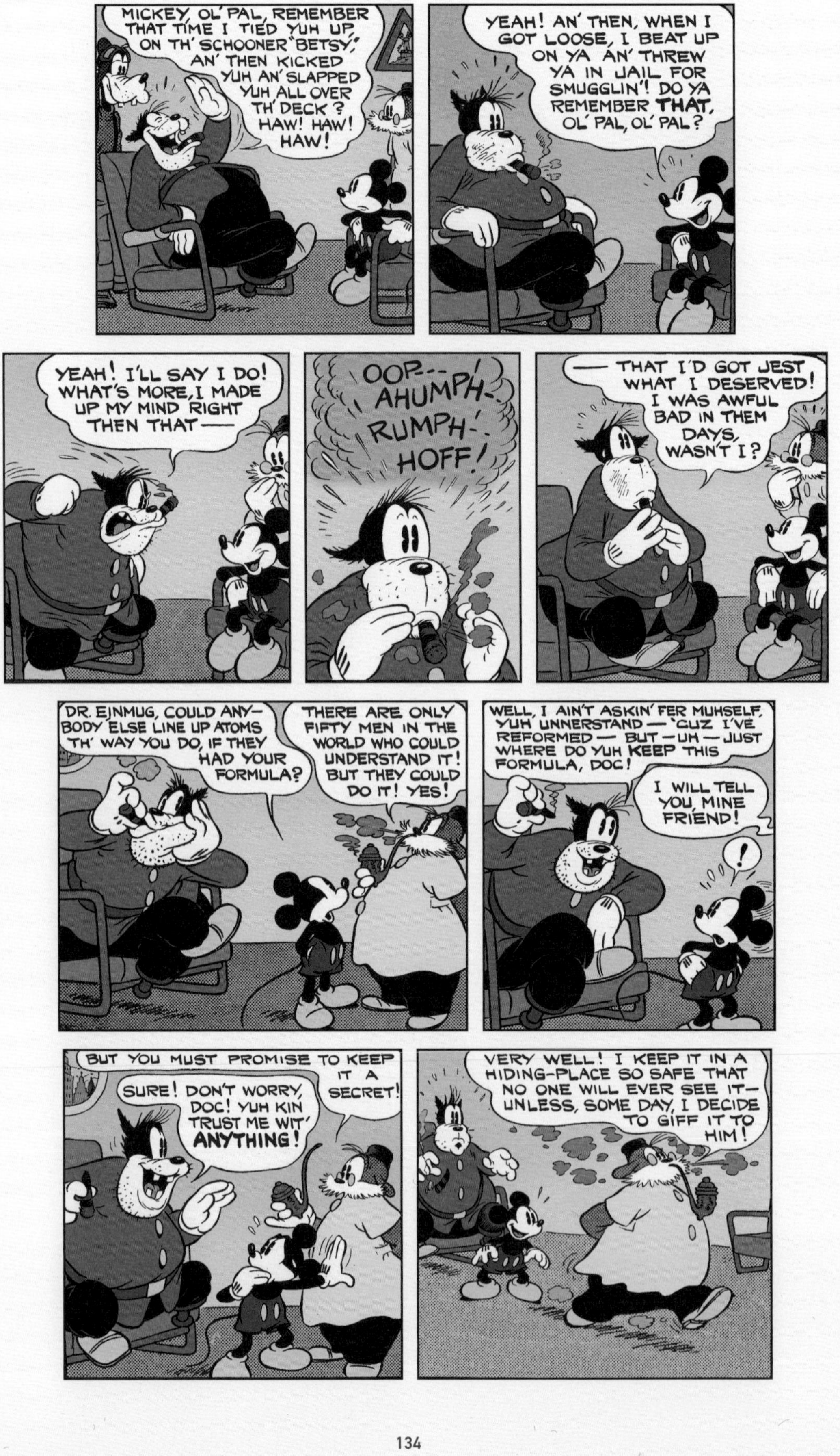
MICKEY, OL' PAL, REMEMBER THAT TIME I TIED YUH UP ON TH' SCHOONER "BETSY," AN' THEN KICKED YUH AN' SLAPPED YUH ALL OVER TH' DECK? HAW! HAW! HAW!
YEAH! AN' THEN, WHEN I GOT LOOSE, I BEAT UP ON YA AN' THREW YA IN JAIL FOR SMUGGLIN'! DO YA REMEMBER THAT, OL' PAL, OL' PAL?
YEAH! I'LL SAY I DO! WHAT'S MORE, I MADE UP MY MIND RIGHT THEN THAT—
OOP-- AHUMPH-- RUMPH-- HOFF!
— THAT I'D GOT JEST WHAT I DESERVED! I WAS AWFUL BAD IN THEM DAYS, WASN'T I?
DR. EJNMUG, COULD ANYBODY ELSE LINE UP ATOMS TH' WAY YOU DO, IF THEY HAD YOUR FORMULA?
THERE ARE ONLY FIFTY MEN IN THE WORLD WHO COULD UNDERSTAND IT! BUT THEY COULD DO IT! YES!
WELL, I AIN'T ASKIN' FER MUHSELF, YUH UNNERSTAND — 'CUZ I'VE REFORMED — BUT — UH — JUST WHERE DO YUH KEEP THIS FORMULA, DOC!
I WILL TELL YOU, MINE FRIEND!
!
BUT YOU MUST PROMISE TO KEEP IT A SECRET!
SURE! DON'T WORRY, DOC! YUH KIN TRUST ME WIT' ANYTHING!
VERY WELL! I KEEP IT IN A HIDING-PLACE SO SAFE THAT NO ONE WILL EVER SEE IT— UNLESS, SOME DAY, I DECIDE TO GIFF IT TO HIM!

HOW ABOUT IT, MICKEY? ARE YUH PLANNIN' TUH GO DOWN HOME TUH-NIGHT, OR——
WHAM!
OH! MINE GOOTNESS!
FOR GOSH SAKES! WHAT HAPPENED?
IT ISS NODDING! IT ISS NODDING! IT ISS NINE O'CLOCK! DOT ISS ALL! THINK ABOUT IT NO MORE!
?
BUT, DOCTOR, WHAT HAS NINE O'CLOCK GOT T'DO WITH THAT SAFE FLYIN' OPEN?
I HAFF A TIME-LOCK ON IT! EFERY NIGHT, AT EXACTLY NINE IT OPENS "ATOMATICALLY"!
I SHUT IT— LIKE DOT! UND NOW NOBODY CAN OPEN IT— NOT MINESELF, EVEN— UNTIL TOMORROW NIGHT! THEN IT FLIES ITSELF OPEN!
YUH MUST HAVE SOMETHIN' PRETTY VALUABLE IN THERE, DOC! WHAT IS IT—MONEY?
NO-NO, NO-NO! NO MONEY! IT ISS NODDING!
IT ISS ONLY— WELL— IT ISS— IT ISS SOME OF MY FAVORITE RECIPES! DOT ISS ALL!

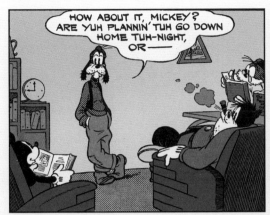

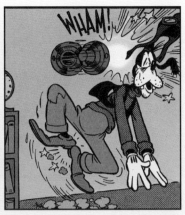

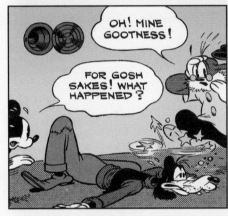

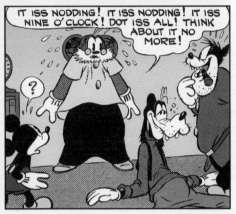

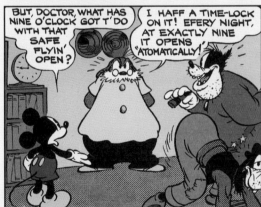

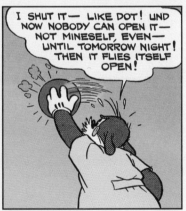

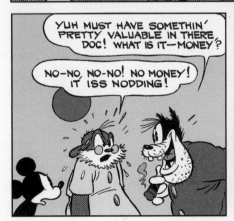

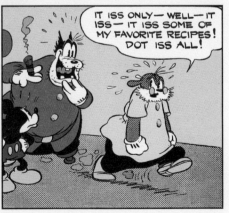

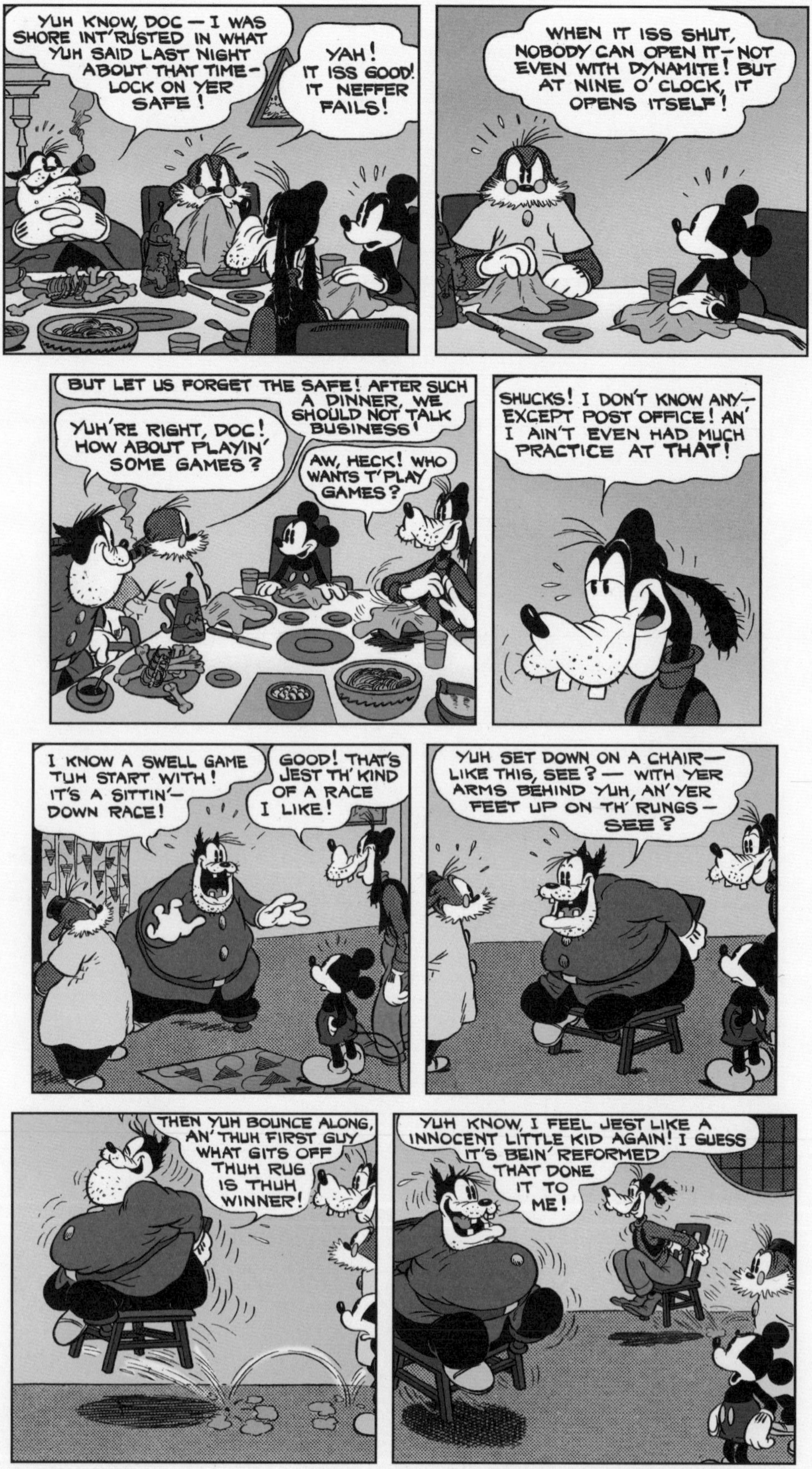
YUH KNOW, DOC — I WAS SHORE INT'RUSTED IN WHAT YUH SAID LAST NIGHT ABOUT THAT TIME-LOCK ON YER SAFE!
YAH! IT ISS GOOD! IT NEFFER FAILS!
WHEN IT ISS SHUT, NOBODY CAN OPEN IT— NOT EVEN WITH DYNAMITE! BUT AT NINE O' CLOCK, IT OPENS ITSELF!
BUT LET US FORGET THE SAFE! AFTER SUCH A DINNER, WE SHOULD NOT TALK BUSINESS!
YUH'RE RIGHT, DOC! HOW ABOUT PLAYIN' SOME GAMES?
AW, HECK! WHO WANTS T'PLAY GAMES?
SHUCKS! I DON'T KNOW ANY— EXCEPT POST OFFICE! AN' I AIN'T EVEN HAD MUCH PRACTICE AT THAT!
I KNOW A SWELL GAME TUH START WITH! IT'S A SITTIN'-DOWN RACE!
GOOD! THAT'S JEST TH' KIND OF A RACE I LIKE!
YUH SET DOWN ON A CHAIR— LIKE THIS, SEE? — WITH YER ARMS BEHIND YUH, AN' YER FEET UP ON TH' RUNGS — SEE?
THEN YUH BOUNCE ALONG, AN' THUH FIRST GUY WHAT GITS OFF THUH RUG IS THUH WINNER!
YUH KNOW, I FEEL JEST LIKE A INNOCENT LITTLE KID AGAIN! I GUESS IT'S BEIN' REFORMED THAT DONE IT TO ME!

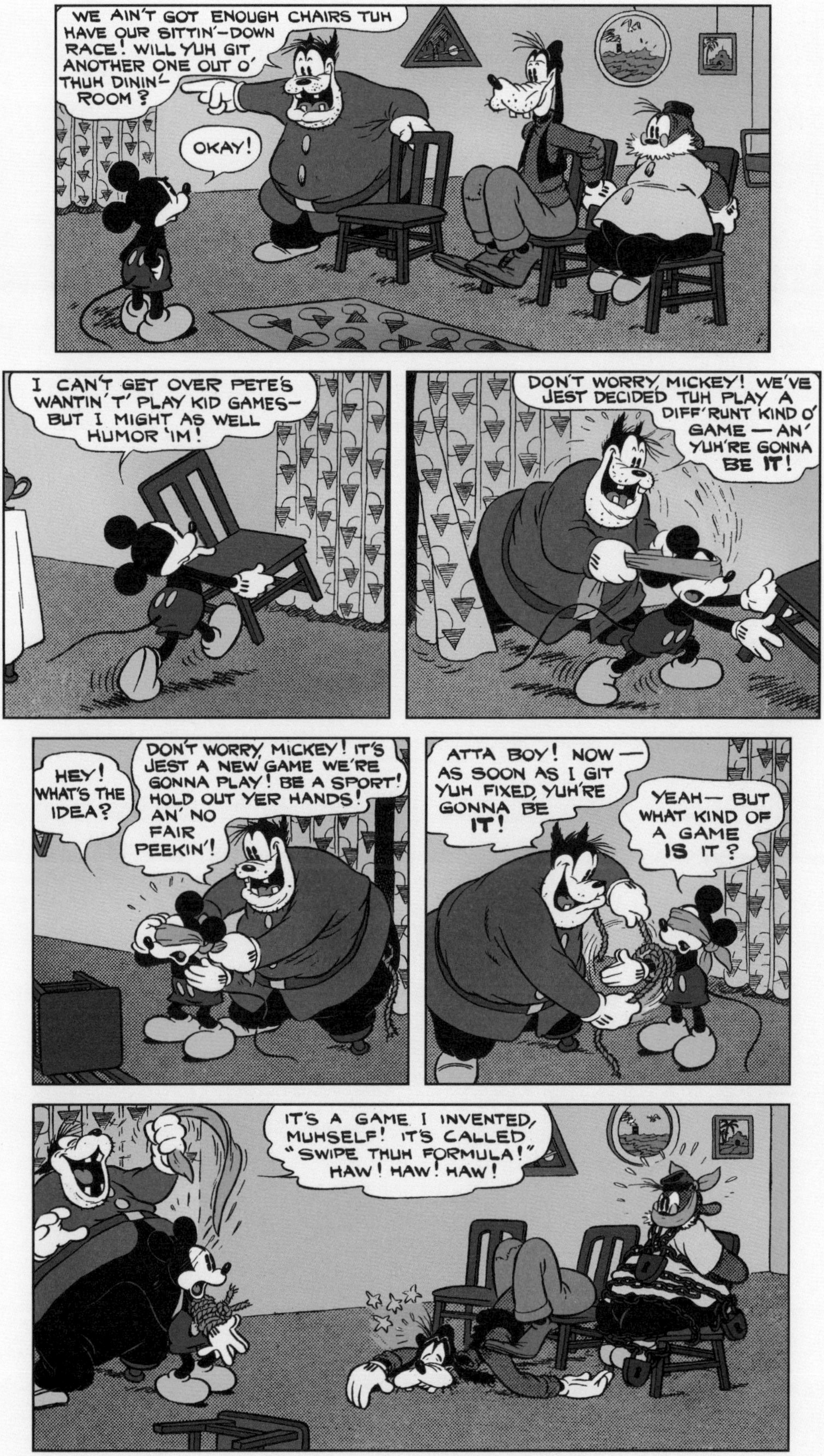
WE AIN'T GOT ENOUGH CHAIRS TUH HAVE OUR SITTIN'-DOWN RACE! WILL YUH GIT ANOTHER ONE OUT O' THUH DININ'-ROOM?
OKAY!
I CAN'T GET OVER PETE'S WANTIN' T' PLAY KID GAMES— BUT I MIGHT AS WELL HUMOR 'IM!
DON'T WORRY, MICKEY! WE'VE JEST DECIDED TUH PLAY A DIFF'RUNT KIND O' GAME — AN' YUH'RE GONNA BE IT!
HEY! WHAT'S THE IDEA?
DON'T WORRY, MICKEY! IT'S JEST A NEW GAME WE'RE GONNA PLAY! BE A SPORT! HOLD OUT YER HANDS! AN' NO FAIR PEEKIN'!
ATTA BOY! NOW — AS SOON AS I GIT YUH FIXED, YUH'RE GONNA BE IT!
YEAH— BUT WHAT KIND OF A GAME IS IT?
IT'S A GAME I INVENTED, MUHSELF! IT'S CALLED "SWIPE THUH FORMULA!" HAW! HAW! HAW!

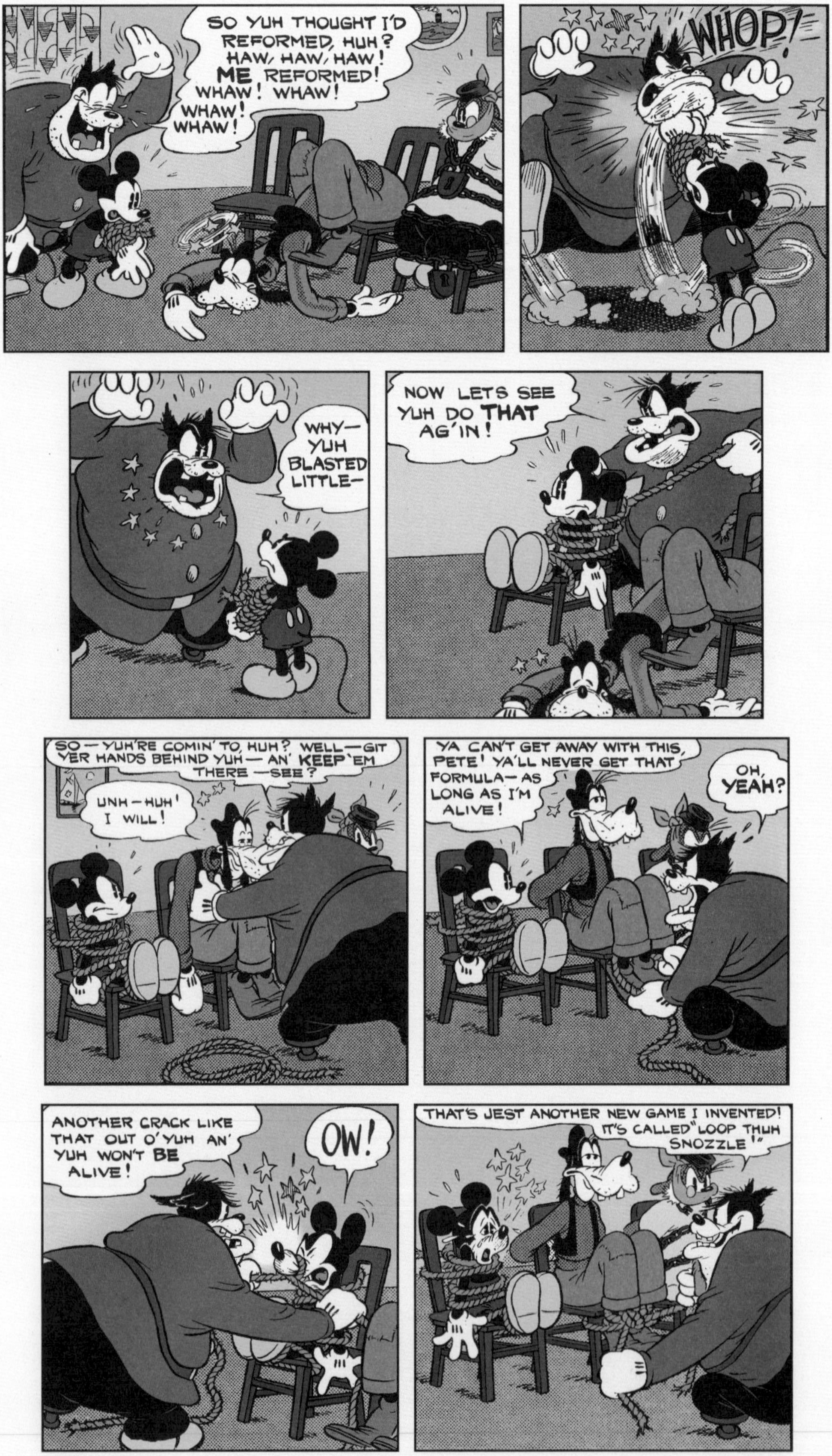
SO YUH THOUGHT I'D REFORMED, HUH? HAW, HAW, HAW! ME REFORMED! WHAW! WHAW! WHAW! WHAW!
WHOP!
WHY— YUH BLASTED LITTLE—
NOW LETS SEE YUH DO THAT AG'IN!
SO—YUH'RE COMIN' TO, HUH? WELL—GIT YER HANDS BEHIND YUH—AN' KEEP 'EM THERE—SEE?
UNH-HUH! I WILL!
YA CAN'T GET AWAY WITH THIS, PETE! YA'LL NEVER GET THAT FORMULA—AS LONG AS I'M ALIVE!
OH, YEAH?
ANOTHER CRACK LIKE THAT OUT O' YUH AN' YUH WON'T BE ALIVE!
OW!
THAT'S JEST ANOTHER NEW GAME I INVENTED! IT'S CALLED "LOOP THUH SNOZZLE!"

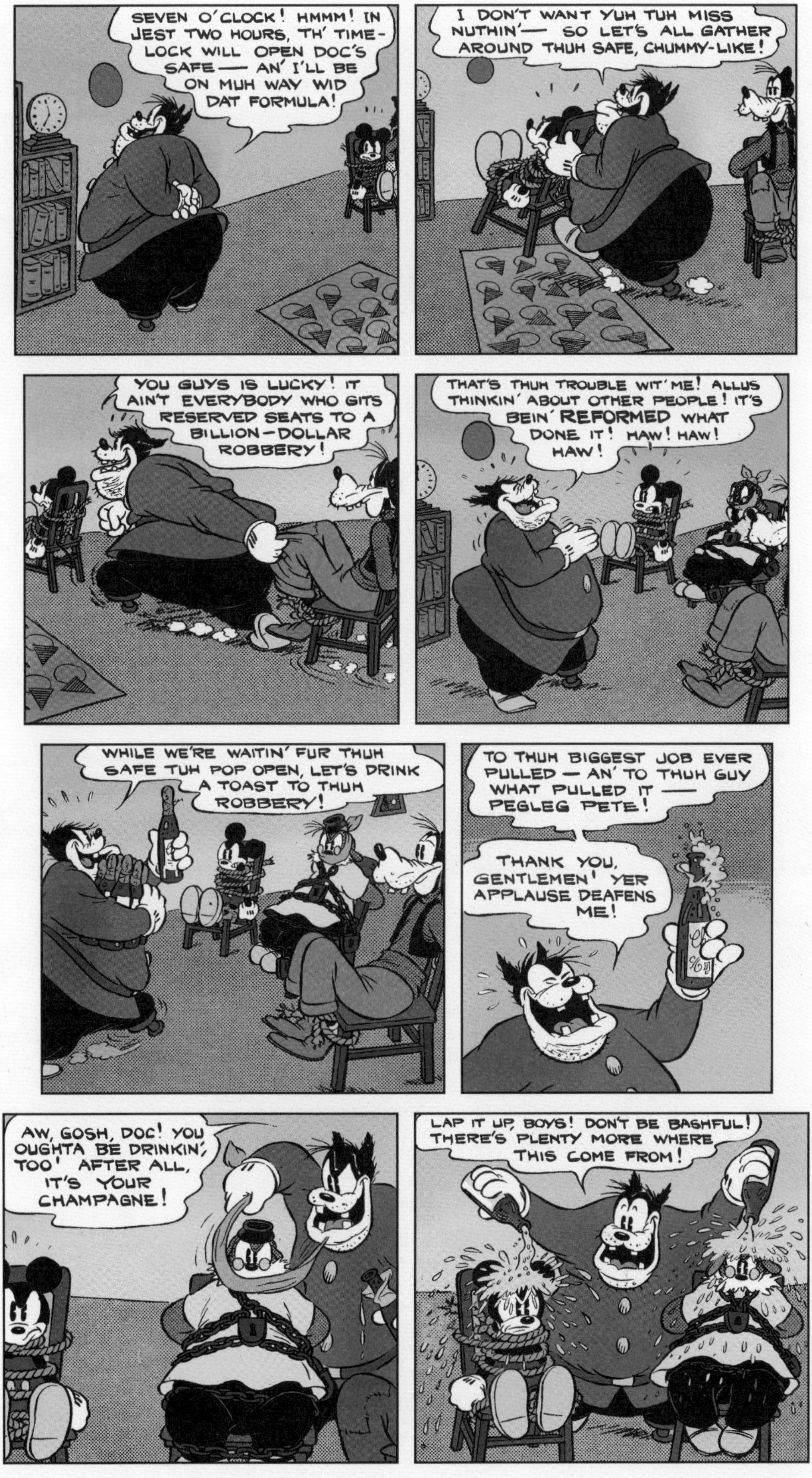
SEVEN O'CLOCK! HMMM! IN JEST TWO HOURS, TH' TIME-LOCK WILL OPEN DOC'S SAFE — AN' I'LL BE ON MUH WAY WID DAT FORMULA!
I DON'T WANT YUH TUH MISS NUTHIN'— SO LET'S ALL GATHER AROUND THUH SAFE, CHUMMY-LIKE!
YOU GUYS IS LUCKY! IT AIN'T EVERYBODY WHO GITS RESERVED SEATS TO A BILLION-DOLLAR ROBBERY!
THAT'S THUH TROUBLE WIT' ME! ALLUS THINKIN' ABOUT OTHER PEOPLE! IT'S BEIN' REFORMED WHAT DONE IT! HAW! HAW! HAW!
WHILE WE'RE WAITIN' FUR THUH SAFE TUH POP OPEN, LET'S DRINK A TOAST TO THUH ROBBERY!
TO THUH BIGGEST JOB EVER PULLED — AN' TO THUH GUY WHAT PULLED IT — PEGLEG PETE!
THANK YOU, GENTLEMEN! YER APPLAUSE DEAFENS ME!
AW, GOSH, DOC! YOU OUGHTA BE DRINKIN', TOO! AFTER ALL, IT'S YOUR CHAMPAGNE!
LAP IT UP, BOYS! DON'T BE BASHFUL! THERE'S PLENTY MORE WHERE THIS COME FROM!

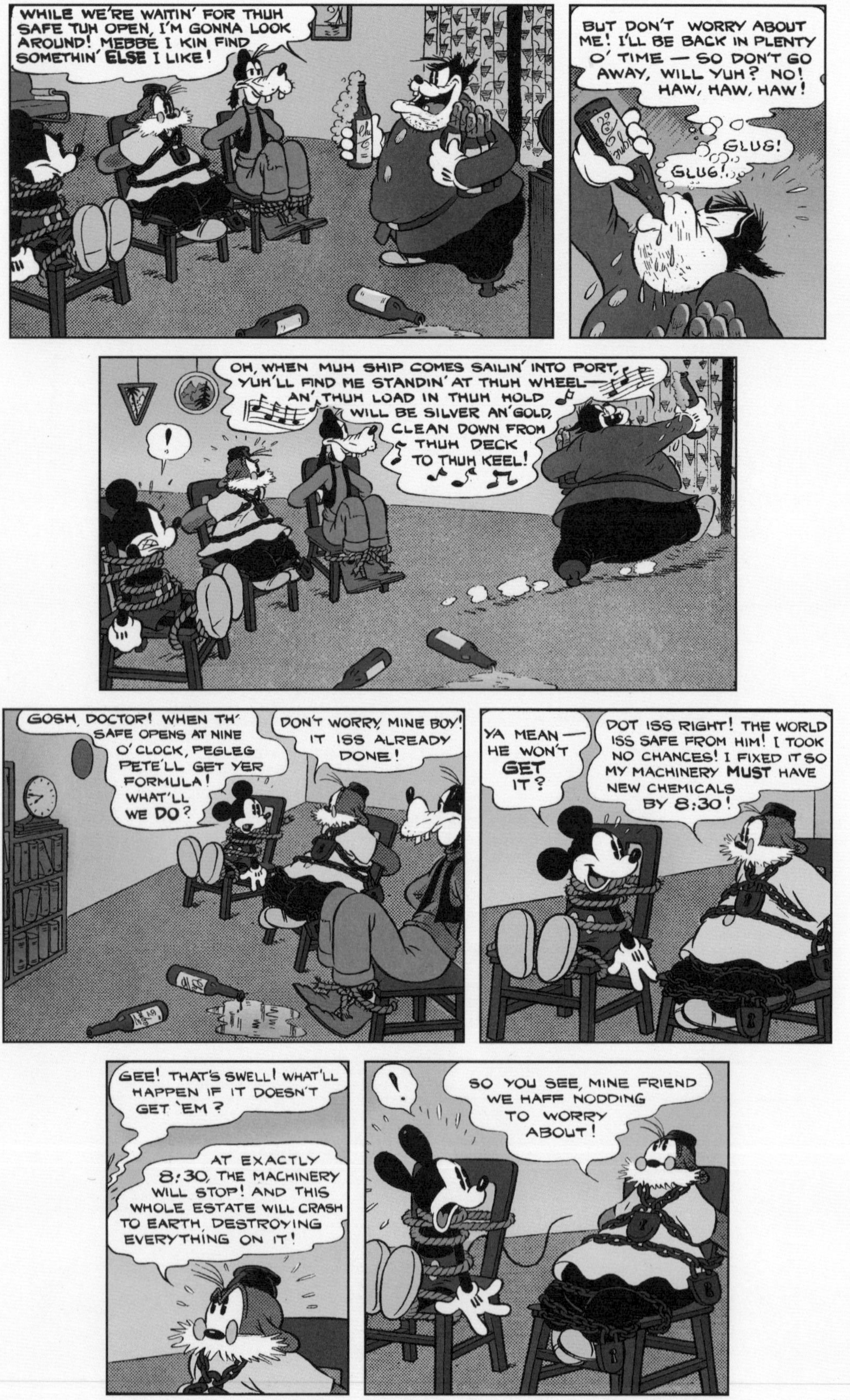
WHILE WE'RE WAITIN' FOR THUH SAFE TUH OPEN, I'M GONNA LOOK AROUND! MEBBE I KIN FIND SOMETHIN' ELSE I LIKE!
BUT DON'T WORRY ABOUT ME! I'LL BE BACK IN PLENTY O' TIME — SO DON'T GO AWAY, WILL YUH? NO! HAW, HAW, HAW!
GLUG!
GLUG!
OH, WHEN MUH SHIP COMES SAILIN' INTO PORT, YUH'LL FIND ME STANDIN' AT THUH WHEEL— AN' THUH LOAD IN THUH HOLD WILL BE SILVER AN' GOLD, CLEAN DOWN FROM THUH DECK TO THUH KEEL!
!
GOSH, DOCTOR! WHEN TH' SAFE OPENS AT NINE O'CLOCK, PEGLEG PETE'LL GET YER FORMULA! WHAT'LL WE DO?
DON'T WORRY, MINE BOY! IT ISS ALREADY DONE!
YA MEAN — HE WON'T GET IT?
DOT ISS RIGHT! THE WORLD ISS SAFE FROM HIM! I TOOK NO CHANCES! I FIXED IT SO MY MACHINERY MUST HAVE NEW CHEMICALS BY 8:30!
GEE! THAT'S SWELL! WHAT'LL HAPPEN IF IT DOESN'T GET 'EM?
AT EXACTLY 8:30, THE MACHINERY WILL STOP! AND THIS WHOLE ESTATE WILL CRASH TO EARTH, DESTROYING EVERYTHING ON IT!
!
SO YOU SEE, MINE FRIEND WE HAFF NODDING TO WORRY ABOUT!

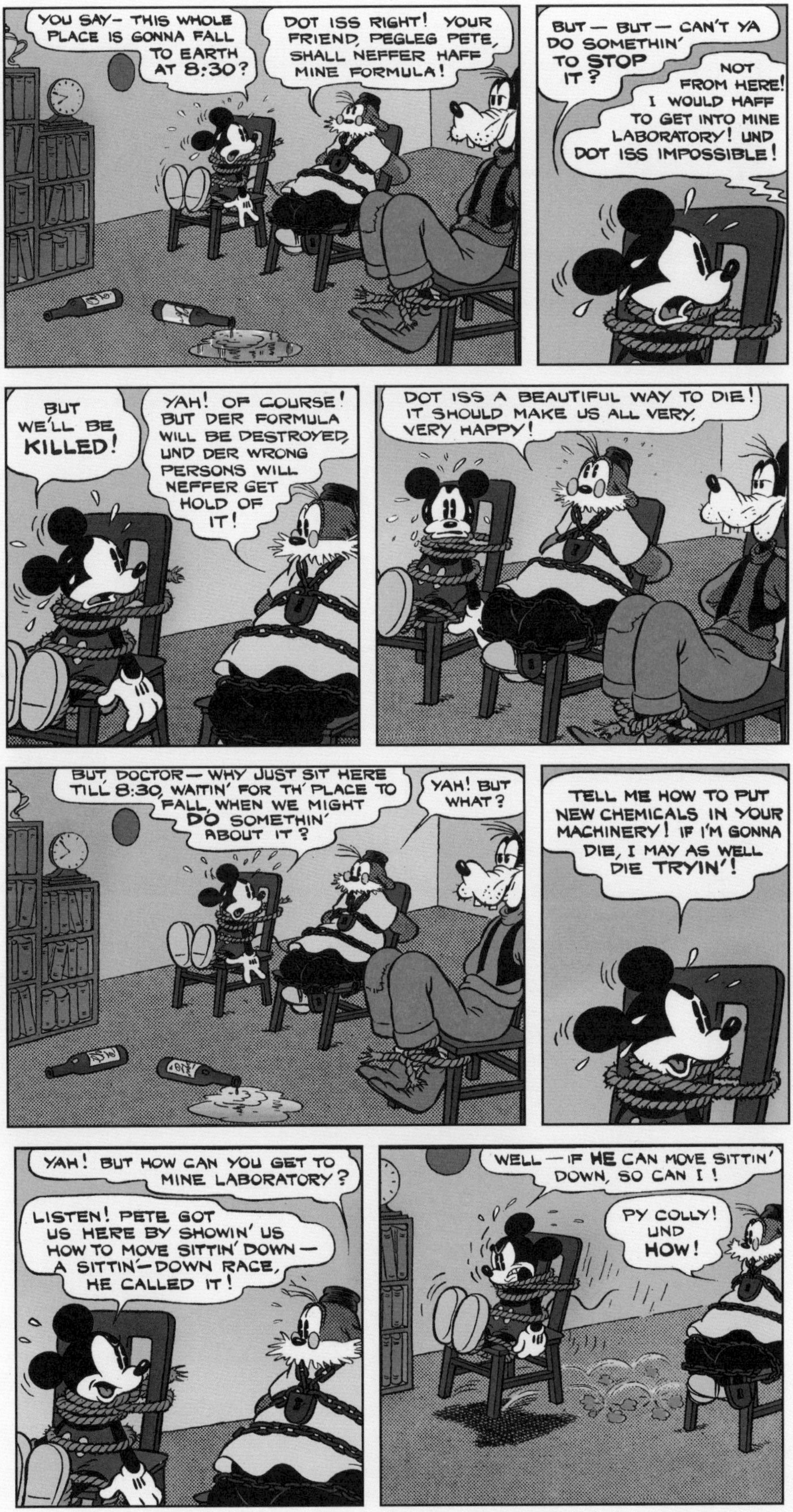
YOU SAY– THIS WHOLE PLACE IS GONNA FALL TO EARTH AT 8:30?
DOT ISS RIGHT! YOUR FRIEND, PEGLEG PETE, SHALL NEFFER HAFF MINE FORMULA!
BUT — BUT — CAN'T YA DO SOMETHIN' TO STOP IT?
NOT FROM HERE! I WOULD HAFF TO GET INTO MINE LABORATORY! UND DOT ISS IMPOSSIBLE!
BUT WE'LL BE KILLED!
YAH! OF COURSE! BUT DER FORMULA WILL BE DESTROYED, UND DER WRONG PERSONS WILL NEFFER GET HOLD OF IT!
DOT ISS A BEAUTIFUL WAY TO DIE! IT SHOULD MAKE US ALL VERY, VERY HAPPY!
BUT, DOCTOR— WHY JUST SIT HERE TILL 8:30, WAITIN' FOR TH' PLACE TO FALL, WHEN WE MIGHT DO SOMETHIN' ABOUT IT?
YAH! BUT WHAT?
TELL ME HOW TO PUT NEW CHEMICALS IN YOUR MACHINERY! IF I'M GONNA DIE, I MAY AS WELL DIE TRYIN'!
YAH! BUT HOW CAN YOU GET TO MINE LABORATORY?
LISTEN! PETE GOT US HERE BY SHOWIN' US HOW TO MOVE SITTIN' DOWN— A SITTIN'-DOWN RACE, HE CALLED IT!
WELL— IF HE CAN MOVE SITTIN' DOWN, SO CAN I!
PY COLLY! UND HOW!

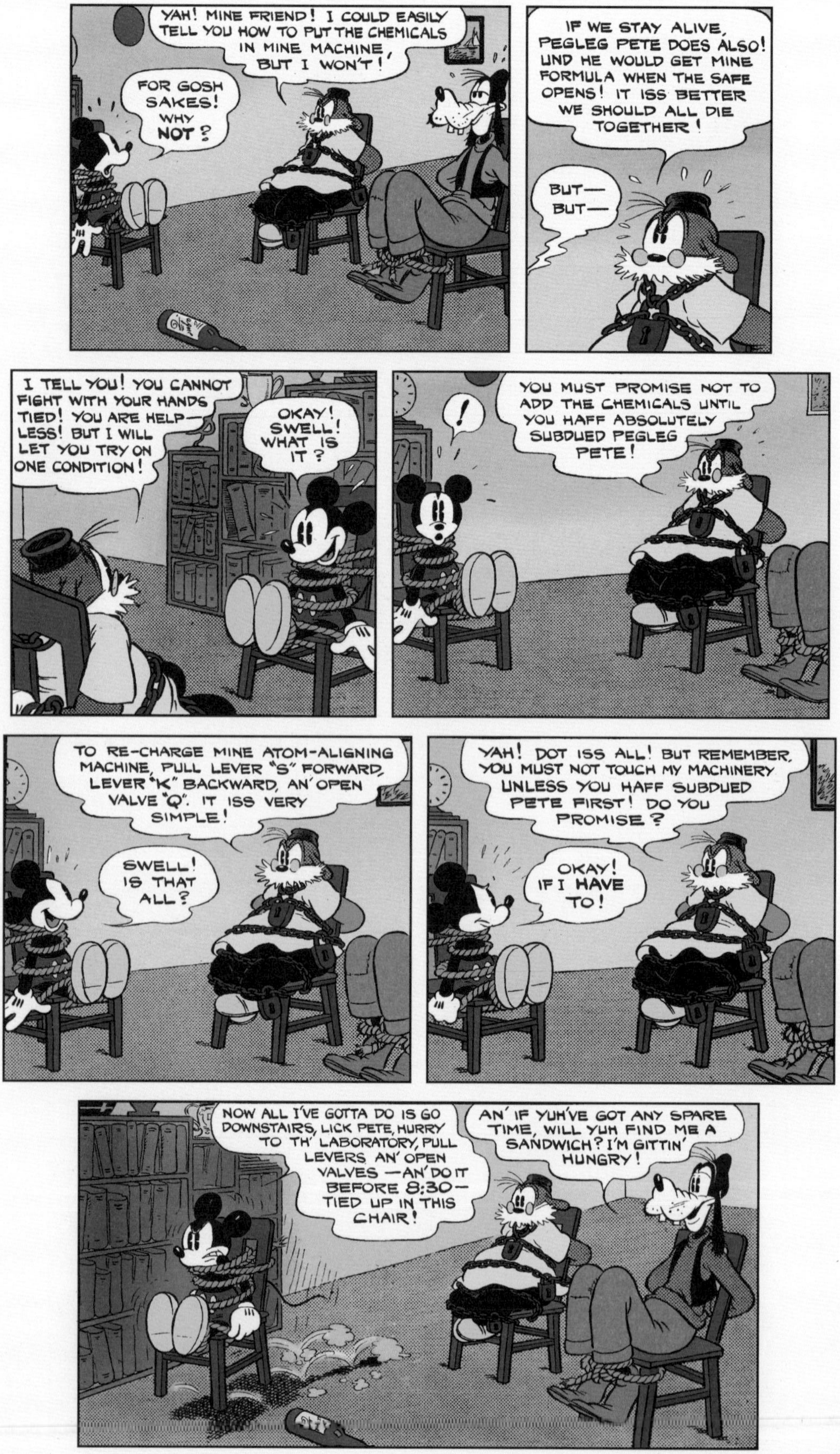
YAH! MINE FRIEND! I COULD EASILY TELL YOU HOW TO PUT THE CHEMICALS IN MINE MACHINE, BUT I WON'T!
FOR GOSH SAKES! WHY NOT?
IF WE STAY ALIVE, PEGLEG PETE DOES ALSO! UND HE WOULD GET MINE FORMULA WHEN THE SAFE OPENS! IT ISS BETTER WE SHOULD ALL DIE TOGETHER!
BUT— BUT—
I TELL YOU! YOU CANNOT FIGHT WITH YOUR HANDS TIED! YOU ARE HELP-LESS! BUT I WILL LET YOU TRY ON ONE CONDITION!
OKAY! SWELL! WHAT IS IT?
!
YOU MUST PROMISE NOT TO ADD THE CHEMICALS UNTIL YOU HAFF ABSOLUTELY SUBDUED PEGLEG PETE!
TO RE-CHARGE MINE ATOM-ALIGNING MACHINE, PULL LEVER "S" FORWARD, LEVER "K" BACKWARD, AN' OPEN VALVE "Q". IT ISS VERY SIMPLE!
SWELL! IS THAT ALL?
YAH! DOT ISS ALL! BUT REMEMBER, YOU MUST NOT TOUCH MY MACHINERY UNLESS YOU HAFF SUBDUED PETE FIRST! DO YOU PROMISE?
OKAY! IF I HAVE TO!
NOW ALL I'VE GOTTA DO IS GO DOWNSTAIRS, LICK PETE, HURRY TO TH' LABORATORY, PULL LEVERS AN' OPEN VALVES —AN' DO IT BEFORE 8:30— TIED UP IN THIS CHAIR!
AN' IF YUH'VE GOT ANY SPARE TIME, WILL YUH FIND ME A SANDWICH? I'M GITTIN' HUNGRY!

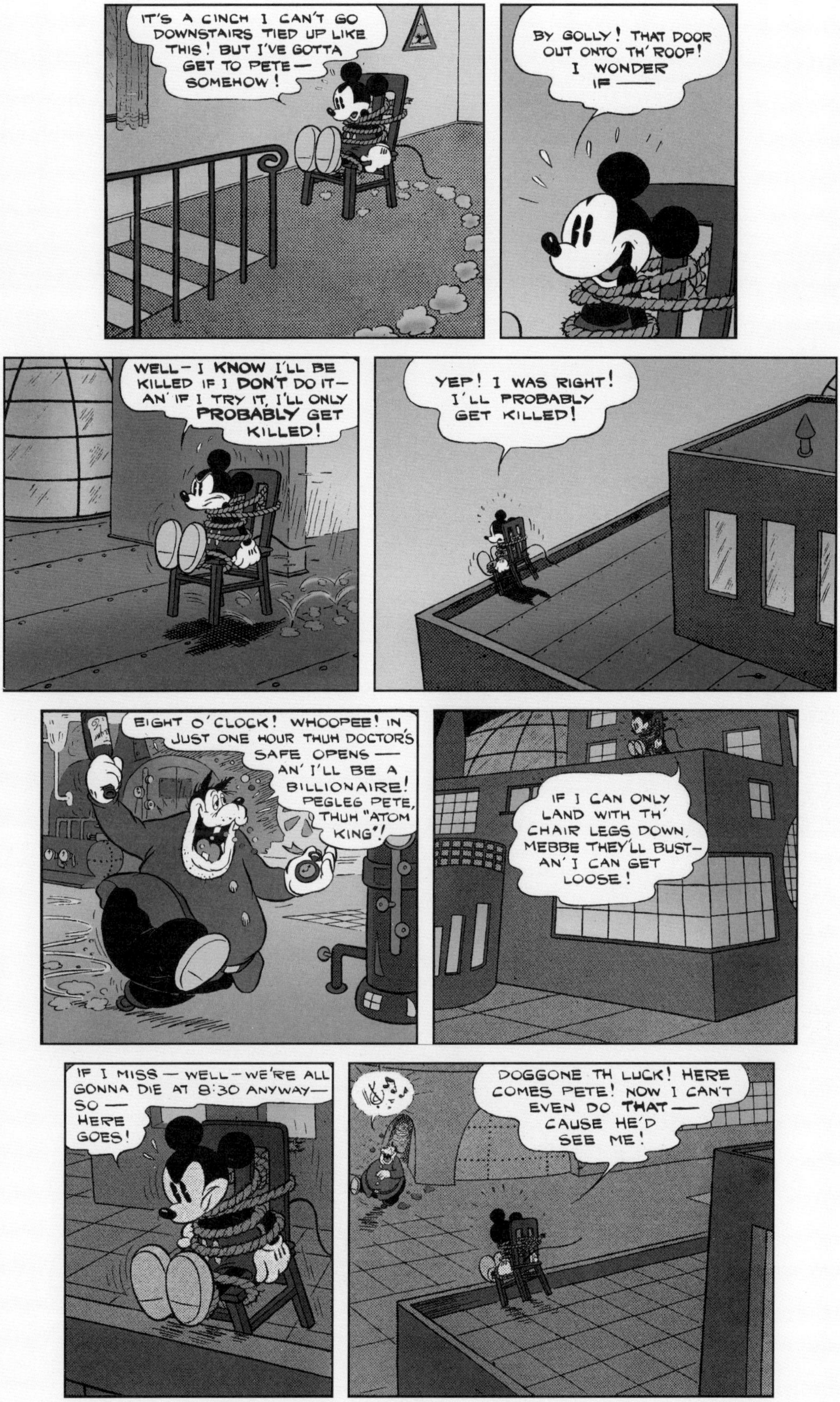
IT'S A CINCH I CAN'T GO DOWNSTAIRS TIED UP LIKE THIS! BUT I'VE GOTTA GET TO PETE — SOMEHOW!
BY GOLLY! THAT DOOR OUT ONTO TH' ROOF! I WONDER IF ——
WELL— I KNOW I'LL BE KILLED IF I DON'T DO IT— AN' IF I TRY IT, I'LL ONLY PROBABLY GET KILLED!
YEP! I WAS RIGHT! I'LL PROBABLY GET KILLED!
EIGHT O'CLOCK! WHOOPEE! IN JUST ONE HOUR THUH DOCTOR'S SAFE OPENS — AN' I'LL BE A BILLIONAIRE! PEGLEG PETE, THUH "ATOM KING"!
IF I CAN ONLY LAND WITH TH' CHAIR LEGS DOWN, MEBBE THEY'LL BUST— AN' I CAN GET LOOSE!
IF I MISS — WELL — WE'RE ALL GONNA DIE AT 8:30 ANYWAY— SO — HERE GOES!
DOGGONE TH LUCK! HERE COMES PETE! NOW I CAN'T EVEN DO THAT — CAUSE HE'D SEE ME!

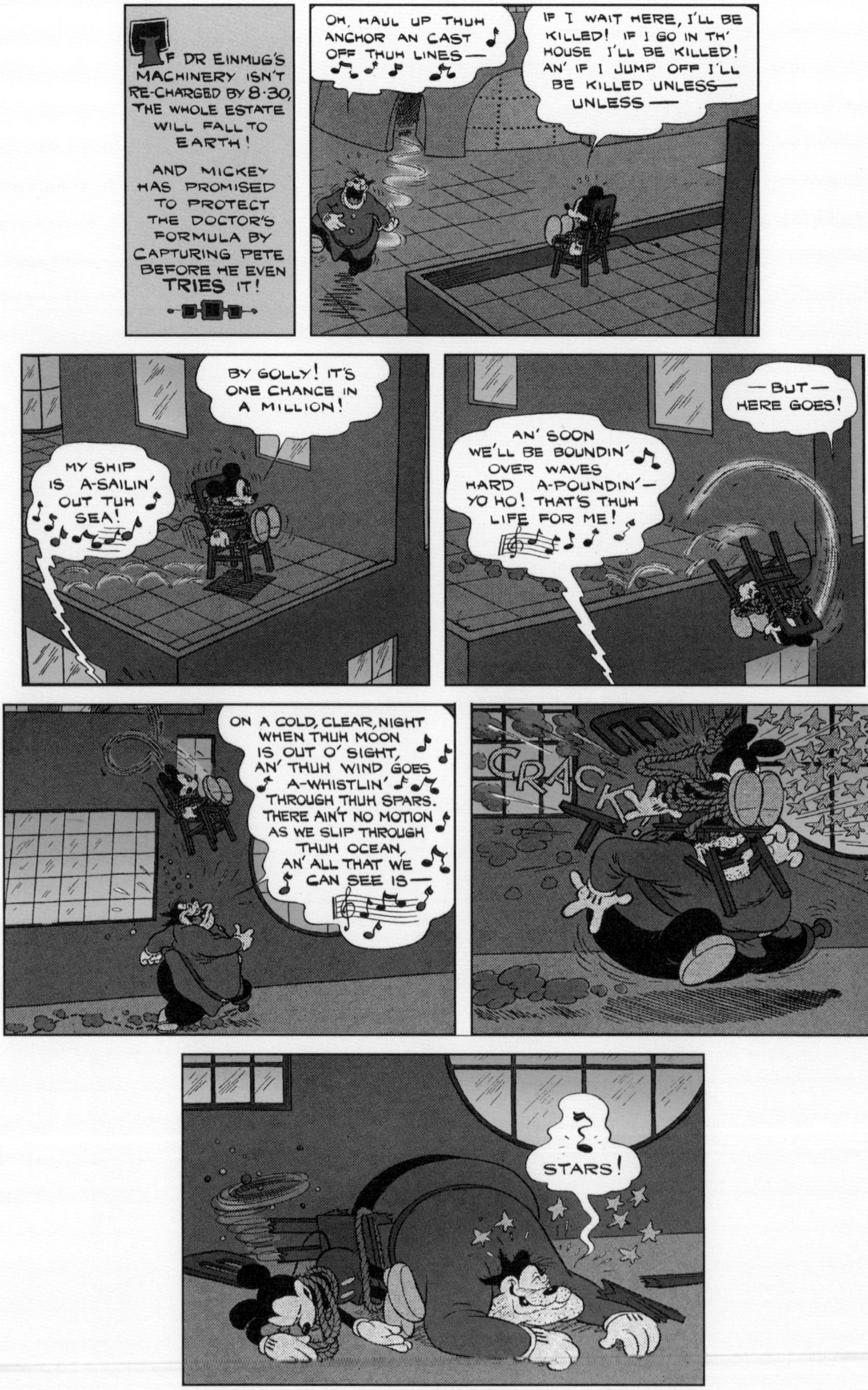
IF DR EINMUG'S MACHINERY ISN'T RE-CHARGED BY 8·30, THE WHOLE ESTATE WILL FALL TO EARTH!
AND MICKEY HAS PROMISED TO PROTECT THE DOCTOR'S FORMULA BY CAPTURING PETE BEFORE HE EVEN TRIES IT!
OH, HAUL UP THUH ANCHOR AN CAST OFF THUH LINES—
IF I WAIT HERE, I'LL BE KILLED! IF I GO IN TH' HOUSE I'LL BE KILLED! AN' IF I JUMP OFF I'LL BE KILLED UNLESS— UNLESS—
MY SHIP IS A-SAILIN' OUT TUH SEA!
BY GOLLY! IT'S ONE CHANCE IN A MILLION!
AN' SOON WE'LL BE BOUNDIN' OVER WAVES HARD A-POUNDIN'— YO HO! THAT'S THUH LIFE FOR ME!
—BUT— HERE GOES!
ON A COLD, CLEAR, NIGHT WHEN THUH MOON IS OUT O' SIGHT, AN' THUH WIND GOES A-WHISTLIN' THROUGH THUH SPARS. THERE AIN'T NO MOTION AS WE SLIP THROUGH THUH OCEAN, AN' ALL THAT WE CAN SEE IS—
CRACK
STARS!

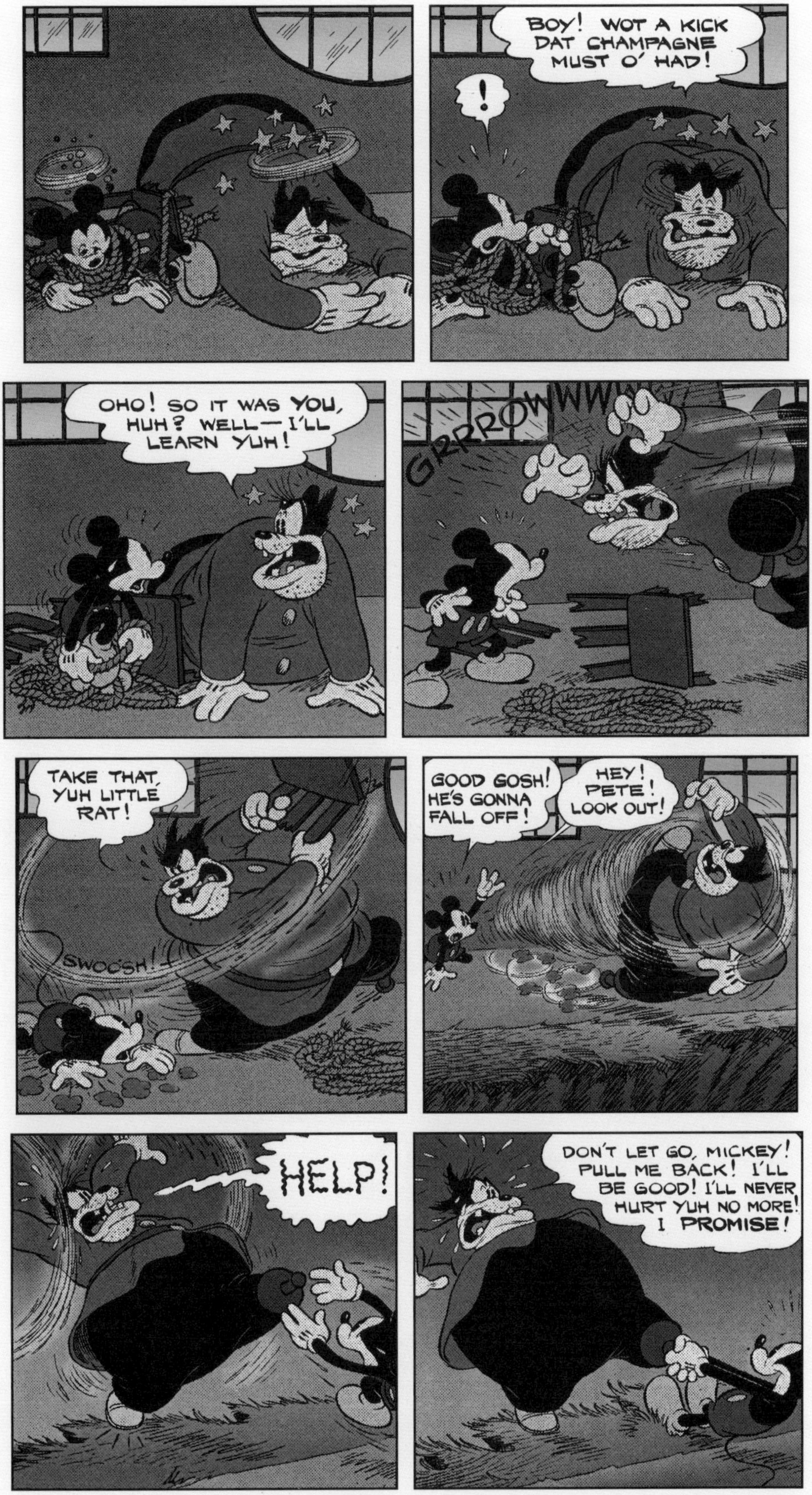
BOY! WOT A KICK DAT CHAMPAGNE MUST O' HAD!
!
OHO! SO IT WAS YOU, HUH? WELL—I'LL LEARN YUH!
GRRROWWW
TAKE THAT, YUH LITTLE RAT!
SWOOSH!
GOOD GOSH! HE'S GONNA FALL OFF!
HEY! PETE! LOOK OUT!
HELP!
DON'T LET GO, MICKEY! PULL ME BACK! I'LL BE GOOD! I'LL NEVER HURT YUH NO MORE! I PROMISE!

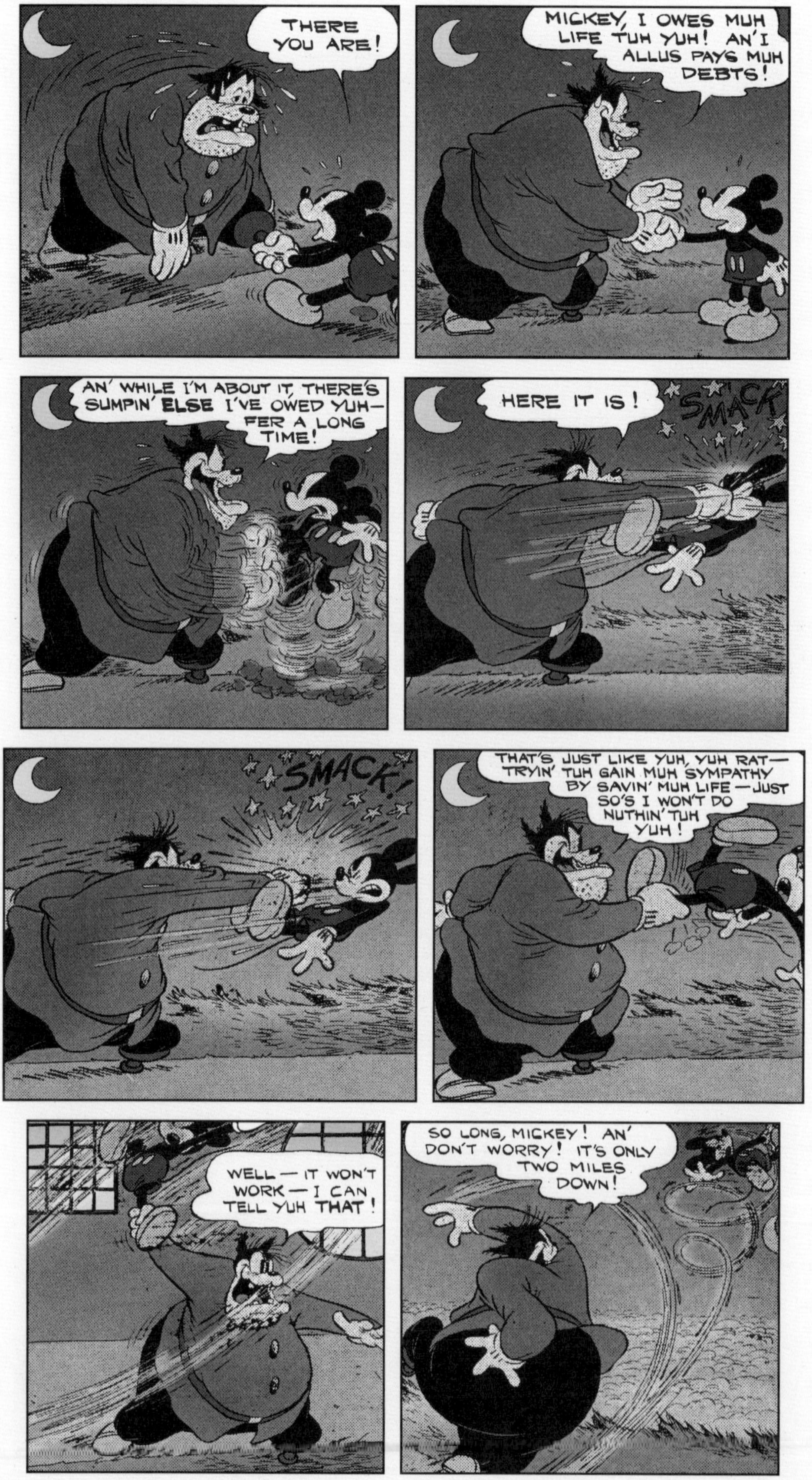
THERE YOU ARE!
MICKEY, I OWES MUH LIFE TUH YUH! AN' I ALLUS PAYS MUH DEBTS!
AN' WHILE I'M ABOUT IT THERE'S SUMPIN' ELSE I'VE OWED YUH— FER A LONG TIME!
HERE IT IS!
SMACK
SMACK!
THAT'S JUST LIKE YUH, YUH RAT— TRYIN' TUH GAIN MUH SYMPATHY BY SAVIN' MUH LIFE—JUST SO'S I WON'T DO NUTHIN' TUH YUH!
WELL—IT WON'T WORK—I CAN TELL YUH THAT!
SO LONG, MICKEY! AN' DON'T WORRY! IT'S ONLY TWO MILES DOWN!

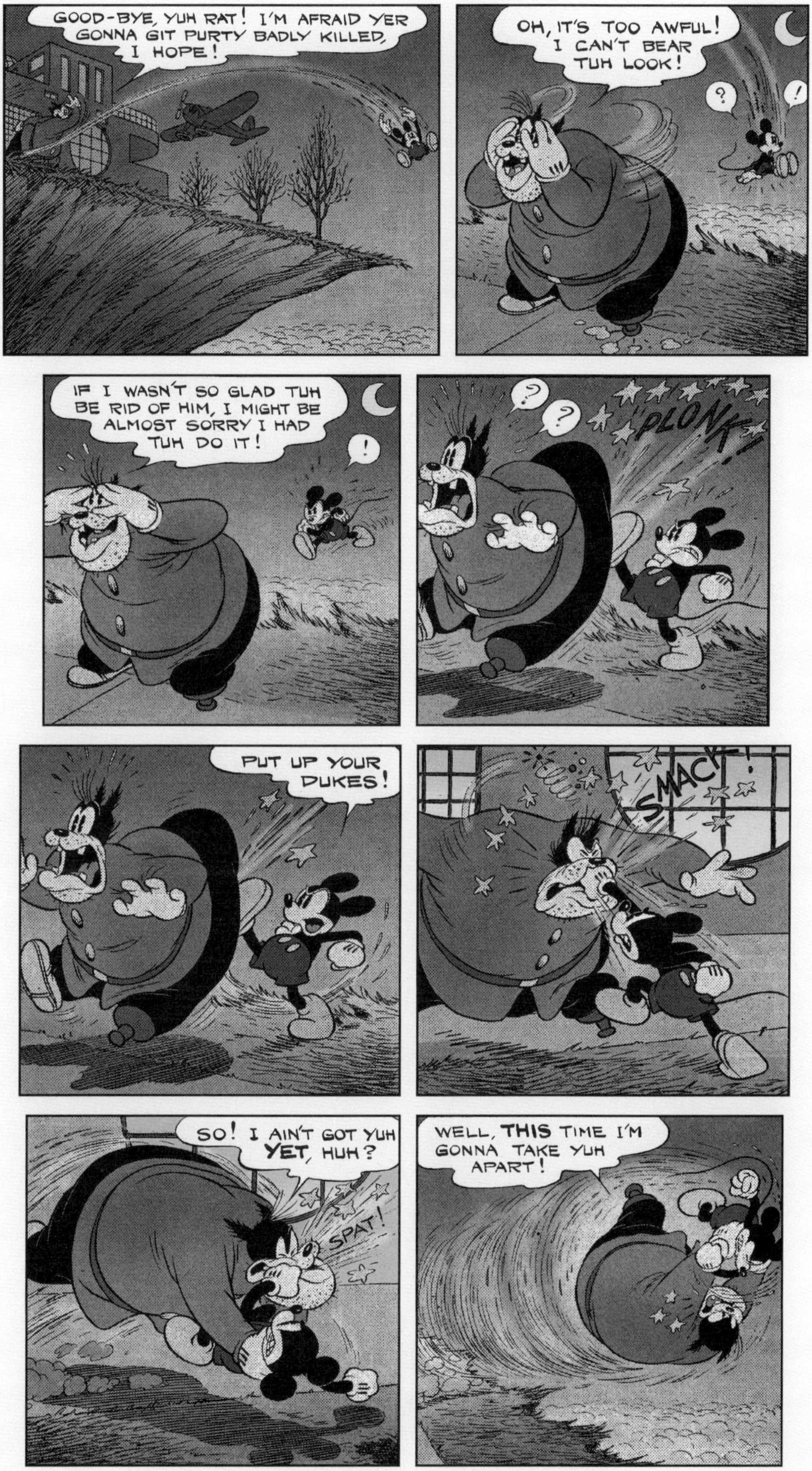
GOOD-BYE, YUH RAT! I'M AFRAID YER GONNA GIT PURTY BADLY KILLED, I HOPE!
OH, IT'S TOO AWFUL! I CAN'T BEAR TUH LOOK!
?
!
IF I WASN'T SO GLAD TUH BE RID OF HIM, I MIGHT BE ALMOST SORRY I HAD TUH DO IT!
!
?
?
PLONK!
PUT UP YOUR DUKES!
SMACK!
SO! I AIN'T GOT YUH YET, HUH?
SPAT!
WELL, THIS TIME I'M GONNA TAKE YUH APART!

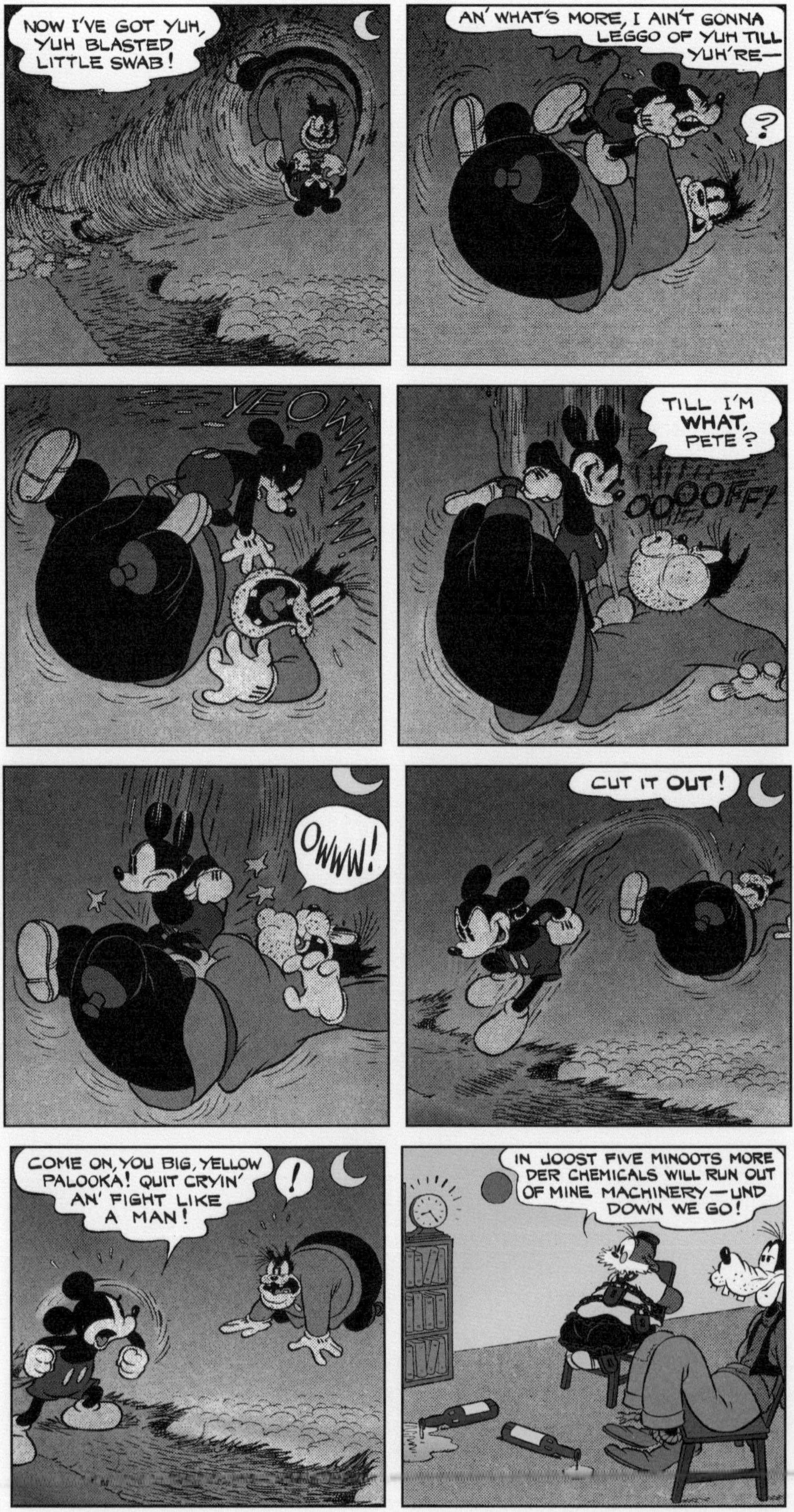
NOW I'VE GOT YUH, YUH BLASTED LITTLE SWAB!
AN' WHAT'S MORE, I AIN'T GONNA LEGGO OF YUH TILL YUH'RE—
?
YEOWWWWW!
TILL I'M WHAT, PETE?
OOOOFF!
OWWW!
CUT IT OUT!
COME ON, YOU BIG, YELLOW PALOOKA! QUIT CRYIN' AN' FIGHT LIKE A MAN!
!
IN JOOST FIVE MINOOTS MORE DER CHEMICALS WILL RUN OUT OF MINE MACHINERY—UND DOWN WE GO!

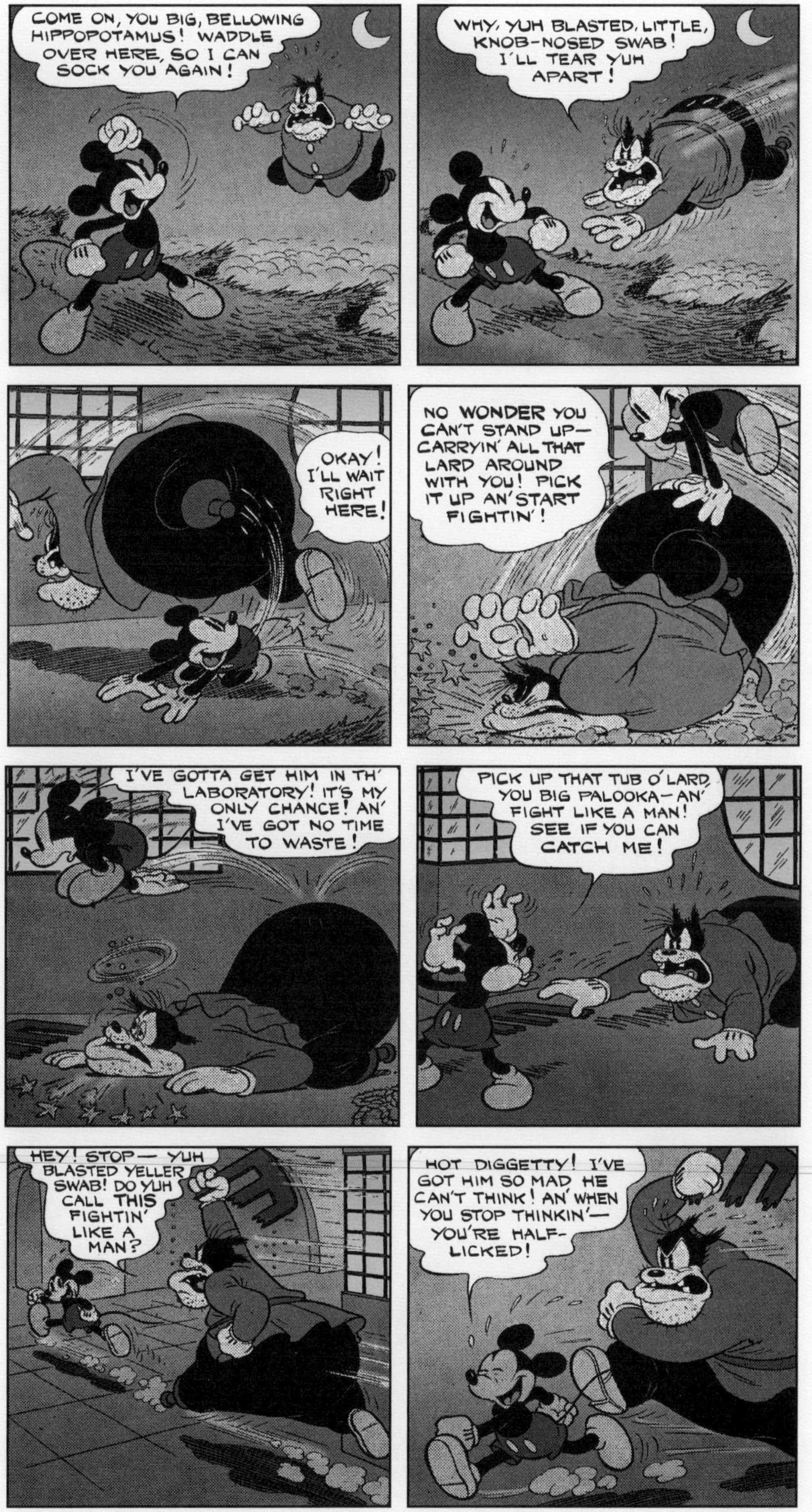
COME ON, YOU BIG, BELLOWING HIPPOPOTAMUS! WADDLE OVER HERE, SO I CAN SOCK YOU AGAIN!
WHY, YUH BLASTED, LITTLE, KNOB-NOSED SWAB! I'LL TEAR YUH APART!
OKAY! I'LL WAIT RIGHT HERE!
NO WONDER YOU CAN'T STAND UP— CARRYIN' ALL THAT LARD AROUND WITH YOU! PICK IT UP AN' START FIGHTIN'!
I'VE GOTTA GET HIM IN TH' LABORATORY! IT'S MY ONLY CHANCE! AN' I'VE GOT NO TIME TO WASTE!
PICK UP THAT TUB O' LARD, YOU BIG PALOOKA— AN' FIGHT LIKE A MAN! SEE IF YOU CAN CATCH ME!
HEY! STOP— YUH BLASTED YELLER SWAB! DO YUH CALL THIS FIGHTIN' LIKE A MAN?
HOT DIGGETTY! I'VE GOT HIM SO MAD HE CAN'T THINK! AN' WHEN YOU STOP THINKIN'— YOU'RE HALF-LICKED!

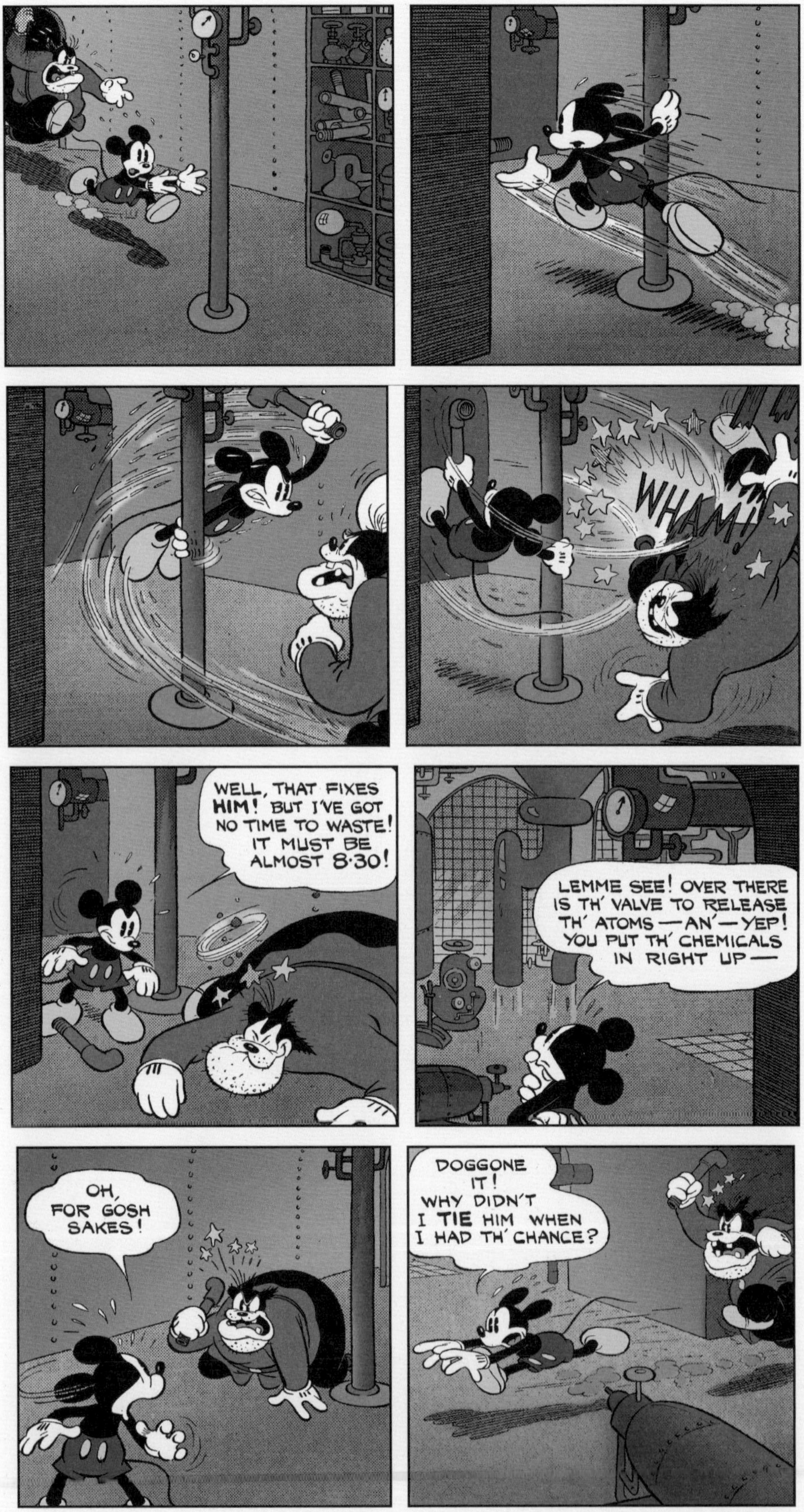
WHAM!
WELL, THAT FIXES HIM! BUT I'VE GOT NO TIME TO WASTE! IT MUST BE ALMOST 8:30!
LEMME SEE! OVER THERE IS TH' VALVE TO RELEASE TH' ATOMS — AN' — YEP! YOU PUT TH' CHEMICALS IN RIGHT UP —
OH, FOR GOSH SAKES!
DOGGONE IT! WHY DIDN'T I TIE HIM WHEN I HAD TH' CHANCE?

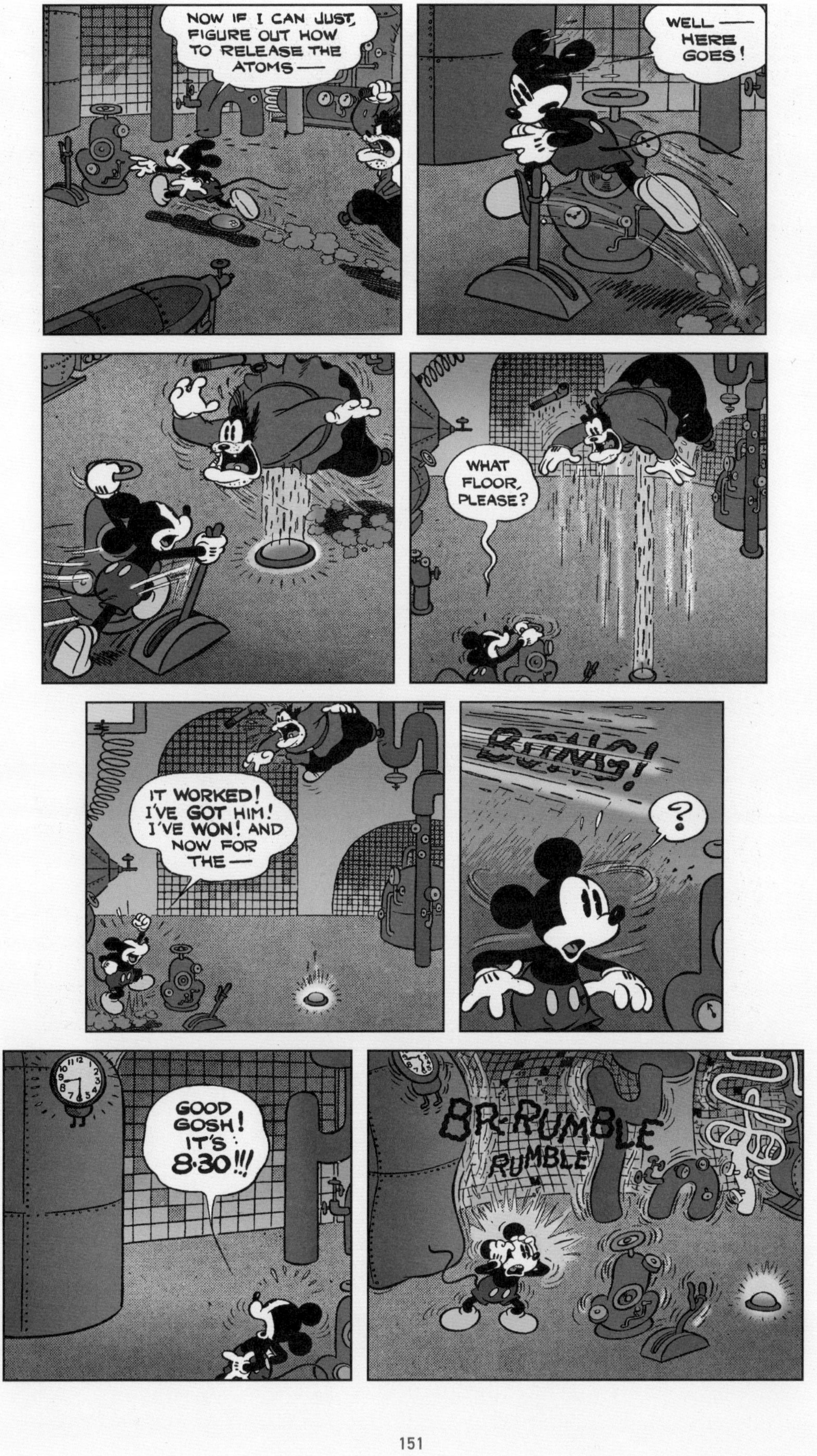
NOW IF I CAN JUST FIGURE OUT HOW TO RELEASE THE ATOMS —
WELL — HERE GOES!
WHAT FLOOR, PLEASE?
IT WORKED! I'VE GOT HIM! I'VE WON! AND NOW FOR THE —
BONG!
?
GOOD GOSH! IT'S 8:30!!!
BR-RUMBLE
RUMBLE

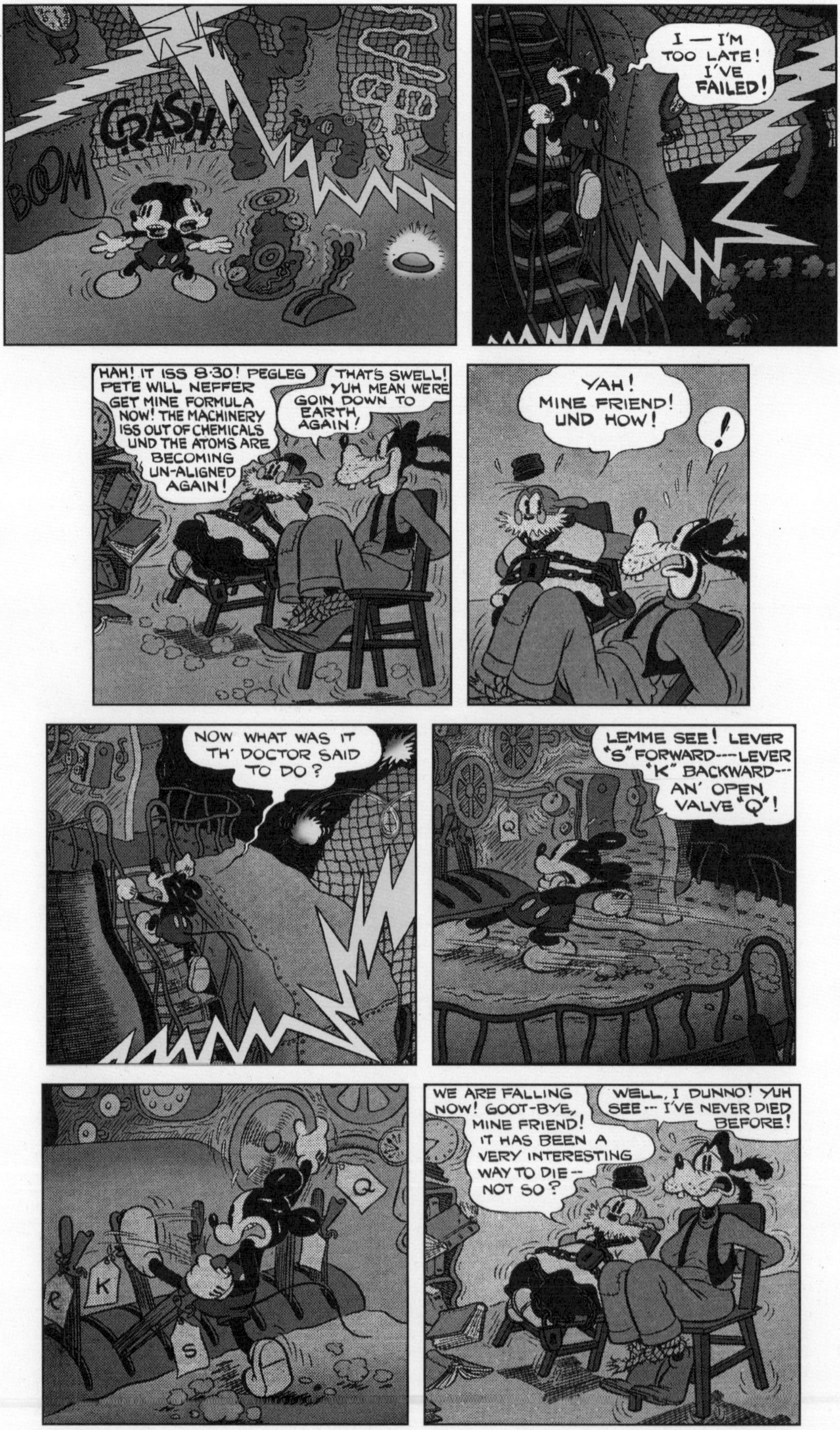
CRASH!
BOOM
I — I'M TOO LATE! I'VE FAILED!
HAH! IT ISS 8:30! PEGLEG PETE WILL NEFFER GET MINE FORMULA NOW! THE MACHINERY ISS OUT OF CHEMICALS UND THE ATOMS ARE BECOMING UN-ALIGNED AGAIN!
THAT'S SWELL! YUH MEAN WE'RE GOIN DOWN TO EARTH AGAIN!
YAH! MINE FRIEND! UND HOW!
!
NOW WHAT WAS IT TH' DOCTOR SAID TO DO?
LEMME SEE! LEVER "S" FORWARD---LEVER "K" BACKWARD--- AN' OPEN VALVE "Q"!
Q
K
S
Q
WE ARE FALLING NOW! GOOT-BYE, MINE FRIEND! IT HAS BEEN A VERY INTERESTING WAY TO DIE-- NOT SO?
WELL, I DUNNO! YUH SEE -- I'VE NEVER DIED BEFORE!

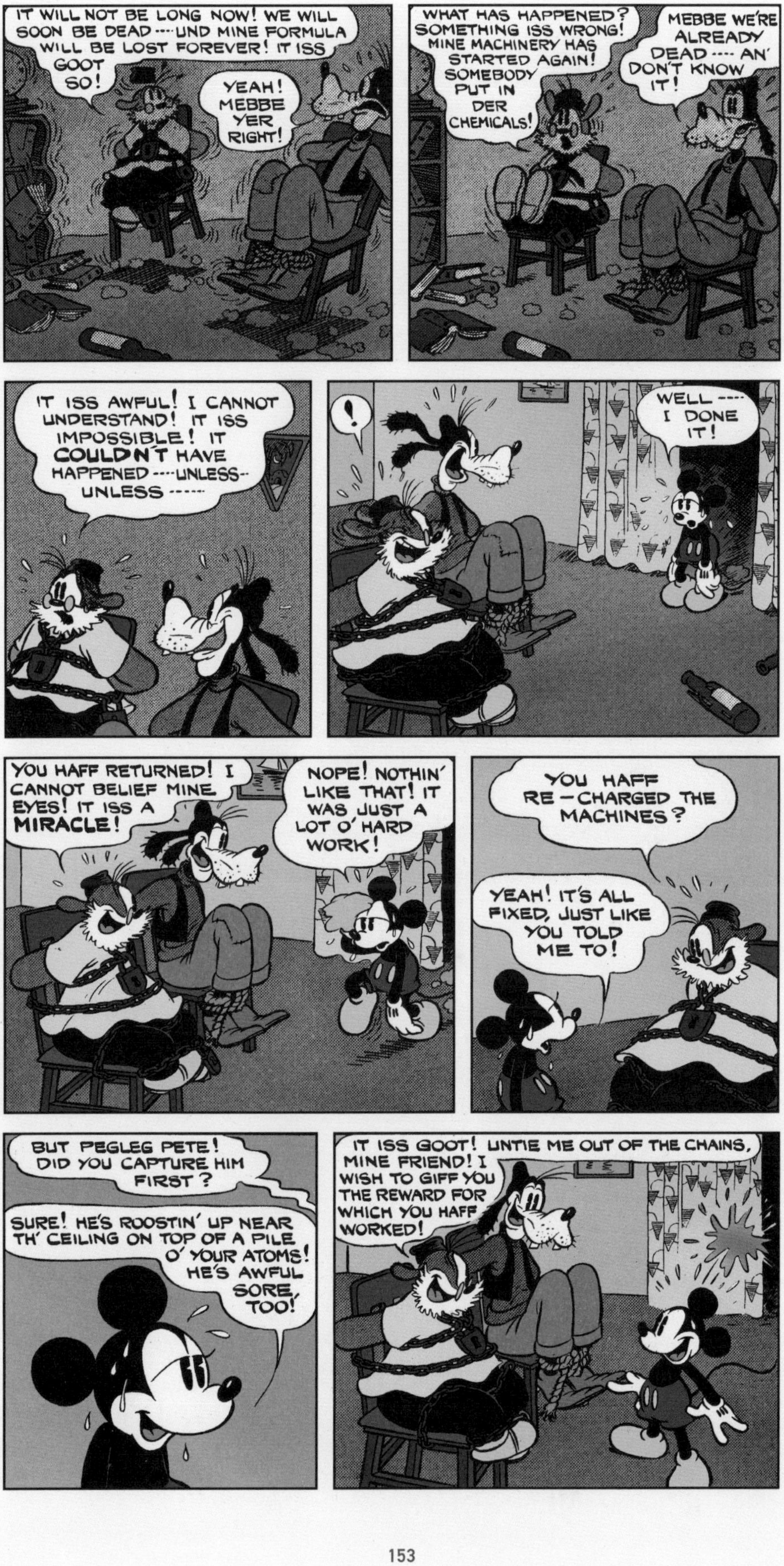
IT WILL NOT BE LONG NOW! WE WILL SOON BE DEAD ---- UND MINE FORMULA WILL BE LOST FOREVER! IT ISS GOOT SO!
YEAH! MEBBE YER RIGHT!
WHAT HAS HAPPENED? SOMETHING ISS WRONG! MINE MACHINERY HAS STARTED AGAIN! SOMEBODY PUT IN DER CHEMICALS!
MEBBE WE'RE ALREADY DEAD ---- AN' DON'T KNOW IT!
IT ISS AWFUL! I CANNOT UNDERSTAND! IT ISS IMPOSSIBLE! IT COULDN'T HAVE HAPPENED ---- UNLESS-- UNLESS -----
!
WELL ---- I DONE IT!
YOU HAFF RETURNED! I CANNOT BELIEF MINE EYES! IT ISS A MIRACLE!
NOPE! NOTHIN' LIKE THAT! IT WAS JUST A LOT O' HARD WORK!
YOU HAFF RE-CHARGED THE MACHINES?
YEAH! IT'S ALL FIXED, JUST LIKE YOU TOLD ME TO!
BUT PEGLEG PETE! DID YOU CAPTURE HIM FIRST?
SURE! HE'S ROOSTIN' UP NEAR TH' CEILING ON TOP OF A PILE O' YOUR ATOMS! HE'S AWFUL SORE, TOO!
IT ISS GOOT! UNTIE ME OUT OF THE CHAINS, MINE FRIEND! I WISH TO GIFF YOU THE REWARD FOR WHICH YOU HAFF WORKED!

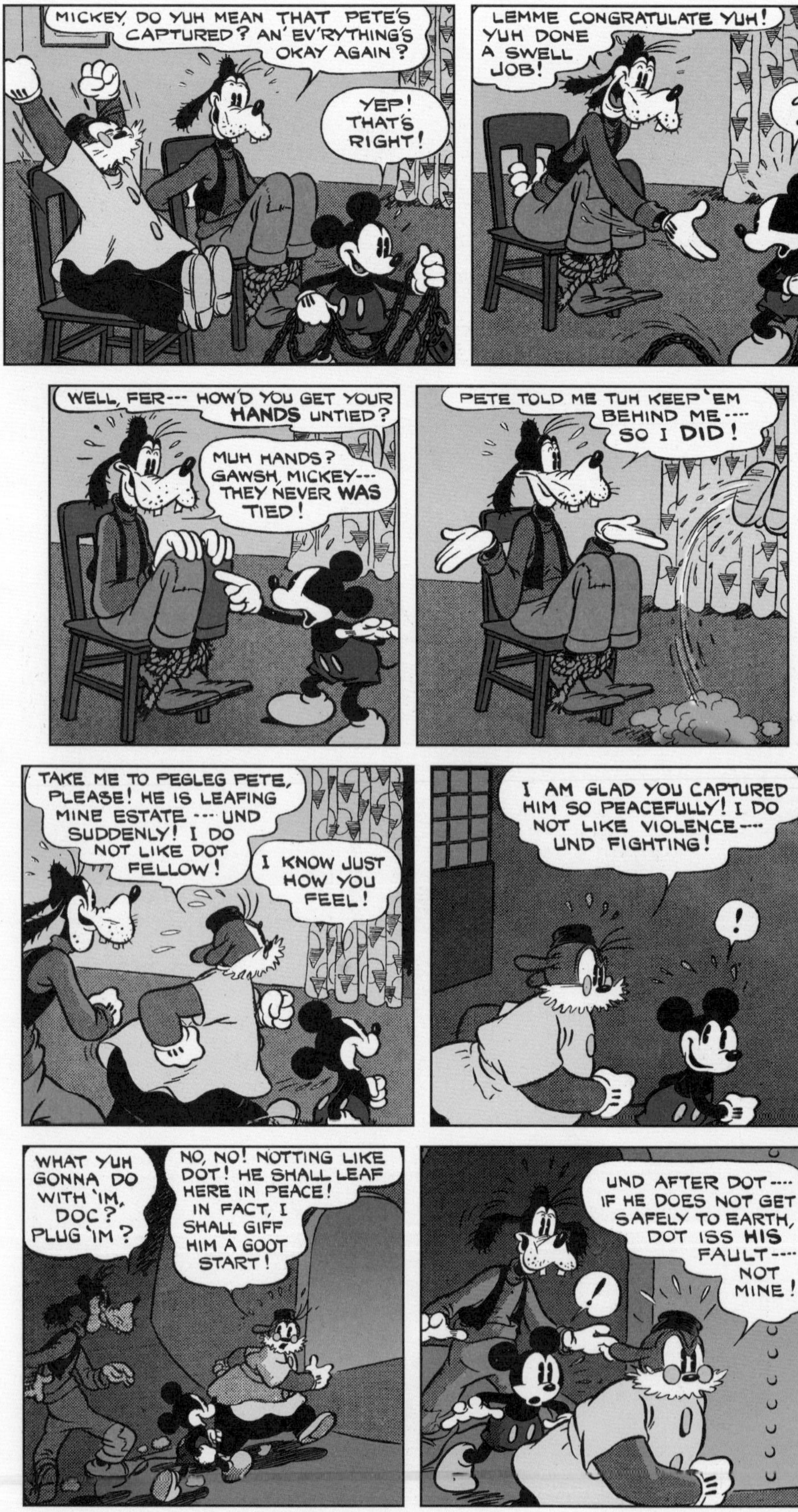
MICKEY, DO YUH MEAN THAT PETE'S CAPTURED? AN' EV'RYTHING'S OKAY AGAIN?
YEP! THAT'S RIGHT!
LEMME CONGRATULATE YUH! YUH DONE A SWELL JOB!
?
WELL, FER--- HOW'D YOU GET YOUR HANDS UNTIED?
MUH HANDS? GAWSH, MICKEY--- THEY NEVER WAS TIED!
PETE TOLD ME TUH KEEP 'EM BEHIND ME---- SO I DID!
TAKE ME TO PEGLEG PETE, PLEASE! HE IS LEAFING MINE ESTATE --- UND SUDDENLY! I DO NOT LIKE DOT FELLOW!
I KNOW JUST HOW YOU FEEL!
I AM GLAD YOU CAPTURED HIM SO PEACEFULLY! I DO NOT LIKE VIOLENCE---- UND FIGHTING!
!
WHAT YUH GONNA DO WITH 'IM, DOC? PLUG 'IM?
NO, NO! NOTTING LIKE DOT! HE SHALL LEAF HERE IN PEACE! IN FACT, I SHALL GIFF HIM A GOOT START!
UND AFTER DOT---- IF HE DOES NOT GET SAFELY TO EARTH, DOT ISS HIS FAULT---- NOT MINE!
!

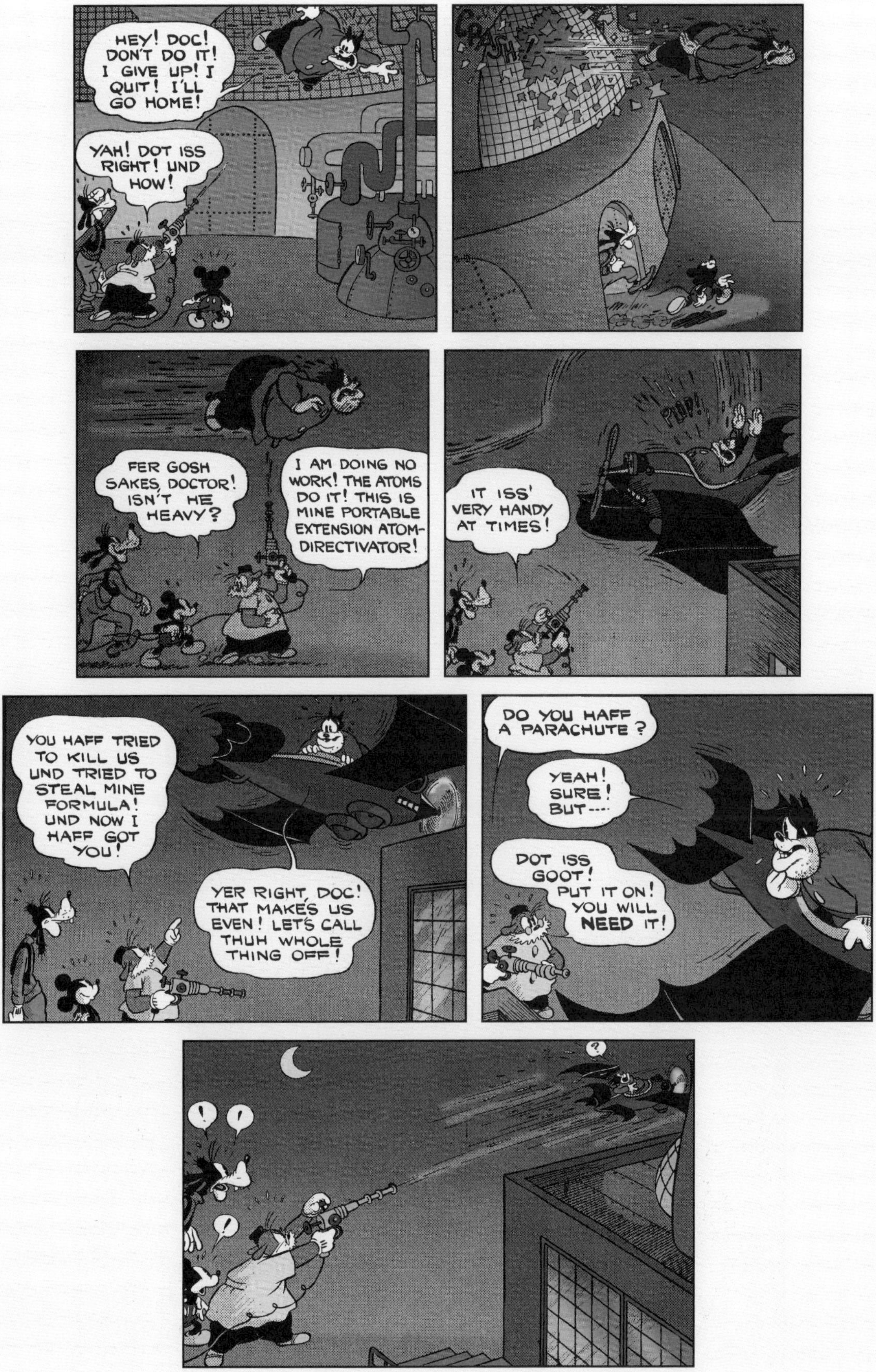
HEY! DOC! DON'T DO IT! I GIVE UP! I QUIT! I'LL GO HOME!
YAH! DOT ISS RIGHT! UND HOW!
CRASH!
FER GOSH SAKES, DOCTOR! ISN'T HE HEAVY?
I AM DOING NO WORK! THE ATOMS DO IT! THIS IS MINE PORTABLE EXTENSION ATOM-DIRECTIVATOR!
IT ISS' VERY HANDY AT TIMES!
YOU HAFF TRIED TO KILL US UND TRIED TO STEAL MINE FORMULA! UND NOW I HAFF GOT YOU!
YER RIGHT, DOC! THAT MAKES US EVEN! LET'S CALL THUH WHOLE THING OFF!
DO YOU HAFF A PARACHUTE?
YEAH! SURE! BUT----
DOT ISS GOOT! PUT IT ON! YOU WILL NEED IT!
!
!
!
?

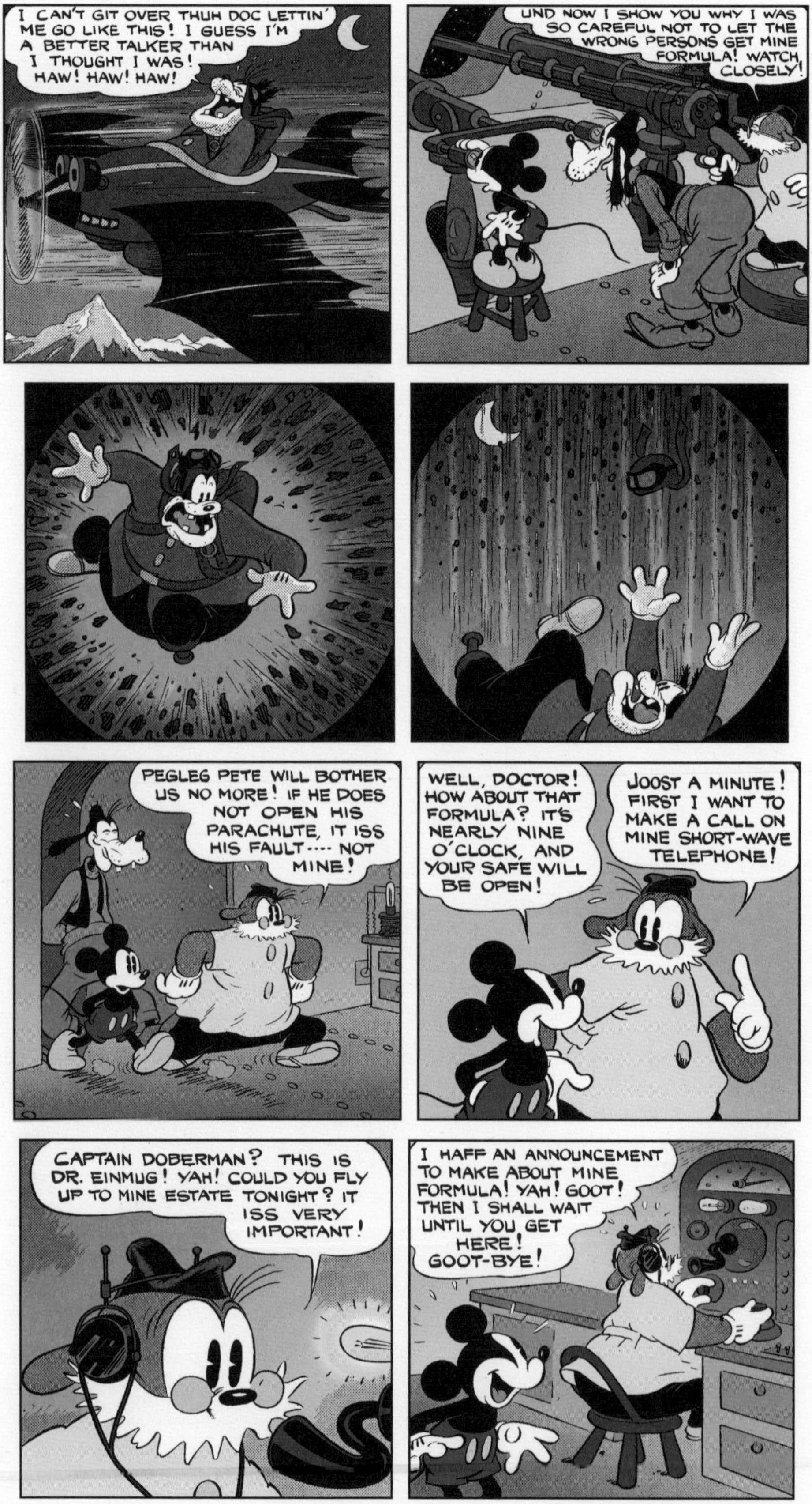
I CAN'T GIT OVER THUH DOC LETTIN' ME GO LIKE THIS! I GUESS I'M A BETTER TALKER THAN I THOUGHT I WAS! HAW! HAW! HAW!
UND NOW I SHOW YOU WHY I WAS SO CAREFUL NOT TO LET THE WRONG PERSONS GET MINE FORMULA! WATCH CLOSELY!
PEGLEG PETE WILL BOTHER US NO MORE! IF HE DOES NOT OPEN HIS PARACHUTE, IT ISS HIS FAULT---- NOT MINE!
WELL, DOCTOR! HOW ABOUT THAT FORMULA? IT'S NEARLY NINE O'CLOCK, AND YOUR SAFE WILL BE OPEN!
JOOST A MINUTE! FIRST I WANT TO MAKE A CALL ON MINE SHORT-WAVE TELEPHONE!
CAPTAIN DOBERMAN? THIS IS DR. EINMUG! YAH! COULD YOU FLY UP TO MINE ESTATE TONIGHT? IT ISS VERY IMPORTANT!
I HAFF AN ANNOUNCEMENT TO MAKE ABOUT MINE FORMULA! YAH! GOOT! THEN I SHALL WAIT UNTIL YOU GET HERE! GOOT-BYE!

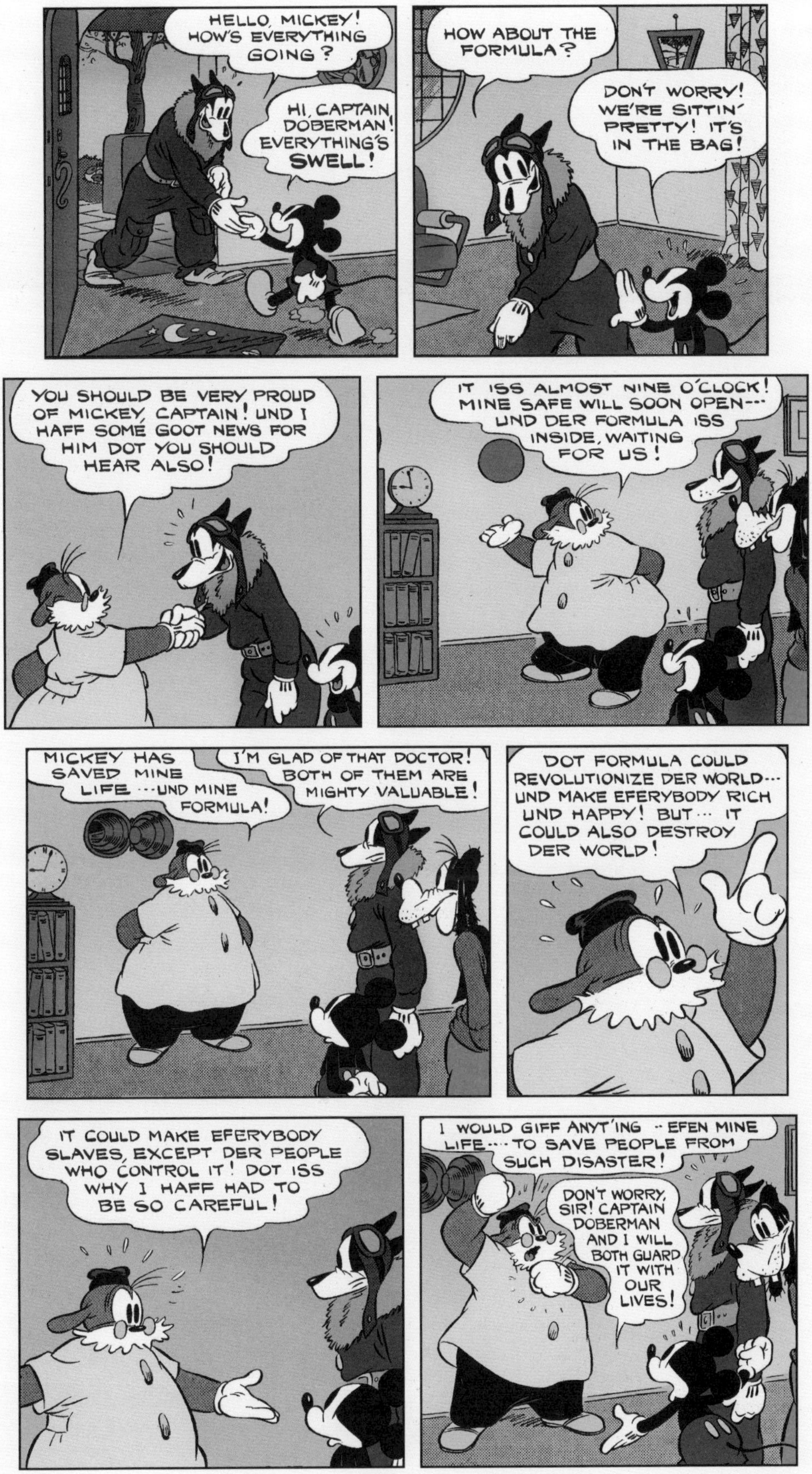
HELLO, MICKEY! HOW'S EVERYTHING GOING?
HI, CAPTAIN DOBERMAN! EVERYTHING'S SWELL!
HOW ABOUT THE FORMULA?
DON'T WORRY! WE'RE SITTIN' PRETTY! IT'S IN THE BAG!
YOU SHOULD BE VERY PROUD OF MICKEY, CAPTAIN! UND I HAFF SOME GOOT NEWS FOR HIM DOT YOU SHOULD HEAR ALSO!
IT ISS ALMOST NINE O'CLOCK! MINE SAFE WILL SOON OPEN--- UND DER FORMULA ISS INSIDE, WAITING FOR US!
MICKEY HAS SAVED MINE LIFE ---UND MINE FORMULA!
I'M GLAD OF THAT DOCTOR! BOTH OF THEM ARE MIGHTY VALUABLE!
DOT FORMULA COULD REVOLUTIONIZE DER WORLD--- UND MAKE EFERYBODY RICH UND HAPPY! BUT--- IT COULD ALSO DESTROY DER WORLD!
IT COULD MAKE EFERYBODY SLAVES, EXCEPT DER PEOPLE WHO CONTROL IT! DOT ISS WHY I HAFF HAD TO BE SO CAREFUL!
I WOULD GIFF ANYT'ING -- EFEN MINE LIFE--- TO SAVE PEOPLE FROM SUCH DISASTER!
DON'T WORRY, SIR! CAPTAIN DOBERMAN AND I WILL BOTH GUARD IT WITH OUR LIVES!

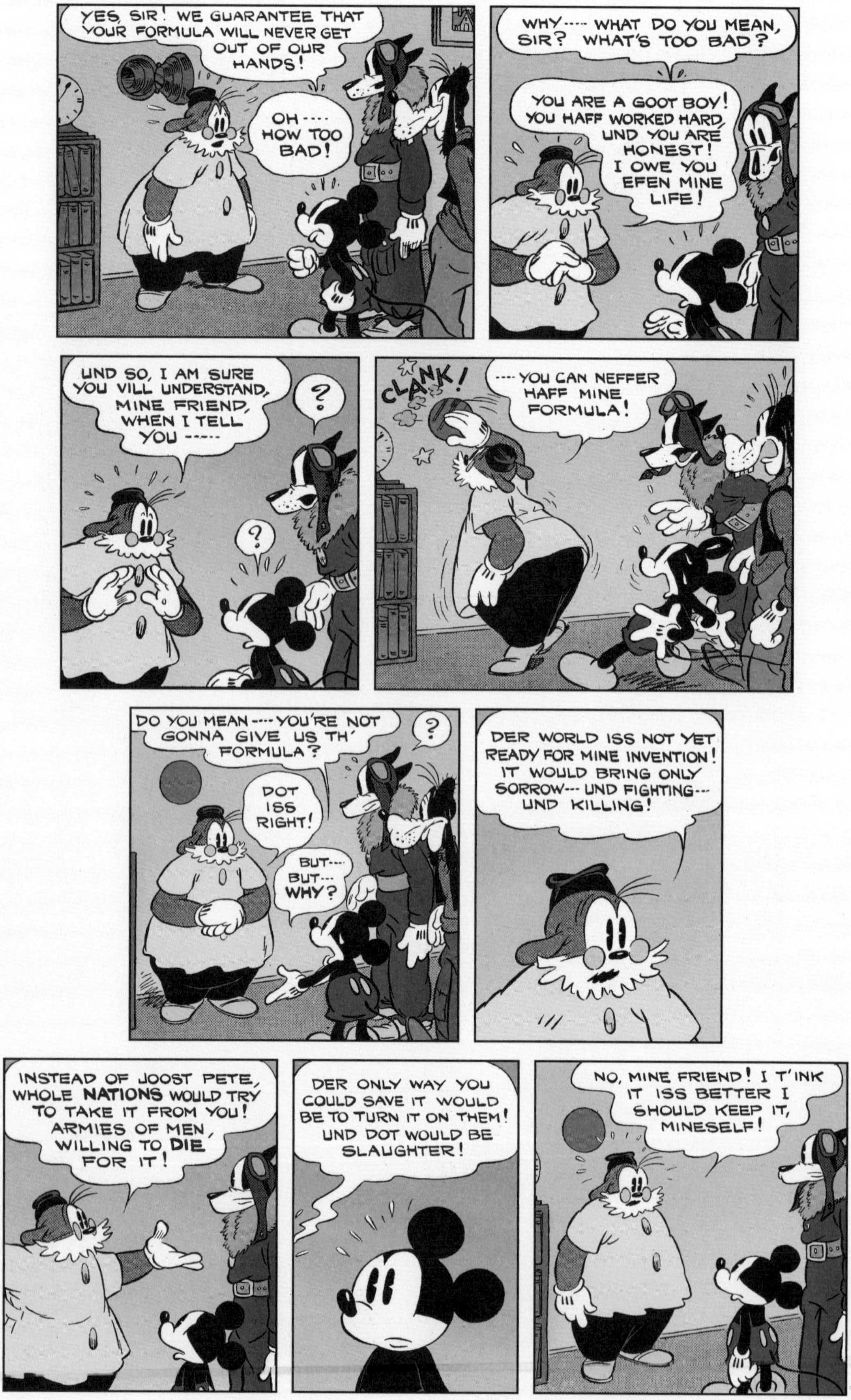
YES, SIR! WE GUARANTEE THAT YOUR FORMULA WILL NEVER GET OUT OF OUR HANDS!
OH ---- HOW TOO BAD!
WHY ---- WHAT DO YOU MEAN, SIR? WHAT'S TOO BAD?
YOU ARE A GOOT BOY! YOU HAFF WORKED HARD, UND YOU ARE HONEST! I OWE YOU EFEN MINE LIFE!
UND SO, I AM SURE YOU VILL UNDERSTAND, MINE FRIEND, WHEN I TELL YOU -----
?
?
CLANK!
---- YOU CAN NEFFER HAFF MINE FORMULA!
DO YOU MEAN ---- YOU'RE NOT GONNA GIVE US TH' FORMULA?
?
DOT ISS RIGHT!
BUT---- BUT--- WHY?
DER WORLD ISS NOT YET READY FOR MINE INVENTION! IT WOULD BRING ONLY SORROW--- UND FIGHTING--- UND KILLING!
INSTEAD OF JOOST PETE, WHOLE NATIONS WOULD TRY TO TAKE IT FROM YOU! ARMIES OF MEN, WILLING TO DIE FOR IT!
DER ONLY WAY YOU COULD SAVE IT WOULD BE TO TURN IT ON THEM! UND DOT WOULD BE SLAUGHTER!
NO, MINE FRIEND! I T'INK IT ISS BETTER I SHOULD KEEP IT, MINESELF!

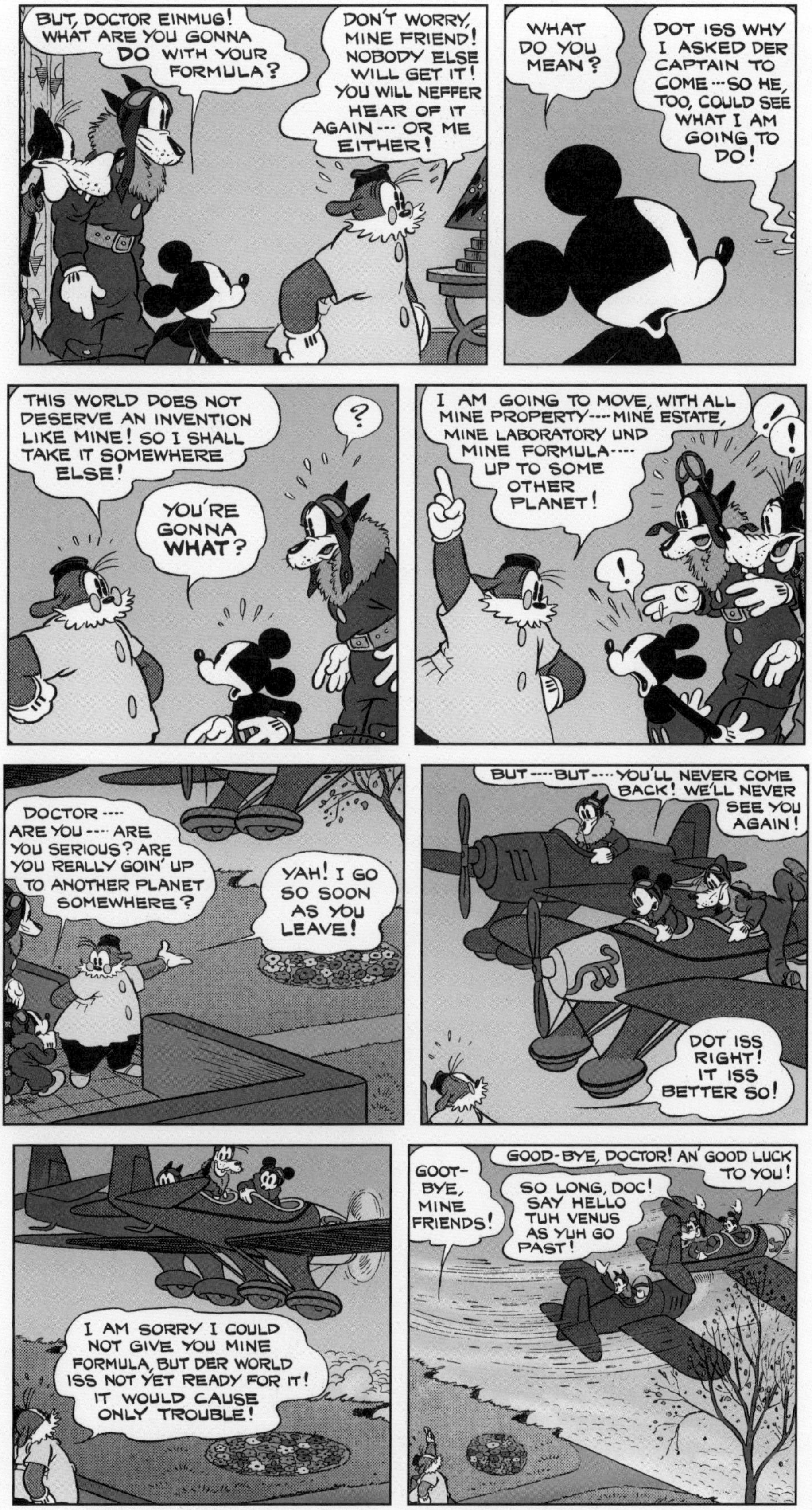
BUT, DOCTOR EINMUG! WHAT ARE YOU GONNA DO WITH YOUR FORMULA?
DON'T WORRY, MINE FRIEND! NOBODY ELSE WILL GET IT! YOU WILL NEFFER HEAR OF IT AGAIN --- OR ME EITHER!
WHAT DO YOU MEAN?
DOT ISS WHY I ASKED DER CAPTAIN TO COME --- SO HE, TOO, COULD SEE WHAT I AM GOING TO DO!
THIS WORLD DOES NOT DESERVE AN INVENTION LIKE MINE! SO I SHALL TAKE IT SOMEWHERE ELSE!
?
YOU'RE GONNA WHAT?
I AM GOING TO MOVE, WITH ALL MINE PROPERTY---- MINE ESTATE, MINE LABORATORY UND MINE FORMULA---- UP TO SOME OTHER PLANET!
!
!
!
DOCTOR ---- ARE YOU ---- ARE YOU SERIOUS? ARE YOU REALLY GOIN' UP TO ANOTHER PLANET SOMEWHERE?
YAH! I GO SO SOON AS YOU LEAVE!
BUT ---- BUT ---- YOU'LL NEVER COME BACK! WE'LL NEVER SEE YOU AGAIN!
DOT ISS RIGHT! IT ISS BETTER SO!
I AM SORRY I COULD NOT GIVE YOU MINE FORMULA, BUT DER WORLD ISS NOT YET READY FOR IT! IT WOULD CAUSE ONLY TROUBLE!
GOOD-BYE, DOCTOR! AN' GOOD LUCK TO YOU!
GOOT-BYE, MINE FRIENDS!
SO LONG, DOC! SAY HELLO TUH VENUS AS YUH GO PAST!

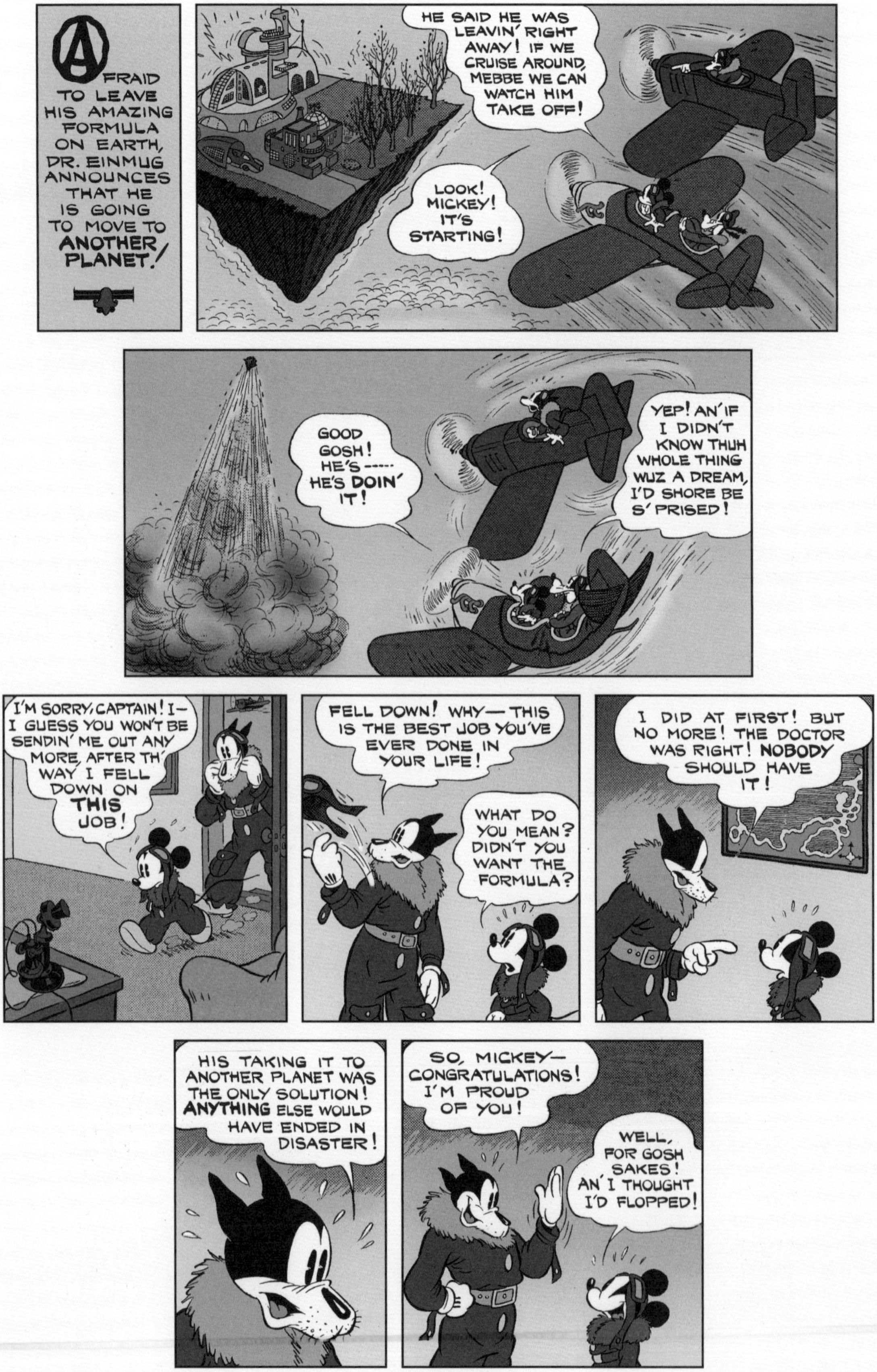
AFRAID TO LEAVE HIS AMAZING FORMULA ON EARTH, DR. EINMUG ANNOUNCES THAT HE IS GOING TO MOVE TO ANOTHER PLANET!
HE SAID HE WAS LEAVIN' RIGHT AWAY! IF WE CRUISE AROUND, MEBBE WE CAN WATCH HIM TAKE OFF!
LOOK! MICKEY! IT'S STARTING!
GOOD GOSH! HE'S ----- HE'S DOIN' IT!
YEP! AN' IF I DIDN'T KNOW THUH WHOLE THING WUZ A DREAM, I'D SHORE BE S'PRISED!
I'M SORRY, CAPTAIN! I— I GUESS YOU WON'T BE SENDIN' ME OUT ANY MORE, AFTER TH' WAY I FELL DOWN ON THIS JOB!
FELL DOWN! WHY— THIS IS THE BEST JOB YOU'VE EVER DONE IN YOUR LIFE!
WHAT DO YOU MEAN? DIDN'T YOU WANT THE FORMULA?
I DID AT FIRST! BUT NO MORE! THE DOCTOR WAS RIGHT! NOBODY SHOULD HAVE IT!
HIS TAKING IT TO ANOTHER PLANET WAS THE ONLY SOLUTION! ANYTHING ELSE WOULD HAVE ENDED IN DISASTER!
SO, MICKEY— CONGRATULATIONS! I'M PROUD OF YOU!
WELL, FOR GOSH SAKES! AN' I THOUGHT I'D FLOPPED!

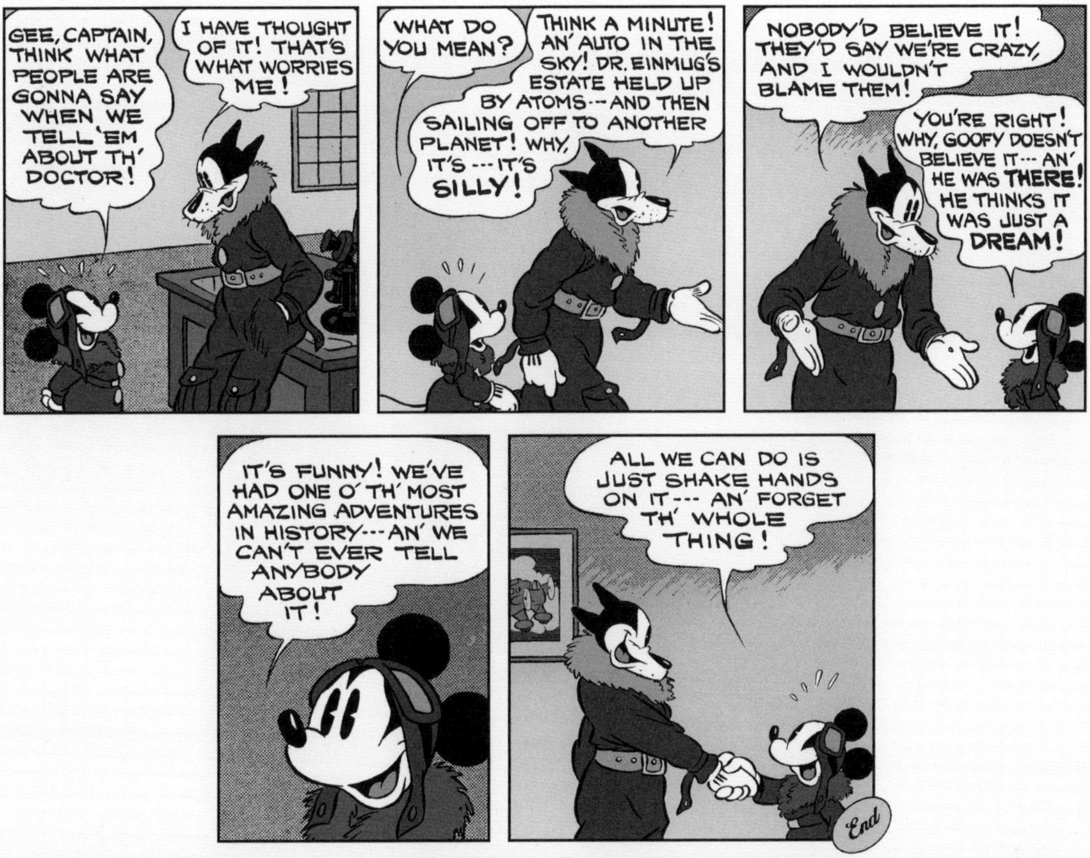
GEE, CAPTAIN, THINK WHAT PEOPLE ARE GONNA SAY WHEN WE TELL 'EM ABOUT TH' DOCTOR!
I HAVE THOUGHT OF IT! THAT'S WHAT WORRIES ME!
WHAT DO YOU MEAN?
THINK A MINUTE! AN' AUTO IN THE SKY! DR. EINMUG'S ESTATE HELD UP BY ATOMS--- AND THEN SAILING OFF TO ANOTHER PLANET! WHY, IT'S --- IT'S SILLY!
NOBODY'D BELIEVE IT! THEY'D SAY WE'RE CRAZY, AND I WOULDN'T BLAME THEM!
YOU'RE RIGHT! WHY, GOOFY DOESN'T BELIEVE IT--- AN' HE WAS THERE! HE THINKS IT WAS JUST A DREAM!
IT'S FUNNY! WE'VE HAD ONE O' TH' MOST AMAZING ADVENTURES IN HISTORY--- AN' WE CAN'T EVER TELL ANYBODY ABOUT IT!
ALL WE CAN DO IS JUST SHAKE HANDS ON IT--- AN' FORGET TH' WHOLE THING!
End

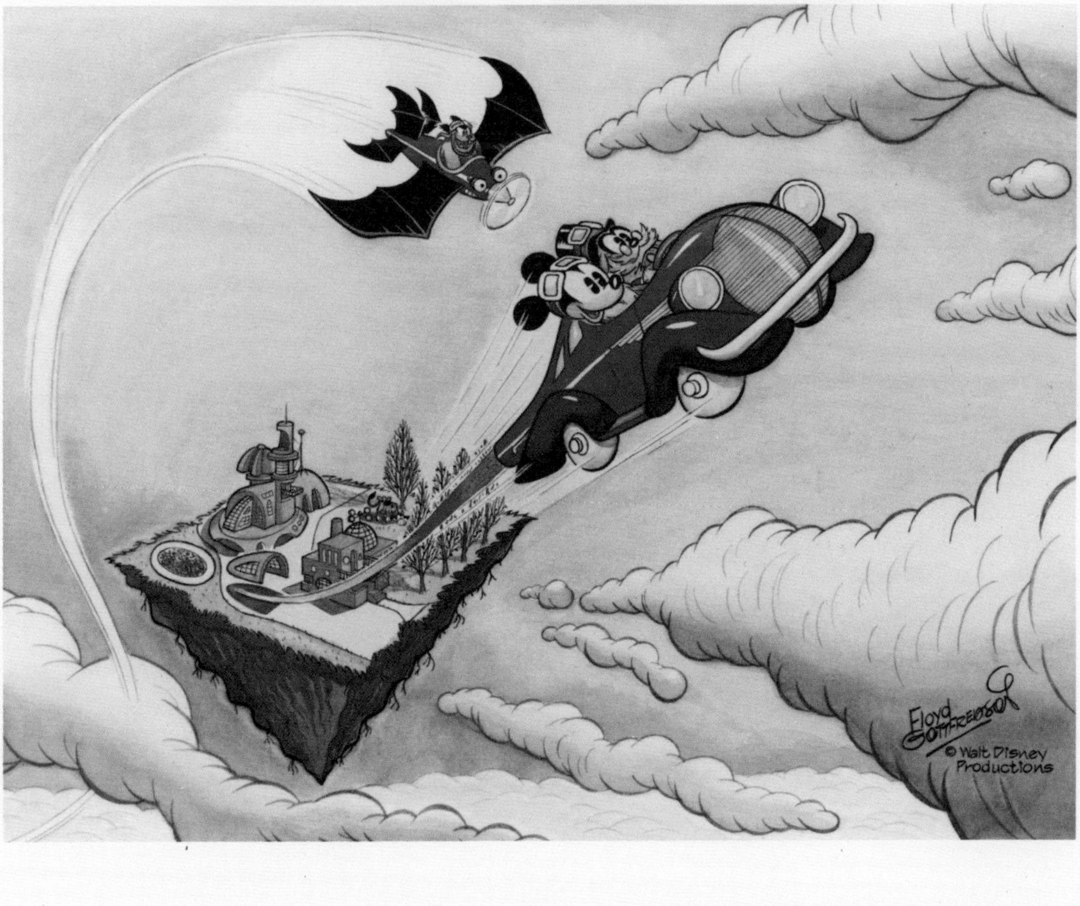
Floyd Gottfredson
© Walt Disney Productions

Now and then Gottfredson would create a special gift drawing of Mickey's whole gang — usually when Disney needed to congratulate a third party for a special event. The image made for the *Honolulu Advertiser*'s 80th anniversary was published in that newspaper July 2, 1936; the birthday greeting for William Randolph Hearst — owner of King Features Syndicate — dates from 1942.

Honolulu Advertiser image courtesy San Francisco Academy of Comic Art; Hearst birthday greeting courtesy The Walt Disney Company Italia.

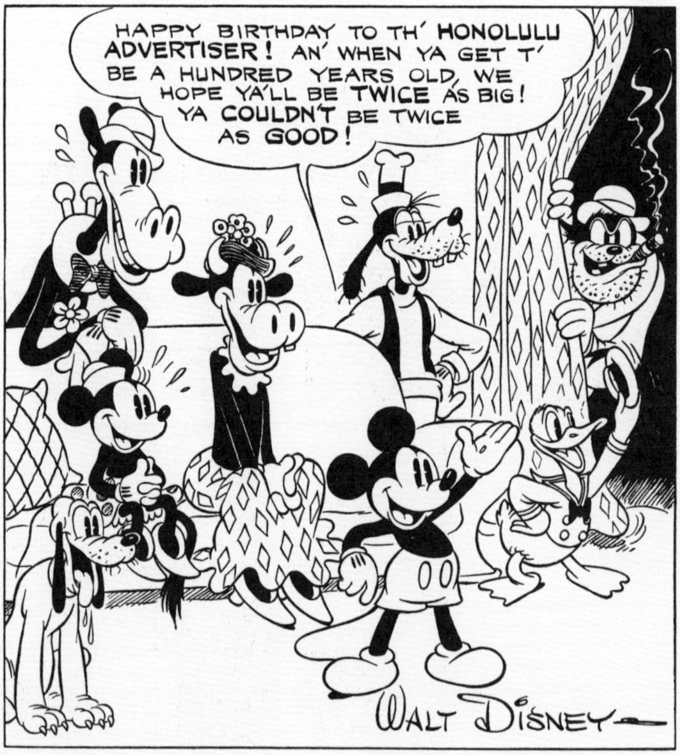
HAPPY BIRTHDAY TO TH' HONOLULU ADVERTISER! AN' WHEN YA GET T' BE A HUNDRED YEARS OLD, WE HOPE YA'LL BE TWICE AS BIG! YA COULDN'T BE TWICE AS GOOD!
WALT DISNEY

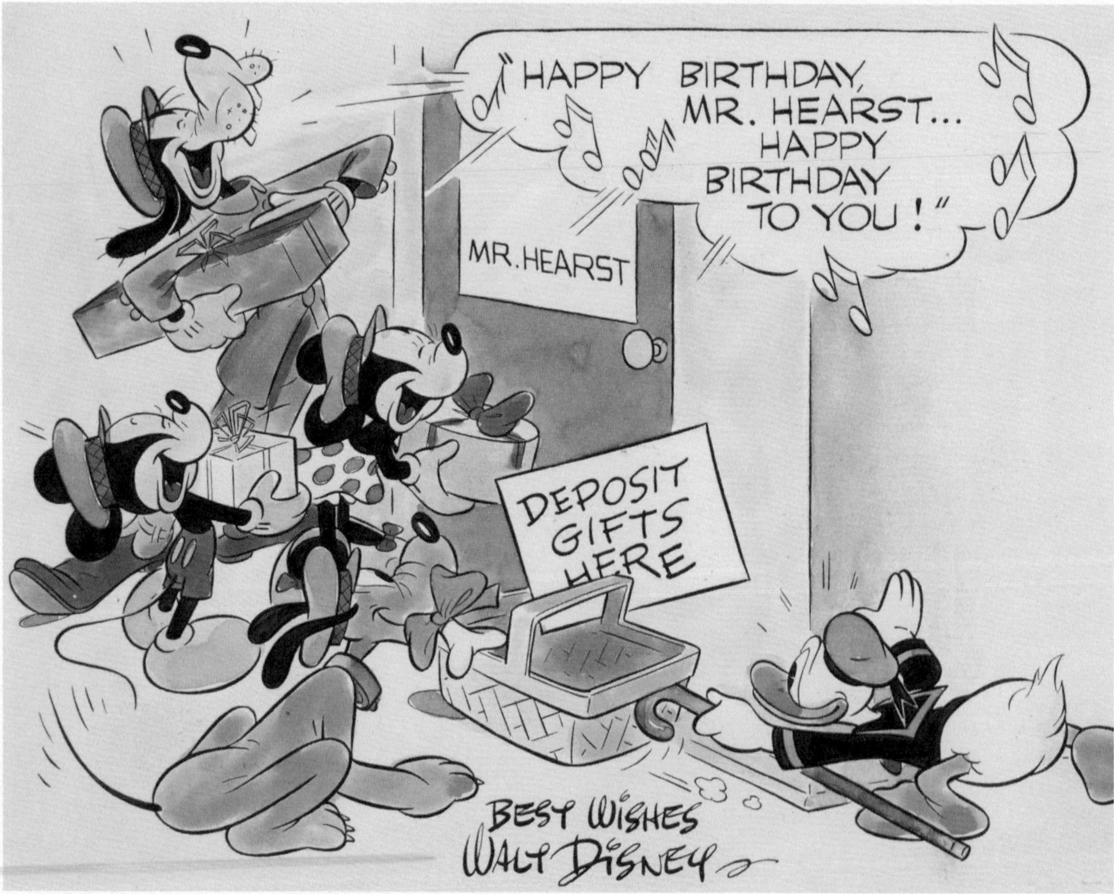
"HAPPY BIRTHDAY, MR. HEARST... HAPPY BIRTHDAY TO YOU!"
MR. HEARST
DEPOSIT GIFTS HERE
BEST WISHES
WALT DISNEY

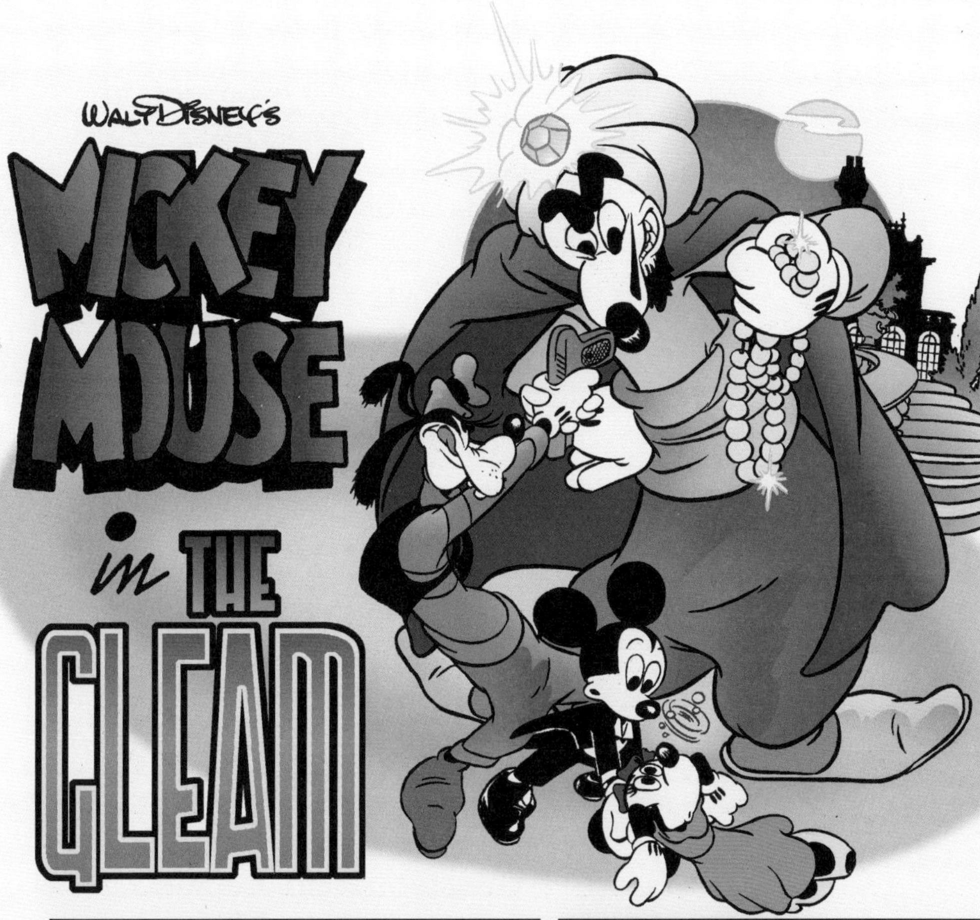
WALT DISNEY'S
MICKEY MOUSE
in THE GLEAM

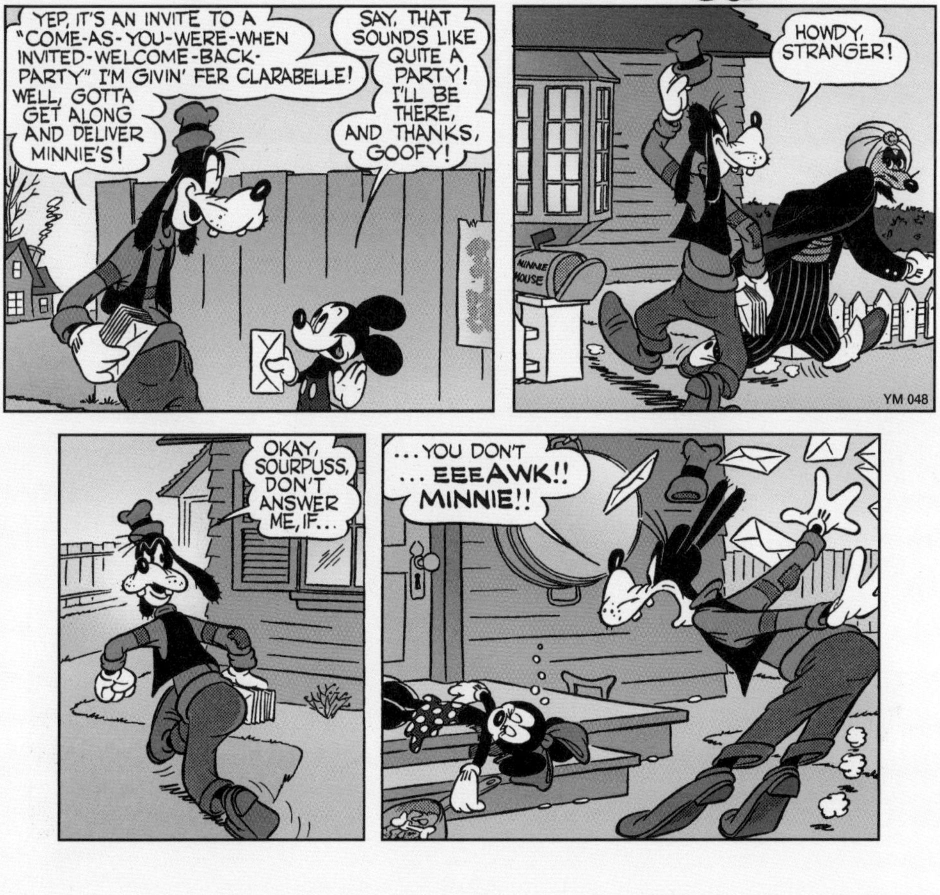
YEP, IT'S AN INVITE TO A "COME-AS-YOU-WERE-WHEN INVITED-WELCOME-BACK-PARTY" I'M GIVIN' FER CLARABELLE! WELL, GOTTA GET ALONG AND DELIVER MINNIE'S!
SAY, THAT SOUNDS LIKE QUITE A PARTY! I'LL BE THERE, AND THANKS, GOOFY!
HOWDY, STRANGER!
MINNIE MOUSE
YM 048
OKAY, SOURPUSS, DON'T ANSWER ME, IF...
...YOU DON'T ...EEEAWK!! MINNIE!!

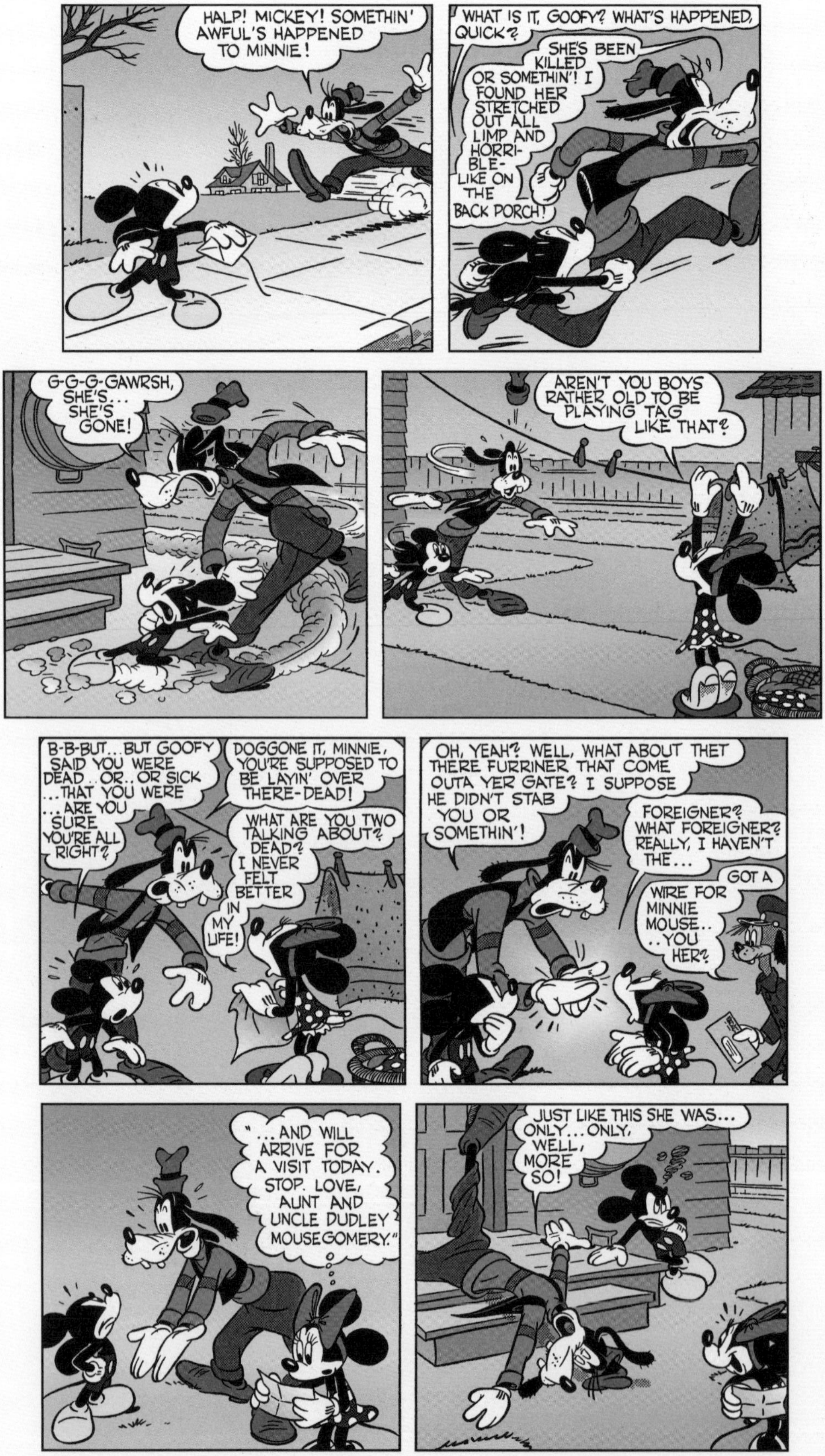
HALP! MICKEY! SOMETHIN' AWFUL'S HAPPENED TO MINNIE!
WHAT IS IT, GOOFY? WHAT'S HAPPENED, QUICK?
SHE'S BEEN KILLED OR SOMETHIN'! I FOUND HER STRETCHED OUT ALL LIMP AND HORRI-BLE-LIKE ON THE BACK PORCH!
G-G-G-GAWRSH, SHE'S... SHE'S GONE!
AREN'T YOU BOYS RATHER OLD TO BE PLAYING TAG LIKE THAT?
B-B-BUT... BUT GOOFY SAID YOU WERE DEAD.. OR.. OR SICK ...THAT YOU WERE ...ARE YOU SURE YOU'RE ALL RIGHT?
DOGGONE IT, MINNIE, YOU'RE SUPPOSED TO BE LAYIN' OVER THERE-DEAD!
WHAT ARE YOU TWO TALKING ABOUT? DEAD? I NEVER FELT BETTER IN MY LIFE!
OH, YEAH? WELL, WHAT ABOUT THET THERE FURRINER THAT COME OUTA YER GATE? I SUPPOSE HE DIDN'T STAB YOU OR SOMETHIN'!
FOREIGNER? WHAT FOREIGNER? REALLY, I HAVEN'T THE...
GOT A WIRE FOR MINNIE MOUSE.. ..YOU HER?
"...AND WILL ARRIVE FOR A VISIT TODAY. STOP. LOVE, AUNT AND UNCLE DUDLEY MOUSEGOMERY."
JUST LIKE THIS SHE WAS... ONLY... ONLY, WELL, MORE SO!

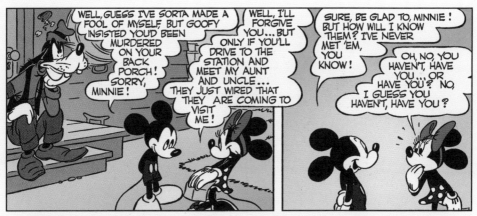

WELL, GUESS I'VE SORTA MADE A FOOL OF MYSELF, BUT GOOFY INSISTED YOU'D BEEN MURDERED ON YOUR BACK PORCH! SORRY, MINNIE!

WELL, I'LL FORGIVE YOU... BUT ONLY IF YOU'LL DRIVE TO THE STATION AND MEET MY AUNT AND UNCLE... THEY JUST WIRED THAT THEY ARE COMING TO VISIT ME!

SURE, BE GLAD TO, MINNIE! BUT HOW WILL I KNOW THEM? I'VE NEVER MET 'EM, YOU KNOW!

OH, NO, YOU HAVEN'T, HAVE YOU... OR HAVE YOU? NO, I GUESS YOU HAVEN'T, HAVE YOU?

WELL, AUNT MARTHA IS SORT OF TALL AND FAT IN A SHORT, SLENDER WAY! AND UNCLE DUDLEY IS RICH, WEARS A CLEAN-SHAVEN BEARD AND IS MUCH TALLER THAN HE IS SHORT!

ER... BY THE WAY, GOOFY, DID WHAT MINNIE SAY SOUND A BIT...WELL, SORT OF CONFUSED TO YOU?

YEP! SHORE DID! SHE SAYS SHE WEREN'T MURDERED, AND I SAYS SHE WERE!

ICKEY AND GOOFY ARE AT THE STATION TO MEET MINNIE'S AUNT MARTHA AND UNCLE DUDLEY MOUSEGOMERY! MINNIE, WHO HAS BEEN ACTING STRANGELY OF LATE, DIDN'T DESCRIBE THEM VERY WELL!

ER...AH...PARDON ME, BUT DO YOU HAPPEN TO BE A FRIEND OF MINNIE'S UNCLE DUDLEY?

THAT I DON'T, SON, AND IF THAT'S THE FRIEND, I'M GLAD OF IT!

IT'S NO USE, GOOFY! THAT'S THE SIXTEENTH COUPLE I'VE TRIED! I GIVE UP! LET'S GO BACK TO THE CAR!

DADGUMMIT, HURRY, DRIVER! WE'VE BEEN WAITING TWENTY MINUTES! DRIVE US TO THE RESIDENCE OF MINERVA MOUSE IMMEDIATELY!

POLKA DOT CAB

CAB STAND

165

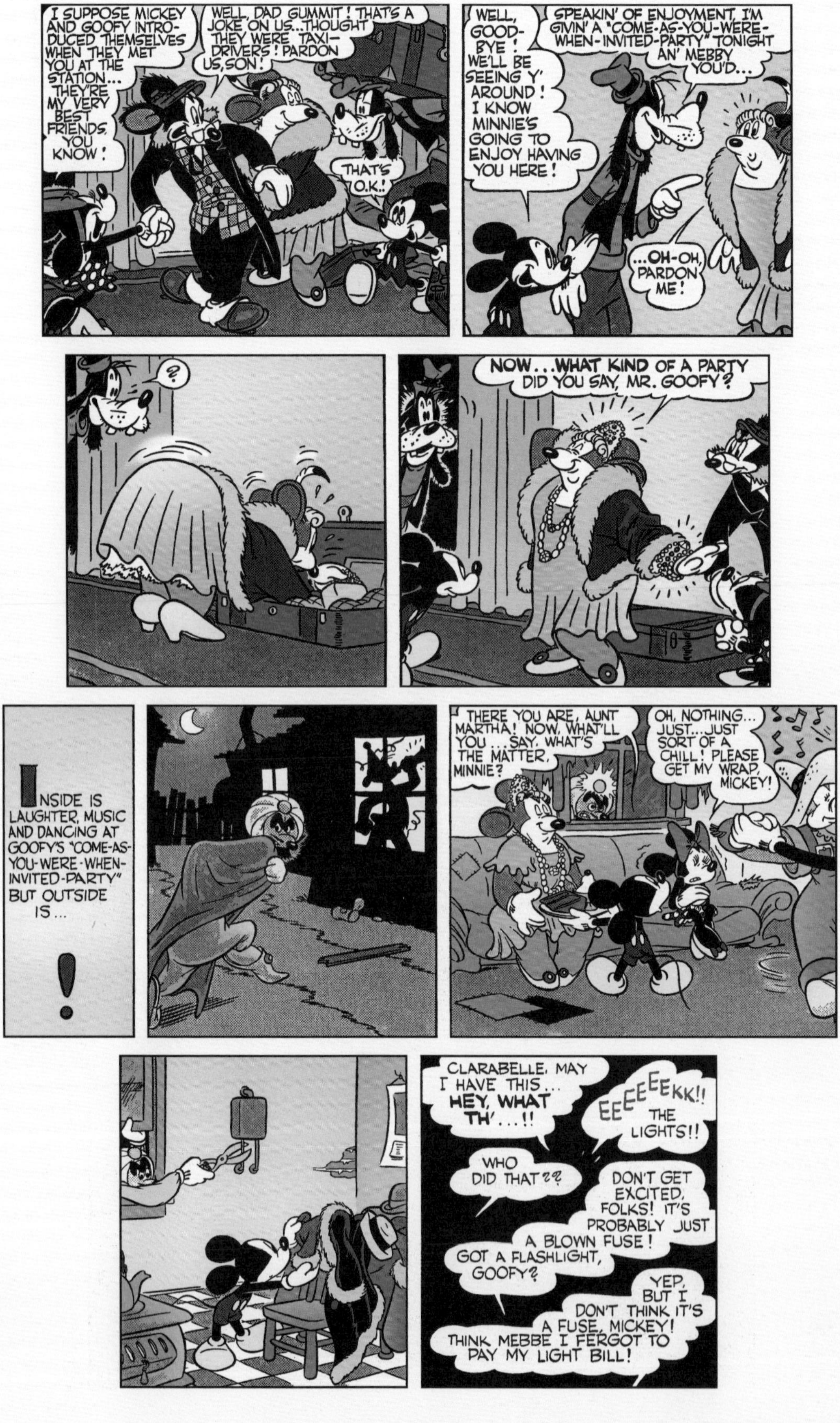
I SUPPOSE MICKEY AND GOOFY INTRO-DUCED THEMSELVES WHEN THEY MET YOU AT THE STATION... THEY'RE MY VERY BEST FRIENDS, YOU KNOW!
WELL, DAD GUMMIT! THAT'S A JOKE ON US...THOUGHT THEY WERE TAXI-DRIVERS! PARDON US, SON!
THAT'S O.K.!
WELL, GOOD-BYE! WE'LL BE SEEING Y' AROUND! I KNOW MINNIE'S GOING TO ENJOY HAVING YOU HERE!
SPEAKIN' OF ENJOYMENT, I'M GIVIN' A "COME-AS-YOU-WERE-WHEN-INVITED-PARTY" TONIGHT AN' MEBBY YOU'D...
...OH-OH, PARDON ME!
?
NOW...WHAT KIND OF A PARTY DID YOU SAY, MR. GOOFY?
INSIDE IS LAUGHTER, MUSIC AND DANCING AT GOOFY'S "COME-AS-YOU-WERE-WHEN-INVITED-PARTY" BUT OUTSIDE IS...
!
THERE YOU ARE, AUNT MARTHA! NOW, WHAT'LL YOU... SAY, WHAT'S THE MATTER, MINNIE?
OH, NOTHING... JUST... JUST SORT OF A CHILL! PLEASE GET MY WRAP, MICKEY!
CLARABELLE, MAY I HAVE THIS... HEY, WHAT TH'...!!
EEEEEEKK!! THE LIGHTS!!
WHO DID THAT??
DON'T GET EXCITED, FOLKS! IT'S PROBABLY JUST A BLOWN FUSE!
GOT A FLASHLIGHT, GOOFY?
YEP, BUT I DON'T THINK IT'S A FUSE, MICKEY! THINK MEBBE I FERGOT TO PAY MY LIGHT BILL!

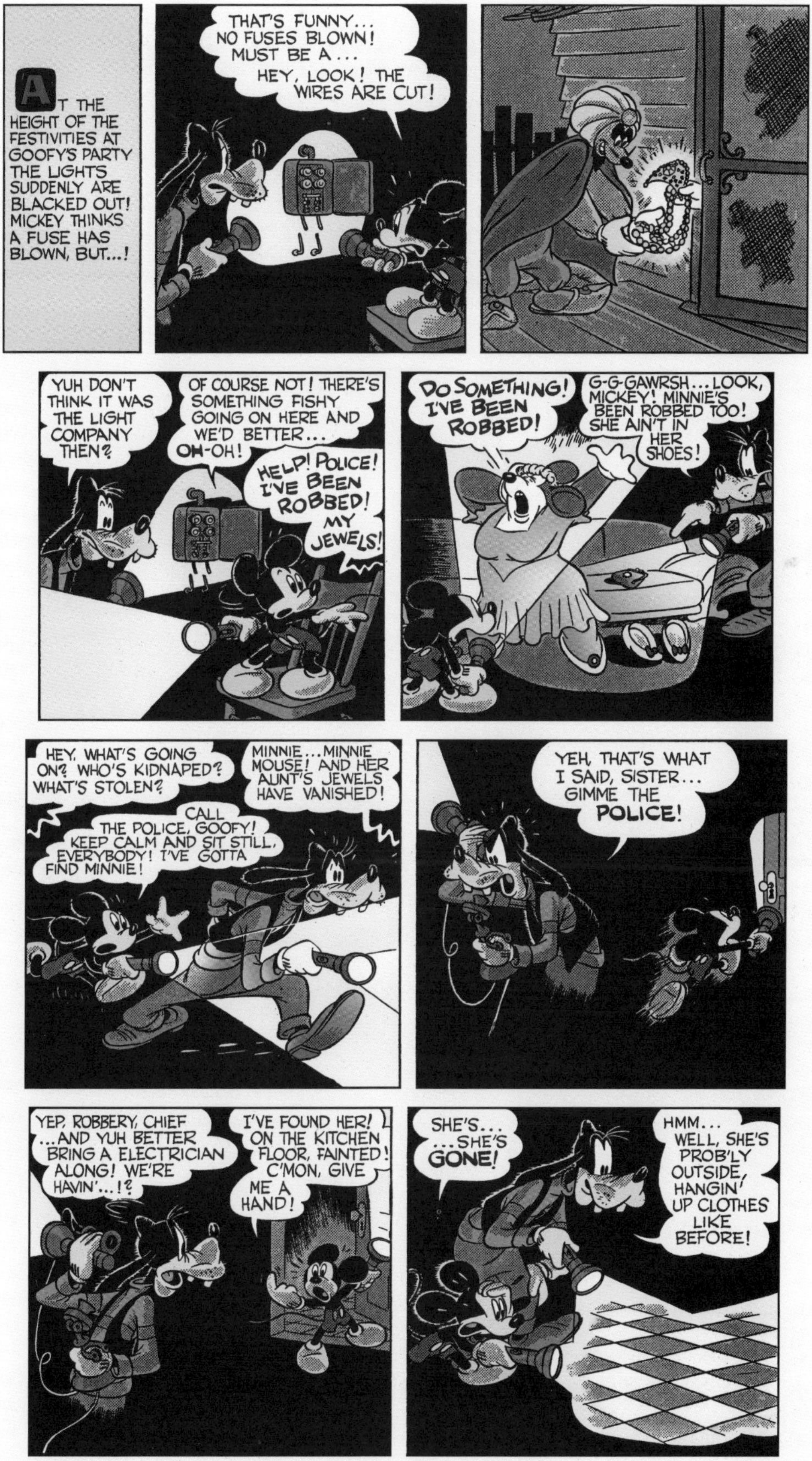
AT THE HEIGHT OF THE FESTIVITIES AT GOOFY'S PARTY THE LIGHTS SUDDENLY ARE BLACKED OUT! MICKEY THINKS A FUSE HAS BLOWN, BUT...!
THAT'S FUNNY... NO FUSES BLOWN! MUST BE A...
HEY, LOOK! THE WIRES ARE CUT!
YUH DON'T THINK IT WAS THE LIGHT COMPANY THEN?
OF COURSE NOT! THERE'S SOMETHING FISHY GOING ON HERE AND WE'D BETTER... OH-OH!
HELP! POLICE! I'VE BEEN ROBBED! MY JEWELS!
DO SOMETHING! I'VE BEEN ROBBED!
G-G-GAWRSH... LOOK, MICKEY! MINNIE'S BEEN ROBBED TOO! SHE AIN'T IN HER SHOES!
HEY, WHAT'S GOING ON? WHO'S KIDNAPED? WHAT'S STOLEN?
MINNIE... MINNIE MOUSE! AND HER AUNT'S JEWELS HAVE VANISHED!
CALL THE POLICE, GOOFY! KEEP CALM AND SIT STILL, EVERYBODY! I'VE GOTTA FIND MINNIE!
YEH, THAT'S WHAT I SAID, SISTER... GIMME THE POLICE!
YEP, ROBBERY, CHIEF ...AND YUH BETTER BRING A ELECTRICIAN ALONG! WE'RE HAVIN'...!?
I'VE FOUND HER! ON THE KITCHEN FLOOR, FAINTED! C'MON, GIVE ME A HAND!
SHE'S... ...SHE'S GONE!
HMM... WELL, SHE'S PROB'LY OUTSIDE, HANGIN' UP CLOTHES LIKE BEFORE!

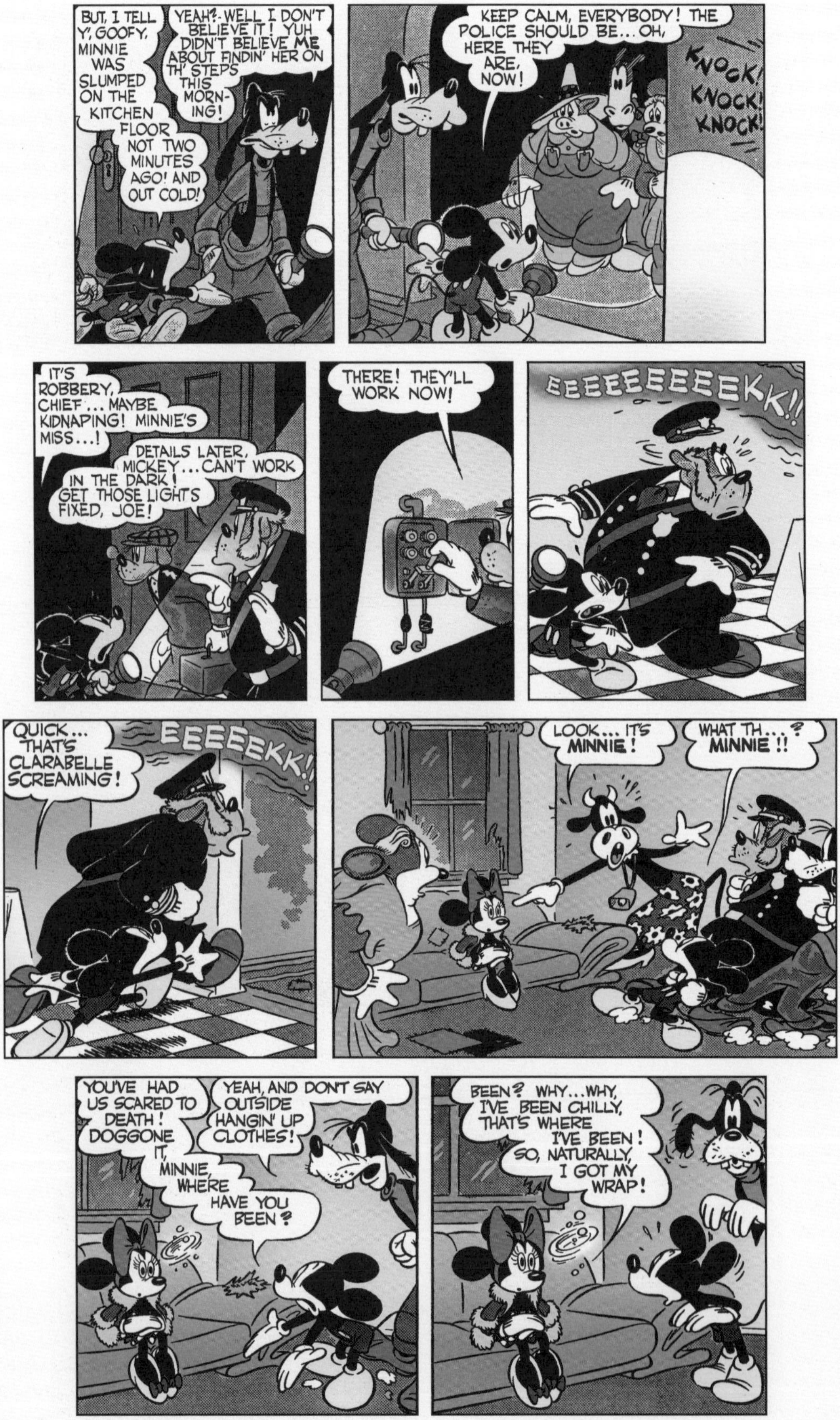
BUT, I TELL Y', GOOFY, MINNIE WAS SLUMPED ON THE KITCHEN FLOOR NOT TWO MINUTES AGO! AND OUT COLD!
YEAH?-WELL I DON'T BELIEVE IT! YUH DIDN'T BELIEVE ME ABOUT FINDIN' HER ON TH' STEPS THIS MORNING!
KEEP CALM, EVERYBODY! THE POLICE SHOULD BE... OH, HERE THEY ARE, NOW!
KNOCK! KNOCK! KNOCK!
IT'S ROBBERY, CHIEF... MAYBE KIDNAPING! MINNIE'S MISS...!
DETAILS LATER, MICKEY... CAN'T WORK IN THE DARK! GET THOSE LIGHTS FIXED, JOE!
THERE! THEY'LL WORK NOW!
EEEEEEEEEKK!!
QUICK... THAT'S CLARABELLE SCREAMING!
EEEEEKK!
LOOK... IT'S MINNIE!
WHAT TH...? MINNIE!!
YOU'VE HAD US SCARED TO DEATH! DOGGONE IT, MINNIE, WHERE HAVE YOU BEEN?
YEAH, AND DON'T SAY OUTSIDE HANGIN' UP CLOTHES!
BEEN? WHY...WHY, I'VE BEEN CHILLY, THAT'S WHERE I'VE BEEN! SO, NATURALLY, I GOT MY WRAP!

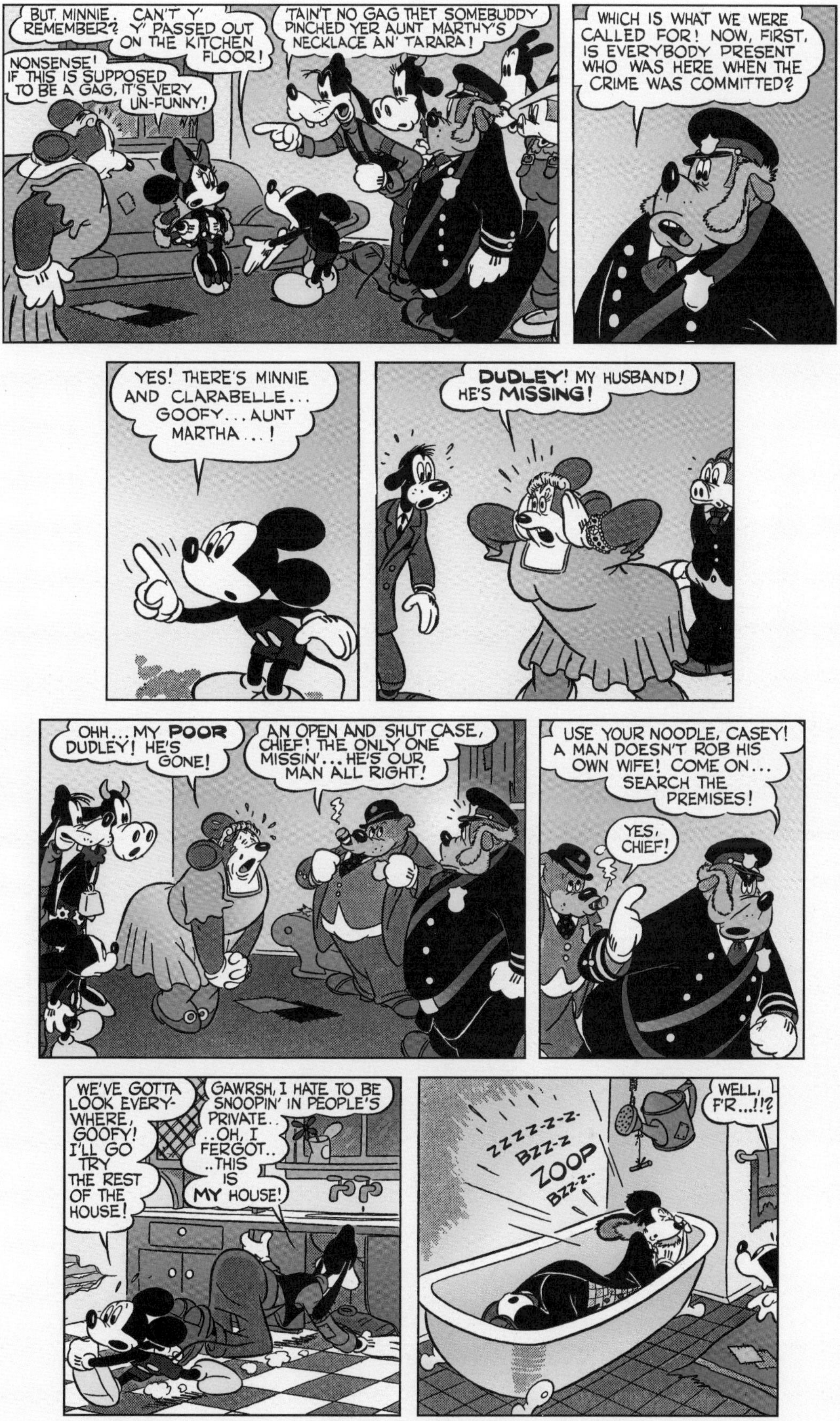
BUT, MINNIE. REMEMBER? CAN'T Y' Y' PASSED OUT ON THE KITCHEN FLOOR!
NONSENSE! IF THIS IS SUPPOSED TO BE A GAG, IT'S VERY UN-FUNNY!
'TAIN'T NO GAG THET SOMEBUDDY PINCHED YER AUNT MARTHY'S NECKLACE AN' TARARA!
WHICH IS WHAT WE WERE CALLED FOR! NOW, FIRST, IS EVERYBODY PRESENT WHO WAS HERE WHEN THE CRIME WAS COMMITTED?
YES! THERE'S MINNIE AND CLARABELLE... GOOFY... AUNT MARTHA...!
DUDLEY! MY HUSBAND! HE'S MISSING!
OHH... MY POOR DUDLEY! HE'S GONE!
AN OPEN AND SHUT CASE, CHIEF! THE ONLY ONE MISSIN'... HE'S OUR MAN ALL RIGHT!
USE YOUR NOODLE, CASEY! A MAN DOESN'T ROB HIS OWN WIFE! COME ON... SEARCH THE PREMISES!
YES, CHIEF!
WE'VE GOTTA LOOK EVERY-WHERE, GOOFY! I'LL GO TRY THE REST OF THE HOUSE!
GAWRSH, I HATE TO BE SNOOPIN' IN PEOPLE'S PRIVATE.. ..OH, I FERGOT.. ..THIS IS MY HOUSE!
ZZZZ-Z-Z-Z- BZZ-Z ZOOP BZZ-Z..
WELL, F'R...!!?

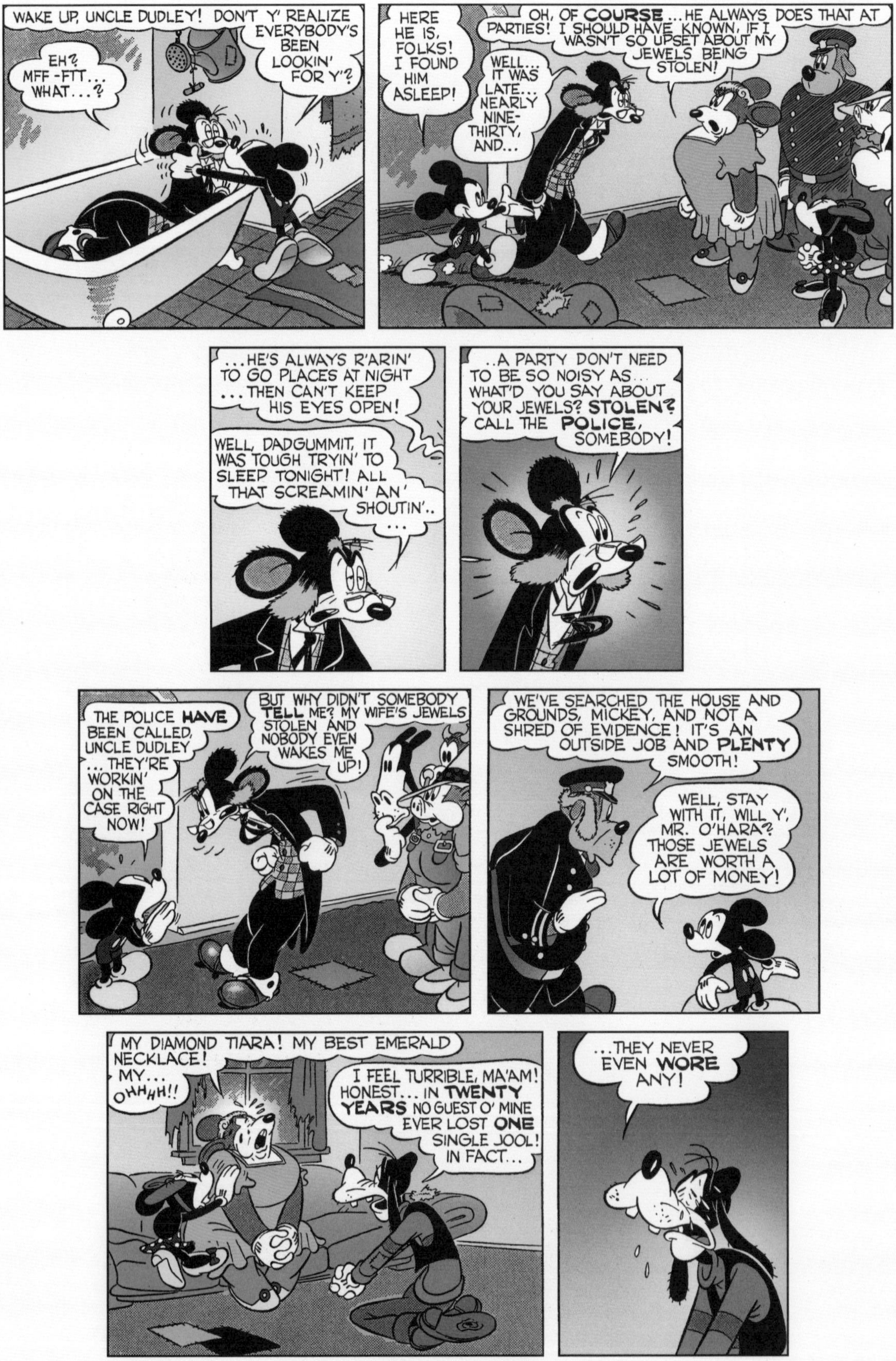
WAKE UP, UNCLE DUDLEY! DON'T Y' REALIZE EVERYBODY'S BEEN LOOKIN' FOR Y'?
EH? MFF-FTT... WHAT...?
HERE HE IS, FOLKS! I FOUND HIM ASLEEP!
WELL... IT WAS LATE... NEARLY NINE-THIRTY, AND...
OH, OF COURSE... HE ALWAYS DOES THAT AT PARTIES! I SHOULD HAVE KNOWN, IF I WASN'T SO UPSET ABOUT MY JEWELS BEING STOLEN!
...HE'S ALWAYS R'ARIN' TO GO PLACES AT NIGHT ...THEN CAN'T KEEP HIS EYES OPEN!
WELL, DADGUMMIT, IT WAS TOUGH TRYIN' TO SLEEP TONIGHT! ALL THAT SCREAMIN' AN' SHOUTIN'.. ...
..A PARTY DON'T NEED TO BE SO NOISY AS... WHAT'D YOU SAY ABOUT YOUR JEWELS? STOLEN? CALL THE POLICE, SOMEBODY!
THE POLICE HAVE BEEN CALLED, UNCLE DUDLEY ... THEY'RE WORKIN' ON THE CASE RIGHT NOW!
BUT WHY DIDN'T SOMEBODY TELL ME? MY WIFE'S JEWELS STOLEN AND NOBODY EVEN WAKES ME UP!
WE'VE SEARCHED THE HOUSE AND GROUNDS, MICKEY, AND NOT A SHRED OF EVIDENCE! IT'S AN OUTSIDE JOB AND PLENTY SMOOTH!
WELL, STAY WITH IT, WILL Y', MR. O'HARA? THOSE JEWELS ARE WORTH A LOT OF MONEY!
MY DIAMOND TIARA! MY BEST EMERALD NECKLACE! MY... OHHHH!!
I FEEL TURRIBLE, MA'AM! HONEST... IN TWENTY YEARS NO GUEST O' MINE EVER LOST ONE SINGLE JOOL! IN FACT...
...THEY NEVER EVEN WORE ANY!

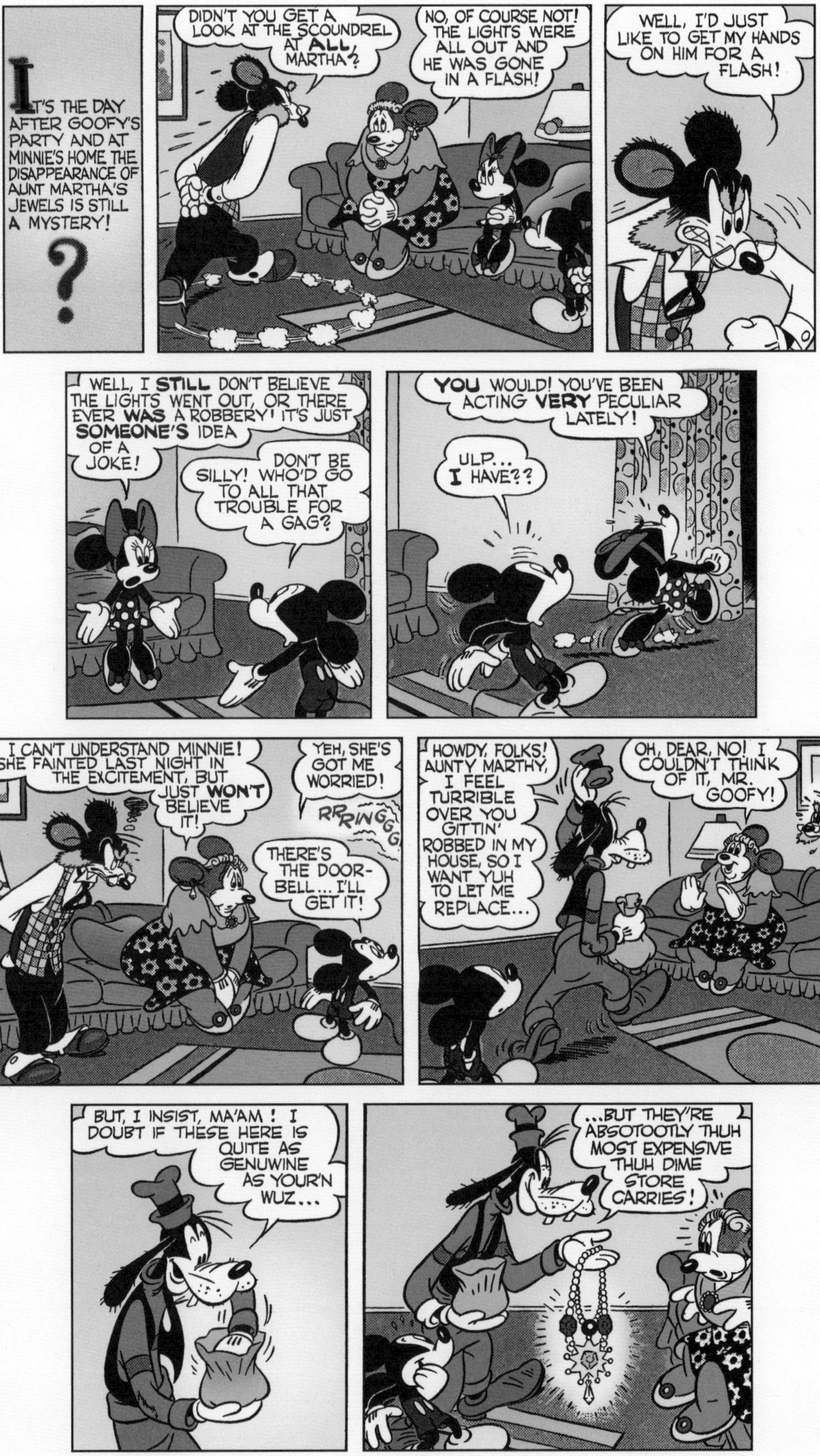
IT'S THE DAY AFTER GOOFY'S PARTY AND AT MINNIE'S HOME THE DISAPPEARANCE OF AUNT MARTHA'S JEWELS IS STILL A MYSTERY!
?
DIDN'T YOU GET A LOOK AT THE SCOUNDREL AT ALL, MARTHA?
NO, OF COURSE NOT! THE LIGHTS WERE ALL OUT AND HE WAS GONE IN A FLASH!
WELL, I'D JUST LIKE TO GET MY HANDS ON HIM FOR A FLASH!
WELL, I STILL DON'T BELIEVE THE LIGHTS WENT OUT, OR THERE EVER WAS A ROBBERY! IT'S JUST SOMEONE'S IDEA OF A JOKE!
DON'T BE SILLY! WHO'D GO TO ALL THAT TROUBLE FOR A GAG?
YOU WOULD! YOU'VE BEEN ACTING VERY PECULIAR LATELY!
ULP... I HAVE??
I CAN'T UNDERSTAND MINNIE! SHE FAINTED LAST NIGHT IN THE EXCITEMENT, BUT JUST WON'T BELIEVE IT!
YEH, SHE'S GOT ME WORRIED!
RRRINGGG
THERE'S THE DOOR-BELL... I'LL GET IT!
HOWDY, FOLKS! AUNTY MARTHY, I FEEL TURRIBLE OVER YOU GITTIN' ROBBED IN MY HOUSE, SO I WANT YUH TO LET ME REPLACE...
OH, DEAR, NO! I COULDN'T THINK OF IT, MR. GOOFY!
BUT, I INSIST, MA'AM! I DOUBT IF THESE HERE IS QUITE AS GENUWINE AS YOUR'N WUZ...
...BUT THEY'RE ABSOTOOTLY THUH MOST EXPENSIVE THUH DIME STORE CARRIES!

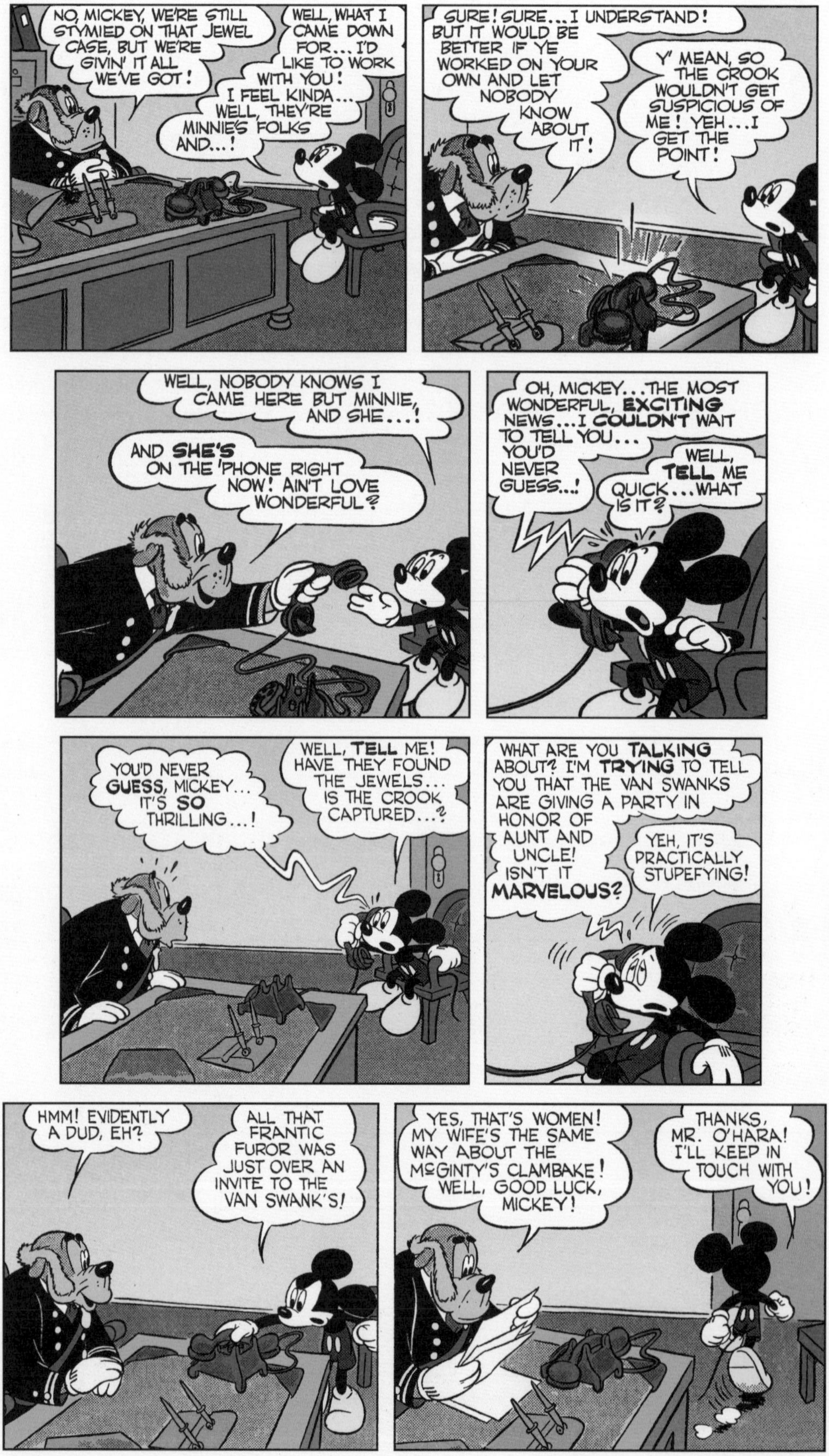
NO, MICKEY, WE'RE STILL STYMIED ON THAT JEWEL CASE, BUT WE'RE GIVIN' IT ALL WE'VE GOT!
WELL, WHAT I CAME DOWN FOR... I'D LIKE TO WORK WITH YOU! I FEEL KINDA... WELL, THEY'RE MINNIE'S FOLKS AND...!
SURE! SURE... I UNDERSTAND! BUT IT WOULD BE BETTER IF YE WORKED ON YOUR OWN AND LET NOBODY KNOW ABOUT IT!
Y' MEAN, SO THE CROOK WOULDN'T GET SUSPICIOUS OF ME! YEH... I GET THE POINT!
WELL, NOBODY KNOWS I CAME HERE BUT MINNIE, AND SHE...!
AND SHE'S ON THE 'PHONE RIGHT NOW! AIN'T LOVE WONDERFUL?
OH, MICKEY... THE MOST WONDERFUL, EXCITING NEWS... I COULDN'T WAIT TO TELL YOU... YOU'D NEVER GUESS...!
WELL, TELL ME QUICK... WHAT IS IT?
YOU'D NEVER GUESS, MICKEY... IT'S SO THRILLING...!
WELL, TELL ME! HAVE THEY FOUND THE JEWELS... IS THE CROOK CAPTURED...?
WHAT ARE YOU TALKING ABOUT? I'M TRYING TO TELL YOU THAT THE VAN SWANKS ARE GIVING A PARTY IN HONOR OF AUNT AND UNCLE! ISN'T IT MARVELOUS?
YEH, IT'S PRACTICALLY STUPEFYING!
HMM! EVIDENTLY A DUD, EH?
ALL THAT FRANTIC FUROR WAS JUST OVER AN INVITE TO THE VAN SWANK'S!
YES, THAT'S WOMEN! MY WIFE'S THE SAME WAY ABOUT THE McGINTY'S CLAMBAKE! WELL, GOOD LUCK, MICKEY!
THANKS, MR. O'HARA! I'LL KEEP IN TOUCH WITH YOU!

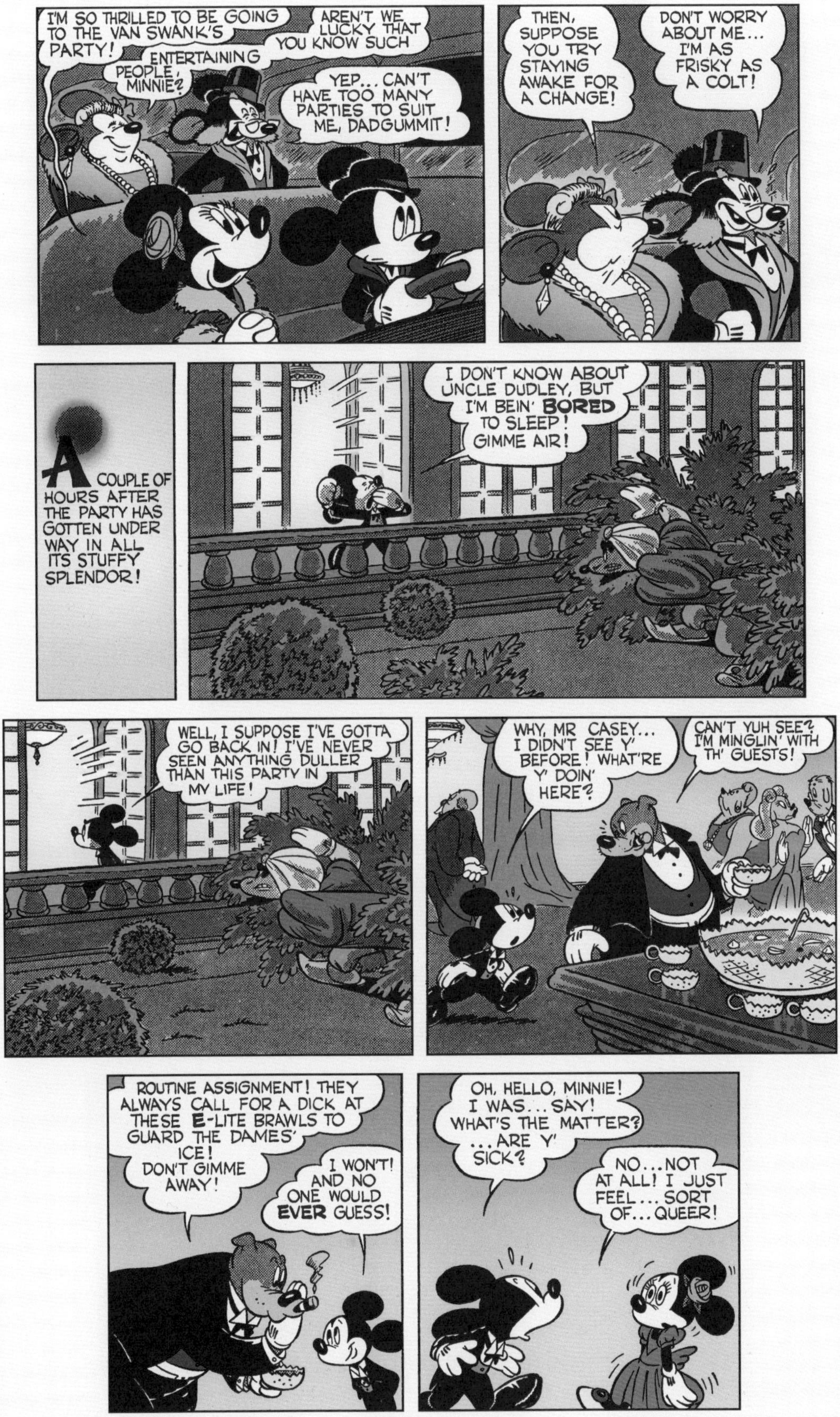
I'M SO THRILLED TO BE GOING TO THE VAN SWANK'S PARTY!
AREN'T WE LUCKY THAT YOU KNOW SUCH ENTERTAINING PEOPLE, MINNIE?
YEP... CAN'T HAVE TOO MANY PARTIES TO SUIT ME, DADGUMMIT!
THEN, SUPPOSE YOU TRY STAYING AWAKE FOR A CHANGE!
DON'T WORRY ABOUT ME... I'M AS FRISKY AS A COLT!
A COUPLE OF HOURS AFTER THE PARTY HAS GOTTEN UNDER WAY IN ALL ITS STUFFY SPLENDOR!
I DON'T KNOW ABOUT UNCLE DUDLEY, BUT I'M BEIN' BORED TO SLEEP! GIMME AIR!
WELL, I SUPPOSE I'VE GOTTA GO BACK IN! I'VE NEVER SEEN ANYTHING DULLER THAN THIS PARTY IN MY LIFE!
WHY, MR CASEY... I DIDN'T SEE Y' BEFORE! WHAT'RE Y' DOIN' HERE?
CAN'T YUH SEE? I'M MINGLIN' WITH TH' GUESTS!
ROUTINE ASSIGNMENT! THEY ALWAYS CALL FOR A DICK AT THESE E-LITE BRAWLS TO GUARD THE DAMES' ICE! DON'T GIMME AWAY!
I WON'T! AND NO ONE WOULD EVER GUESS!
OH, HELLO, MINNIE! I WAS... SAY! WHAT'S THE MATTER? ...ARE Y' SICK?
NO... NOT AT ALL! I JUST FEEL... SORT OF... QUEER!

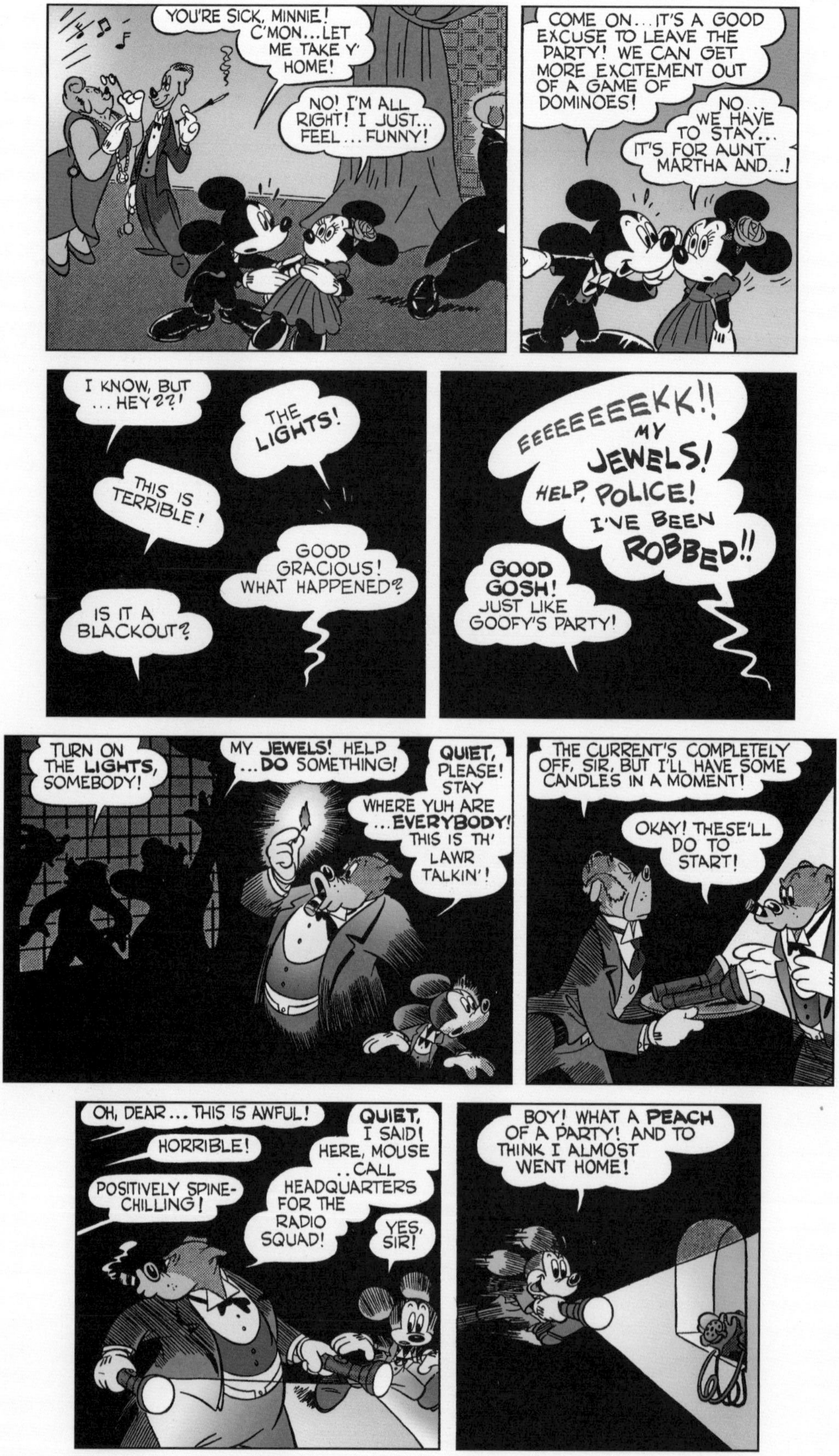
YOU'RE SICK, MINNIE! C'MON...LET ME TAKE Y' HOME!
NO! I'M ALL RIGHT! I JUST... FEEL... FUNNY!
COME ON... IT'S A GOOD EXCUSE TO LEAVE THE PARTY! WE CAN GET MORE EXCITEMENT OUT OF A GAME OF DOMINOES!
NO... WE HAVE TO STAY... IT'S FOR AUNT MARTHA AND...!
I KNOW, BUT ... HEY??!
THE LIGHTS!
THIS IS TERRIBLE!
GOOD GRACIOUS! WHAT HAPPENED?
IS IT A BLACKOUT?
EEEEEEEEKK!! MY JEWELS! HELP, POLICE! I'VE BEEN ROBBED!!
GOOD GOSH! JUST LIKE GOOFY'S PARTY!
TURN ON THE LIGHTS, SOMEBODY!
MY JEWELS! HELP ...DO SOMETHING!
QUIET, PLEASE! STAY WHERE YUH ARE ...EVERYBODY! THIS IS TH' LAWR TALKIN'!
THE CURRENT'S COMPLETELY OFF, SIR, BUT I'LL HAVE SOME CANDLES IN A MOMENT!
OKAY! THESE'LL DO TO START!
OH, DEAR... THIS IS AWFUL!
HORRIBLE!
POSITIVELY SPINE-CHILLING!
QUIET, I SAID! HERE, MOUSE ..CALL HEADQUARTERS FOR THE RADIO SQUAD!
YES, SIR!
BOY! WHAT A PEACH OF A PARTY! AND TO THINK I ALMOST WENT HOME!

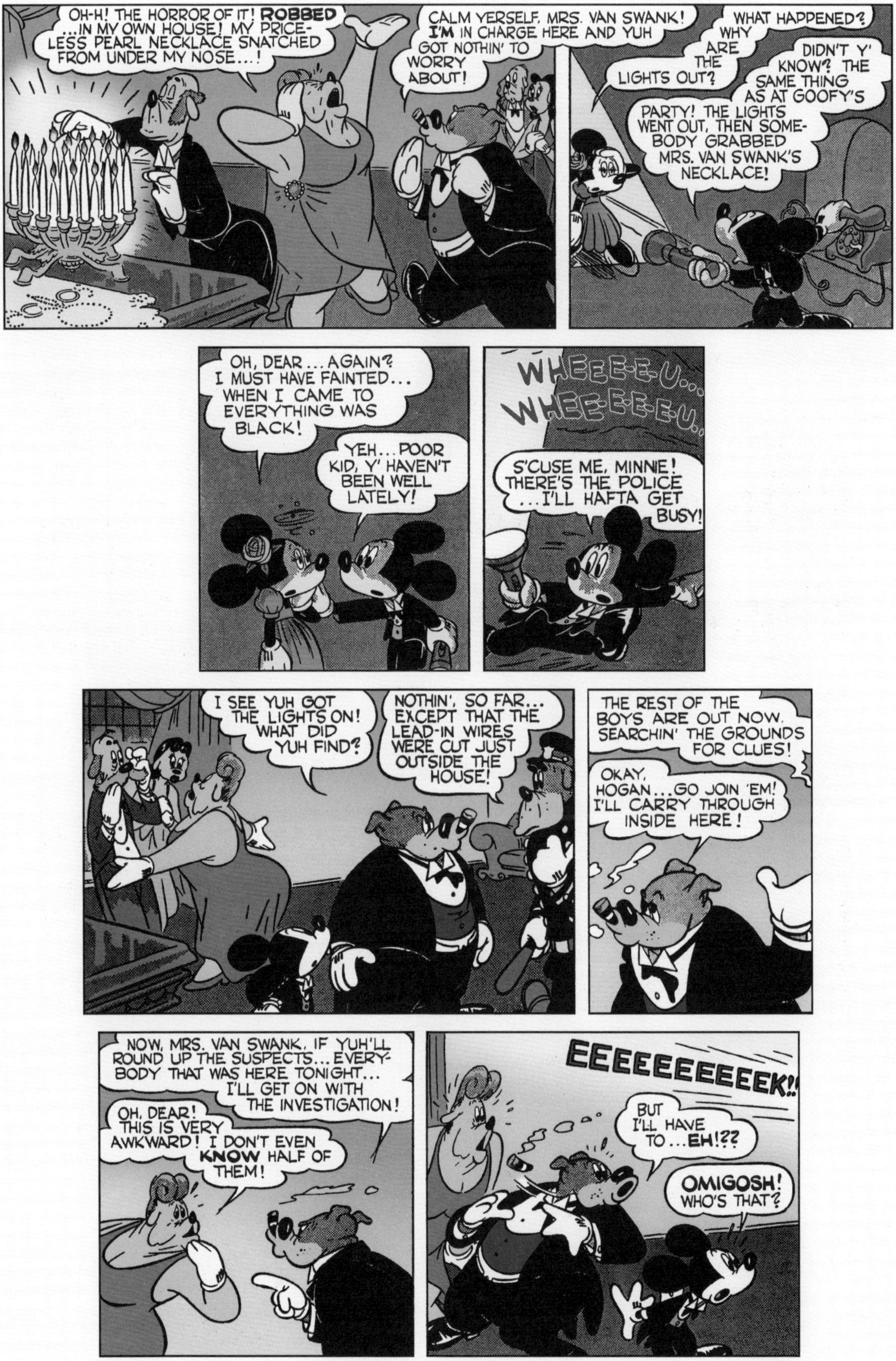
OH-H! THE HORROR OF IT! ROBBED ...IN MY OWN HOUSE! MY PRICE-LESS PEARL NECKLACE SNATCHED FROM UNDER MY NOSE...!
CALM YERSELF, MRS. VAN SWANK! I'M IN CHARGE HERE AND YUH GOT NOTHIN' TO WORRY ABOUT!
WHAT HAPPENED? WHY ARE THE LIGHTS OUT?
DIDN'T Y' KNOW? THE SAME THING AS AT GOOFY'S PARTY! THE LIGHTS WENT OUT, THEN SOME-BODY GRABBED MRS. VAN SWANK'S NECKLACE!
OH, DEAR... AGAIN? I MUST HAVE FAINTED... WHEN I CAME TO EVERYTHING WAS BLACK!
YEH... POOR KID, Y' HAVEN'T BEEN WELL LATELY!
WHEEE-E-U... WHEE-E-E-E-U...
S'CUSE ME, MINNIE! THERE'S THE POLICE ...I'LL HAFTA GET BUSY!
I SEE YUH GOT THE LIGHTS ON! WHAT DID YUH FIND?
NOTHIN', SO FAR... EXCEPT THAT THE LEAD-IN WIRES WERE CUT JUST OUTSIDE THE HOUSE!
THE REST OF THE BOYS ARE OUT NOW, SEARCHIN' THE GROUNDS FOR CLUES!
OKAY, HOGAN... GO JOIN 'EM! I'LL CARRY THROUGH INSIDE HERE!
NOW, MRS. VAN SWANK, IF YUH'LL ROUND UP THE SUSPECTS... EVERY-BODY THAT WAS HERE TONIGHT... I'LL GET ON WITH THE INVESTIGATION!
OH, DEAR! THIS IS VERY AWKWARD! I DON'T EVEN KNOW HALF OF THEM!
EEEEEEEEEEK!!
BUT I'LL HAVE TO ...EH!??
OMIGOSH! WHO'S THAT?

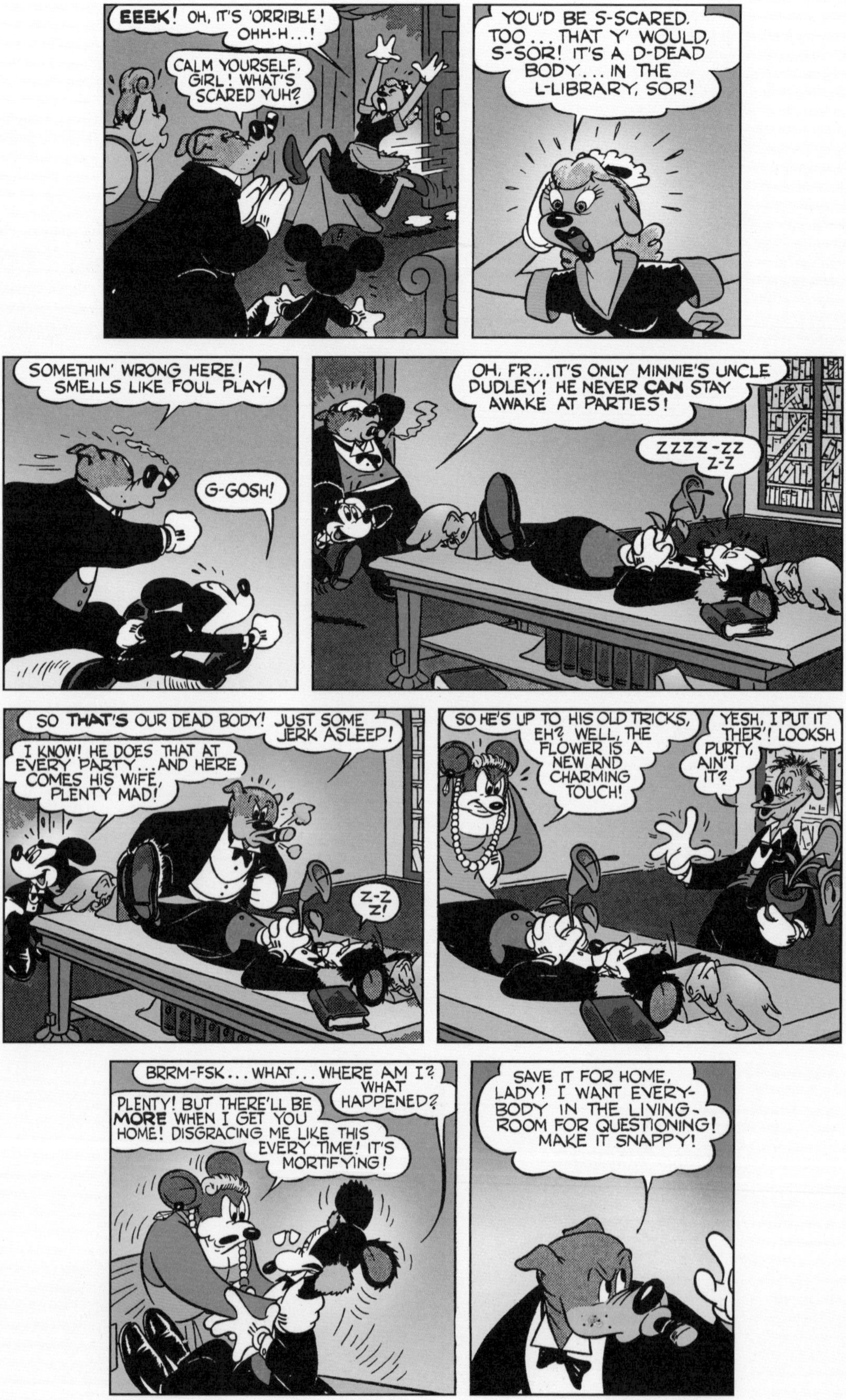
EEEK! OH, IT'S 'ORRIBLE! OHH-H...!
CALM YOURSELF, GIRL! WHAT'S SCARED YUH?
YOU'D BE S-SCARED, TOO... THAT Y' WOULD, S-SOR! IT'S A D-DEAD BODY... IN THE L-LIBRARY, SOR!
SOMETHIN' WRONG HERE! SMELLS LIKE FOUL PLAY!
G-GOSH!
OH, F'R... IT'S ONLY MINNIE'S UNCLE DUDLEY! HE NEVER CAN STAY AWAKE AT PARTIES!
ZZZZ-ZZ Z-Z
SO THAT'S OUR DEAD BODY! JUST SOME JERK ASLEEP!
I KNOW! HE DOES THAT AT EVERY PARTY... AND HERE COMES HIS WIFE, PLENTY MAD!
Z-Z Z!
SO HE'S UP TO HIS OLD TRICKS, EH? WELL, THE FLOWER IS A NEW AND CHARMING TOUCH!
YESH, I PUT IT THER'! LOOKSH PURTY, AIN'T IT?
BRRM-FSK... WHAT... WHERE AM I? WHAT HAPPENED?
PLENTY! BUT THERE'LL BE MORE WHEN I GET YOU HOME! DISGRACING ME LIKE THIS EVERY TIME! IT'S MORTIFYING!
SAVE IT FOR HOME, LADY! I WANT EVERY-BODY IN THE LIVING-ROOM FOR QUESTIONING! MAKE IT SNAPPY!

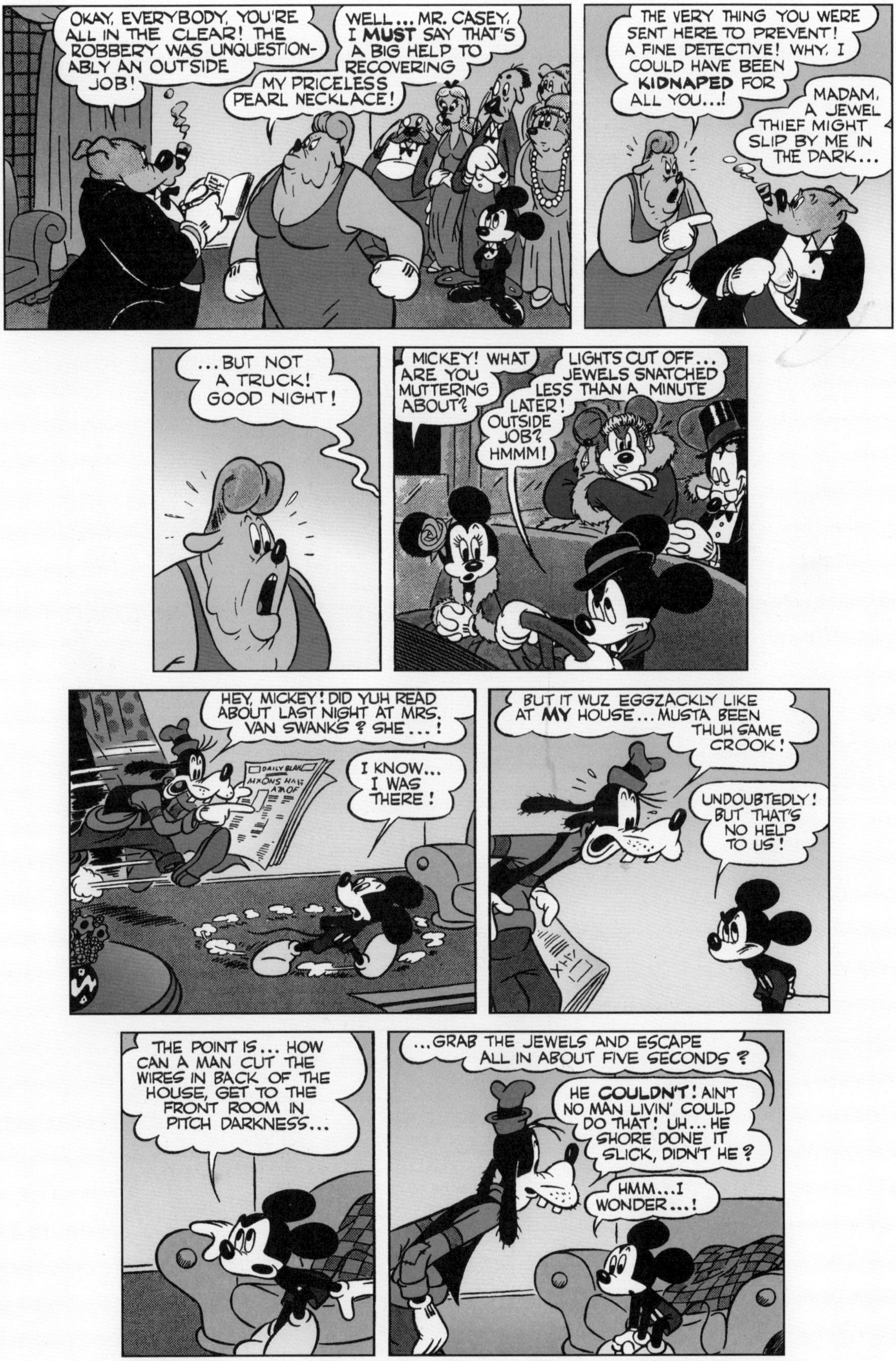
OKAY, EVERYBODY, YOU'RE ALL IN THE CLEAR! THE ROBBERY WAS UNQUESTIONABLY AN OUTSIDE JOB!
WELL... MR. CASEY, I **MUST** SAY THAT'S A BIG HELP TO RECOVERING
MY PRICELESS PEARL NECKLACE!
THE VERY THING YOU WERE SENT HERE TO PREVENT! A FINE DETECTIVE! WHY, I COULD HAVE BEEN **KIDNAPED** FOR ALL YOU...!
MADAM, A JEWEL THIEF MIGHT SLIP BY ME IN THE DARK...
...BUT NOT A TRUCK! GOOD NIGHT!
MICKEY! WHAT ARE YOU MUTTERING ABOUT?
LIGHTS CUT OFF... JEWELS SNATCHED LESS THAN A MINUTE LATER! OUTSIDE JOB? HMMM!
HEY, MICKEY! DID YUH READ ABOUT LAST NIGHT AT MRS. VAN SWANKS? SHE...!
I KNOW... I WAS THERE!
BUT IT WUZ EGGZACKLY LIKE AT **MY** HOUSE... MUSTA BEEN THUH SAME CROOK!
UNDOUBTEDLY! BUT THAT'S NO HELP TO US!
THE POINT IS... HOW CAN A MAN CUT THE WIRES IN BACK OF THE HOUSE, GET TO THE FRONT ROOM IN PITCH DARKNESS...
...GRAB THE JEWELS AND ESCAPE ALL IN ABOUT FIVE SECONDS?
HE **COULDN'T**! AIN'T NO MAN LIVIN' COULD DO THAT! UH... HE SHORE DONE IT SLICK, DIDN'T HE?
HMM...I WONDER...!

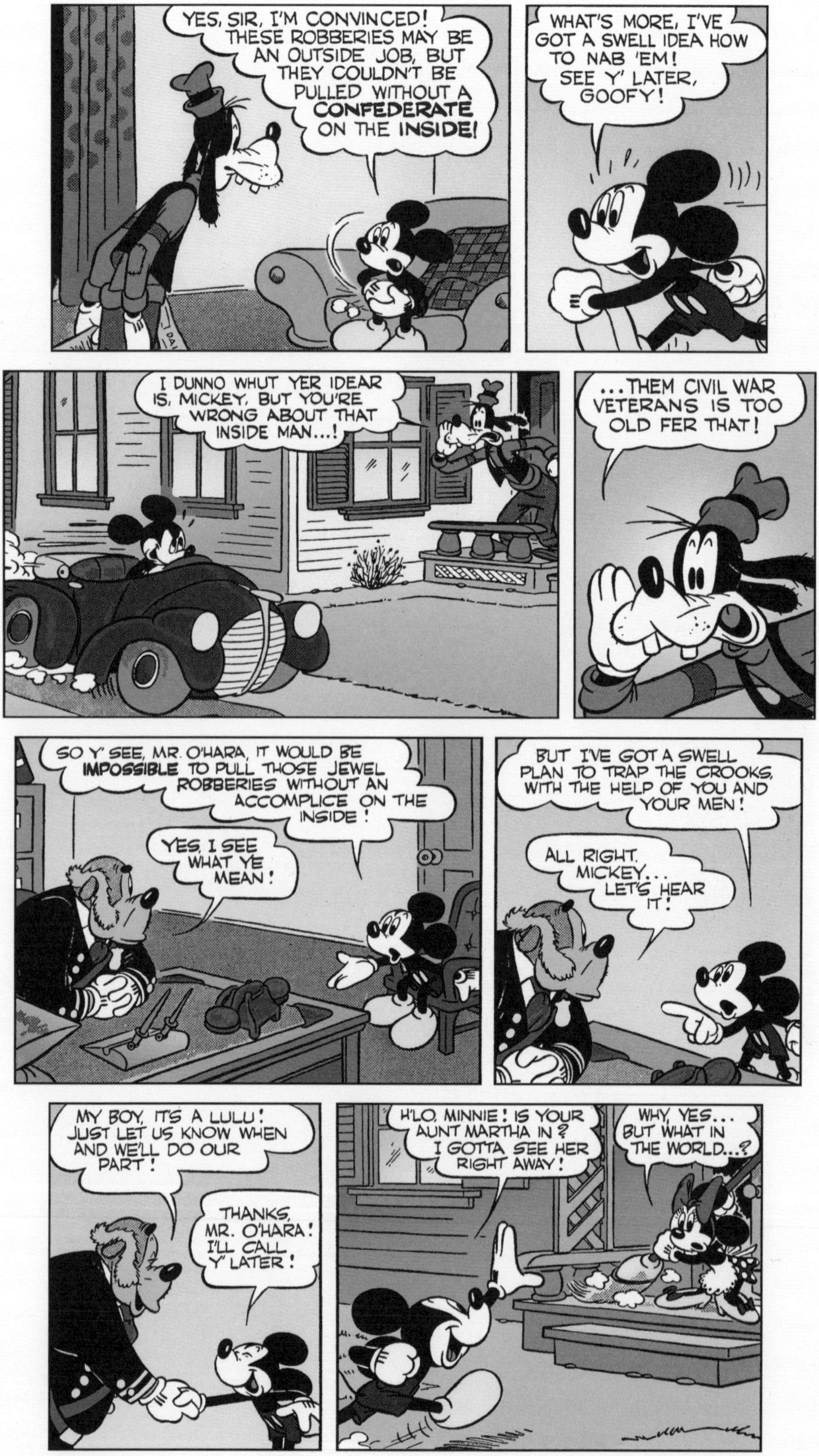
YES, SIR, I'M CONVINCED! THESE ROBBERIES MAY BE AN OUTSIDE JOB, BUT THEY COULDN'T BE PULLED WITHOUT A CONFEDERATE ON THE INSIDE!
WHAT'S MORE, I'VE GOT A SWELL IDEA HOW TO NAB 'EM! SEE Y' LATER, GOOFY!
I DUNNO WHUT YER IDEAR IS, MICKEY, BUT YOU'RE WRONG ABOUT THAT INSIDE MAN...!
...THEM CIVIL WAR VETERANS IS TOO OLD FER THAT!
SO Y' SEE, MR. O'HARA, IT WOULD BE IMPOSSIBLE TO PULL THOSE JEWEL ROBBERIES WITHOUT AN ACCOMPLICE ON THE INSIDE!
YES, I SEE WHAT YE MEAN!
BUT I'VE GOT A SWELL PLAN TO TRAP THE CROOKS, WITH THE HELP OF YOU AND YOUR MEN!
ALL RIGHT, MICKEY... LET'S HEAR IT!
MY BOY, IT'S A LULU! JUST LET US KNOW WHEN AND WE'LL DO OUR PART!
THANKS, MR. O'HARA! I'LL CALL Y' LATER!
H'LO, MINNIE! IS YOUR AUNT MARTHA IN? I GOTTA SEE HER RIGHT AWAY!
WHY, YES... BUT WHAT IN THE WORLD...?

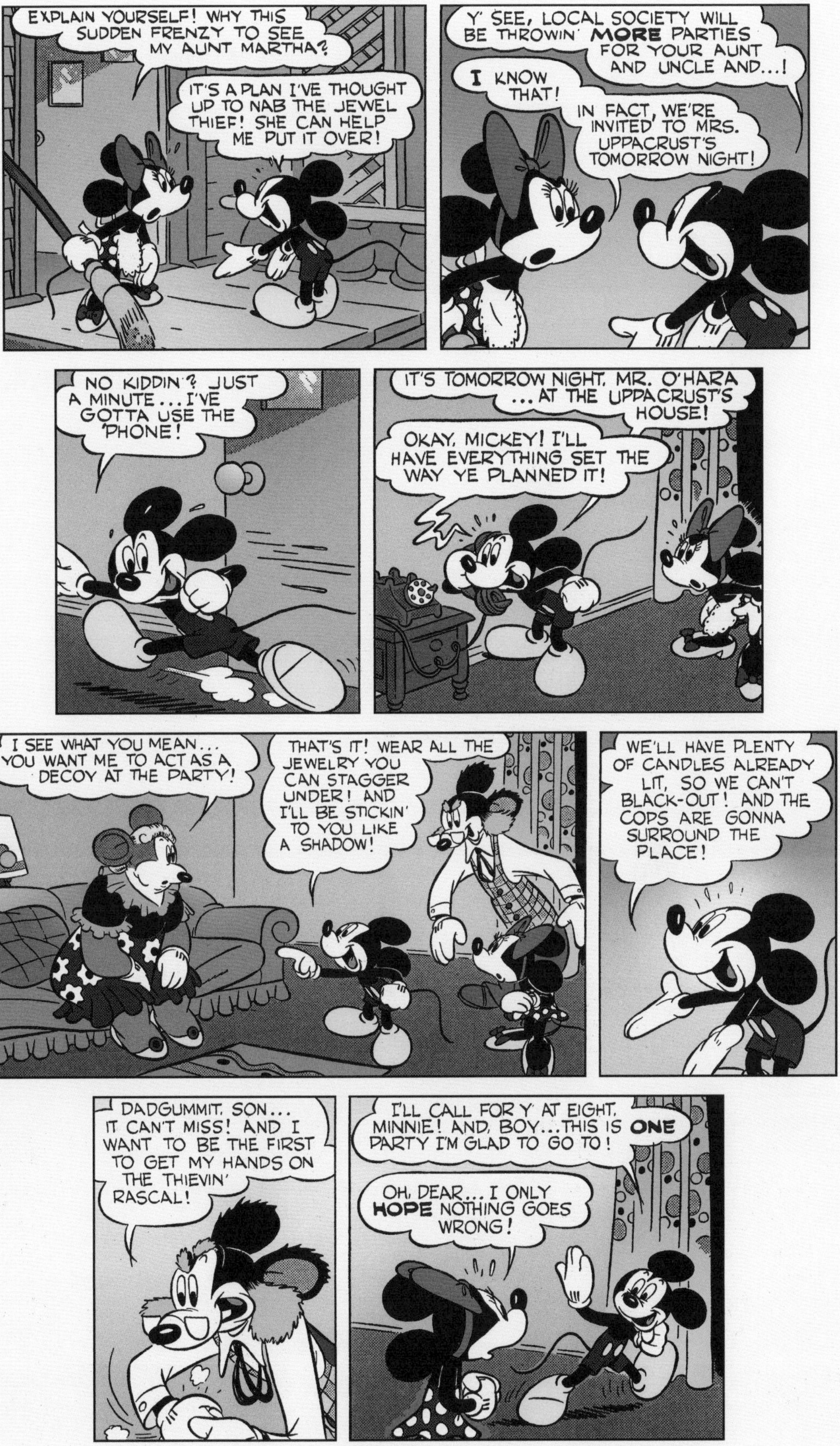
EXPLAIN YOURSELF! WHY THIS SUDDEN FRENZY TO SEE MY AUNT MARTHA?
IT'S A PLAN I'VE THOUGHT UP TO NAB THE JEWEL THIEF! SHE CAN HELP ME PUT IT OVER!
Y' SEE, LOCAL SOCIETY WILL BE THROWIN' MORE PARTIES FOR YOUR AUNT AND UNCLE AND...!
I KNOW THAT!
IN FACT, WE'RE INVITED TO MRS. UPPACRUST'S TOMORROW NIGHT!
NO KIDDIN'? JUST A MINUTE...I'VE GOTTA USE THE 'PHONE!
IT'S TOMORROW NIGHT, MR. O'HARA ...AT THE UPPACRUST'S HOUSE!
OKAY, MICKEY! I'LL HAVE EVERYTHING SET THE WAY YE PLANNED IT!
I SEE WHAT YOU MEAN... YOU WANT ME TO ACT AS A DECOY AT THE PARTY!
THAT'S IT! WEAR ALL THE JEWELRY YOU CAN STAGGER UNDER! AND I'LL BE STICKIN' TO YOU LIKE A SHADOW!
WE'LL HAVE PLENTY OF CANDLES ALREADY LIT, SO WE CAN'T BLACK-OUT! AND THE COPS ARE GONNA SURROUND THE PLACE!
DADGUMMIT, SON... IT CAN'T MISS! AND I WANT TO BE THE FIRST TO GET MY HANDS ON THE THIEVIN' RASCAL!
I'LL CALL FOR Y' AT EIGHT, MINNIE! AND, BOY...THIS IS ONE PARTY I'M GLAD TO GO TO!
OH, DEAR...I ONLY HOPE NOTHING GOES WRONG!

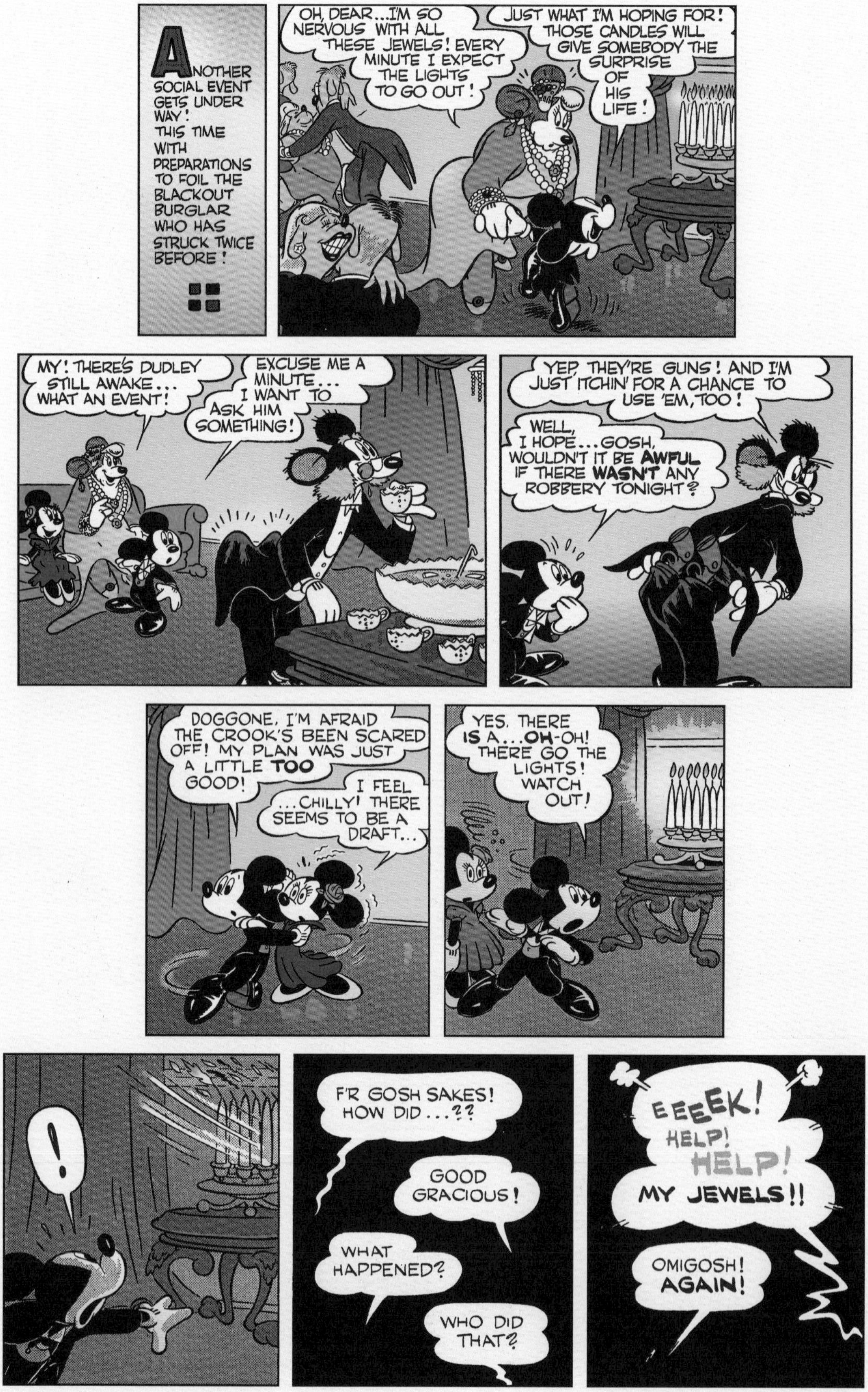
ANOTHER SOCIAL EVENT GETS UNDER WAY! THIS TIME WITH PREPARATIONS TO FOIL THE BLACKOUT BURGLAR WHO HAS STRUCK TWICE BEFORE!
OH, DEAR...I'M SO NERVOUS WITH ALL THESE JEWELS! EVERY MINUTE I EXPECT THE LIGHTS TO GO OUT!
JUST WHAT I'M HOPING FOR! THOSE CANDLES WILL GIVE SOMEBODY THE SURPRISE OF HIS LIFE!
MY! THERE'S DUDLEY STILL AWAKE... WHAT AN EVENT!
EXCUSE ME A MINUTE... I WANT TO ASK HIM SOMETHING!
YEP, THEY'RE GUNS! AND I'M JUST ITCHIN' FOR A CHANCE TO USE 'EM, TOO!
WELL, I HOPE...GOSH, WOULDN'T IT BE **AWFUL** IF THERE **WASN'T** ANY ROBBERY TONIGHT?
DOGGONE, I'M AFRAID THE CROOK'S BEEN SCARED OFF! MY PLAN WAS JUST A LITTLE **TOO** GOOD!
I FEEL ...CHILLY! THERE SEEMS TO BE A DRAFT...
YES. THERE **IS** A...**OH**-OH! THERE GO THE LIGHTS! WATCH OUT!
!
F'R GOSH SAKES! HOW DID...??
GOOD GRACIOUS!
WHAT HAPPENED?
WHO DID THAT?
EEEEK! HELP! HELP! MY JEWELS!!
OMIGOSH! AGAIN!

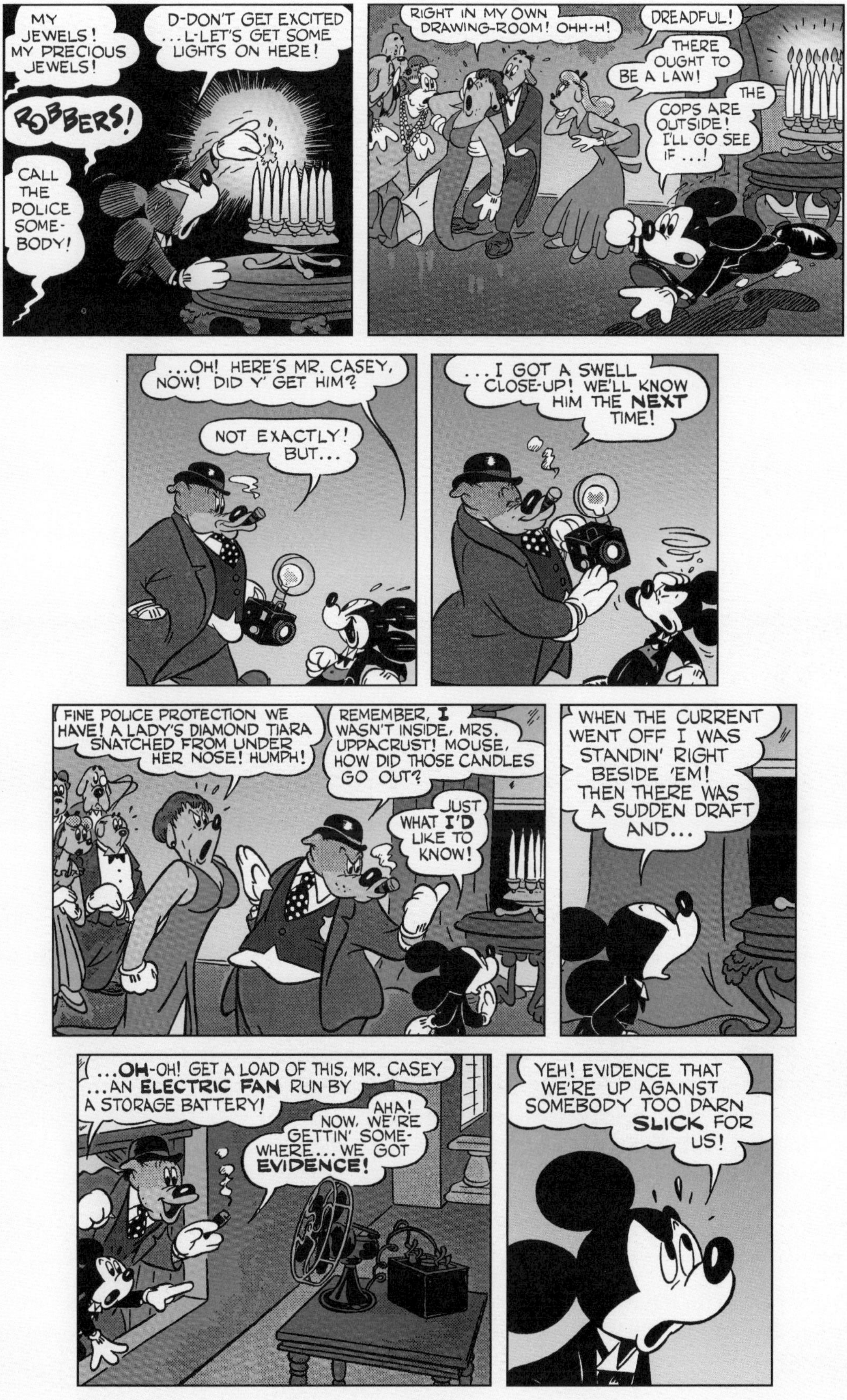
MY JEWELS! MY PRECIOUS JEWELS!
ROBBERS!
CALL THE POLICE SOMEBODY!
D-DON'T GET EXCITED ... L-LET'S GET SOME LIGHTS ON HERE!
RIGHT IN MY OWN DRAWING-ROOM! OHH-H!
DREADFUL!
THERE OUGHT TO BE A LAW!
THE COPS ARE OUTSIDE! I'LL GO SEE IF ...!
...OH! HERE'S MR. CASEY, NOW! DID Y' GET HIM?
NOT EXACTLY! BUT...
...I GOT A SWELL CLOSE-UP! WE'LL KNOW HIM THE NEXT TIME!
FINE POLICE PROTECTION WE HAVE! A LADY'S DIAMOND TIARA SNATCHED FROM UNDER HER NOSE! HUMPH!
REMEMBER, I WASN'T INSIDE, MRS. UPPACRUST! MOUSE, HOW DID THOSE CANDLES GO OUT?
JUST WHAT I'D LIKE TO KNOW!
WHEN THE CURRENT WENT OFF I WAS STANDIN' RIGHT BESIDE 'EM! THEN THERE WAS A SUDDEN DRAFT AND...
...OH-OH! GET A LOAD OF THIS, MR. CASEY ...AN ELECTRIC FAN RUN BY A STORAGE BATTERY!
AHA! NOW, WE'RE GETTIN' SOMEWHERE... WE GOT EVIDENCE!
YEH! EVIDENCE THAT WE'RE UP AGAINST SOMEBODY TOO DARN SLICK FOR US!

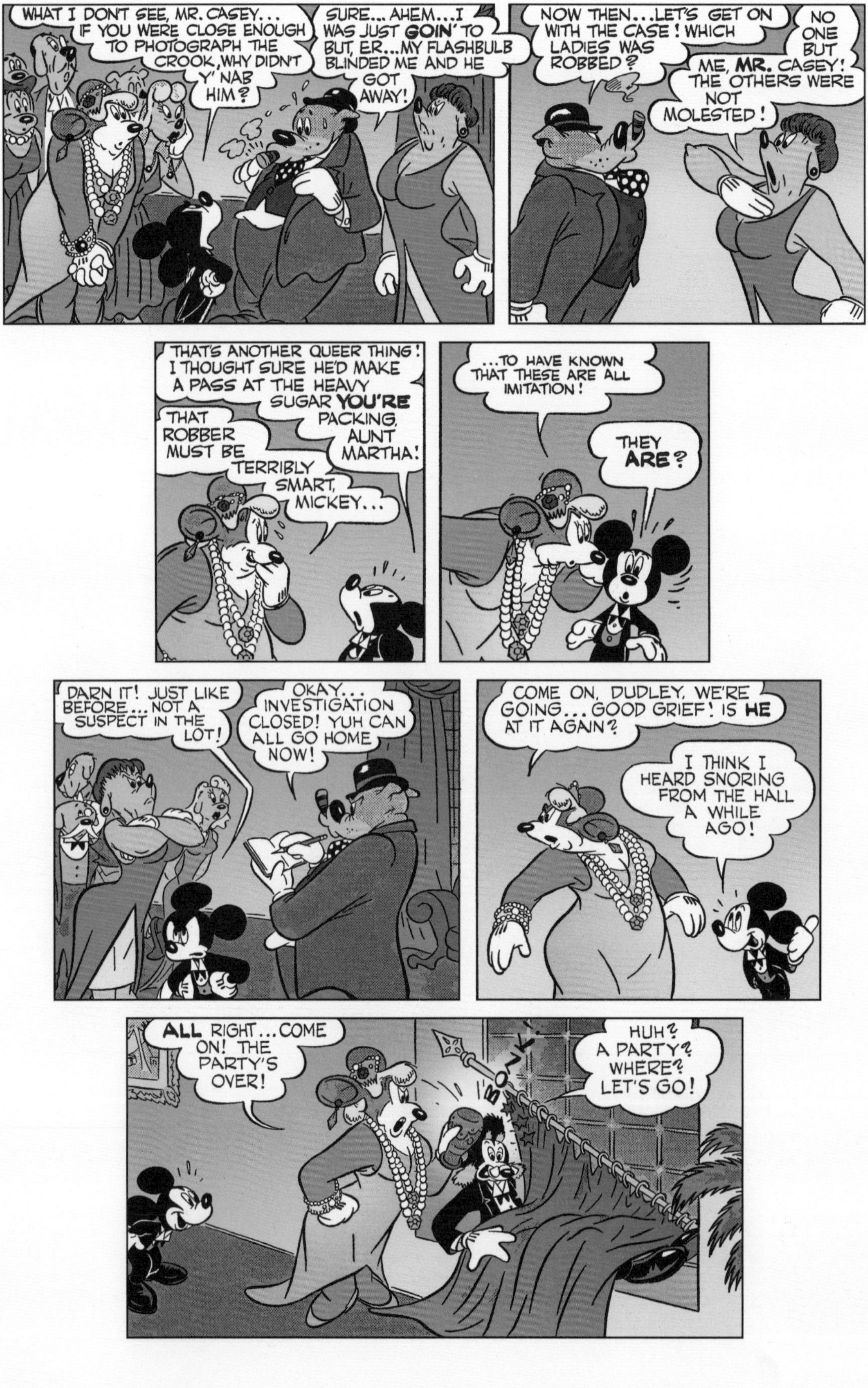
WHAT I DON'T SEE, MR. CASEY... IF YOU WERE CLOSE ENOUGH TO PHOTOGRAPH THE CROOK, WHY DIDN'T Y' NAB HIM?
SURE... AHEM... I WAS JUST GOIN' TO BUT, ER... MY FLASHBULB BLINDED ME AND HE GOT AWAY!
NOW THEN... LET'S GET ON WITH THE CASE! WHICH LADIES WAS ROBBED?
NO ONE BUT ME, MR. CASEY! THE OTHERS WERE NOT MOLESTED!
THAT'S ANOTHER QUEER THING! I THOUGHT SURE HE'D MAKE A PASS AT THE HEAVY SUGAR YOU'RE PACKING, AUNT MARTHA!
THAT ROBBER MUST BE TERRIBLY SMART, MICKEY...
...TO HAVE KNOWN THAT THESE ARE ALL IMITATION!
THEY ARE?
DARN IT! JUST LIKE BEFORE... NOT A SUSPECT IN THE LOT!
OKAY... INVESTIGATION CLOSED! YUH CAN ALL GO HOME NOW!
COME ON, DUDLEY, WE'RE GOING... GOOD GRIEF! IS HE AT IT AGAIN?
I THINK I HEARD SNORING FROM THE HALL A WHILE AGO!
ALL RIGHT... COME ON! THE PARTY'S OVER!
BONK
HUH? A PARTY? WHERE? LET'S GO!

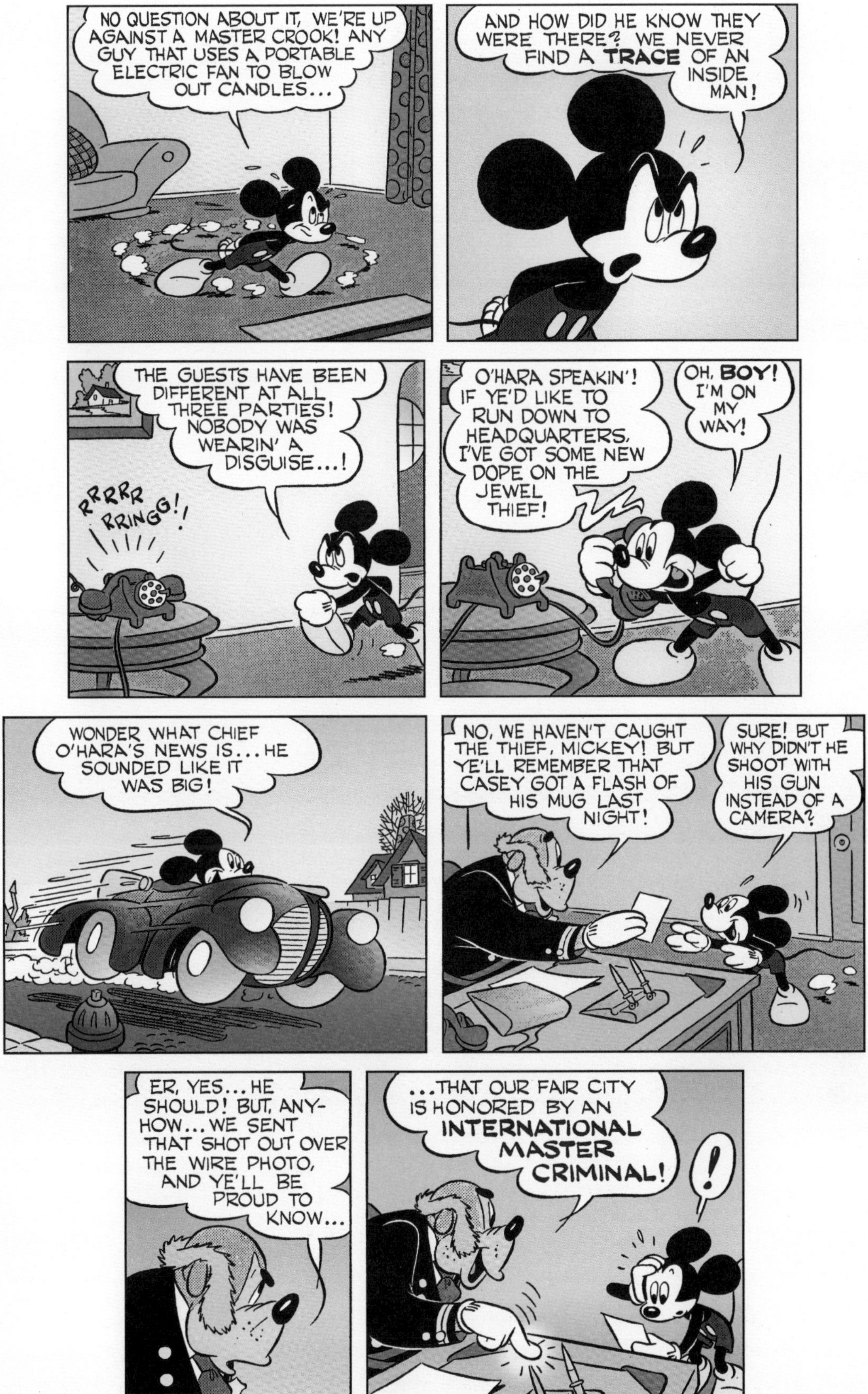
NO QUESTION ABOUT IT, WE'RE UP AGAINST A MASTER CROOK! ANY GUY THAT USES A PORTABLE ELECTRIC FAN TO BLOW OUT CANDLES...
AND HOW DID HE KNOW THEY WERE THERE? WE NEVER FIND A TRACE OF AN INSIDE MAN!
THE GUESTS HAVE BEEN DIFFERENT AT ALL THREE PARTIES! NOBODY WAS WEARIN' A DISGUISE...!
RRRRR RRINGG!!
O'HARA SPEAKIN'! IF YE'D LIKE TO RUN DOWN TO HEADQUARTERS, I'VE GOT SOME NEW DOPE ON THE JEWEL THIEF!
OH, BOY! I'M ON MY WAY!
WONDER WHAT CHIEF O'HARA'S NEWS IS... HE SOUNDED LIKE IT WAS BIG!
NO, WE HAVEN'T CAUGHT THE THIEF, MICKEY! BUT YE'LL REMEMBER THAT CASEY GOT A FLASH OF HIS MUG LAST NIGHT!
SURE! BUT WHY DIDN'T HE SHOOT WITH HIS GUN INSTEAD OF A CAMERA?
ER, YES... HE SHOULD! BUT, ANYHOW... WE SENT THAT SHOT OUT OVER THE WIRE PHOTO, AND YE'LL BE PROUD TO KNOW...
...THAT OUR FAIR CITY IS HONORED BY AN INTERNATIONAL MASTER CRIMINAL!
!

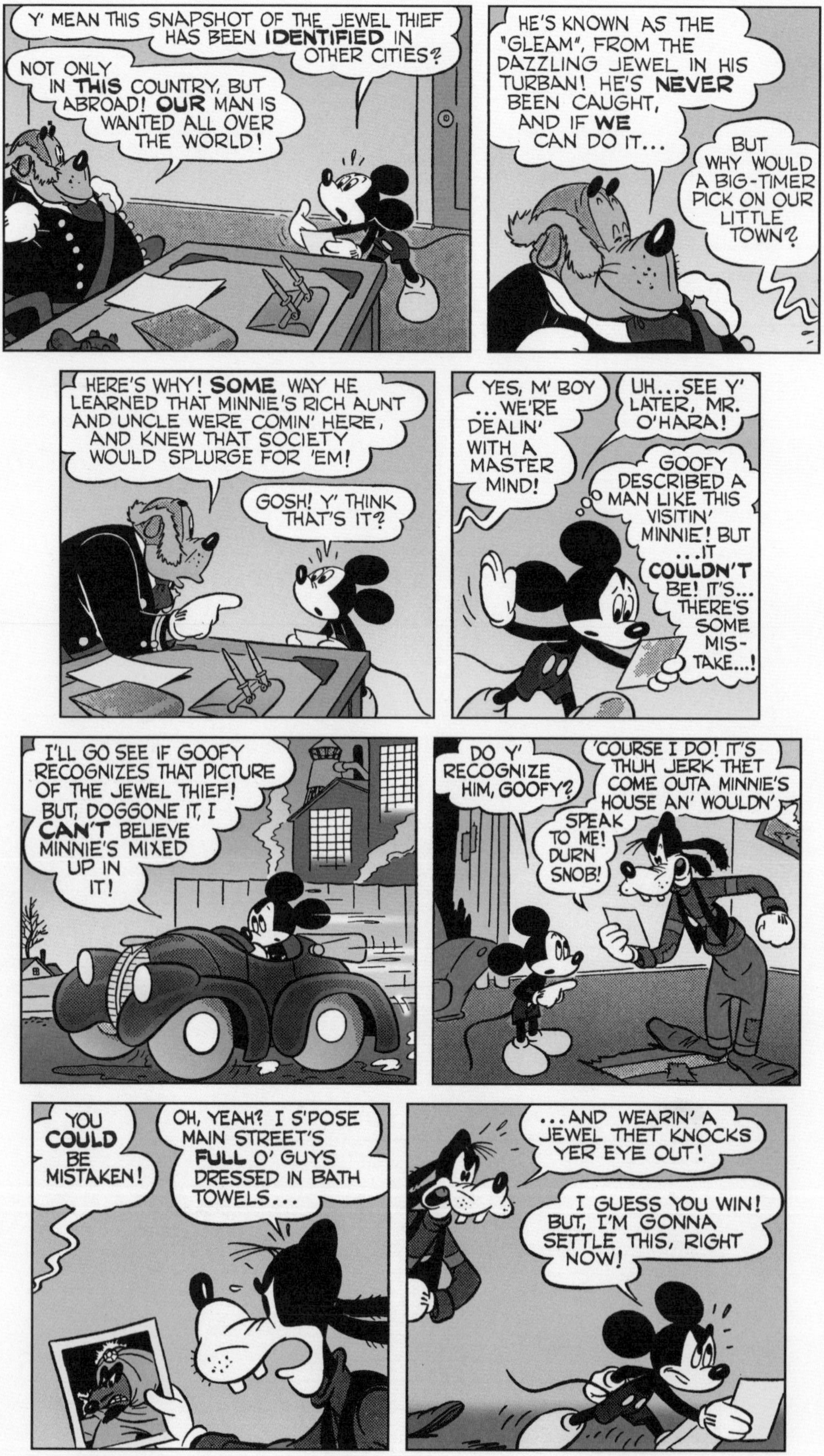
Y' MEAN THIS SNAPSHOT OF THE JEWEL THIEF HAS BEEN IDENTIFIED IN OTHER CITIES?
NOT ONLY IN THIS COUNTRY, BUT ABROAD! OUR MAN IS WANTED ALL OVER THE WORLD!
HE'S KNOWN AS THE "GLEAM", FROM THE DAZZLING JEWEL IN HIS TURBAN! HE'S NEVER BEEN CAUGHT, AND IF WE CAN DO IT...
BUT WHY WOULD A BIG-TIMER PICK ON OUR LITTLE TOWN?
HERE'S WHY! SOME WAY HE LEARNED THAT MINNIE'S RICH AUNT AND UNCLE WERE COMIN' HERE, AND KNEW THAT SOCIETY WOULD SPLURGE FOR 'EM!
GOSH! Y' THINK THAT'S IT?
YES, M' BOY ...WE'RE DEALIN' WITH A MASTER MIND!
UH...SEE Y' LATER, MR. O'HARA!
GOOFY DESCRIBED A MAN LIKE THIS VISITIN' MINNIE! BUT ...IT COULDN'T BE! IT'S... THERE'S SOME MIS-TAKE...!
I'LL GO SEE IF GOOFY RECOGNIZES THAT PICTURE OF THE JEWEL THIEF! BUT, DOGGONE IT, I CAN'T BELIEVE MINNIE'S MIXED UP IN IT!
DO Y' RECOGNIZE HIM, GOOFY?
'COURSE I DO! IT'S THUH JERK THET COME OUTA MINNIE'S HOUSE AN' WOULDN'
SPEAK TO ME! DURN SNOB!
YOU COULD BE MISTAKEN!
OH, YEAH? I S'POSE MAIN STREET'S FULL O' GUYS DRESSED IN BATH TOWELS...
...AND WEARIN' A JEWEL THET KNOCKS YER EYE OUT!
I GUESS YOU WIN! BUT, I'M GONNA SETTLE THIS, RIGHT NOW!

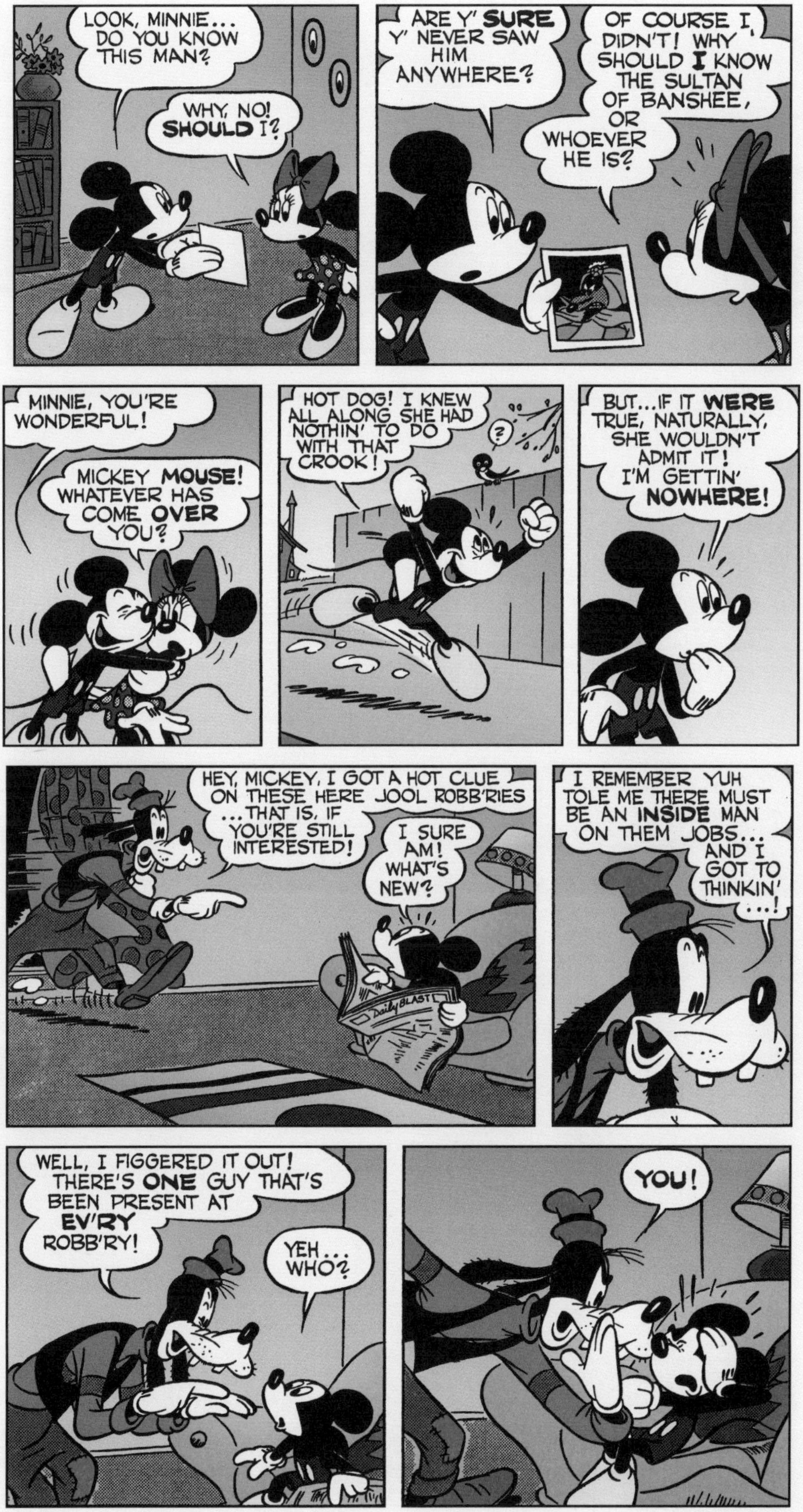
LOOK, MINNIE... DO YOU KNOW THIS MAN?
WHY, NO! SHOULD I?
ARE Y' SURE Y' NEVER SAW HIM ANYWHERE?
OF COURSE I DIDN'T! WHY SHOULD I KNOW THE SULTAN OF BANSHEE, OR WHOEVER HE IS?
MINNIE, YOU'RE WONDERFUL!
MICKEY MOUSE! WHATEVER HAS COME OVER YOU?
HOT DOG! I KNEW ALL ALONG SHE HAD NOTHIN' TO DO WITH THAT CROOK!
?
BUT...IF IT WERE TRUE, NATURALLY, SHE WOULDN'T ADMIT IT! I'M GETTIN' NOWHERE!
HEY, MICKEY, I GOT A HOT CLUE ON THESE HERE JOOL ROBB'RIES ...THAT IS, IF YOU'RE STILL INTERESTED!
I SURE AM! WHAT'S NEW?
Daily BLAST
I REMEMBER YUH TOLE ME THERE MUST BE AN INSIDE MAN ON THEM JOBS... AND I GOT TO THINKIN' ...!
WELL, I FIGGERED IT OUT! THERE'S ONE GUY THAT'S BEEN PRESENT AT EV'RY ROBB'RY!
YEH... WHO?
YOU!

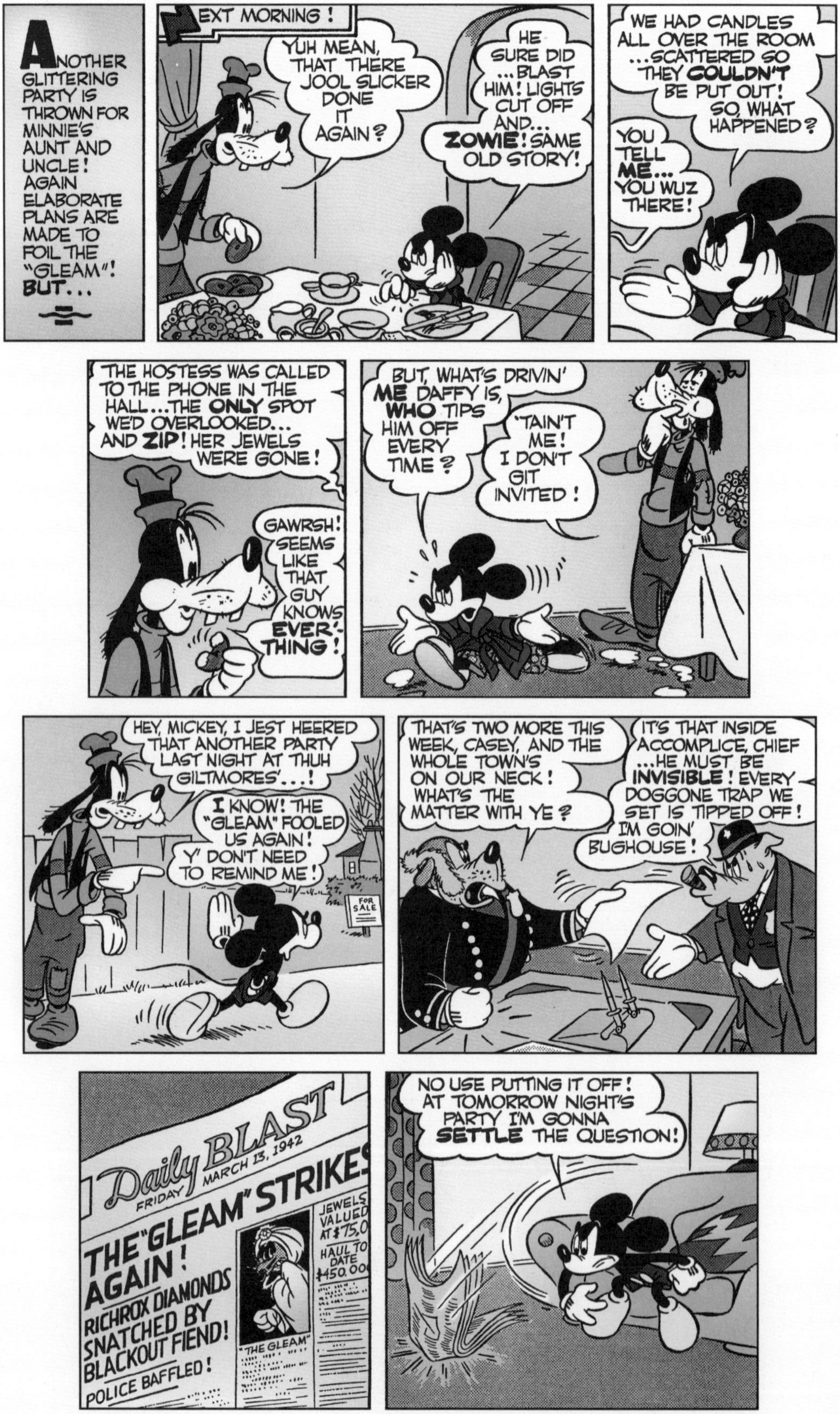
ANOTHER GLITTERING PARTY IS THROWN FOR MINNIE'S AUNT AND UNCLE! AGAIN ELABORATE PLANS ARE MADE TO FOIL THE "GLEAM"! BUT...
NEXT MORNING!
YUH MEAN, THAT THERE JOOL SLICKER DONE IT AGAIN?
HE SURE DID ...BLAST HIM! LIGHTS CUT OFF AND... ZOWIE! SAME OLD STORY!
WE HAD CANDLES ALL OVER THE ROOM ...SCATTERED SO THEY COULDN'T BE PUT OUT!
SO, WHAT HAPPENED?
YOU TELL ME... YOU WUZ THERE!
THE HOSTESS WAS CALLED TO THE PHONE IN THE HALL...THE ONLY SPOT WE'D OVERLOOKED... AND ZIP! HER JEWELS WERE GONE!
GAWRSH! SEEMS LIKE THAT GUY KNOWS EVER'-THING!
BUT, WHAT'S DRIVIN' ME DAFFY IS, WHO TIPS HIM OFF EVERY TIME?
'TAIN'T ME! I DON'T GIT INVITED!
HEY, MICKEY, I JEST HEERED THAT ANOTHER PARTY LAST NIGHT AT THUH GILTMORES'...!
I KNOW! THE "GLEAM" FOOLED US AGAIN! Y' DON'T NEED TO REMIND ME!
FOR SALE
THAT'S TWO MORE THIS WEEK, CASEY, AND THE WHOLE TOWN'S ON OUR NECK! WHAT'S THE MATTER WITH YE?
IT'S THAT INSIDE ACCOMPLICE, CHIEF ...HE MUST BE INVISIBLE! EVERY DOGGONE TRAP WE SET IS TIPPED OFF! I'M GOIN' BUGHOUSE!
Daily BLAST
FRIDAY MARCH 13, 1942
"GLEAM" STRIKES
THE "GLEAM" AGAIN!
RICHROX DIAMONDS SNATCHED BY BLACKOUT FIEND!
POLICE BAFFLED!
JEWELS VALUED AT $75,0
HAUL TO DATE $450,00
"THE GLEAM"
NO USE PUTTING IT OFF! AT TOMORROW NIGHT'S PARTY I'M GONNA SETTLE THE QUESTION!

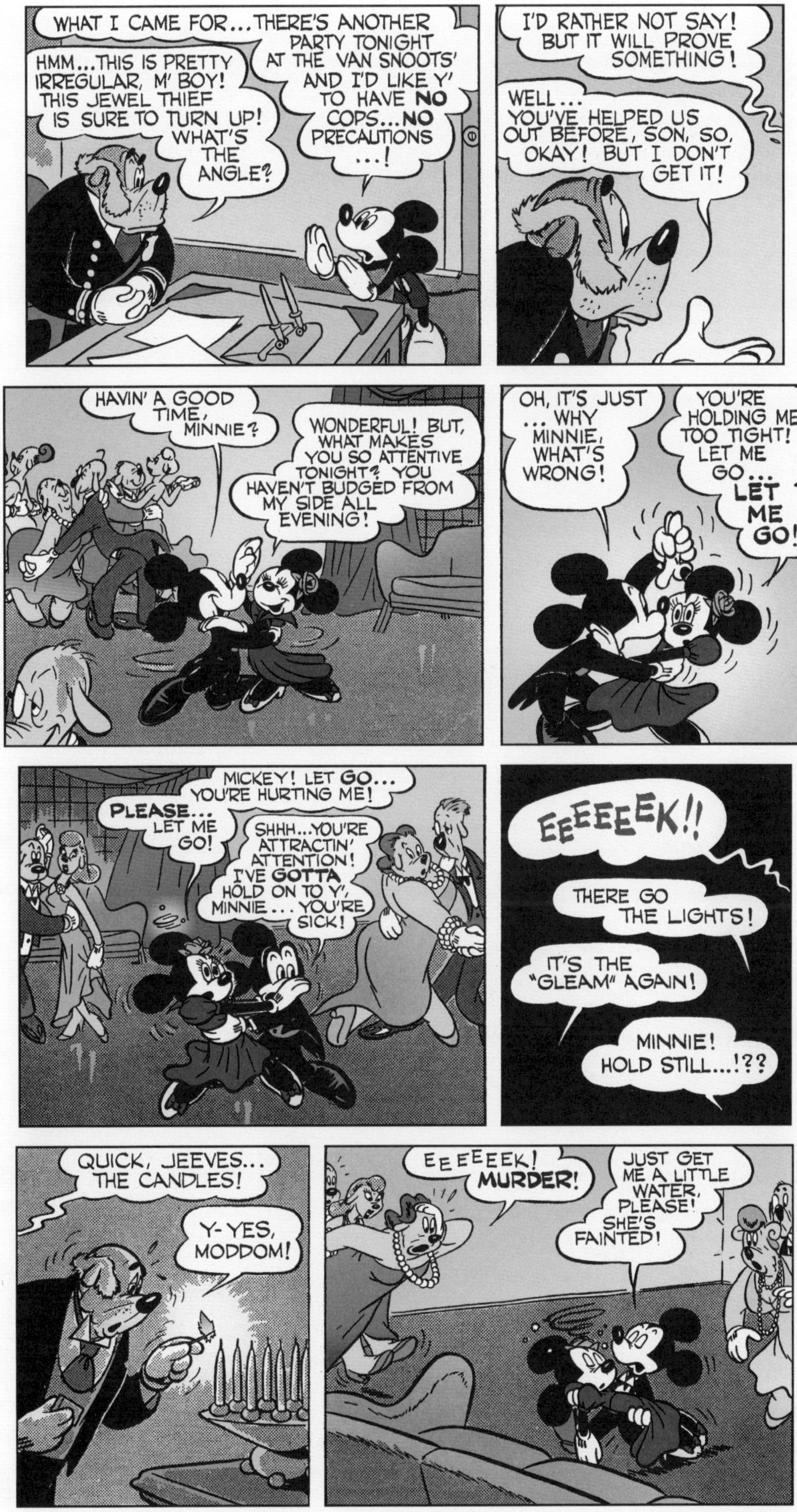
WHAT I CAME FOR... THERE'S ANOTHER PARTY TONIGHT AT THE VAN SNOOTS' AND I'D LIKE Y' TO HAVE NO COPS... NO PRECAUTIONS ...!
HMM... THIS IS PRETTY IRREGULAR, M' BOY! THIS JEWEL THIEF IS SURE TO TURN UP! WHAT'S THE ANGLE?
I'D RATHER NOT SAY! BUT IT WILL PROVE SOMETHING!
WELL... YOU'VE HELPED US OUT BEFORE, SON, SO, OKAY! BUT I DON'T GET IT!
HAVIN' A GOOD TIME, MINNIE?
WONDERFUL! BUT, WHAT MAKES YOU SO ATTENTIVE TONIGHT? YOU HAVEN'T BUDGED FROM MY SIDE ALL EVENING!
OH, IT'S JUST ... WHY MINNIE, WHAT'S WRONG!
YOU'RE HOLDING ME TOO TIGHT! LET ME GO... LET ME GO!
MICKEY! LET GO... YOU'RE HURTING ME!
PLEASE... LET ME GO!
SHHH... YOU'RE ATTRACTIN' ATTENTION! I'VE GOTTA HOLD ON TO Y', MINNIE... YOU'RE SICK!
EEEEEEK!!
THERE GO THE LIGHTS!
IT'S THE "GLEAM" AGAIN!
MINNIE! HOLD STILL...!??
QUICK, JEEVES... THE CANDLES!
Y-YES, MODDOM!
EEEEEEK! MURDER!
JUST GET ME A LITTLE WATER, PLEASE! SHE'S FAINTED!

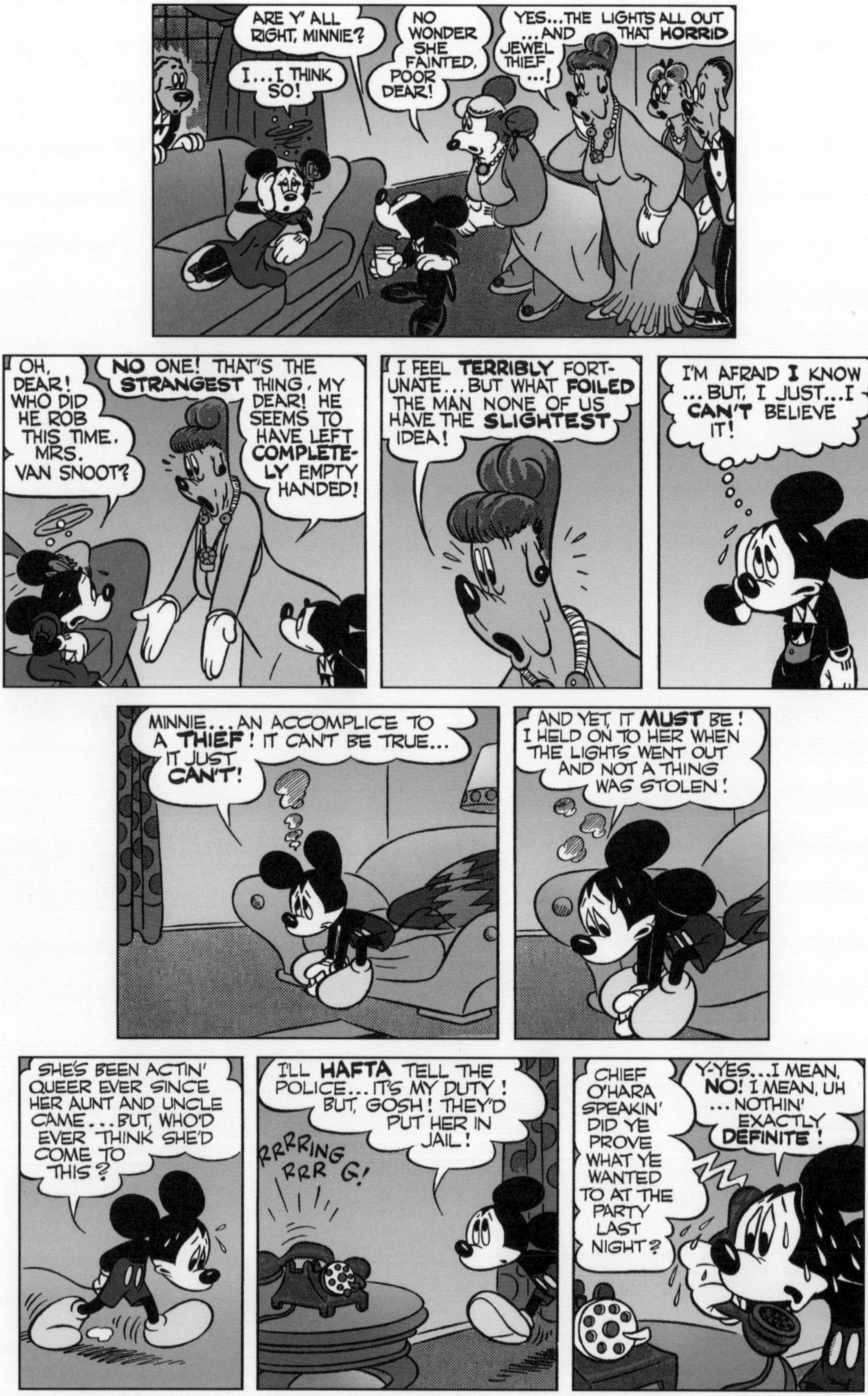
ARE Y' ALL RIGHT, MINNIE?
I...I THINK SO!
NO WONDER SHE FAINTED, POOR DEAR!
YES...THE LIGHTS ALL OUT ...AND THAT HORRID JEWEL THIEF ...!
OH, DEAR! WHO DID HE ROB THIS TIME. MRS. VAN SNOOT?
NO ONE! THAT'S THE STRANGEST THING, MY DEAR! HE SEEMS TO HAVE LEFT COMPLETE-LY EMPTY HANDED!
I FEEL TERRIBLY FORT-UNATE...BUT WHAT FOILED THE MAN NONE OF US HAVE THE SLIGHTEST IDEA!
I'M AFRAID I KNOW ...BUT, I JUST...I CAN'T BELIEVE IT!
MINNIE...AN ACCOMPLICE TO A THIEF! IT CAN'T BE TRUE... IT JUST CAN'T!
AND YET, IT MUST BE! I HELD ON TO HER WHEN THE LIGHTS WENT OUT AND NOT A THING WAS STOLEN!
SHE'S BEEN ACTIN' QUEER EVER SINCE HER AUNT AND UNCLE CAME...BUT, WHO'D EVER THINK SHE'D COME TO THIS?
I'LL HAFTA TELL THE POLICE...IT'S MY DUTY! BUT, GOSH! THEY'D PUT HER IN JAIL!
RRRRING RRR G!
CHIEF O'HARA SPEAKIN' DID YE PROVE WHAT YE WANTED TO AT THE PARTY LAST NIGHT?
Y-YES...I MEAN, NO! I MEAN, UH ...NOTHIN' EXACTLY DEFINITE!

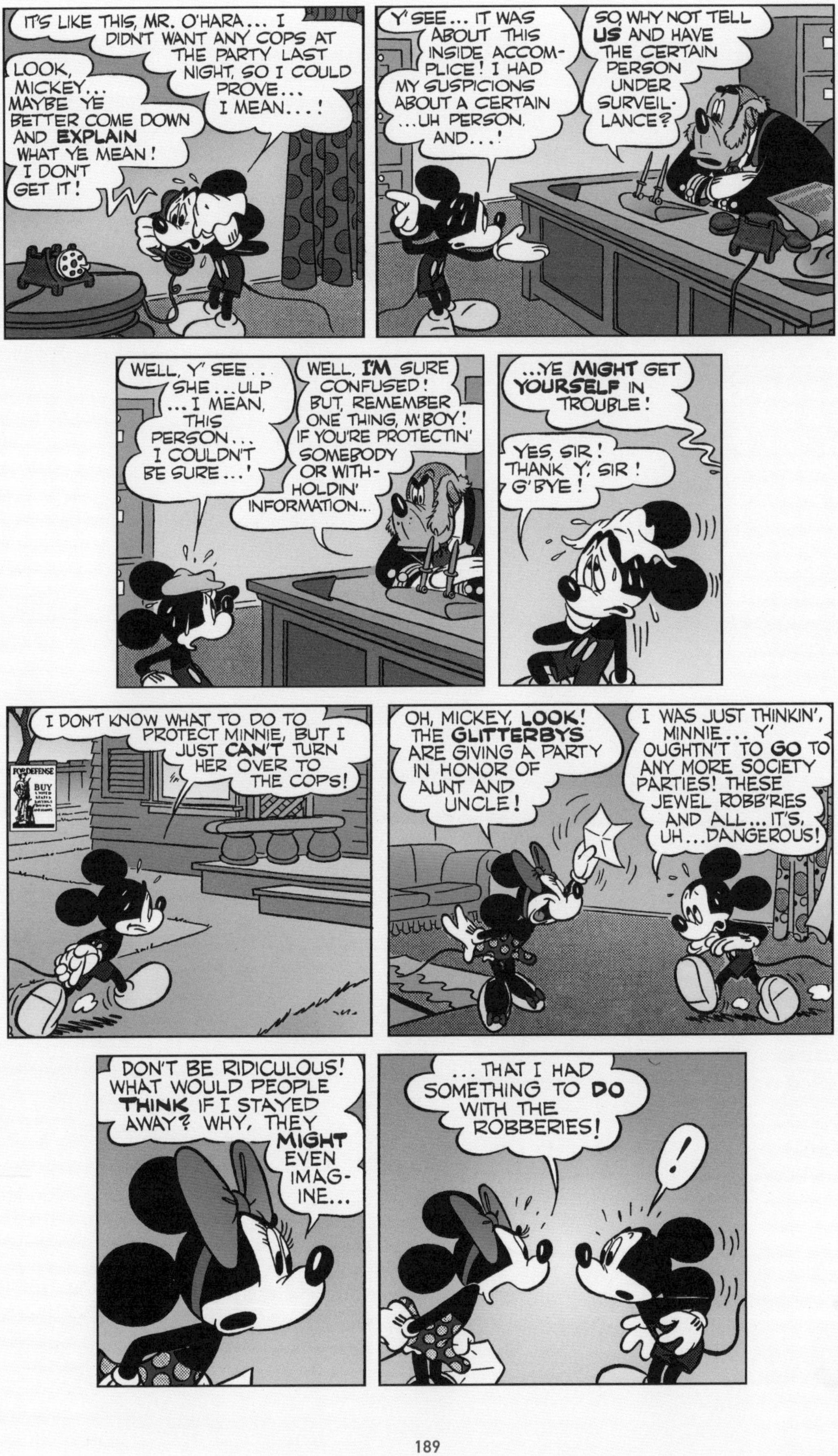
IT'S LIKE THIS, MR. O'HARA... I DIDN'T WANT ANY COPS AT THE PARTY LAST NIGHT, SO I COULD PROVE... I MEAN...!
LOOK, MICKEY... MAYBE YE BETTER COME DOWN AND EXPLAIN WHAT YE MEAN! I DON'T GET IT!
Y' SEE... IT WAS ABOUT THIS INSIDE ACCOMPLICE! I HAD MY SUSPICIONS ABOUT A CERTAIN ...UH PERSON, AND...!
SO, WHY NOT TELL US AND HAVE THE CERTAIN PERSON UNDER SURVEILLANCE?
WELL, Y' SEE... SHE... ULP ... I MEAN, THIS PERSON... I COULDN'T BE SURE...'
WELL, I'M SURE CONFUSED! BUT, REMEMBER ONE THING, M'BOY! IF YOU'RE PROTECTIN' SOMEBODY OR WITHHOLDIN' INFORMATION...
...YE MIGHT GET YOURSELF IN TROUBLE!
YES, SIR! THANK Y', SIR! G'BYE!
I DON'T KNOW WHAT TO DO TO PROTECT MINNIE, BUT I JUST CAN'T TURN HER OVER TO THE COPS!
FOR DEFENSE
BUY
OH, MICKEY, LOOK! THE GLITTERBYS ARE GIVING A PARTY IN HONOR OF AUNT AND UNCLE!
I WAS JUST THINKIN', MINNIE... Y' OUGHTN'T TO GO TO ANY MORE SOCIETY PARTIES! THESE JEWEL ROBB'RIES AND ALL... IT'S, UH... DANGEROUS!
DON'T BE RIDICULOUS! WHAT WOULD PEOPLE THINK IF I STAYED AWAY? WHY, THEY MIGHT EVEN IMAGINE...
...THAT I HAD SOMETHING TO DO WITH THE ROBBERIES!
!

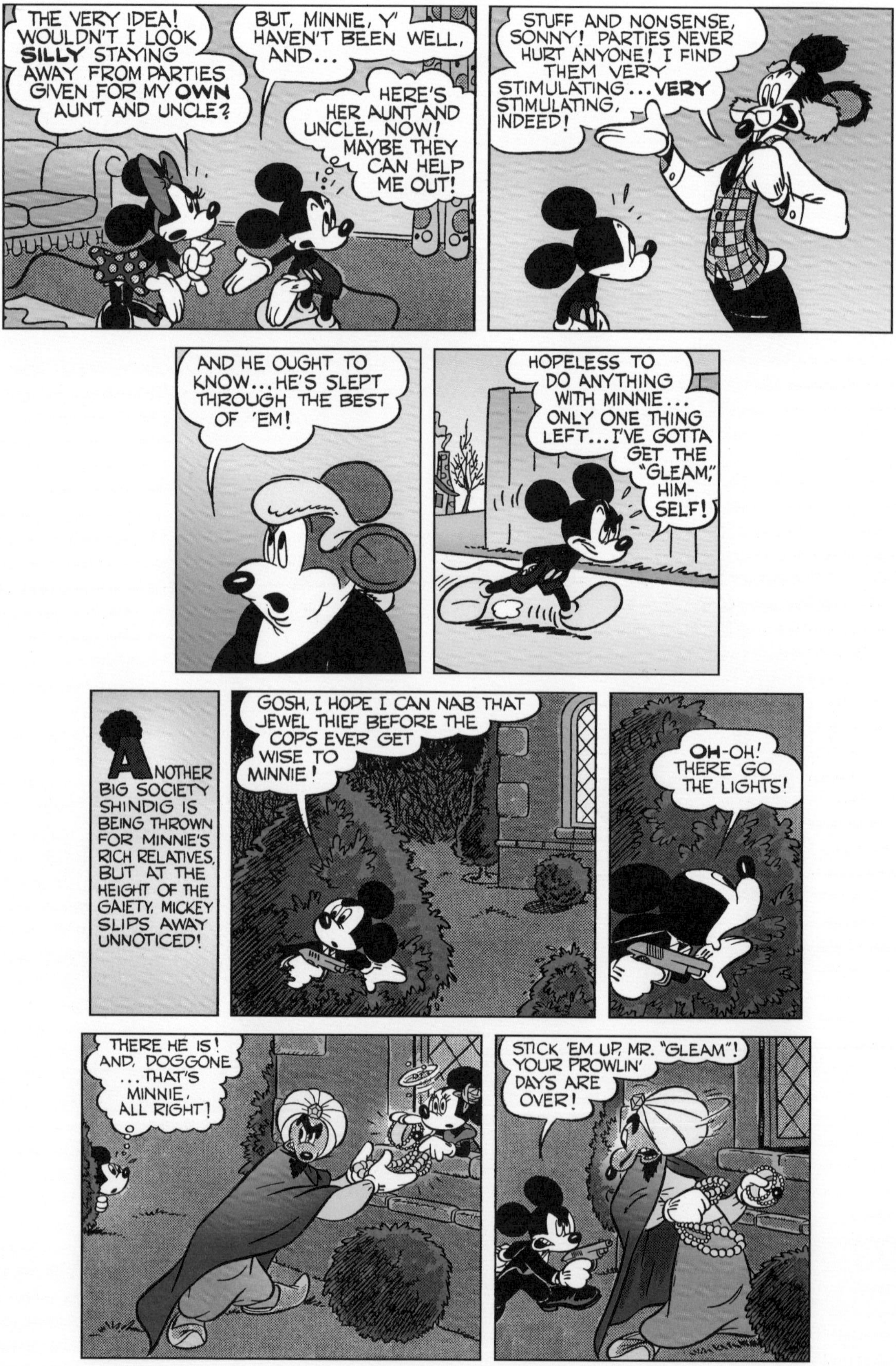
THE VERY IDEA! WOULDN'T I LOOK SILLY STAYING AWAY FROM PARTIES GIVEN FOR MY OWN AUNT AND UNCLE?
BUT, MINNIE, Y' HAVEN'T BEEN WELL, AND...
HERE'S HER AUNT AND UNCLE, NOW! MAYBE THEY CAN HELP ME OUT!
STUFF AND NONSENSE, SONNY! PARTIES NEVER HURT ANYONE! I FIND THEM VERY STIMULATING... VERY STIMULATING, INDEED!
AND HE OUGHT TO KNOW... HE'S SLEPT THROUGH THE BEST OF 'EM!
HOPELESS TO DO ANYTHING WITH MINNIE... ONLY ONE THING LEFT... I'VE GOTTA GET THE "GLEAM," HIMSELF!
ANOTHER BIG SOCIETY SHINDIG IS BEING THROWN FOR MINNIE'S RICH RELATIVES, BUT AT THE HEIGHT OF THE GAIETY, MICKEY SLIPS AWAY UNNOTICED!
GOSH, I HOPE I CAN NAB THAT JEWEL THIEF BEFORE THE COPS EVER GET WISE TO MINNIE!
OH-OH! THERE GO THE LIGHTS!
THERE HE IS! AND, DOGGONE ... THAT'S MINNIE, ALL RIGHT!
STICK 'EM UP, MR. "GLEAM"! YOUR PROWLIN' DAYS ARE OVER!

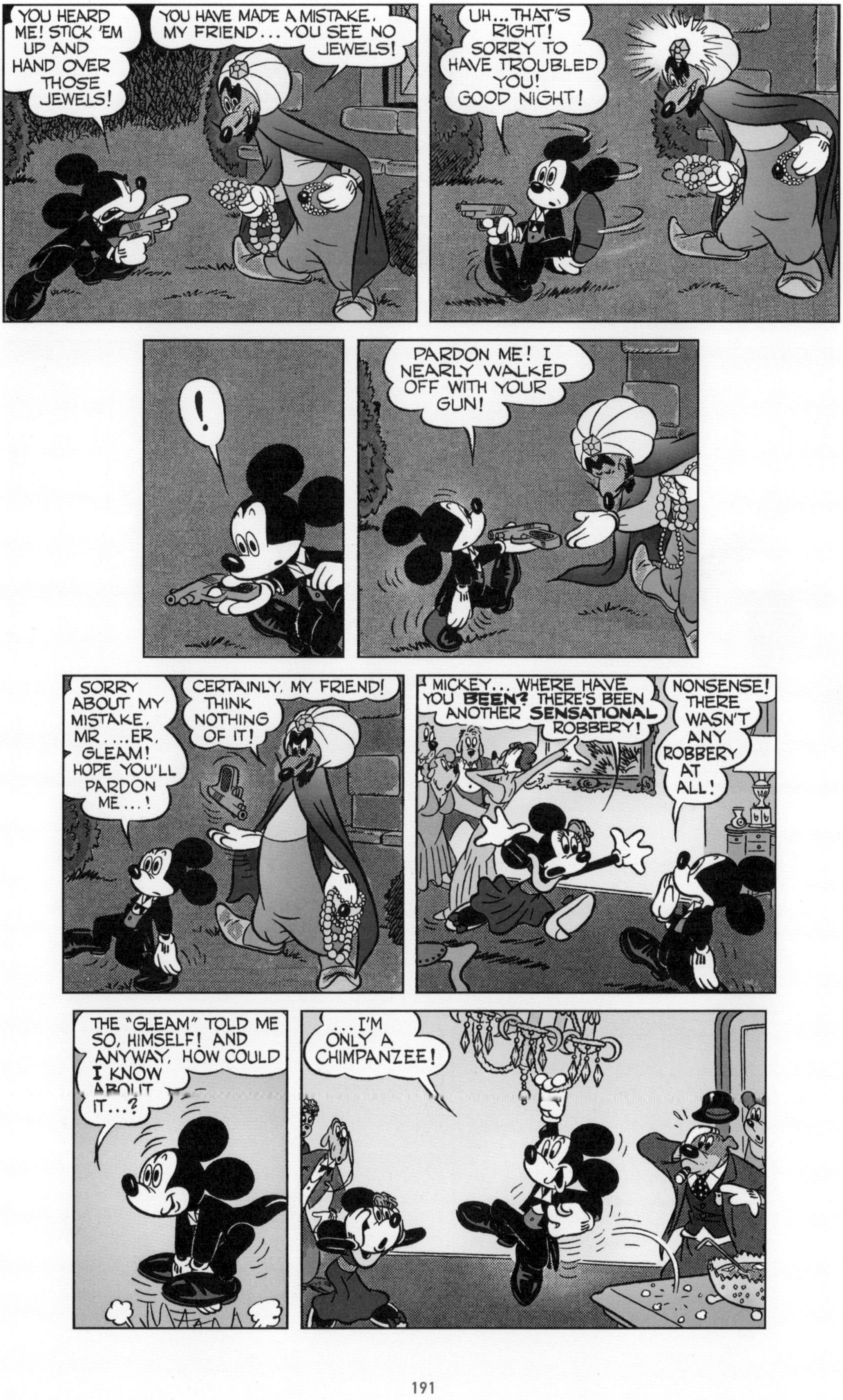
YOU HEARD ME! STICK 'EM UP AND HAND OVER THOSE JEWELS!
YOU HAVE MADE A MISTAKE, MY FRIEND... YOU SEE NO JEWELS!
UH...THAT'S RIGHT! SORRY TO HAVE TROUBLED YOU! GOOD NIGHT!
!
PARDON ME! I NEARLY WALKED OFF WITH YOUR GUN!
SORRY ABOUT MY MISTAKE, MR....ER, GLEAM! HOPE YOU'LL PARDON ME...!
CERTAINLY, MY FRIEND! THINK NOTHING OF IT!
MICKEY... WHERE HAVE YOU **BEEN?** THERE'S BEEN ANOTHER **SENSATIONAL** ROBBERY!
NONSENSE! THERE WASN'T ANY ROBBERY AT ALL!
THE "GLEAM" TOLD ME SO, HIMSELF! AND ANYWAY, HOW COULD **I** KNOW ABOUT IT...?
...I'M ONLY A CHIMPANZEE!

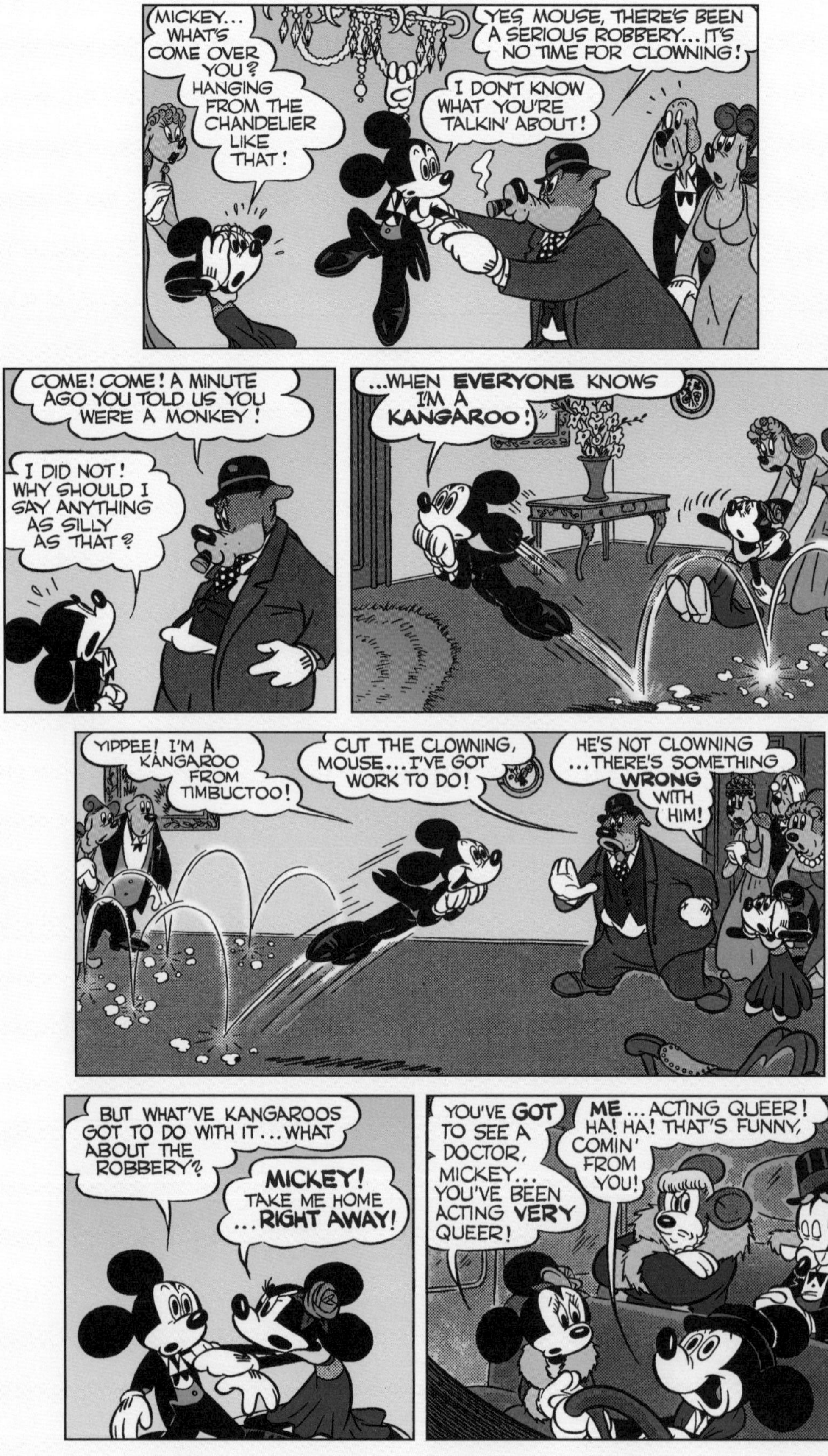
MICKEY... WHAT'S COME OVER YOU? HANGING FROM THE CHANDELIER LIKE THAT!
YES, MOUSE, THERE'S BEEN A SERIOUS ROBBERY... IT'S NO TIME FOR CLOWNING!
I DON'T KNOW WHAT YOU'RE TALKIN' ABOUT!
COME! COME! A MINUTE AGO YOU TOLD US YOU WERE A MONKEY!
I DID NOT! WHY SHOULD I SAY ANYTHING AS SILLY AS THAT?
...WHEN EVERYONE KNOWS I'M A KANGAROO!
YIPPEE! I'M A KANGAROO FROM TIMBUCTOO!
CUT THE CLOWNING, MOUSE... I'VE GOT WORK TO DO!
HE'S NOT CLOWNING ...THERE'S SOMETHING WRONG WITH HIM!
BUT WHAT'VE KANGAROOS GOT TO DO WITH IT... WHAT ABOUT THE ROBBERY?
MICKEY! TAKE ME HOME ...RIGHT AWAY!
YOU'VE GOT TO SEE A DOCTOR, MICKEY... YOU'VE BEEN ACTING VERY QUEER!
ME... ACTING QUEER! HA! HA! THAT'S FUNNY, COMIN' FROM YOU!

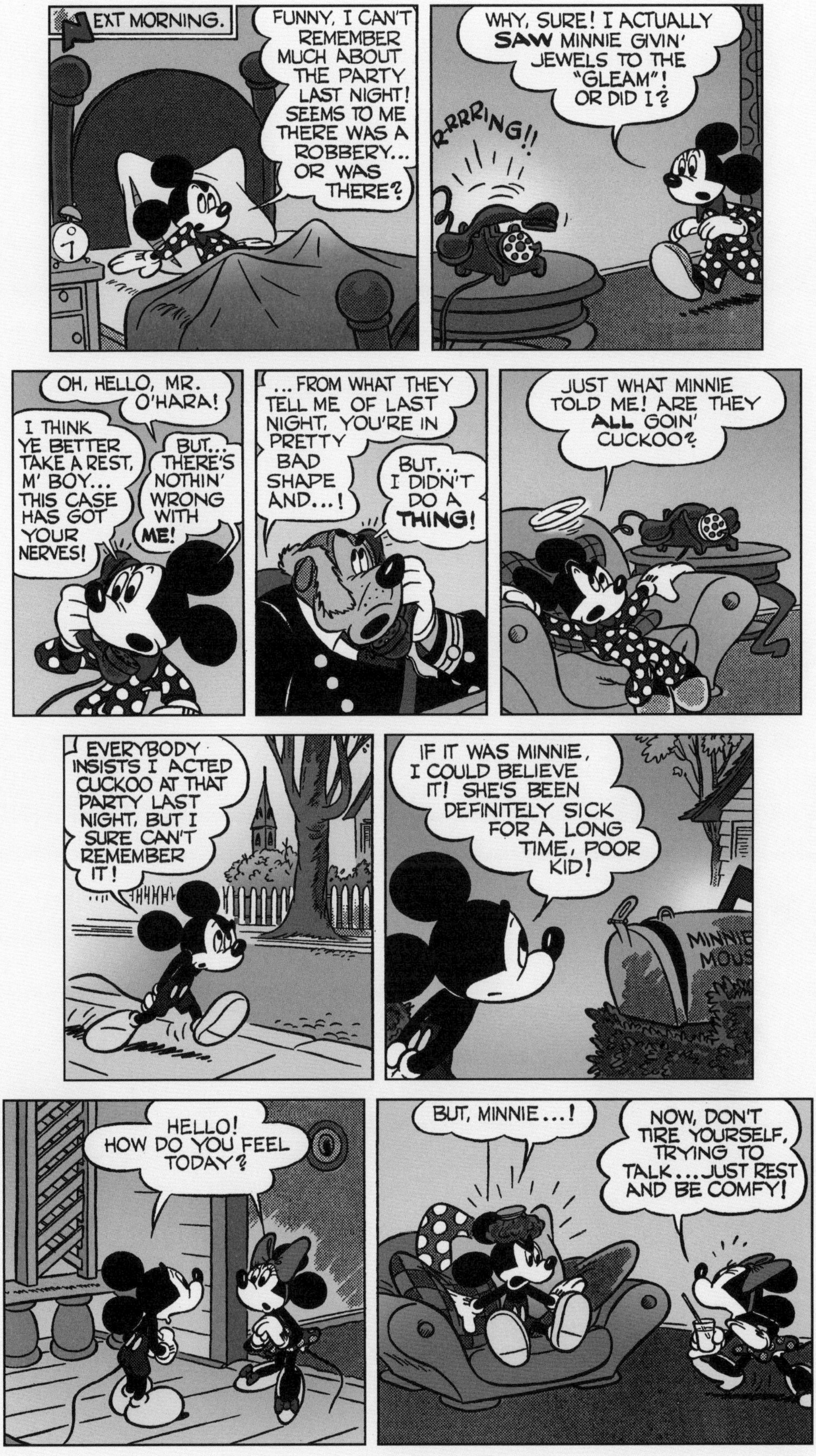
NEXT MORNING.
FUNNY, I CAN'T REMEMBER MUCH ABOUT THE PARTY LAST NIGHT! SEEMS TO ME THERE WAS A ROBBERY... OR WAS THERE?
WHY, SURE! I ACTUALLY SAW MINNIE GIVIN' JEWELS TO THE "GLEAM"! OR DID I?
R-RRRING!!
OH, HELLO, MR. O'HARA!
I THINK YE BETTER TAKE A REST, M' BOY... THIS CASE HAS GOT YOUR NERVES!
BUT... THERE'S NOTHIN' WRONG WITH ME!
... FROM WHAT THEY TELL ME OF LAST NIGHT, YOU'RE IN PRETTY BAD SHAPE AND...!
BUT... I DIDN'T DO A THING!
JUST WHAT MINNIE TOLD ME! ARE THEY ALL GOIN' CUCKOO?
EVERYBODY INSISTS I ACTED CUCKOO AT THAT PARTY LAST NIGHT, BUT I SURE CAN'T REMEMBER IT!
IF IT WAS MINNIE, I COULD BELIEVE IT! SHE'S BEEN DEFINITELY SICK FOR A LONG TIME, POOR KID!
MINNIE MOUS
HELLO! HOW DO YOU FEEL TODAY?
BUT, MINNIE...!
NOW, DON'T TIRE YOURSELF, TRYING TO TALK... JUST REST AND BE COMFY!

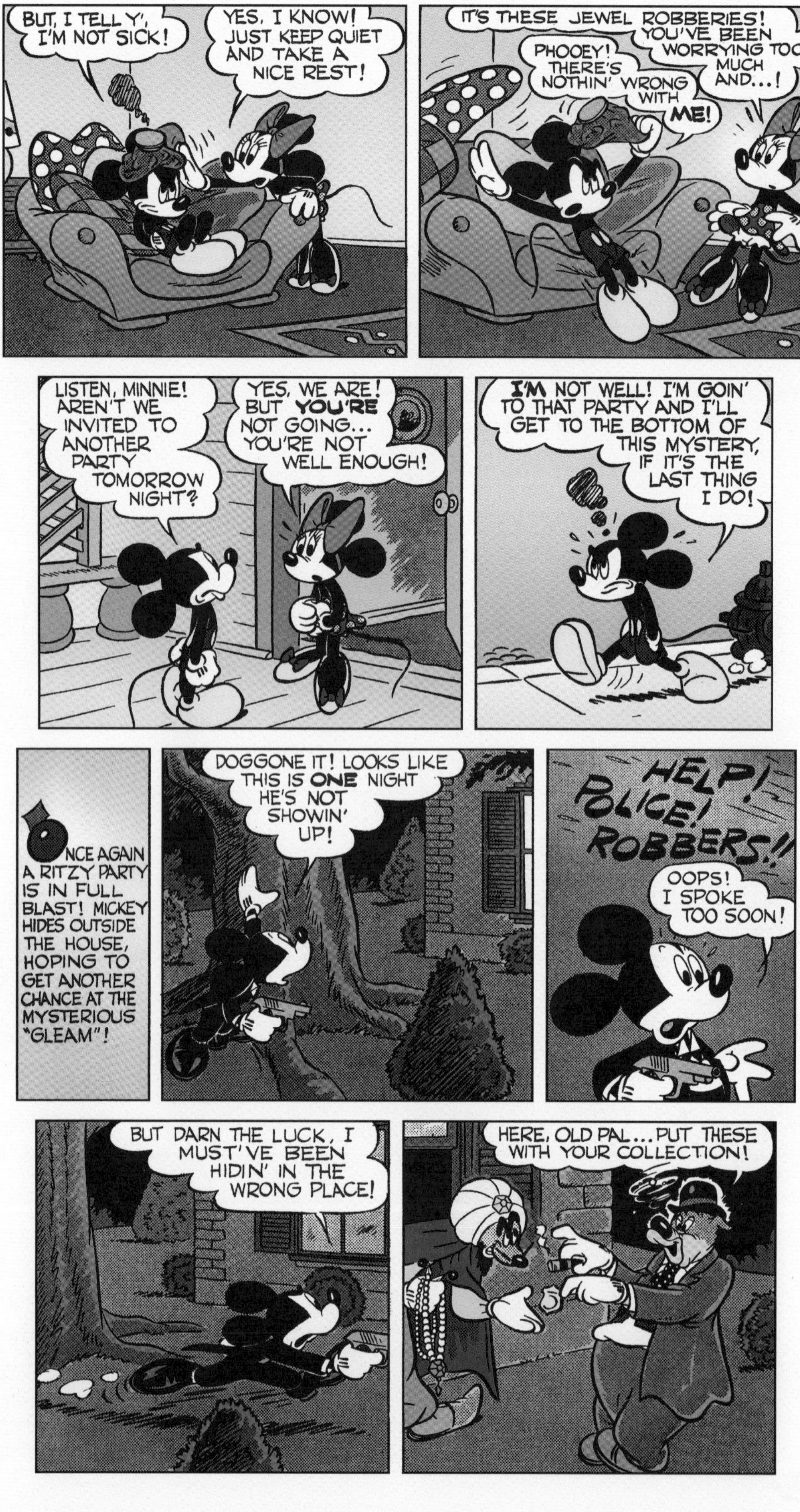
BUT, I TELL Y', I'M NOT SICK!
YES, I KNOW! JUST KEEP QUIET AND TAKE A NICE REST!
IT'S THESE JEWEL ROBBERIES! YOU'VE BEEN WORRYING TOO MUCH AND...!
PHOOEY! THERE'S NOTHIN' WRONG WITH ME!
LISTEN, MINNIE! AREN'T WE INVITED TO ANOTHER PARTY TOMORROW NIGHT?
YES, WE ARE! BUT YOU'RE NOT GOING... YOU'RE NOT WELL ENOUGH!
I'M NOT WELL! I'M GOIN' TO THAT PARTY AND I'LL GET TO THE BOTTOM OF THIS MYSTERY, IF IT'S THE LAST THING I DO!
ONCE AGAIN A RITZY PARTY IS IN FULL BLAST! MICKEY HIDES OUTSIDE THE HOUSE, HOPING TO GET ANOTHER CHANCE AT THE MYSTERIOUS "GLEAM"!
DOGGONE IT! LOOKS LIKE THIS IS ONE NIGHT HE'S NOT SHOWIN' UP!
HELP! POLICE! ROBBERS!!
OOPS! I SPOKE TOO SOON!
BUT DARN THE LUCK, I MUST'VE BEEN HIDIN' IN THE WRONG PLACE!
HERE, OLD PAL... PUT THESE WITH YOUR COLLECTION!

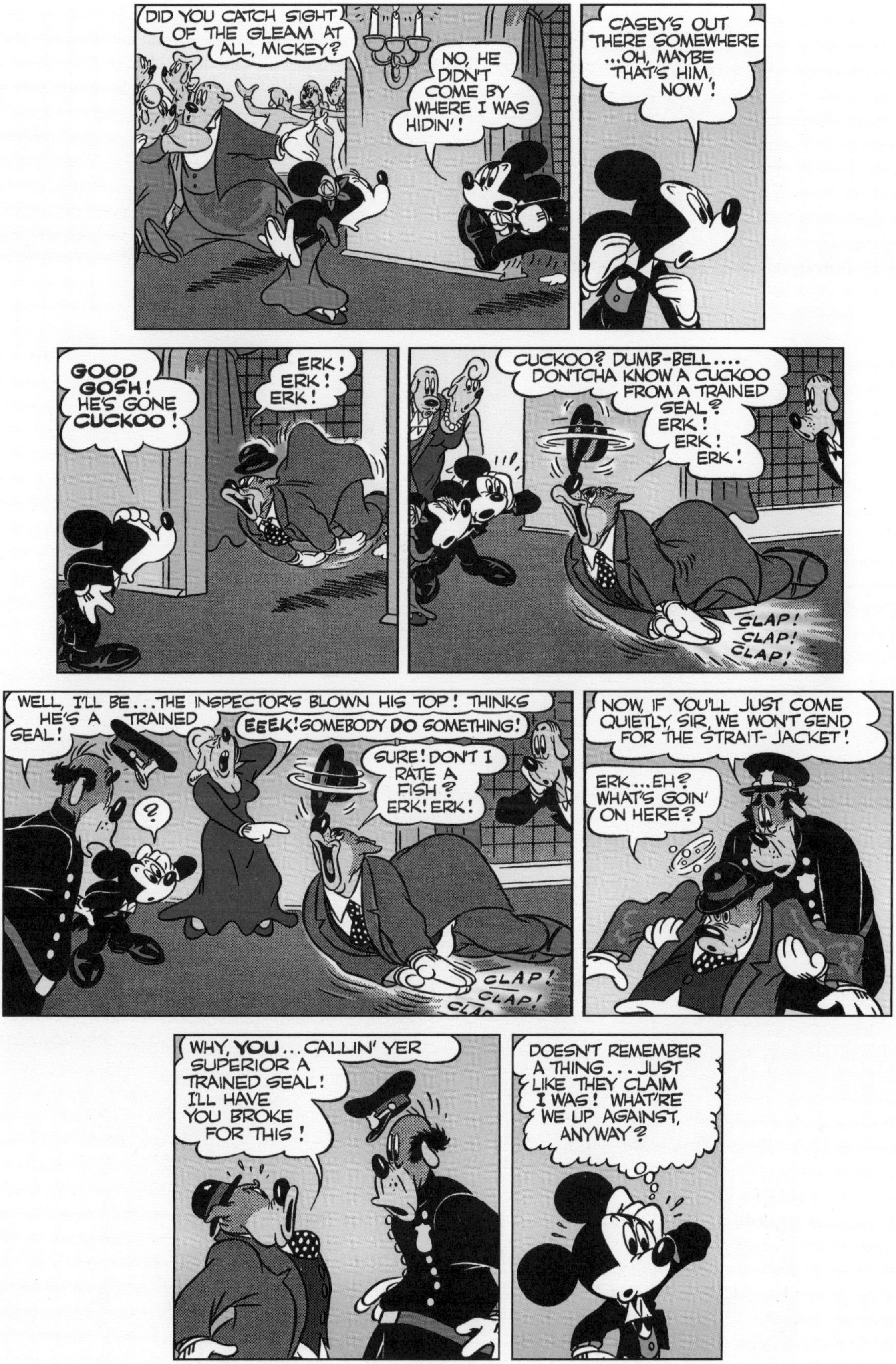
DID YOU CATCH SIGHT OF THE GLEAM AT ALL, MICKEY?
NO, HE DIDN'T COME BY WHERE I WAS HIDIN'!
CASEY'S OUT THERE SOMEWHERE ...OH, MAYBE THAT'S HIM, NOW!
GOOD GOSH! HE'S GONE CUCKOO!
ERK! ERK! ERK!
CUCKOO? DUMB-BELL.... DON'TCHA KNOW A CUCKOO FROM A TRAINED SEAL? ERK! ERK! ERK!
CLAP! CLAP! CLAP!
WELL, I'LL BE...THE INSPECTOR'S BLOWN HIS TOP! THINKS HE'S A TRAINED SEAL!
EEEK! SOMEBODY DO SOMETHING!
?
SURE! DON'T I RATE A FISH? ERK! ERK!
CLAP! CLAP!
NOW, IF YOU'LL JUST COME QUIETLY, SIR, WE WON'T SEND FOR THE STRAIT-JACKET!
ERK...EH? WHAT'S GOIN' ON HERE?
WHY, YOU...CALLIN' YER SUPERIOR A TRAINED SEAL! I'LL HAVE YOU BROKE FOR THIS!
DOESN'T REMEMBER A THING... JUST LIKE THEY CLAIM I WAS! WHAT'RE WE UP AGAINST, ANYWAY?

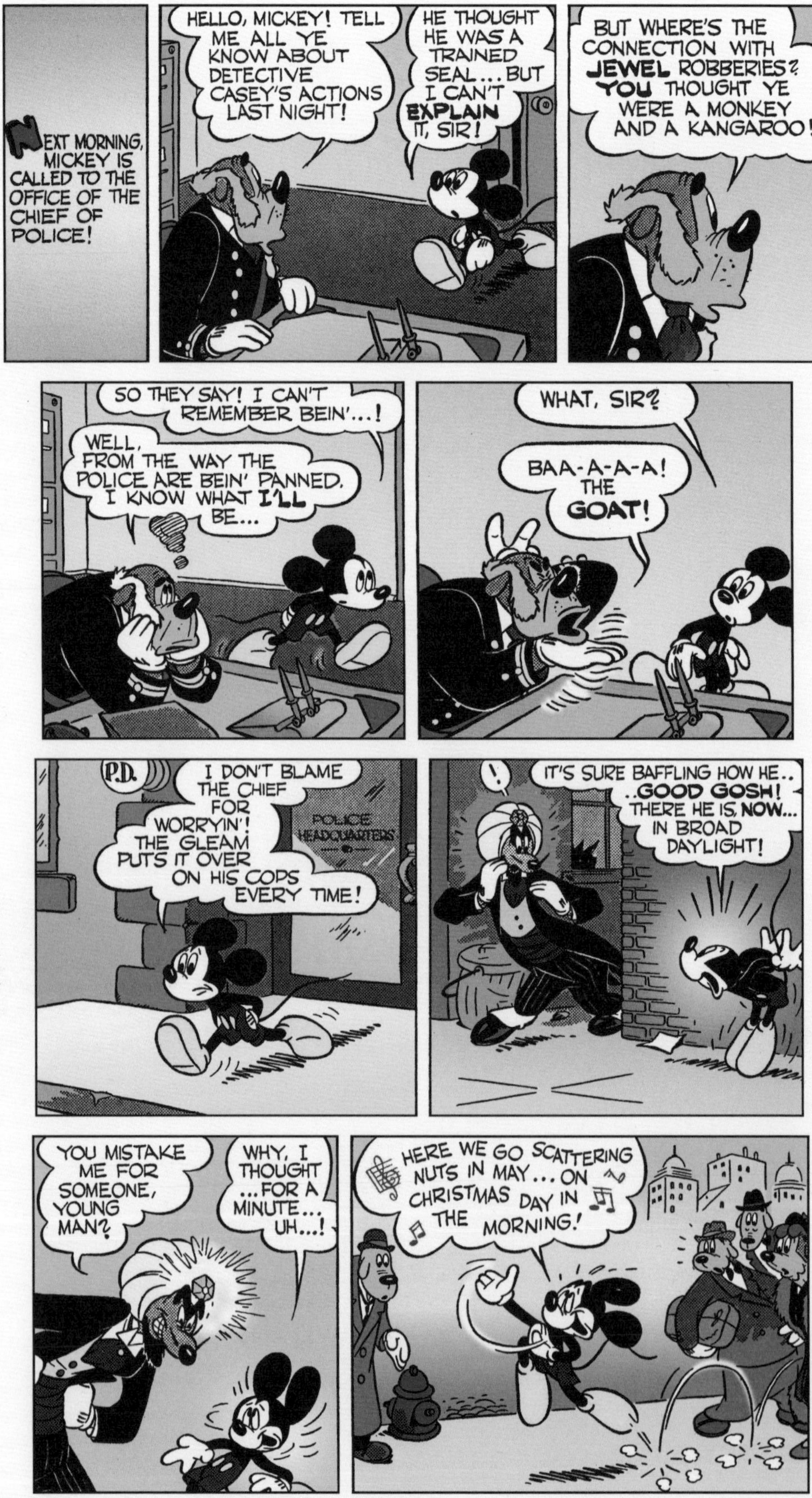
NEXT MORNING, MICKEY IS CALLED TO THE OFFICE OF THE CHIEF OF POLICE!
HELLO, MICKEY! TELL ME ALL YE KNOW ABOUT DETECTIVE CASEY'S ACTIONS LAST NIGHT!
HE THOUGHT HE WAS A TRAINED SEAL... BUT I CAN'T EXPLAIN IT, SIR!
BUT WHERE'S THE CONNECTION WITH JEWEL ROBBERIES? YOU THOUGHT YE WERE A MONKEY AND A KANGAROO!
SO THEY SAY! I CAN'T REMEMBER BEIN'...!
WELL, FROM THE WAY THE POLICE ARE BEIN' PANNED, I KNOW WHAT I'LL BE...
WHAT, SIR?
BAA-A-A-A! THE GOAT!
P.D.
I DON'T BLAME THE CHIEF FOR WORRYIN'! THE GLEAM PUTS IT OVER ON HIS COPS EVERY TIME!
POLICE HEADQUARTERS
!
IT'S SURE BAFFLING HOW HE.. ..GOOD GOSH! THERE HE IS, NOW... IN BROAD DAYLIGHT!
YOU MISTAKE ME FOR SOMEONE, YOUNG MAN?
WHY, I THOUGHT ...FOR A MINUTE... UH...!
HERE WE GO SCATTERING NUTS IN MAY... ON CHRISTMAS DAY IN THE MORNING!

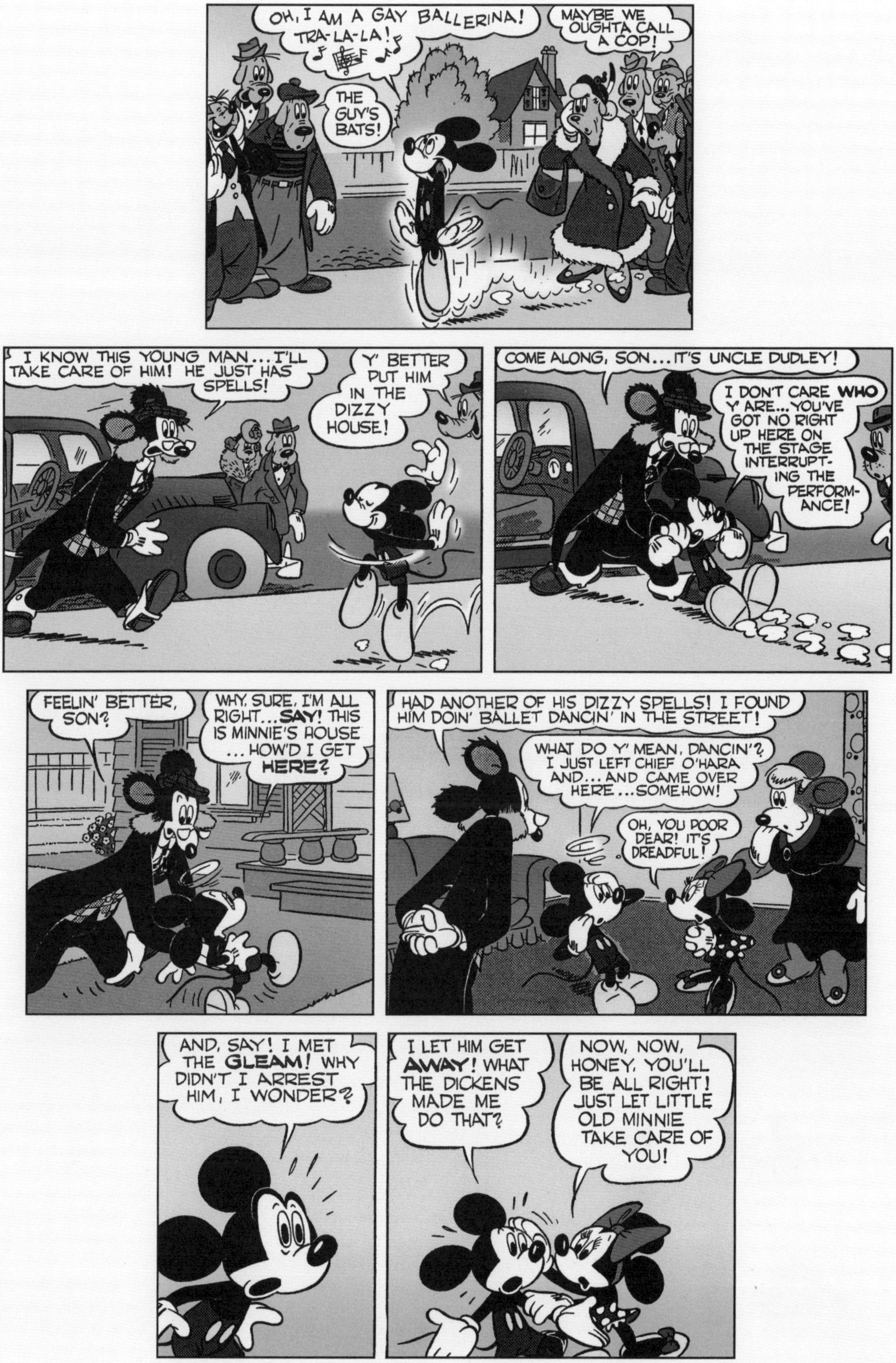
OH, I AM A GAY BALLERINA! TRA-LA-LA!
MAYBE WE OUGHTA CALL A COP!
THE GUY'S BATS!
I KNOW THIS YOUNG MAN... I'LL TAKE CARE OF HIM! HE JUST HAS SPELLS!
Y' BETTER PUT HIM IN THE DIZZY HOUSE!
COME ALONG, SON... IT'S UNCLE DUDLEY!
I DON'T CARE WHO Y' ARE... YOU'VE GOT NO RIGHT UP HERE ON THE STAGE INTERRUPTING THE PERFORMANCE!
FEELIN' BETTER, SON?
WHY, SURE, I'M ALL RIGHT... SAY! THIS IS MINNIE'S HOUSE ... HOW'D I GET HERE?
HAD ANOTHER OF HIS DIZZY SPELLS! I FOUND HIM DOIN' BALLET DANCIN' IN THE STREET!
WHAT DO Y' MEAN, DANCIN'? I JUST LEFT CHIEF O'HARA AND... AND CAME OVER HERE... SOMEHOW!
OH, YOU POOR DEAR! IT'S DREADFUL!
AND, SAY! I MET THE GLEAM! WHY DIDN'T I ARREST HIM, I WONDER?
I LET HIM GET AWAY! WHAT THE DICKENS MADE ME DO THAT?
NOW, NOW, HONEY, YOU'LL BE ALL RIGHT! JUST LET LITTLE OLD MINNIE TAKE CARE OF YOU!

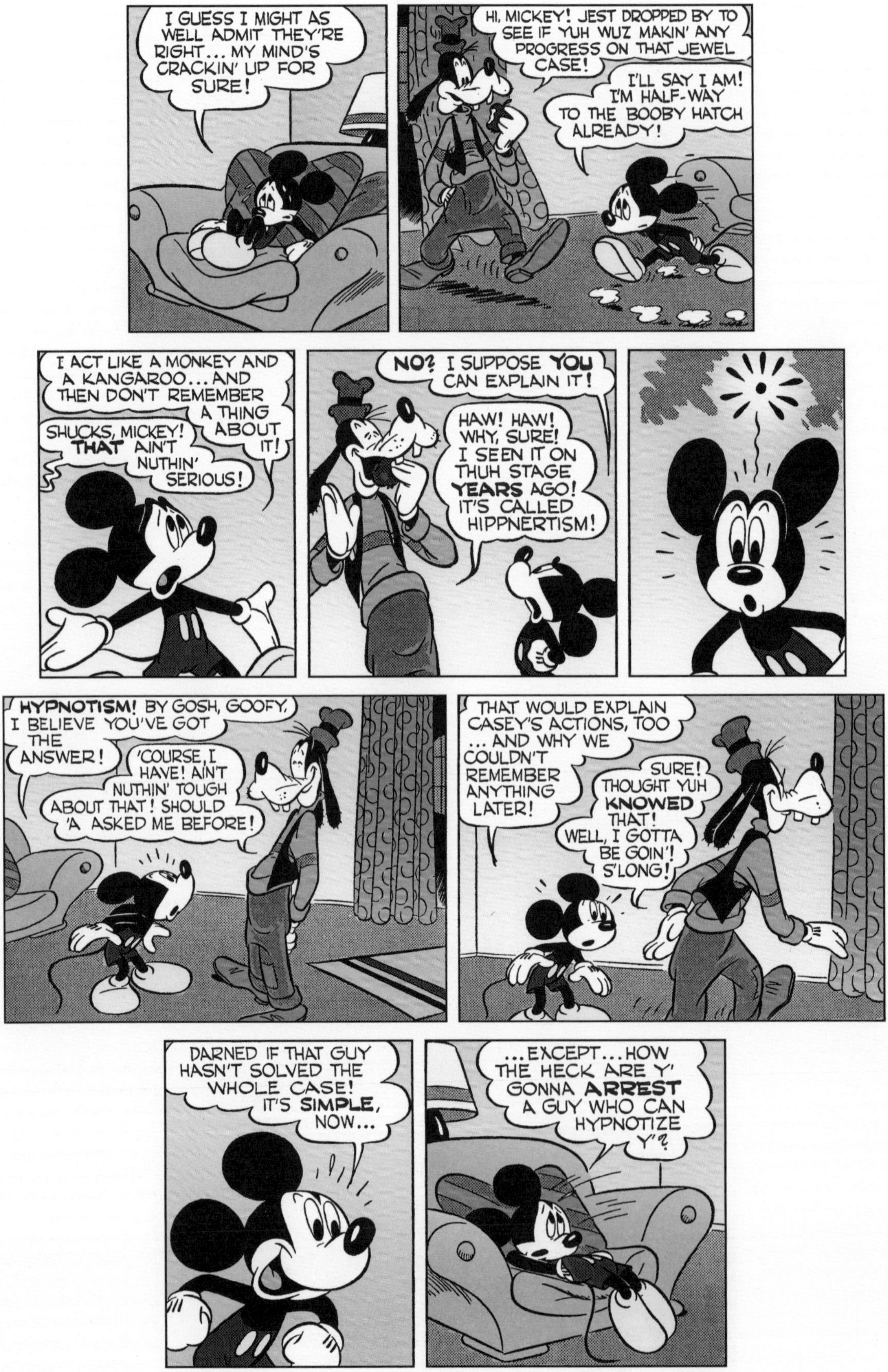
I GUESS I MIGHT AS WELL ADMIT THEY'RE RIGHT... MY MIND'S CRACKIN' UP FOR SURE!
HI, MICKEY! JEST DROPPED BY TO SEE IF YUH WUZ MAKIN' ANY PROGRESS ON THAT JEWEL CASE!
I'LL SAY I AM! I'M HALF-WAY TO THE BOOBY HATCH ALREADY!
I ACT LIKE A MONKEY AND A KANGAROO... AND THEN DON'T REMEMBER A THING ABOUT IT!
SHUCKS, MICKEY! THAT AIN'T NUTHIN' SERIOUS!
NO? I SUPPOSE YOU CAN EXPLAIN IT!
HAW! HAW! WHY, SURE! I SEEN IT ON THUH STAGE YEARS AGO! IT'S CALLED HIPPNERTISM!
HYPNOTISM! BY GOSH, GOOFY, I BELIEVE YOU'VE GOT THE ANSWER!
'COURSE, I HAVE! AIN'T NUTHIN' TOUGH ABOUT THAT! SHOULD 'A ASKED ME BEFORE!
THAT WOULD EXPLAIN CASEY'S ACTIONS, TOO ... AND WHY WE COULDN'T REMEMBER ANYTHING LATER!
SURE! THOUGHT YUH KNOWED THAT! WELL, I GOTTA BE GOIN'! S'LONG!
DARNED IF THAT GUY HASN'T SOLVED THE WHOLE CASE! IT'S SIMPLE, NOW...
...EXCEPT...HOW THE HECK ARE Y' GONNA ARREST A GUY WHO CAN HYPNOTIZE Y'?

THERE MUST BE A WAY TO **PREVENT** BEIN' HYPNOTIZED, IF I CAN ONLY FIND IT!

PUBLIC LIBRARY

HOT DOG! PLENTY OF BOOKS ON THE SUBJECT! I'LL FOOL THAT OLD GLEAM YET!

"H"

MY, MY! DOES THIS MEAN YOU'RE GOING TO START A NEW CAREER, MICKEY?

NO, MA'AM! AS A MATTER OF FACT...

...I MEAN TO **END** SOMEBODY'S CAREER ...I HOPE!

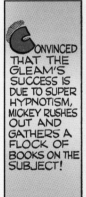

CONVINCED THAT THE GLEAM'S SUCCESS IS DUE TO SUPER HYPNOTISM, MICKEY RUSHES OUT AND GATHERS A FLOCK OF BOOKS ON THE SUBJECT!

BOY! ALL I HAFTA DO IS LEARN HOW TO **PREVENT** BEIN' HYPNOTIZED AND I'VE GOT HIM!

...MMM-MUMBLE..."STARE FIXEDLY AT THE SUBJECT AND IN A LOW, STEADY VOICE SAY, 'SLEEP...SLEEP'..." NO, THAT'S NOT IT!

"...AND IF PRACTISED FAITHFULLY, CANNOT FAIL! THE SUBJECT WILL BELIEVE HIMSELF A RABBIT OR..." AW, PHOOEY!

EVERY ONE THE SAME! NOT A **WORD** FROM THE **RABBIT'S** ANGLE!

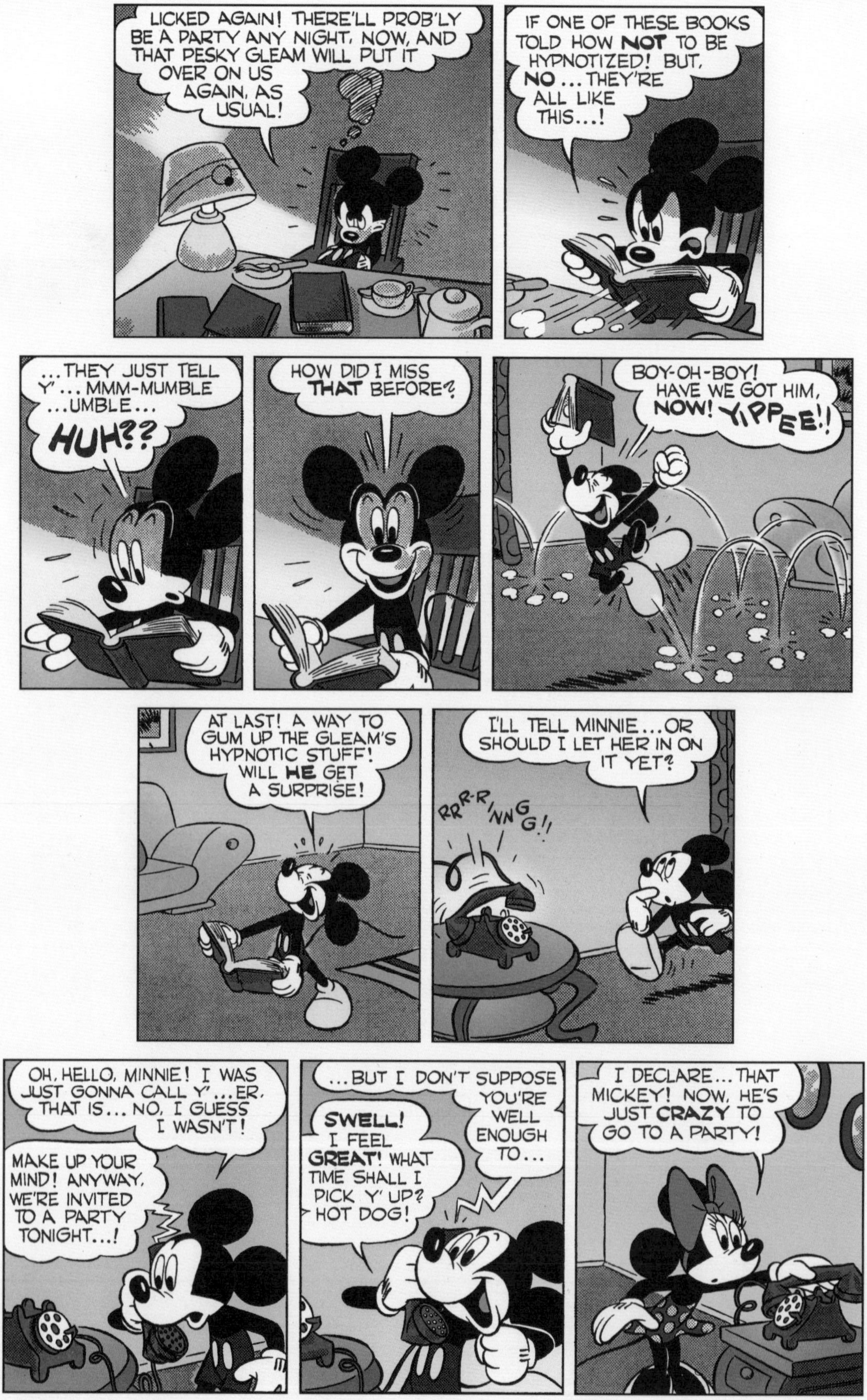
LICKED AGAIN! THERE'LL PROB'LY BE A PARTY ANY NIGHT, NOW, AND THAT PESKY GLEAM WILL PUT IT OVER ON US AGAIN, AS USUAL!
IF ONE OF THESE BOOKS TOLD HOW NOT TO BE HYPNOTIZED! BUT, NO... THEY'RE ALL LIKE THIS...!
...THEY JUST TELL Y'... MMM-MUMBLE ...UMBLE...
HUH??
HOW DID I MISS THAT BEFORE?
BOY-OH-BOY! HAVE WE GOT HIM, NOW! YIPPEE!!
AT LAST! A WAY TO GUM UP THE GLEAM'S HYPNOTIC STUFF! WILL HE GET A SURPRISE!
I'LL TELL MINNIE...OR SHOULD I LET HER IN ON IT YET?
RRR-RINNG!!
OH, HELLO, MINNIE! I WAS JUST GONNA CALL Y'...ER, THAT IS... NO, I GUESS I WASN'T!
MAKE UP YOUR MIND! ANYWAY, WE'RE INVITED TO A PARTY TONIGHT...!
...BUT I DON'T SUPPOSE YOU'RE WELL ENOUGH TO...
SWELL! I FEEL GREAT! WHAT TIME SHALL I PICK Y' UP? HOT DOG!
I DECLARE... THAT MICKEY! NOW, HE'S JUST CRAZY TO GO TO A PARTY!

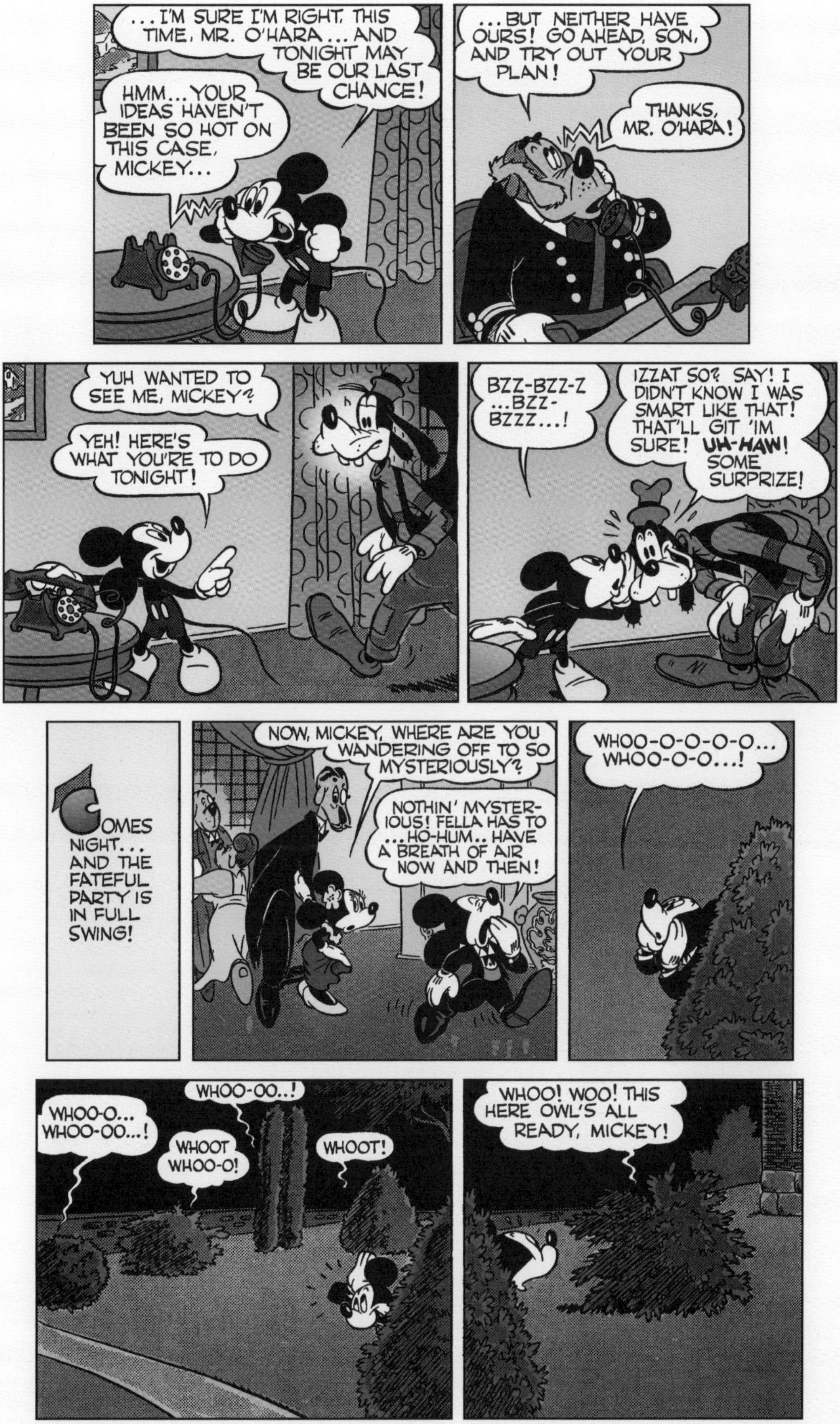
...I'M SURE I'M RIGHT, THIS TIME, MR. O'HARA... AND TONIGHT MAY BE OUR LAST CHANCE!
HMM... YOUR IDEAS HAVEN'T BEEN SO HOT ON THIS CASE, MICKEY...
...BUT NEITHER HAVE OURS! GO AHEAD, SON, AND TRY OUT YOUR PLAN!
THANKS, MR. O'HARA!
YUH WANTED TO SEE ME, MICKEY?
YEH! HERE'S WHAT YOU'RE TO DO TONIGHT!
BZZ-BZZ-Z ...BZZ-BZZZ...!
IZZAT SO? SAY! I DIDN'T KNOW I WAS SMART LIKE THAT! THAT'LL GIT 'IM SURE! UH-HAW! SOME SURPRIZE!
COMES NIGHT... AND THE FATEFUL PARTY IS IN FULL SWING!
NOW, MICKEY, WHERE ARE YOU WANDERING OFF TO SO MYSTERIOUSLY?
NOTHIN' MYSTERIOUS! FELLA HAS TO ...HO-HUM.. HAVE A BREATH OF AIR NOW AND THEN!
WHOO-O-O-O-O... WHOO-O-O...!
WHOO-O... WHOO-OO...!
WHOO-OO..!
WHOOT WHOO-O!
WHOOT!
WHOO! WOO! THIS HERE OWL'S ALL READY, MICKEY!

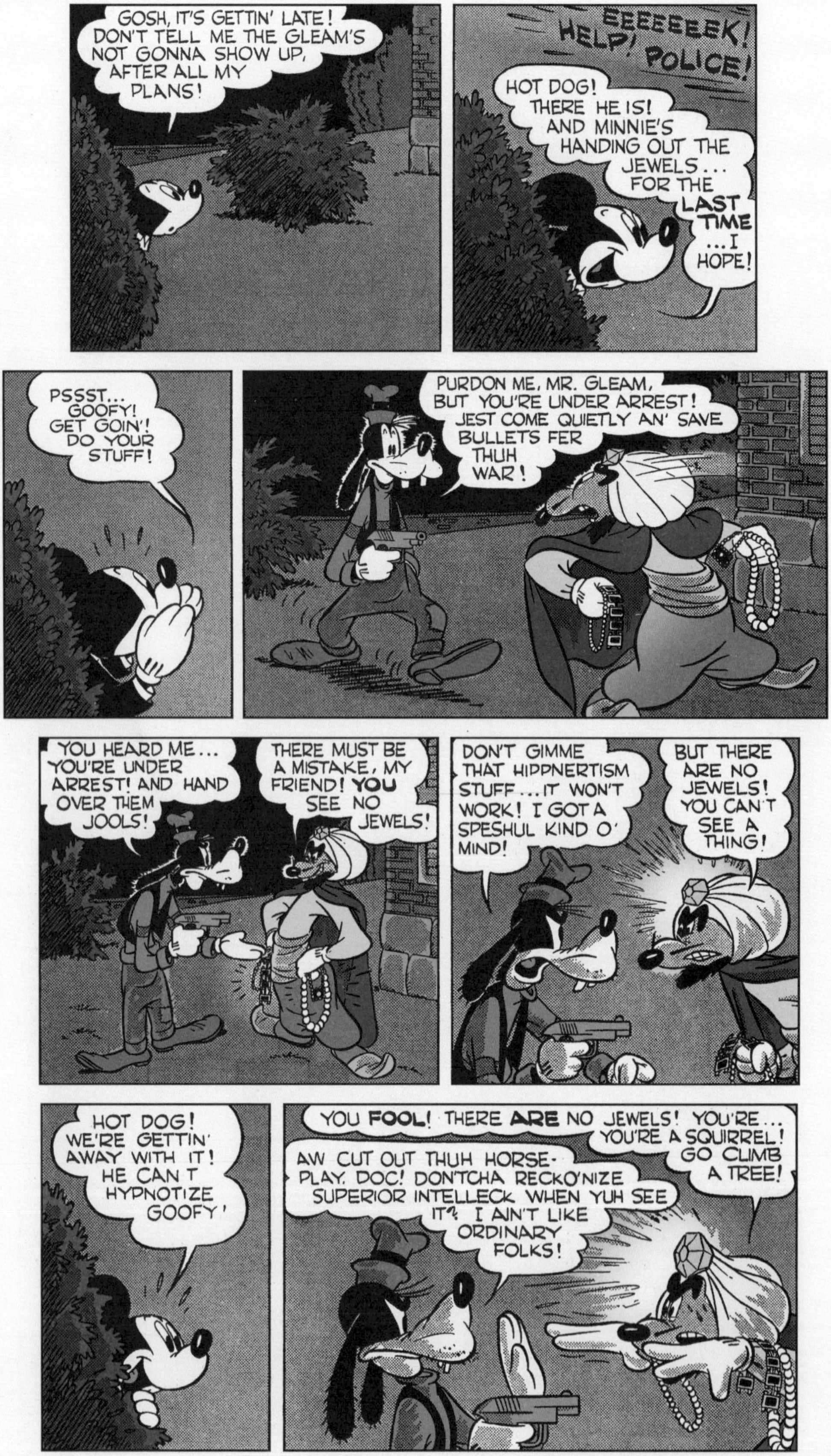
GOSH, IT'S GETTIN' LATE! DON'T TELL ME THE GLEAM'S NOT GONNA SHOW UP, AFTER ALL MY PLANS!
EEEEEEEK! HELP! POLICE!
HOT DOG! THERE HE IS! AND MINNIE'S HANDING OUT THE JEWELS... FOR THE LAST TIME ...I HOPE!
PSSST... GOOFY! GET GOIN'! DO YOUR STUFF!
PURDON ME, MR. GLEAM, BUT YOU'RE UNDER ARREST! JEST COME QUIETLY AN' SAVE BULLETS FER THUH WAR!
YOU HEARD ME... YOU'RE UNDER ARREST! AND HAND OVER THEM JOOLS!
THERE MUST BE A MISTAKE, MY FRIEND! YOU SEE NO JEWELS!
DON'T GIMME THAT HIPPNERTISM STUFF... IT WON'T WORK! I GOT A SPESHUL KIND O' MIND!
BUT THERE ARE NO JEWELS! YOU CAN'T SEE A THING!
HOT DOG! WE'RE GETTIN' AWAY WITH IT! HE CAN T HYPNOTIZE GOOFY'
YOU FOOL! THERE ARE NO JEWELS! YOU'RE... YOU'RE A SQUIRREL! GO CLIMB A TREE!
AW CUT OUT THUH HORSE-PLAY, DOC! DON'TCHA RECKO'NIZE SUPERIOR INTELLECK WHEN YUH SEE IT? I AIN'T LIKE ORDINARY FOLKS!

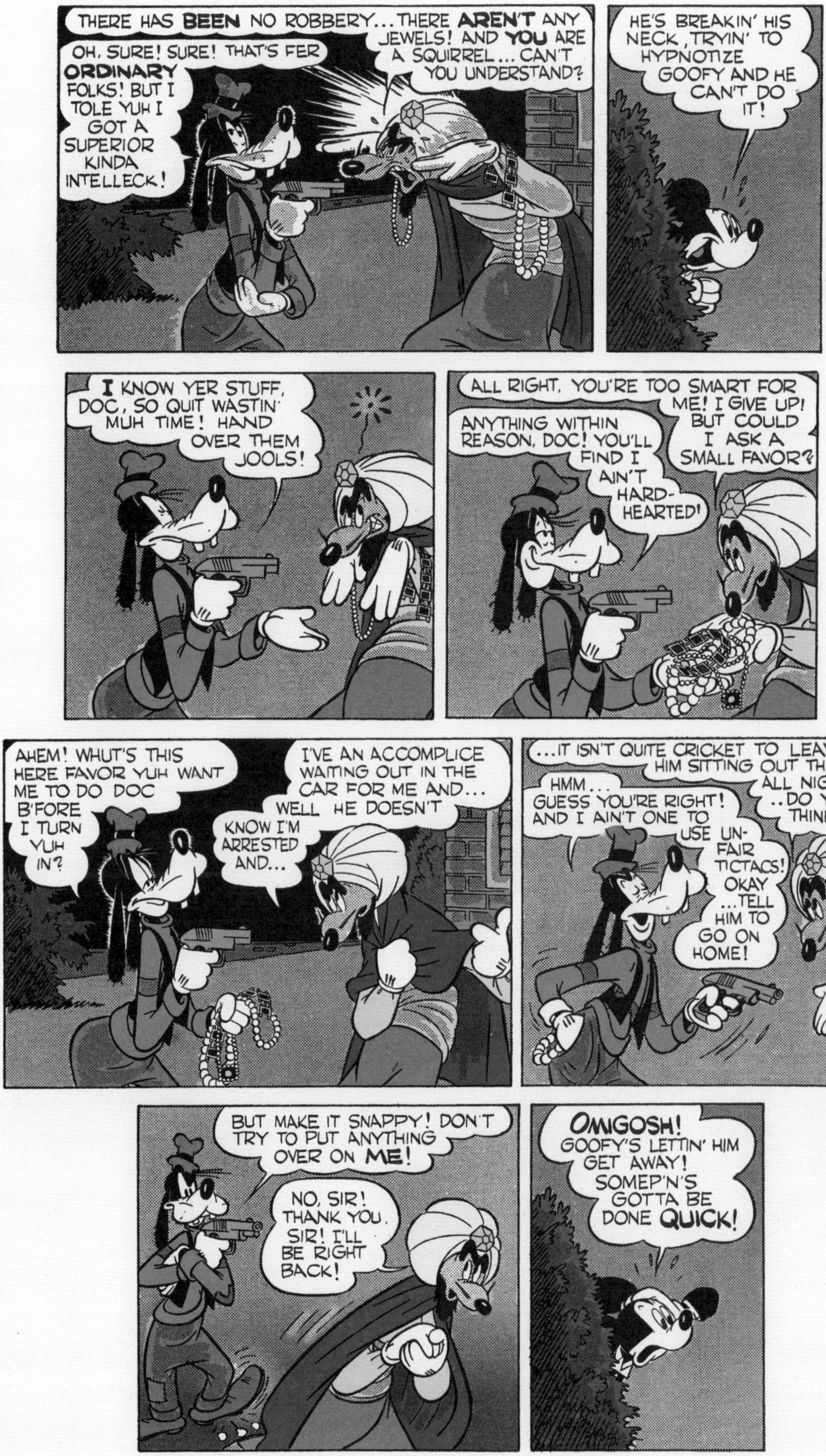
THERE HAS BEEN NO ROBBERY... THERE AREN'T ANY JEWELS! AND YOU ARE A SQUIRREL... CAN'T YOU UNDERSTAND?
OH, SURE! SURE! THAT'S FER ORDINARY FOLKS! BUT I TOLE YUH I GOT A SUPERIOR KINDA INTELLECK!
HE'S BREAKIN' HIS NECK, TRYIN' TO HYPNOTIZE GOOFY AND HE CAN'T DO IT!
I KNOW YER STUFF, DOC, SO QUIT WASTIN' MUH TIME! HAND OVER THEM JOOLS!
ALL RIGHT, YOU'RE TOO SMART FOR ME! I GIVE UP! BUT COULD I ASK A SMALL FAVOR?
ANYTHING WITHIN REASON, DOC! YOU'LL FIND I AIN'T HARD-HEARTED!
AHEM! WHUT'S THIS HERE FAVOR YUH WANT ME TO DO DOC B'FORE I TURN YUH IN?
I'VE AN ACCOMPLICE WAITING OUT IN THE CAR FOR ME AND... WELL HE DOESN'T KNOW I'M ARRESTED AND...
...IT ISN'T QUITE CRICKET TO LEAVE HIM SITTING OUT THERE ALL NIGHT... ..DO YOU THINK?
HMM... GUESS YOU'RE RIGHT! AND I AIN'T ONE TO USE UN-FAIR TICTACS! OKAY ...TELL HIM TO GO ON HOME!
BUT MAKE IT SNAPPY! DON'T TRY TO PUT ANYTHING OVER ON ME!
NO, SIR! THANK YOU, SIR! I'LL BE RIGHT BACK!
OMIGOSH! GOOFY'S LETTIN' HIM GET AWAY! SOMEP'N'S GOTTA BE DONE QUICK!

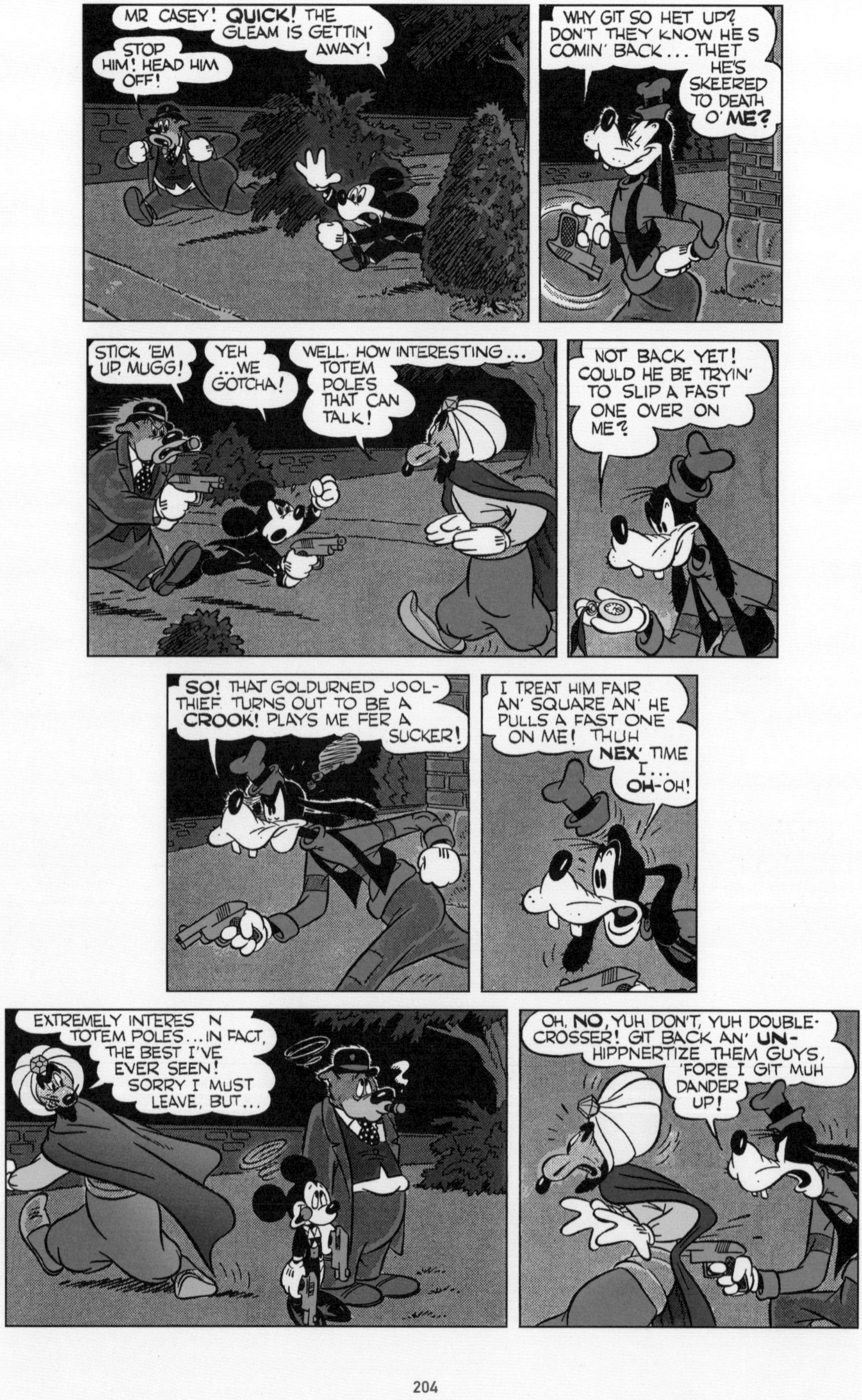
MR CASEY! QUICK! THE GLEAM IS GETTIN' AWAY!
STOP HIM! HEAD HIM OFF!
WHY GIT SO HET UP? DON'T THEY KNOW HE'S COMIN' BACK... THET HE'S SKEERED TO DEATH O' ME?
STICK 'EM UP, MUGG!
YEH ...WE GOTCHA!
WELL, HOW INTERESTING... TOTEM POLES THAT CAN TALK!
NOT BACK YET! COULD HE BE TRYIN' TO SLIP A FAST ONE OVER ON ME?
SO! THAT GOLDURNED JOOL-THIEF TURNS OUT TO BE A CROOK! PLAYS ME FER A SUCKER!
I TREAT HIM FAIR AN' SQUARE AN' HE PULLS A FAST ONE ON ME! THUH NEX' TIME I... OH-OH!
EXTREMELY INTERES N TOTEM POLES... IN FACT, THE BEST I'VE EVER SEEN! SORRY I MUST LEAVE, BUT...
OH, NO, YUH DON'T, YUH DOUBLE-CROSSER! GIT BACK AN' UN-HIPPNERTIZE THEM GUYS, 'FORE I GIT MUH DANDER UP!

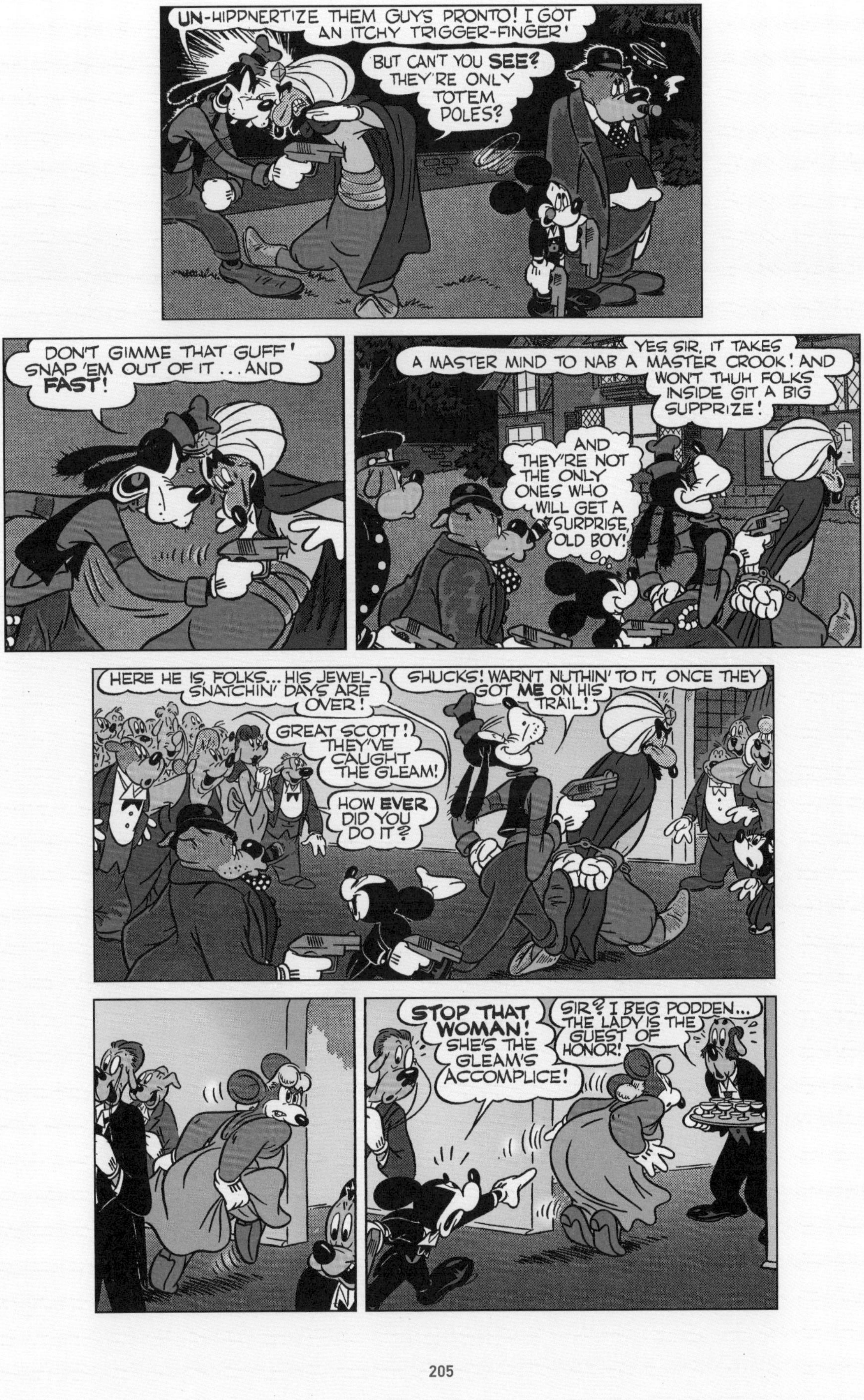
UN-HIPPNERTIZE THEM GUYS PRONTO! I GOT AN ITCHY TRIGGER-FINGER!
BUT CAN'T YOU SEE? THEY'RE ONLY TOTEM POLES?
DON'T GIMME THAT GUFF! SNAP 'EM OUT OF IT . . . AND FAST!
YES SIR, IT TAKES A MASTER MIND TO NAB A MASTER CROOK! AND WON'T THUH FOLKS INSIDE GIT A BIG SUPPRIZE!
AND THEY'RE NOT THE ONLY ONES WHO WILL GET A SURPRISE, OLD BOY!
HERE HE IS, FOLKS... HIS JEWEL-SNATCHIN' DAYS ARE OVER!
SHUCKS! WARN'T NUTHIN' TO IT, ONCE THEY GOT ME ON HIS TRAIL!
GREAT SCOTT! THEY'VE CAUGHT THE GLEAM!
HOW EVER DID YOU DO IT?
STOP THAT WOMAN! SHE'S THE GLEAM'S ACCOMPLICE!
SIR? I BEG PODDEN... THE LADY IS THE GUEST OF HONOR!

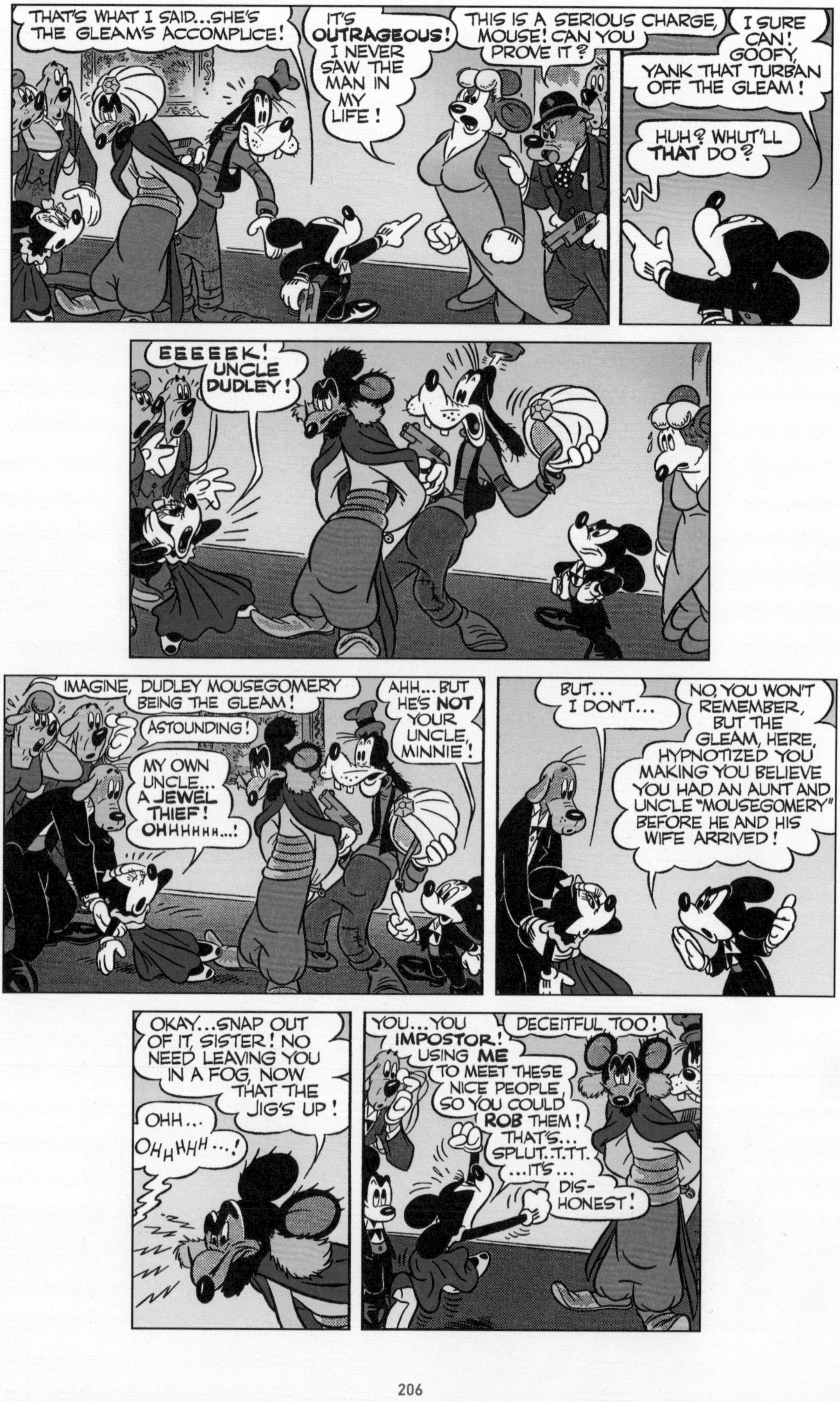
THAT'S WHAT I SAID...SHE'S THE GLEAM'S ACCOMPLICE!
IT'S OUTRAGEOUS! I NEVER SAW THE MAN IN MY LIFE!
THIS IS A SERIOUS CHARGE, MOUSE! CAN YOU PROVE IT?
I SURE CAN! GOOFY, YANK THAT TURBAN OFF THE GLEAM!
HUH? WHUT'LL THAT DO?
EEEEEK! UNCLE DUDLEY!
IMAGINE, DUDLEY MOUSEGOMERY BEING THE GLEAM!
ASTOUNDING!
MY OWN UNCLE... A JEWEL THIEF! OHHHHHH...!
AHH...BUT HE'S NOT YOUR UNCLE, MINNIE!
BUT... I DON'T...
NO, YOU WON'T REMEMBER, BUT THE GLEAM, HERE, HYPNOTIZED YOU MAKING YOU BELIEVE YOU HAD AN AUNT AND UNCLE "MOUSEGOMERY" BEFORE HE AND HIS WIFE ARRIVED!
OKAY...SNAP OUT OF IT, SISTER! NO NEED LEAVING YOU IN A FOG, NOW THAT THE JIG'S UP!
OHH... OHHHHH...!
YOU...YOU IMPOSTOR! USING ME TO MEET THESE NICE PEOPLE, SO YOU COULD ROB THEM! THAT'S... SPLUT..T.TT. ...IT'S... DIS-HONEST!
DECEITFUL, TOO!

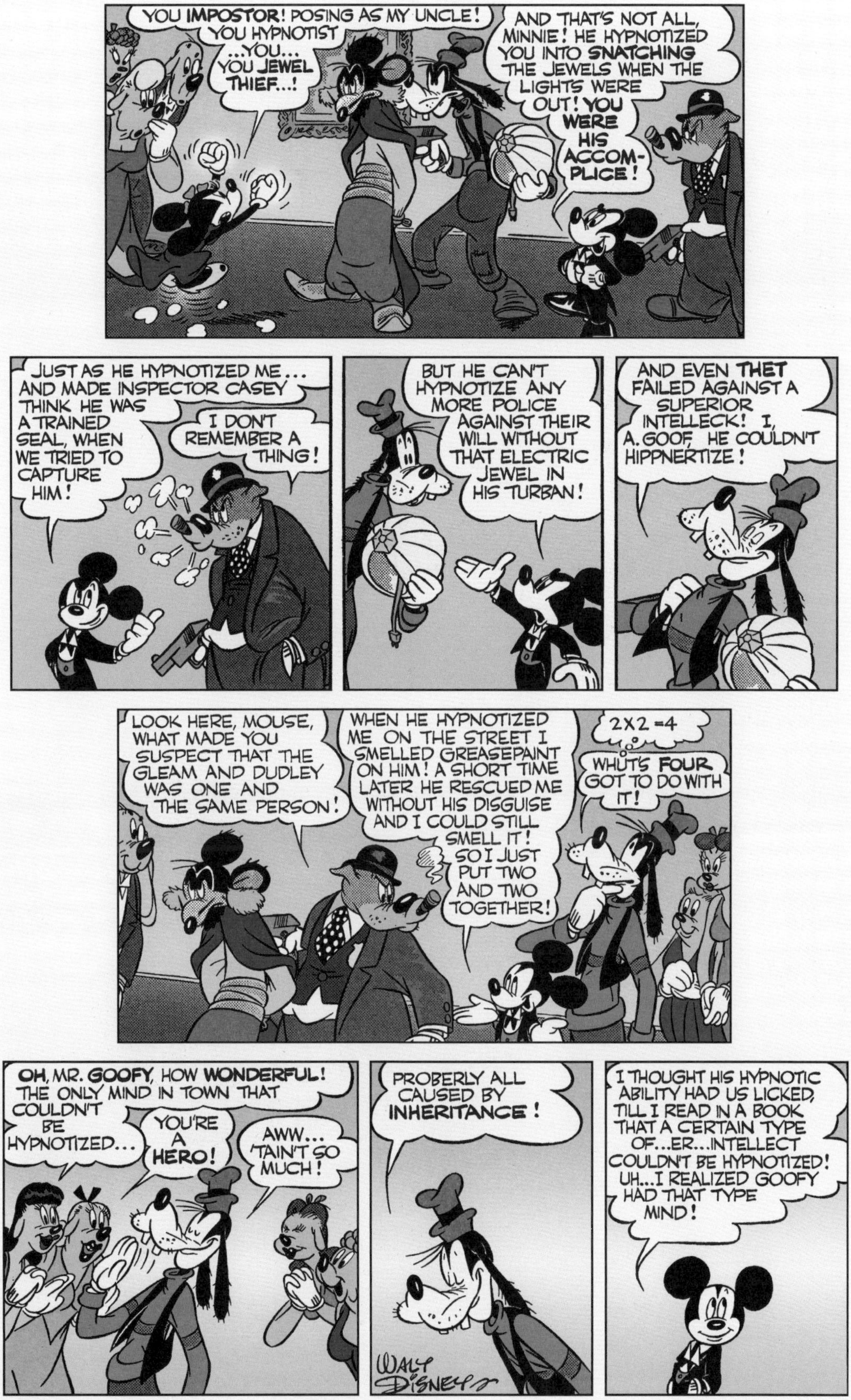
YOU IMPOSTOR! POSING AS MY UNCLE! YOU HYPNOTIST ...YOU... YOU JEWEL THIEF...!
AND THAT'S NOT ALL, MINNIE! HE HYPNOTIZED YOU INTO SNATCHING THE JEWELS WHEN THE LIGHTS WERE OUT! YOU WERE HIS ACCOMPLICE!
JUST AS HE HYPNOTIZED ME... AND MADE INSPECTOR CASEY THINK HE WAS A TRAINED SEAL, WHEN WE TRIED TO CAPTURE HIM!
I DON'T REMEMBER A THING!
BUT HE CAN'T HYPNOTIZE ANY MORE POLICE AGAINST THEIR WILL WITHOUT THAT ELECTRIC JEWEL IN HIS TURBAN!
AND EVEN THET FAILED AGAINST A SUPERIOR INTELLECK! I, A. GOOF, HE COULDN'T HIPPNERTIZE!
LOOK HERE, MOUSE, WHAT MADE YOU SUSPECT THAT THE GLEAM AND DUDLEY WAS ONE AND THE SAME PERSON!
WHEN HE HYPNOTIZED ME ON THE STREET I SMELLED GREASEPAINT ON HIM! A SHORT TIME LATER HE RESCUED ME WITHOUT HIS DISGUISE AND I COULD STILL SMELL IT! SO I JUST PUT TWO AND TWO TOGETHER!
2X2 =4
WHUT'S FOUR GOT TO DO WITH IT!
OH, MR. GOOFY, HOW WONDERFUL! THE ONLY MIND IN TOWN THAT COULDN'T BE HYPNOTIZED...
YOU'RE A HERO!
AWW... 'TAIN'T SO MUCH!
PROBERLY ALL CAUSED BY INHERITANCE!
WALT DISNEY
I THOUGHT HIS HYPNOTIC ABILITY HAD US LICKED, TILL I READ IN A BOOK THAT A CERTAIN TYPE OF...ER...INTELLECT COULDN'T BE HYPNOTIZED! UH...I REALIZED GOOFY HAD THAT TYPE MIND!

OKAY, YOU TWO, YOU GO ON ICE FOR THE NIGHT!
NICE WORK, MOUSE! SEE Y' TOMORROW!
WAIT A MINUTE! IF THOSE CROOKS ARE NOT MY RELATIVES, THEY OWE ME FOUR MONTHS' BOARD BILL! I DEMAND AN ACCOUNTING!
WHOA, MINNIE! THEY'RE INTERNATIONAL JEWEL THIEVES AND THERE'S A REWARD THAT OUGHT TO EVEN EVERYTHING UP!
I'VE GOT A HUNCH WE'LL FIND ALL THE STOLEN JEWELRY AT MINNIE'S HOUSE, SO NOBODY'LL LOSE ANYTHING!

I'M AWFULLY SORRY I'VE CAUSED SUCH A FLURRY IN THE SOCIAL WORLD, MRS. RHINESTONE!
SORRY? MY DEAR, YOU'VE GIVEN US THE MOST EXCITING SEASON I'VE EVER KNOWN! WE'LL NEVER FORGET IT!
IMAGINE! THE ONLY MIND IN TOWN THET COULDN'T BE HIPPNERTIZED! WHO'D EVER SUSPECTED THET I HAD SUCH A SUPERIOR INTELLECK!
The End

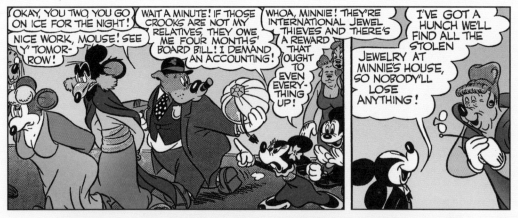

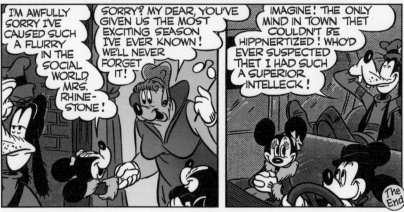

The cover to *Better Little Book* #1464, 1949, featuring a retitled version of "The Gleam." Artist unknown. Image courtesy Larry Lowery.

WALT DISNEY'S
MICKEY MOUSE
and the
STOLEN
JEWELS

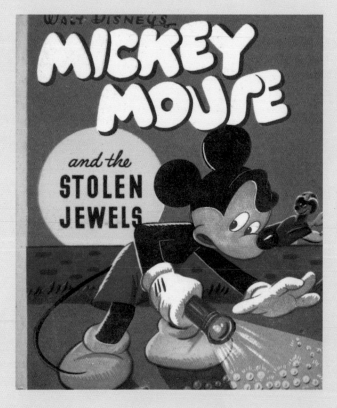

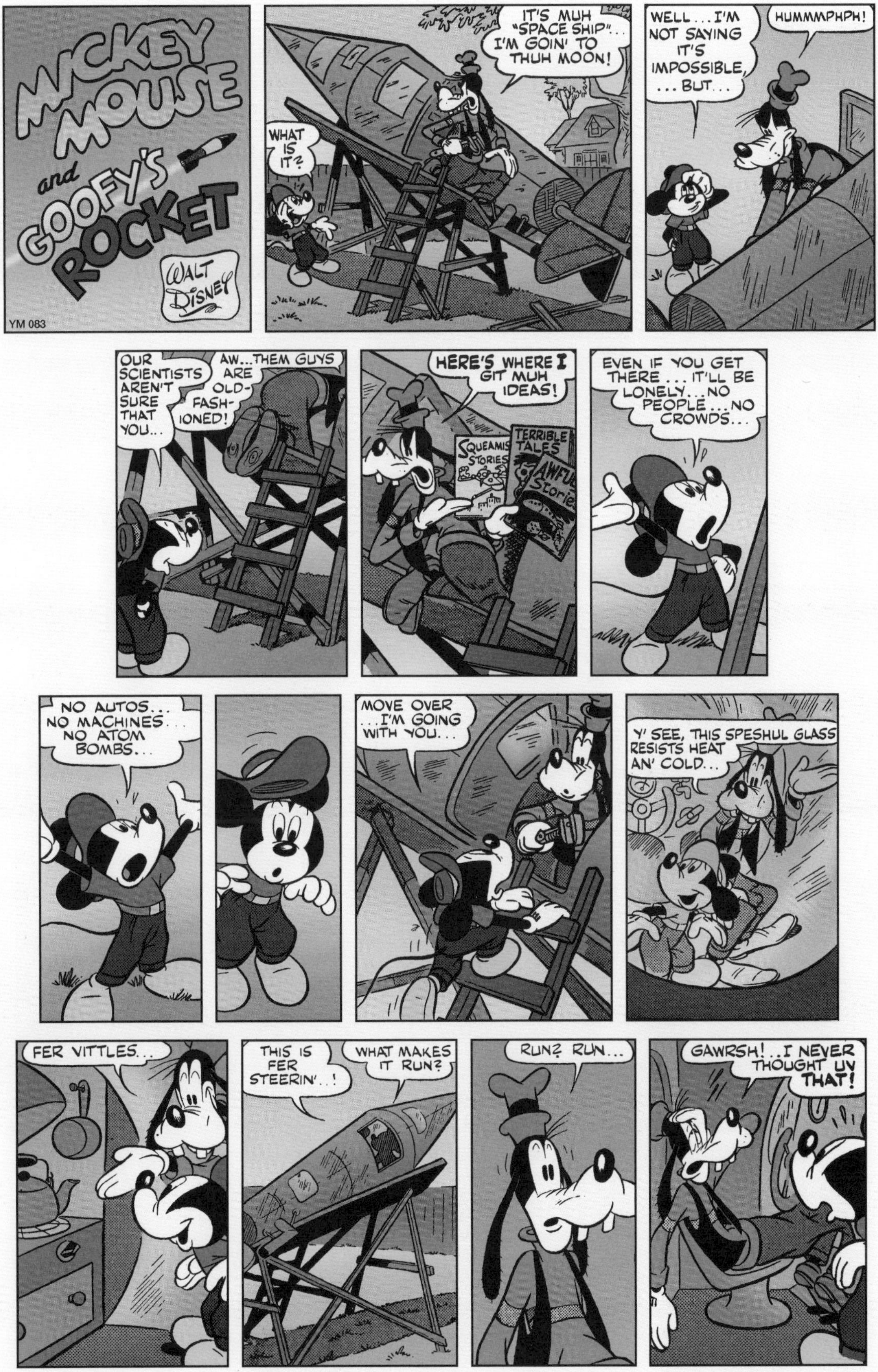
MICKEY MOUSE
and
GOOFY'S ROCKET
WALT DISNEY
YM 083
IT'S MUH "SPACE SHIP"... I'M GOIN' TO THUH MOON!
WHAT IS IT?
WELL... I'M NOT SAYING IT'S IMPOSSIBLE, ... BUT...
HUMMMPHPH!
OUR SCIENTISTS AREN'T SURE THAT YOU...
AW...THEM GUYS ARE OLD-FASHIONED!
HERE'S WHERE I GIT MUH IDEAS!
TERRIBLE TALES
EVEN IF YOU GET THERE... IT'LL BE LONELY... NO PEOPLE... NO CROWDS...
NO AUTOS... NO MACHINES... NO ATOM BOMBS...
MOVE OVER ...I'M GOING WITH YOU...
Y' SEE, THIS SPESHUL GLASS RESISTS HEAT AN' COLD...
FER VITTLES...
THIS IS FER STEERIN'..!
WHAT MAKES IT RUN?
RUN? RUN...
GAWRSH!..I NEVER THOUGHT UV THAT!

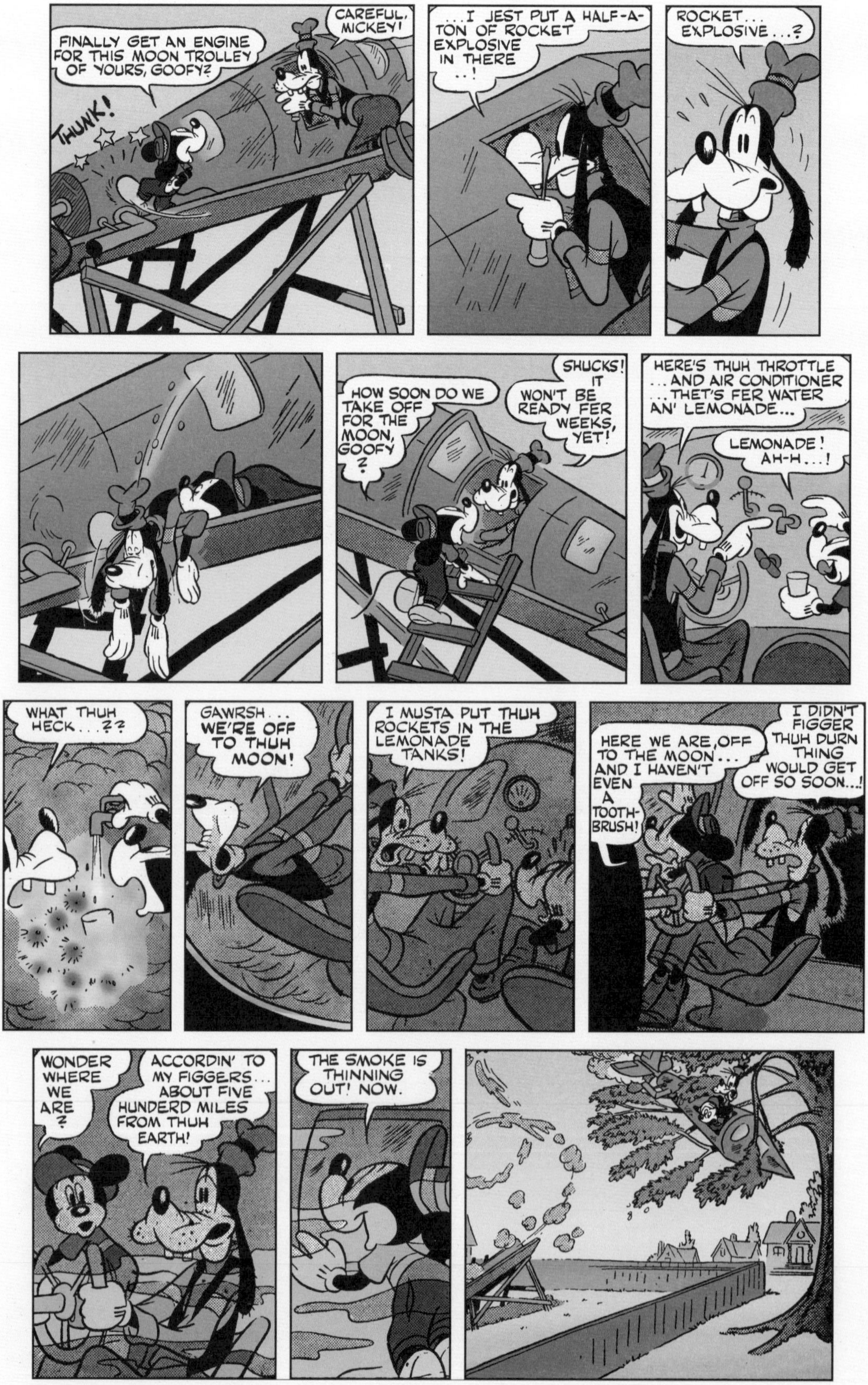
FINALLY GET AN ENGINE FOR THIS MOON TROLLEY OF YOURS, GOOFY?
CAREFUL, MICKEY!
THUNK!
...I JEST PUT A HALF-A-TON OF ROCKET EXPLOSIVE IN THERE ..!
ROCKET... EXPLOSIVE ...?
HOW SOON DO WE TAKE OFF FOR THE MOON, GOOFY ?
SHUCKS! IT WON'T BE READY FER WEEKS, YET!
HERE'S THUH THROTTLE ...AND AIR CONDITIONER ...THET'S FER WATER AN' LEMONADE...
LEMONADE! AH-H...!
WHAT THUH HECK...??
GAWRSH... WE'RE OFF TO THUH MOON!
I MUSTA PUT THUH ROCKETS IN THE LEMONADE TANKS!
HERE WE ARE, OFF TO THE MOON... AND I HAVEN'T EVEN A TOOTH-BRUSH!
I DIDN'T FIGGER THUH DURN THING WOULD GET OFF SO SOON...!
WONDER WHERE WE ARE ?
ACCORDIN' TO MY FIGGERS... ABOUT FIVE HUNDERD MILES FROM THUH EARTH!
THE SMOKE IS THINNING OUT! NOW.

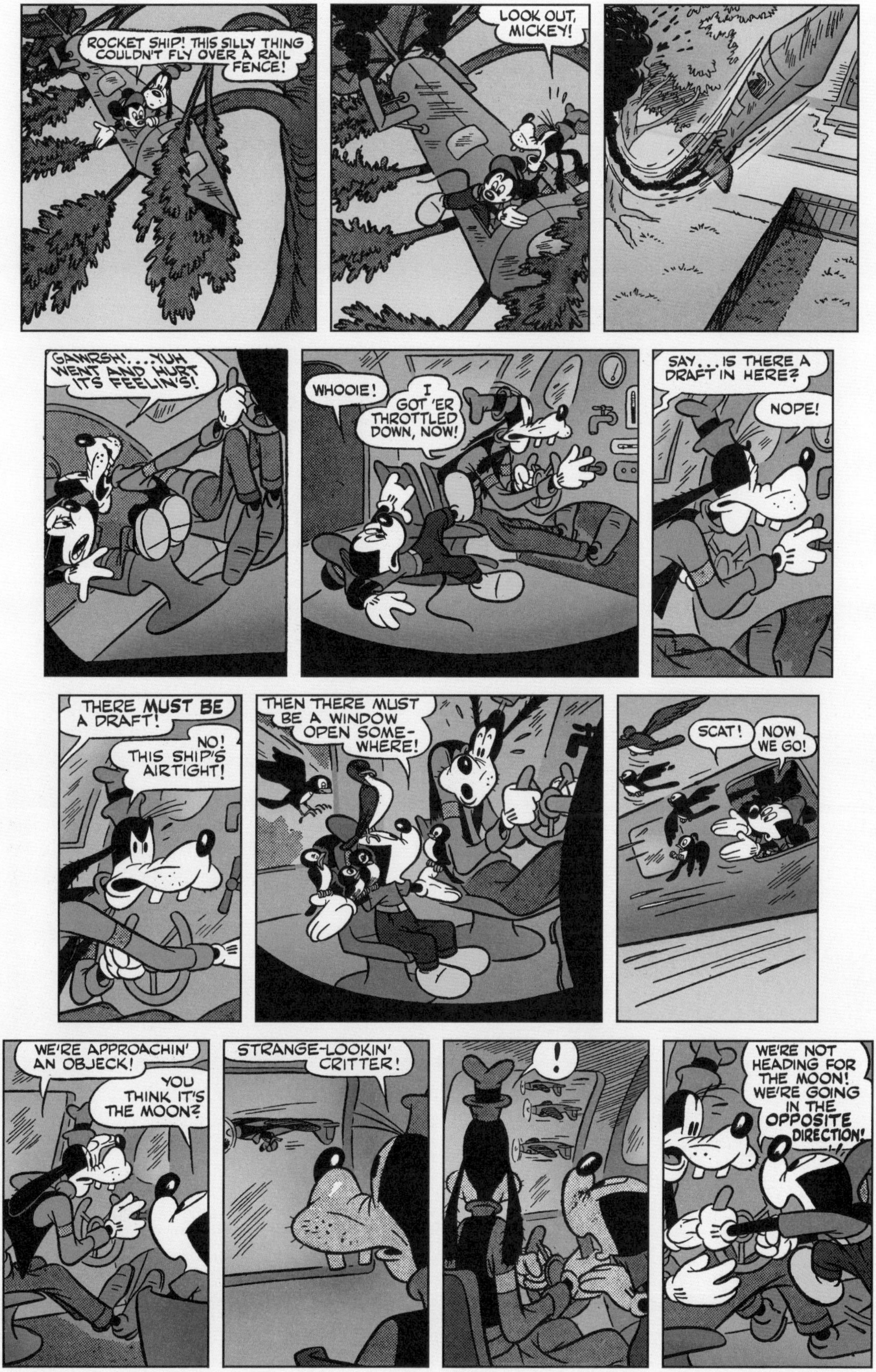
ROCKET SHIP! THIS SILLY THING COULDN'T FLY OVER A RAIL FENCE!
LOOK OUT, MICKEY!
GAWRSH!...YUH WENT AND HURT ITS FEELIN'S!
WHOOIE!
I GOT 'ER THROTTLED DOWN, NOW!
SAY... IS THERE A DRAFT IN HERE?
NOPE!
THERE MUST BE A DRAFT!
NO! THIS SHIP'S AIRTIGHT!
THEN THERE MUST BE A WINDOW OPEN SOME-WHERE!
SCAT!
NOW WE GO!
WE'RE APPROACHIN' AN OBJECK!
YOU THINK IT'S THE MOON?
STRANGE-LOOKIN' CRITTER!
!
WE'RE NOT HEADING FOR THE MOON! WE'RE GOING IN THE OPPOSITE DIRECTION!

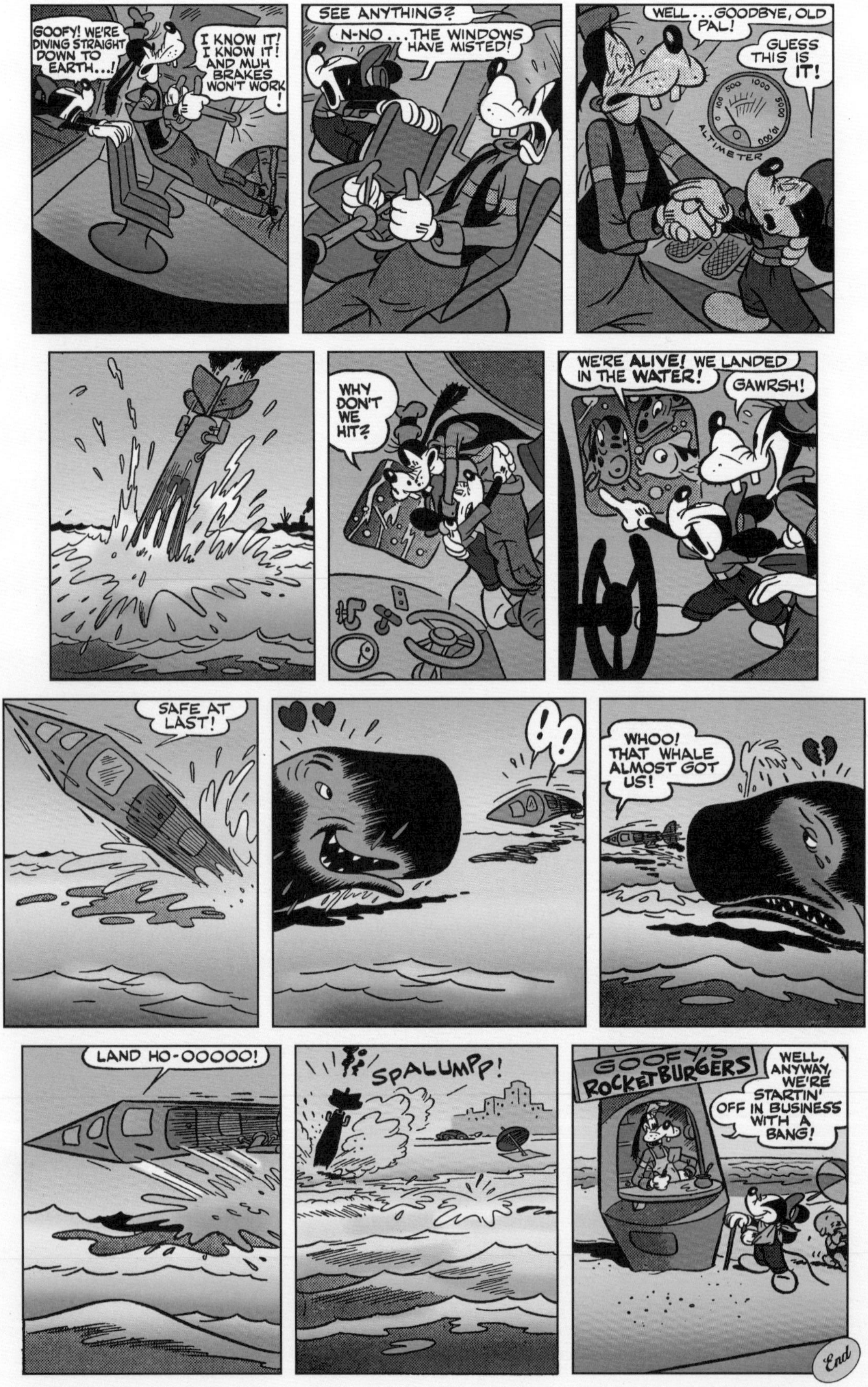
GOOFY! WE'RE DIVING STRAIGHT DOWN TO EARTH...!
I KNOW IT! I KNOW IT! AND MUH BRAKES WON'T WORK!
SEE ANYTHING?
N-NO...THE WINDOWS HAVE MISTED!
WELL...GOODBYE, OLD PAL!
GUESS THIS IS IT!
ALTIMETER
WHY DON'T WE HIT?
WE'RE ALIVE! WE LANDED IN THE WATER!
GAWRSH!
SAFE AT LAST!
WHOO! THAT WHALE ALMOST GOT US!
LAND HO-OOOOO!
SPALUMPP!
GOOFY'S ROCKETBURGERS
WELL, ANYWAY, WE'RE STARTIN' OFF IN BUSINESS WITH A BANG!
End

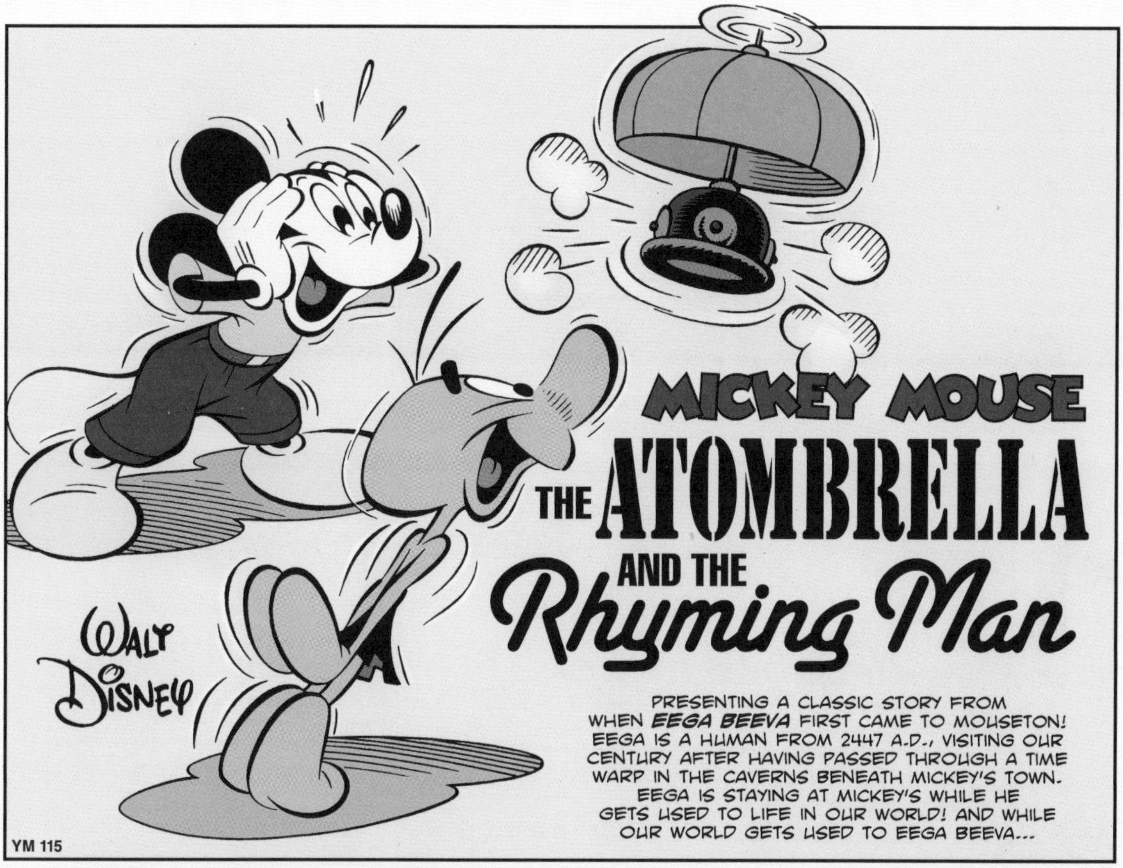
MICKEY MOUSE
THE ATOMBRELLA
AND THE
Rhyming Man
WALT DISNEY
PRESENTING A CLASSIC STORY FROM WHEN EEGA BEEVA FIRST CAME TO MOUSETON! EEGA IS A HUMAN FROM 2447 A.D., VISITING OUR CENTURY AFTER HAVING PASSED THROUGH A TIME WARP IN THE CAVERNS BENEATH MICKEY'S TOWN. EEGA IS STAYING AT MICKEY'S WHILE HE GETS USED TO LIFE IN OUR WORLD! AND WHILE OUR WORLD GETS USED TO EEGA BEEVA...
YM 115

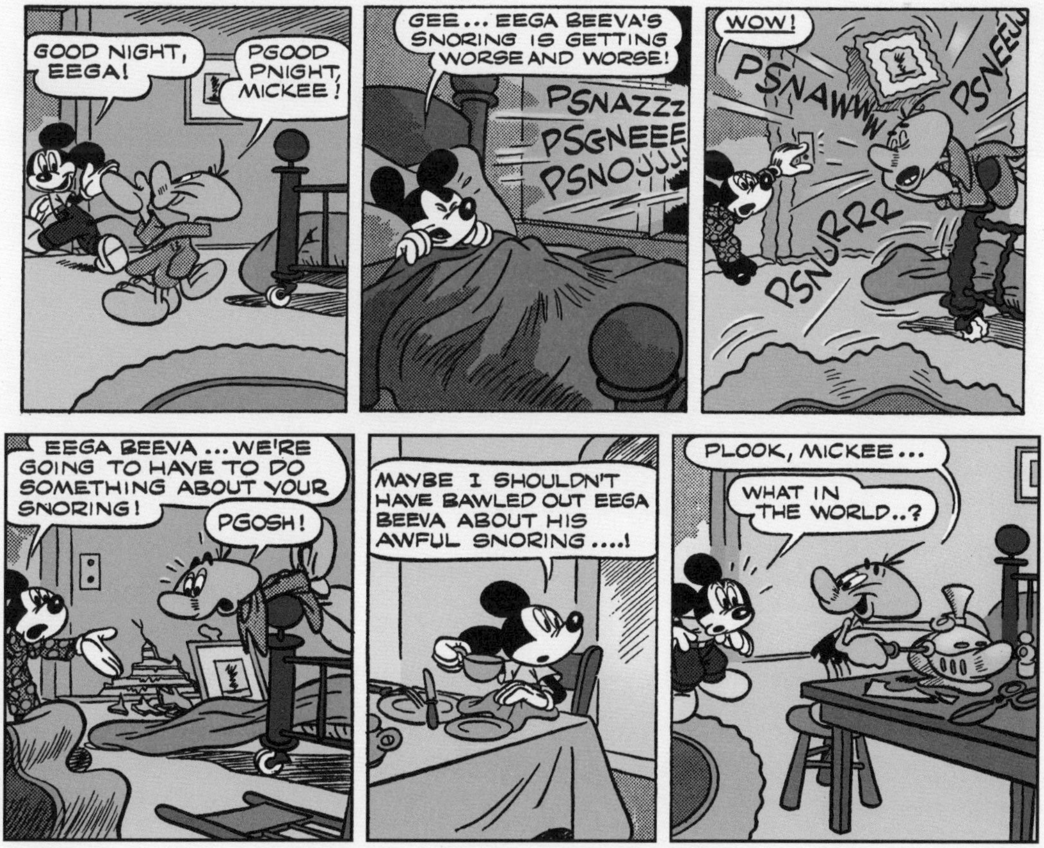
GOOD NIGHT, EEGA!
PGOOD PNIGHT, MICKEE!
GEE... EEGA BEEVA'S SNORING IS GETTING WORSE AND WORSE!
PSNAZZz
PSGNEEE
PSNOJJJJ
WOW!
PSNAWWW
PSNEEE
PSNURRR
EEGA BEEVA ... WE'RE GOING TO HAVE TO DO SOMETHING ABOUT YOUR SNORING!
PGOSH!
MAYBE I SHOULDN'T HAVE BAWLED OUT EEGA BEEVA ABOUT HIS AWFUL SNORING ....!
PLOOK, MICKEE...
WHAT IN THE WORLD..?

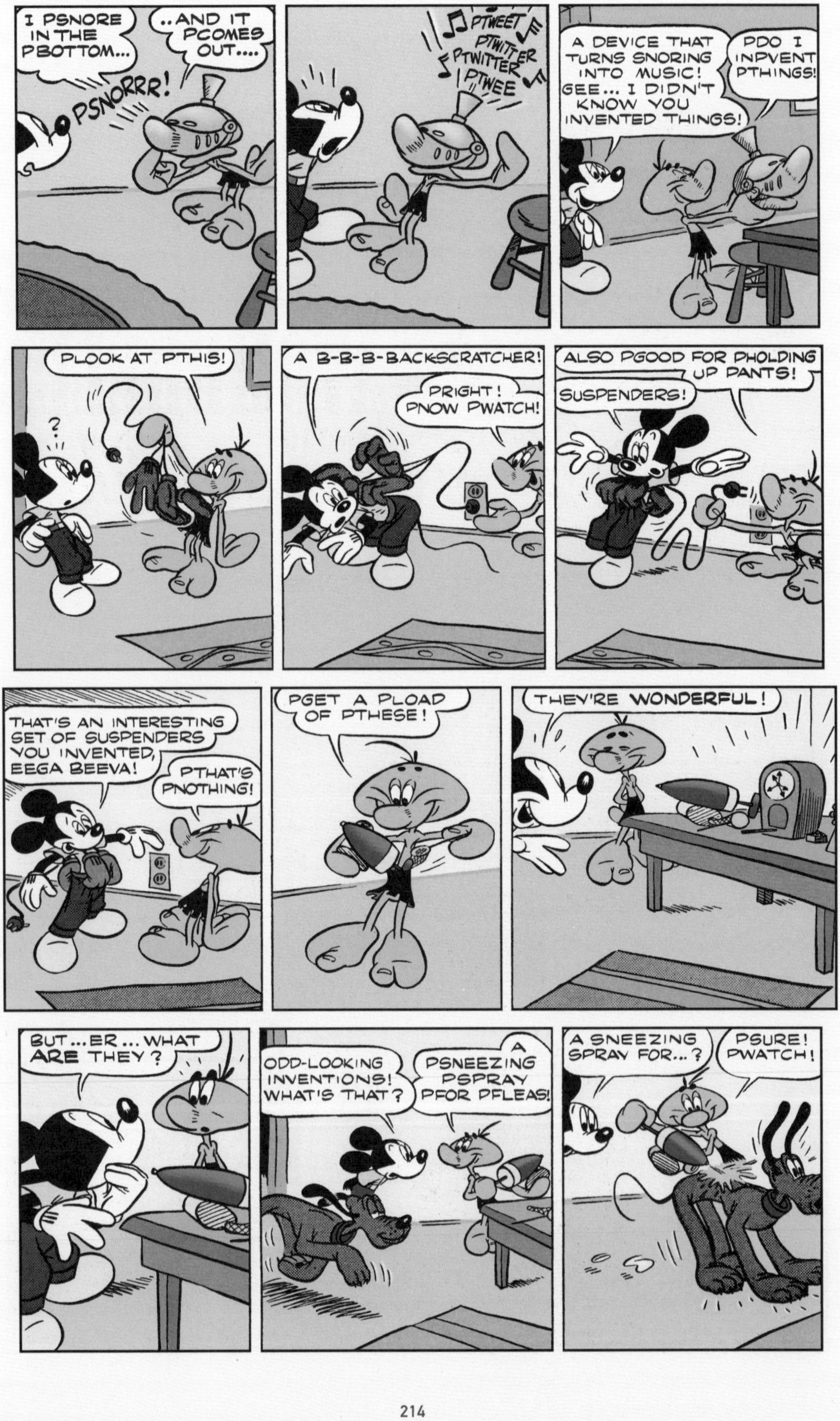
I PSNORE IN THE PBOTTOM...
..AND IT PCOMES OUT....
PSNORRR!
PTWEET
PTWITTER
PTWITTER
PTWEE
A DEVICE THAT TURNS SNORING INTO MUSIC! GEE... I DIDN'T KNOW YOU INVENTED THINGS!
PDO I INPVENT PTHINGS!
PLOOK AT PTHIS!
?
A B-B-B-BACKSCRATCHER!
PRIGHT! PNOW PWATCH!
ALSO PGOOD FOR PHOLDING UP PANTS!
SUSPENDERS!
THAT'S AN INTERESTING SET OF SUSPENDERS YOU INVENTED, EEGA BEEVA!
PTHAT'S PNOTHING!
PGET A PLOAD OF PTHESE!
THEY'RE WONDERFUL!
BUT... ER ... WHAT ARE THEY?
ODD-LOOKING INVENTIONS! WHAT'S THAT?
A PSNEEZING PSPRAY PFOR PFLEAS!
A SNEEZING SPRAY FOR...?
PSURE! PWATCH!

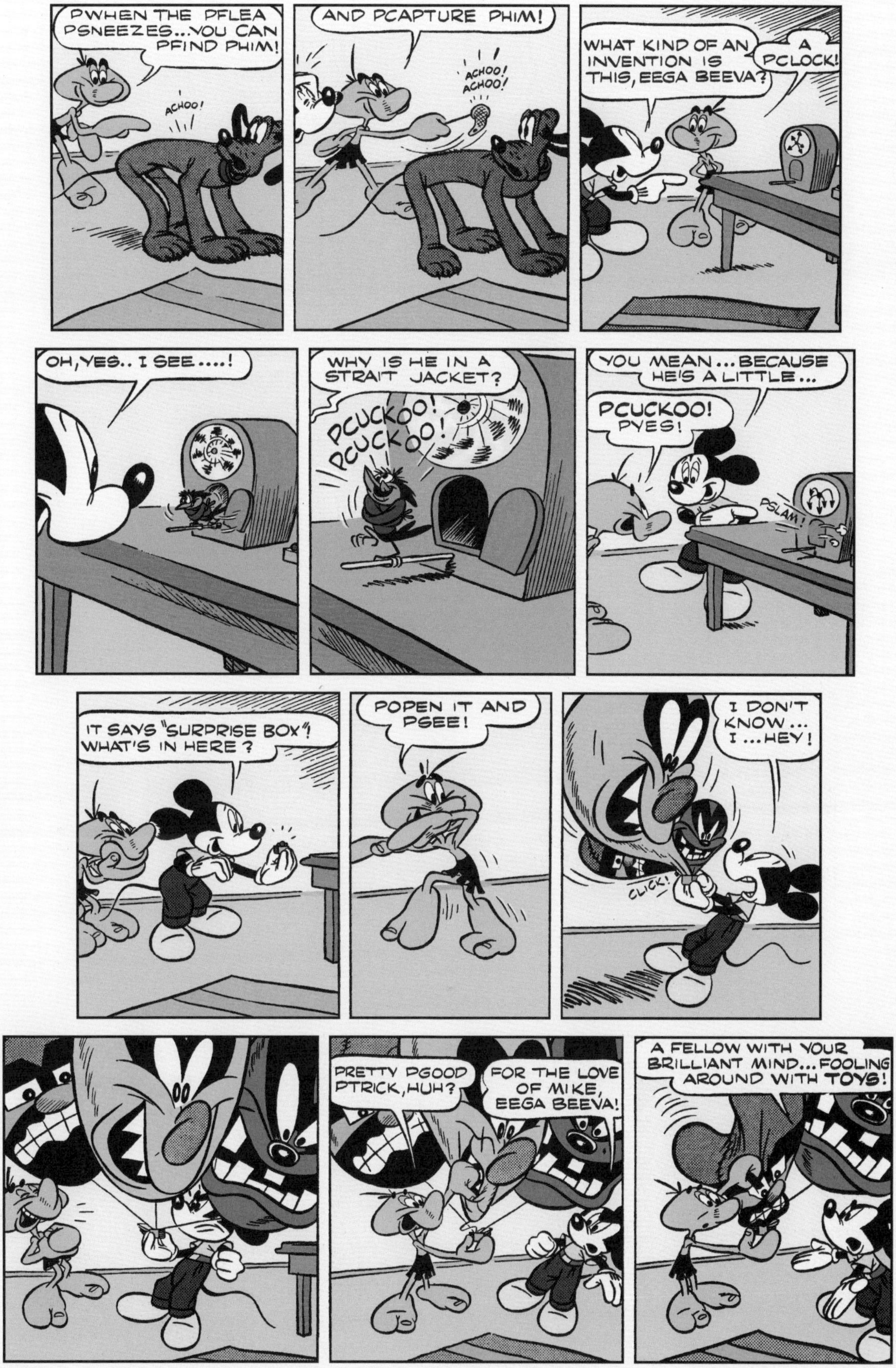
PWHEN THE PFLEA PSNEEZES...YOU CAN PFIND PHIM!
ACHOO!
AND PCAPTURE PHIM!
ACHOO! ACHOO!
WHAT KIND OF AN INVENTION IS THIS, EEGA BEEVA?
A PCLOCK!
OH, YES.. I SEE....!
WHY IS HE IN A STRAIT JACKET?
PCUCKOO! PCUCKOO!
YOU MEAN...BECAUSE HE'S A LITTLE...
PCUCKOO! PYES!
PSLAM!
IT SAYS "SURPRISE BOX"! WHAT'S IN HERE?
POPEN IT AND PSEE!
I DON'T KNOW... I...HEY!
CLICK!
PRETTY PGOOD PTRICK, HUH?
FOR THE LOVE OF MIKE, EEGA BEEVA!
A FELLOW WITH YOUR BRILLIANT MIND...FOOLING AROUND WITH TOYS!

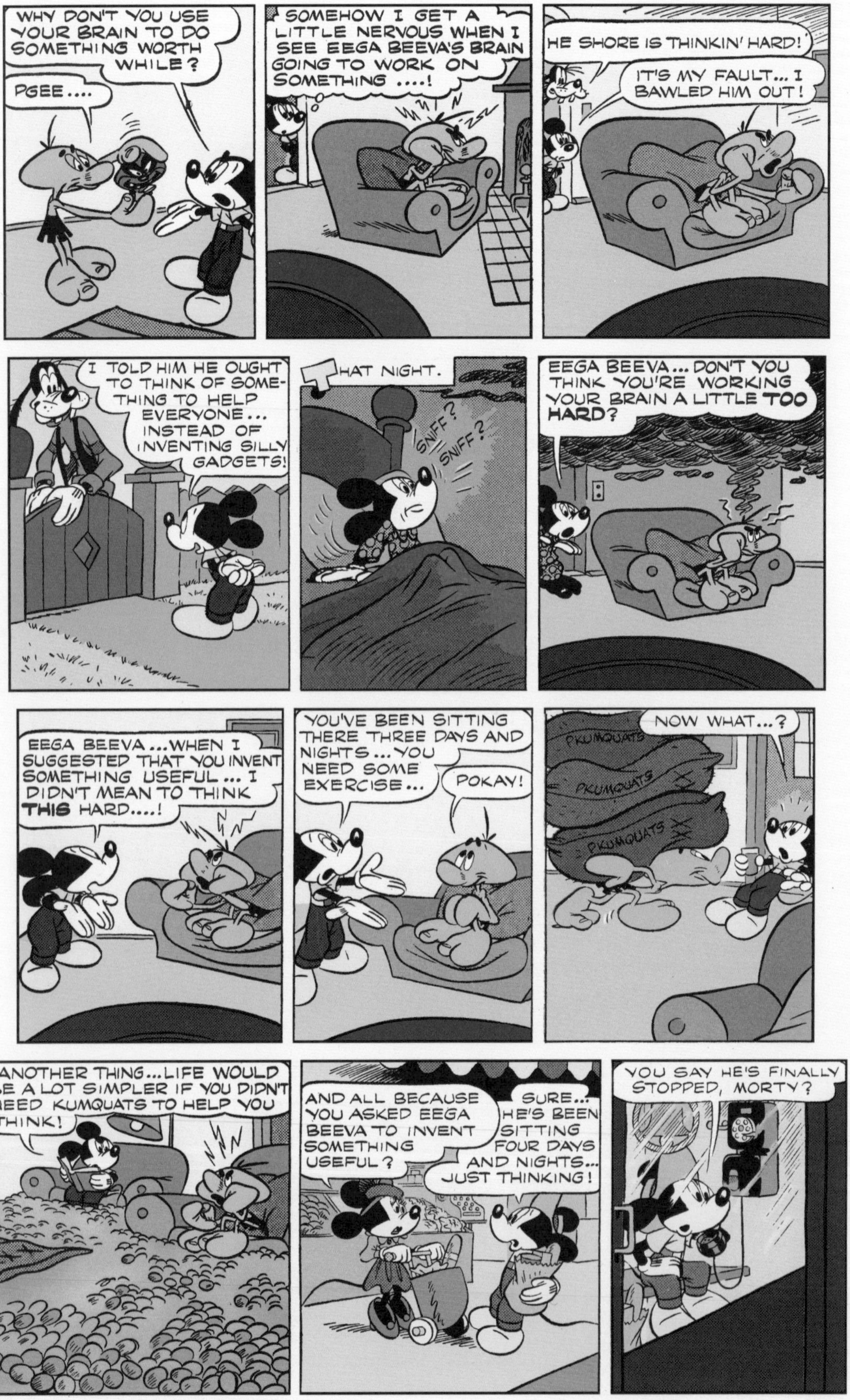
WHY DON'T YOU USE YOUR BRAIN TO DO SOMETHING WORTH WHILE?
PGEE....
SOMEHOW I GET A LITTLE NERVOUS WHEN I SEE EEGA BEEVA'S BRAIN GOING TO WORK ON SOMETHING ....!
HE SHORE IS THINKIN' HARD!
IT'S MY FAULT... I BAWLED HIM OUT!
I TOLD HIM HE OUGHT TO THINK OF SOMETHING TO HELP EVERYONE... INSTEAD OF INVENTING SILLY GADGETS!
THAT NIGHT.
SNIFF?
SNIFF?
EEGA BEEVA... DON'T YOU THINK YOU'RE WORKING YOUR BRAIN A LITTLE TOO HARD?
EEGA BEEVA...WHEN I SUGGESTED THAT YOU INVENT SOMETHING USEFUL... I DIDN'T MEAN TO THINK THIS HARD....!
YOU'VE BEEN SITTING THERE THREE DAYS AND NIGHTS...YOU NEED SOME EXERCISE...
POKAY!
PKUMQUATS
PKUMQUATS
PKUMQUATS
NOW WHAT...?
ANOTHER THING...LIFE WOULD BE A LOT SIMPLER IF YOU DIDN'T NEED KUMQUATS TO HELP YOU THINK!
AND ALL BECAUSE YOU ASKED EEGA BEEVA TO INVENT SOMETHING USEFUL?
SURE... HE'S BEEN SITTING FOUR DAYS AND NIGHTS... JUST THINKING!
YOU SAY HE'S FINALLY STOPPED, MORTY?

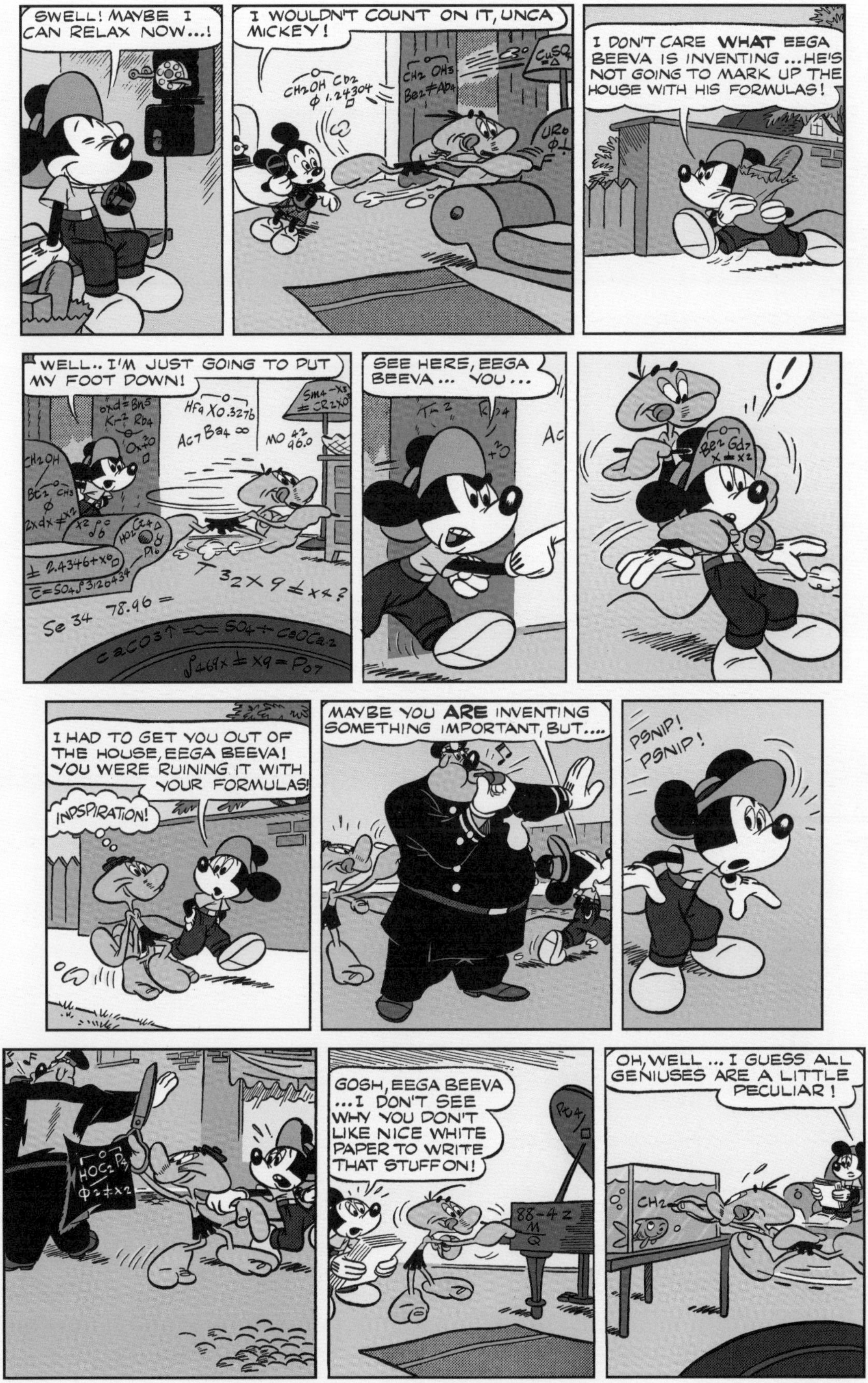
SWELL! MAYBE I CAN RELAX NOW...!
I WOULDN'T COUNT ON IT, UNCA MICKEY!
I DON'T CARE WHAT EEGA BEEVA IS INVENTING ...HE'S NOT GOING TO MARK UP THE HOUSE WITH HIS FORMULAS!
WELL.. I'M JUST GOING TO PUT MY FOOT DOWN!
SEE HERE, EEGA BEEVA... YOU...
!
I HAD TO GET YOU OUT OF THE HOUSE, EEGA BEEVA! YOU WERE RUINING IT WITH YOUR FORMULAS!
INSPIRATION!
MAYBE YOU ARE INVENTING SOMETHING IMPORTANT, BUT....
PSNIP! PSNIP!
GOSH, EEGA BEEVA ...I DON'T SEE WHY YOU DON'T LIKE NICE WHITE PAPER TO WRITE THAT STUFF ON!
OH, WELL ... I GUESS ALL GENIUSES ARE A LITTLE PECULIAR!

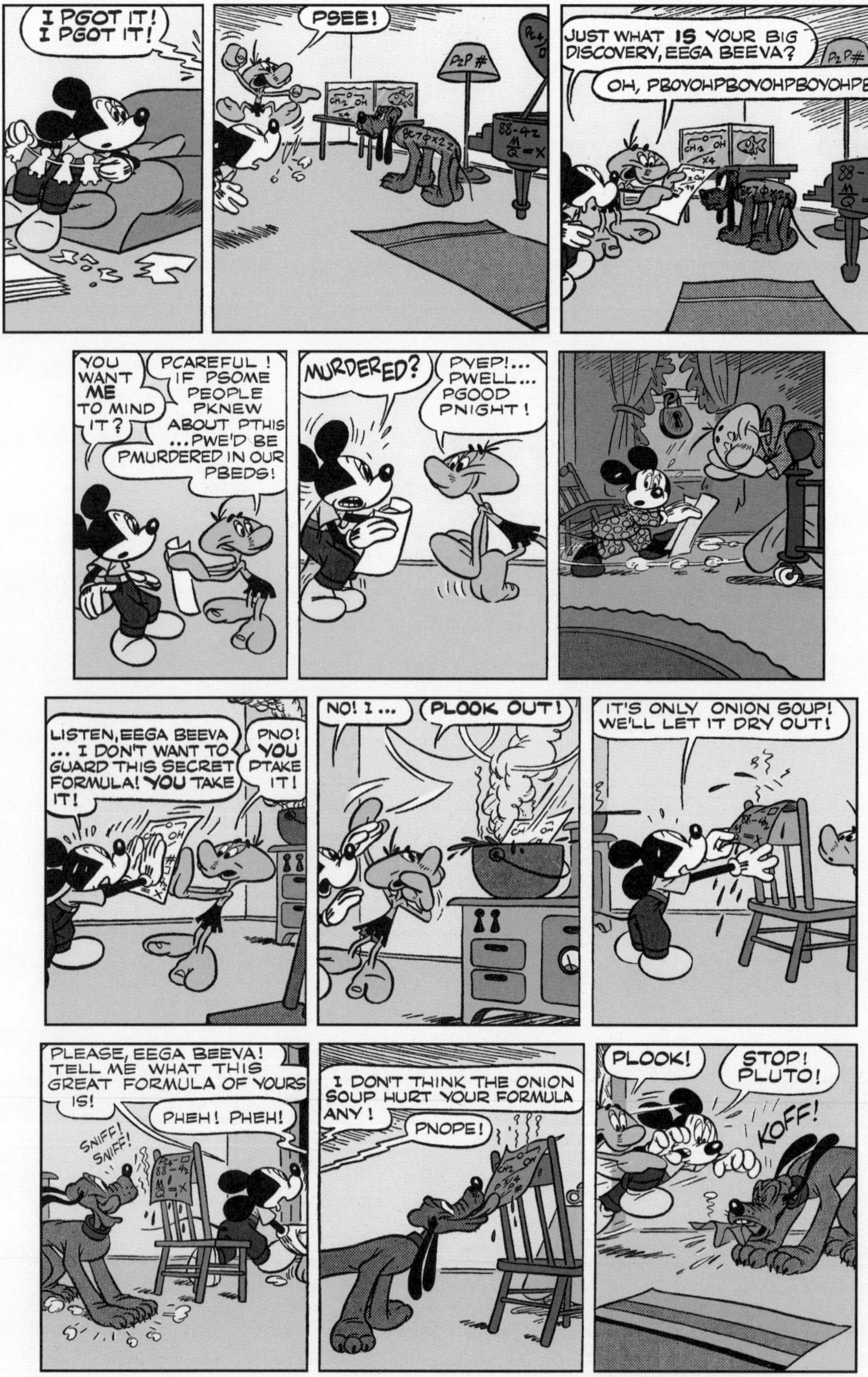
I PGOT IT! I PGOT IT!
PSEE!
JUST WHAT IS YOUR BIG DISCOVERY, EEGA BEEVA?
OH, PBOYOHPBOYOHPBOYOHPBOY!
YOU WANT ME TO MIND IT?
PCAREFUL! IF PSOME PEOPLE PKNEW ABOUT PTHIS ...PWE'D BE PMURDERED IN OUR PBEDS!
MURDERED?
PYEP!... PWELL... PGOOD PNIGHT!
LISTEN, EEGA BEEVA ... I DON'T WANT TO GUARD THIS SECRET FORMULA! YOU TAKE IT!
PNO! YOU PTAKE IT!
NO! I ...
PLOOK OUT!
IT'S ONLY ONION SOUP! WE'LL LET IT DRY OUT!
PLEASE, EEGA BEEVA! TELL ME WHAT THIS GREAT FORMULA OF YOURS IS!
PHEH! PHEH!
SNIFF! SNIFF!
I DON'T THINK THE ONION SOUP HURT YOUR FORMULA ANY!
PNOPE!
PLOOK!
STOP! PLUTO!
KOFF!

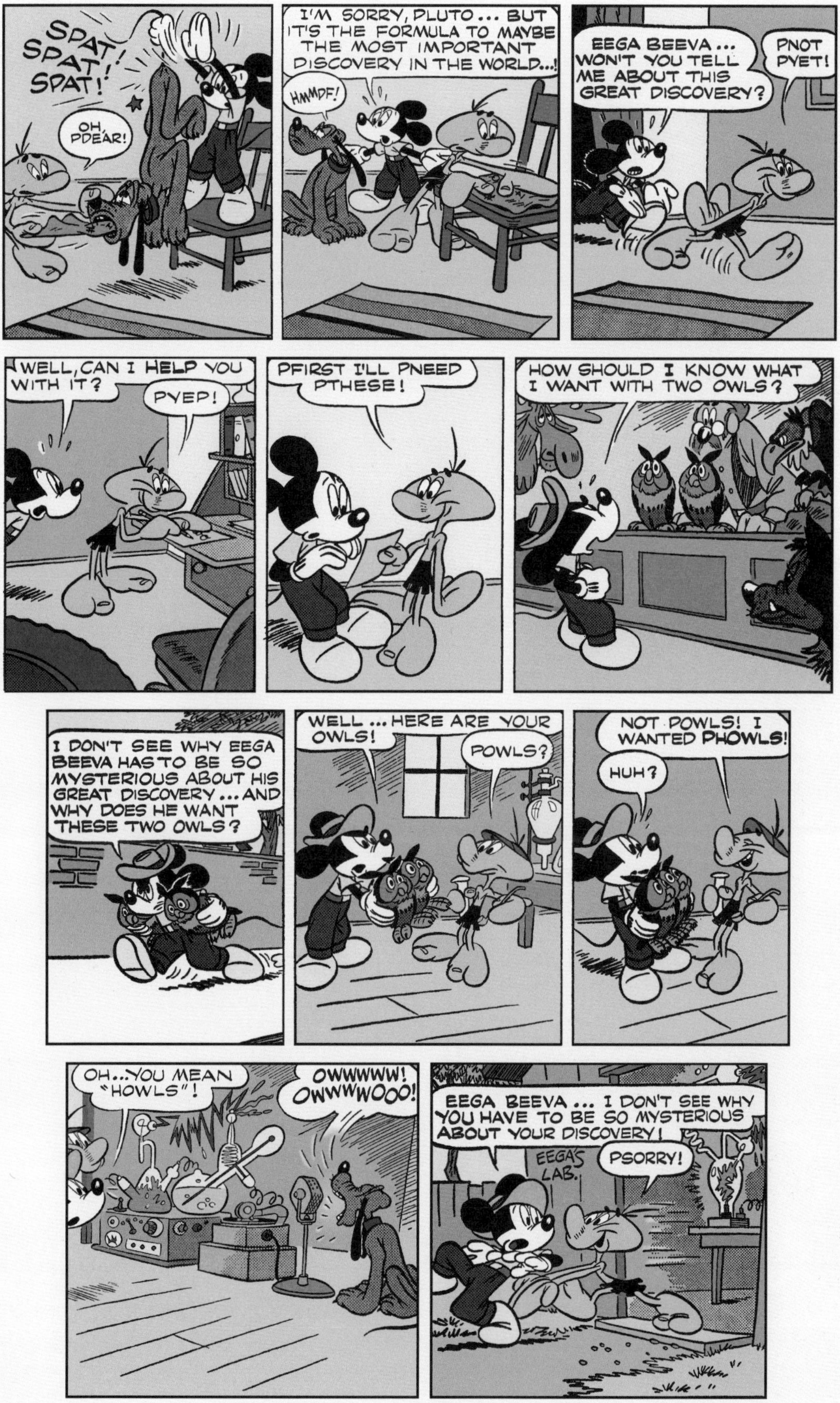
SPAT! SPAT! SPAT!
OH, PDEAR!
I'M SORRY, PLUTO... BUT IT'S THE FORMULA TO MAYBE THE MOST IMPORTANT DISCOVERY IN THE WORLD...!
HMMPF!
EEGA BEEVA... WON'T YOU TELL ME ABOUT THIS GREAT DISCOVERY?
PNOT PYET!
WELL, CAN I HELP YOU WITH IT?
PYEP!
PFIRST I'LL PNEED PTHESE!
HOW SHOULD I KNOW WHAT I WANT WITH TWO OWLS?
I DON'T SEE WHY EEGA BEEVA HAS TO BE SO MYSTERIOUS ABOUT HIS GREAT DISCOVERY... AND WHY DOES HE WANT THESE TWO OWLS?
WELL... HERE ARE YOUR OWLS!
POWLS?
NOT POWLS! I WANTED PHOWLS!
HUH?
OH... YOU MEAN "HOWLS"!
OWWWWW! OWWWWOOO!
EEGA BEEVA... I DON'T SEE WHY YOU HAVE TO BE SO MYSTERIOUS ABOUT YOUR DISCOVERY!
EEGA'S LAB.
PSORRY!

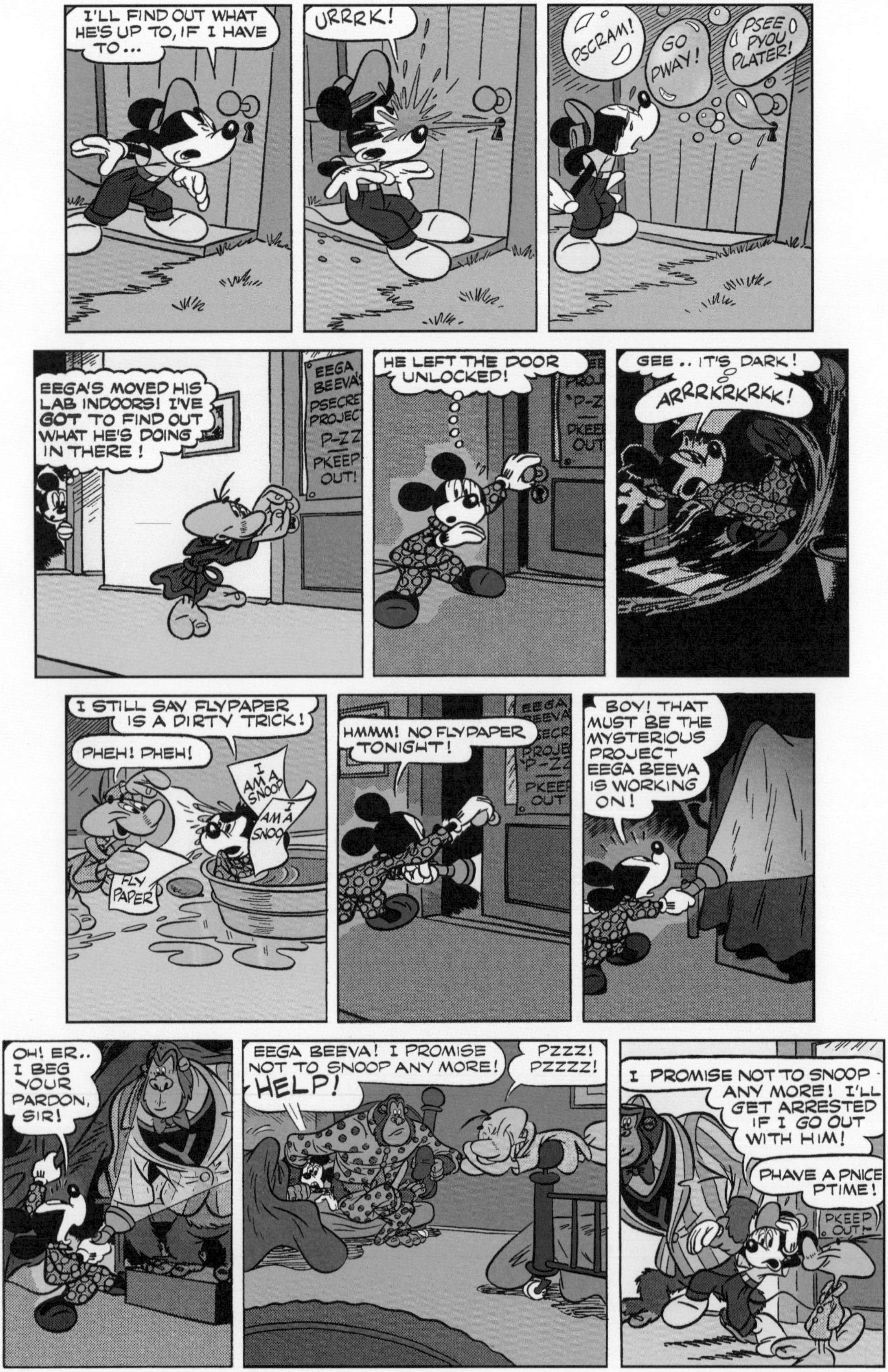
I'LL FIND OUT WHAT HE'S UP TO, IF I HAVE TO...
URRRK!
PSCRAM!
GO PWAY!
PSEE PYOU PLATER!
EEGA'S MOVED HIS LAB INDOORS! I'VE GOT TO FIND OUT WHAT HE'S DOING IN THERE!
EEGA BEEVA'S PSECRET PROJECT P-ZZ PKEEP OUT!
HE LEFT THE DOOR UNLOCKED!
GEE.. IT'S DARK!
ARRRKRKRKK!
I STILL SAY FLYPAPER IS A DIRTY TRICK!
PHEH! PHEH!
I AM A SNOOP
I AM A SNOO
FLY PAPER
HMMM! NO FLYPAPER TONIGHT!
BOY! THAT MUST BE THE MYSTERIOUS PROJECT EEGA BEEVA IS WORKING ON!
OH! ER.. I BEG YOUR PARDON, SIR!
EEGA BEEVA! I PROMISE NOT TO SNOOP ANY MORE! HELP!
PZZZ! PZZZZ!
I PROMISE NOT TO SNOOP ANY MORE! I'LL GET ARRESTED IF I GO OUT WITH HIM!
PHAVE A PNICE PTIME!
PKEEP OUT!

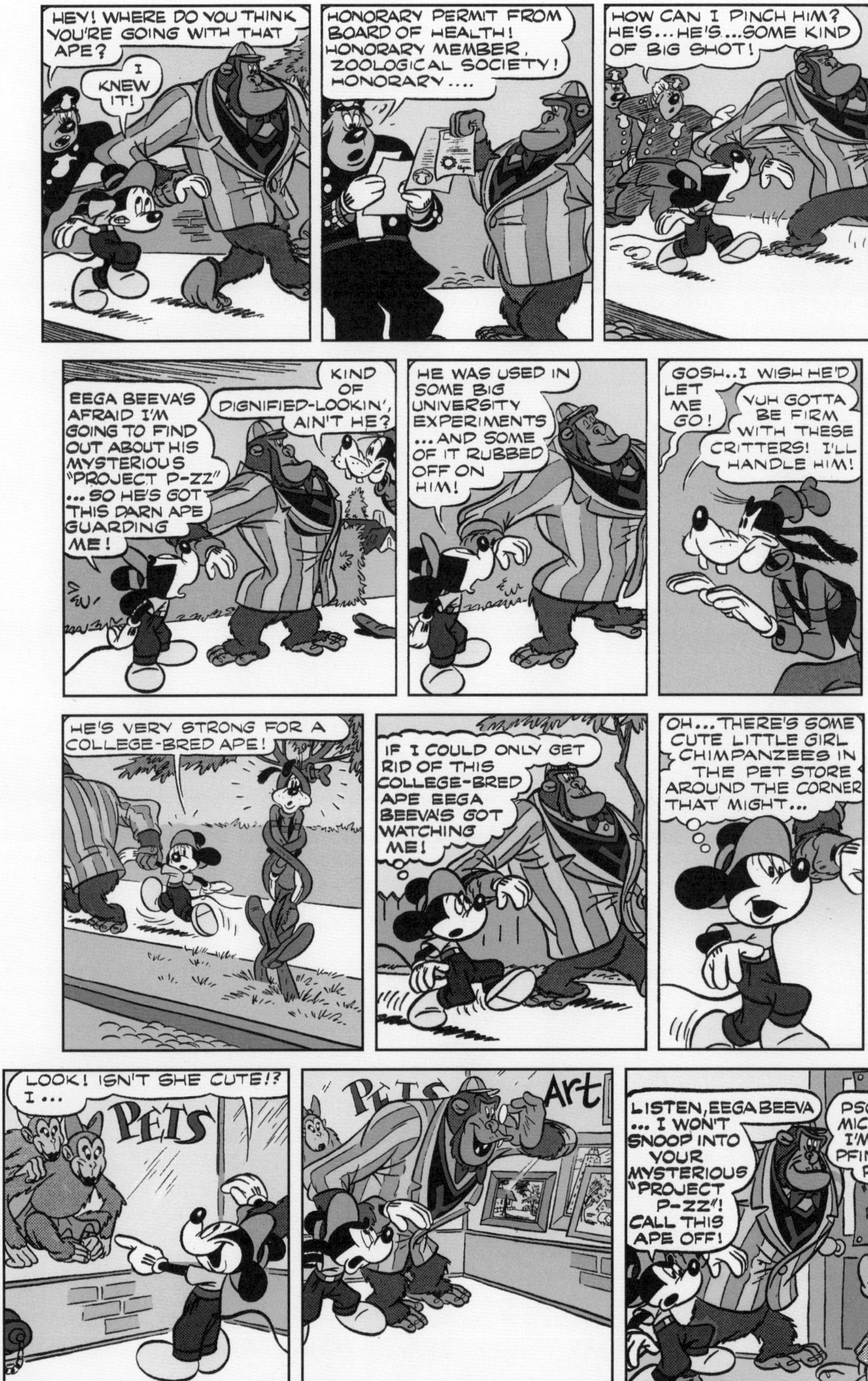
HEY! WHERE DO YOU THINK YOU'RE GOING WITH THAT APE?
I KNEW IT!
HONORARY PERMIT FROM BOARD OF HEALTH! HONORARY MEMBER, ZOOLOGICAL SOCIETY! HONORARY....
HOW CAN I PINCH HIM? HE'S...HE'S...SOME KIND OF BIG SHOT!
EEGA BEEVA'S AFRAID I'M GOING TO FIND OUT ABOUT HIS MYSTERIOUS "PROJECT P-ZZ" ...SO HE'S GOT THIS DARN APE GUARDING ME!
KIND OF DIGNIFIED-LOOKIN', AIN'T HE?
HE WAS USED IN SOME BIG UNIVERSITY EXPERIMENTS ...AND SOME OF IT RUBBED OFF ON HIM!
GOSH..I WISH HE'D LET ME GO!
YUH GOTTA BE FIRM WITH THESE CRITTERS! I'LL HANDLE HIM!
HE'S VERY STRONG FOR A COLLEGE-BRED APE!
IF I COULD ONLY GET RID OF THIS COLLEGE-BRED APE EEGA BEEVA'S GOT WATCHING ME!
OH...THERE'S SOME CUTE LITTLE GIRL CHIMPANZEES IN THE PET STORE AROUND THE CORNER THAT MIGHT...
LOOK! ISN'T SHE CUTE!? I...
PETS
PETS
Art
LISTEN, EEGA BEEVA ...I WON'T SNOOP INTO YOUR MYSTERIOUS "PROJECT P-ZZ"! CALL THIS APE OFF!
PSORRY, MICKEE! I'M NOT PFINISHED PYET!
EEGA
P-ZZ
PKEEP OUT!

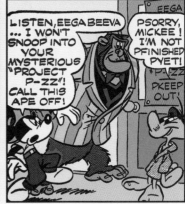

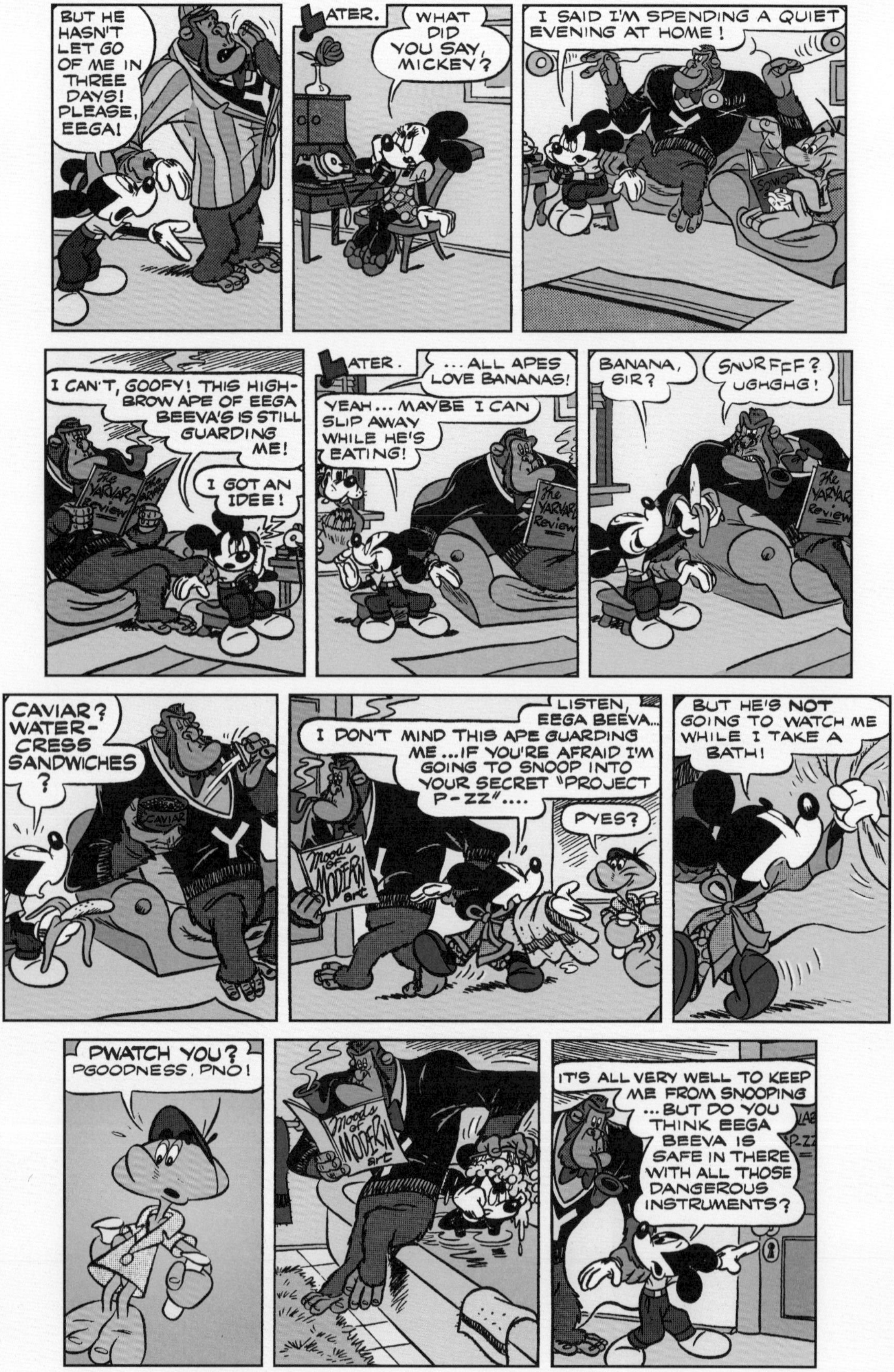
BUT HE HASN'T LET GO OF ME IN THREE DAYS! PLEASE, EEGA!
LATER.
WHAT DID YOU SAY, MICKEY?
I SAID I'M SPENDING A QUIET EVENING AT HOME!
I CAN'T, GOOFY! THIS HIGH-BROW APE OF EEGA BEEVA'S IS STILL GUARDING ME!
I GOT AN IDEE!
LATER.
...ALL APES LOVE BANANAS!
YEAH... MAYBE I CAN SLIP AWAY WHILE HE'S EATING!
BANANA, SIR?
SNURFFF? UGHGHG!
CAVIAR? WATER-CRESS SANDWICHES?
CAVIAR
LISTEN, EEGA BEEVA...
I DON'T MIND THIS APE GUARDING ME... IF YOU'RE AFRAID I'M GOING TO SNOOP INTO YOUR SECRET "PROJECT P-ZZ"....
PYES?
BUT HE'S NOT GOING TO WATCH ME WHILE I TAKE A BATH!
PWATCH YOU? PGOODNESS, PNO!
IT'S ALL VERY WELL TO KEEP ME FROM SNOOPING ... BUT DO YOU THINK EEGA BEEVA IS SAFE IN THERE WITH ALL THOSE DANGEROUS INSTRUMENTS?

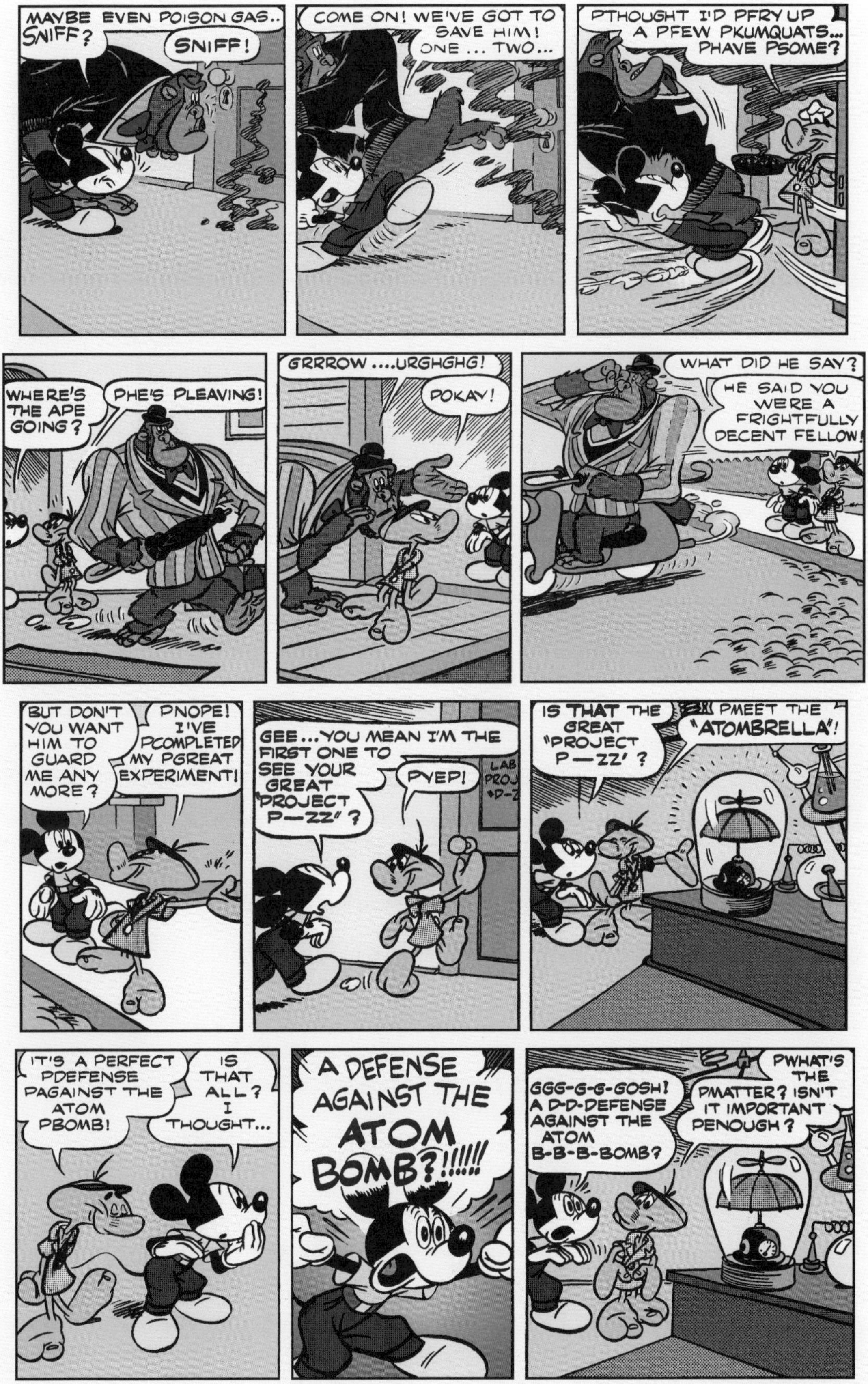
MAYBE EVEN POISON GAS.. SNIFF?
SNIFF!
COME ON! WE'VE GOT TO SAVE HIM! ONE ... TWO...
PTHOUGHT I'D PFRY UP A PFEW PKUMQUATS... PHAVE PSOME?
WHERE'S THE APE GOING?
PHE'S PLEAVING!
GRRROW ....URGHGHG!
POKAY!
WHAT DID HE SAY?
HE SAID YOU WERE A FRIGHTFULLY DECENT FELLOW!
BUT DON'T YOU WANT HIM TO GUARD ME ANY MORE?
PNOPE! I'VE PCOMPLETED MY PGREAT EXPERIMENT!
GEE...YOU MEAN I'M THE FIRST ONE TO SEE YOUR GREAT "PROJECT P—ZZ"?
PYEP!
IS THAT THE GREAT "PROJECT P—ZZ'?
PMEET THE "ATOMBRELLA"!
IT'S A PERFECT PDEFENSE PAGAINST THE ATOM PBOMB!
IS THAT ALL? I THOUGHT...
A DEFENSE AGAINST THE ATOM BOMB?!!!!!!
GGG-G-G-GOSH! A D-D-DEFENSE AGAINST THE ATOM B-B-B-BOMB?
PWHAT'S THE PMATTER? ISN'T IT IMPORTANT PENOUGH?

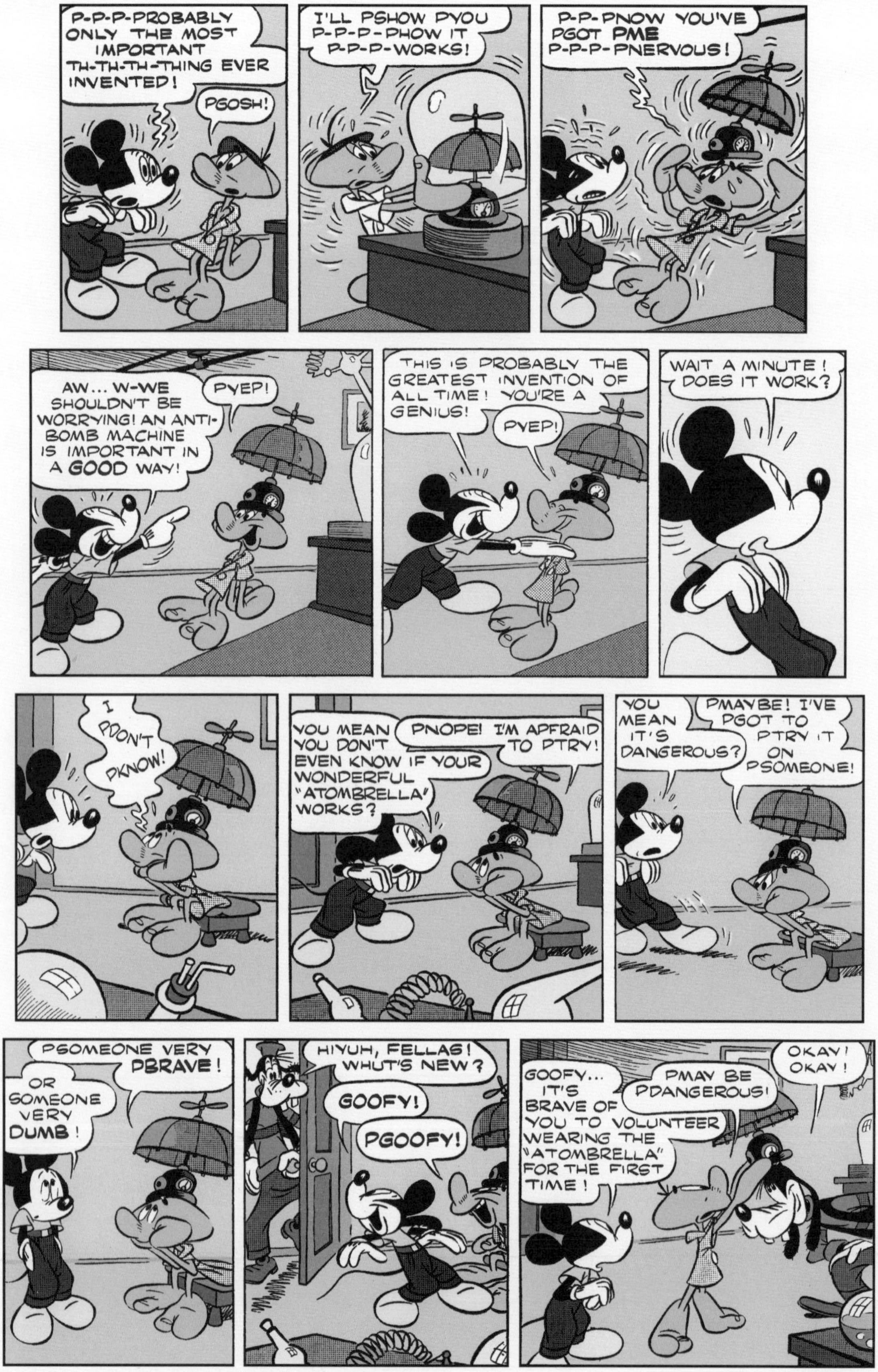
P-P-P-PROBABLY ONLY THE MOST IMPORTANT TH-TH-TH-THING EVER INVENTED!
PGOSH!
I'LL PSHOW PYOU P-P-P-PHOW IT P-P-P-WORKS!
P-P-PNOW YOU'VE PGOT PME P-P-P-PNERVOUS!
AW... W-WE SHOULDN'T BE WORRYING! AN ANTI-BOMB MACHINE IS IMPORTANT IN A GOOD WAY!
PYEP!
THIS IS PROBABLY THE GREATEST INVENTION OF ALL TIME! YOU'RE A GENIUS!
PYEP!
WAIT A MINUTE! DOES IT WORK?
I PDON'T PKNOW!
YOU MEAN YOU DON'T EVEN KNOW IF YOUR WONDERFUL "ATOMBRELLA" WORKS?
PNOPE! I'M APFRAID TO PTRY!
YOU MEAN IT'S DANGEROUS?
PMAYBE! I'VE PGOT TO PTRY IT ON PSOMEONE!
PSOMEONE VERY PBRAVE!
OR SOMEONE VERY DUMB!
HIYUH, FELLAS! WHUT'S NEW?
GOOFY!
PGOOFY!
GOOFY... IT'S BRAVE OF YOU TO VOLUNTEER WEARING THE "ATOMBRELLA" FOR THE FIRST TIME!
PMAY BE PDANGEROUS!
OKAY! OKAY!

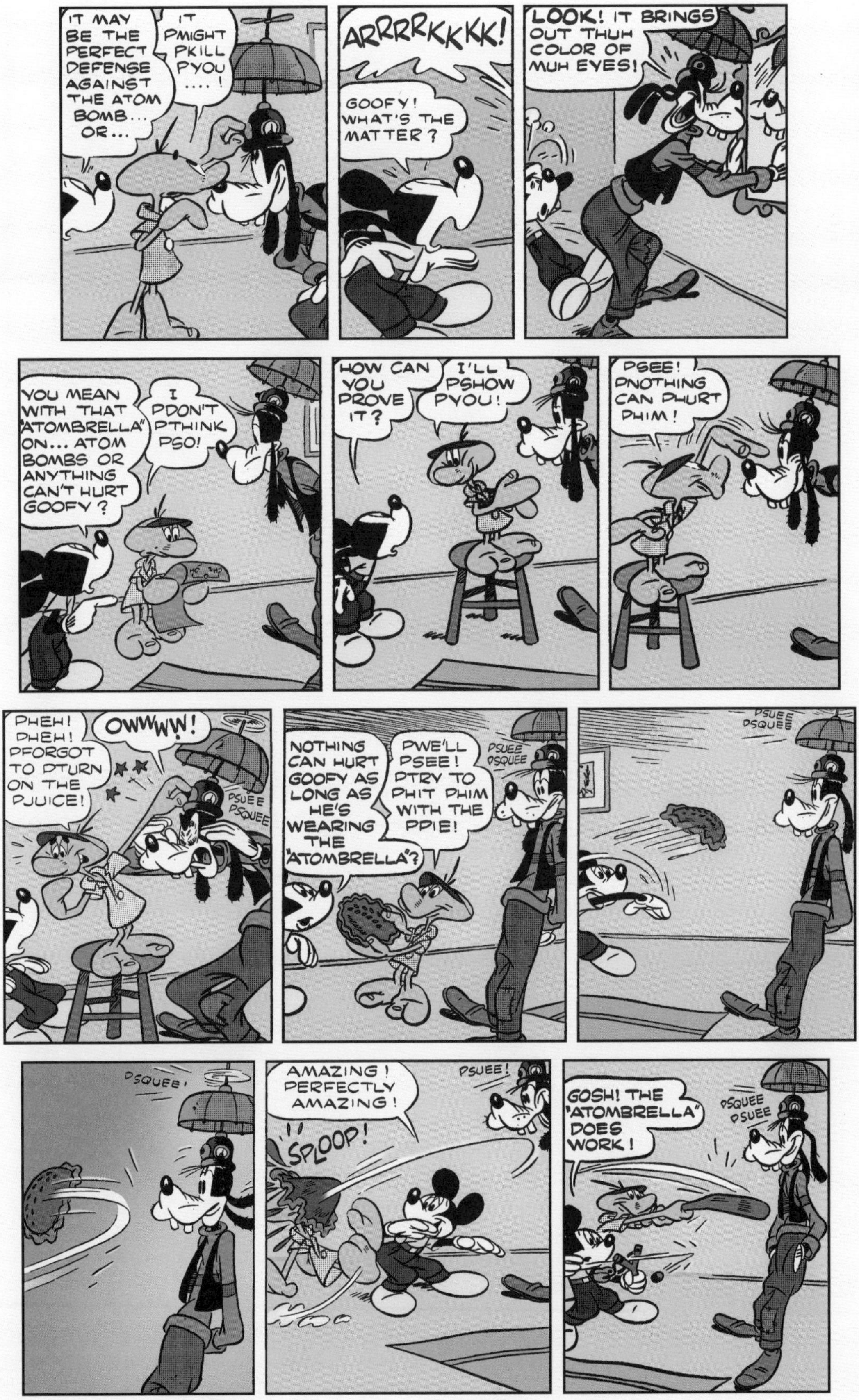
IT MAY BE THE PERFECT DEFENSE AGAINST THE ATOM BOMB... OR...
IT PMIGHT PKILL PYOU ....!
ARRRRKKKK!
GOOFY! WHAT'S THE MATTER?
LOOK! IT BRINGS OUT THUH COLOR OF MUH EYES!
YOU MEAN WITH THAT "ATOMBRELLA" ON... ATOM BOMBS OR ANYTHING CAN'T HURT GOOFY?
I PDON'T PTHINK PSO!
HOW CAN YOU PROVE IT?
I'LL PSHOW PYOU!
PSEE! PNOTHING CAN PHURT PHIM!
PHEH! PHEH! PFORGOT TO PTURN ON THE PJUICE!
OWWWW!
PSUEE PSQUEE
NOTHING CAN HURT GOOFY AS LONG AS HE'S WEARING THE "ATOMBRELLA"?
PWE'LL PSEE! PTRY TO PHIT PHIM WITH THE PPIE!
PSUEE PSQUEE
PSUEE PSQUEE
PSQUEE!
AMAZING! PERFECTLY AMAZING!
PSUEE!
SPLOOP!
GOSH! THE "ATOMBRELLA" DOES WORK!
PSQUEE PSUEE

WATER DOESN'T WORK, EITHER!

HOW'M I DOIN'?

YOU KNOW, EEGA BEEVA... I THINK YOU'VE GOT SOMETHING HERE!

EEGA!

SO FAR SO GOOD! NOW WE NEED A FAMOUS SCIENTIFIC AUTHORITY TO PROVE THE ATOMBRELLA IS PROOF AGAINST ATOMS!

LATER.

IT'S GREAT, PROFESSOR! AND EEGA BEEVA IS THE GREATEST INVENTIVE MIND IN THE WORLD! SUCH GENIUS!

SUCH BRAIN POWER! SUCH....

IS THAT YOUR GREAT SCIENTIST?

BAH!

PDID I PDO PSOMETHING PWRONG?

SLAM!

NO WONDER I CAN'T GET THE ATOM EXPERTS INTERESTED IN YOUR ATOMBRELLA! LOOK AT YOU!

PSIGH!

IF WE'RE GOING TO CONVINCE THE WORLD YOU'RE A GREAT SCIENTIST, YOU'VE GOT TO LOOK THE PART!

PTHEN PCAN I PHAVE MY PYO-PYO PBACK?

Le Swank
MEN'S SHOP

NOW WE'RE GETTING SOMEWHERE!

NOW YOU LOOK LIKE SOMETHING!

I PFEEL AWPFUL!

PCAN I PHAVE PBACK MY PYO-PYO?

Le Swank
MEN'S SHOP

PLEASE, PCAN I PHAVE PBACK MY PYO-PYO?

NO... I'VE MADE AN APPOINTMENT TO SEE THE GREAT DR. KOPPENHOOPER ABOUT YOUR ATOMBRELLA! YOU'VE GOT TO LOOK DIGNIFIED!

UNIVERSITY

ELECTRON AND RESEARC BUILDING

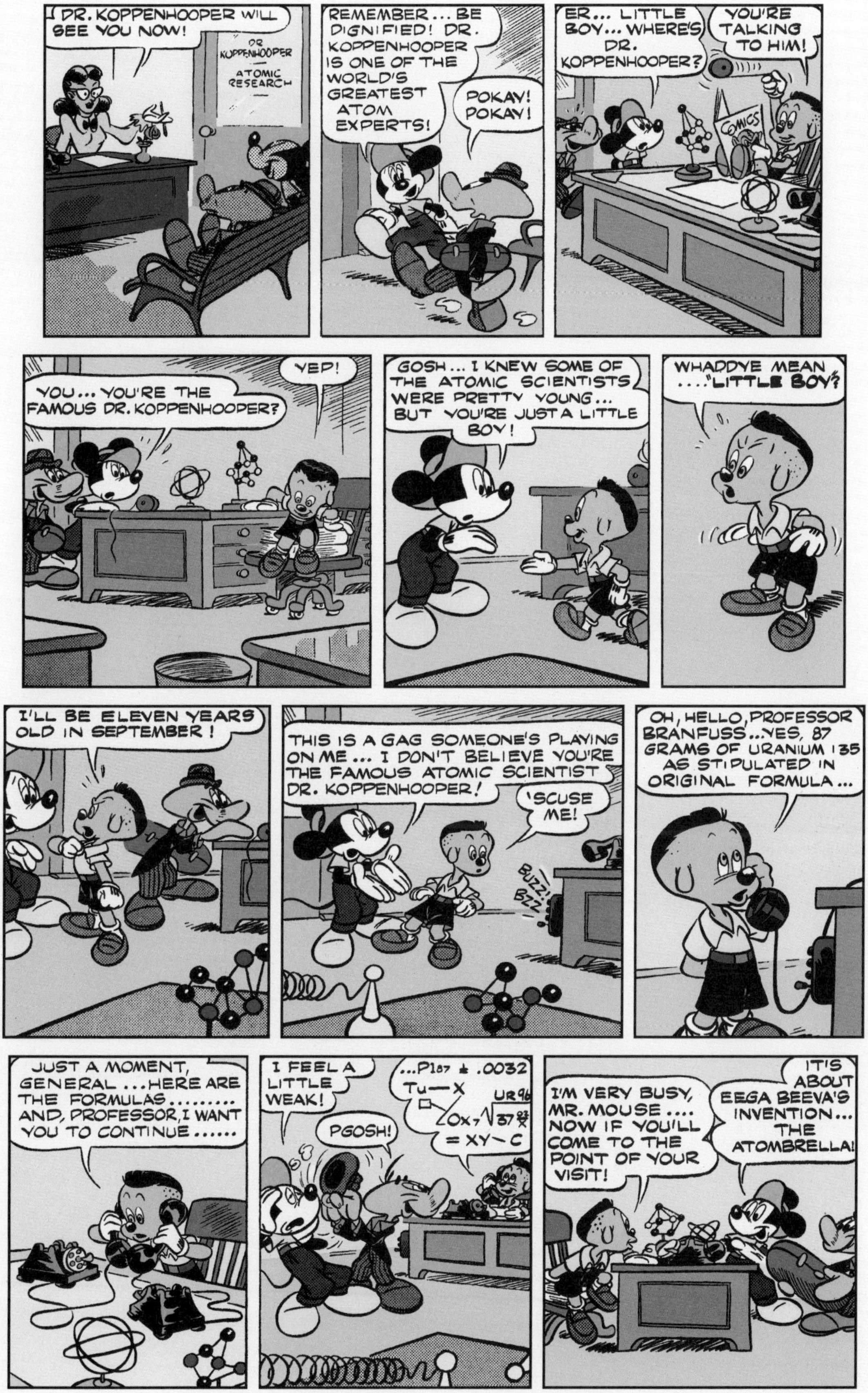
DR. KOPPENHOOPER WILL SEE YOU NOW!
DR KOPPENHOOPER — ATOMIC RESEARCH
REMEMBER ... BE DIGNIFIED! DR. KOPPENHOOPER IS ONE OF THE WORLD'S GREATEST ATOM EXPERTS!
POKAY! POKAY!
ER... LITTLE BOY... WHERE'S DR. KOPPENHOOPER?
YOU'RE TALKING TO HIM!
COMICS
YOU... YOU'RE THE FAMOUS DR. KOPPENHOOPER?
YEP!
GOSH ... I KNEW SOME OF THE ATOMIC SCIENTISTS WERE PRETTY YOUNG... BUT YOU'RE JUST A LITTLE BOY!
WHADDYE MEAN ...."LITTLE BOY"?
I'LL BE ELEVEN YEARS OLD IN SEPTEMBER!
THIS IS A GAG SOMEONE'S PLAYING ON ME ... I DON'T BELIEVE YOU'RE THE FAMOUS ATOMIC SCIENTIST DR. KOPPENHOOPER!
'SCUSE ME!
BUZZ! BZZ!
OH, HELLO, PROFESSOR BRANFUSS...YES, 87 GRAMS OF URANIUM 135 AS STIPULATED IN ORIGINAL FORMULA...
JUST A MOMENT, GENERAL ...HERE ARE THE FORMULAS......... AND, PROFESSOR, I WANT YOU TO CONTINUE......
I FEEL A LITTLE WEAK!
PGOSH!
I'M VERY BUSY, MR. MOUSE .... NOW IF YOU'LL COME TO THE POINT OF YOUR VISIT!
IT'S ABOUT EEGA BEEVA'S INVENTION... THE ATOMBRELLA!

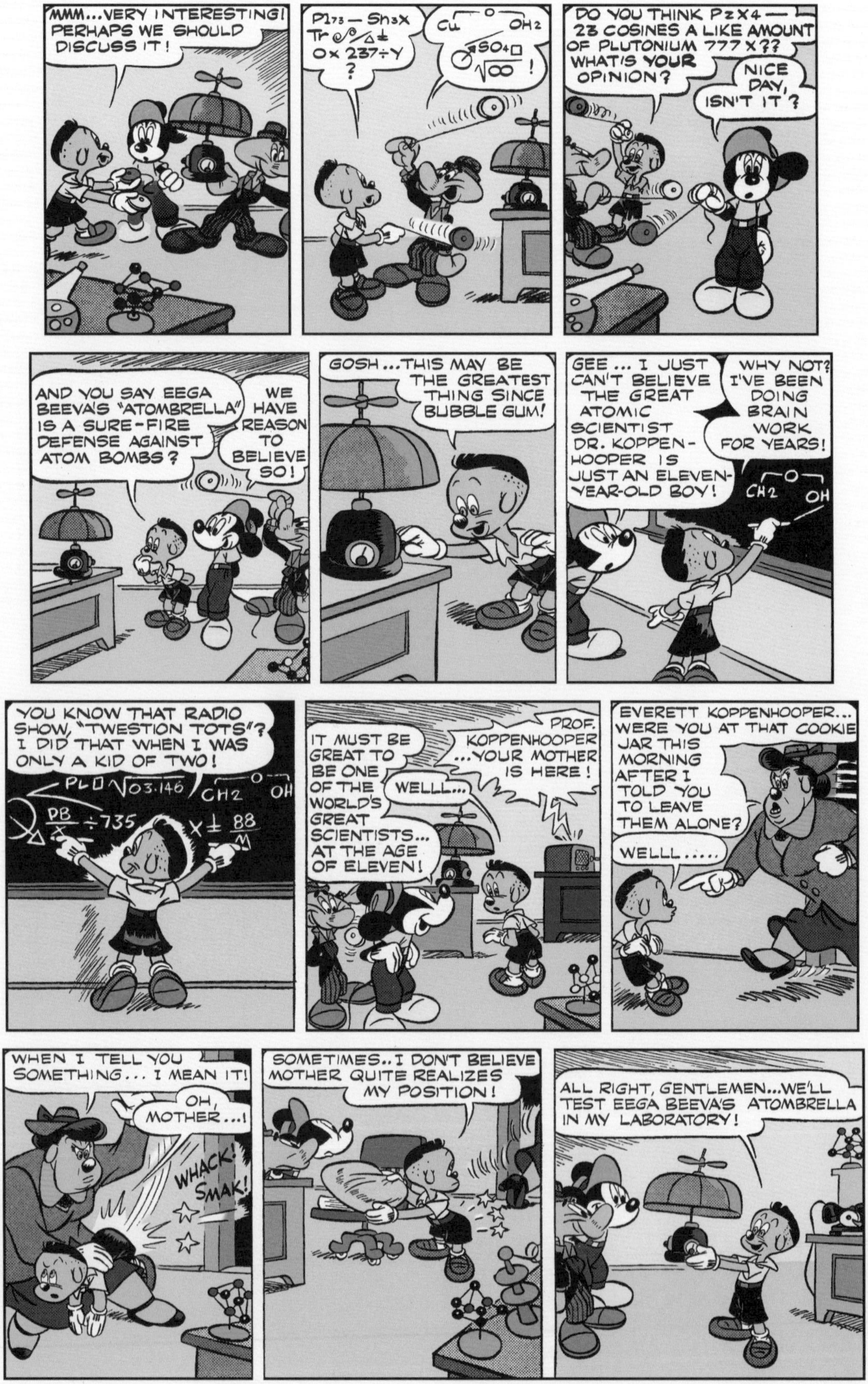
MMM...VERY INTERESTING! PERHAPS WE SHOULD DISCUSS IT!
DO YOU THINK P z X 4 — 23 COSINES A LIKE AMOUNT OF PLUTONIUM 777 X?? WHAT'S YOUR OPINION?
NICE DAY, ISN'T IT?
AND YOU SAY EEGA BEEVA'S "ATOMBRELLA" IS A SURE-FIRE DEFENSE AGAINST ATOM BOMBS?
WE HAVE REASON TO BELIEVE SO!
GOSH...THIS MAY BE THE GREATEST THING SINCE BUBBLE GUM!
GEE... I JUST CAN'T BELIEVE THE GREAT ATOMIC SCIENTIST DR. KOPPEN-HOOPER IS JUST AN ELEVEN-YEAR-OLD BOY!
WHY NOT? I'VE BEEN DOING BRAIN WORK FOR YEARS!
YOU KNOW THAT RADIO SHOW, "TWESTION TOTS"? I DID THAT WHEN I WAS ONLY A KID OF TWO!
IT MUST BE GREAT TO BE ONE OF THE WORLD'S GREAT SCIENTISTS... AT THE AGE OF ELEVEN!
WELLL...
PROF. KOPPENHOOPER ...YOUR MOTHER IS HERE!
EVERETT KOPPENHOOPER... WERE YOU AT THAT COOKIE JAR THIS MORNING AFTER I TOLD YOU TO LEAVE THEM ALONE?
WELLL.....
WHEN I TELL YOU SOMETHING... I MEAN IT!
OH, MOTHER...!
WHACK! SMAK!
SOMETIMES..I DON'T BELIEVE MOTHER QUITE REALIZES MY POSITION!
ALL RIGHT, GENTLEMEN...WE'LL TEST EEGA BEEVA'S ATOMBRELLA IN MY LABORATORY!

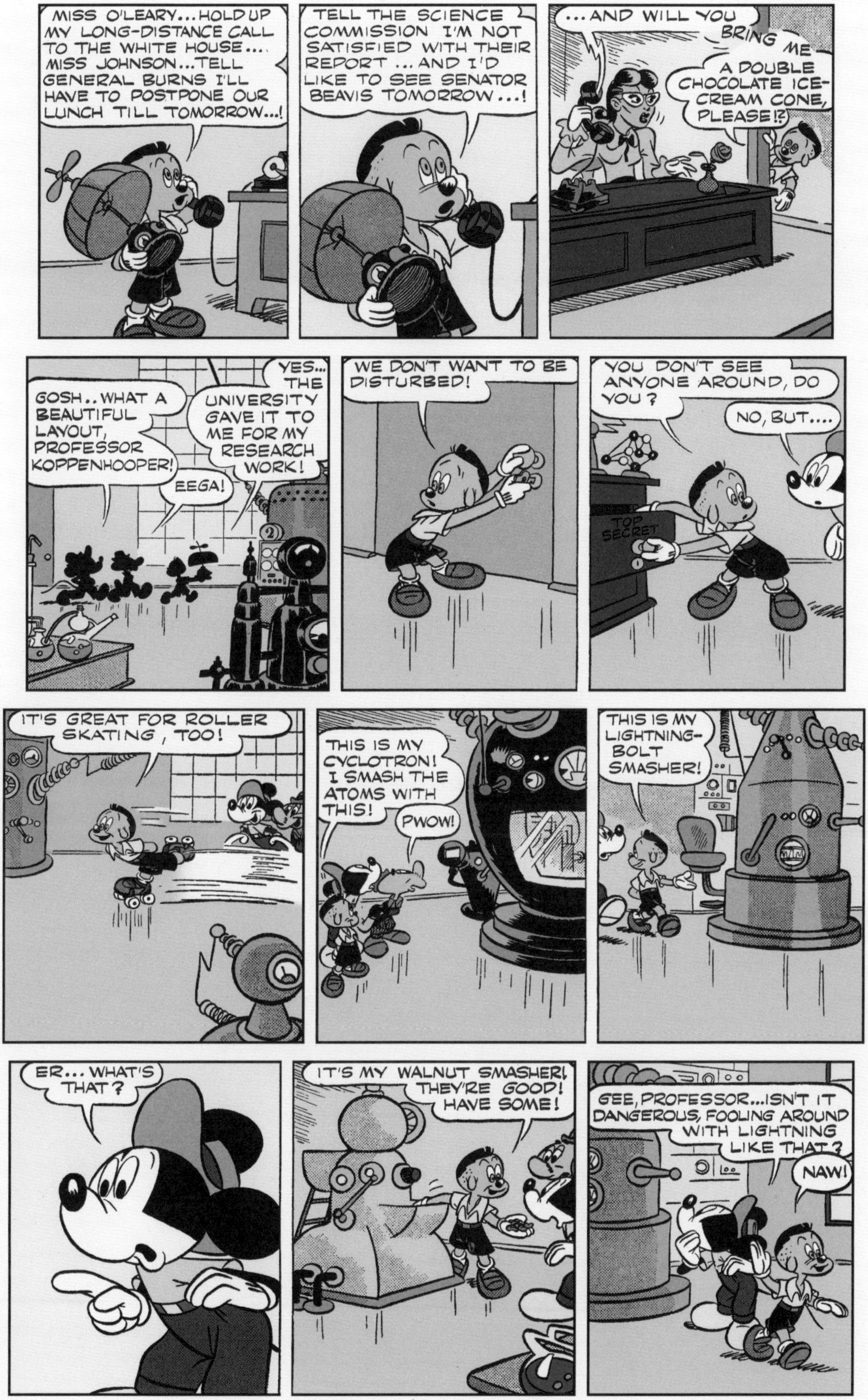
MISS O'LEARY...HOLD UP MY LONG-DISTANCE CALL TO THE WHITE HOUSE.... MISS JOHNSON...TELL GENERAL BURNS I'LL HAVE TO POSTPONE OUR LUNCH TILL TOMORROW...!
TELL THE SCIENCE COMMISSION I'M NOT SATISFIED WITH THEIR REPORT ... AND I'D LIKE TO SEE SENATOR BEAVIS TOMORROW...!
...AND WILL YOU BRING ME
A DOUBLE CHOCOLATE ICE-CREAM CONE, PLEASE!?
GOSH..WHAT A BEAUTIFUL LAYOUT, PROFESSOR KOPPENHOOPER!
YES... THE UNIVERSITY GAVE IT TO ME FOR MY RESEARCH WORK!
EEGA!
WE DON'T WANT TO BE DISTURBED!
YOU DON'T SEE ANYONE AROUND, DO YOU?
NO, BUT....
TOP SECRET
IT'S GREAT FOR ROLLER SKATING, TOO!
THIS IS MY CYCLOTRON! I SMASH THE ATOMS WITH THIS!
PWOW!
THIS IS MY LIGHTNING-BOLT SMASHER!
ER... WHAT'S THAT?
IT'S MY WALNUT SMASHER! THEY'RE GOOD! HAVE SOME!
GEE, PROFESSOR...ISN'T IT DANGEROUS, FOOLING AROUND WITH LIGHTNING LIKE THAT?
NAW!

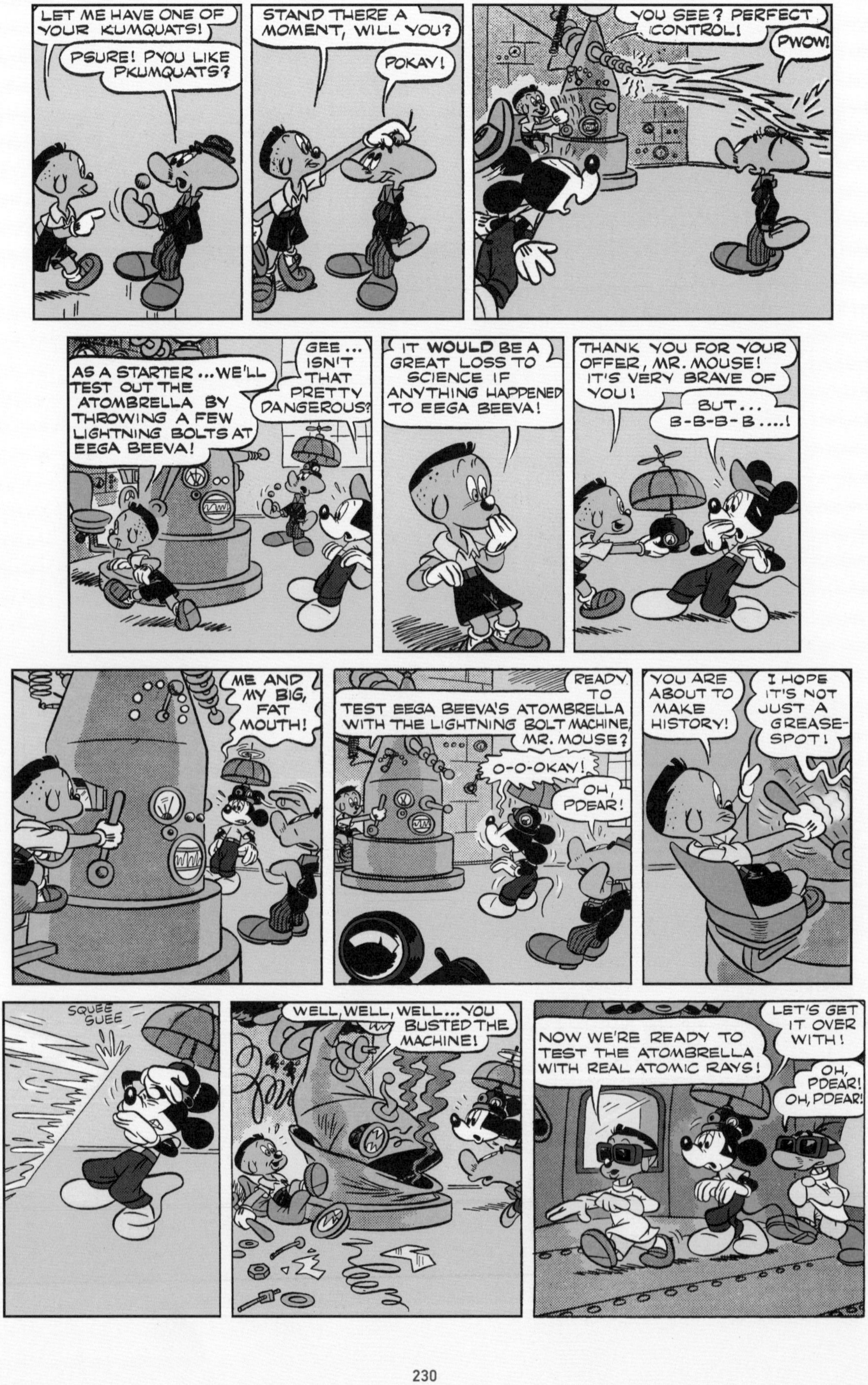
LET ME HAVE ONE OF YOUR KUMQUATS!
PSURE! PYOU LIKE PKUMQUATS?
STAND THERE A MOMENT, WILL YOU?
POKAY!
YOU SEE? PERFECT CONTROL!
PWOW!
AS A STARTER ... WE'LL TEST OUT THE ATOMBRELLA BY THROWING A FEW LIGHTNING BOLTS AT EEGA BEEVA!
GEE ... ISN'T THAT PRETTY DANGEROUS?
IT WOULD BE A GREAT LOSS TO SCIENCE IF ANYTHING HAPPENED TO EEGA BEEVA!
THANK YOU FOR YOUR OFFER, MR. MOUSE! IT'S VERY BRAVE OF YOU!
BUT... B-B-B-B ....!
ME AND MY BIG, FAT MOUTH!
READY TO TEST EEGA BEEVA'S ATOMBRELLA WITH THE LIGHTNING BOLT MACHINE, MR. MOUSE?
O-O-OKAY!
OH, PDEAR!
YOU ARE ABOUT TO MAKE HISTORY!
I HOPE IT'S NOT JUST A GREASE-SPOT!
SQUEE SUEE
WELL, WELL, WELL... YOU BUSTED THE MACHINE!
NOW WE'RE READY TO TEST THE ATOMBRELLA WITH REAL ATOMIC RAYS!
LET'S GET IT OVER WITH!
OH, PDEAR! OH, PDEAR!

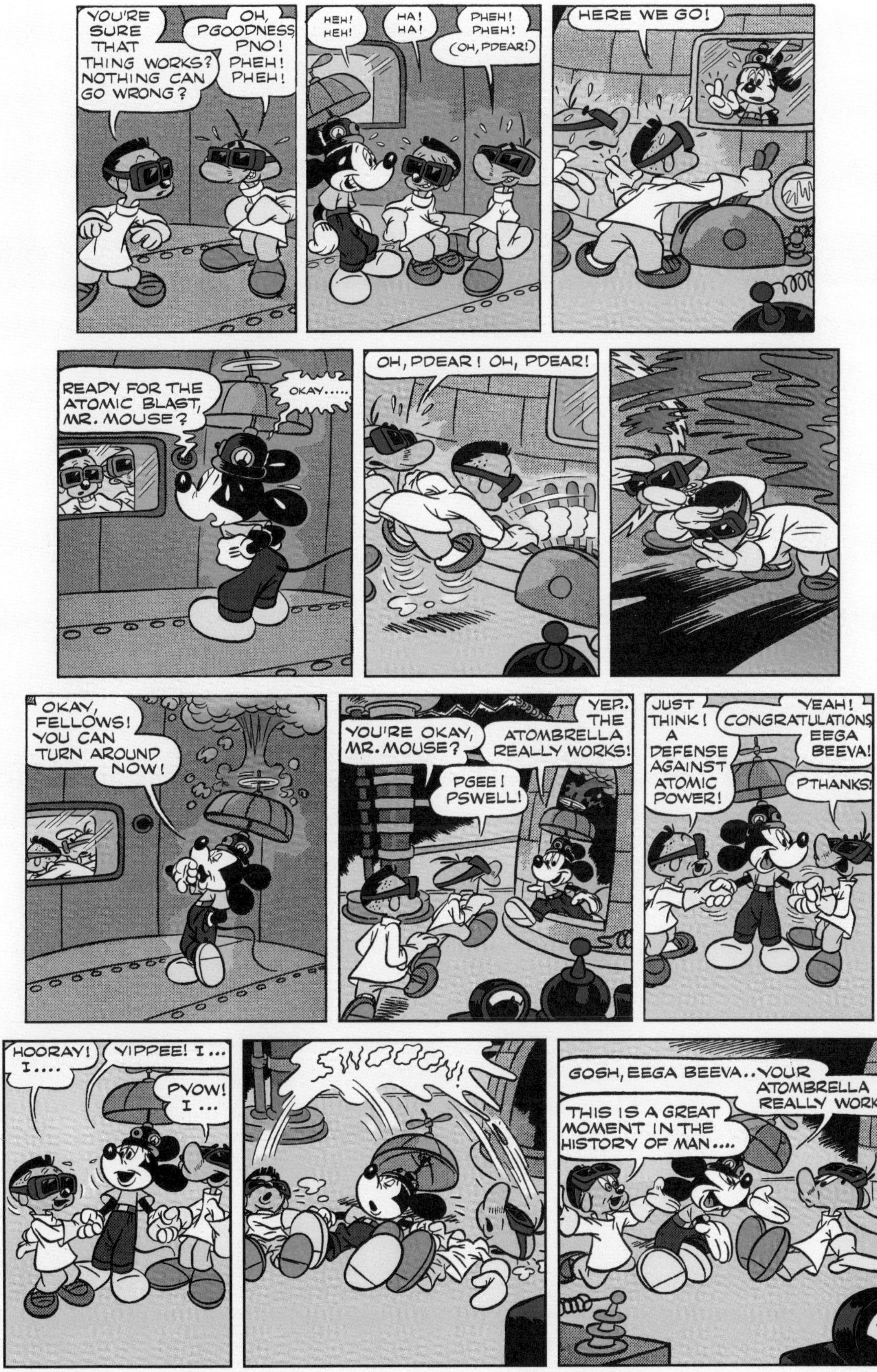
YOU'RE SURE THAT THING WORKS? NOTHING CAN GO WRONG?
OH, PGOODNESS, PNO! PHEH! PHEH!
HEH! HEH!
HA! HA!
PHEH! PHEH! (OH, PDEAR!)
HERE WE GO!
READY FOR THE ATOMIC BLAST, MR. MOUSE?
OKAY.....
OH, PDEAR! OH, PDEAR!
OKAY, FELLOWS! YOU CAN TURN AROUND NOW!
YOU'RE OKAY, MR. MOUSE?
YEP. THE ATOMBRELLA REALLY WORKS!
PGEE! PSWELL!
JUST THINK! A DEFENSE AGAINST ATOMIC POWER!
YEAH! CONGRATULATIONS, EEGA BEEVA!
PTHANKS!
HOORAY! I....
YIPPEE! I...
PYOW! I...
SWOOOSH!
GOSH, EEGA BEEVA.. YOUR ATOMBRELLA REALLY WORKS!
THIS IS A GREAT MOMENT IN THE HISTORY OF MAN....

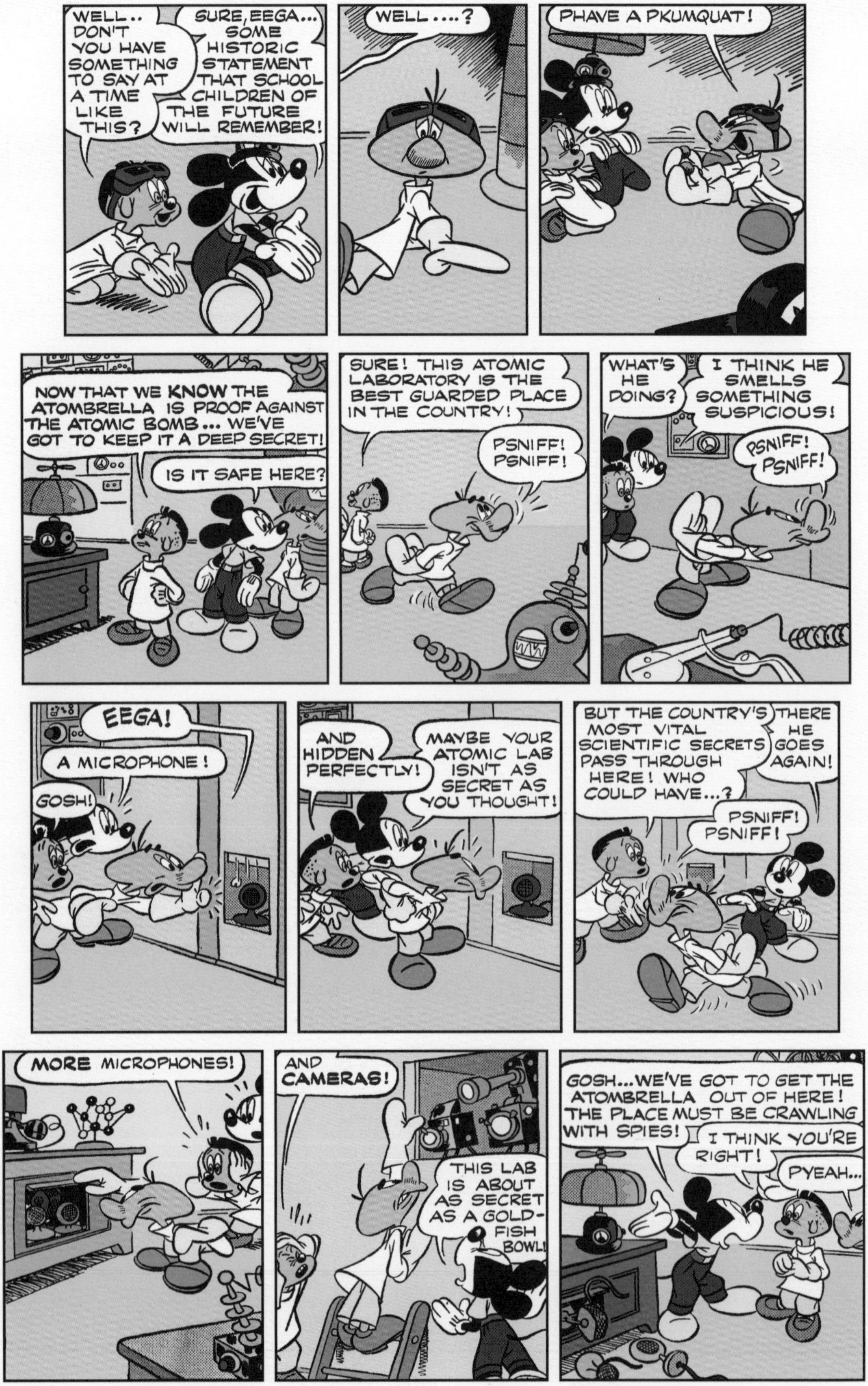
WELL.. DON'T YOU HAVE SOMETHING TO SAY AT A TIME LIKE THIS?
SURE, EEGA... SOME HISTORIC STATEMENT THAT SCHOOL CHILDREN OF THE FUTURE WILL REMEMBER!
WELL....?
PHAVE A PKUMQUAT!
NOW THAT WE KNOW THE ATOMBRELLA IS PROOF AGAINST THE ATOMIC BOMB... WE'VE GOT TO KEEP IT A DEEP SECRET!
IS IT SAFE HERE?
SURE! THIS ATOMIC LABORATORY IS THE BEST GUARDED PLACE IN THE COUNTRY!
PSNIFF! PSNIFF!
WHAT'S HE DOING?
I THINK HE SMELLS SOMETHING SUSPICIOUS!
PSNIFF! PSNIFF!
EEGA!
A MICROPHONE!
GOSH!
AND HIDDEN PERFECTLY!
MAYBE YOUR ATOMIC LAB ISN'T AS SECRET AS YOU THOUGHT!
BUT THE COUNTRY'S MOST VITAL SCIENTIFIC SECRETS PASS THROUGH HERE! WHO COULD HAVE...?
THERE HE GOES AGAIN!
PSNIFF! PSNIFF!
MORE MICROPHONES!
AND CAMERAS!
THIS LAB IS ABOUT AS SECRET AS A GOLD-FISH BOWL!
GOSH...WE'VE GOT TO GET THE ATOMBRELLA OUT OF HERE! THE PLACE MUST BE CRAWLING WITH SPIES!
I THINK YOU'RE RIGHT!
PYEAH...

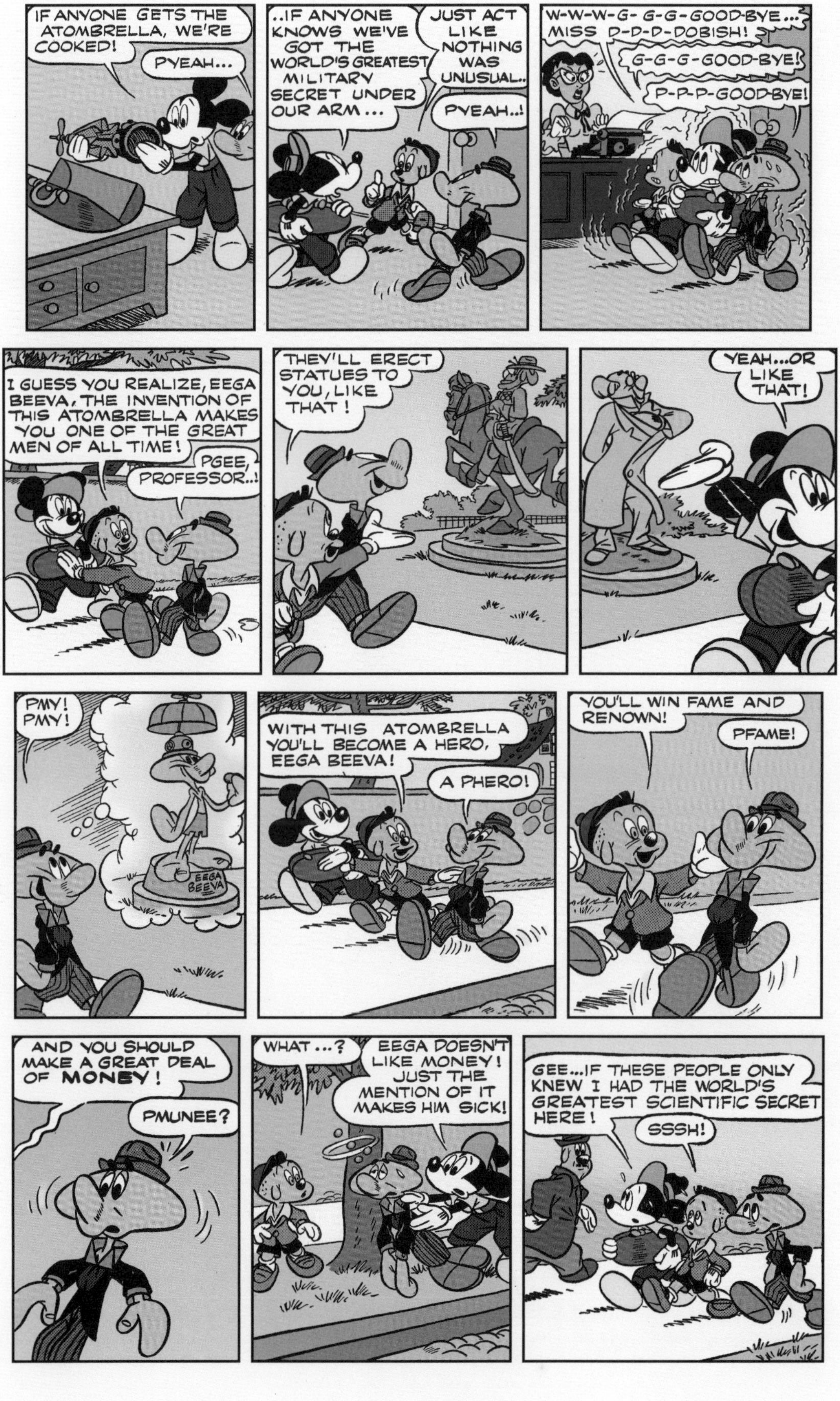
IF ANYONE GETS THE ATOMBRELLA, WE'RE COOKED!
PYEAH...
..IF ANYONE KNOWS WE'VE GOT THE WORLD'S GREATEST MILITARY SECRET UNDER OUR ARM ...
JUST ACT LIKE NOTHING WAS UNUSUAL..
PYEAH..!
W-W-W-G- G-G-GOOD-BYE... MISS D-D-D-DOBISH!
G-G-G-GOOD-BYE!
P-P-P-GOOD-BYE!
I GUESS YOU REALIZE, EEGA BEEVA, THE INVENTION OF THIS ATOMBRELLA MAKES YOU ONE OF THE GREAT MEN OF ALL TIME!
PGEE, PROFESSOR..!
THEY'LL ERECT STATUES TO YOU, LIKE THAT!
YEAH...OR LIKE THAT!
PMY! PMY!
EEGA BEEVA
WITH THIS ATOMBRELLA YOU'LL BECOME A HERO, EEGA BEEVA!
A PHERO!
YOU'LL WIN FAME AND RENOWN!
PFAME!
AND YOU SHOULD MAKE A GREAT DEAL OF MONEY!
PMUNEE?
WHAT ...?
EEGA DOESN'T LIKE MONEY! JUST THE MENTION OF IT MAKES HIM SICK!
GEE...IF THESE PEOPLE ONLY KNEW I HAD THE WORLD'S GREATEST SCIENTIFIC SECRET HERE!
SSSH!

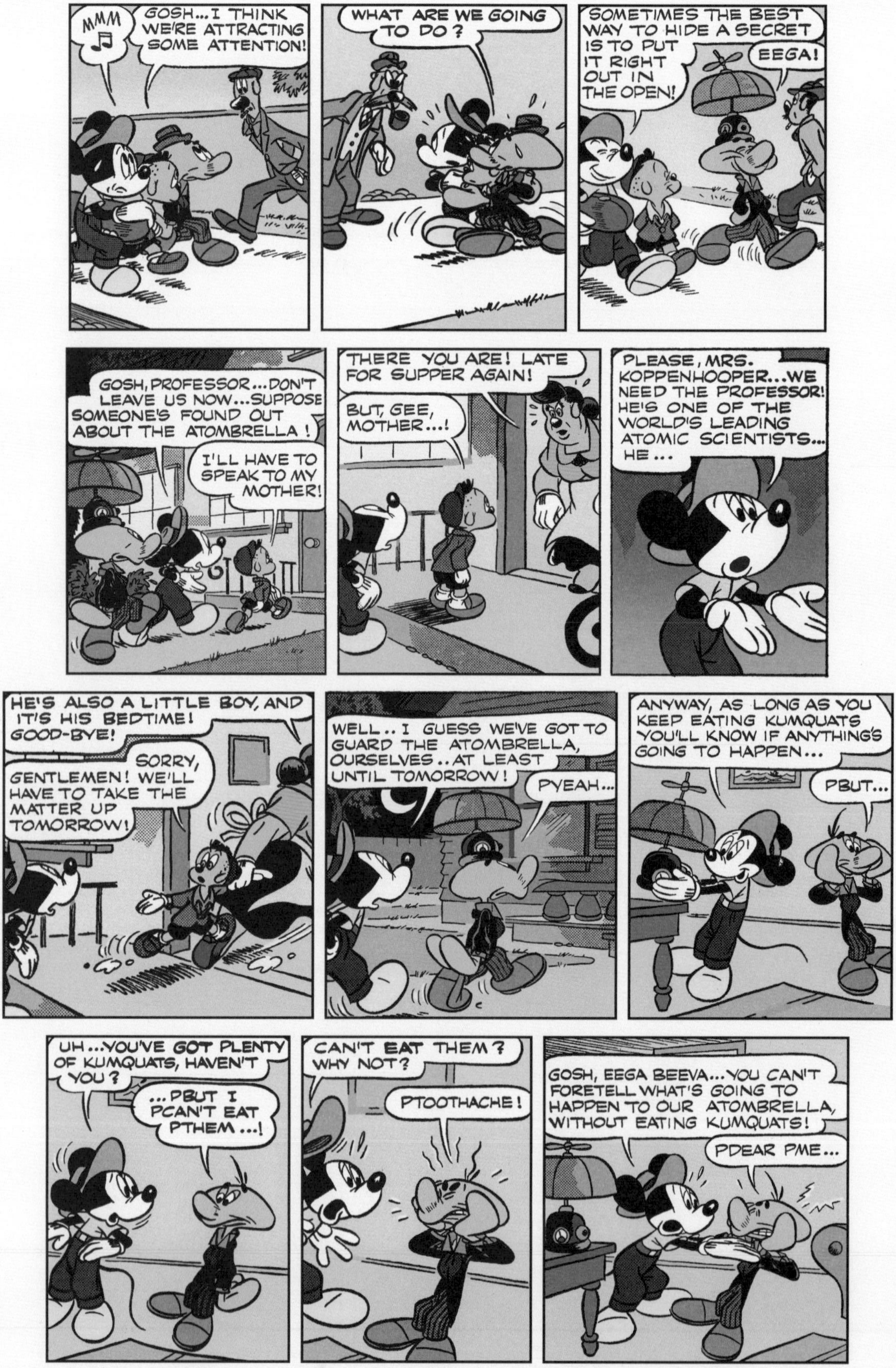
MMM ♫
GOSH...I THINK WE'RE ATTRACTING SOME ATTENTION!
WHAT ARE WE GOING TO DO ?
SOMETIMES THE BEST WAY TO HIDE A SECRET IS TO PUT IT RIGHT OUT IN THE OPEN!
EEGA!
GOSH, PROFESSOR...DON'T LEAVE US NOW...SUPPOSE SOMEONE'S FOUND OUT ABOUT THE ATOMBRELLA !
I'LL HAVE TO SPEAK TO MY MOTHER!
THERE YOU ARE! LATE FOR SUPPER AGAIN!
BUT, GEE, MOTHER...!
PLEASE, MRS. KOPPENHOOPER...WE NEED THE PROFESSOR! HE'S ONE OF THE WORLD'S LEADING ATOMIC SCIENTISTS... HE...
HE'S ALSO A LITTLE BOY, AND IT'S HIS BEDTIME! GOOD-BYE!
SORRY, GENTLEMEN! WE'LL HAVE TO TAKE THE MATTER UP TOMORROW!
WELL.. I GUESS WE'VE GOT TO GUARD THE ATOMBRELLA, OURSELVES..AT LEAST UNTIL TOMORROW!
PYEAH...
ANYWAY, AS LONG AS YOU KEEP EATING KUMQUATS YOU'LL KNOW IF ANYTHING'S GOING TO HAPPEN...
PBUT...
UH...YOU'VE GOT PLENTY OF KUMQUATS, HAVEN'T YOU ?
...PBUT I PCAN'T EAT PTHEM...!
CAN'T EAT THEM ? WHY NOT?
PTOOTHACHE!
GOSH, EEGA BEEVA...YOU CAN'T FORETELL WHAT'S GOING TO HAPPEN TO OUR ATOMBRELLA, WITHOUT EATING KUMQUATS!
PDEAR PME...

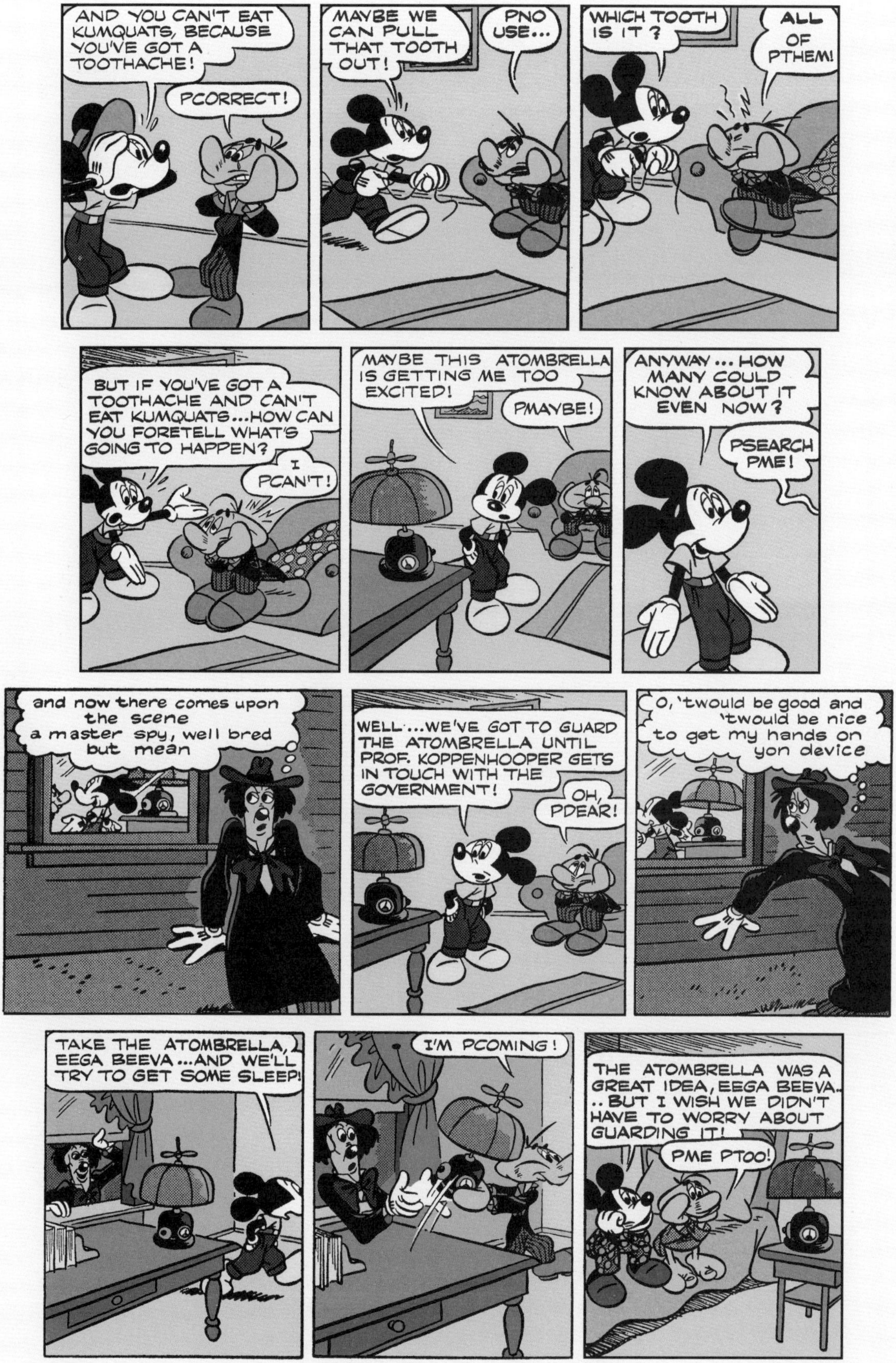
AND YOU CAN'T EAT KUMQUATS, BECAUSE YOU'VE GOT A TOOTHACHE!
PCORRECT!
MAYBE WE CAN PULL THAT TOOTH OUT!
PNO USE...
WHICH TOOTH IS IT ?
ALL OF PTHEM!
BUT IF YOU'VE GOT A TOOTHACHE AND CAN'T EAT KUMQUATS...HOW CAN YOU FORETELL WHAT'S GOING TO HAPPEN?
I PCAN'T!
MAYBE THIS ATOMBRELLA IS GETTING ME TOO EXCITED!
PMAYBE!
ANYWAY... HOW MANY COULD KNOW ABOUT IT EVEN NOW?
PSEARCH PME!
and now there comes upon the scene a master spy, well bred but mean
WELL...WE'VE GOT TO GUARD THE ATOMBRELLA UNTIL PROF. KOPPENHOOPER GETS IN TOUCH WITH THE GOVERNMENT!
OH, PDEAR!
O, 'twould be good and 'twould be nice to get my hands on yon device
TAKE THE ATOMBRELLA, EEGA BEEVA...AND WE'LL TRY TO GET SOME SLEEP!
I'M PCOMING!
THE ATOMBRELLA WAS A GREAT IDEA, EEGA BEEVA.. ..BUT I WISH WE DIDN'T HAVE TO WORRY ABOUT GUARDING IT!
PME PTOO!

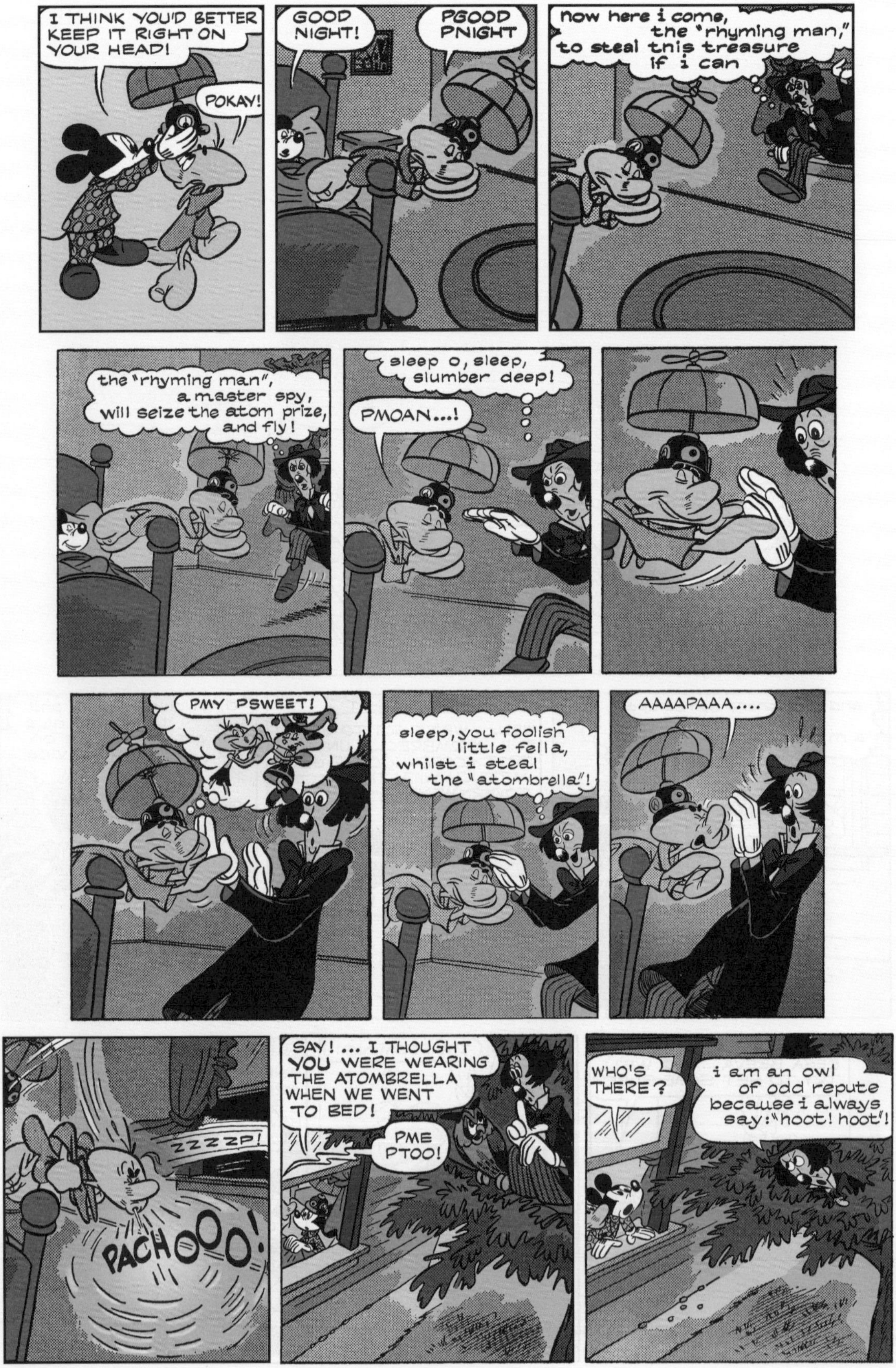
I THINK YOU'D BETTER KEEP IT RIGHT ON YOUR HEAD!
POKAY!
GOOD NIGHT!
PGOOD PNIGHT
now here i come, the "rhyming man," to steal this treasure if i can
the "rhyming man", a master spy, will seize the atom prize, and fly!
sleep o, sleep, slumber deep!
PMOAN...!
PMY PSWEET!
sleep, you foolish little fella, whilst i steal the "atombrella"!
AAAAPAAA....
ZZZZP!
PACHOOO!
SAY! ... I THOUGHT YOU WERE WEARING THE ATOMBRELLA WHEN WE WENT TO BED!
PME PTOO!
WHO'S THERE?
i am an owl of odd repute because i always say: "hoot! hoot"!

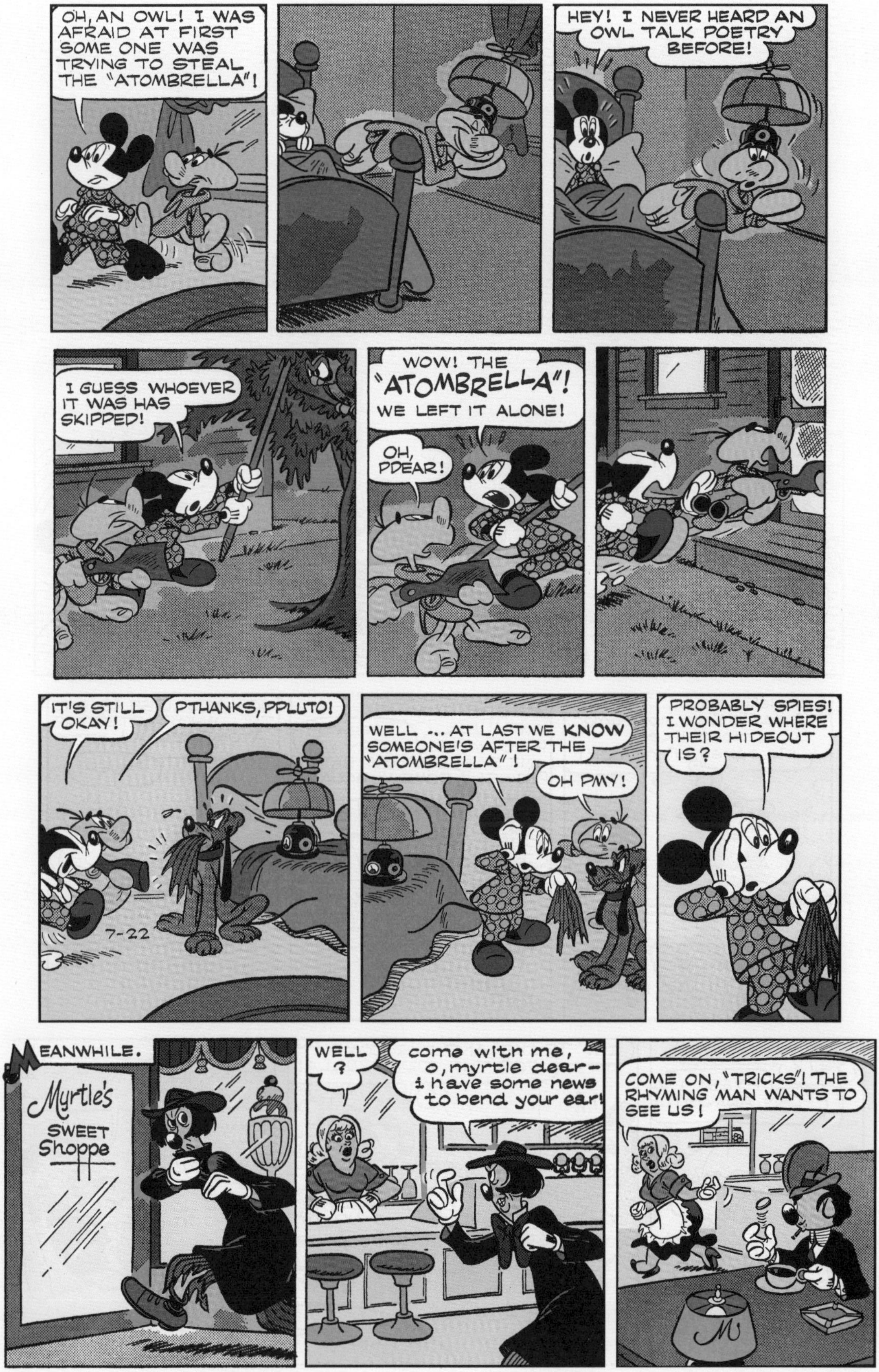
OH, AN OWL! I WAS AFRAID AT FIRST SOME ONE WAS TRYING TO STEAL THE "ATOMBRELLA"!
HEY! I NEVER HEARD AN OWL TALK POETRY BEFORE!
I GUESS WHOEVER IT WAS HAS SKIPPED!
WOW! THE "ATOMBRELLA"! WE LEFT IT ALONE!
OH, PDEAR!
IT'S STILL OKAY!
PTHANKS, PPLUTO!
7-22
WELL -.. AT LAST WE KNOW SOMEONE'S AFTER THE "ATOMBRELLA"!
OH PMY!
PROBABLY SPIES! I WONDER WHERE THEIR HIDEOUT IS?
MEANWHILE.
Myrtle's SWEET Shoppe
WELL ?
come with me, o, myrtle dear- i have some news to bend your ear!
COME ON, "TRICKS"! THE RHYMING MAN WANTS TO SEE US!

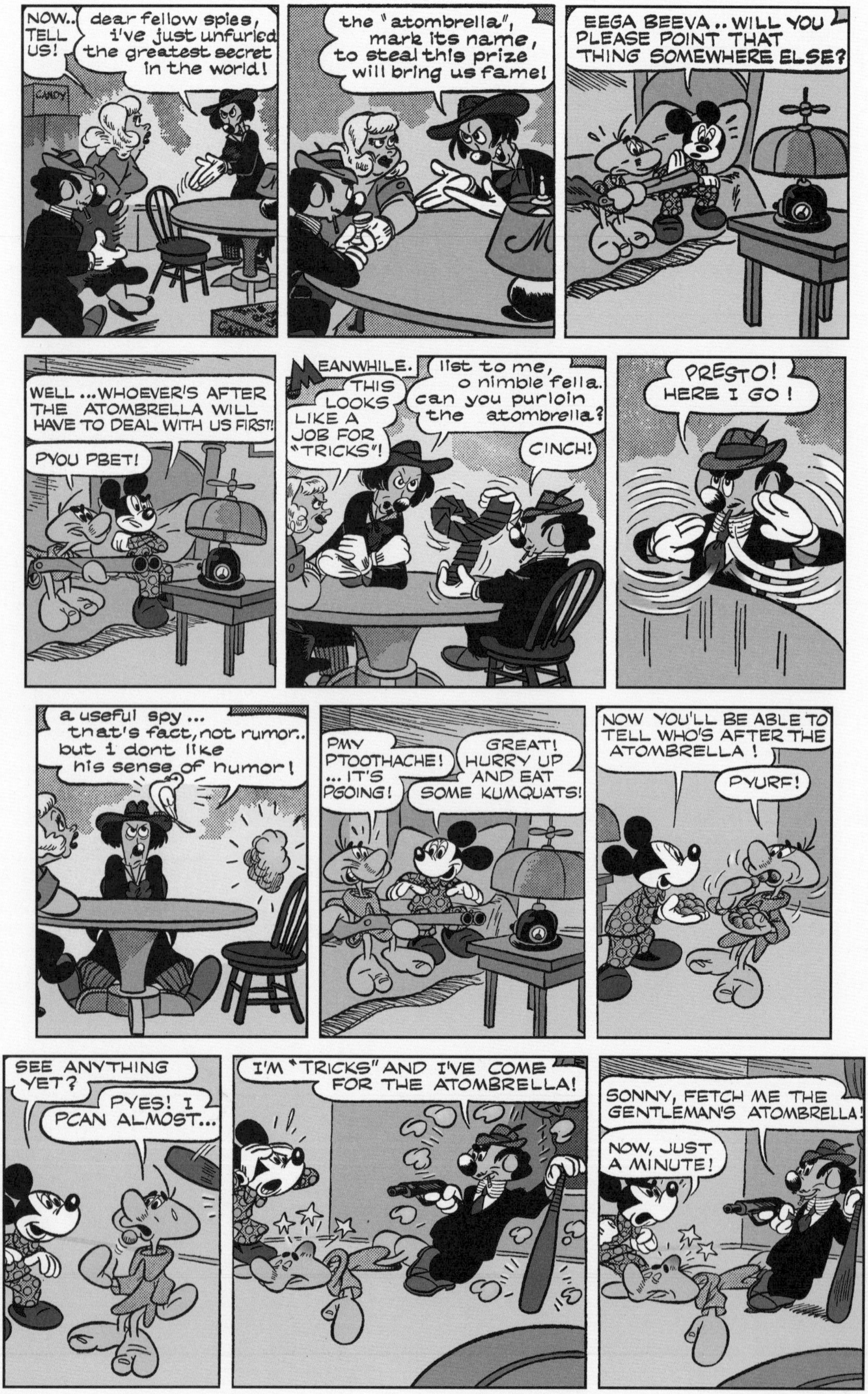
NOW.. TELL US!
dear fellow spies, i've just unfurled the greatest secret in the world!
the "atombrella", mark its name, to steal this prize will bring us fame!
EEGA BEEVA.. WILL YOU PLEASE POINT THAT THING SOMEWHERE ELSE?
WELL ...WHOEVER'S AFTER THE ATOMBRELLA WILL HAVE TO DEAL WITH US FIRST!
PYOU PBET!
MEANWHILE.
THIS LOOKS LIKE A JOB FOR "TRICKS"!
list to me, o nimble fella. can you purloin the atombrella?
CINCH!
PRESTO! HERE I GO!
a useful spy ... that's fact, not rumor.. but i dont like his sense of humor!
PMY PTOOTHACHE! ...IT'S PGOING!
GREAT! HURRY UP AND EAT SOME KUMQUATS!
NOW YOU'LL BE ABLE TO TELL WHO'S AFTER THE ATOMBRELLA!
PYURF!
SEE ANYTHING YET?
PYES! I PCAN ALMOST...
I'M "TRICKS" AND I'VE COME FOR THE ATOMBRELLA!
SONNY, FETCH ME THE GENTLEMAN'S ATOMBRELLA!
NOW, JUST A MINUTE!

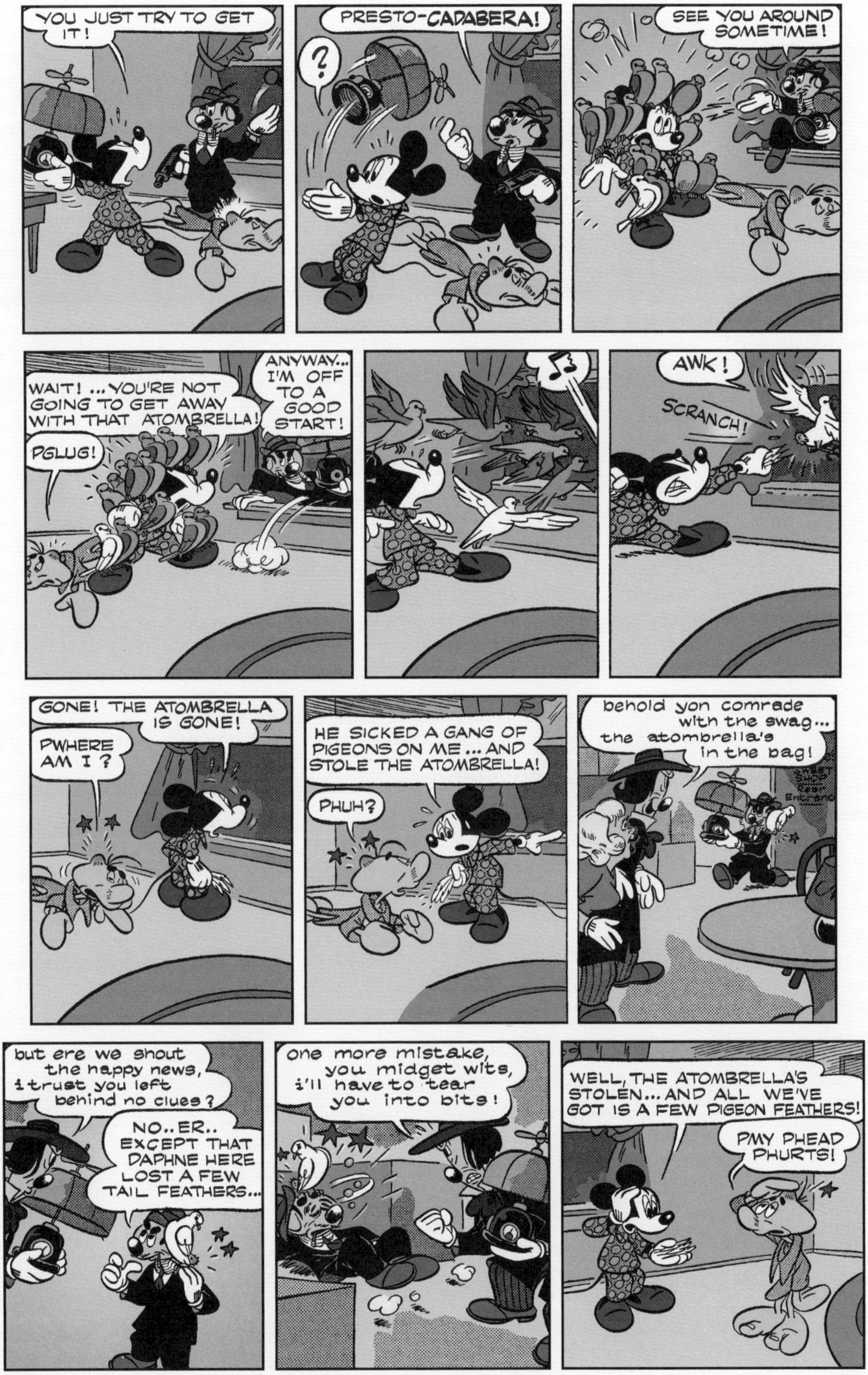
YOU JUST TRY TO GET IT!
PRESTO-CADABERA!
?
SEE YOU AROUND SOMETIME!
WAIT! ...YOU'RE NOT GOING TO GET AWAY WITH THAT ATOMBRELLA!
PGLUG!
ANYWAY... I'M OFF TO A GOOD START!
AWK!
SCRANCH!
GONE! THE ATOMBRELLA IS GONE!
PWHERE AM I?
HE SICKED A GANG OF PIGEONS ON ME ... AND STOLE THE ATOMBRELLA!
PHUH?
behold yon comrade with the swag... the atombrella's in the bag!
but ere we shout the happy news, i trust you left behind no clues?
NO..ER.. EXCEPT THAT DAPHNE HERE LOST A FEW TAIL FEATHERS...
one more mistake, you midget wits, i'll have to tear you into bits!
WELL, THE ATOMBRELLA'S STOLEN... AND ALL WE'VE GOT IS A FEW PIGEON FEATHERS!
PMY PHEAD PHURTS!

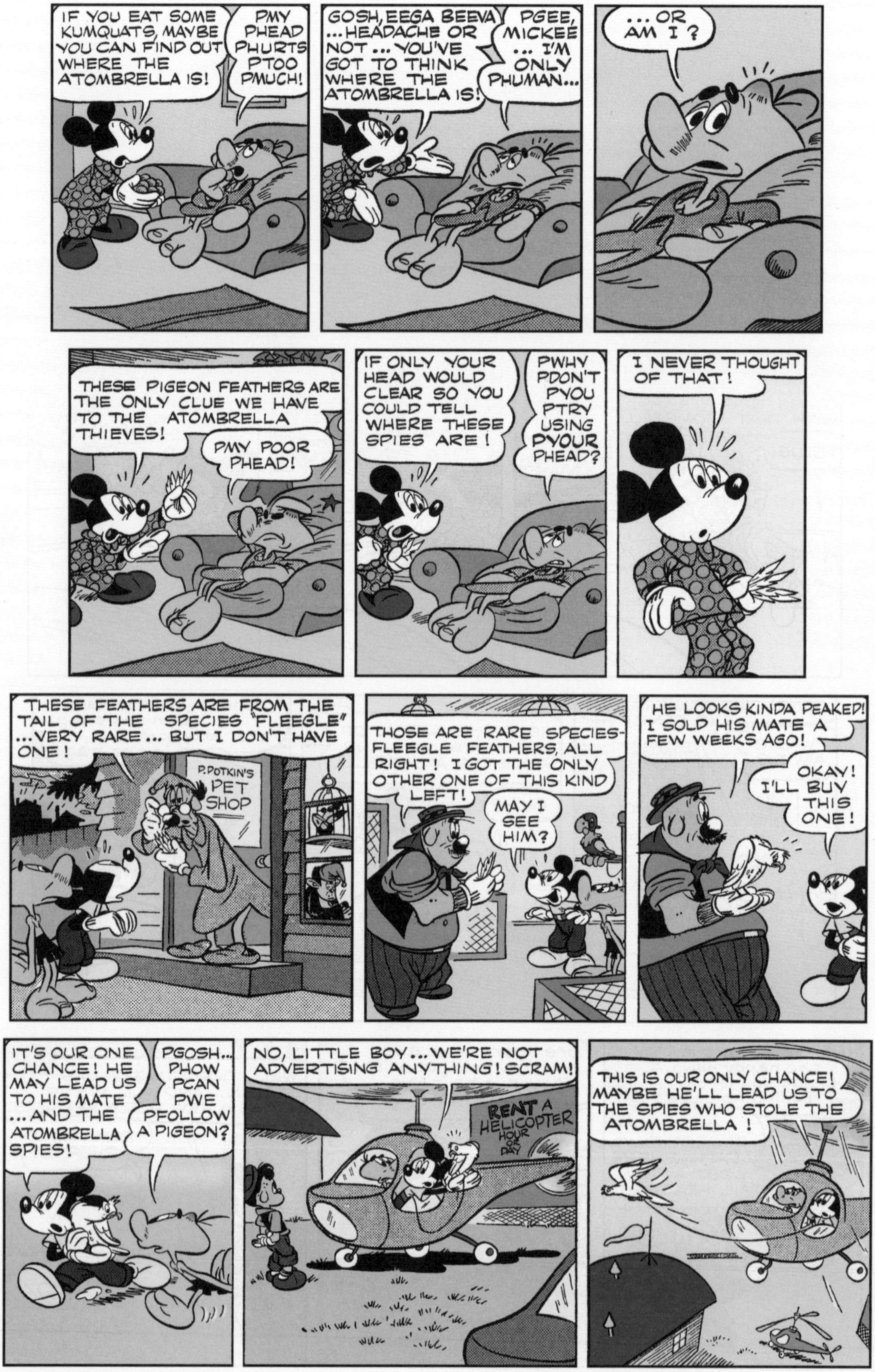
IF YOU EAT SOME KUMQUATS, MAYBE YOU CAN FIND OUT WHERE THE ATOMBRELLA IS!
PMY PHEAD PHURTS PTOO PMUCH!
GOSH, EEGA BEEVA ... HEADACHE OR NOT ... YOU'VE GOT TO THINK WHERE THE ATOMBRELLA IS!
PGEE, MICKEE ... I'M ONLY PHUMAN...
... OR AM I ?
THESE PIGEON FEATHERS ARE THE ONLY CLUE WE HAVE TO THE ATOMBRELLA THIEVES!
PMY POOR PHEAD!
IF ONLY YOUR HEAD WOULD CLEAR SO YOU COULD TELL WHERE THESE SPIES ARE!
PWHY PDON'T PYOU PTRY USING PYOUR PHEAD?
I NEVER THOUGHT OF THAT!
THESE FEATHERS ARE FROM THE TAIL OF THE SPECIES "FLEEGLE" ...VERY RARE ... BUT I DON'T HAVE ONE!
P. POTKIN'S PET SHOP
THOSE ARE RARE SPECIES-FLEEGLE FEATHERS, ALL RIGHT! I GOT THE ONLY OTHER ONE OF THIS KIND LEFT!
MAY I SEE HIM?
HE LOOKS KINDA PEAKED! I SOLD HIS MATE A FEW WEEKS AGO!
OKAY! I'LL BUY THIS ONE!
IT'S OUR ONE CHANCE! HE MAY LEAD US TO HIS MATE ... AND THE ATOMBRELLA SPIES!
PGOSH... PHOW PCAN PWE PFOLLOW A PIGEON?
NO, LITTLE BOY ... WE'RE NOT ADVERTISING ANYTHING! SCRAM!
RENT A HELICOPTER HOUR OR DAY
THIS IS OUR ONLY CHANCE! MAYBE HE'LL LEAD US TO THE SPIES WHO STOLE THE ATOMBRELLA!

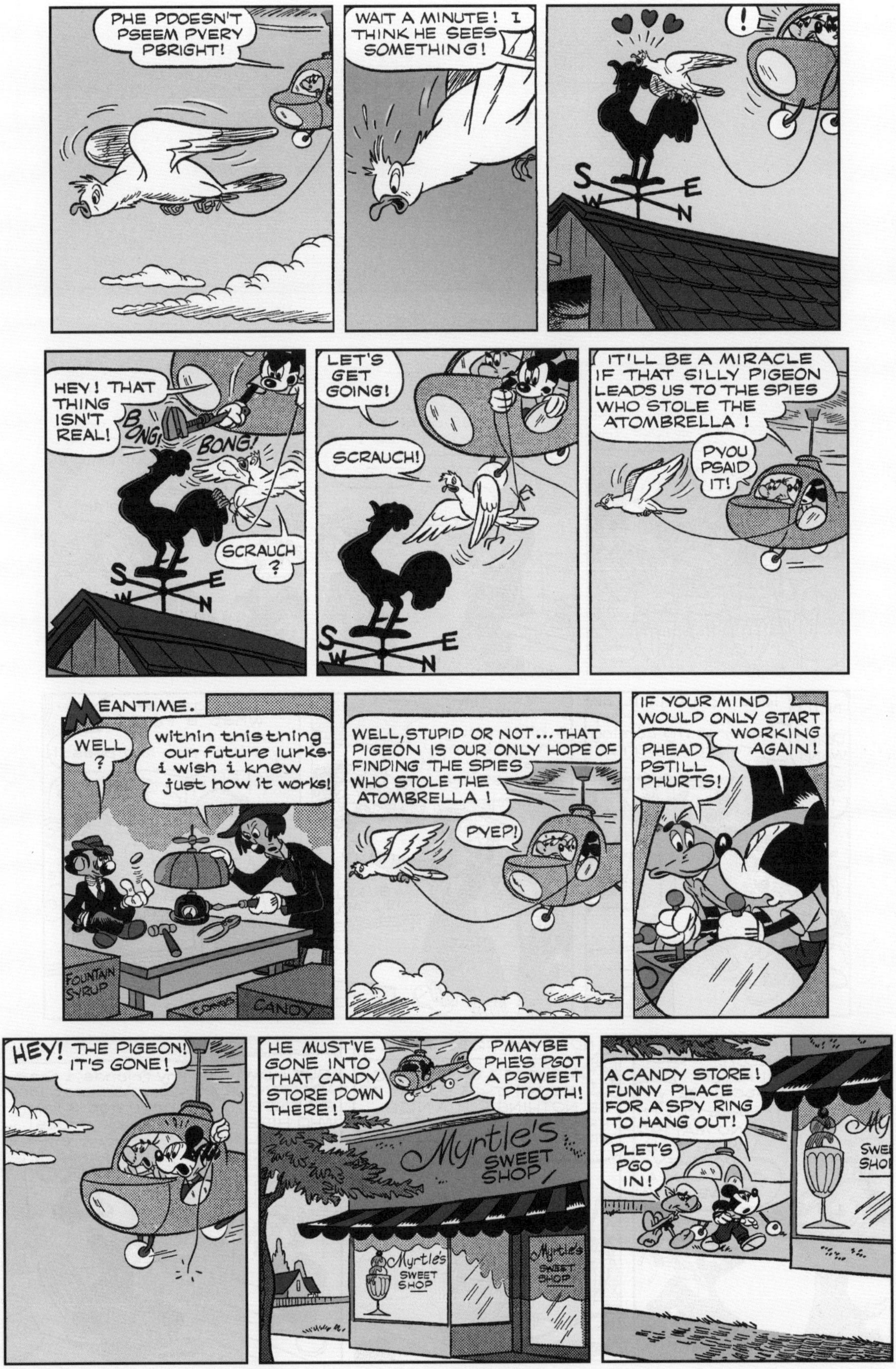
PHE PDOESN'T PSEEM PVERY PBRIGHT!
WAIT A MINUTE! I THINK HE SEES SOMETHING!
!
S W E N
HEY! THAT THING ISN'T REAL!
BONG!
BONG!
SCRAUCH ?
LET'S GET GOING!
SCRAUCH!
IT'LL BE A MIRACLE IF THAT SILLY PIGEON LEADS US TO THE SPIES WHO STOLE THE ATOMBRELLA!
PYOU PSAID IT!
MEANTIME.
WELL ?
within this thing our future lurks- i wish i knew just how it works!
FOUNTAIN SYRUP
CANDY
WELL, STUPID OR NOT... THAT PIGEON IS OUR ONLY HOPE OF FINDING THE SPIES WHO STOLE THE ATOMBRELLA!
PYEP!
IF YOUR MIND WOULD ONLY START WORKING AGAIN!
PHEAD PSTILL PHURTS!
HEY! THE PIGEON! IT'S GONE!
HE MUST'VE GONE INTO THAT CANDY STORE DOWN THERE!
PMAYBE PHE'S PGOT A PSWEET PTOOTH!
Myrtle's SWEET SHOP
A CANDY STORE! FUNNY PLACE FOR A SPY RING TO HANG OUT!
PLET'S PGO IN!

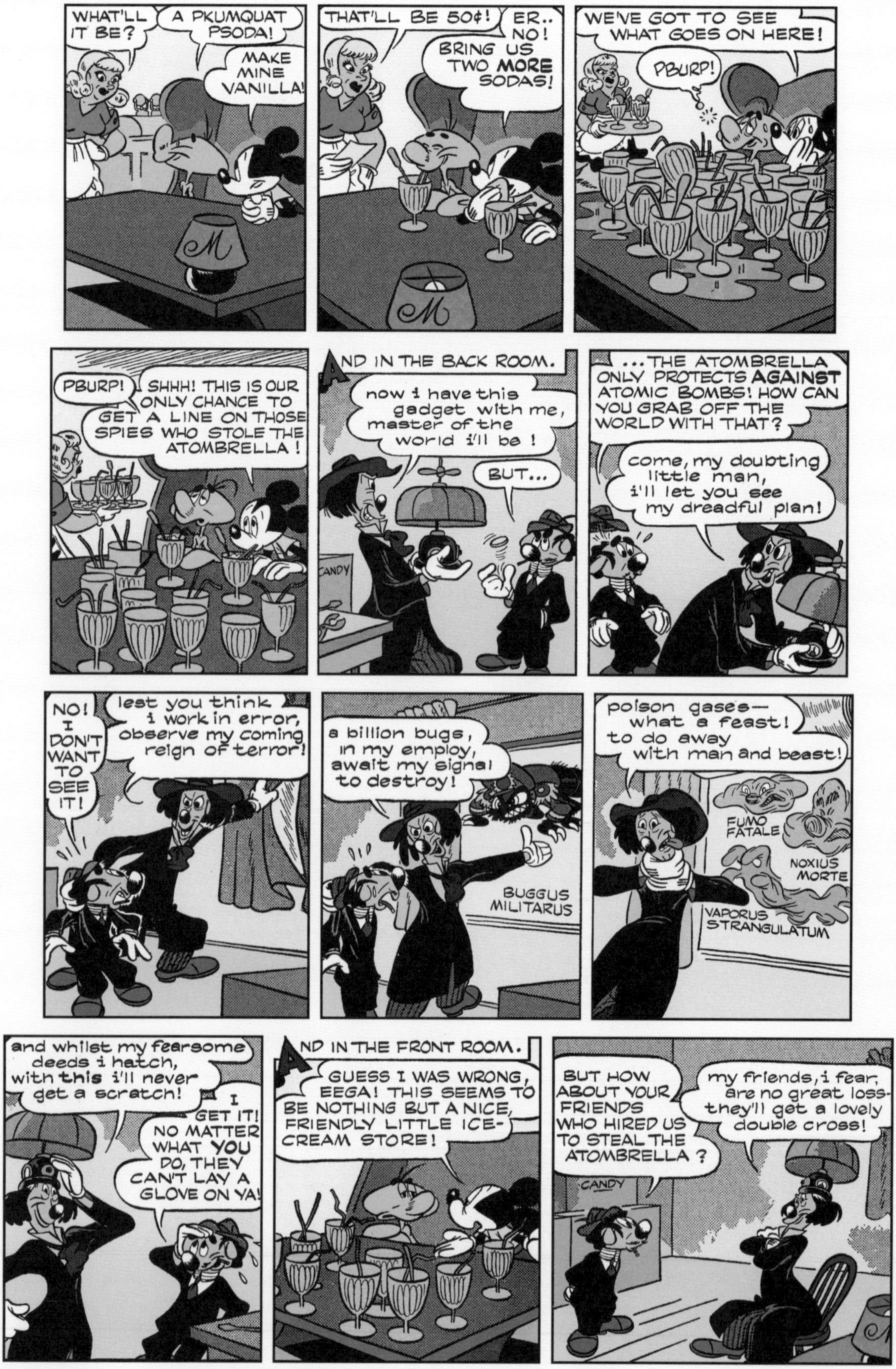
WHAT'LL IT BE?
A PKUMQUAT PSODA!
MAKE MINE VANILLA!
THAT'LL BE 50¢!
ER.. NO! BRING US TWO MORE SODAS!
WE'VE GOT TO SEE WHAT GOES ON HERE!
PBURP!
PBURP!
SHHH! THIS IS OUR ONLY CHANCE TO GET A LINE ON THOSE SPIES WHO STOLE THE ATOMBRELLA!
AND IN THE BACK ROOM.
now i have this gadget with me, master of the world i'll be!
BUT...
CANDY
...THE ATOMBRELLA ONLY PROTECTS AGAINST ATOMIC BOMBS! HOW CAN YOU GRAB OFF THE WORLD WITH THAT?
come, my doubting little man, i'll let you see my dreadful plan!
NO! I DON'T WANT TO SEE IT!
lest you think i work in error, observe my coming reign of terror!
a billion bugs, in my employ, await my signal to destroy!
BUGGUS MILITARUS
poison gases— what a feast! to do away with man and beast!
FUMO FATALE
NOXIUS MORTE
VAPORUS STRANGULATUM
and whilst my fearsome deeds i hatch, with this i'll never get a scratch!
I GET IT! NO MATTER WHAT YOU DO, THEY CAN'T LAY A GLOVE ON YA!
AND IN THE FRONT ROOM.
GUESS I WAS WRONG, EEGA! THIS SEEMS TO BE NOTHING BUT A NICE, FRIENDLY LITTLE ICE-CREAM STORE!
BUT HOW ABOUT YOUR FRIENDS WHO HIRED US TO STEAL THE ATOMBRELLA?
my friends, i fear, are no great loss-they'll get a lovely double cross!
CANDY

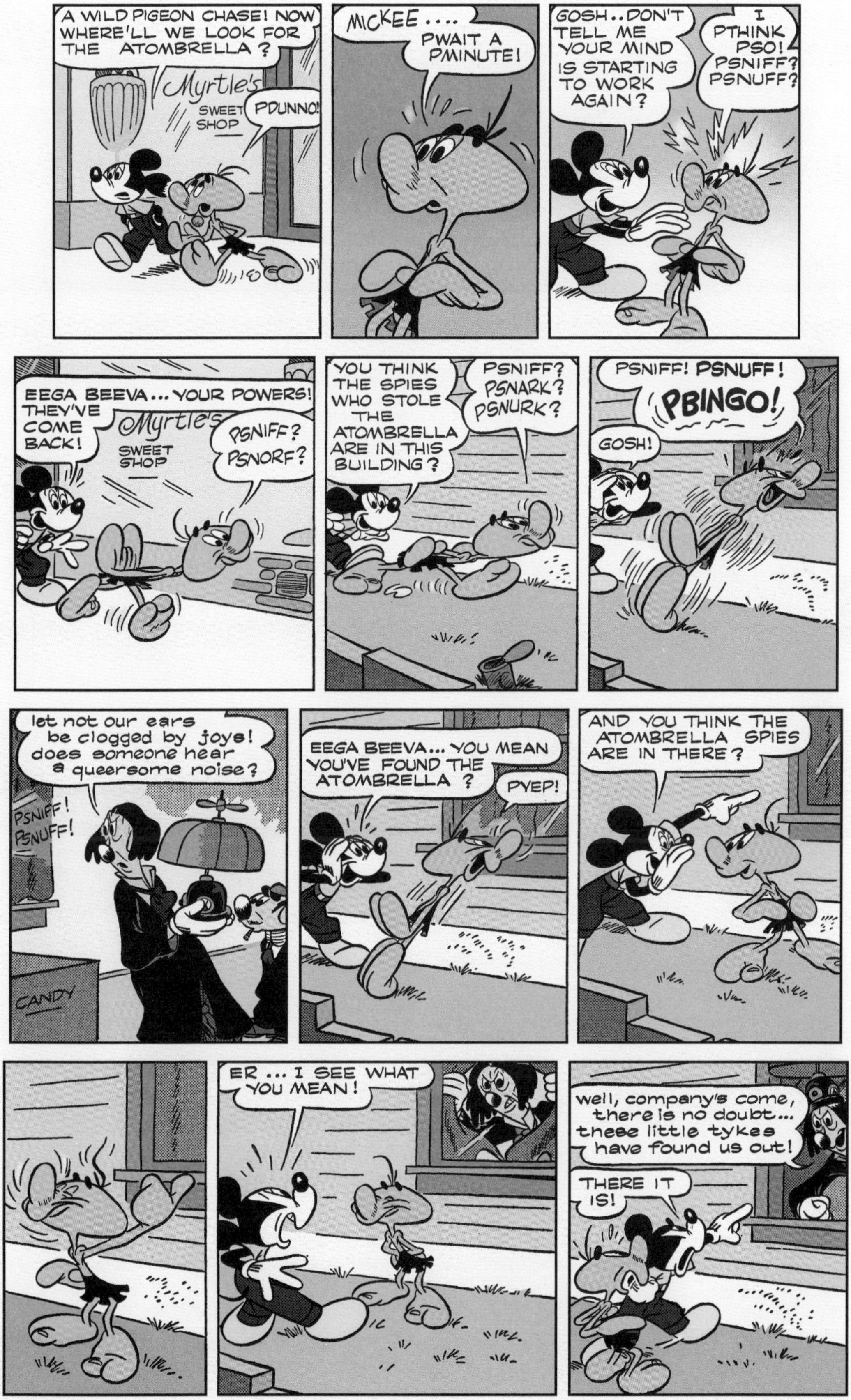
A WILD PIGEON CHASE! NOW WHERE'LL WE LOOK FOR THE ATOMBRELLA?
Myrtle's SWEET SHOP
PDUNNO!
MICKEE....
PWAIT A PMINUTE!
GOSH..DON'T TELL ME YOUR MIND IS STARTING TO WORK AGAIN?
I PTHINK PSO! PSNIFF? PSNUFF?
EEGA BEEVA... YOUR POWERS! THEY'VE COME BACK!
Myrtle's SWEET SHOP
PSNIFF? PSNORF?
YOU THINK THE SPIES WHO STOLE THE ATOMBRELLA ARE IN THIS BUILDING?
PSNIFF? PSNARK? PSNURK?
PSNIFF! PSNUFF!
PBINGO!
GOSH!
let not our ears be clogged by joys! does someone hear a queersome noise?
PSNIFF! PSNUFF!
CANDY
EEGA BEEVA... YOU MEAN YOU'VE FOUND THE ATOMBRELLA?
PYEP!
AND YOU THINK THE ATOMBRELLA SPIES ARE IN THERE?
ER... I SEE WHAT YOU MEAN!
well, company's come, there is no doubt... these little tykes have found us out!
THERE IT IS!

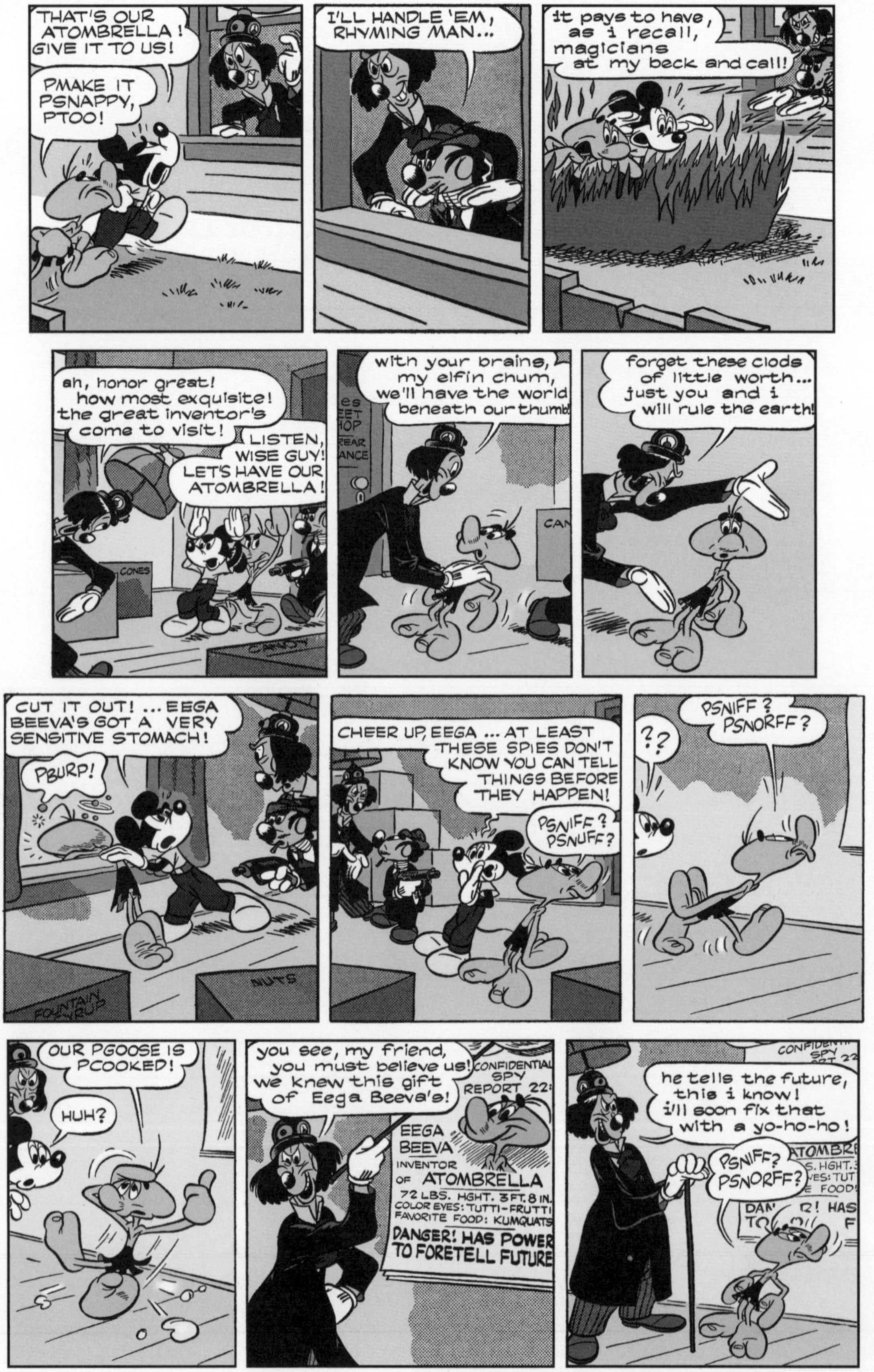
THAT'S OUR ATOMBRELLA! GIVE IT TO US!
PMAKE IT PSNAPPY, PTOO!
I'LL HANDLE 'EM, RHYMING MAN...
it pays to have, as i recall, magicians at my beck and call!
ah, honor great! how most exquisite! the great inventor's come to visit!
LISTEN, WISE GUY! LET'S HAVE OUR ATOMBRELLA!
CONES
with your brains, my elfin chum, we'll have the world beneath our thumb!
forget these clods of little worth... just you and i will rule the earth!
CUT IT OUT! ... EEGA BEEVA'S GOT A VERY SENSITIVE STOMACH!
PBURP!
NUTS
FOUNTAIN SYRUP
CHEER UP, EEGA ... AT LEAST THESE SPIES DON'T KNOW YOU CAN TELL THINGS BEFORE THEY HAPPEN!
PSNIFF? PSNUFF?
??
PSNIFF? PSNORFF?
OUR PGOOSE IS PCOOKED!
HUH?
you see, my friend, you must believe us! we knew this gift of Eega Beeva's!
CONFIDENTIAL SPY REPORT 22:
EEGA BEEVA INVENTOR OF ATOMBRELLA
72 LBS. HGHT. 3FT. 8 IN. COLOR EYES: TUTTI-FRUTTI FAVORITE FOOD: KUMQUATS
DANGER! HAS POWER TO FORETELL FUTURE
he tells the future, this i know! i'll soon fix that with a yo-ho-ho!
PSNIFF? PSNORFF?

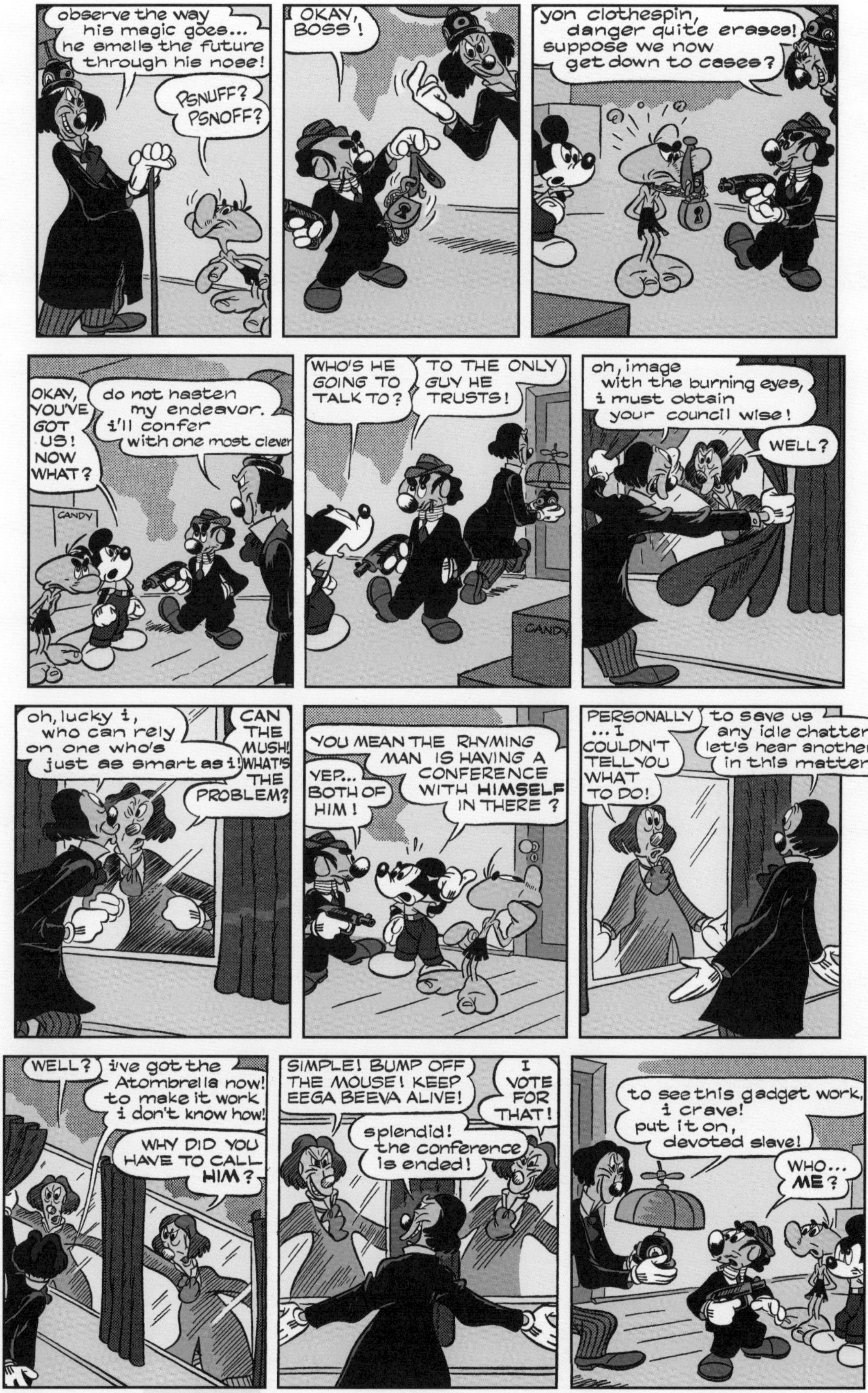
observe the way his magic goes... he smells the future through his nose!
PSNUFF? PSNOFF?
OKAY, BOSS!
yon clothespin, danger quite erases! suppose we now get down to cases?
OKAY, YOU'VE GOT US! NOW WHAT?
do not hasten my endeavor. i'll confer with one most clever
CANDY
WHO'S HE GOING TO TALK TO?
TO THE ONLY GUY HE TRUSTS!
CANDY
oh, image with the burning eyes, i must obtain your council wise!
WELL?
oh, lucky i, who can rely on one who's just as smart as i!
CAN THE MUSH! WHAT'S THE PROBLEM?
YOU MEAN THE RHYMING MAN IS HAVING A CONFERENCE WITH HIMSELF IN THERE?
YEP... BOTH OF HIM!
PERSONALLY ... I COULDN'T TELL YOU WHAT TO DO!
to save us any idle chatter, let's hear another in this matter!
WELL?
i've got the Atombrella now! to make it work i don't know how!
WHY DID YOU HAVE TO CALL HIM?
SIMPLE! BUMP OFF THE MOUSE! KEEP EEGA BEEVA ALIVE!
I VOTE FOR THAT!
splendid! the conference is ended!
to see this gadget work, i crave! put it on, devoted slave!
WHO... ME?

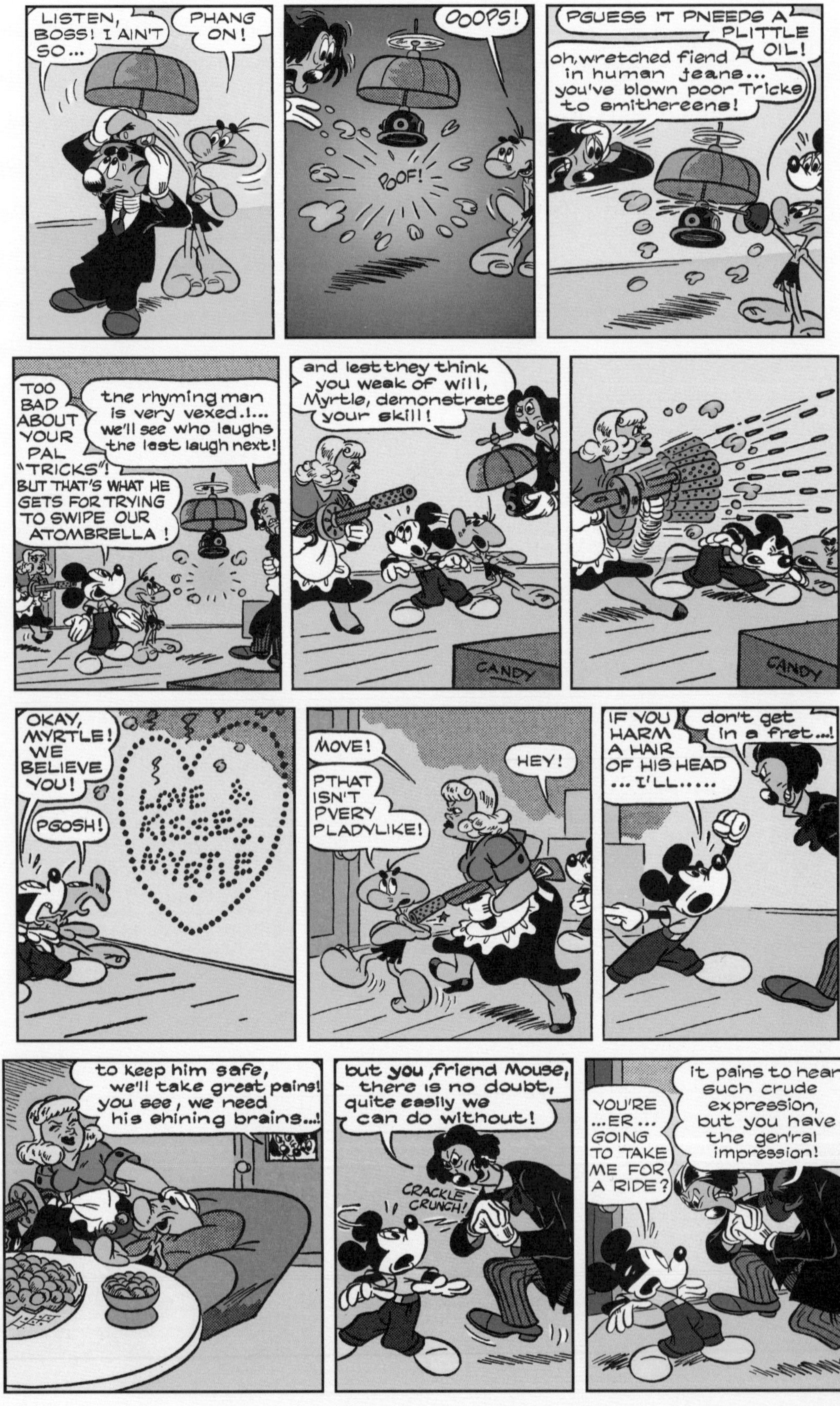
LISTEN, BOSS! I AIN'T SO...
PHANG ON!
OOOPS!
POOF!
PGUESS IT PNEEDS A PLITTLE OIL!
oh, wretched fiend in human jeans... you've blown poor Tricks to smithereens!
TOO BAD ABOUT YOUR PAL "TRICKS"!
the rhyming man is very vexed.!... we'll see who laughs the last laugh next!
BUT THAT'S WHAT HE GETS FOR TRYING TO SWIPE OUR ATOMBRELLA!
and lest they think you weak of will, Myrtle, demonstrate your skill!
CANDY
CANDY
OKAY, MYRTLE! WE BELIEVE YOU!
PGOSH!
LOVE & KISSES. MYRTLE
MOVE!
PTHAT ISN'T PVERY PLADYLIKE!
HEY!
IF YOU HARM A HAIR OF HIS HEAD ... I'LL.....
don't get in a fret...!
to keep him safe, we'll take great pains! you see, we need his shining brains...!
but you, friend Mouse, there is no doubt, quite easily we can do without!
CRACKLE CRUNCH!
YOU'RE ...ER... GOING TO TAKE ME FOR A RIDE?
it pains to hear such crude expression, but you have the gen'ral impression!

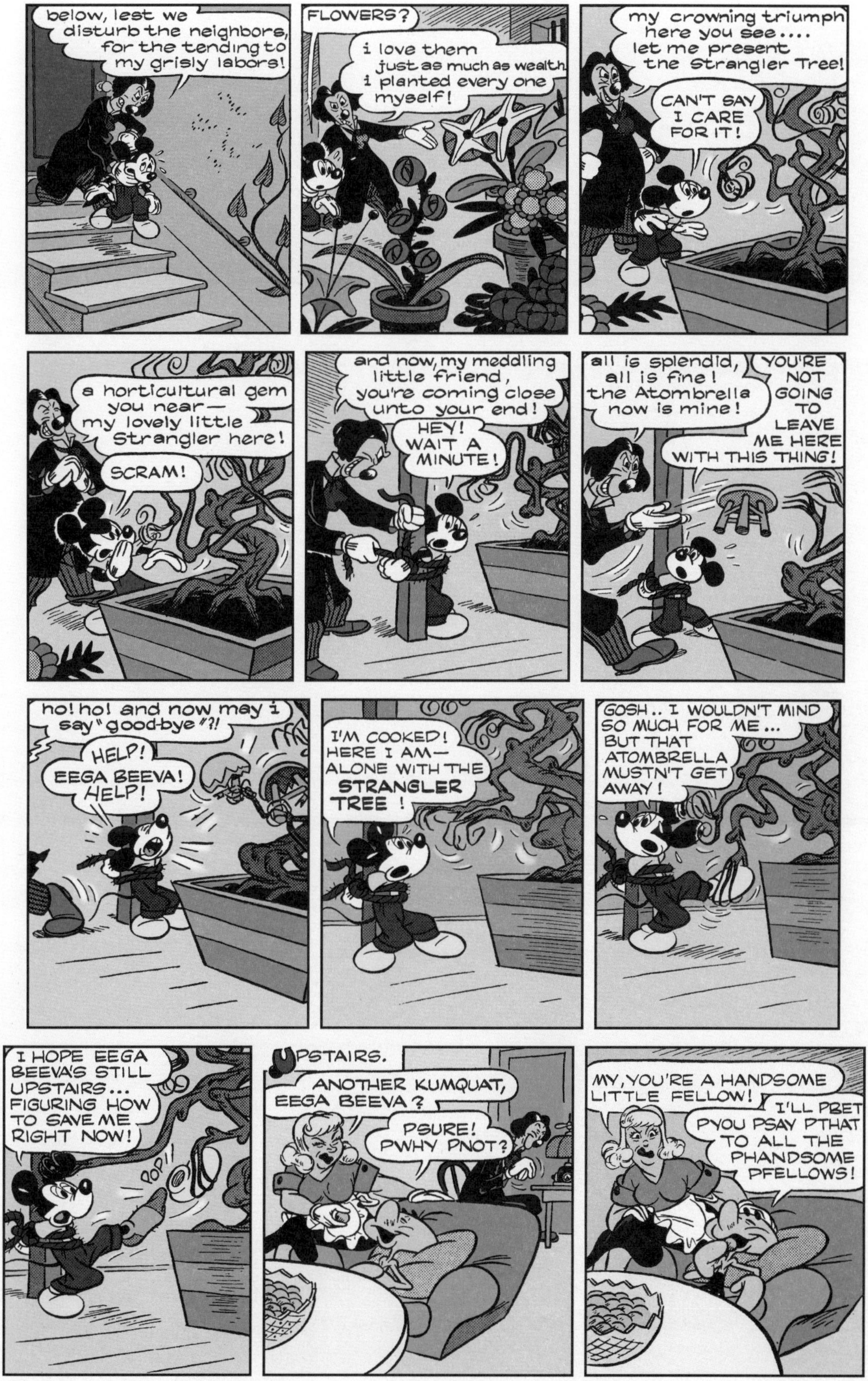
below, lest we disturb the neighbors, for the tending to my grisly labors!
FLOWERS?
i love them just as much as wealth. i planted every one myself!
my crowning triumph here you see.... let me present the Strangler Tree!
CAN'T SAY I CARE FOR IT!
a horticultural gem you near— my lovely little Strangler here!
SCRAM!
and now, my meddling little friend, you're coming close unto your end!
HEY! WAIT A MINUTE!
all is splendid, all is fine! the Atombrella now is mine!
YOU'RE NOT GOING TO LEAVE ME HERE WITH THIS THING!
ho! ho! and now may i say "good-bye"?!
HELP! EEGA BEEVA! HELP!
I'M COOKED! HERE I AM— ALONE WITH THE STRANGLER TREE!
GOSH.. I WOULDN'T MIND SO MUCH FOR ME... BUT THAT ATOMBRELLA MUSTN'T GET AWAY!
I HOPE EEGA BEEVA'S STILL UPSTAIRS... FIGURING HOW TO SAVE ME RIGHT NOW!
POP!!
UPSTAIRS.
ANOTHER KUMQUAT, EEGA BEEVA?
PSURE! PWHY PNOT?
MY, YOU'RE A HANDSOME LITTLE FELLOW!
I'LL PBET PYOU PSAY PTHAT TO ALL THE PHANDSOME PFELLOWS!

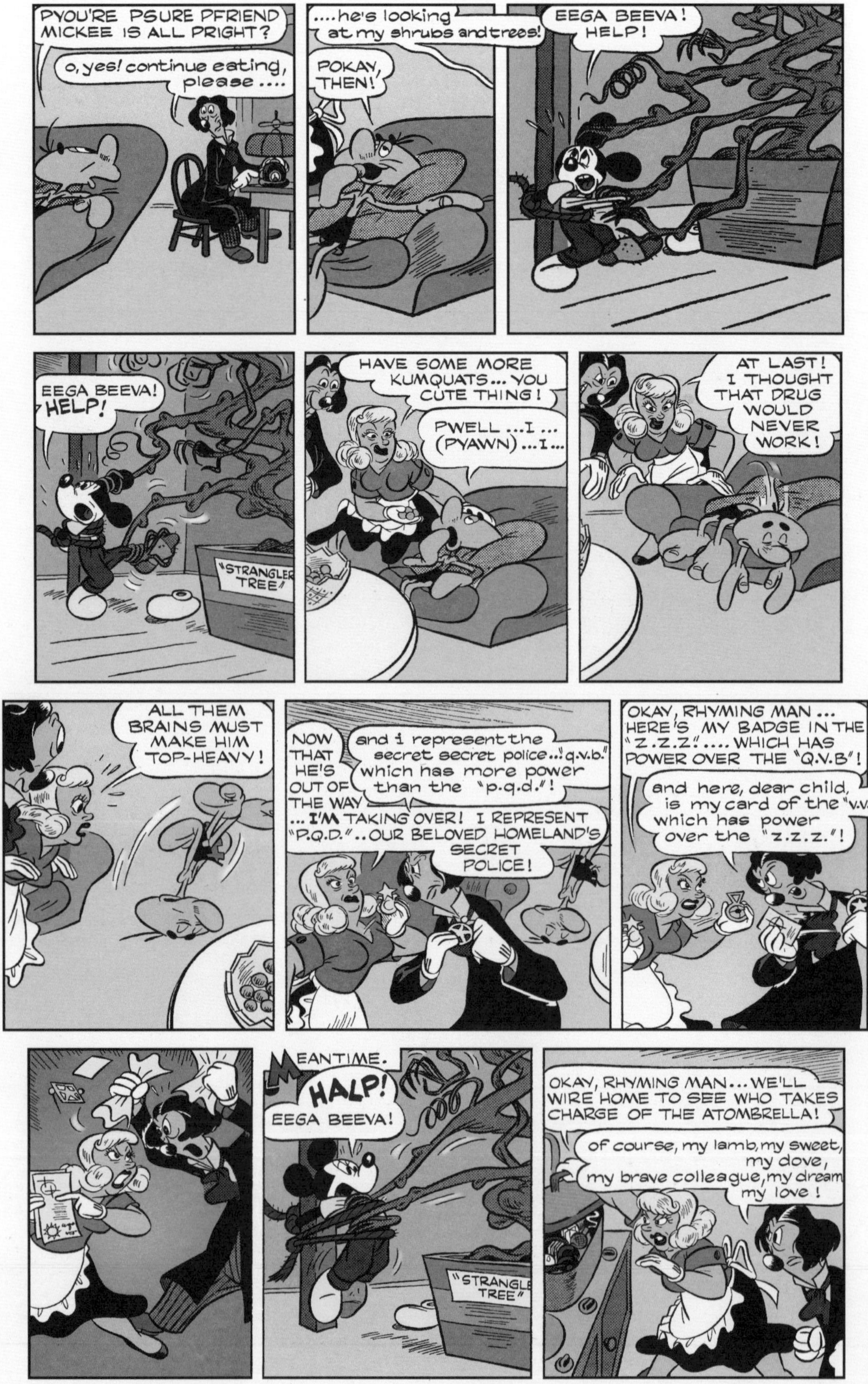
PYOU'RE PSURE PFRIEND MICKEE IS ALL PRIGHT?
o, yes! continue eating, please ....
....he's looking at my shrubs and trees!
POKAY, THEN!
EEGA BEEVA! HELP!
EEGA BEEVA! HELP!
HAVE SOME MORE KUMQUATS... YOU CUTE THING!
PWELL ...I ... (PYAWN) ...I...
"STRANGLER TREE"
AT LAST! I THOUGHT THAT DRUG WOULD NEVER WORK!
ALL THEM BRAINS MUST MAKE HIM TOP-HEAVY!
NOW THAT HE'S OUT OF THE WAY ... I'M TAKING OVER! I REPRESENT "P.Q.D."..OUR BELOVED HOMELAND'S SECRET POLICE!
and i represent the secret secret police..! "q.v.b." which has more power than the "p.q.d."!
OKAY, RHYMING MAN ... HERE'S MY BADGE IN THE "Z.Z.Z."..... WHICH HAS POWER OVER THE "Q.V.B"!
and here, dear child, is my card of the "v.v.v." which has power over the "z.z.z."!
MEANTIME.
HALP!
EEGA BEEVA!
"STRANGLE TREE"
OKAY, RHYMING MAN... WE'LL WIRE HOME TO SEE WHO TAKES CHARGE OF THE ATOMBRELLA!
of course, my lamb, my sweet, my dove, my brave colleague, my dream my love!

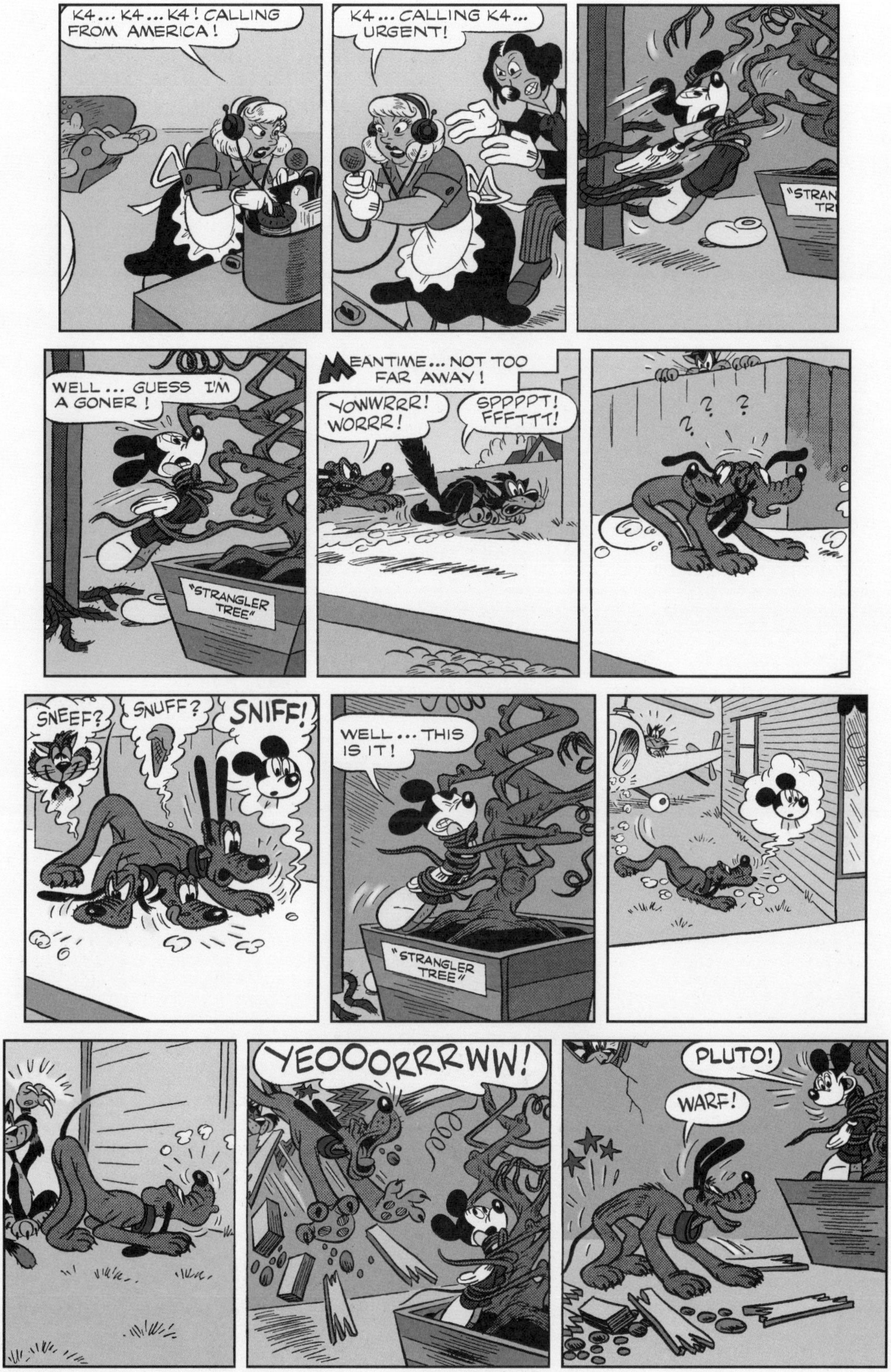
K4... K4... K4! CALLING FROM AMERICA!
K4... CALLING K4... URGENT!
"STRAN TR
WELL... GUESS I'M A GONER!
"STRANGLER TREE"
MEANTIME... NOT TOO FAR AWAY!
YOWWRRR! WORRR!
SPPPPT! FFFTTT!
? ? ?
SNEEF?
SNUFF?
SNIFF!
WELL... THIS IS IT!
"STRANGLER TREE"
YEOOORRRWW!
PLUTO!
WARF!

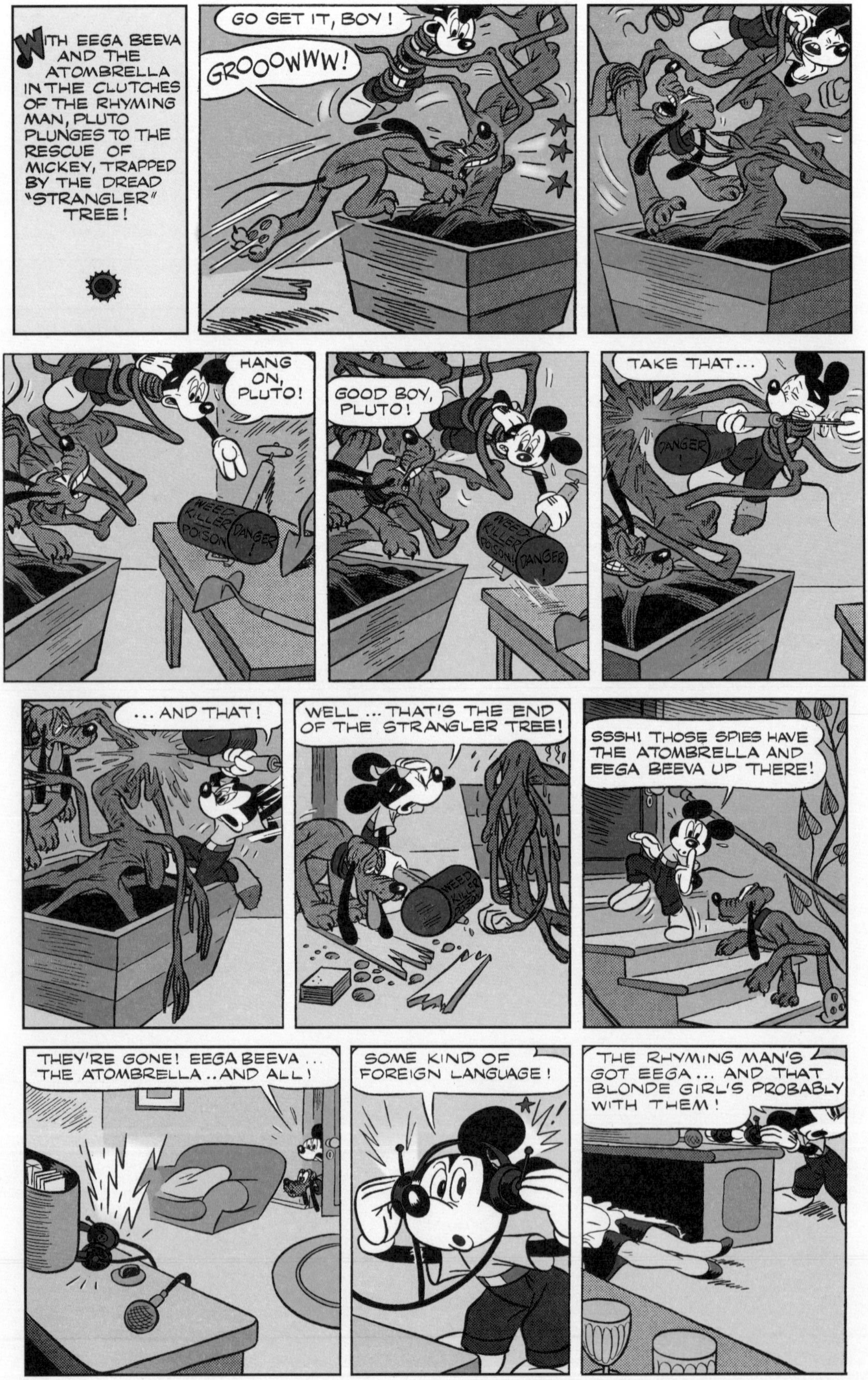
WITH EEGA BEEVA AND THE ATOMBRELLA IN THE CLUTCHES OF THE RHYMING MAN, PLUTO PLUNGES TO THE RESCUE OF MICKEY, TRAPPED BY THE DREAD "STRANGLER" TREE!
GO GET IT, BOY!
GROOOWWW!
HANG ON, PLUTO!
GOOD BOY, PLUTO!
WEED KILLER POISON
DANGER!
TAKE THAT...
DANGER!
... AND THAT!
WELL ... THAT'S THE END OF THE STRANGLER TREE!
SSSH! THOSE SPIES HAVE THE ATOMBRELLA AND EEGA BEEVA UP THERE!
THEY'RE GONE! EEGA BEEVA ... THE ATOMBRELLA .. AND ALL!
SOME KIND OF FOREIGN LANGUAGE!
THE RHYMING MAN'S GOT EEGA ... AND THAT BLONDE GIRL'S PROBABLY WITH THEM!

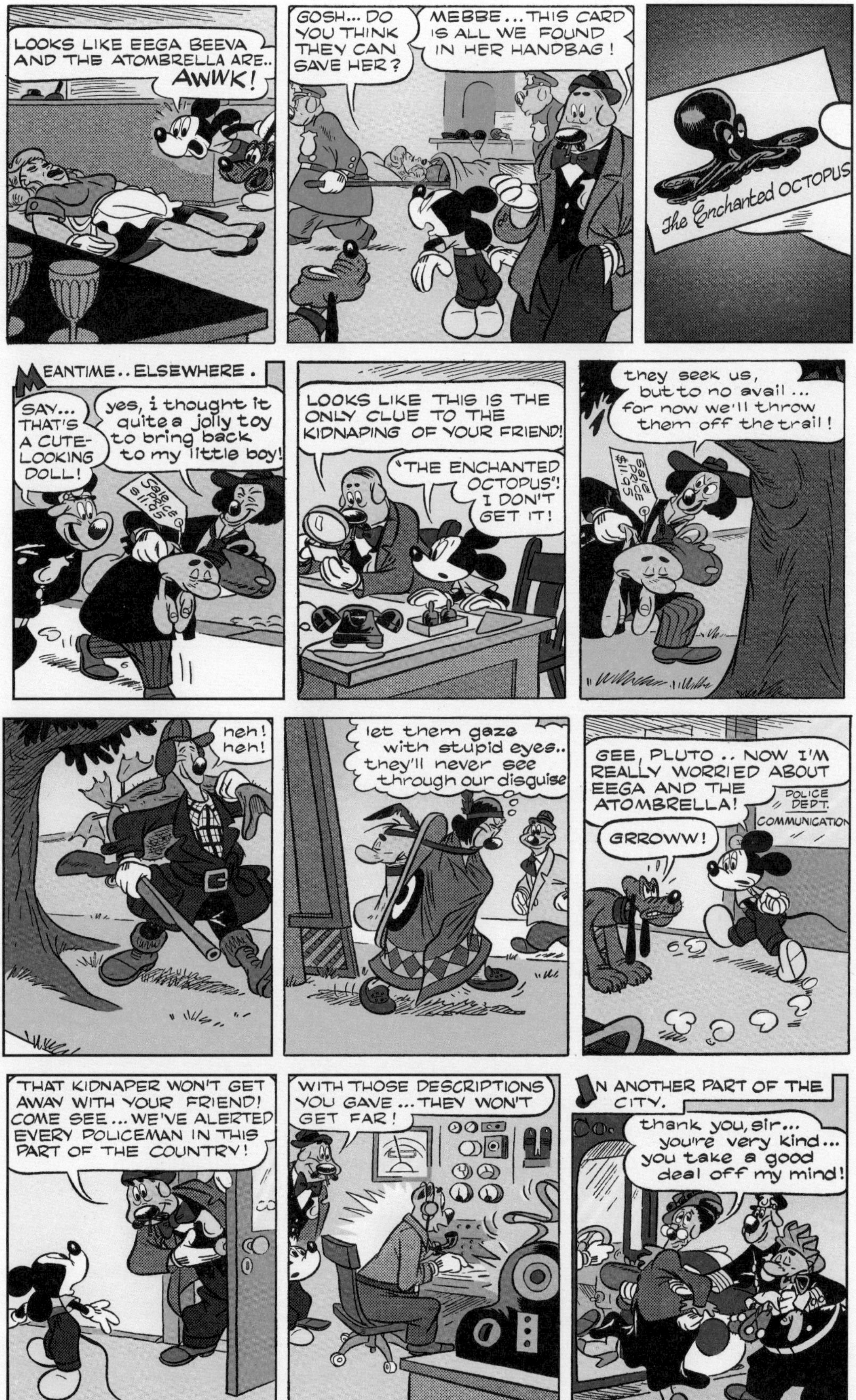
LOOKS LIKE EEGA BEEVA AND THE ATOMBRELLA ARE.. AWWK!
GOSH... DO YOU THINK THEY CAN SAVE HER?
MEBBE... THIS CARD IS ALL WE FOUND IN HER HANDBAG!
The Enchanted OCTOPUS
MEANTIME.. ELSEWHERE.
SAY... THAT'S A CUTE-LOOKING DOLL!
yes, i thought it quite a jolly toy to bring back to my little boy!
LOOKS LIKE THIS IS THE ONLY CLUE TO THE KIDNAPING OF YOUR FRIEND!
"THE ENCHANTED OCTOPUS"! I DON'T GET IT!
they seek us, but to no avail... for now we'll throw them off the trail!
heh! heh!
let them gaze with stupid eyes.. they'll never see through our disguise
GEE, PLUTO.. NOW I'M REALLY WORRIED ABOUT EEGA AND THE ATOMBRELLA!
POLICE DEPT.
COMMUNICATION
GRROWW!
THAT KIDNAPER WON'T GET AWAY WITH YOUR FRIEND! COME SEE... WE'VE ALERTED EVERY POLICEMAN IN THIS PART OF THE COUNTRY!
WITH THOSE DESCRIPTIONS YOU GAVE... THEY WON'T GET FAR!
IN ANOTHER PART OF THE CITY.
thank you, sir... you're very kind... you take a good deal off my mind!

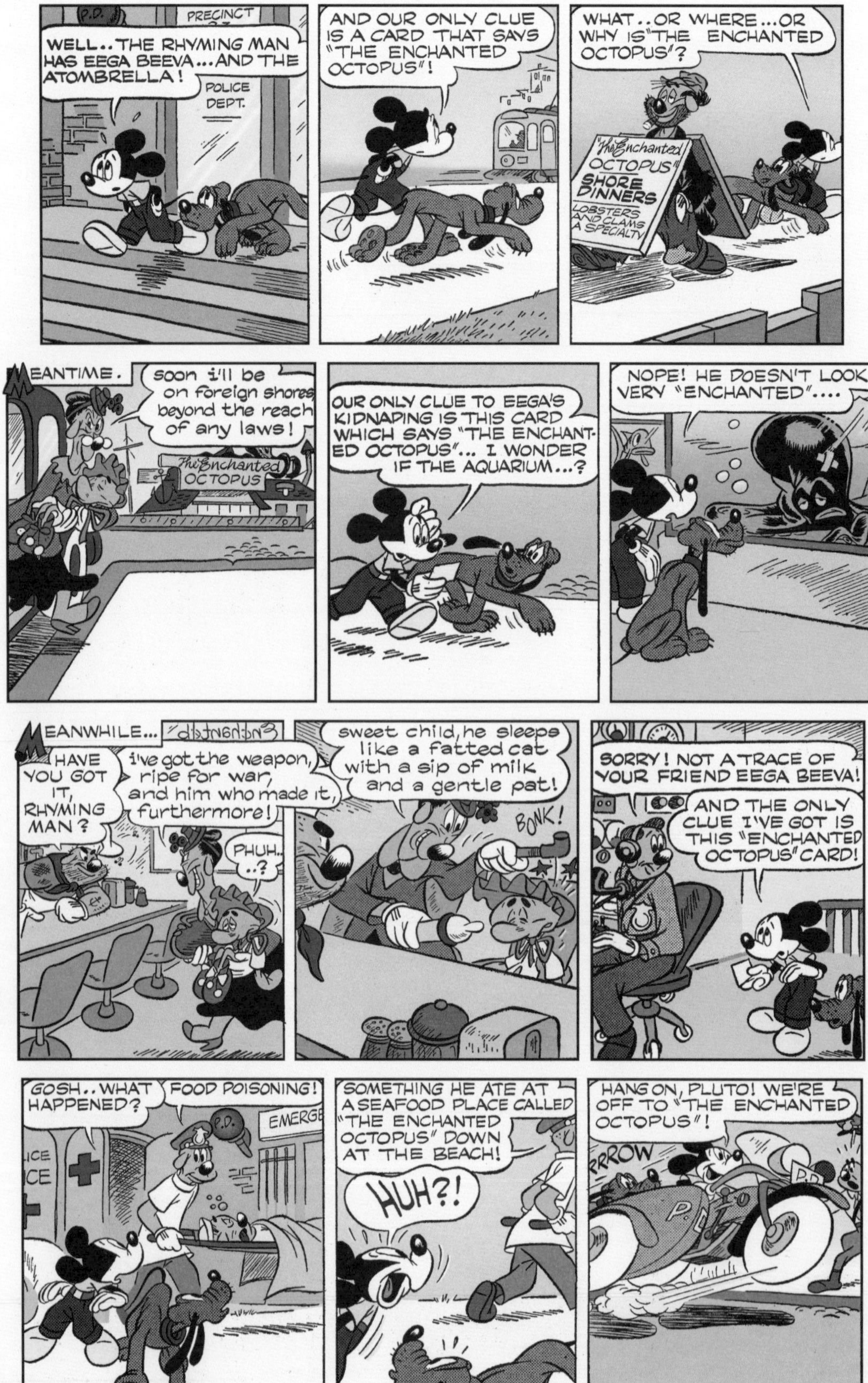
P.D.
PRECINCT
WELL..THE RHYMING MAN HAS EEGA BEEVA...AND THE ATOMBRELLA!
POLICE DEPT.
AND OUR ONLY CLUE IS A CARD THAT SAYS "THE ENCHANTED OCTOPUS"!
WHAT..OR WHERE...OR WHY IS "THE ENCHANTED OCTOPUS"?
"The Enchanted OCTOPUS" SHORE DINNERS LOBSTERS AND CLAMS A SPECIALTY
MEANTIME.
soon i'll be on foreign shores beyond the reach of any laws!
The Enchanted OCTOPUS
OUR ONLY CLUE TO EEGA'S KIDNAPING IS THIS CARD WHICH SAYS "THE ENCHANTED OCTOPUS"... I WONDER IF THE AQUARIUM...?
NOPE! HE DOESN'T LOOK VERY "ENCHANTED"....
MEANWHILE...
HAVE YOU GOT IT, RHYMING MAN?
i've got the weapon, ripe for war, and him who made it, furthermore!
PHUH.. ..?
sweet child, he sleeps like a fatted cat with a sip of milk and a gentle pat!
BONK!
SORRY! NOT A TRACE OF YOUR FRIEND EEGA BEEVA!
AND THE ONLY CLUE I'VE GOT IS THIS "ENCHANTED OCTOPUS" CARD!
GOSH..WHAT HAPPENED?
FOOD POISONING!
P.D.
EMERGE
SOMETHING HE ATE AT A SEAFOOD PLACE CALLED "THE ENCHANTED OCTOPUS" DOWN AT THE BEACH!
HUH?!
HANG ON, PLUTO! WE'RE OFF TO "THE ENCHANTED OCTOPUS"!
RRROW

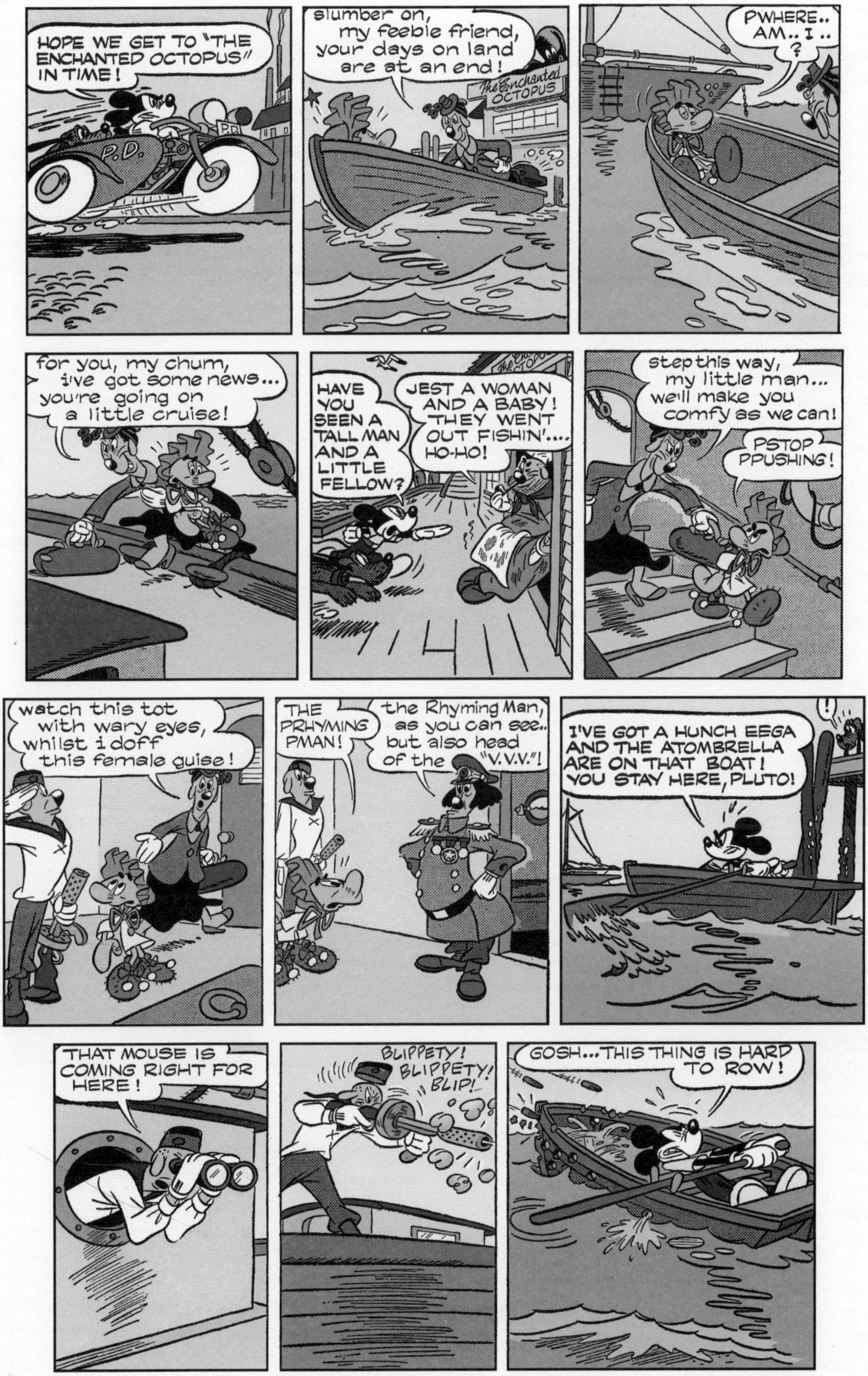
HOPE WE GET TO "THE ENCHANTED OCTOPUS" IN TIME!
P.D.
slumber on, my feeble friend, your days on land are at an end!
The Enchanted OCTOPUS
PWHERE.. AM.. I.. ?
for you, my chum, i've got some news... you're going on a little cruise!
HAVE YOU SEEN A TALL MAN AND A LITTLE FELLOW?
JEST A WOMAN AND A BABY! THEY WENT OUT FISHIN'.... HO-HO!
step this way, my little man... we'll make you comfy as we can!
PSTOP PPUSHING!
watch this tot with wary eyes, whilst i doff this female guise!
THE PRHYMING PMAN!
the Rhyming Man, as you can see.. but also head of the "V.V.V."!
I'VE GOT A HUNCH EEGA AND THE ATOMBRELLA ARE ON THAT BOAT! YOU STAY HERE, PLUTO!
!
THAT MOUSE IS COMING RIGHT FOR HERE!
BLIPPETY! BLIPPETY! BLIP!
GOSH...THIS THING IS HARD TO ROW!

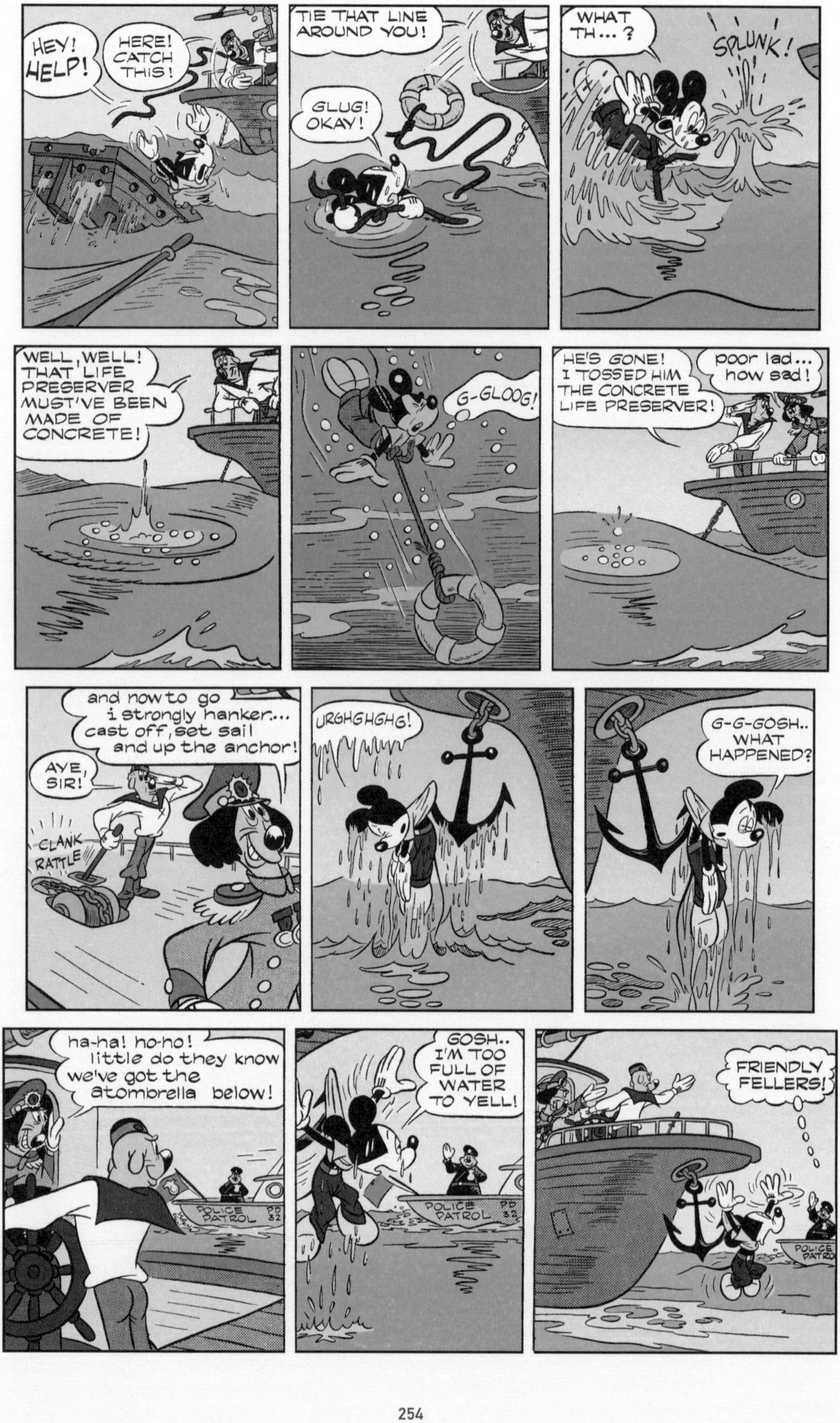
HEY! HELP!
HERE! CATCH THIS!
TIE THAT LINE AROUND YOU!
GLUG! OKAY!
WHAT TH...?
SPLUNK!
WELL, WELL! THAT LIFE PRESERVER MUST'VE BEEN MADE OF CONCRETE!
G-GLOOG!
HE'S GONE! I TOSSED HIM THE CONCRETE LIFE PRESERVER!
poor lad... how sad!
and now to go i strongly hanker... cast off, set sail and up the anchor!
AYE, SIR!
CLANK RATTLE
URGHGHGHG!
G-G-GOSH.. WHAT HAPPENED?
ha-ha! ho-ho! little do they know we've got the atombrella below!
POLICE PATROL PD 32
GOSH.. I'M TOO FULL OF WATER TO YELL!
POLICE PATROL PD 32
FRIENDLY FELLERS!

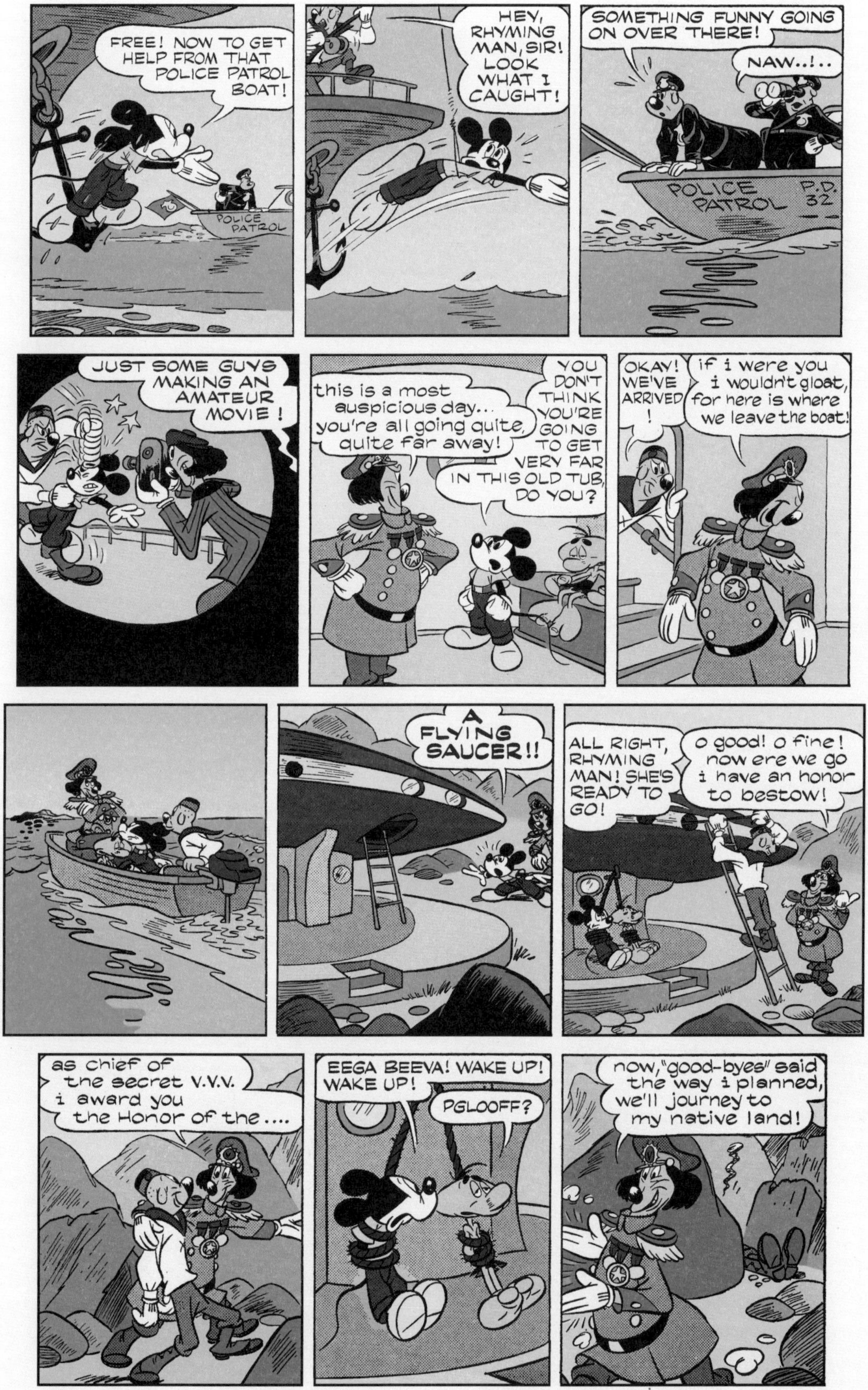
FREE! NOW TO GET HELP FROM THAT POLICE PATROL BOAT!
POLICE PATROL
HEY, RHYMING MAN, SIR! LOOK WHAT I CAUGHT!
SOMETHING FUNNY GOING ON OVER THERE!
NAW..!..
POLICE PATROL P.D. 32
JUST SOME GUYS MAKING AN AMATEUR MOVIE!
this is a most auspicious day... you're all going quite, quite far away!
YOU DON'T THINK YOU'RE GOING TO GET VERY FAR IN THIS OLD TUB, DO YOU?
OKAY! WE'VE ARRIVED!
if i were you i wouldn't gloat, for here is where we leave the boat!
A FLYING SAUCER!!
ALL RIGHT, RHYMING MAN! SHE'S READY TO GO!
o good! o fine! now ere we go i have an honor to bestow!
as chief of the secret V.V.V. i award you the Honor of the....
EEGA BEEVA! WAKE UP! WAKE UP!
PGLOOFF?
now, "good-byes" said the way i planned, we'll journey to my native land!

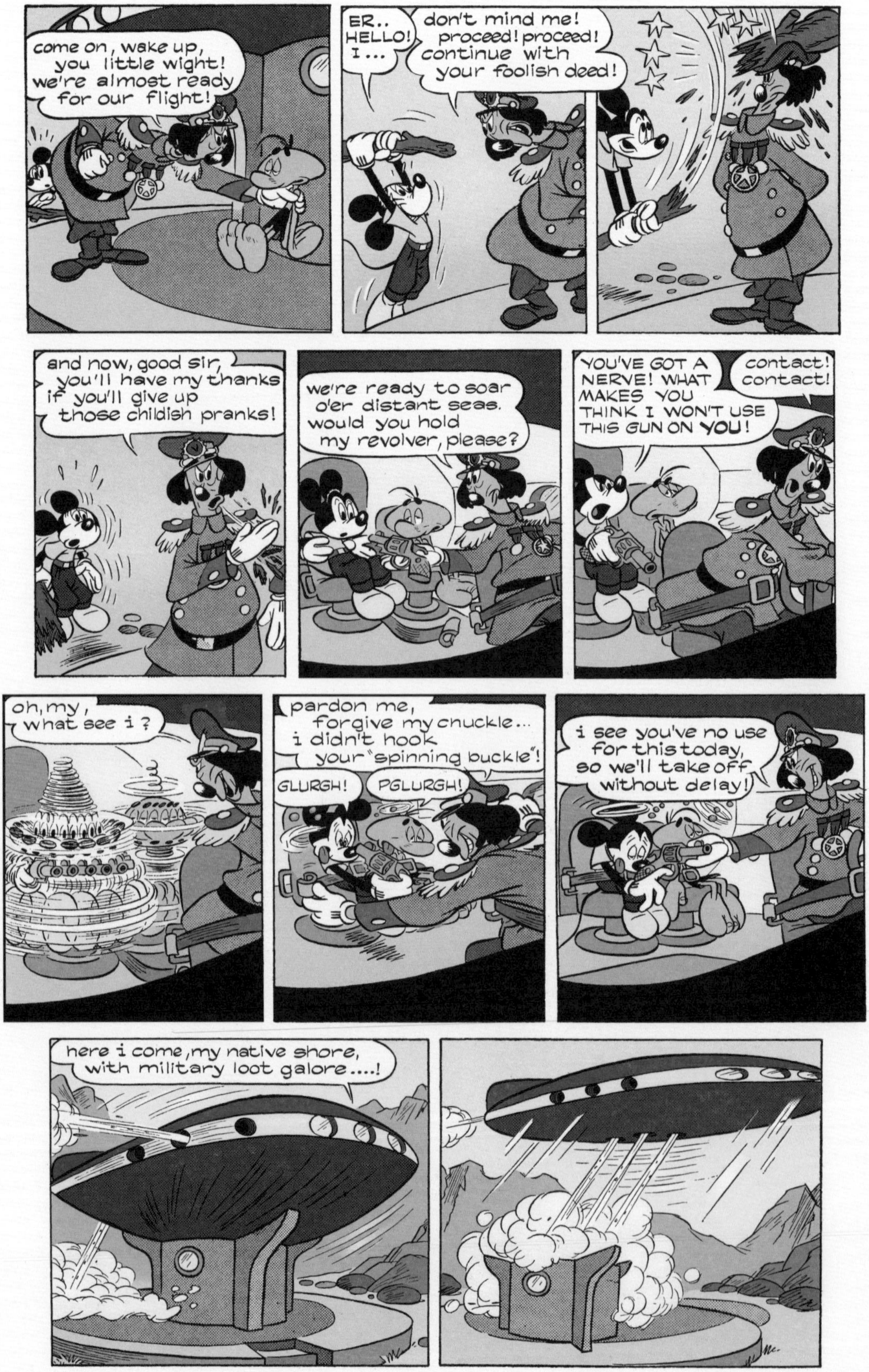
come on, wake up, you little wight! we're almost ready for our flight!
ER.. HELLO! I...
don't mind me! proceed! proceed! continue with your foolish deed!
and now, good sir, you'll have my thanks if you'll give up those childish pranks!
we're ready to soar o'er distant seas. would you hold my revolver, please?
YOU'VE GOT A NERVE! WHAT MAKES YOU THINK I WON'T USE THIS GUN ON YOU!
contact! contact!
oh, my, what see i?
pardon me, forgive my chuckle... i didn't hook your "spinning buckle"!
GLURGH!
PGLURGH!
i see you've no use for this today, so we'll take off without delay!
here i come, my native shore, with military loot galore....!

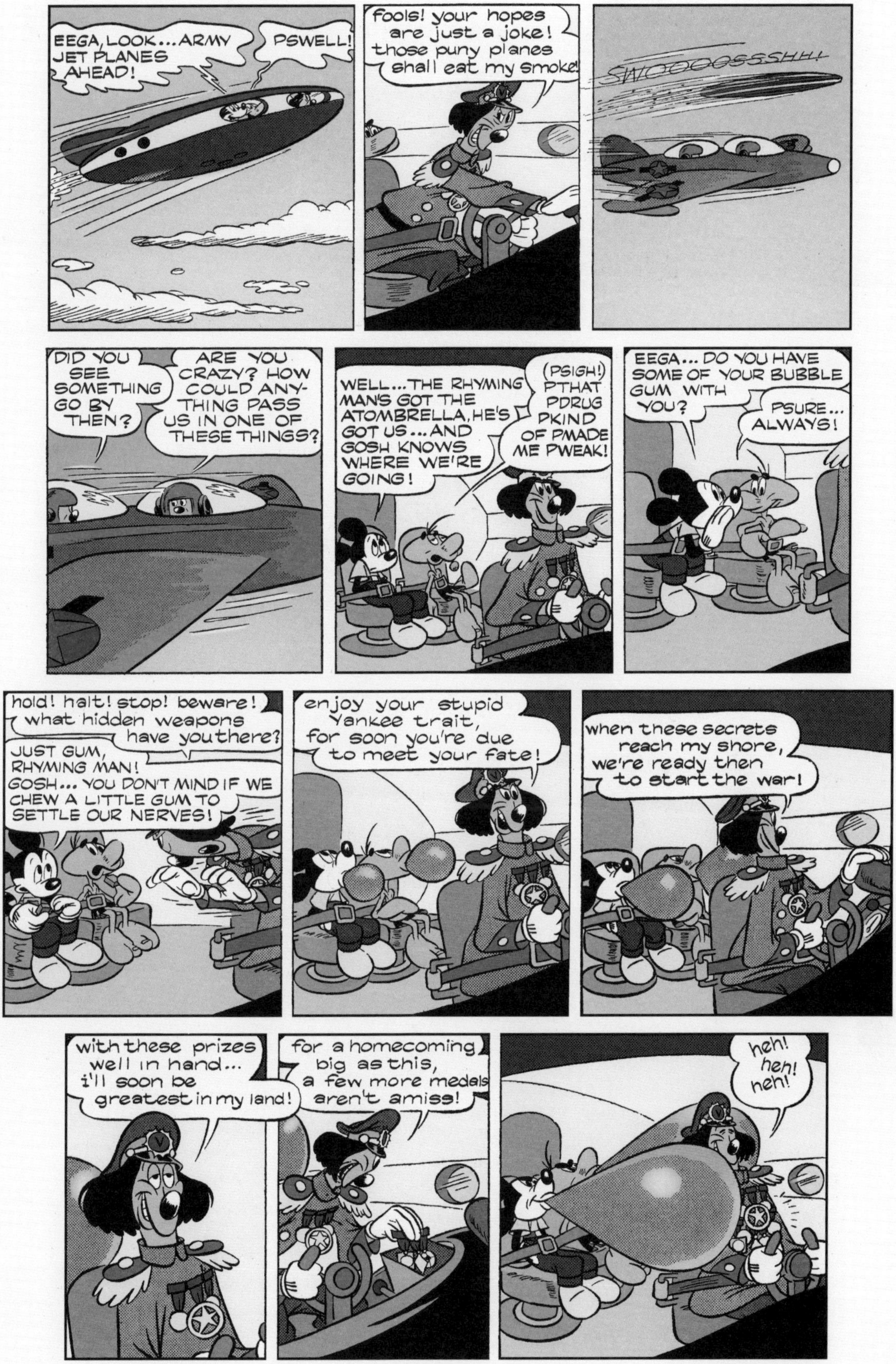
EEGA, LOOK... ARMY JET PLANES AHEAD!
PSWELL!
fools! your hopes are just a joke! those puny planes shall eat my smoke!
SWOOOOOSSSHH!
DID YOU SEE SOMETHING GO BY THEN?
ARE YOU CRAZY? HOW COULD ANYTHING PASS US IN ONE OF THESE THINGS?
WELL... THE RHYMING MAN'S GOT THE ATOMBRELLA, HE'S GOT US... AND GOSH KNOWS WHERE WE'RE GOING!
(PSIGH!) PTHAT PDRUG PKIND OF PMADE ME PWEAK!
EEGA... DO YOU HAVE SOME OF YOUR BUBBLE GUM WITH YOU?
PSURE... ALWAYS!
hold! halt! stop! beware! what hidden weapons have you there?
JUST GUM, RHYMING MAN! GOSH... YOU DON'T MIND IF WE CHEW A LITTLE GUM TO SETTLE OUR NERVES!
enjoy your stupid Yankee trait, for soon you're due to meet your fate!
when these secrets reach my shore, we're ready then to start the war!
with these prizes well in hand... i'll soon be greatest in my land!
for a homecoming big as this, a few more medals aren't amiss!
heh! heh! heh!

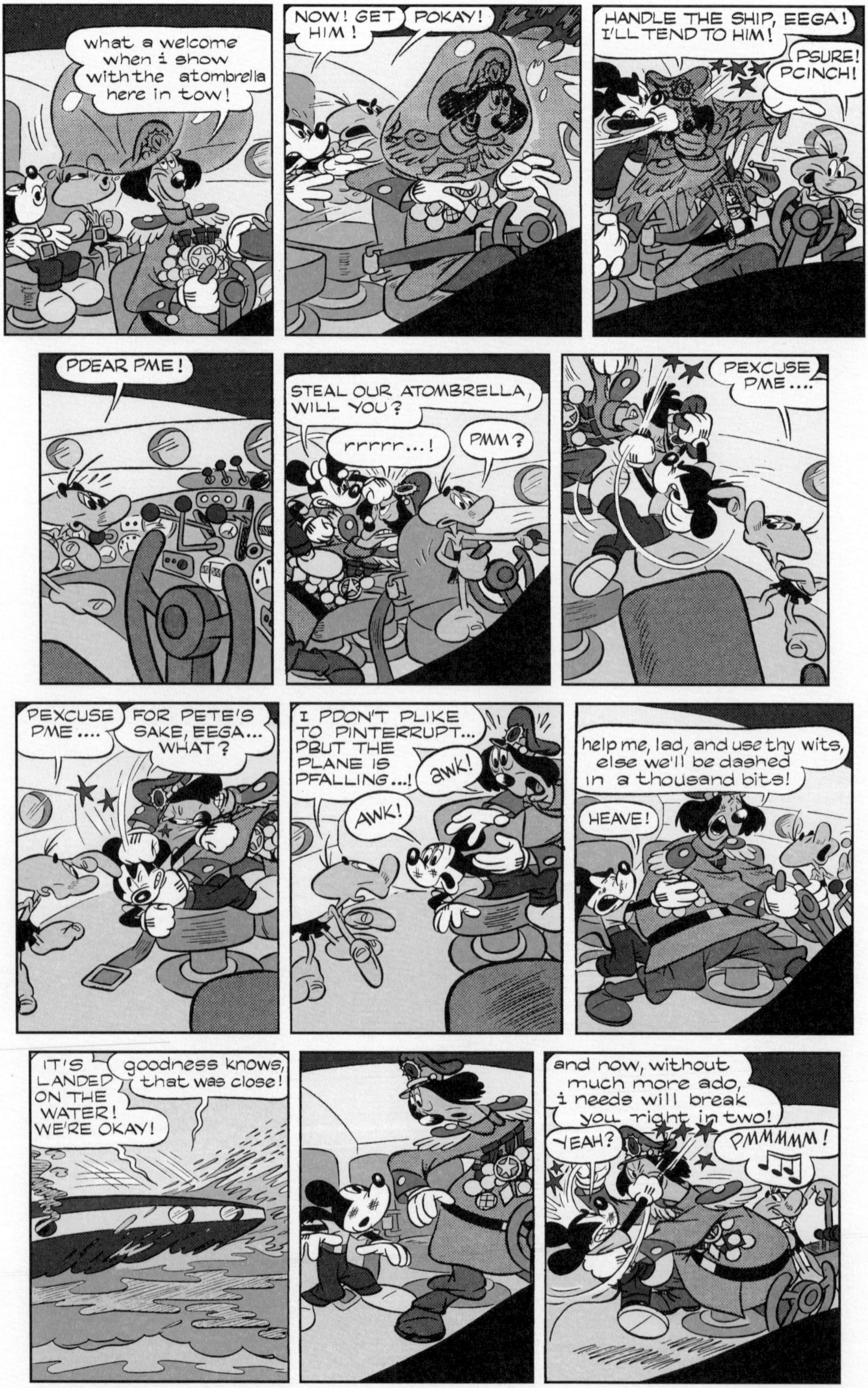
what a welcome when i show with the atombrella here in tow!
NOW! GET HIM!
POKAY!
HANDLE THE SHIP, EEGA! I'LL TEND TO HIM!
PSURE! PCINCH!
PDEAR PME!
STEAL OUR ATOMBRELLA, WILL YOU?
rrrrr...!
PMM?
PEXCUSE PME....
PEXCUSE PME....
FOR PETE'S SAKE, EEGA... WHAT?
I PDON'T PLIKE TO PINTERRUPT... PBUT THE PLANE IS PFALLING...!
awk!
AWK!
help me, lad, and use thy wits, else we'll be dashed in a thousand bits!
HEAVE!
IT'S LANDED ON THE WATER! WE'RE OKAY!
goodness knows, that was close!
and now, without much more ado, i needs will break you right in two!
YEAH?
PMMMMM!

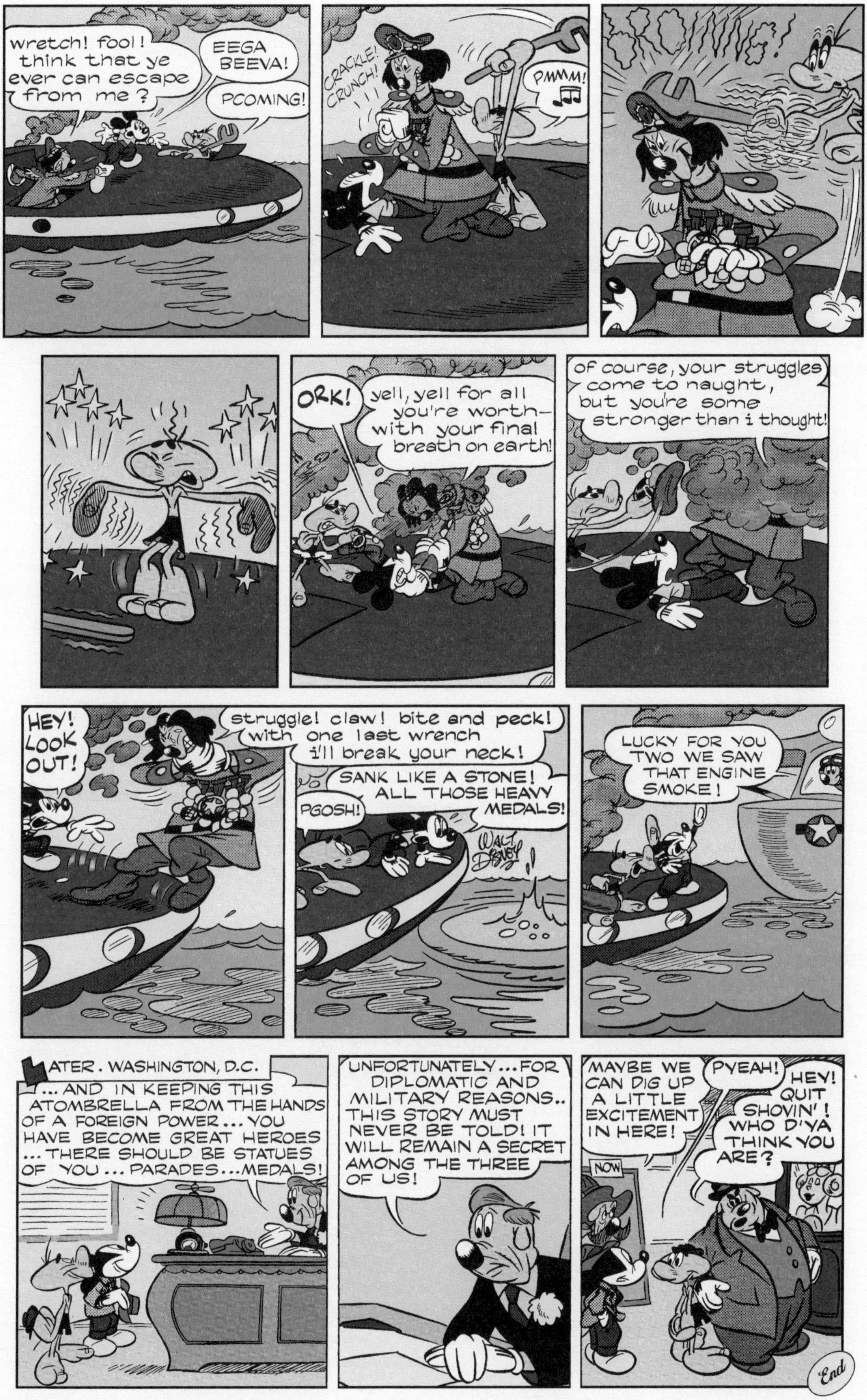
wretch! fool! think that ye ever can escape from me?
EEGA BEEVA!
PCOMING!
CRACKLE! CRUNCH!
PMMM!
KOIIIING!
ORK!
yell, yell for all you're worth— with your final breath on earth!
of course, your struggles come to naught, but you're some stronger than i thought!
HEY! LOOK OUT!
struggle! claw! bite and peck! with one last wrench i'll break your neck!
SANK LIKE A STONE! ALL THOSE HEAVY MEDALS!
PGOSH!
WALT DISNEY
LUCKY FOR YOU TWO WE SAW THAT ENGINE SMOKE!
LATER. WASHINGTON, D.C.
...AND IN KEEPING THIS ATOMBRELLA FROM THE HANDS OF A FOREIGN POWER... YOU HAVE BECOME GREAT HEROES ...THERE SHOULD BE STATUES OF YOU... PARADES...MEDALS!
UNFORTUNATELY...FOR DIPLOMATIC AND MILITARY REASONS.. THIS STORY MUST NEVER BE TOLD! IT WILL REMAIN A SECRET AMONG THE THREE OF US!
MAYBE WE CAN DIG UP A LITTLE EXCITEMENT IN HERE!
PYEAH!
HEY! QUIT SHOVIN'! WHO D'YA THINK YOU ARE?
NOW
End

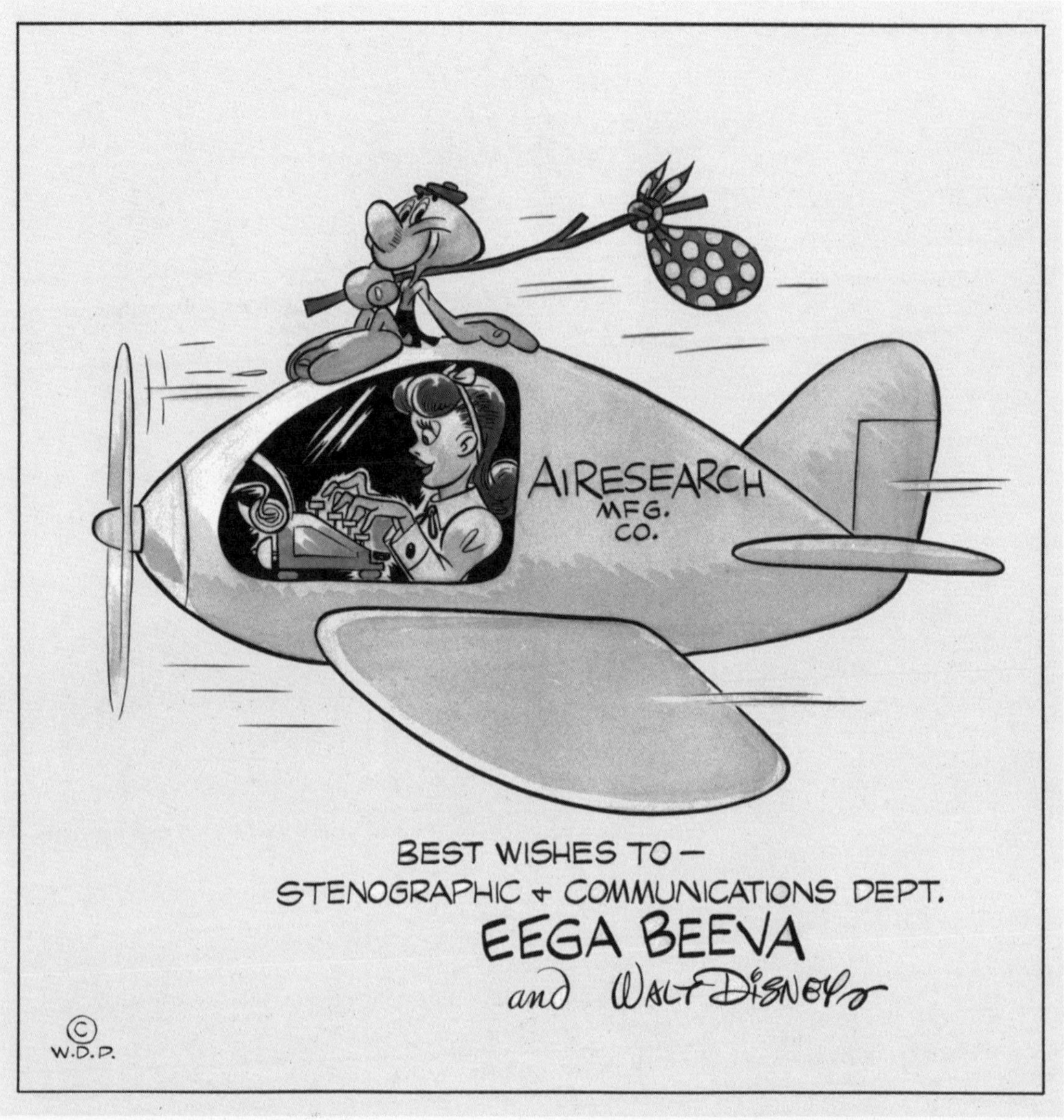
AIRESEARCH
MFG.
CO.
BEST WISHES TO —
STENOGRAPHIC + COMMUNICATIONS DEPT.
EEGA BEEVA
and WALT DISNEY
© W.D.P.

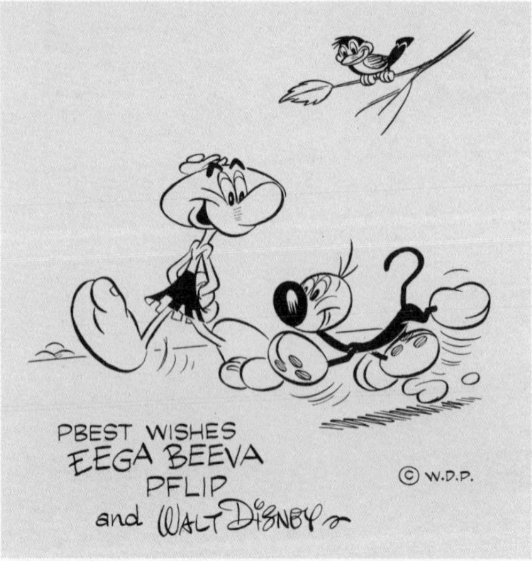
PBEST WISHES
EEGA BEEVA
PFLIP
and WALT DISNEY
© W.D.P.

Gottfredson even made special drawings of Mickey's futuristic pal Eega Beeva, both to promote Eega's Mickey Mouse strip appearances and to greet Disney corporate partners. The airplane image was created in November 1947 as a Disney studio gift for the Stenographic and Communications Department of AiResearch Manufacturing Company, a Los Angeles-based research firm. The image of Eega with his pet "thnuckle-booh" Pflip was a 1949 fan card.

Images courtesy Walt Disney Photo Library.

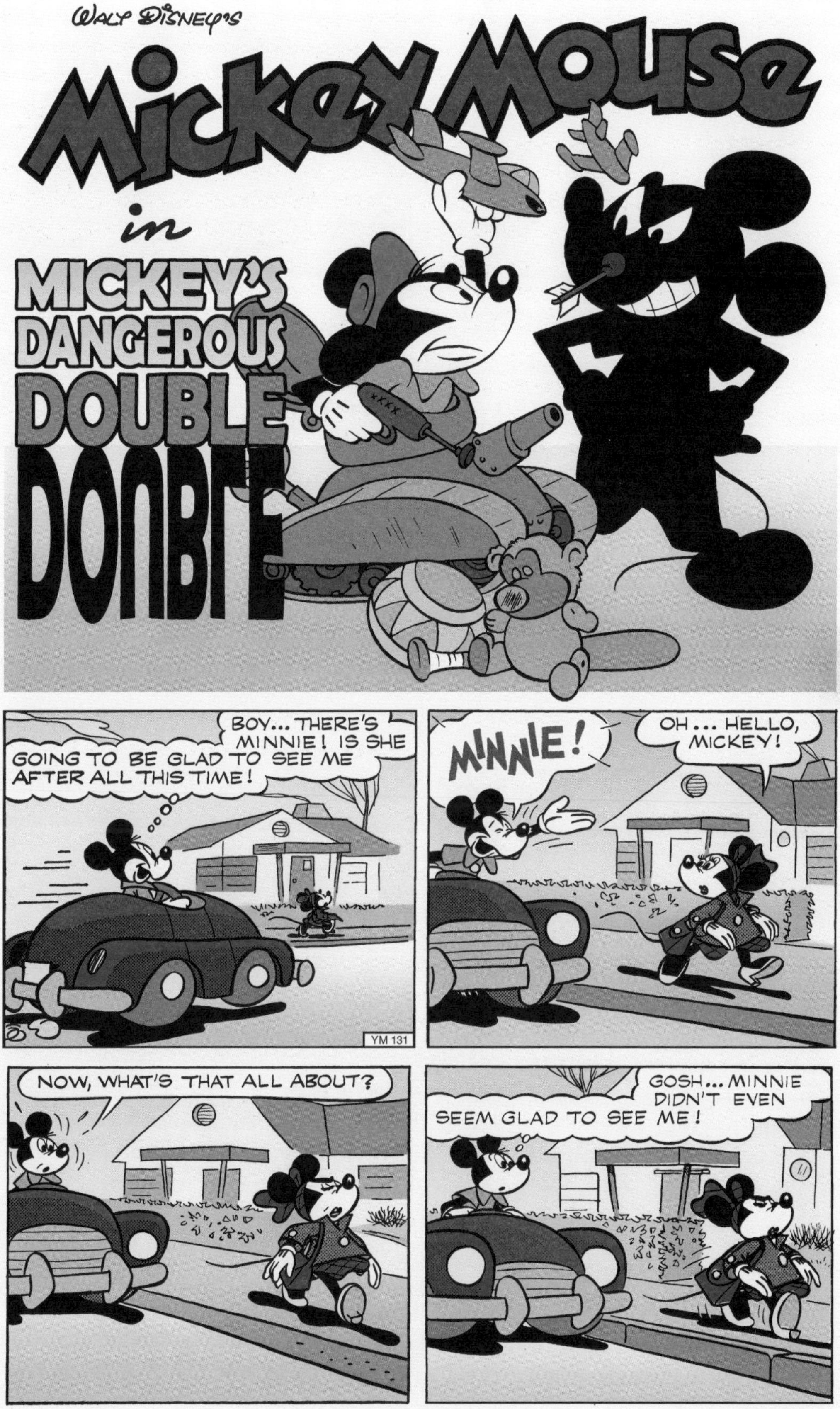
WALT DISNEY'S
MICKEY MOUSE
in
MICKEY'S DANGEROUS DOUBLE
BOY... THERE'S MINNIE! IS SHE GOING TO BE GLAD TO SEE ME AFTER ALL THIS TIME!
YM 131
MINNIE!
OH... HELLO, MICKEY!
NOW, WHAT'S THAT ALL ABOUT?
GOSH... MINNIE DIDN'T EVEN SEEM GLAD TO SEE ME!

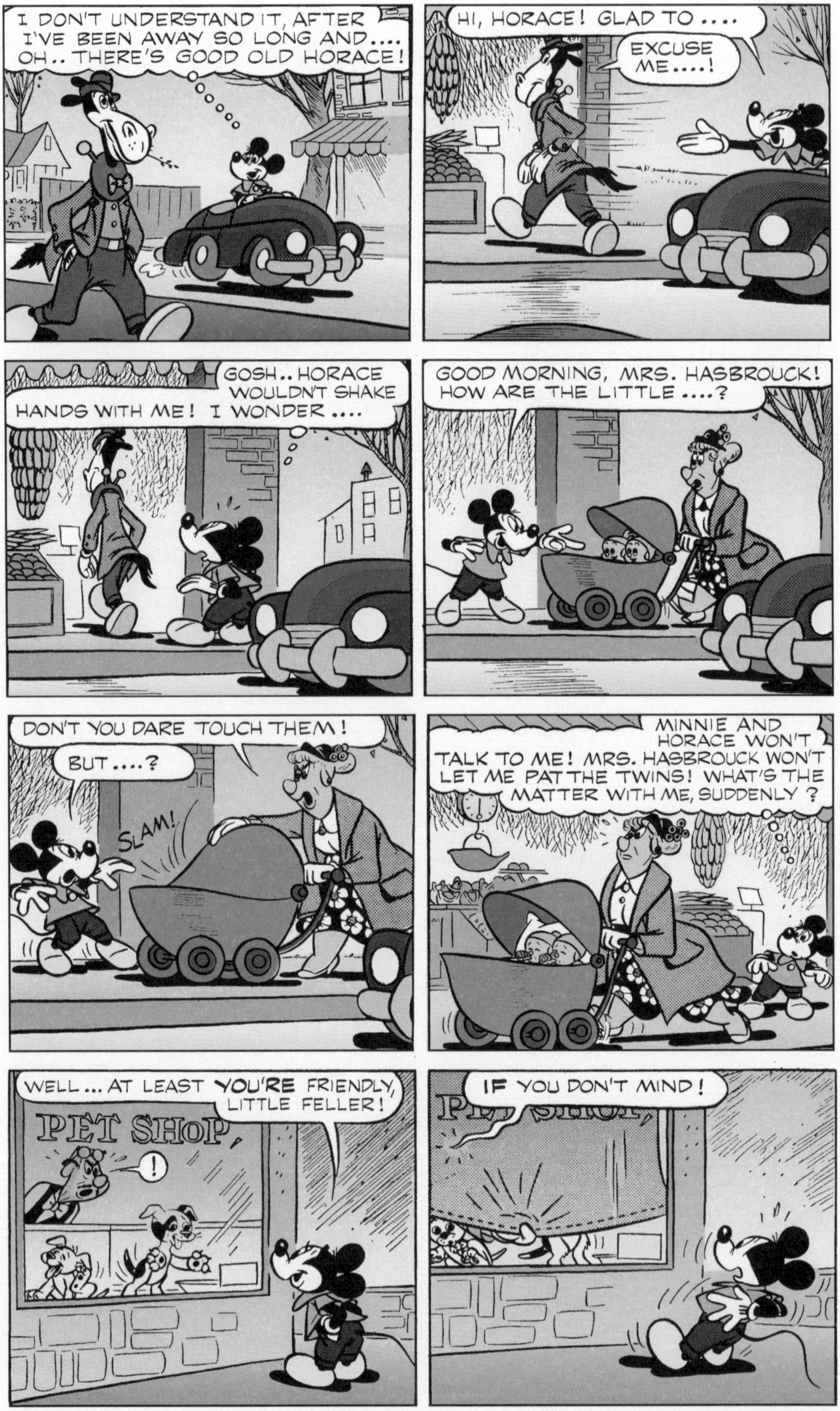
I DON'T UNDERSTAND IT, AFTER I'VE BEEN AWAY SO LONG AND.... OH.. THERE'S GOOD OLD HORACE!
HI, HORACE! GLAD TO ....
EXCUSE ME....!
GOSH.. HORACE WOULDN'T SHAKE HANDS WITH ME! I WONDER ....
GOOD MORNING, MRS. HASBROUCK! HOW ARE THE LITTLE ....?
DON'T YOU DARE TOUCH THEM!
BUT....?
SLAM!
MINNIE AND HORACE WON'T TALK TO ME! MRS. HASBROUCK WON'T LET ME PAT THE TWINS! WHAT'S THE MATTER WITH ME, SUDDENLY ?
WELL... AT LEAST YOU'RE FRIENDLY, LITTLE FELLER!
PET SHOP
!
IF YOU DON'T MIND!

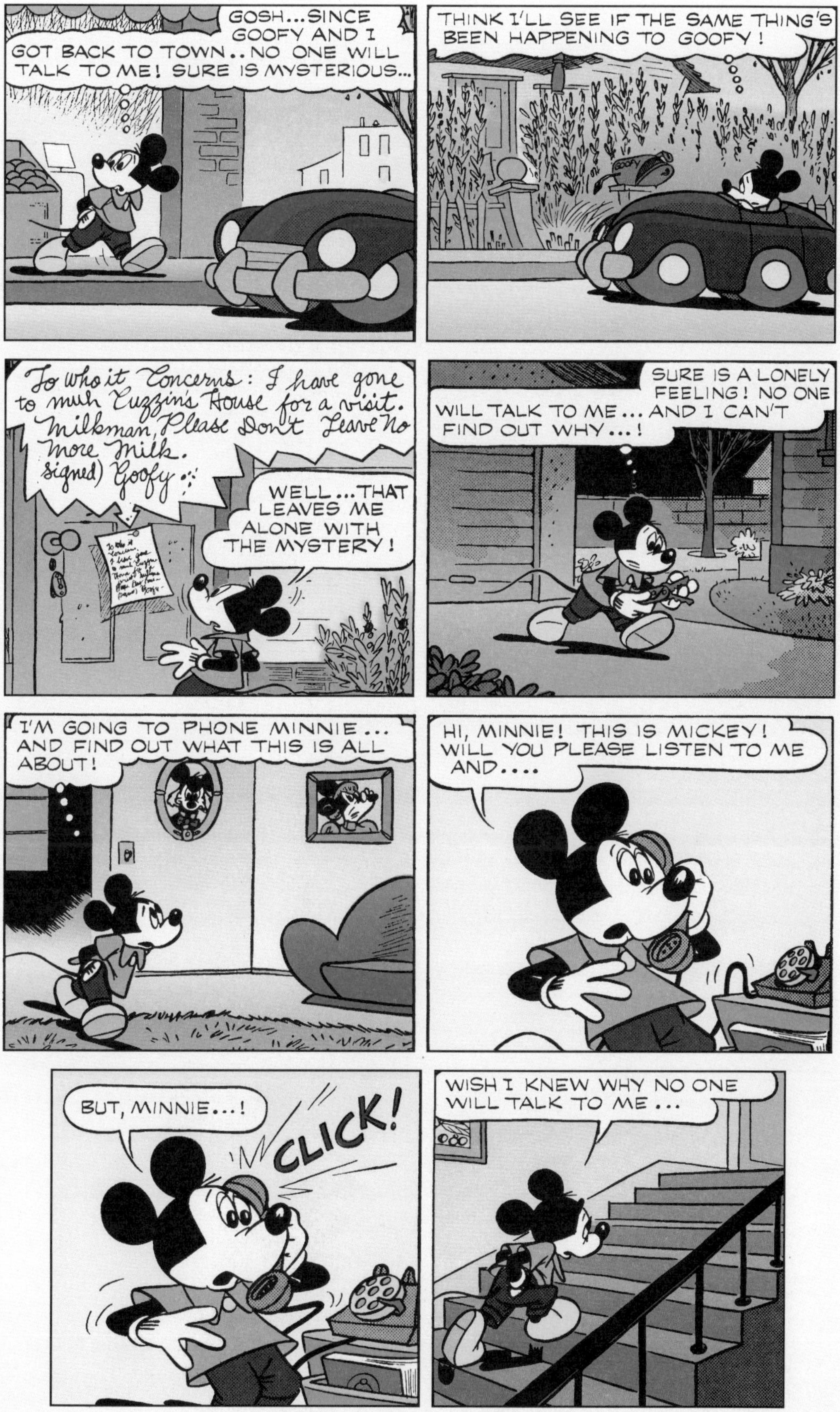
GOSH...SINCE GOOFY AND I GOT BACK TO TOWN..NO ONE WILL TALK TO ME! SURE IS MYSTERIOUS...
THINK I'LL SEE IF THE SAME THING'S BEEN HAPPENING TO GOOFY!
GOOFY
To Who it Concerns: I have gone to muh Cuzzin's House for a visit. Milkman, Please Don't Leave No more Milk. signed) Goofy
WELL...THAT LEAVES ME ALONE WITH THE MYSTERY!
SURE IS A LONELY FEELING! NO ONE WILL TALK TO ME... AND I CAN'T FIND OUT WHY...!
I'M GOING TO PHONE MINNIE... AND FIND OUT WHAT THIS IS ALL ABOUT!
HI, MINNIE! THIS IS MICKEY! WILL YOU PLEASE LISTEN TO ME AND....
BUT, MINNIE...!
CLICK!
WISH I KNEW WHY NO ONE WILL TALK TO ME...

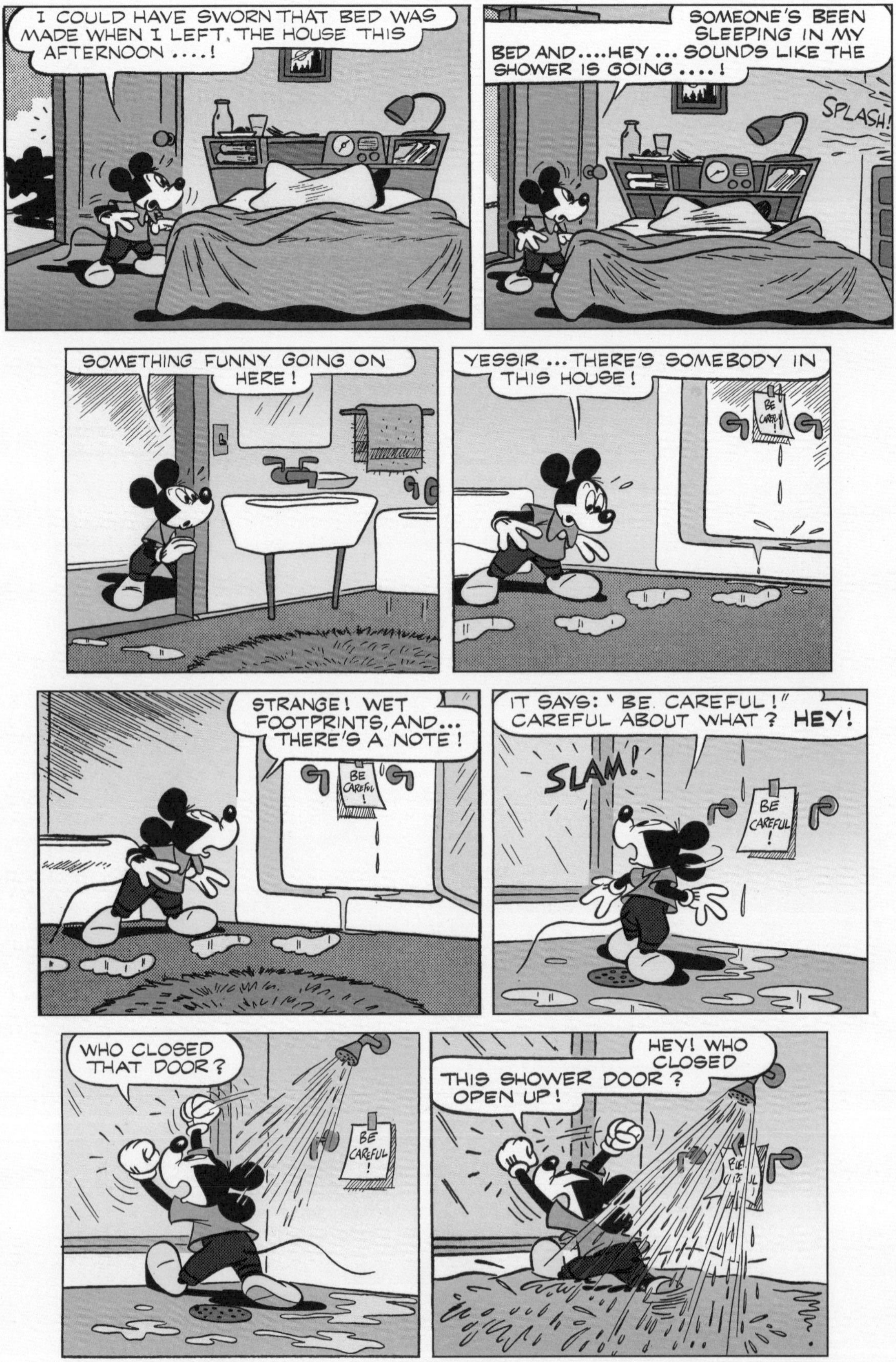
I COULD HAVE SWORN THAT BED WAS MADE WHEN I LEFT THE HOUSE THIS AFTERNOON ....!
SOMEONE'S BEEN SLEEPING IN MY BED AND....HEY ... SOUNDS LIKE THE SHOWER IS GOING ....!
SPLASH!
SOMETHING FUNNY GOING ON HERE!
YESSIR ...THERE'S SOMEBODY IN THIS HOUSE!
STRANGE! WET FOOTPRINTS, AND... THERE'S A NOTE!
BE CAREFUL!
IT SAYS: "BE CAREFUL!" CAREFUL ABOUT WHAT? HEY!
SLAM!
BE CAREFUL!
WHO CLOSED THAT DOOR?
BE CAREFUL!
HEY! WHO CLOSED THIS SHOWER DOOR? OPEN UP!

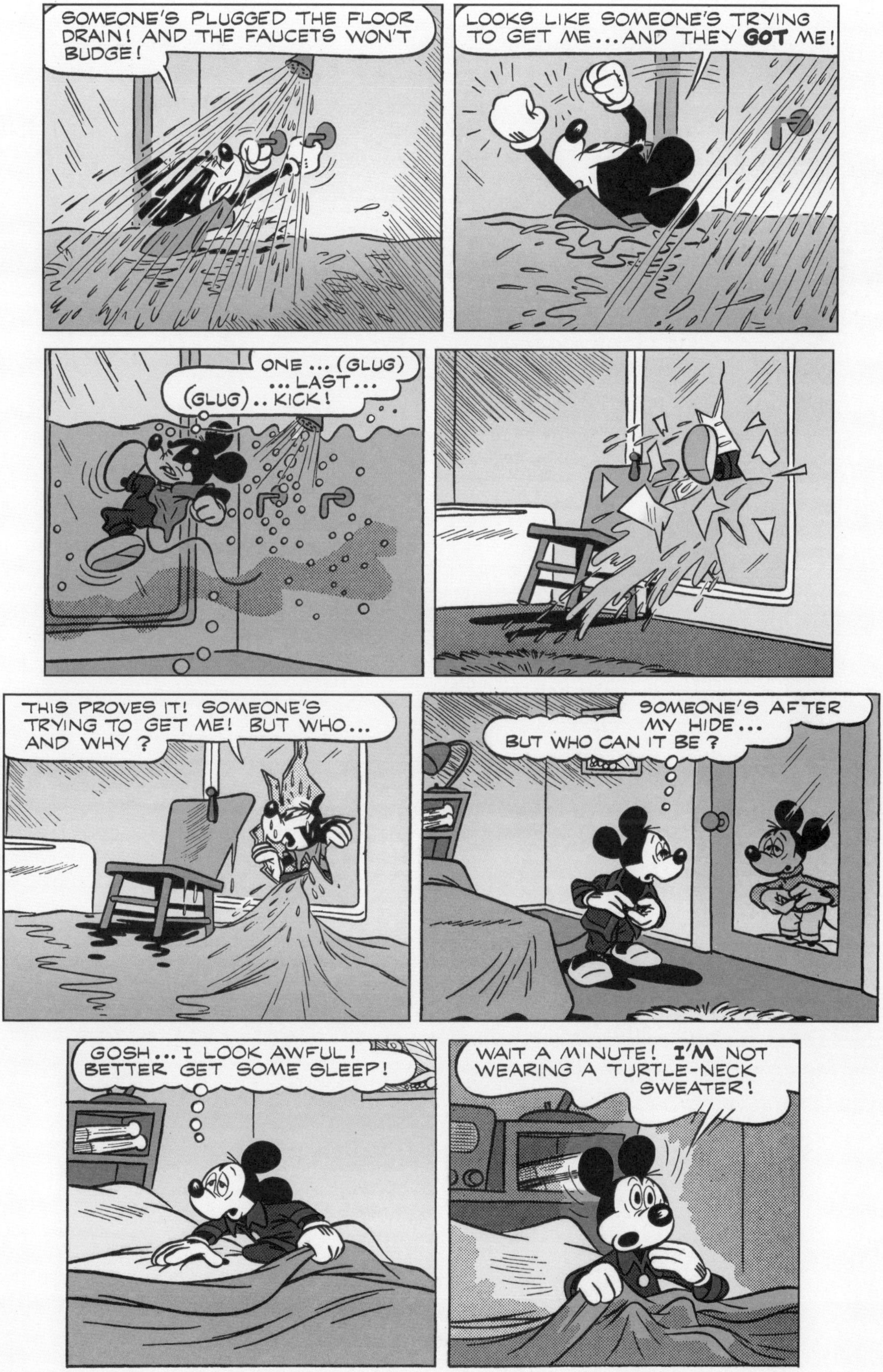
SOMEONE'S PLUGGED THE FLOOR DRAIN! AND THE FAUCETS WON'T BUDGE!
LOOKS LIKE SOMEONE'S TRYING TO GET ME... AND THEY GOT ME!
ONE ... (GLUG) ... LAST ... (GLUG) .. KICK!
THIS PROVES IT! SOMEONE'S TRYING TO GET ME! BUT WHO... AND WHY?
SOMEONE'S AFTER MY HIDE... BUT WHO CAN IT BE?
GOSH... I LOOK AWFUL! BETTER GET SOME SLEEP!
WAIT A MINUTE! I'M NOT WEARING A TURTLE-NECK SWEATER!

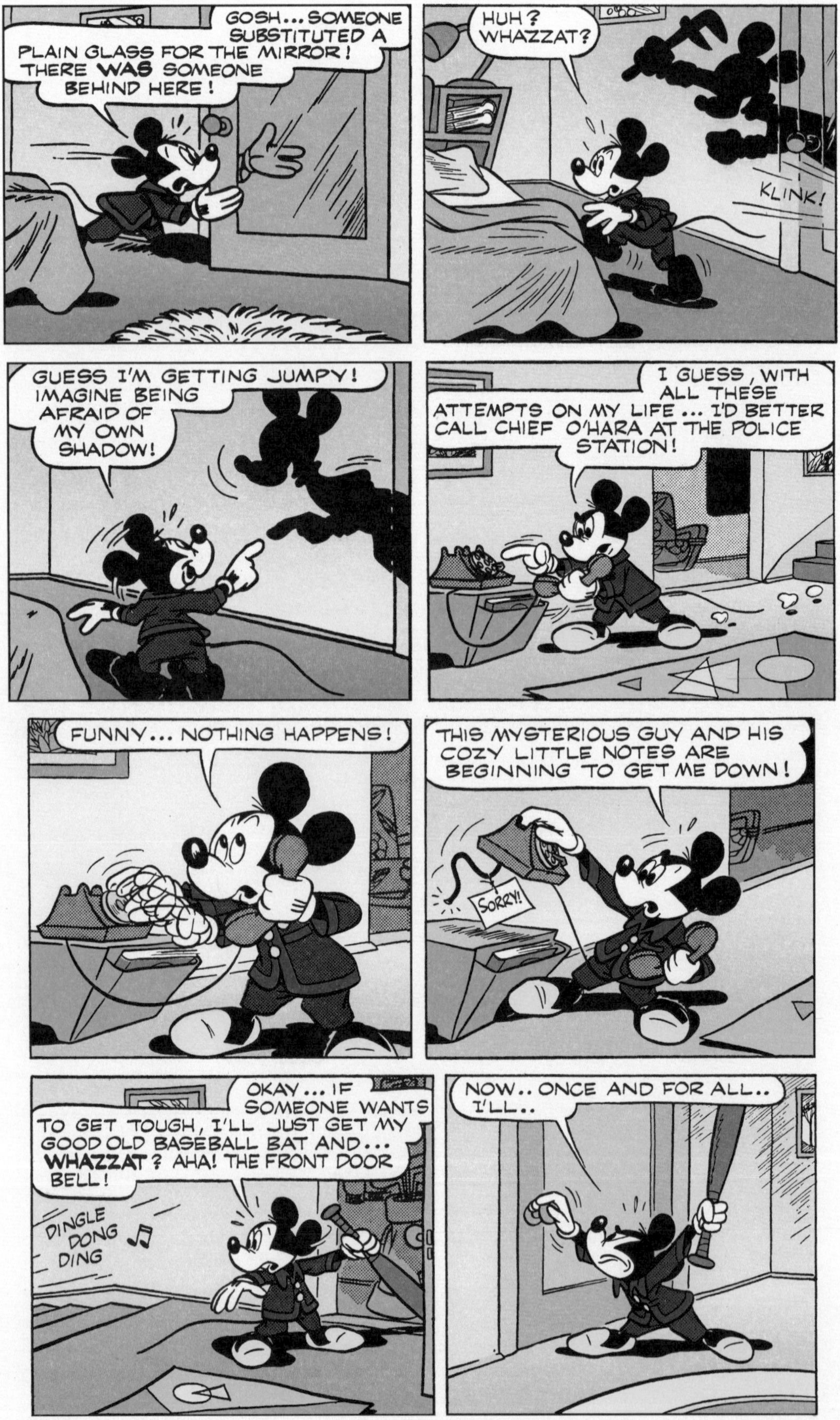
GOSH... SOMEONE SUBSTITUTED A PLAIN GLASS FOR THE MIRROR! THERE WAS SOMEONE BEHIND HERE!
HUH? WHAZZAT?
KLINK!
GUESS I'M GETTING JUMPY! IMAGINE BEING AFRAID OF MY OWN SHADOW!
I GUESS, WITH ALL THESE ATTEMPTS ON MY LIFE... I'D BETTER CALL CHIEF O'HARA AT THE POLICE STATION!
FUNNY... NOTHING HAPPENS!
THIS MYSTERIOUS GUY AND HIS COZY LITTLE NOTES ARE BEGINNING TO GET ME DOWN!
SORRY!
OKAY... IF SOMEONE WANTS TO GET TOUGH, I'LL JUST GET MY GOOD OLD BASEBALL BAT AND... WHAZZAT? AHA! THE FRONT DOOR BELL!
DINGLE DONG DING
NOW.. ONCE AND FOR ALL.. I'LL..

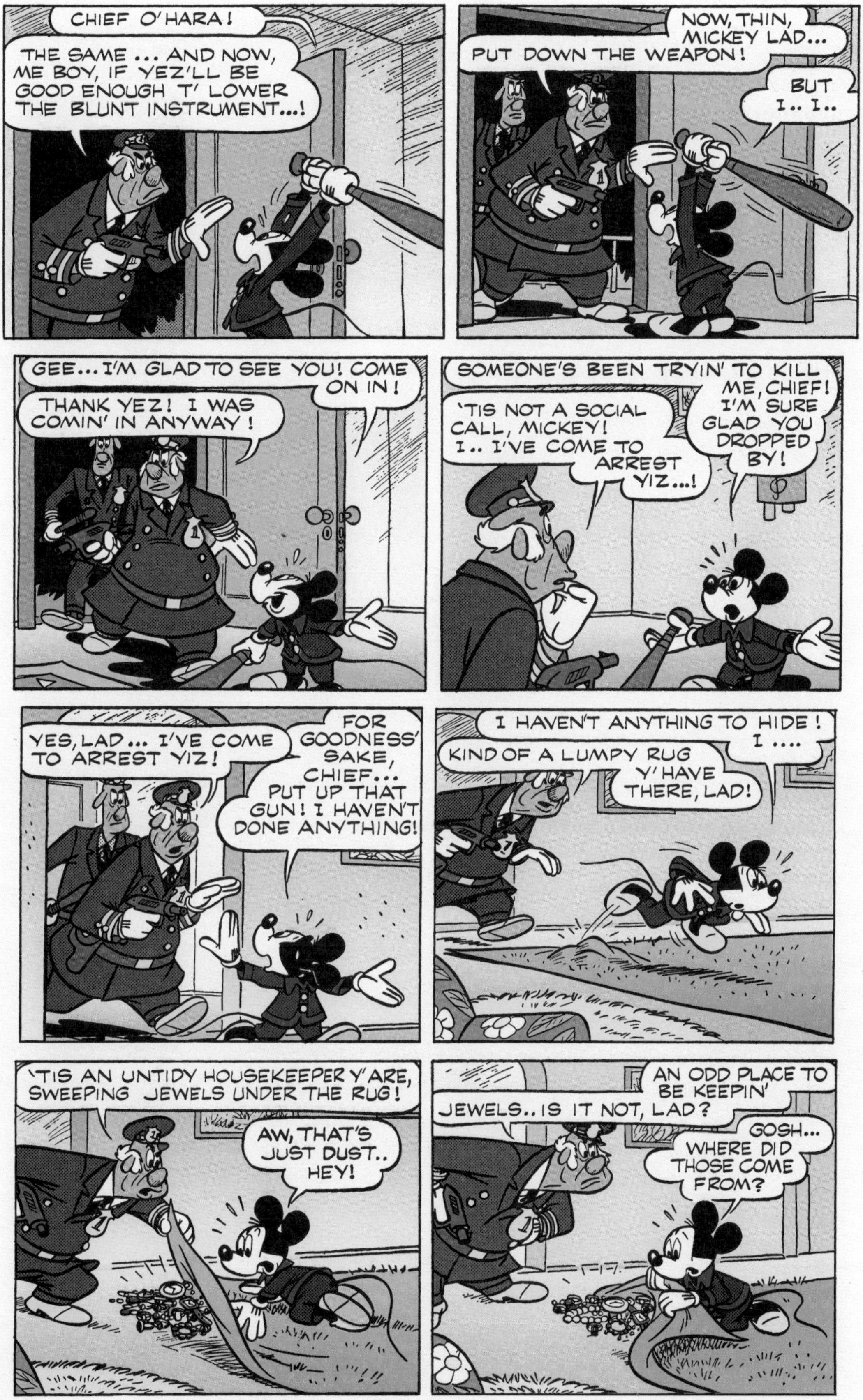
CHIEF O'HARA!
THE SAME ... AND NOW, ME BOY, IF YEZ'LL BE GOOD ENOUGH T' LOWER THE BLUNT INSTRUMENT...!
NOW, THIN, MICKEY LAD... PUT DOWN THE WEAPON!
BUT I.. I..
GEE... I'M GLAD TO SEE YOU! COME ON IN!
THANK YEZ! I WAS COMIN' IN ANYWAY!
SOMEONE'S BEEN TRYIN' TO KILL ME, CHIEF! I'M SURE GLAD YOU DROPPED BY!
'TIS NOT A SOCIAL CALL, MICKEY! I.. I'VE COME TO ARREST YIZ...!
YES, LAD... I'VE COME TO ARREST YIZ!
FOR GOODNESS' SAKE, CHIEF... PUT UP THAT GUN! I HAVEN'T DONE ANYTHING!
I HAVEN'T ANYTHING TO HIDE! I ....
KIND OF A LUMPY RUG Y' HAVE THERE, LAD!
'TIS AN UNTIDY HOUSEKEEPER Y' ARE, SWEEPING JEWELS UNDER THE RUG!
AW, THAT'S JUST DUST.. HEY!
AN ODD PLACE TO BE KEEPIN' JEWELS.. IS IT NOT, LAD?
GOSH... WHERE DID THOSE COME FROM?

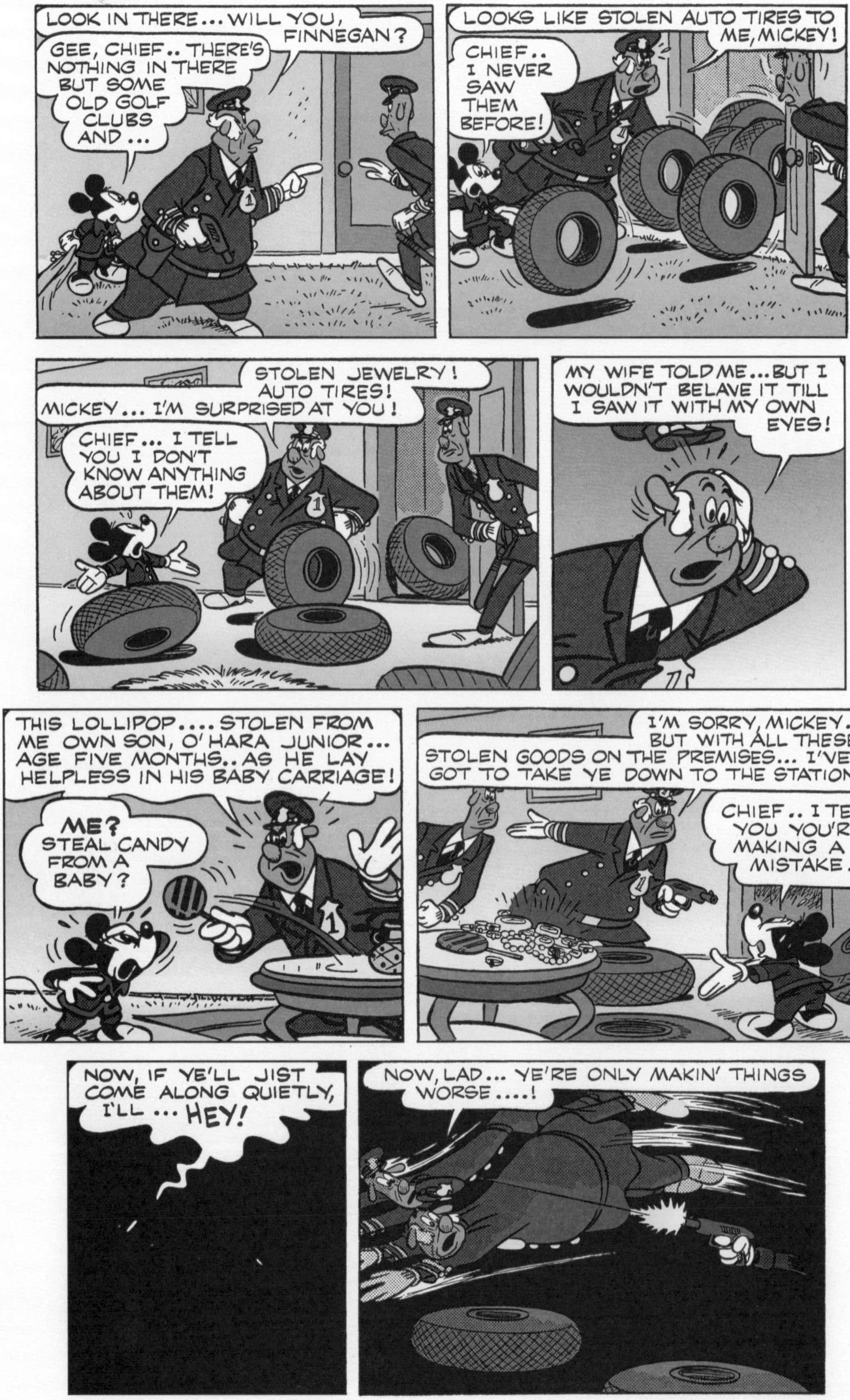
LOOK IN THERE... WILL YOU, FINNEGAN?
GEE, CHIEF.. THERE'S NOTHING IN THERE BUT SOME OLD GOLF CLUBS AND...
LOOKS LIKE STOLEN AUTO TIRES TO ME, MICKEY!
CHIEF.. I NEVER SAW THEM BEFORE!
STOLEN JEWELRY! AUTO TIRES!
MICKEY... I'M SURPRISED AT YOU!
CHIEF... I TELL YOU I DON'T KNOW ANYTHING ABOUT THEM!
MY WIFE TOLD ME... BUT I WOULDN'T BELAVE IT TILL I SAW IT WITH MY OWN EYES!
THIS LOLLIPOP.... STOLEN FROM ME OWN SON, O'HARA JUNIOR... AGE FIVE MONTHS.. AS HE LAY HELPLESS IN HIS BABY CARRIAGE!
ME? STEAL CANDY FROM A BABY?
I'M SORRY, MICKEY... BUT WITH ALL THESE STOLEN GOODS ON THE PREMISES... I'VE GOT TO TAKE YE DOWN TO THE STATION!
CHIEF.. I TELL YOU YOU'RE MAKING A MISTAKE...!
NOW, IF YE'LL JIST COME ALONG QUIETLY, I'LL ... HEY!
NOW, LAD... YE'RE ONLY MAKIN' THINGS WORSE....!

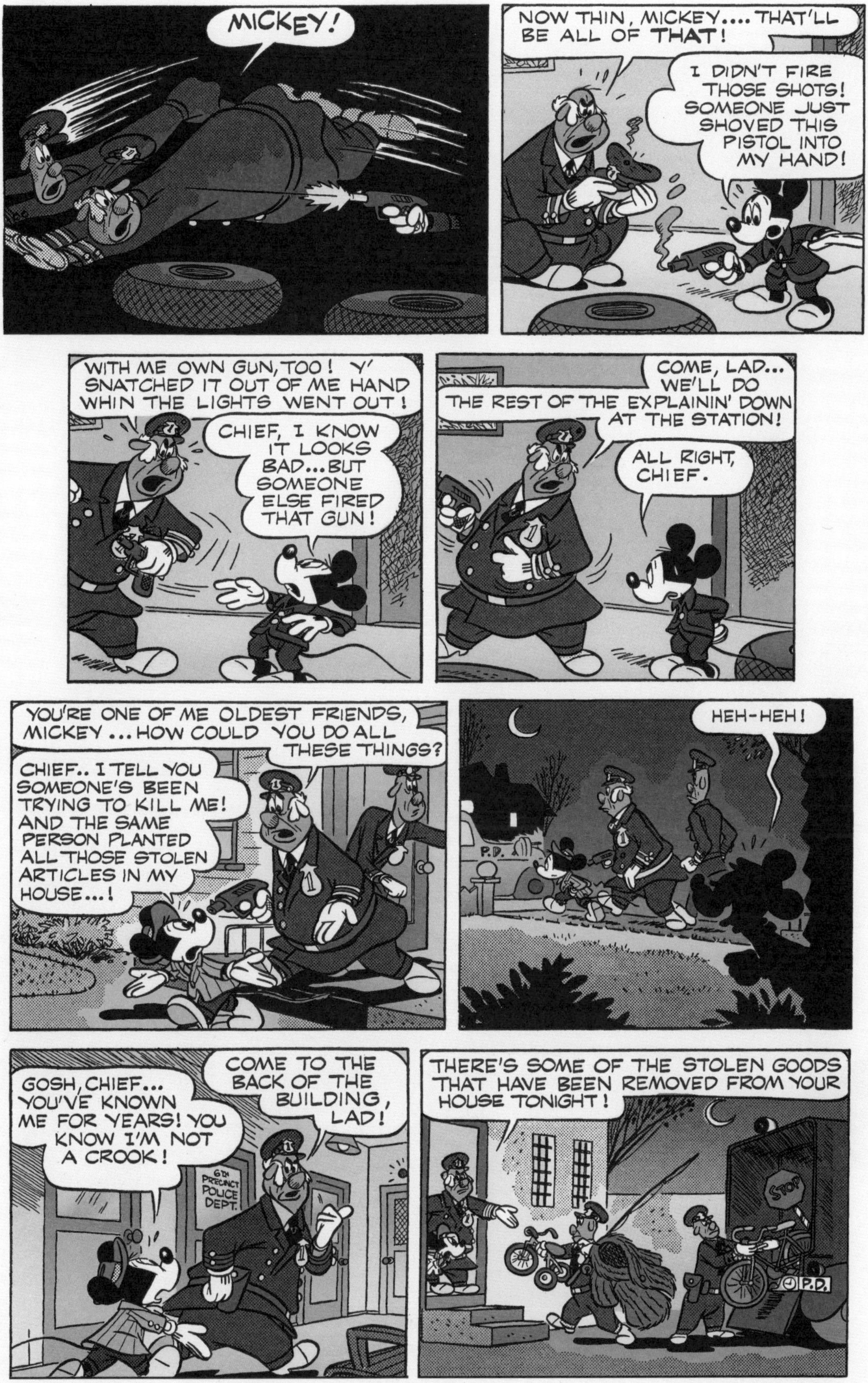
MICKEY!
NOW THIN, MICKEY.... THAT'LL BE ALL OF THAT!
I DIDN'T FIRE THOSE SHOTS! SOMEONE JUST SHOVED THIS PISTOL INTO MY HAND!
WITH ME OWN GUN, TOO! Y' SNATCHED IT OUT OF ME HAND WHIN THE LIGHTS WENT OUT!
CHIEF, I KNOW IT LOOKS BAD...BUT SOMEONE ELSE FIRED THAT GUN!
COME, LAD... WE'LL DO THE REST OF THE EXPLAININ' DOWN AT THE STATION!
ALL RIGHT, CHIEF.
YOU'RE ONE OF ME OLDEST FRIENDS, MICKEY ... HOW COULD YOU DO ALL THESE THINGS?
CHIEF.. I TELL YOU SOMEONE'S BEEN TRYING TO KILL ME! AND THE SAME PERSON PLANTED ALL THOSE STOLEN ARTICLES IN MY HOUSE...!
P.D.
HEH-HEH!
GOSH, CHIEF... YOU'VE KNOWN ME FOR YEARS! YOU KNOW I'M NOT A CROOK!
COME TO THE BACK OF THE BUILDING, LAD!
6TH PRECINCT POLICE DEPT.
THERE'S SOME OF THE STOLEN GOODS THAT HAVE BEEN REMOVED FROM YOUR HOUSE TONIGHT!
STOP
P.D.

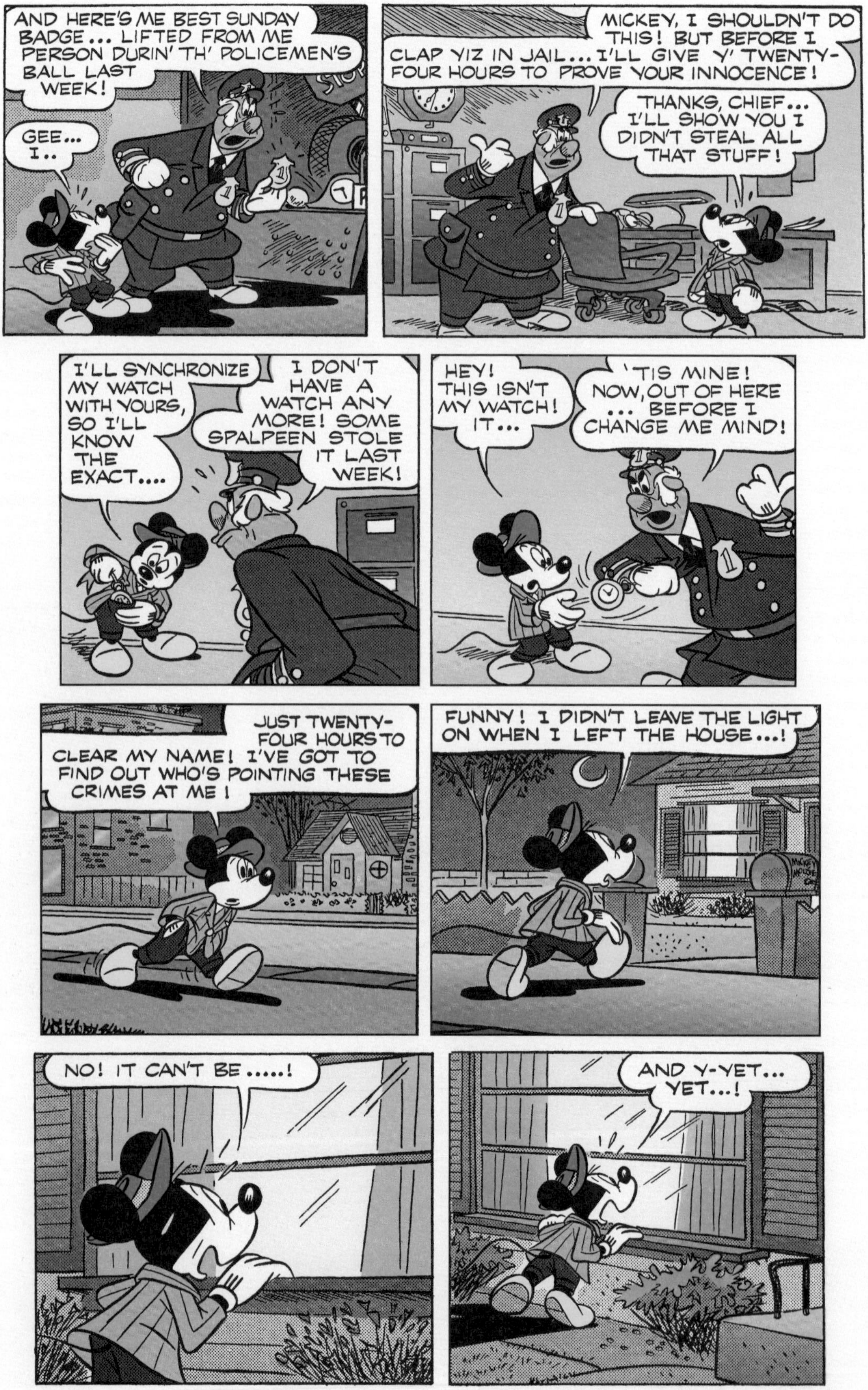
AND HERE'S ME BEST SUNDAY BADGE... LIFTED FROM ME PERSON DURIN' TH' POLICEMEN'S BALL LAST WEEK!
GEE... I..
MICKEY, I SHOULDN'T DO THIS! BUT BEFORE I CLAP YIZ IN JAIL... I'LL GIVE Y' TWENTY-FOUR HOURS TO PROVE YOUR INNOCENCE!
THANKS, CHIEF... I'LL SHOW YOU I DIDN'T STEAL ALL THAT STUFF!
I'LL SYNCHRONIZE MY WATCH WITH YOURS, SO I'LL KNOW THE EXACT....
I DON'T HAVE A WATCH ANY MORE! SOME SPALPEEN STOLE IT LAST WEEK!
HEY! THIS ISN'T MY WATCH! IT...
'TIS MINE! NOW, OUT OF HERE ... BEFORE I CHANGE ME MIND!
JUST TWENTY-FOUR HOURS TO CLEAR MY NAME! I'VE GOT TO FIND OUT WHO'S POINTING THESE CRIMES AT ME!
FUNNY! I DIDN'T LEAVE THE LIGHT ON WHEN I LEFT THE HOUSE...!
NO! IT CAN'T BE .....!
AND Y-YET... YET...!

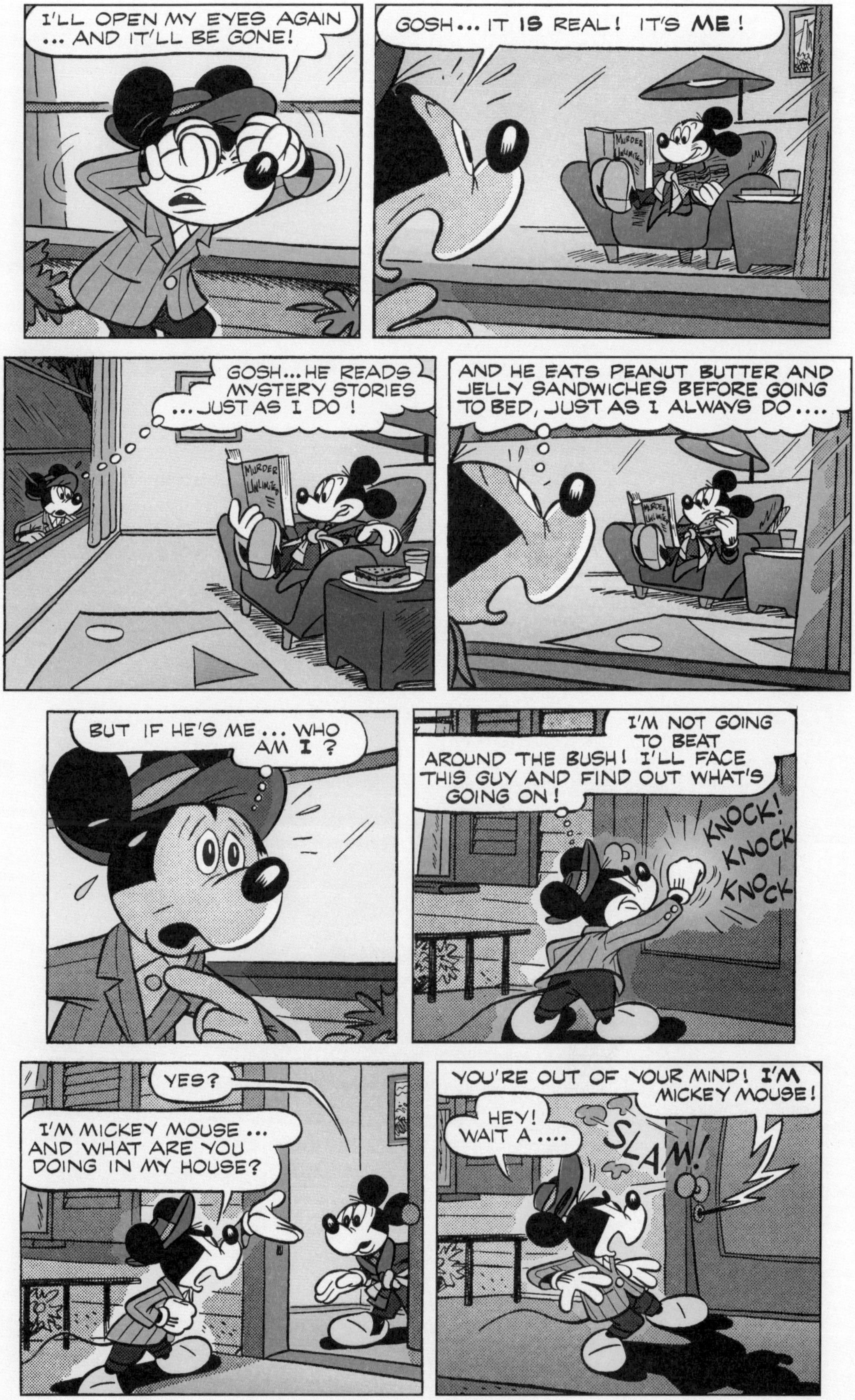
I'LL OPEN MY EYES AGAIN ... AND IT'LL BE GONE!
GOSH... IT IS REAL! IT'S ME!
MURDER UNLIMITED
GOSH... HE READS MYSTERY STORIES ... JUST AS I DO!
MURDER UNLIMITED
AND HE EATS PEANUT BUTTER AND JELLY SANDWICHES BEFORE GOING TO BED, JUST AS I ALWAYS DO....
BUT IF HE'S ME... WHO AM I?
I'M NOT GOING TO BEAT AROUND THE BUSH! I'LL FACE THIS GUY AND FIND OUT WHAT'S GOING ON!
KNOCK! KNOCK KNOCK
YES?
I'M MICKEY MOUSE ... AND WHAT ARE YOU DOING IN MY HOUSE?
YOU'RE OUT OF YOUR MIND! I'M MICKEY MOUSE!
HEY! WAIT A....
SLAM!

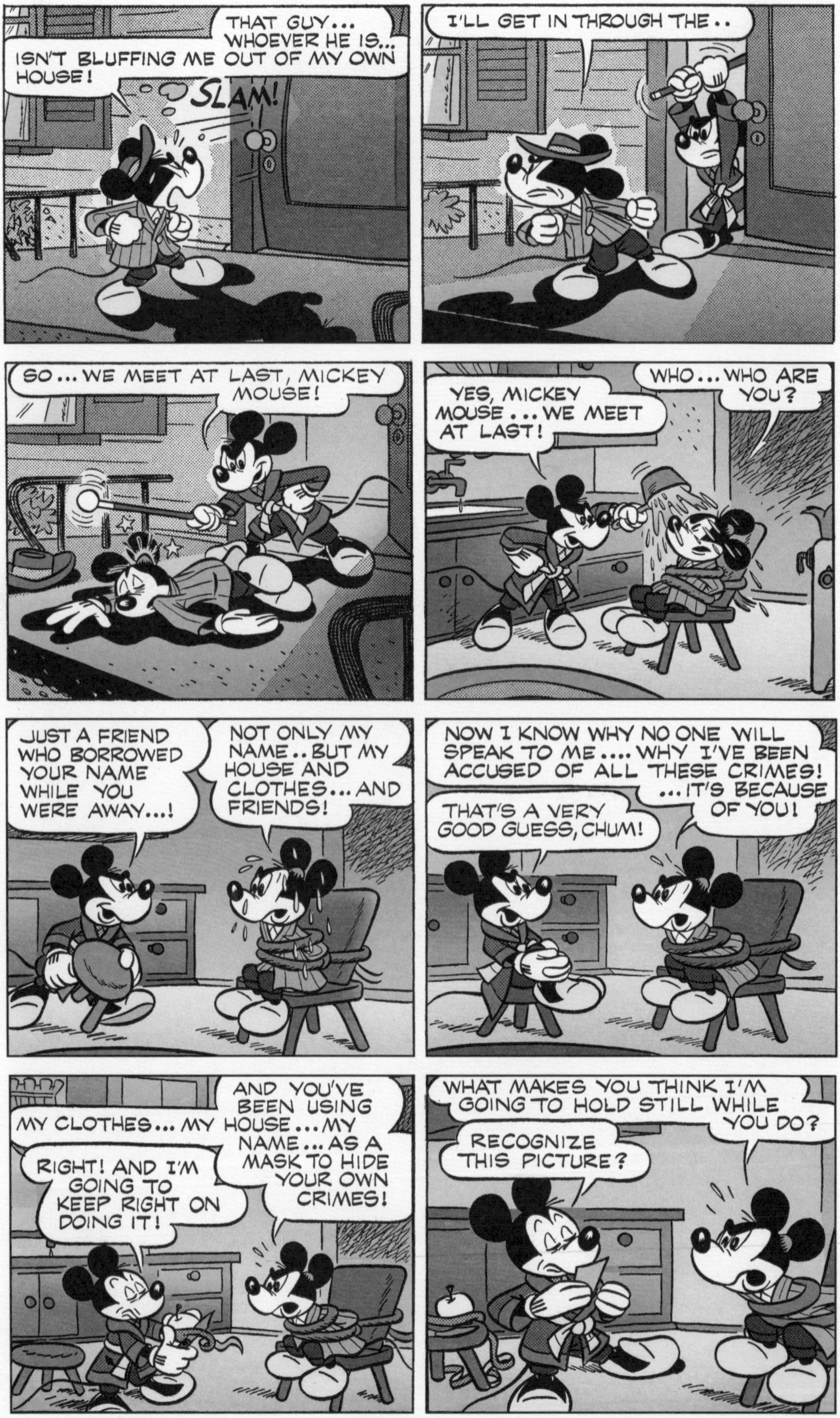
THAT GUY... WHOEVER HE IS... ISN'T BLUFFING ME OUT OF MY OWN HOUSE!
SLAM!
I'LL GET IN THROUGH THE..
SO... WE MEET AT LAST, MICKEY MOUSE!
YES, MICKEY MOUSE... WE MEET AT LAST!
WHO... WHO ARE YOU?
JUST A FRIEND WHO BORROWED YOUR NAME WHILE YOU WERE AWAY...!
NOT ONLY MY NAME.. BUT MY HOUSE AND CLOTHES... AND FRIENDS!
NOW I KNOW WHY NO ONE WILL SPEAK TO ME.... WHY I'VE BEEN ACCUSED OF ALL THESE CRIMES! ...IT'S BECAUSE OF YOU!
THAT'S A VERY GOOD GUESS, CHUM!
AND YOU'VE BEEN USING MY CLOTHES... MY HOUSE... MY NAME... AS A MASK TO HIDE YOUR OWN CRIMES!
RIGHT! AND I'M GOING TO KEEP RIGHT ON DOING IT!
WHAT MAKES YOU THINK I'M GOING TO HOLD STILL WHILE YOU DO?
RECOGNIZE THIS PICTURE?

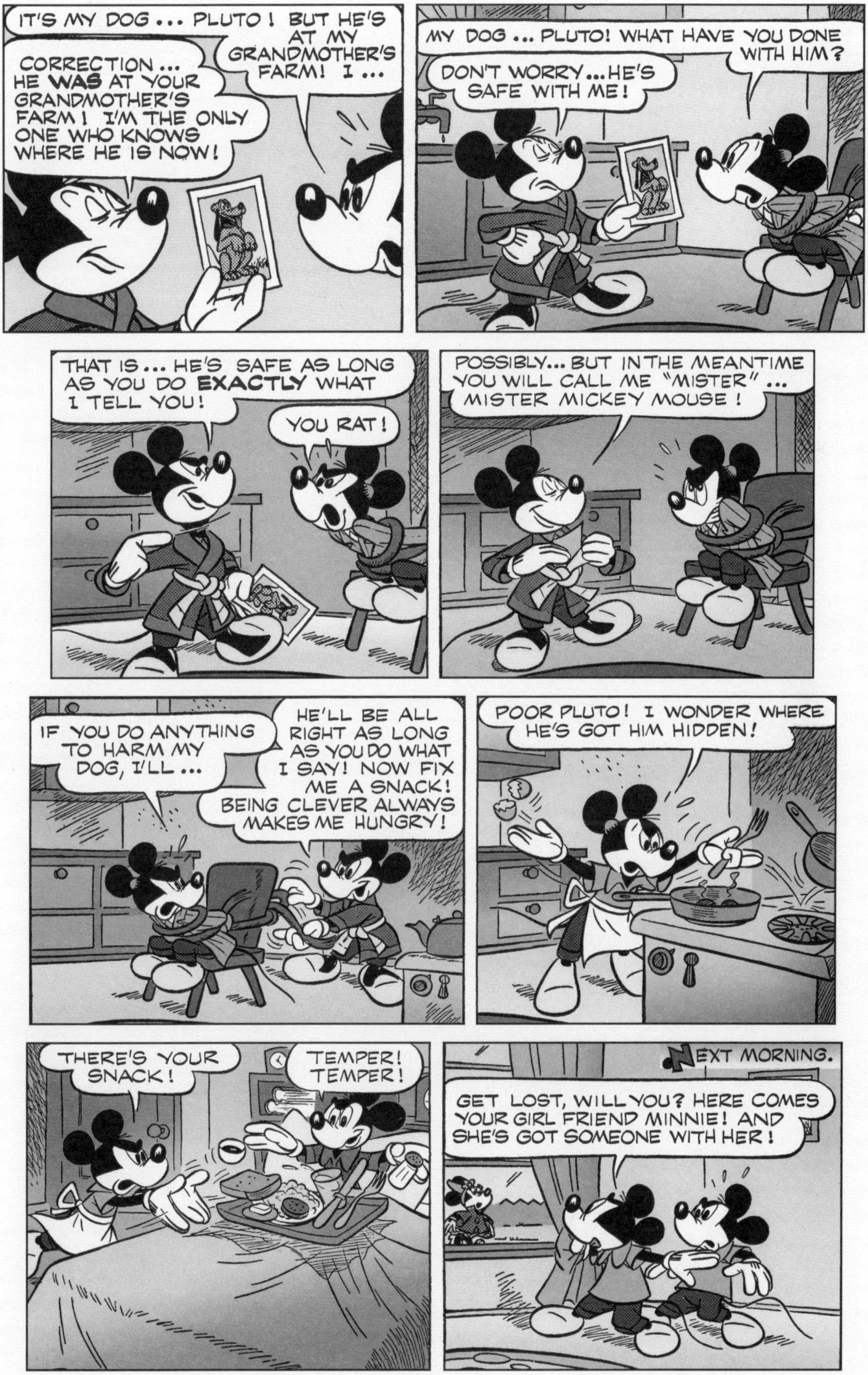
IT'S MY DOG ... PLUTO! BUT HE'S AT MY GRANDMOTHER'S FARM! I ...
CORRECTION ... HE WAS AT YOUR GRANDMOTHER'S FARM! I'M THE ONLY ONE WHO KNOWS WHERE HE IS NOW!
MY DOG ... PLUTO! WHAT HAVE YOU DONE WITH HIM?
DON'T WORRY ... HE'S SAFE WITH ME!
THAT IS ... HE'S SAFE AS LONG AS YOU DO EXACTLY WHAT I TELL YOU!
YOU RAT!
POSSIBLY... BUT IN THE MEANTIME YOU WILL CALL ME "MISTER" ... MISTER MICKEY MOUSE!
IF YOU DO ANYTHING TO HARM MY DOG, I'LL ...
HE'LL BE ALL RIGHT AS LONG AS YOU DO WHAT I SAY! NOW FIX ME A SNACK! BEING CLEVER ALWAYS MAKES ME HUNGRY!
POOR PLUTO! I WONDER WHERE HE'S GOT HIM HIDDEN!
THERE'S YOUR SNACK!
TEMPER! TEMPER!
NEXT MORNING.
GET LOST, WILL YOU? HERE COMES YOUR GIRL FRIEND MINNIE! AND SHE'S GOT SOMEONE WITH HER!

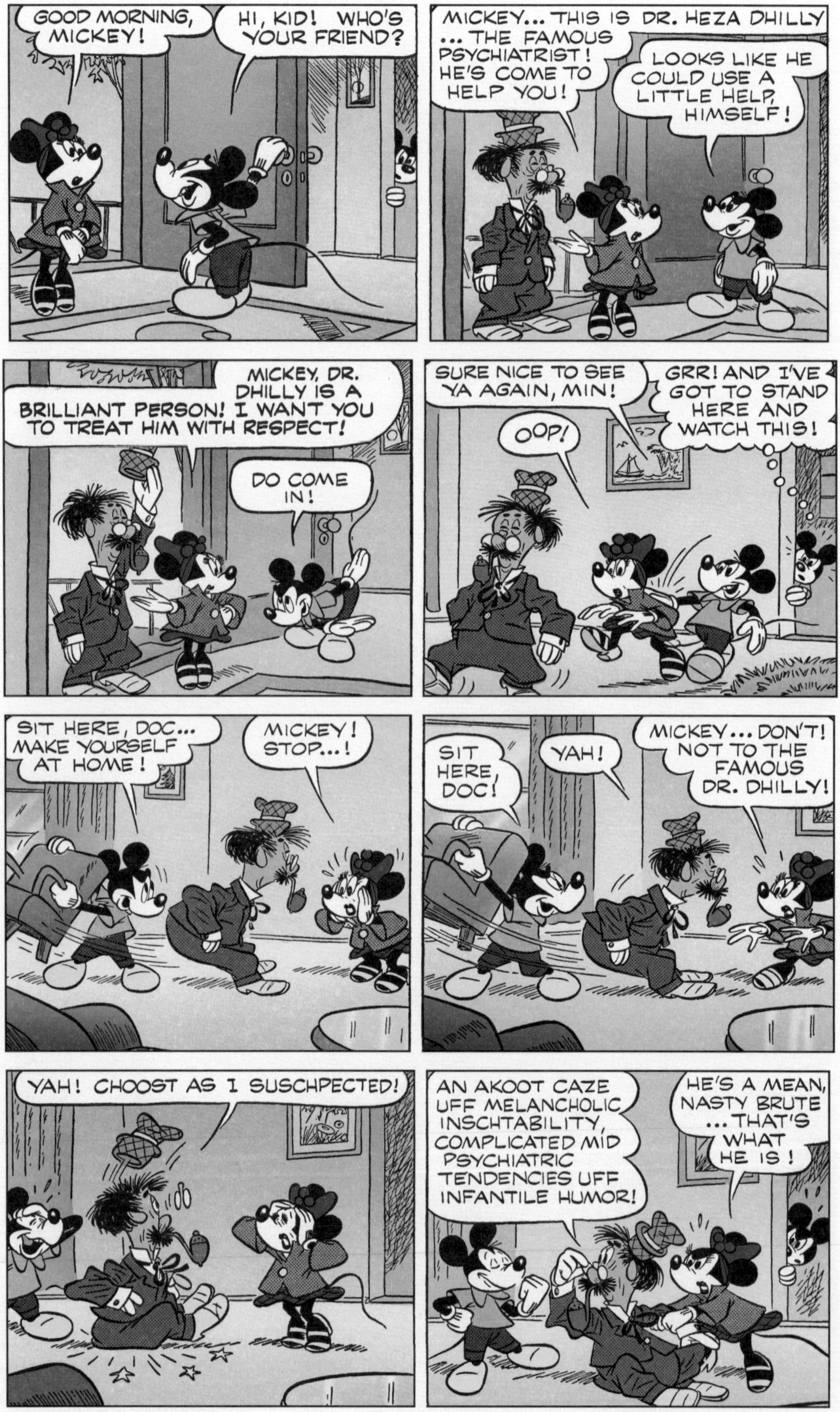
GOOD MORNING, MICKEY!
HI, KID! WHO'S YOUR FRIEND?
MICKEY... THIS IS DR. HEZA DHILLY ... THE FAMOUS PSYCHIATRIST! HE'S COME TO HELP YOU!
LOOKS LIKE HE COULD USE A LITTLE HELP, HIMSELF!
MICKEY, DR. DHILLY IS A BRILLIANT PERSON! I WANT YOU TO TREAT HIM WITH RESPECT!
DO COME IN!
SURE NICE TO SEE YA AGAIN, MIN!
OOP!
GRR! AND I'VE GOT TO STAND HERE AND WATCH THIS!
SIT HERE, DOC... MAKE YOURSELF AT HOME!
MICKEY! STOP...!
SIT HERE, DOC!
YAH!
MICKEY... DON'T! NOT TO THE FAMOUS DR. DHILLY!
YAH! CHOOST AS I SUSCHPECTED!
AN AKOOT CAZE UFF MELANCHOLIC INSCHTABILITY, COMPLICATED MID PSYCHIATRIC TENDENCIES UFF INFANTILE HUMOR!
HE'S A MEAN, NASTY BRUTE ...THAT'S WHAT HE IS!

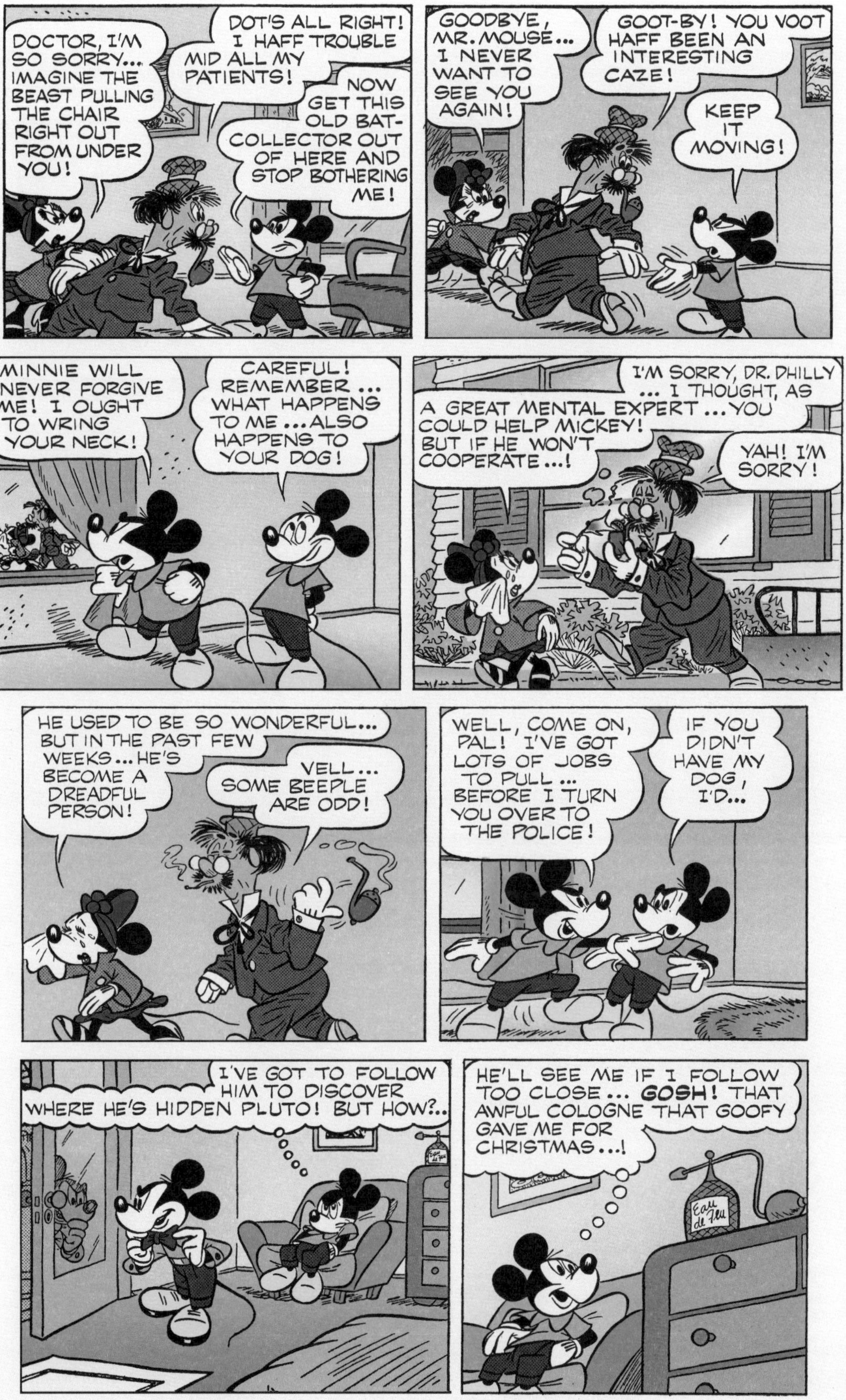
DOCTOR, I'M SO SORRY... IMAGINE THE BEAST PULLING THE CHAIR RIGHT OUT FROM UNDER YOU!
DOT'S ALL RIGHT! I HAFF TROUBLE MID ALL MY PATIENTS!
NOW GET THIS OLD BAT-COLLECTOR OUT OF HERE AND STOP BOTHERING ME!
GOODBYE, MR. MOUSE... I NEVER WANT TO SEE YOU AGAIN!
GOOT-BY! YOU VOOT HAFF BEEN AN INTERESTING CAZE!
KEEP IT MOVING!
MINNIE WILL NEVER FORGIVE ME! I OUGHT TO WRING YOUR NECK!
CAREFUL! REMEMBER... WHAT HAPPENS TO ME... ALSO HAPPENS TO YOUR DOG!
I'M SORRY, DR. DHILLY ... I THOUGHT, AS A GREAT MENTAL EXPERT... YOU COULD HELP MICKEY! BUT IF HE WON'T COOPERATE...!
YAH! I'M SORRY!
HE USED TO BE SO WONDERFUL... BUT IN THE PAST FEW WEEKS... HE'S BECOME A DREADFUL PERSON!
VELL... SOME BEEPLE ARE ODD!
WELL, COME ON, PAL! I'VE GOT LOTS OF JOBS TO PULL... BEFORE I TURN YOU OVER TO THE POLICE!
IF YOU DIDN'T HAVE MY DOG, I'D...!
I'VE GOT TO FOLLOW HIM TO DISCOVER WHERE HE'S HIDDEN PLUTO! BUT HOW?..
HE'LL SEE ME IF I FOLLOW TOO CLOSE... GOSH! THAT AWFUL COLOGNE THAT GOOFY GAVE ME FOR CHRISTMAS...!
Eau de Feu

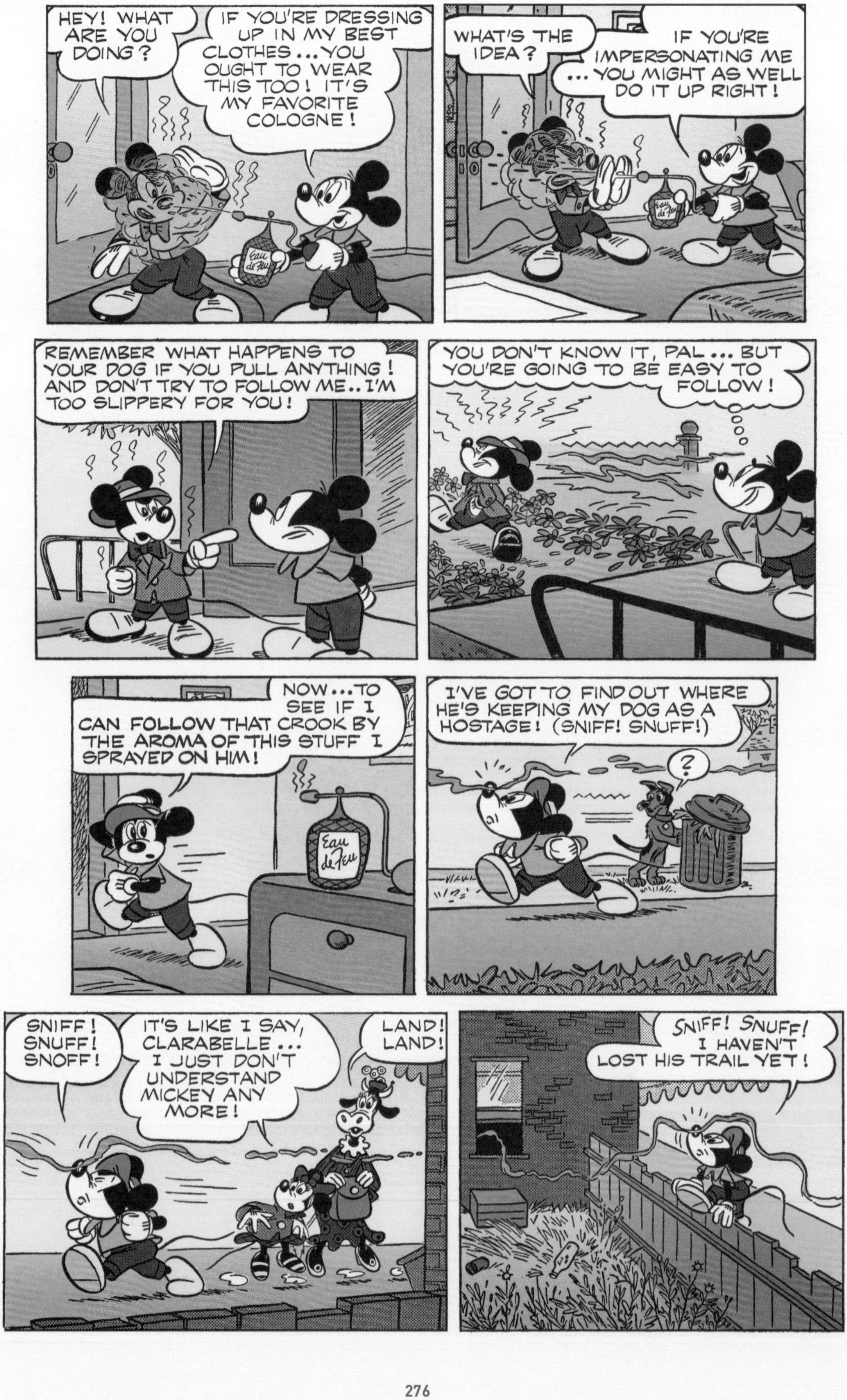
HEY! WHAT ARE YOU DOING?
IF YOU'RE DRESSING UP IN MY BEST CLOTHES ... YOU OUGHT TO WEAR THIS TOO! IT'S MY FAVORITE COLOGNE!
Eau de Feu
WHAT'S THE IDEA?
IF YOU'RE IMPERSONATING ME ... YOU MIGHT AS WELL DO IT UP RIGHT!
Eau de Feu
REMEMBER WHAT HAPPENS TO YOUR DOG IF YOU PULL ANYTHING! AND DON'T TRY TO FOLLOW ME.. I'M TOO SLIPPERY FOR YOU!
YOU DON'T KNOW IT, PAL ... BUT YOU'RE GOING TO BE EASY TO FOLLOW!
NOW ... TO SEE IF I CAN FOLLOW THAT CROOK BY THE AROMA OF THIS STUFF I SPRAYED ON HIM!
Eau de Feu
I'VE GOT TO FIND OUT WHERE HE'S KEEPING MY DOG AS A HOSTAGE! (SNIFF! SNUFF!)
?
SNIFF! SNUFF! SNOFF!
IT'S LIKE I SAY, CLARABELLE ... I JUST DON'T UNDERSTAND MICKEY ANY MORE!
LAND! LAND!
SNIFF! SNUFF! I HAVEN'T LOST HIS TRAIL YET!

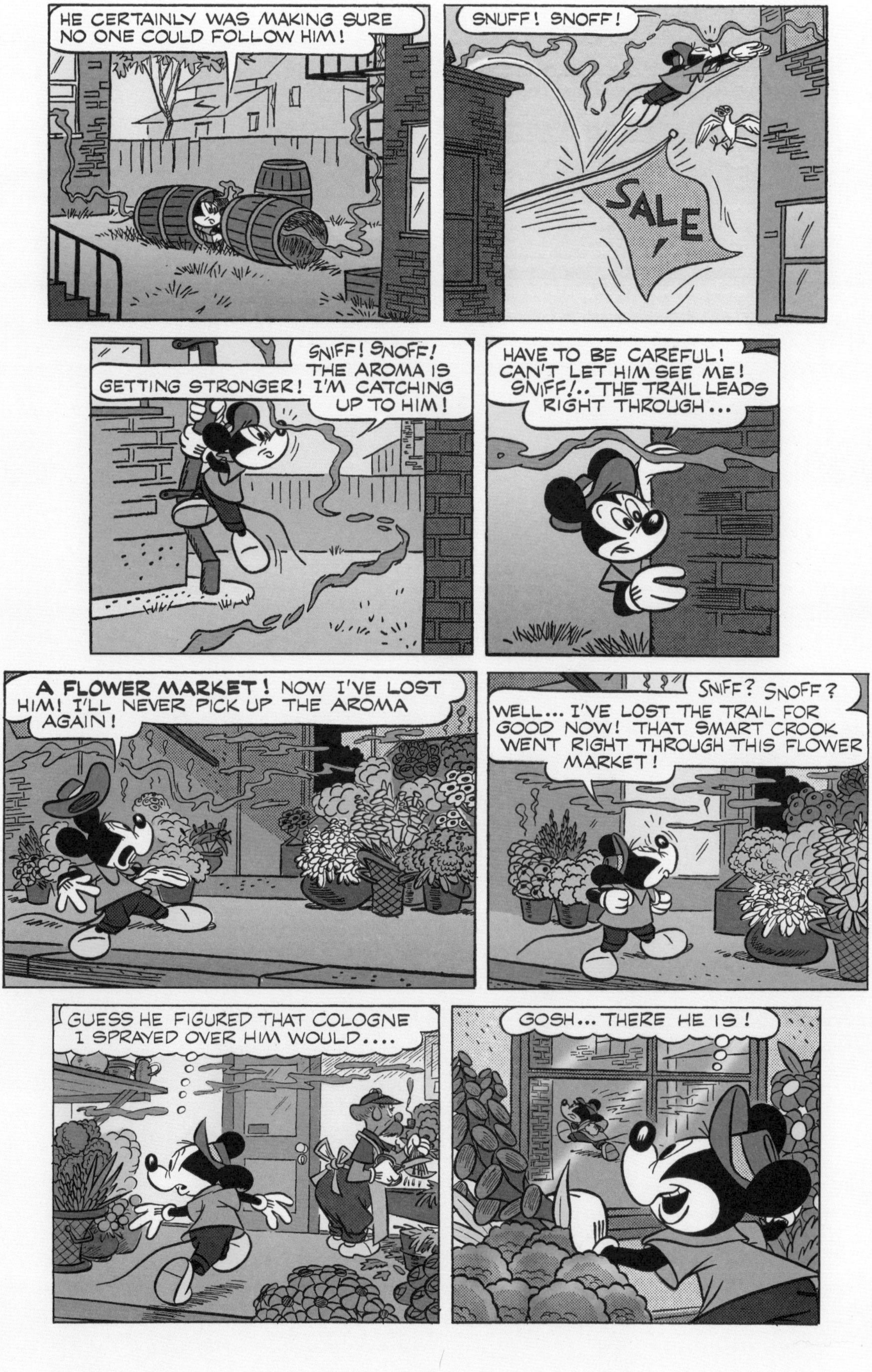
HE CERTAINLY WAS MAKING SURE NO ONE COULD FOLLOW HIM!
SNUFF! SNOFF!
SALE
SNIFF! SNOFF! THE AROMA IS GETTING STRONGER! I'M CATCHING UP TO HIM!
HAVE TO BE CAREFUL! CAN'T LET HIM SEE ME! SNIFF!.. THE TRAIL LEADS RIGHT THROUGH...
A FLOWER MARKET! NOW I'VE LOST HIM! I'LL NEVER PICK UP THE AROMA AGAIN!
SNIFF? SNOFF?
WELL... I'VE LOST THE TRAIL FOR GOOD NOW! THAT SMART CROOK WENT RIGHT THROUGH THIS FLOWER MARKET!
GUESS HE FIGURED THAT COLOGNE I SPRAYED OVER HIM WOULD....
GOSH... THERE HE IS!

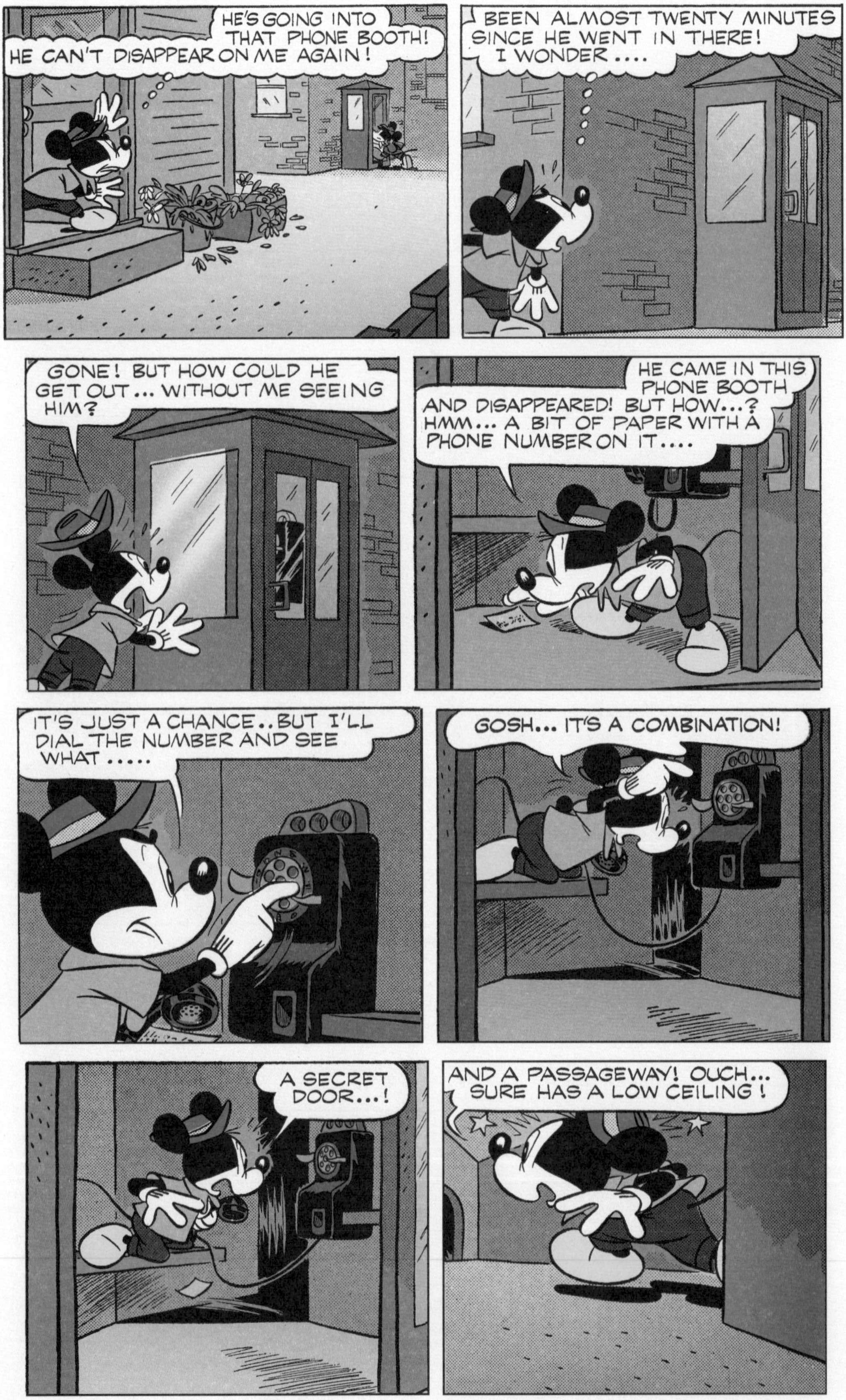
HE'S GOING INTO THAT PHONE BOOTH! HE CAN'T DISAPPEAR ON ME AGAIN!
BEEN ALMOST TWENTY MINUTES SINCE HE WENT IN THERE! I WONDER....
GONE! BUT HOW COULD HE GET OUT... WITHOUT ME SEEING HIM?
HE CAME IN THIS PHONE BOOTH AND DISAPPEARED! BUT HOW...? HMM... A BIT OF PAPER WITH A PHONE NUMBER ON IT....
IT'S JUST A CHANCE..BUT I'LL DIAL THE NUMBER AND SEE WHAT.....
GOSH... IT'S A COMBINATION!
A SECRET DOOR...!
AND A PASSAGEWAY! OUCH... SURE HAS A LOW CEILING!

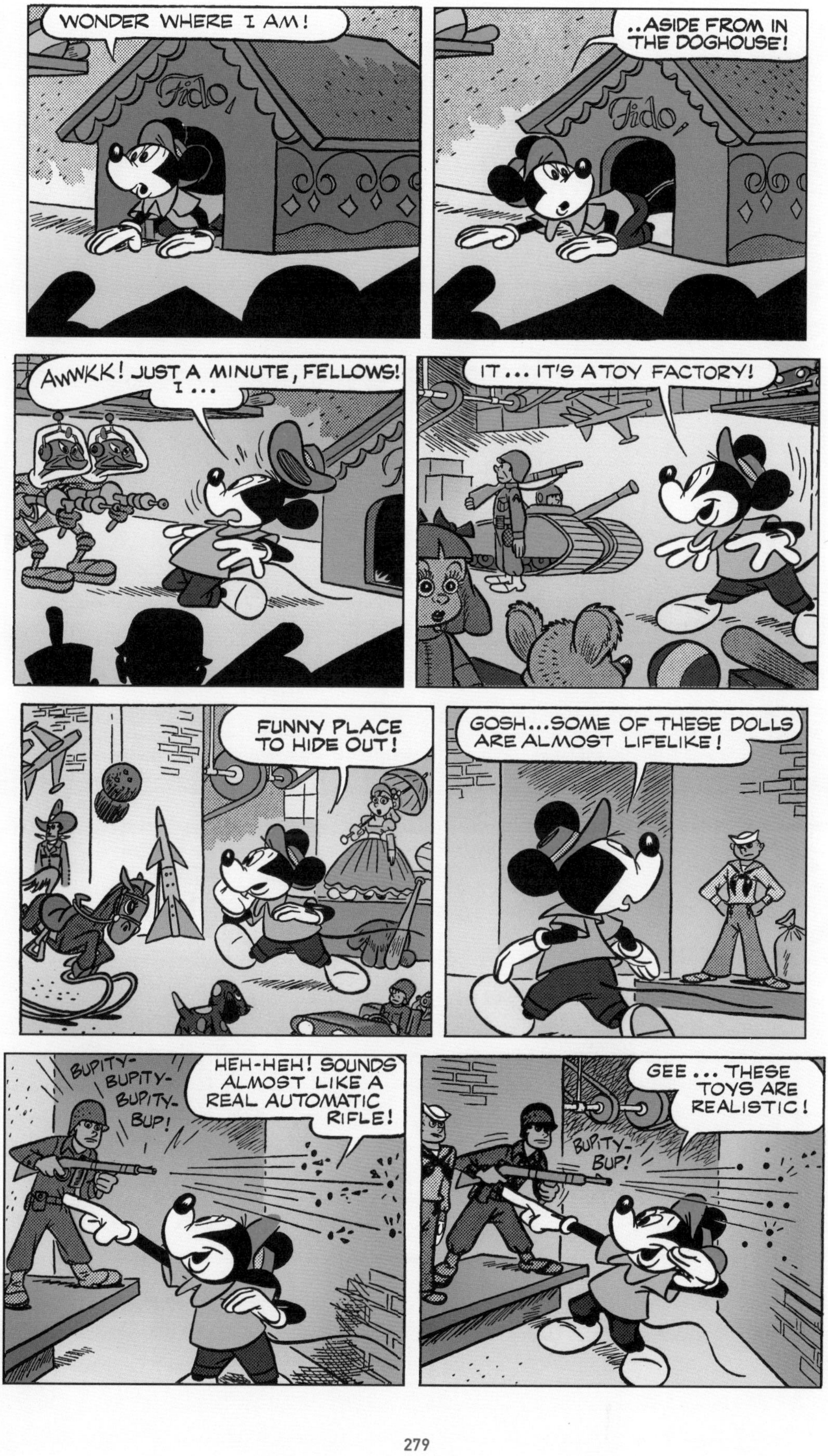
WONDER WHERE I AM!
Fido
..ASIDE FROM IN THE DOGHOUSE!
Fido
AWWKK! JUST A MINUTE, FELLOWS! I ...
IT ... IT'S A TOY FACTORY!
FUNNY PLACE TO HIDE OUT!
GOSH...SOME OF THESE DOLLS ARE ALMOST LIFELIKE!
BUPITY-BUPITY-BUPITY-BUP!
HEH-HEH! SOUNDS ALMOST LIKE A REAL AUTOMATIC RIFLE!
BUPITY-BUP!
GEE ... THESE TOYS ARE REALISTIC!

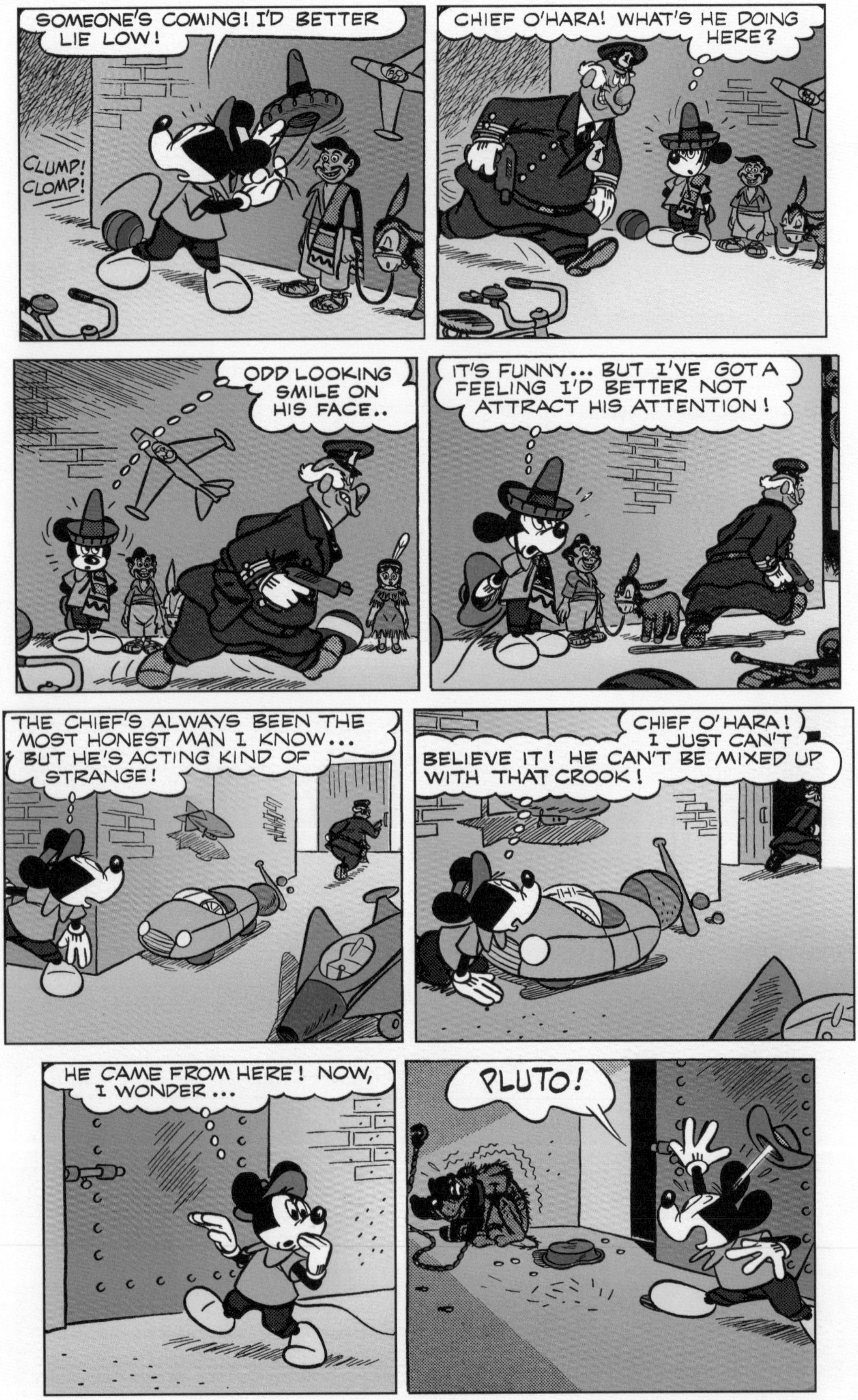
SOMEONE'S COMING! I'D BETTER LIE LOW!
CLUMP! CLOMP!
CHIEF O'HARA! WHAT'S HE DOING HERE?
ODD LOOKING SMILE ON HIS FACE..
IT'S FUNNY... BUT I'VE GOT A FEELING I'D BETTER NOT ATTRACT HIS ATTENTION!
THE CHIEF'S ALWAYS BEEN THE MOST HONEST MAN I KNOW... BUT HE'S ACTING KIND OF STRANGE!
CHIEF O'HARA! I JUST CAN'T BELIEVE IT! HE CAN'T BE MIXED UP WITH THAT CROOK!
HE CAME FROM HERE! NOW, I WONDER...
PLUTO!

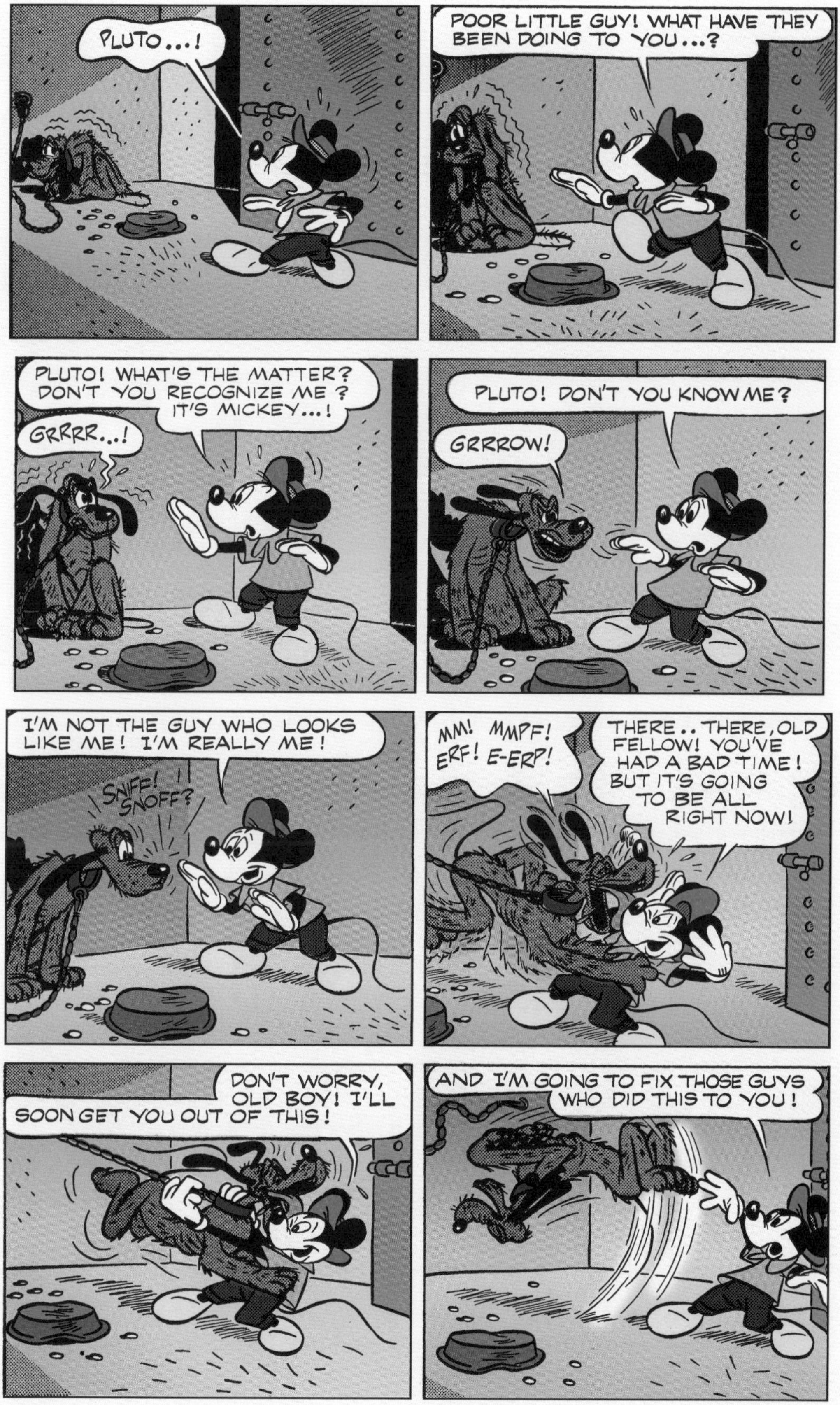
PLUTO...!
POOR LITTLE GUY! WHAT HAVE THEY BEEN DOING TO YOU...?
PLUTO! WHAT'S THE MATTER? DON'T YOU RECOGNIZE ME? IT'S MICKEY...!
GRRRR...!
PLUTO! DON'T YOU KNOW ME?
GRRROW!
I'M NOT THE GUY WHO LOOKS LIKE ME! I'M REALLY ME!
SNIFF! SNOFF?
MM! MMPF! ERF! E-ERP!
THERE.. THERE, OLD FELLOW! YOU'VE HAD A BAD TIME! BUT IT'S GOING TO BE ALL RIGHT NOW!
DON'T WORRY, OLD BOY! I'LL SOON GET YOU OUT OF THIS!
AND I'M GOING TO FIX THOSE GUYS WHO DID THIS TO YOU!

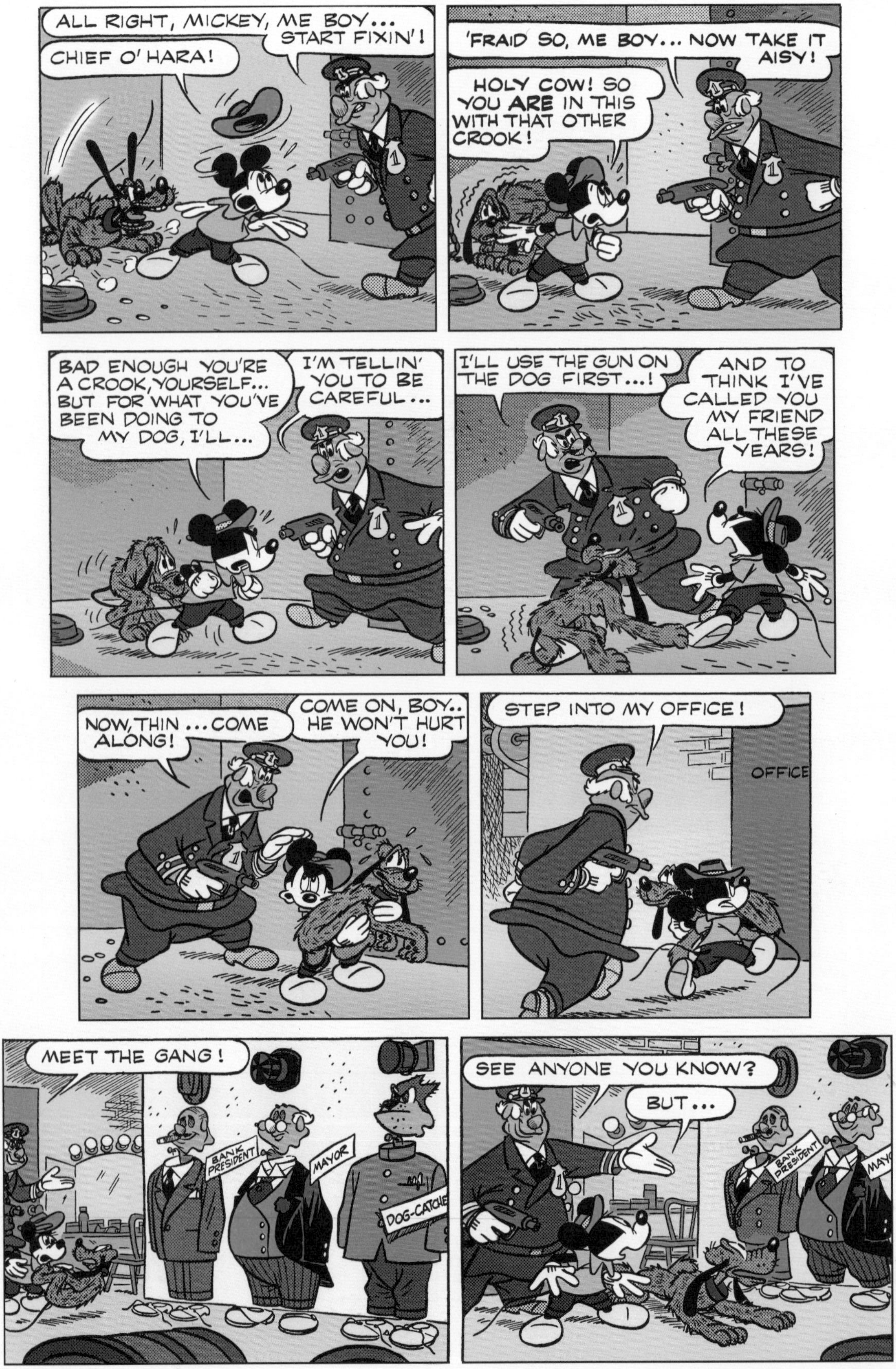
ALL RIGHT, MICKEY, ME BOY... START FIXIN'!
CHIEF O' HARA!
'FRAID SO, ME BOY... NOW TAKE IT AISY!
HOLY COW! SO YOU **ARE** IN THIS WITH THAT OTHER CROOK!
BAD ENOUGH YOU'RE A CROOK, YOURSELF... BUT FOR WHAT YOU'VE BEEN DOING TO MY DOG, I'LL...
I'M TELLIN' YOU TO BE CAREFUL...
I'LL USE THE GUN ON THE DOG FIRST...!
AND TO THINK I'VE CALLED YOU MY FRIEND ALL THESE YEARS!
NOW, THIN ... COME ALONG!
COME ON, BOY.. HE WON'T HURT YOU!
STEP INTO MY OFFICE!
OFFICE
MEET THE GANG!
BANK PRESIDENT
MAYOR
DOG-CATCHE
SEE ANYONE YOU KNOW?
BUT...
BANK PRESIDENT
MAYO

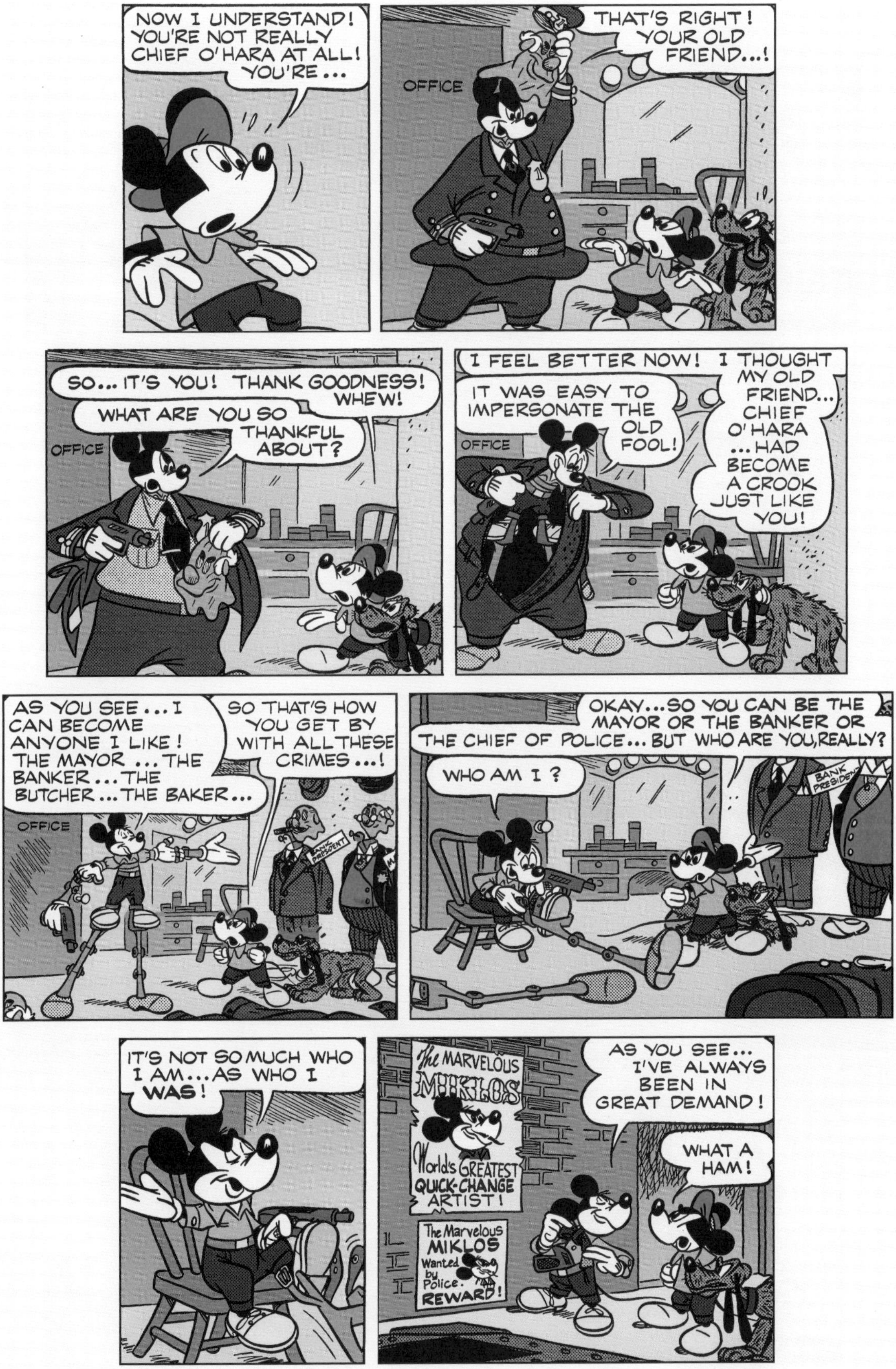
NOW I UNDERSTAND! YOU'RE NOT REALLY CHIEF O'HARA AT ALL! YOU'RE...
THAT'S RIGHT! YOUR OLD FRIEND...!
OFFICE
SO... IT'S YOU! THANK GOODNESS! WHEW!
WHAT ARE YOU SO THANKFUL ABOUT?
OFFICE
I FEEL BETTER NOW! I THOUGHT MY OLD FRIEND... CHIEF O'HARA ...HAD BECOME A CROOK JUST LIKE YOU!
IT WAS EASY TO IMPERSONATE THE OLD FOOL!
OFFICE
AS YOU SEE... I CAN BECOME ANYONE I LIKE! THE MAYOR ... THE BANKER... THE BUTCHER... THE BAKER...
SO THAT'S HOW YOU GET BY WITH ALL THESE CRIMES...!
OFFICE
BANK PRESIDENT
OKAY... SO YOU CAN BE THE MAYOR OR THE BANKER OR THE CHIEF OF POLICE... BUT WHO ARE YOU, REALLY?
WHO AM I?
BANK PRESIDENT
IT'S NOT SO MUCH WHO I AM... AS WHO I WAS!
The MARVELOUS MIKLOS World's GREATEST QUICK-CHANGE ARTIST!
The Marvelous MIKLOS Wanted by Police. REWARD!
AS YOU SEE... I'VE ALWAYS BEEN IN GREAT DEMAND!
WHAT A HAM!

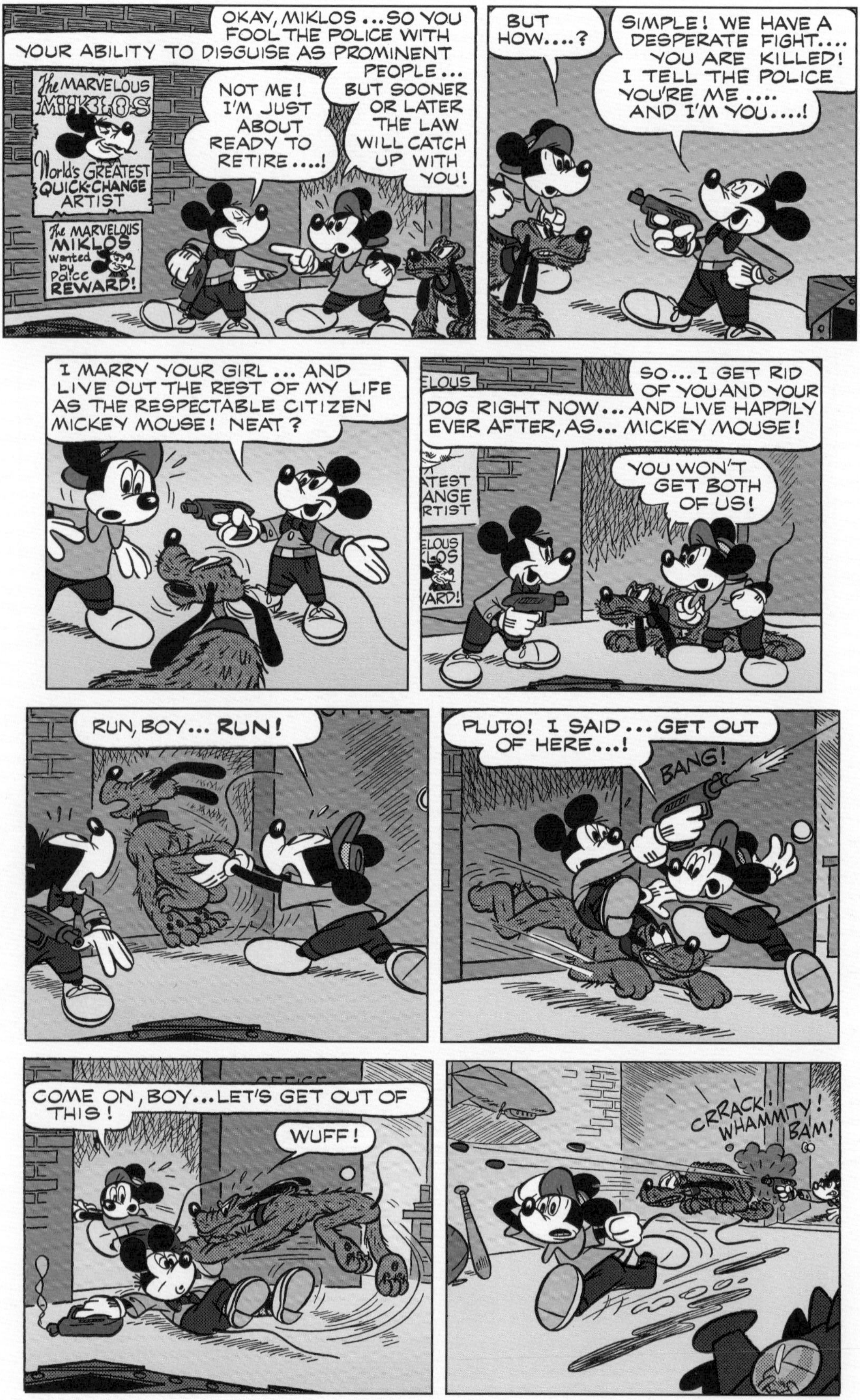
OKAY, MIKLOS ...SO YOU FOOL THE POLICE WITH YOUR ABILITY TO DISGUISE AS PROMINENT PEOPLE...
The MARVELOUS MIKLOS World's GREATEST QUICK-CHANGE ARTIST
The MARVELOUS MIKLOS Wanted by Police REWARD!
NOT ME! I'M JUST ABOUT READY TO RETIRE....!
BUT SOONER OR LATER THE LAW WILL CATCH UP WITH YOU!
BUT HOW....?
SIMPLE! WE HAVE A DESPERATE FIGHT.... YOU ARE KILLED! I TELL THE POLICE YOU'RE ME .... AND I'M YOU....!
I MARRY YOUR GIRL ... AND LIVE OUT THE REST OF MY LIFE AS THE RESPECTABLE CITIZEN MICKEY MOUSE! NEAT?
SO... I GET RID OF YOU AND YOUR DOG RIGHT NOW... AND LIVE HAPPILY EVER AFTER, AS... MICKEY MOUSE!
YOU WON'T GET BOTH OF US!
RUN, BOY... RUN!
PLUTO! I SAID... GET OUT OF HERE...!
BANG!
COME ON, BOY...LET'S GET OUT OF THIS!
WUFF!
CRRACK! WHAMMITY! BAM!

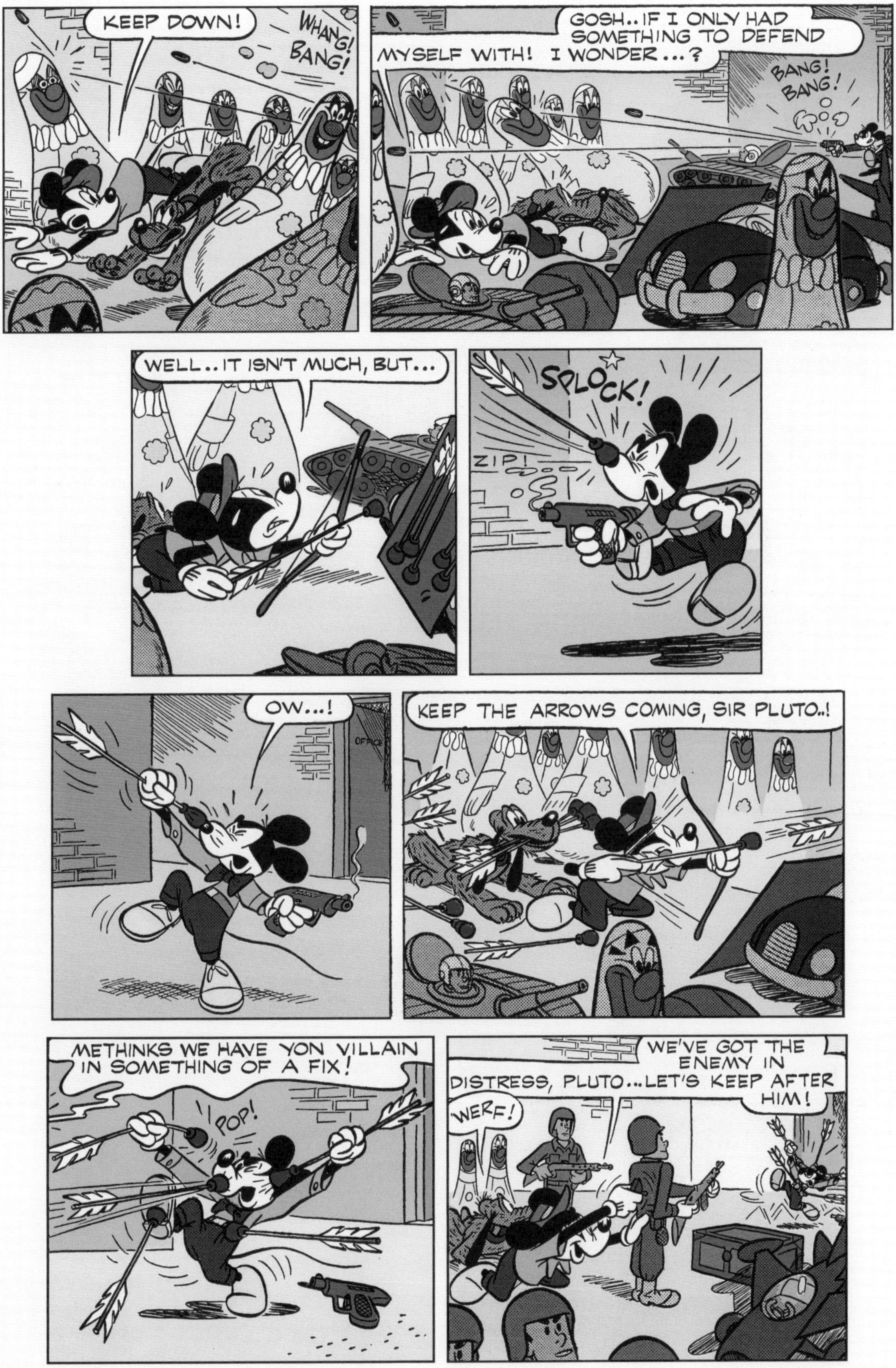
KEEP DOWN!
WHANG! BANG!
GOSH.. IF I ONLY HAD SOMETHING TO DEFEND MYSELF WITH! I WONDER...?
BANG! BANG!
WELL.. IT ISN'T MUCH, BUT...
SPLOCK!
ZIP!
OW...!
KEEP THE ARROWS COMING, SIR PLUTO..!
METHINKS WE HAVE YON VILLAIN IN SOMETHING OF A FIX!
POP!
WE'VE GOT THE ENEMY IN DISTRESS, PLUTO... LET'S KEEP AFTER HIM!
WERF!

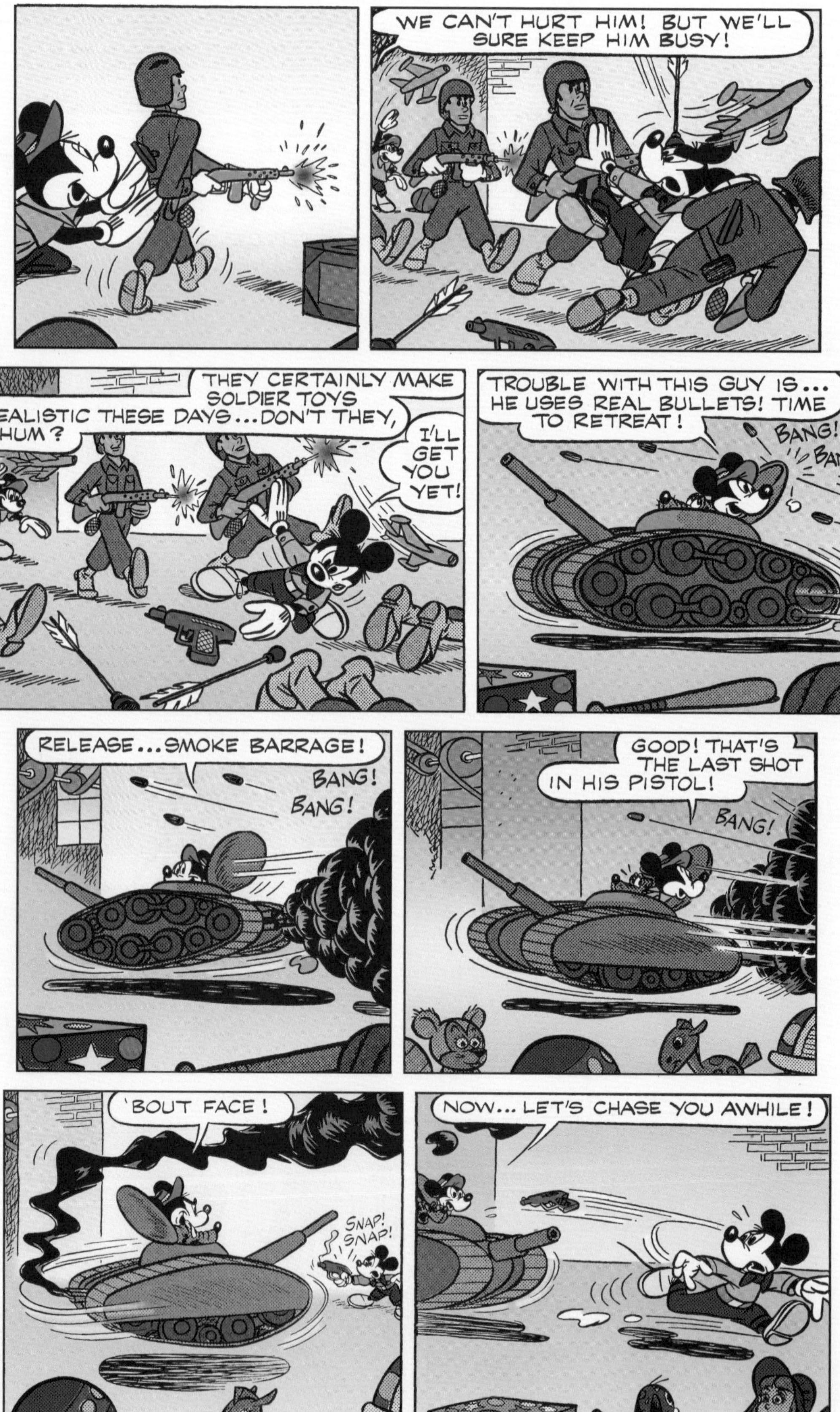
WE CAN'T HURT HIM! BUT WE'LL SURE KEEP HIM BUSY!
THEY CERTAINLY MAKE SOLDIER TOYS REALISTIC THESE DAYS...DON'T THEY, CHUM?
I'LL GET YOU YET!
TROUBLE WITH THIS GUY IS... HE USES REAL BULLETS! TIME TO RETREAT!
BANG!
BANG
RELEASE...SMOKE BARRAGE!
BANG!
BANG!
GOOD! THAT'S THE LAST SHOT IN HIS PISTOL!
BANG!
'BOUT FACE!
SNAP! SNAP!
NOW... LET'S CHASE YOU AWHILE!

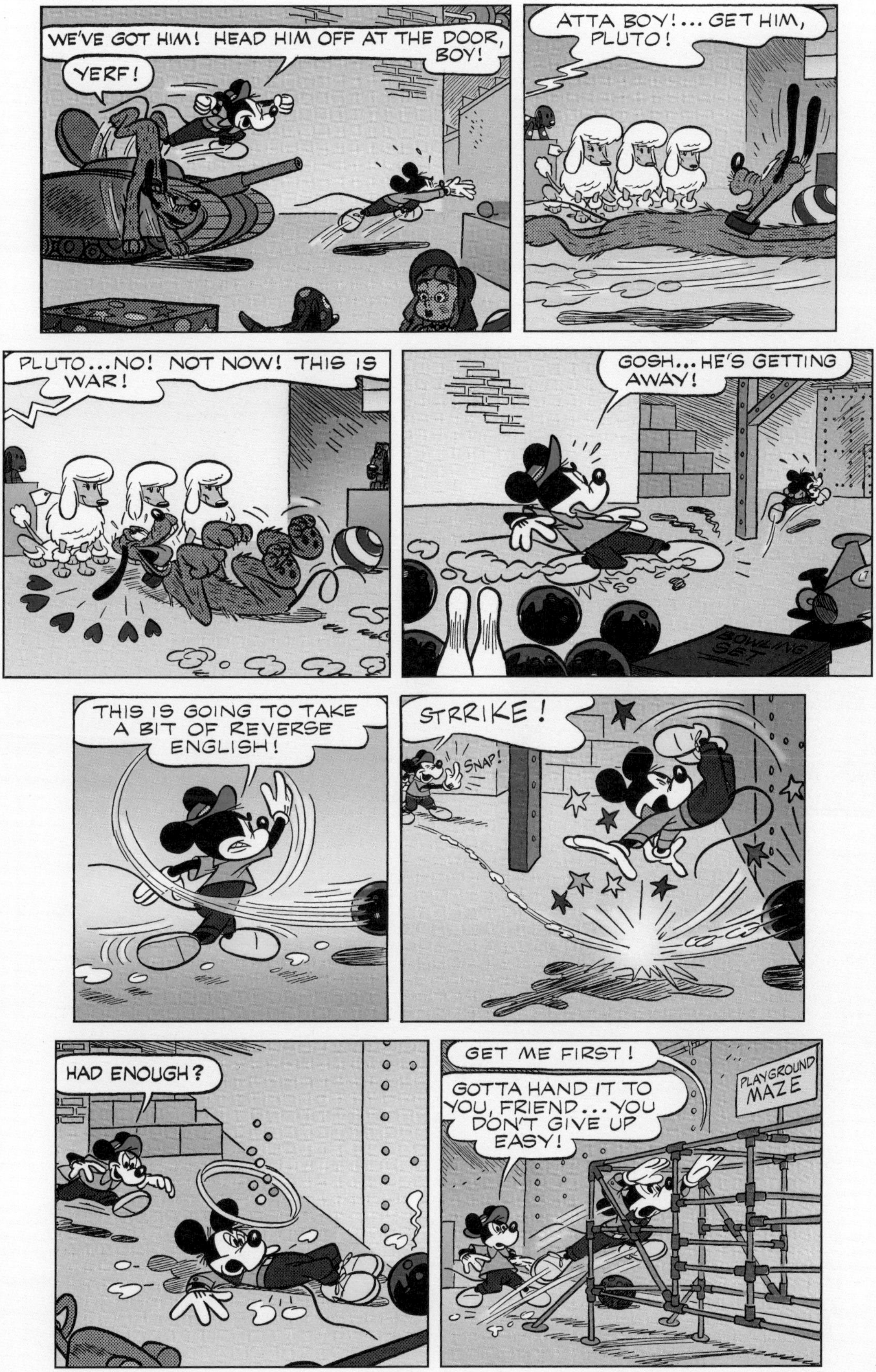
WE'VE GOT HIM! HEAD HIM OFF AT THE DOOR, BOY!
YERF!
ATTA BOY!... GET HIM, PLUTO!
PLUTO...NO! NOT NOW! THIS IS WAR!
GOSH... HE'S GETTING AWAY!
BOWLING SET
THIS IS GOING TO TAKE A BIT OF REVERSE ENGLISH!
STRRIKE!
SNAP!
HAD ENOUGH?
GET ME FIRST!
GOTTA HAND IT TO YOU, FRIEND... YOU DON'T GIVE UP EASY!
PLAYGROUND MAZE

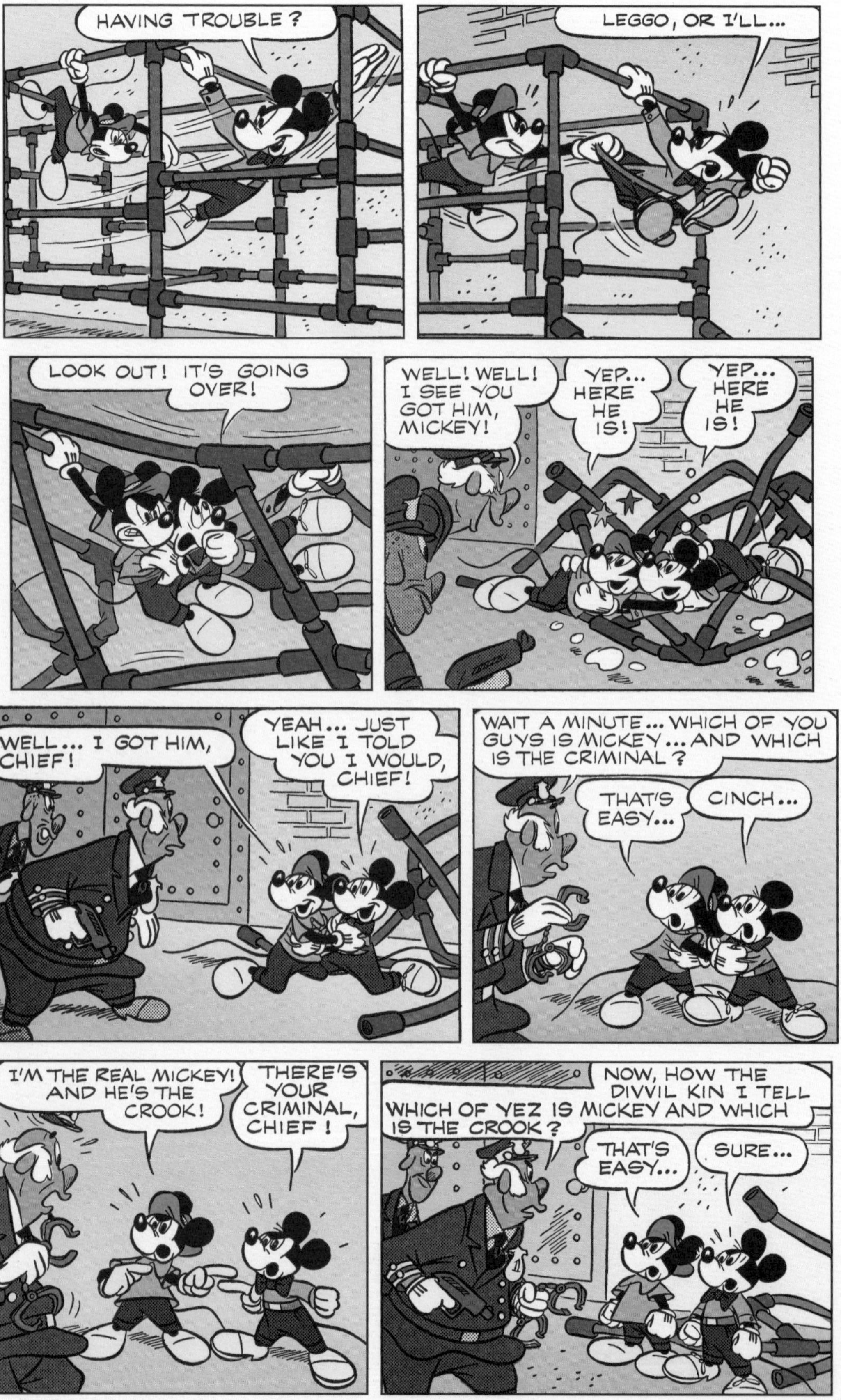
HAVING TROUBLE?
LEGGO, OR I'LL...
LOOK OUT! IT'S GOING OVER!
WELL! WELL! I SEE YOU GOT HIM, MICKEY!
YEP... HERE HE IS!
YEP... HERE HE IS!
WELL... I GOT HIM, CHIEF!
YEAH... JUST LIKE I TOLD YOU I WOULD, CHIEF!
WAIT A MINUTE... WHICH OF YOU GUYS IS MICKEY... AND WHICH IS THE CRIMINAL?
THAT'S EASY...
CINCH...
I'M THE REAL MICKEY! AND HE'S THE CROOK!
THERE'S YOUR CRIMINAL, CHIEF!
NOW, HOW THE DIVVIL KIN I TELL WHICH OF YEZ IS MICKEY AND WHICH IS THE CROOK?
THAT'S EASY...
SURE...

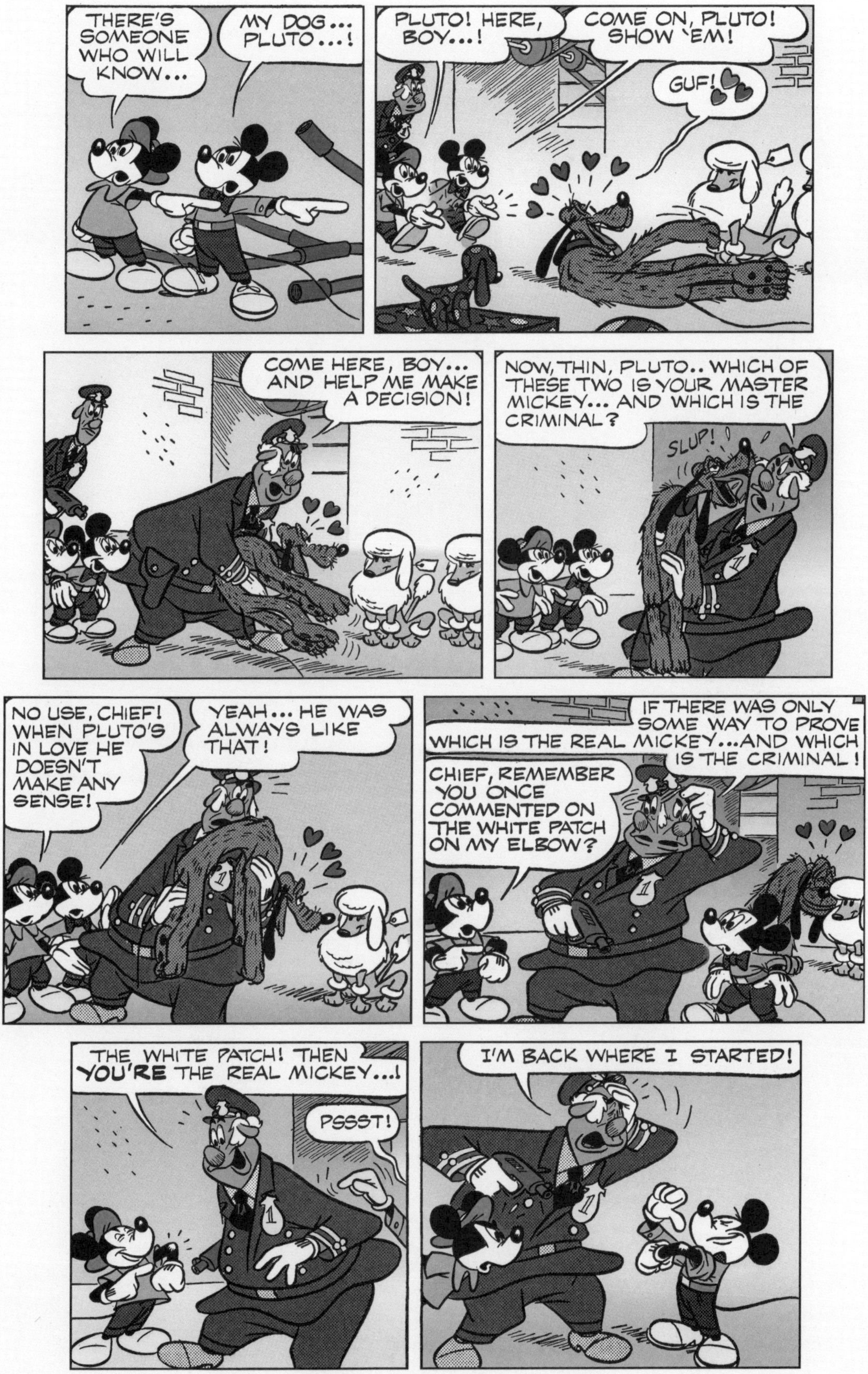
THERE'S SOMEONE WHO WILL KNOW...
MY DOG... PLUTO...!
PLUTO! HERE, BOY...!
COME ON, PLUTO! SHOW 'EM!
GUF!
COME HERE, BOY... AND HELP ME MAKE A DECISION!
NOW, THIN, PLUTO.. WHICH OF THESE TWO IS YOUR MASTER MICKEY... AND WHICH IS THE CRIMINAL?
SLUP!
NO USE, CHIEF! WHEN PLUTO'S IN LOVE HE DOESN'T MAKE ANY SENSE!
YEAH... HE WAS ALWAYS LIKE THAT!
IF THERE WAS ONLY SOME WAY TO PROVE WHICH IS THE REAL MICKEY...AND WHICH IS THE CRIMINAL!
CHIEF, REMEMBER YOU ONCE COMMENTED ON THE WHITE PATCH ON MY ELBOW?
THE WHITE PATCH! THEN **YOU'RE** THE REAL MICKEY...!
PSSST!
I'M BACK WHERE I STARTED!

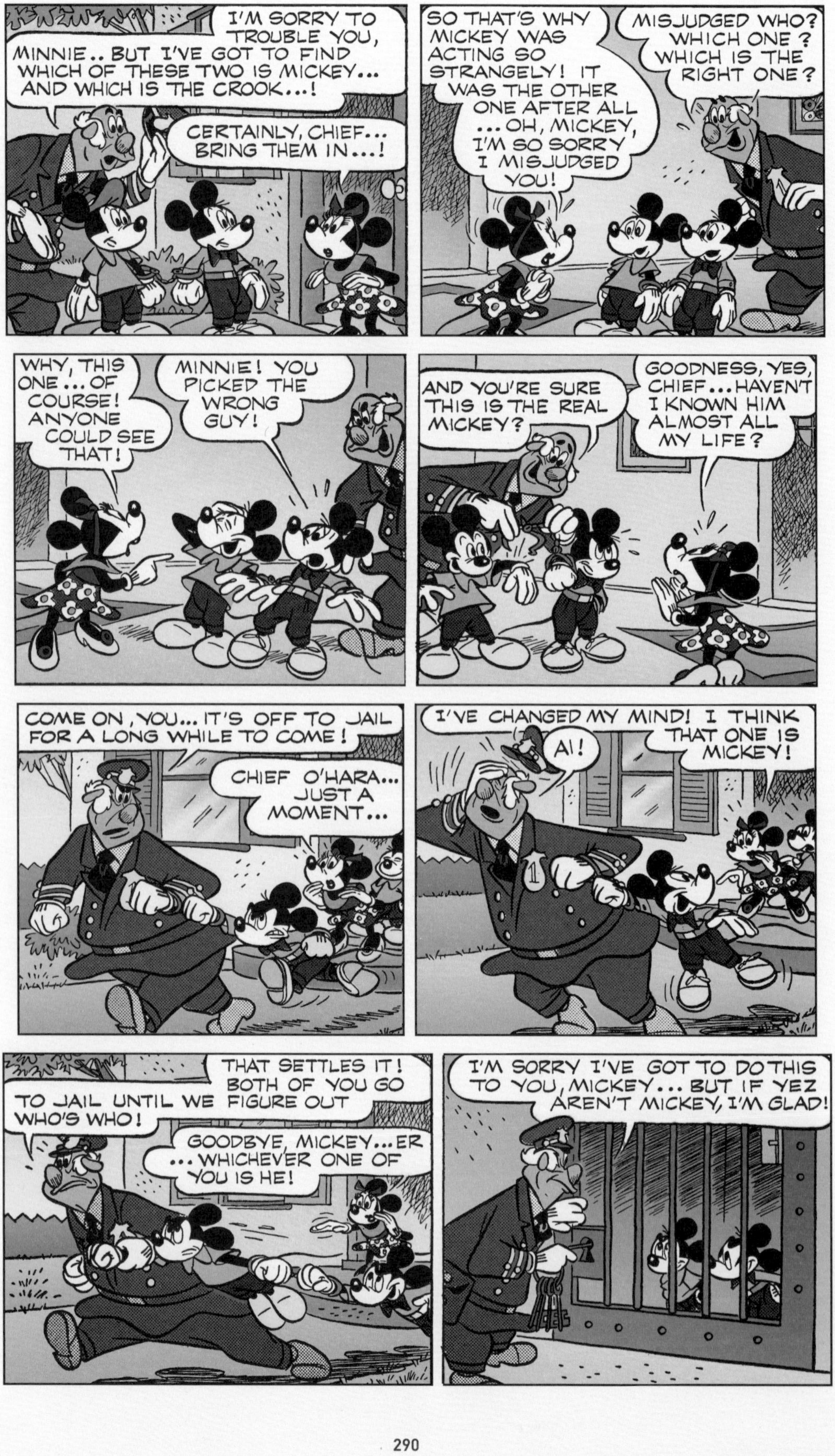
I'M SORRY TO TROUBLE YOU, MINNIE.. BUT I'VE GOT TO FIND WHICH OF THESE TWO IS MICKEY... AND WHICH IS THE CROOK...!
CERTAINLY, CHIEF... BRING THEM IN...!
SO THAT'S WHY MICKEY WAS ACTING SO STRANGELY! IT WAS THE OTHER ONE AFTER ALL ...OH, MICKEY, I'M SO SORRY I MISJUDGED YOU!
MISJUDGED WHO? WHICH ONE? WHICH IS THE RIGHT ONE?
WHY, THIS ONE... OF COURSE! ANYONE COULD SEE THAT!
MINNIE! YOU PICKED THE WRONG GUY!
AND YOU'RE SURE THIS IS THE REAL MICKEY?
GOODNESS, YES, CHIEF... HAVEN'T I KNOWN HIM ALMOST ALL MY LIFE?
COME ON, YOU... IT'S OFF TO JAIL FOR A LONG WHILE TO COME!
CHIEF O'HARA... JUST A MOMENT...
I'VE CHANGED MY MIND! I THINK THAT ONE IS MICKEY!
AI!
THAT SETTLES IT! BOTH OF YOU GO TO JAIL UNTIL WE FIGURE OUT WHO'S WHO!
GOODBYE, MICKEY... ER ... WHICHEVER ONE OF YOU IS HE!
I'M SORRY I'VE GOT TO DO THIS TO YOU, MICKEY... BUT IF YEZ AREN'T MICKEY, I'M GLAD!

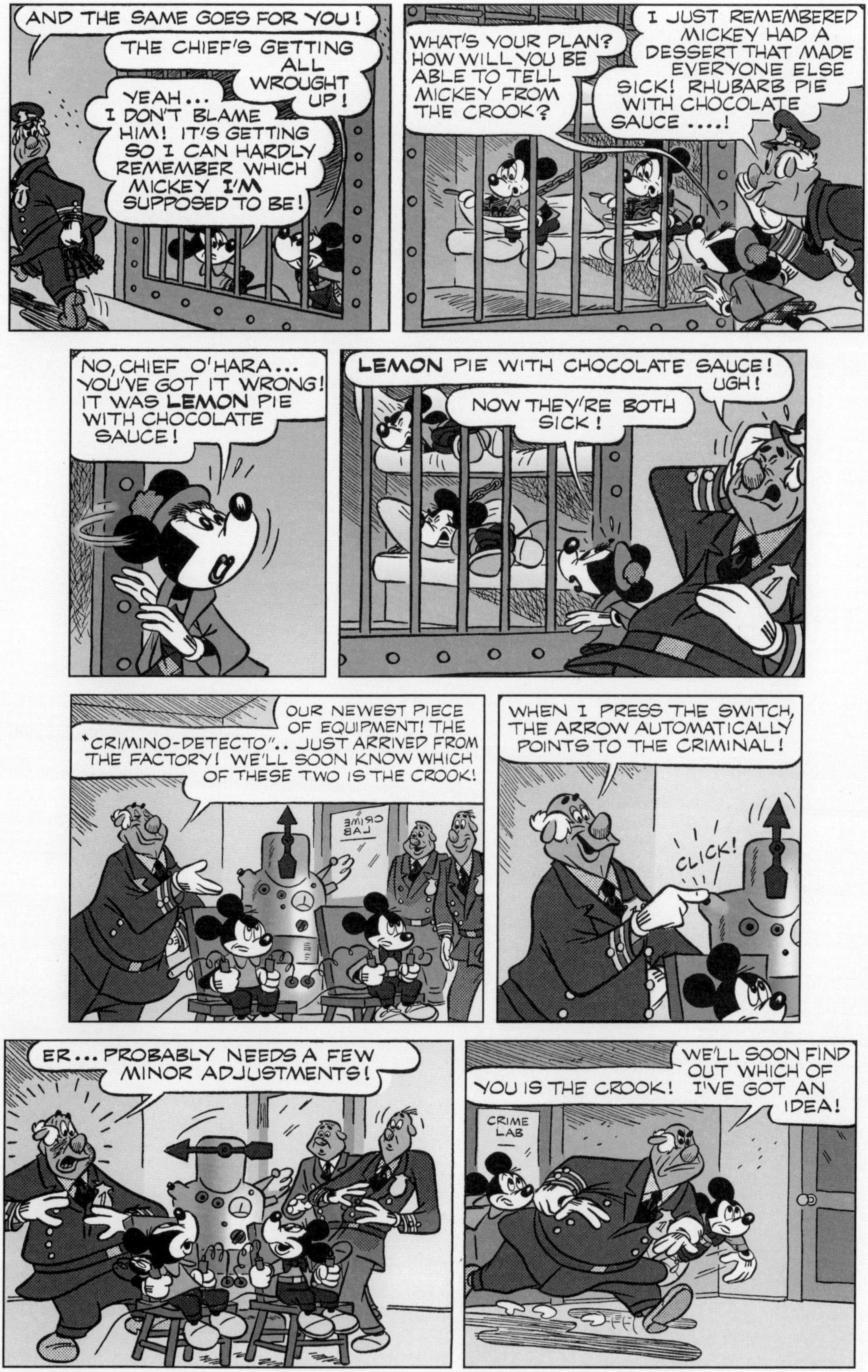
AND THE SAME GOES FOR YOU!
THE CHIEF'S GETTING ALL WROUGHT UP!
YEAH... I DON'T BLAME HIM! IT'S GETTING SO I CAN HARDLY REMEMBER WHICH MICKEY I'M SUPPOSED TO BE!
WHAT'S YOUR PLAN? HOW WILL YOU BE ABLE TO TELL MICKEY FROM THE CROOK?
I JUST REMEMBERED MICKEY HAD A DESSERT THAT MADE EVERYONE ELSE SICK! RHUBARB PIE WITH CHOCOLATE SAUCE....!
NO, CHIEF O'HARA... YOU'VE GOT IT WRONG! IT WAS LEMON PIE WITH CHOCOLATE SAUCE!
LEMON PIE WITH CHOCOLATE SAUCE! UGH!
NOW THEY'RE BOTH SICK!
OUR NEWEST PIECE OF EQUIPMENT! THE "CRIMINO-DETECTO".. JUST ARRIVED FROM THE FACTORY! WE'LL SOON KNOW WHICH OF THESE TWO IS THE CROOK!
CRIME LAB
WHEN I PRESS THE SWITCH, THE ARROW AUTOMATICALLY POINTS TO THE CRIMINAL!
CLICK!
ER... PROBABLY NEEDS A FEW MINOR ADJUSTMENTS!
WE'LL SOON FIND OUT WHICH OF YOU IS THE CROOK! I'VE GOT AN IDEA!
CRIME LAB

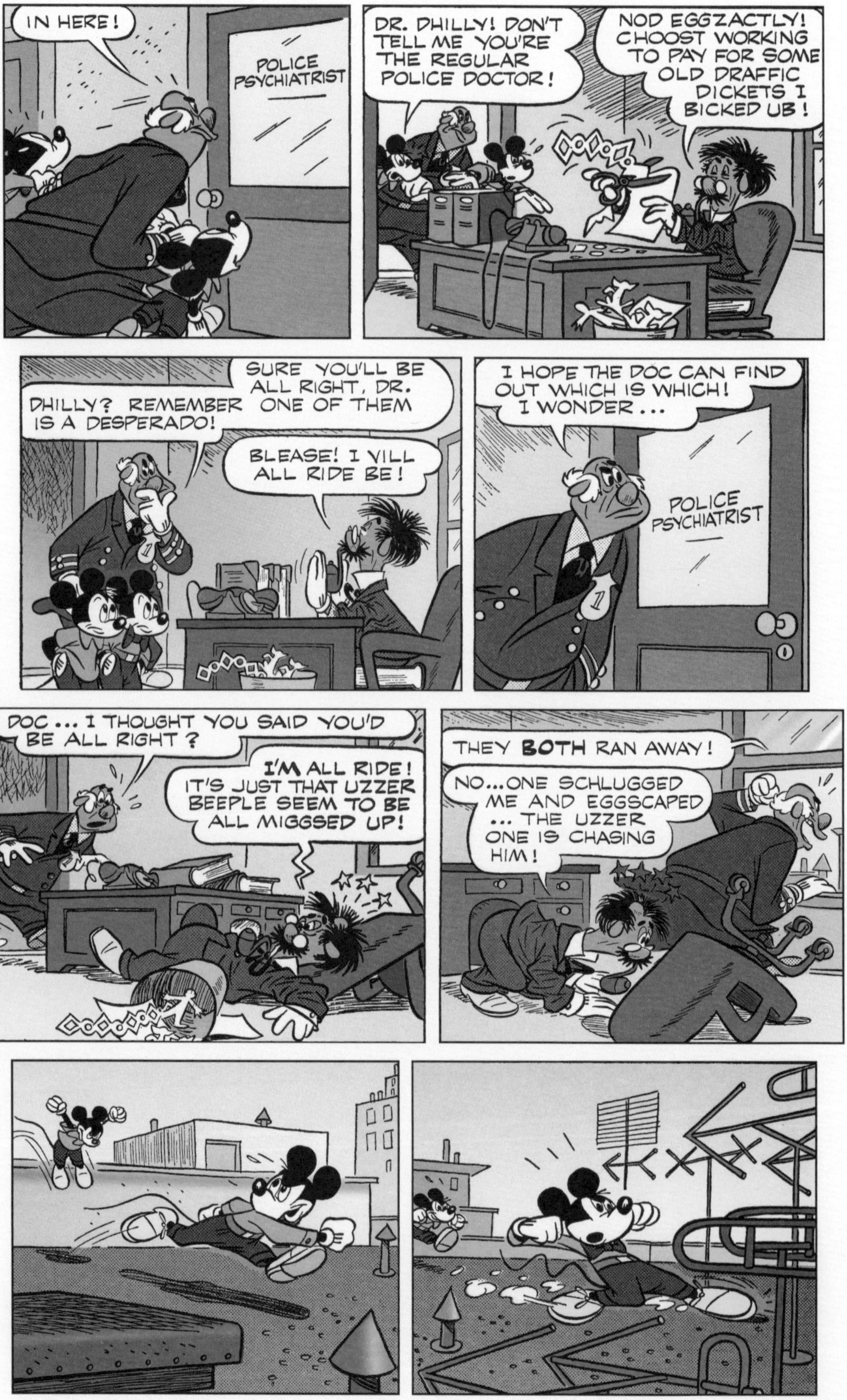
IN HERE!
POLICE PSYCHIATRIST
DR. DHILLY! DON'T TELL ME YOU'RE THE REGULAR POLICE DOCTOR!
NOD EGGZACTLY! CHOOST WORKING TO PAY FOR SOME OLD DRAFFIC DICKETS I BICKED UB!
SURE YOU'LL BE ALL RIGHT, DR. DHILLY? REMEMBER ONE OF THEM IS A DESPERADO!
BLEASE! I VILL ALL RIDE BE!
I HOPE THE DOC CAN FIND OUT WHICH IS WHICH! I WONDER...
POLICE PSYCHIATRIST
DOC... I THOUGHT YOU SAID YOU'D BE ALL RIGHT?
I'M ALL RIDE! IT'S JUST THAT UZZER BEEPLE SEEM TO BE ALL MIGGSED UP!
THEY BOTH RAN AWAY!
NO...ONE SCHLUGGED ME AND EGGSCAPED ... THE UZZER ONE IS CHASING HIM!

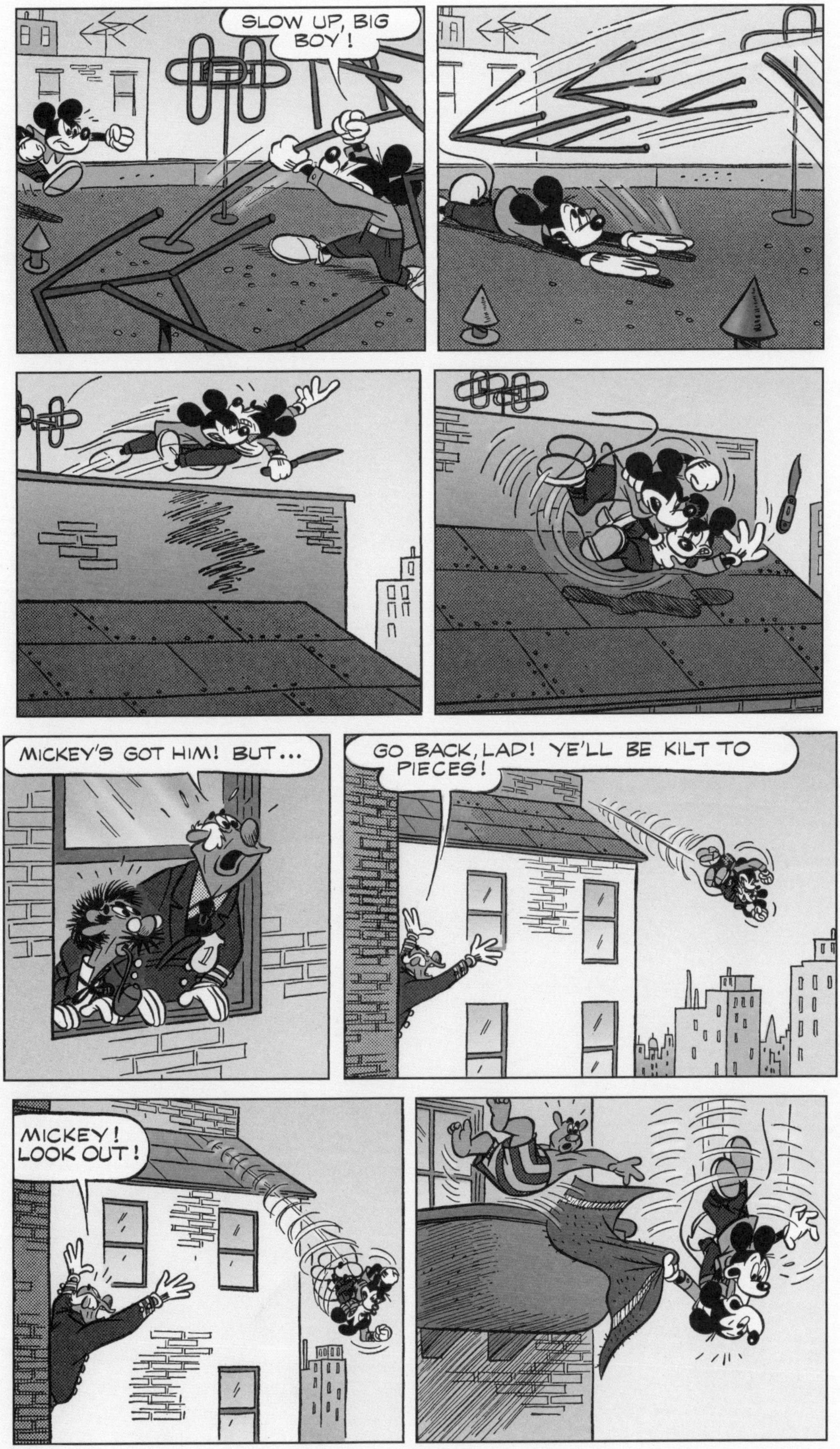
SLOW UP, BIG BOY!
MICKEY'S GOT HIM! BUT...
GO BACK, LAD! YE'LL BE KILT TO PIECES!
MICKEY! LOOK OUT!

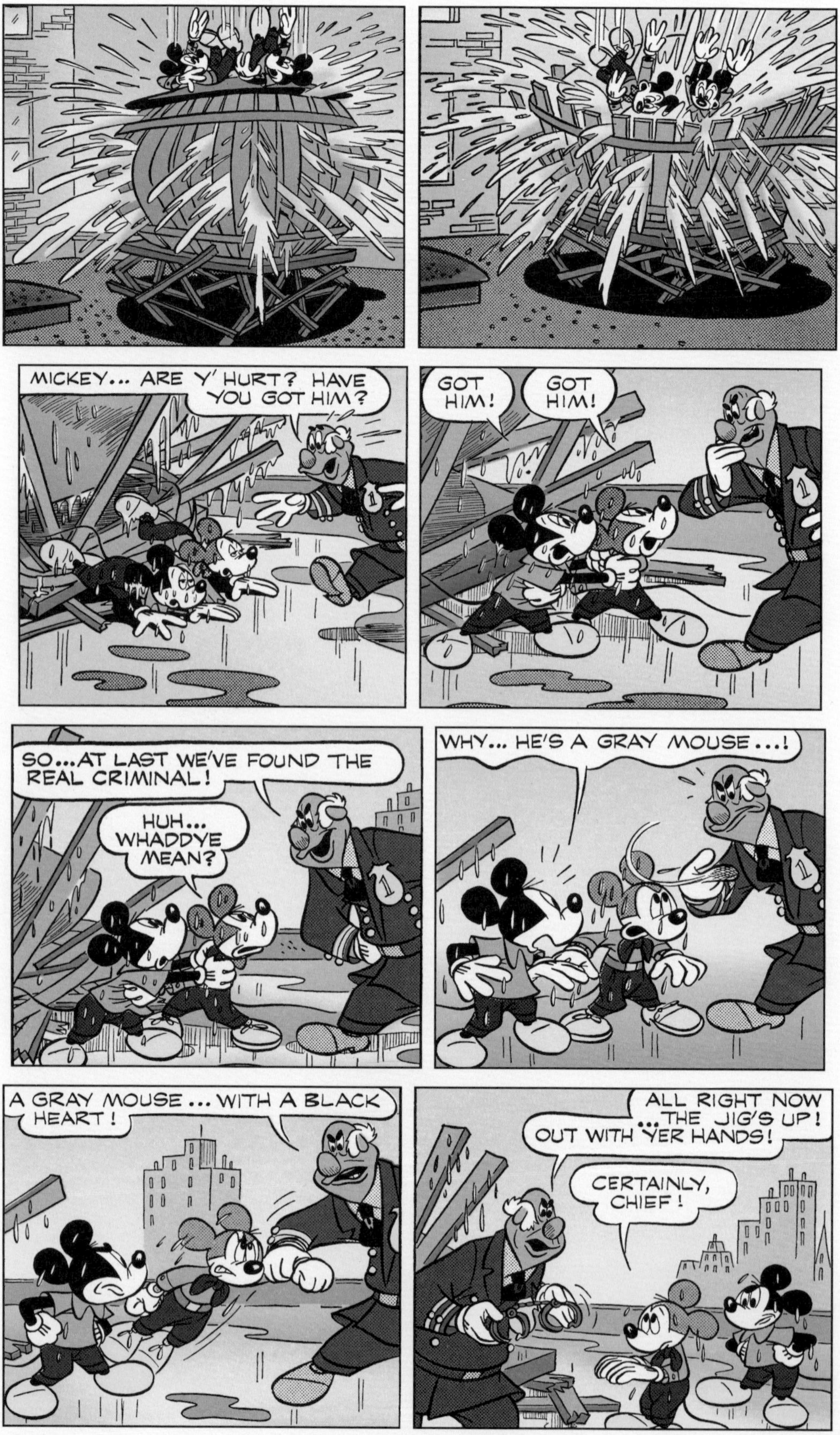
MICKEY... ARE Y' HURT? HAVE YOU GOT HIM?
GOT HIM!
GOT HIM!
SO...AT LAST WE'VE FOUND THE REAL CRIMINAL!
HUH... WHADDYE MEAN?
WHY... HE'S A GRAY MOUSE...!
A GRAY MOUSE... WITH A BLACK HEART!
ALL RIGHT NOW ...THE JIG'S UP! OUT WITH YER HANDS!
CERTAINLY, CHIEF!

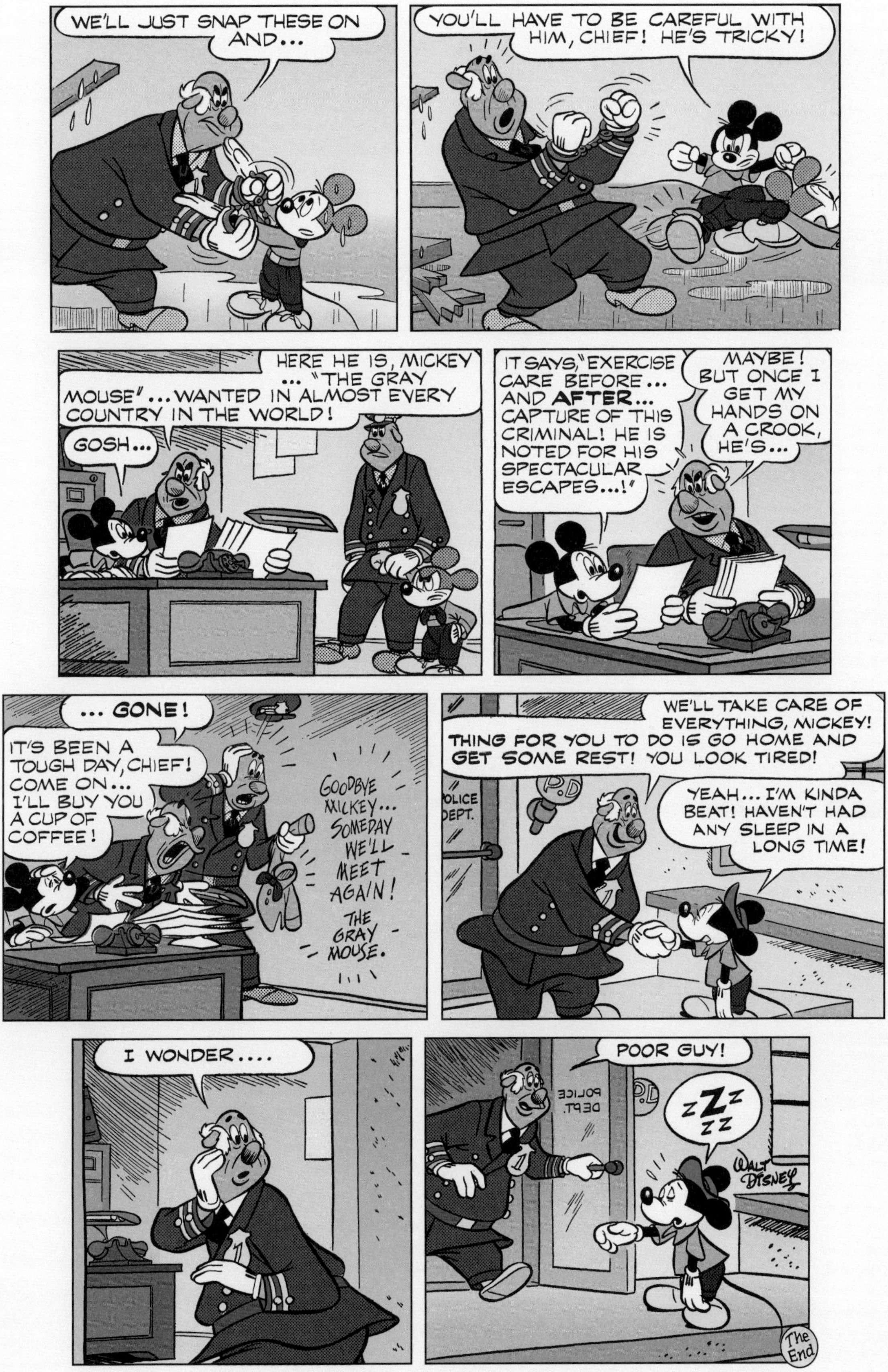
WE'LL JUST SNAP THESE ON AND...
YOU'LL HAVE TO BE CAREFUL WITH HIM, CHIEF! HE'S TRICKY!
HERE HE IS, MICKEY ... "THE GRAY MOUSE"...WANTED IN ALMOST EVERY COUNTRY IN THE WORLD!
GOSH...
IT SAYS, "EXERCISE CARE BEFORE... AND **AFTER**... CAPTURE OF THIS CRIMINAL! HE IS NOTED FOR HIS SPECTACULAR ESCAPES...!"
MAYBE! BUT ONCE I GET MY HANDS ON A CROOK, HE'S...
... **GONE**!
IT'S BEEN A TOUGH DAY, CHIEF! COME ON... I'LL BUY YOU A CUP OF COFFEE!
GOODBYE MICKEY... SOMEDAY WE'LL MEET AGAIN! THE GRAY MOUSE.
WE'LL TAKE CARE OF EVERYTHING, MICKEY! THING FOR YOU TO DO IS GO HOME AND GET SOME REST! YOU LOOK TIRED!
POLICE DEPT.
YEAH... I'M KINDA BEAT! HAVEN'T HAD ANY SLEEP IN A LONG TIME!
I WONDER....
POOR GUY!
ZZZ ZZ
WALT DISNEY
The End

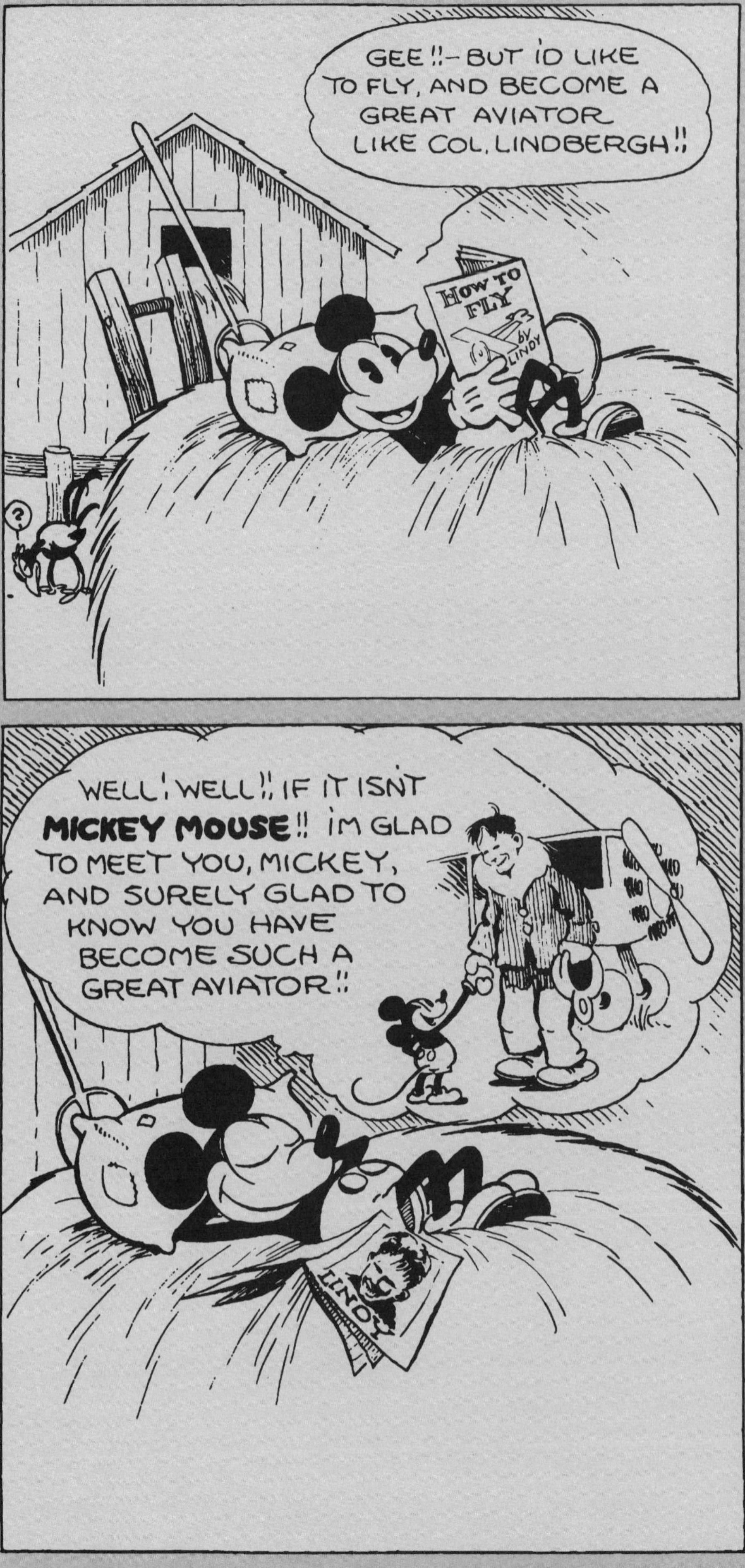
GEE!!- BUT I'D LIKE TO FLY, AND BECOME A GREAT AVIATOR LIKE COL. LINDBERGH!!
HOW TO FLY by LINDY
?
WELL! WELL!! IF IT ISN'T MICKEY MOUSE!! I'M GLAD TO MEET YOU, MICKEY, AND SURELY GLAD TO KNOW YOU HAVE BECOME SUCH A GREAT AVIATOR!!
LINDY

MICKEY MOUSE:
THE HERO

Afterword by David Gerstein

What kind of star character did Walt Disney and Ub Iwerks create? And what kind of hero did Floyd Gottfredson inherit? As we noted in this book's opening pages, Mickey *became* inquisitive, adventurous, trailblazing, selfless, and funny, but the earliest Mickey, like any newly created fictional figure, was less consistent at the start.

Mickey was quickly defined as young and ambitious — his dreams of flight and fame in Walt's pre-Gottfredson comic strip serial, "Lost on a Desert Island" (1930), mirrored his bold goals in the primal cartoon that inspired that strip, *Plane Crazy* (1928). But how Mickey dealt with his ambitions varied wildly from one moment to the next. Some strips showed a go-getter mouse full of genuine bravado, while others showed a boy too

confused, clumsy, or even cowardly to accomplish his goals. At one moment, Mickey might bravely bluff a whole gang of enemies. On another day, coconut-throwing monkeys might be enough to send him fleeing in fear.

On some level, the shifting personality of Mickey Mouse in his earliest adventures parallels that of many early comedy stars. In quest of laughs first and foremost, screen stars and fictional figures alike tossed consistency aside — nothing was out of character as long as it was funny at the moment. Cartoons like *The Jazz Fool* (1929) could even show Mickey outsmarted by inanimate objects.

Floyd Gottfredson would help guide our hero past this early, unsettled state. By late in the story of "Mickey Mouse in Death Valley" (p. 1), Mickey was

1.

CHUG!!
POP!
BANG!
HA! HAW!! HA!!!
OH, MICKEY— ARE YOU HURT ? I TOLD YOU TO GIVE UP AND TURN BACK!!
GIVE UP ?? NEVER!! I MAY BE DOWN, BUT I'M NOT OUT!!

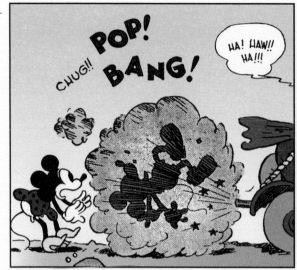

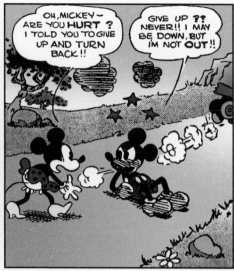

less likely to flee unless it was part of his strategy, more likely to bound back after a setback. (1) He was now a young man determined not to let a bad moment keep him down. Gottfredson had grown up with Horatio Alger's boys' novels — stories of overwhelmed lads pushing back at Dickensian hardship — and he noted how "the world was so much bigger than" Mickey, too. Animation soon took the same stance — in *The Gorilla Mystery* (1930), Mickey initially panics at every threat, but repeatedly steels himself and returns to the fray.

A braver Mickey also made sense with other behaviors seen on the screen. From the beginning, Disney films showed Mickey as a part-time authority figure, sometimes acting as the master of ceremonies for concerts and public events. How could Mickey be both this pillar of society and, in other shorts and comics, an irrepressible kid?

The films didn't deal with the discrepancy, but Gottfredson did. At the end of "Death Valley" and other early serials, Mickey emerges as a public hero: finding a gold mine, winning a boxing match, and generally setting the whole town talking. While Gottfredson always took care to remind us that Mickey was still young and fun loving, Mickey was also increasingly aware of his potential for adult accomplishment — and his struggle to achieve was often placed front and center.

This book's third story, "Island in the Sky" (p. 107), exemplifies this trend. Mickey's boyish glee at acquiring his own plane reminds us of his thrill at discovering the "Death Valley" treasure

2.

IT'S UP TO YOU AN' ME T' FIND OUT— AN' TRY T' GET HIS FORMULA!
BUT WHAT IF HE DON'T WANT TUH GIVE IT TO US ?
?
WELL — AT LEAST WE'LL KNOW WE DIED FOR A SWELL CAUSE !

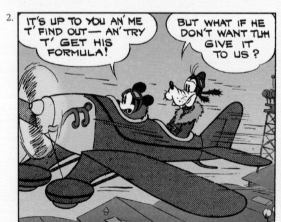

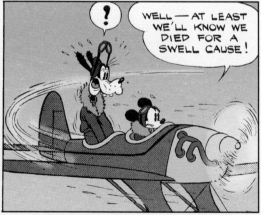

3.

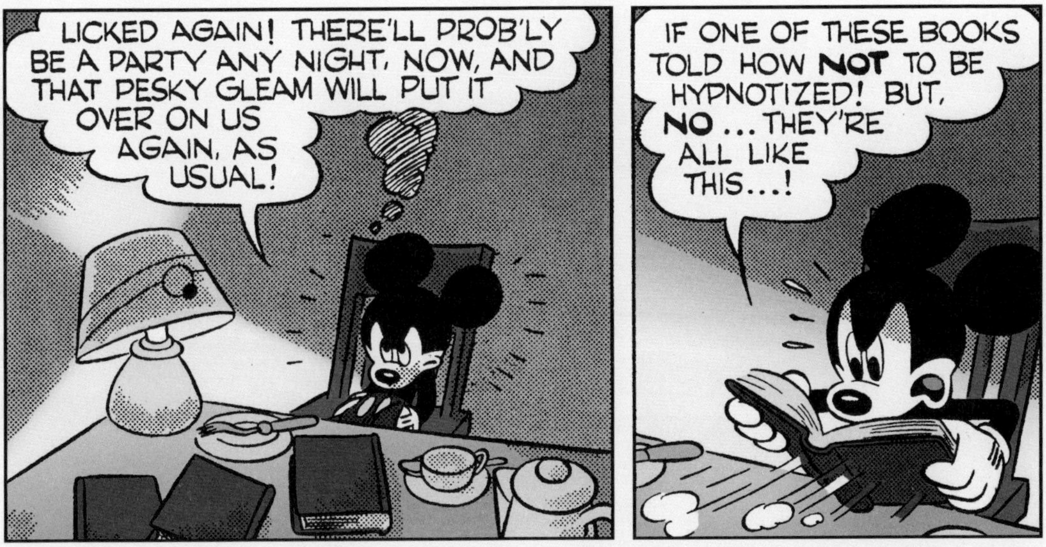
LICKED AGAIN! THERE'LL PROB'LY BE A PARTY ANY NIGHT, NOW, AND THAT PESKY GLEAM WILL PUT IT OVER ON US AGAIN, AS USUAL!
IF ONE OF THESE BOOKS TOLD HOW **NOT** TO BE HYPNOTIZED! BUT, **NO** ... THEY'RE ALL LIKE THIS...!

map.(2) But while the earlier Mickey leapt into danger and constantly lost control, now Mickey reacts to the discovery of Dr. Einmug's atomic power — to circumstances getting serious, that is — by becoming more cautious, more aware of the potential gains and threats. Mickey strategizes internally while wrestling with Pete. He acts the idealistic naïf, in an effort to pacify Einmug, with actual idealism but very little naïveté. When this Mickey loses control — when he strains, for instance, to keep Sky Island afloat — it is now a more dramatic event.

Or a more comical one — because a more mature Mickey is also a funnier straight man for comedic crises. In 1930, when Mickey faced silly setbacks with mules in "Death Valley," his own immaturity and impulsive choices were quite often the source of the humor. But by the mid-1930s, as Horace and Goofy become better-developed sidekicks, this situation changes. Goofy, in particular, is so eccentric, so unpredictable (in "Island in the Sky," Pete can incapacitate Goofy without tying him up!) that Mickey comes across as more mature by default. Gottfredson evolves from laughing *at* Mickey to laughing *with* Mickey — or, just as often, groaning with him — *at* everything else.

By the early 1940s, when a savvier Mickey struggles with his own hypnotized state in "The Gleam" (p. 163), his angst is fully relatable, even as the hypnosis makes him look ridiculous.(3) As a thoughtful detective in whom Chief O'Hara has vested some authority, Mickey knows his silliest actions are the fault of his circumstances, not himself. We feel for Mickey as we would for any unlucky young person "surrounded by idiots," as the saying goes — even when the "idiot" is a role played by Mickey's own hypnotized brain.

After Bill Walsh, in 1943, replaced Gottfredson as plotter on the *Mickey Mouse* daily strip, Mickey adopts another behavior, symbolized by the fedora hat he begins wearing (as in "Mickey Mouse and Goofy's Rocket," p. 209).(4) The 1940s were "an almost mythical age," culture critic Gary Kamiya observed, "the fedora-hat era, when a sweaty glamor hovered over the whole sidewalk-pounding enterprise of being a daily [newspaper] man," or a radio crooner, or a G-man. Fedoras were linked to the 1940s rituals of the macho, the seen-it-all, and the firmly grown up. When Gottfredson's Mickey — hitherto a rather ageless fellow — began to wear a fedora, it seemed not only to define him more clearly as an adult, but as a *realistic* adult, trading his Horatio Alger idealism for a worldly-wise resignation to postwar suburban life.

This is not to say that Mickey, fifteen years into his comics career, did not preserve a fair amount of his original character description. Hustled from adventure to adventure — quite often out of his own control — and oppressed

4.

IT'S MUH "SPACE SHIP"... I'M GOIN' TO THUH MOON!
WHAT IS IT?
WELL ... I'M NOT SAYING IT'S IMPOSSIBLE, ... BUT...
HUMMMPHPH!

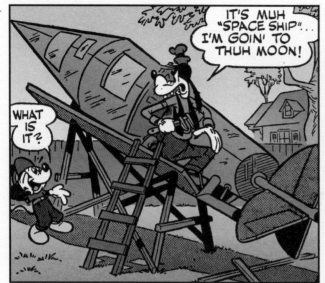

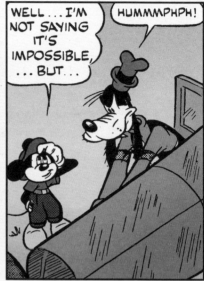

by power players from dogcatchers to dictators, Mickey was still the archetypal "little guy" — still striving to do good, make good, and make the best of a world much larger than him. And in a pinch, Mickey still had finely honed fight-or-flight instincts.

Yet in the postwar years, some pinches seemed unavoidable. While adventure continued to find Mickey in the Walsh-era stories, Mickey himself sought it out less often. Middle-aged, workaday men (the type often played by comedians like George Burns, for whom Walsh had written) weren't usually the type to go looking for excitement. When Mickey pushes time traveler Eega Beeva into inventing something important in "The Atombrella and the Rhyming Man" (p. 213), it was the first example of Mickey taking the initiative in a while. (5) More often, we see Eega take the lead — handling certain bits of business (like the mischievous use of booby traps to protect his lab) that would obviously have been Mickey's bailiwick just a few years before.

Indeed, if Mickey was sidelined in the humor department by the maturing Goofy, Mickey's relationship with Eega — the closest thing to an intellectual match he had had in years — sidelined Mickey in other ways. Eega gave Mickey a myriad of new challenges and opportunities for adventure. Yet as Eega got used to life in Mickey's time period, he felt less like a nutty future man and more like a second Mickey — or, now and then, more like the eager pre-war Mickey.

5.

WHY DON'T YOU USE YOUR BRAIN TO DO SOMETHING WORTH WHILE?
PGEE....
SOMEHOW I GET A LITTLE NERVOUS WHEN I SEE EEGA BEEVA'S BRAIN GOING TO WORK ON SOMETHING ....!
HE SHORE IS THINKIN' HARD!
IT'S MY FAULT... I BAWLED HIM OUT!

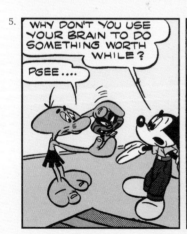

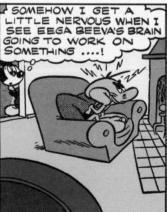

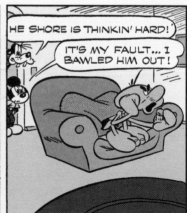

6.

REMEMBER WHAT HAPPENS TO YOUR DOG IF YOU PULL ANYTHING ! AND DON'T TRY TO FOLLOW ME.. I'M TOO SLIPPERY FOR YOU !
YOU DON'T KNOW IT, PAL ... BUT YOU'RE GOING TO BE EASY TO FOLLOW !

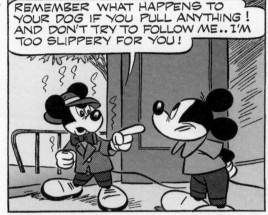

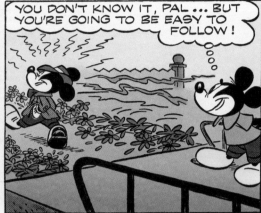

So what becomes of Mickey once Eega leaves the scene? This book's post-Eega tale, "Mickey's Dangerous Double" (p. 261), shows our hero retaking center stage at his dashing best — yanked into an adventure with no choice in the matter, but, once yanked, grabbing the moment with bumptious savoir faire. In his effort to keep his evil twin, Miklos, from replacing him, Mickey doesn't actually need to spray Miklos with stinky cologne and track him singlehandedly — but that's his boyish, exciting plan.

Alas, it is among the last boyish plans for a Mickey who, even without Eega at his side, soon reverts to once again being more reactive than proactive. While still generally portrayed as daring, snarky, and ready to rise to any occasion, by 1953 even a mid-adventure Mickey occasionally shows his years — becoming almost blasé, in fact, as Minnie later tries to distinguish him from Miklos. The evil twin is himself nicknamed "The Gray Mouse," but one wonders if Minnie glimpsed Mickey, too, graying around the temples.

Jokes aside, Mickey's temporary 1950s devolution did little to dampen the overall strengths of his portrayal in the greater Gottfredson canon — one that, by the 1970s, was being recognized and celebrated by comics scholars. When historian Bill Blackbeard celebrated the "death-defying, tough, steel-gutted Mickey Mouse ... who held the kids of 1933 rapt with his adventures on pirate dirigibles, cannibal islands, and bullet-tattered fighter planes," there was no question about which Mickey he meant. Soon, that Mickey was being collected and anthologized around the world — including, ultimately, in the volumes of the complete *Floyd Gottfredson Library of Walt Disney's Mickey Mouse* (Fantagraphics Books, 2011–2017).

Today, the influence of Gottfredson's Mickey Mouse extends beyond the comics canon. As the star of new short cartoons and video games, the animated Mickey has long since reclaimed a lot of that gung-ho Gottfredson gumption. Modern audiences are once again used to seeing Mickey Mouse explore challenges that seem too big, take on threats that are clearly too dangerous, and race through a world that looms too large for a little guy.

Floyd Gottfredson would recognize it all.

P.296: A Walt Disney-scripted Mickey expounds on his ambitions in "Lost on a Desert Island" (1930). Ub Iwerks (pencils), Win Smith (inks).